Rachel

DAHVEED

ALSO BY TERRI L. FIVASH
Historical Biblical Fiction

Joseph: A Story
Ruth and Boaz: Strangers in the Land

THE DAHVEED SERIES

Book 1: *Yahweh's Chosen*
Book 2: *Yahweh's Warrior*
Book 3: *Yahweh's Fugitive*

Forthcoming in the series:

Book 4: *Yahweh's Soldier*
Book 5: *Yahweh's General*
Book 6: *Yahweh's King*

Devotional and Spiritual Life

Myrie's Lord's Prayer
Your Spiritual Toolbox

Visit my web site to order and learn more.
www.terrifivash.com

DAHVEED

YAHWEH'S FUGITIVE

BOOK THREE

BY

TERRI L. FIVASH

The author assumes full responsibility for the accuracy of all facts and quotations as cited in this book.

This book was
Edited by Gerald Wheeler
Cover Designed by Rhonda Root - Copyright 2011
Cover art by Raoul Vitale
Interior Design Copyright 2011

First printing November 2011
Second printing December 2011

List of Maps

Maps are found at the end of the book.

Land of Israel

Central Israel

South Israel

¥ ¥ ¥ ¥ ¥ ¥

DEDICATION

This book is dedicated to
Via
who knows what it is to wander in the wilderness.

ACKNOWLEDGMENTS

As always I am indebted to many people for their help in the creation of this book. Among them are:

Roy Gane for reviewing my translations of the Psalms.

Bethany Bolduc for her last-minute suggestions that sharpened the story.

All my advanced readers, my editors, and

Rhonda Root for her hours of tedious work in preparing the maps and illustrations for both this book and the one before it.

Thank you.

To Parents of Young Readers

The story of David is one of the best known in the Bible. However, David lived a violent life, and warfare back then was very up-close and personal. You will, therefore, find combat in this book. While I do not feel that I must wallow in blood and gore, a certain amount of it is unavoidable if I am to remain faithful to the culture of biblical times and the biblical narrative itself. Please keep this in mind if you choose to read this book to your children.

Another aspect of David's story which you may want to consider is polygamy. David had several wives, and he begins collecting them in this book. Please also keep this in mind for younger readers.

To the Reader

The two previous books in the Dahveed series have, for the most part, been in chronological sequence. However, this book when written in a straight chronological manner can be hard to follow, so I have adopted a more thematic approach. Therefore, please pay special attention to time comments when the character point-of-view changes. There are at least two major time shifts, and I believe that Tamar's comments cover these, but be aware that time can slip backward or forward at other places in the story.

Three main story lines interweave in this book: Jonathan, Dahveed, and Abigail of Carmel. To begin with, Dahveed and Jonathan's stories are intricately intertwined as they are in the previous books. Abigail remains separate until the end, when her story merges with Dahveed's. But, in the middle, the three story lines go their own separate ways, with occasional touch-points between them. I have tried to make following each story line as easy as possible, since events in one can affect what happened in the others whether or not the characters interact.

And, unavoidably, there are a multitude of characters! Many are familiar from the previous books, but during this time of his life Dahveed builds up the core of his army, collecting around him an entire band of mercenaries. At one point, I wanted to introduce each of the 30 mighty men with a background story about them, but I quickly realized that was too much to do. I have, therefore, concentrated on characters who will be important to Dahveed in later books.

Character names are also--um--interesting at times! And I apologize for the duplicate names. I am, however, constrained by the biblical records. I especially ask your patience with the names Jonathan and Shammah. There are, I believe, six different Jonathan's connected to Dahveed in the Bible and at least three Shammah's. I will do my best to keep them separate!

There are also other duplicate names, such as Jaasiel, and many names that are similar in spelling and pronunciation. If I have a choice, I try to keep names as different as possible to aid in keeping characters separate. For instance, Bunah and Bunni are scribes. Mebunnai is one of Dahveed's men, but Mebunnai has an alternate name, Sibbecai, the one I use in the book. Other times I'm not so lucky, and I have to use the names given, no matter how confusing.

And just as a reminder, I am following Dahveed's story as recorded in 1 and 2 Samuel, translations of psalms in the book are my own, and numbers in Dahveed's time were very mushy! See "A Word About . . ." on my web site for further discussion of the above.

Characters in Dahveed 3

Names in **Bold** appear in this book.
Names with an asterisk (*) are biblical characters

Abiadan--Sahrah of Ammon, daughter of King Nahash, wife of Jesse, and mother of Abigail and Zeruiah. Deceased.

***Abiathar**--Son of Hakkohen Haggadol Ahimelech. A priest.

Abiaz--Trouble-maker in Heshbon when Ruth was a young woman.

***Abiezer**--Member of Hassar Jonathan's personal guard.

***Abigail**--Dahveed's half sister, and full sister to Zeruiah. Daughter of Abiadan.

***Abigail of Carmel**--Wife of Nabal. Gebirah to the Carmel Calebite clans.

***Abinadab**--Jesse's second son by Miriam, his Israelite wife. Half-brother to Dahveed.

***Abishai**--Dahveed's nephew, first born of Zeruiah, half-sister to Dahveed.

***Abner**--General of Shaul's armies and his cousin.

Achsah--Maid to Michal.

*Adriel--Son of Barzillai. Marries Merab.

Ahaz--Elder of Bethlehem.

***Ahiam**--Habiru sworn to Dahveed.

***Ahibaal**--Puzzling man on a mule looking for Dahveed whom Dahveed asks about.

***Ahimelech**--High priest in Nob during Shaul's reign.

***Ahinoam**--Shaul's wife.

***Ahinoam of Jezreel**--Daughter of Ahlai. Sister of Zabad. Marries Dahveed.

***Ahlai**--Father of Zabad, Ahinoam, and Lael. Rival to Nabal.

***Ahor**--Canaanite landowner near Shechem. Grandfather to Hushai the Archite.

*Aiah--Father of Rizpah, Shaul's concubine. Lives in Jabesh.

***Akish**--Son of Maoch of Gath, who becomes Seren of Gath when his father dies.

Ala--Zelek's sister. Taken by Manani in Ekron and tries to stop her brother from assassinating Hassar Jonathan. Half Ammonite, half Cushite, and blood cousin to Abigail and Zeruiah.

Amarel of Dibon--Man who took Moab's throne during the time of Ruth.

***Amasa**--Son of Dahveed's sister Abigail.

***Armoni**--Rizpah's first son.

***Araunah**--Title for king of Jebus. Used as a name.

Areli--Man from Naphtali in the second unit. Cousin to Cheran.

***Asahel**--Dahveed's nephew, third son of Zeruiah.

Asaiah--Boyhood friend of Dahveed in Bethlehem, son of Telah.

Atarah--Jebusite woman rescued by Dahveed and Ethan. Sister to Ornan.

***Azmaveth**--Bodyguard to the hassar and father of Pelet. Forced to spy on Jonathan.

***Balak**--Man of Bethlehem, four years older than Dahveed and who dislikes him.

Baqqush--Envoy from the kingdom of Mari who makes a covenant with Shaul.

*Barzillai--Man from Jabesh in Gilead who buys a lamb from Ruth.

Father to Adriel.
Basemath--Maid to Rizpah.
Ben-Geber--Dahveed's childhood name.
*__Bichri__--Man of Benjamin who tries to bully a beggar and is stopped.
'Bijah--Boy in Navyoth who watches the soldiers prophesy.
*__Boaz__--Dahveed's great-grandfather. Ruth's husband.
Bodbaal--Philistine member of Ethan's band. Mute. Brother to Geresh and Peleth.
Bukki--Lahab's father. Landowner in Bethlehem.
Bunah--Scribe to Jonathan Hassar.
Bunni--Scribe to Jonathan Hassar.
Caleb--Habiru member of Ethan's band with twin daughters, Leah and Rachel.
Carmi--Homesteader north of Bethlehem. Comes to the gate for Jesse.
*__Cheran__--Newest personal attendant to Shaul. Cousin of Areli.
*__Dahveed__--Jesse's eighth son, anointed to be king for Yahweh. (Dahveed is also a title.)
*__Dara__--Hassar Jonathan's shield bearer.
Dathan--Nagid of the Hebron Calebite clans. Supports Abigail of Carmel.
David--See Dahveed.
Debir--Adon in Jebus who stages a palace coup and becomes Araunah.
Dishon--Commander of the eighth unit.
*Dodo--Father of Eleazar of Benjamin.
*Dodo--Father of Dahveed's childhood friend Elhanan.
*__Doeg__--Edomite in Shaul's service who kills the priests.
Dumah--Kin of Ornan and Atarah, who betrays them.
*El--Mighty One, God.
*El Elyon--God Most High.
*El Shaddai--God Almighty.
*__Eleazar__--Left-handed swordsman who becomes shield-bearer to Sar Ishvi.
*__Elhanan__--son of Bethlehem's innkeeper. Dahveed's childhood friend and member of his band.
*__Eliab__--Jesse's first born child, his bekor. Can be greedy. Half-brother to Dahveed.
*__Eliam__--Son to Ahibaal. Joins Dahveed's band at his father's command.
*__Elihu__--Jesse's seventh son. Trains to be a scribe. Half-brother to

Dahveed.
***Elika**--One of Dahveed's men. From En-harod. Friend of Shammah.
***Eliphelet ben Ahasbai**--Steals from Dahveed. Then joins him. From Abel Beth-Maacah.
Elyaton--Name that Dahveed uses when he goes to Jonathan's wedding.
***Eshbaal**--Shaul's fourth son, younger than Michal. Very good administrator.
Ethan--Grandson of Patah and Gaddi. Bodyguard for Ruth. Leader of the Habiru near Bethlehem and Dahveed's teacher.
Ezra--Man from Judah whose family needs help. Deceased.
Gabri--Honest jewel merchant in Jebus.
***Gad**--Roeh Shamuel's servant.
Gaddi--Grandfather to Ethan. Life-time slave to Boaz's house.
Gareb--Man of Judah who joins Dahveed.
Gedor--Man of the second unit who died saving Sar Malchi.
***Gera**--Benjamite whose clan does not like Dahveed.
Geresh--Philistine Habiru of Ethan's band. Brother to Bodbaal and Peleth.
***Goliath**--Traditional name of the champion of the Philistines whom Dahveed kills.
Hadar--Ishmaelite merchant with Gebirah Abigail for a customer.
***Hanan**--Habiru youth affiliated with Joel's band near Keilah. One of Yahweh's Arrows.
(the) Hassarah--Title of respect given to Ruth, Dahveed's great-grandmother.
Hazzel--Akish of Gath's sister. Ittai's mother.
Heber--A Habiru dahveed near the ravines of Gaash.
***Hezro**--Commander of the guard to Nabal. Loyal to Gebirah Abigail.
***Hiddai**--unsavory man who tries to use Dahveed before joining him.
Hod--Balak's father. A Moabite landowner in Bethlehem.
***Hushai**--The Archite. Grandson of Ahor and who likes Dahveed.
***Igal**--Man from Zobah who exasperates Dahveed, but joins him.
*Ira--Great-grandson of Shamuel, who asked for a song. Brother to Hannah.
***Ira**--Man of Judah who joins Dahveed.
Iscah--Woman in Shaul's clan with a very helpful son.
***Ishvi**--Shaul's second son. A sar.
Ishvi ben Ezra--Only survivor of his house. Foster son to Sar Ishvi.

*__Ishvi-benob__--Kin to Goliath of Gath with four relatives all of whom hate Dahveed.
*__Ithmah__--Man of Moab who joins Dahveed.
*__Ittai__--Philistine/Israelite youth bound to Dahveed through circumcision.
*__Jaasiel__--Abner's son.
*__Jaasiel__--Friend to Igal, who also joins Dahveed.
Jalam--Overseer to Abigail of Carmel.
Jamin--Ethan's younger brother. A Habiru and one of Yahweh's Arrows.
Jarib--Demoted Commander of the second unit. Executed by Dahveed for his part in the Gibeonite crime.
*Jashobeam--See Josheb.
Jerioth--Sister of Asaiah, and wife of Elhanan. Deceased.
Jemima--Sister of Palti of Gallim who marries Ahiam.
Jeshua--Leader of the Gibeah band of Habiru.
*__Jesse__--Dahveed's father. Elder and rich landowner in Bethlehem.
*__Jether__--Abigail's husband. Ishmaelite trader.
*__Joab__--Dahveed's nephew. Second son of Zeruiah. Wanted by the Egyptians.
Joel--Habiru dahveed of the Keilah band. Supporter of Ethan. Yahweh's Arrow.
*__Jonadab__--Second son of Shammah, and Dahveed's nephew.
*__Jonathan__--Dahveed's uncle (brother of his mother).
*__Jonathan__--Shaul's oldest son. The Hassar.
*__Jonathan__--Dahveed's nephew, son of Shammah.
*__Jonathan__--Son of the Habiru Shagay. Yahweh's Arrow.
Jonathan ben Ezra--Son of Ezra who died.
*__Joseph ben Jacob__--favorite son of Jacob who became Tate of Egypt.
*__Josheb-Basshebeth ben Zabdiel__--Former bodyguard to Hassar Jonathan. One of Dahveed's men.
*__Jotbah__--Handmaid and scribe to Gebirah Abigail.
Judith--Maid to Ahinoam and abandoned wife of Balak.
*__Kemosh__--god of Moab.
Kemosh-dan--Overlord of Moab when Ruth was a young woman.
*__Keren__--Dahveed's mother and Jesse's wife.
Keturah--Gibeonite woman dependent on Dahveed. Sister to Naharai.
*__Keziah__--Wife of Dahveed's half-brother Shammah.
*Kish--Shaul's father.

Kohath--Head scribe under Eshbaal. Killed himself over the Gibeonite crime.
Lael ben Ahlai--Young man who cannot seem to control his spending.
Lahab--Vintner of Bethlehem and son of Bukki. Sets up shop with Raddai.
*__Lahmi__--Kin to Goliath of Gath. Brother of Ishvi-Benob. Hates Dahveed.
Leah--One of Caleb's twins. Habiru.
Libni--Commander of the tenth unit. Supports Abner.
Lotan--Man of the second unit. A Hittite mastersmith.
*__Maacah bat Talmai__--Young daughter of Geshur's king who is amused by Dahveed.
Malcath bat Talmai--Older sister of Maacah who is getting married.
Malchi--See Malchi-shua.
*__Malchi-shua__--Shaul's third son. A sar.
Manani--Chief seren in Ekron. A cruel man, universally hated and feared.
*Maoch--Father of Akish. Former seren of Gath.
Mari--Messenger sent to Shaul, who is murdered on the way. Also a city-state north of Israel.
*__Matred__--Handmaid to Gebirah Abigail.
Mattan--Meshullam's son and dahveed after him. Swore his band to Boaz and Boaz's bloodline.
*Mephibosheth--Rizpah's second son.
*__Merab__--Shaul's oldest child, his bekorah. Wife of Adriel.
Merab bat Ezra--daughter of Ezra of Judah. Deceased.
*__Meribbaal__--Son of Jonathan Hassar.
Meshullam--Habiru dahveed of Boaz's time.
*__Mibhar ben Hagri__--Shepherd to Nabal of Carmel who recognizes Dahveed.
*__Michal__--Shaul's younger daughter and Dahveed's wife.
Milcom--God of Ammon.
Minelek--Philistine merchant of Chephirah, whom Dahveed appoints as Gibeonite overseer.
Miriam--Jesse's Israelite wife.
*__Nabal__--Nagid of Carmel's Calebite clans. Husband to Abigail. Greedy for honor.
Nadab--Quartermaster of Shaul's army.
*__Naharai__--Gibeonite man of the second unit. Keturah's brother.

***Nahash**--King of Ammon and grandfather of Abigail and Zeruiah. Saves Dahveed.
***Namea**--Handmaid to Gebirah Abigail.
Natan--Commander of the fifth unit.
Negbi--Treasurer of Keilah. Not necessarily honest.
Nemuel--Jonathan's boyhood friend. Killed by Philistines.
***Ner**--Abner's father. Uncle to Shaul.
***Nethanel**--Jesse's fourth son, Dahveed's half-brother.
Nimshi--Ethan's youngest son.
***Obed**--Ruth's son, Jesse's father. Deceased.
***Oholah**--Handmaid and scribe to Gebirah Abigail.
***Ornan**--Jebusite youth rescued by Dahveed and Ethan. Brother to Atarah.
***Ozem**--Jesse's sixth son. Younger twin to Raddai, Dahveed's half brother.
Pallu--Man of the second unit. Good archer.
***Palti of Gallim**--Scribe to Sar Ishvi. Brother of Jemima. Is given Michal Sahrah.
***Parai**--Slave to Gebirah Abigail who runs away. A tanner. Joins Dahveed.
Pasach--Commander of the eleventh unit.
Pashur--Habiru of Boaz's time and life-time friend of Boaz.
Patah--Old dahveed of the Habiru when Ben-geber is a child. Grandson of Meshullam and grandfather of Ethan and Jamin.
Pekah--Son of Zalmon.
Pelet--Son of Azmaveth. Taken by Abner.
Peleth--Former Philistine slave to Hassar Jonathan and overseer for him. Brother of Bodbaal and Geresh.
Puah--Wife of Shagay and mother to Jonathan.
Qausa--Habiru who accepted money to kill King Shaul. Deceased, but won't stay dead.
Rachel--One of Caleb's twins. Habiru.
***Raddai**--Jesse's fifth son. Older twin to Ozem, Dahveed's half-brother.
Ram--Commander of the first unit in King Shaul's permanent forces.
*Recheb--Gibeonite from Beeroth. Son of Rimmon to whom Jonathan Hassar gives hesed.
Reu--Man of the second unit. Good engineer.
***Ribai**--Israelite slave who married Akish's sister Hazzel. Father of

Ittai. Deceased.
*Rimmon--Gibeonite from Beeroth who tried to kill Jonathan Hassar.
***Rinnah**--Man of Ziph who doesn't want Dahveed around.
***Rizpah**--Concubine to King Shaul, from Jabesh in Gilead.
***Ruth**--The Hassarah. Wife of Boaz and great-grandmother of Dahveed.
Sakar ben Hissil--Prince of Heshbon and husband of Orpah in Ruth's time.
Samlah--Merchant who is not too picky about where he gets his wares.
***Samson**--Judge in Israel who was captured by the Philistines after betrayal by Delilah.
Samuel--See Shamuel.
***Saph**--Kin to Goliath of Gath, Ishvi-benob and Lahmi. Hates Dahveed.
Saul--See Shaul.
***Shagay**--Habiru and Yahweh's Arrow. Dahveed's first retainer.
***Shammah**--Jesse's third son, Dahveed's half-brother.
***Shammah**--One of Dahveed's men. Friend of Elika. From En-harod.
*Shammah ben Agee--See Shagay.
***Shamuel**--Roeh, seer, in Israel. Anoints Shaul and Dahveed.
***Shaul**--King of Israel, Jonathan and Michal's father.
Shemel--A Philistine. Dahveed's commander in Gath. Shows Dahveed hesed.
Sheva--Commander of King Shaul's guard.
*Shimei--Cousin to Jonathan Hassar. Banned from appearing at court. Of Gera's clan.
Shoher--Father of Ethan. Deceased.
***Sibbecai**--Bitter man from Hushah who takes Dahveed's sword. Then joins him.
Sithri--Man of the second unit who can sharpen things well.
Steward of the House of Tahat--Man whom Jonathan Hassar finally finds.
Tahan--Man of the second unit who knows jewelry.
Tahat--Business associate of Dahveed's great-grandfather Boaz.
***Talmai**--Father of Maacah and Malcath. Tries to use Dahveed.
Tamakel--Son of Nahash, father of Ala and Zelek. Deceased.
Tanhum--Hiddeous cripple saved by Dahveed, and appreciated by Jonathan. Father of Ziba.
***Taphath**--wife of Jonathan and mother of Meribbaal. From Jabesh.

Cousin to Azmaveth.
Telah--Elder in Bethlehem.
Teman--Head elder of Keilah.
Tiras--Very tall Habiru dahveed who finds the Lion of Judah. Brother to Uzzia.
*__Tirzah__--Plump handmaid to Gebirah Abigail.
Tokhath--Nabal's intelligent and ambitious scribe.
*__Uriah the Hittite__--Neighbor of Dahveed who joins him and who can teach. A lot.
*__Uzzia__--Tiras' taller brother who is hostage to Dahveed. From Ashterath in Bashan.
Yah--Short form of Yahweh.
Yahas--Balak's great-grandfather. Son of Abiaz.
Yahoadan--Jamin's daughter. Habiru.
*__Yahweh__--Israel's God. Has chosen Dahveed.
Yahweh's Arrows--Habiru who have affiliated with Ethan and his band to protect and serve Boaz's bloodline.
*__Yira__--King of Moab and very wary of Dahveed.
*__Zabad ben Ahlai__--Disowned son of Ahlai. Brother of Ahinoam. Good fighter. Given to Dahveed.
*__Zalmon__--Benjamite who finds Dahveed by descending on him. Father of Pekah.
*__Zelek__--Ammonite/Cushite who tried to assassinate Hassar Jonathan. Brother to Ala. Blood kin to Abigail and Zeruiah.
Zemirah--head elder in Bethlehem.
Zeri--Habiru from the Gibeah band. Yahweh's Arrow. Refuses to hunt Dahveed.
*__Zeruiah__--Jesse's oldest daughter by Abiadan. Mother of Abishai, Joab, and Asahel.
*__Ziba__--Son of Tanhum. Brother to Atarah. Unhappy with Jonathan Hassar.
Zorath--Commander of the third unit and supporter of Dahveed.

Habiru lineage:
Meshullam-Mattan-Patah-Shoher-Ethan-Nimshi

Dahveed's lineage:
Salmon--Boaz--Obed--Jesse--Dahveed

Masculine titles of respect in Israel--least to most
Geber--Adon/Baal--Sar--Nahsi--Nagid--Melek

Feminine titles of respect--least to most
Geberet--Baalah--Sahrah--Hassarah

Vocabulary

Pronunciations:
A pronounced "Ah." Spelled "ah;" occasionally pronounced as short "A." Spelled "a."
E pronounced as long A. Spelled "ay;" occasionally as short "e." Spelled "eh."
I pronounced as long E. Spelled "ee."
O pronounced as long O. Spelled "oh."
U pronounced as "oo." Spelled "oo."
AI pronounced as long I. Spelled "aye."

Italics indicate the stressed syllable.

Abbi--(*ah*-bee), my father, term of endearment, i.e. Daddy.
Adon--(ah-*dohn*), masculine title of respect: Lord.
Adonai--(Ah-dohn-*naye*), plural of adoni--used exclusively for Yahweh.
Adoni--(ah-dohn-*ee*), my lord.
Aijalon--(Aye-yah-*lohn*), a pass from the hills into the Shephelah about 15 miles west of Jebus.
Baalah--(bah-*ah*-lah), feminine title of respect: Lady.
Bat--(baht), daughter of, or female descendent of.
Bekor--(beh-*kohr*), first born, masculine.
Bekorah--(beh-kohr-*ah*), first born, feminine.
Ben--(bayn), son of, or male descendent of.
Chinnereth--See Sea of Chinnereth.
Couscous--(*koos*-koos), cooked cracked wheat.
Cuirass--(kwee-*rahs*), armored "shirt" for heavy infantry.
Dagon--fish god of the Philistines.

Dahveed--(dah-*veed*), probably "Beloved one." May have been used to designate an important or "beloved" leader in war. It is used in this context in this book, although there is much argument over the word's ancient usage and meaning.
Dod--(dohd), kinsman, uncle, indicates close kinsman relationship.
Dodi--(doh-*dee*), my uncle.
Geber--(*gehb*-behr), masculine title of respect: master or sir.
Geberet--(geh-*behr*-eht), feminine title of respect: mistress or ma'm.
Gebirah--(geh-*beer*-ah), the woman in whom the kingdom is embodied. She is also called the "Handmaid." Whomever the gebirah marries will have the right to rule the kingdom. The gebirah was normally of the same clan as the royal family, if not the royal family itself. Girdle--wide wrap of cloth or soft leather wrapped around the waist to hold a robe together and provide a place to put things.
Great Sea--Ancient name for the Mediterranean Sea.
Habiru--(hah-*bee*-roo), name for bands of nomads, usually small, which roamed Israel during the time of David. They were composed of landless family units or displaced persons from the twelve tribes or any of the surrounding nations. Their main occupation was as mercenaries, but many bands simply supported themselves by robbery and murder. Habiru can refer to the entire band, or a single member of it.
Hakkohen Haggadol--(hah-koh-*hayn* hah-gah-*dohl*), the High Priest.
Hallelu--(hahl-lay-*loo*), second person plural command. "You (all of you) praise."
Hamsin--(hahm-*seen*), harsh dry east wind from the desert.
Hassar--(hah-*sahr*), *The* prince, hence first or crown prince.
Hassarah--(hah-sahr-*ah*), *The* princess/queen, hence most important princess/queen.
Henna--reddish stain from plants used to decorate nails and skin.
Hesed--(*hes*-ed), voluntary kindness on the life-saving level provided by the only one able to give it.
Jebus--ancient name for the city which became Jerusalem.
Kohen--(koh-*hayn*), priest.
Leben--(*leh*-behn), curdled milk, churned in a skin bag and used for food.
Mashiah--(mah-shee-*ah*), anointed one.
Meil--(may-*eel*), expensive, richly embroidered tunic worn only by

royalty.

Melek--(*mel*-ek) King. Dahveed was anointed as melek.

Nahsi--(nah-*see*), also Nasi, masculine title of respect: high/governing lord. Carries the connotation of political/judicial authority.

Nagid--(*nah*-geed) Prince, captain or leader. Used in this book as the next step down from king. Shaul was anointed as nagid.

Pithoi–Plural of pithos

Pithos–Large pottery jars used for storage. They were wide at the top and tapered to a near point at the bottom.. A grain pithos could be six feet tall and 30 inches across at the widest point, just under the neck.

Roeh--(Roh-*eh*), seer or prophet.

Sahrah--(sah-*rah*), feminine title of respect: princess, queen.

Sar--(sahr), masculine title of respect: prince. In Philistia it means "commander".

Salt Sea--Ancient name for the Dead Sea.

Sea of Chinnereth--Ancient name for the Sea of Galilee.

Seren--(*seh*-rehn), Philistine title equivalent to Sar/Nagid.

Sereni--(Seh-rehn-*ee*), my seren.

Shephelah--the gently rolling hills between the coastal plain by the Mediterranean Sea and the central hills of Palestine west of the Jordan River.

Shobeh--(sho-*beh*), captor.

Yah's fire--Lightning. Lightning was considered fire from the god of the land.

Zammar-(zah-*mahr*), singer.

Cultural Notes

Blood Guilt--The murder of a person always brought the curse of blood-guilt, which could only be cleared with blood. If someone murdered or killed a person, the victim's family would appoint a "redeemer (goel) of the blood" to track down and execute the individual responsible, creating the need for the cities of refuge. A person who caused accidental death could flee to them and be safe from the avenging Goel of the Blood.

As for someone found murdered out in the forest or on the road somewhere, the land itself had incurred blood-guilt, and there was a specific sacrifice and ritual associated with cleansing the land of the murdered person's blood, and thus removing the curse from the land and/or any nearby towns. Curses were terrible punishments and greatly feared since the gods or Yahweh enforced them, and there was no protection from Yahweh's curse.

Clothing and Honor--Clothing was a social signal of status. In addition, it literally bestowed authority. To this day, we still have investiture ceremonies wherein those assuming certain offices receive the clothing (the vestments) symbolizing the position. We just don't continue to wear that costume every day!

The opposite of "invest" is "divest," and if we divest someone of something, we strip away the associated vestments, and thus the authority (as when a dishonored soldier will have his insignia of rank torn off). The possession of a high office brought with it the obligation to wear the clothing of that office, so people would know who held what position. By wearing the garments associated with an office, a person laid claim to that authority. Because of this, simply wearing the king's clothing could be an act of treason.

Family Relationships--Family was of primary importance in the ancient Near East. However, families were organized differently than they are today. The closest bond a person had was with siblings, not parents. Society expected brothers and sisters to look out for each other and be each other's confidants and advisors. The husband-wife relationship was more of a business/contractual partnership than anything else. The ancient world did not assume that a wife must love her husband. While she should be loyal to him, her supportive relationships would come from her family of origin, and she would not be counted part of her husband's family until she bore a son. The closest bond for a married woman was with her son, who was expected to stand up for her against all comers, even his father if necessary, and who would care for her in her old age. The function of a father (as we understand it today) was not performed by the man who sired you, but by your mother's brother, your maternal uncle. He was the one responsible for emotional support, teaching, and guidance.

Forever--In biblical times, forever meant "as long as one or other of the parties swearing live." Since Jonathan asked for hesed for his "house" and his family would presumably continue for generations, Dahveed must swear for as long as he (Dahveed) shall live, as he would not expect to outlive the generations in Jonathan's family. This is why Joab later flees to the tabernacle altar when he hears that Dahveed has died. Any covenant of protection given to him "forever" ceases to be, since with Dahveed's death, "forever" is over. That is also why the death of an overlord king demanded that all the under-kings renew their allegiance even though they swore to be faithful forever. The other party had died, so forever had ended. Of course, not all the under-kings would want to renew a covenant, which usually precipitated war.

Gebirah--The Gebirah was the woman who owned the land, and so embodied that land. Whoever married her "married" the land and became its ruler. The idea of the Gebirah had several variations in ancient times. In Egypt any woman in the palace could be named Gebirah, so to be safe the Pharoah married them all. However in Edom, one woman was Gebirah, (and her daughter probably became the next Gebirah) and whoever married her became the next king of Edom. The Hittites had a position similar to the Gebirah that also carried religious duties. The woman was appointed to the position, and held it for life independently of other political changes. The institution of Gebirah existed in Israel until King Asa, as attested in 1 Kings 15:13 and 2 Chronicles 15:16. The word is usually translated as "queen mother" in these verses.

Gibeonites-- The Gibeonites lived in four cities occupying the heart of the territory of Ephraim west of Jebus/Jerusalem--Gibeon, Beeroth, Chephirah, and Kiriath Jearim. See Joshua 9 for the beginning of their service to the tabernacle. The genealogies in 1 Chronicles 8: 29-34 and 9:35-40 give clear indication that Shaul's clan descended from Gibeon.

Harp or Lyre--The ancient Israelites had two stringed instruments that scholars have been able to identify as a harp or a lyre. Unfortunately, they have not be able to determine which Hebrew name goes with which instrument! Therefore, some say the instrument Dahveed played for Shaul was a lyre, others say a harp. Since "common knowledge" regards Dahveed as playing a harp, I chose that term.

Hesed--Most modern translation render the Hebrew word as "loving-kindness." Sometimes it is translated "mercy," but both renderings leave out some of the important connotations of the Hebrew idea. Hesed can only come from the one person who must act in order to preserve another's life. This makes it the perfect word to describe what God does for us. If He didn't act, we'd all die, and He is the only one whose action will give us life. Therefore, He gives hesed.

Honor--Honor was the grease that made ancient society work, much as money does in Western societies. We can think of honor as the respect and approval of one's community. To understand honor, imagine it as a credit rating. Without honor, the avenues open to a man to support himself and his family were severely limited, much as a bad credit rating hampers a person today. Anything that would make people think less of a person or their family reduced the family honor. Keeping and maintaining honor, therefore, was of primary importance, and one had to measure every action against what people would think of it.

Generally speaking for people on the same status level, older persons had more honor than younger ones. All honor belonged to someone, and gaining honor meant that someone else lost it. Where honor came from was very important, and being greedy about honor brought dishonor! Also generally speaking, richer people had more honor than poorer ones, but only relatively so. The most honorable man in town didn't have to be the one with the most possessions. To be rich without honor meant a person was greedy, and so society despised them. But to be rich with honor meant a person was wealthy, and therefore blessed and honored.

Honor Wars--Honor wars involved what we today call "disrespecting" someone. Such wars could only develop between persons of the same status. Therefore, a householder could not have an honor war with a servant--only with another householder who held the same amount of honor in the eyes of the community. Servants could have honor wars with each other, but not with their master/employer. One could show disrespect in either overt or subtle ways. Deliberately not bowing low enough to someone would slight their honor. Refusing to look at another person could do the same, as well as the order in which you spoke to people when in their presence. If an honor slight was given, the person slighted was obligated to either protest the slight or return it in some way, or else lose honor in the eyes of the community. Wars could also develop, though, over compliments and gift giving. Any gift/compliment received brought the obligation to return a gift/compliment of equal value, otherwise one lost honor to the giver. Any and all society interaction, therefore, had to be carefully viewed and calculated to take honor into account.

Israel and Judah Separate--During the time of Shaul and Dahveed, Israel and Judah were considered distinct political entities, which is the reason that the Bible names them separately in so much of Scripture. This may hark back to Genesis 38:1 which tells us that Judah separated himself from his brothers and lived around Adullam. What was involved in this separation, how long it lasted, and how it affected his relationship with Jacob and the rest of his family we don't know. In any case, Judah was apart from the rest, and many of the stories in Judges never mention the tribe. Archaeology reveals that during the time of Shaul and Dahveed, Judah was very sparsely populated and people lived at subsistence level. Only around Hebron do we find some measure of wealth. The separation between Israel and Judah continued during the "United Monarchy," preserved in the differing political arrangements between the two countries and their king, who simply happened to be the same person.

Marriage--Attitudes toward marriage were very different in the ancient Near East. Marriage was more of a business partnership/political partnership than a relationship of love and trust. A woman was not expected to love her husband or to look to him for emotional support. His job was to supply her physical needs and give her children, particularly sons, who would then support her in her old age. Emotional support came from the woman's siblings/family of origin. Pre-nuptial agreements were the norm, with everything expected from each side of the union spelled out. This included what would happen in case of divorce. Rights for the woman and her children were explicitly stated.

Given the above attitudes, having more than one wife was simply a matter of how many you could support. And only those who were rich/of high status could support more than one. Thus multiple wives was a sign of status.

From the political side of things, almost any alliance with a neighboring country/king necessitated a marriage. Thus God's prohibition that Israel's kings were not to multiply wives had a very strong political side to it. Israel was not to have a lot of alliances with surrounding countries.

However, by the time of Dahveed, much, if not most, of God's counsel on these matters had been lost. Remember, Shamuel had to write up a book of judgments when Shaul became king. Therefore, the cultural attitudes in Israel matched those of the surrounding peoples.

Marriage was a rather easy-come, easy-go affair with one exception. The woman must always be provided with support to sustain her life and that of her children if there were any. This concern seems to have remained even when other parts of God's counsel didn't. These attitudes explain why Shaul could so easily sever the union between Dahveed and Michal, why he could give Michal to another man, why Dahveed felt free to marry other women, and why concubinage was accepted. As long as the woman was provided for, her "social security" was in place, things were fine.

Honorable men could have what we would term an affair today, and no one blinked an eye. Indeed, if the woman involved was from a lower status family, her connection to a higher status man was a distinct advantage to her house and clan, one not to be despised. (For example, Atarah's connection to Hassar Jonathan in Book 2.) However, if the affair ended, for whatever reason, the woman must be decently provided for, on pain of loss of honor to the man. (And remember, loss of honor was a very serious thing.)

Money--People in Israel in Dahveed's time didn't have money or even coins as we know them. They had pieces of precious metals, and traded them for goods, although most "buying and selling" was actually trading for goods in kind. (For instance, "I'll give you this goat for that much grain.") As a result, jewelry was as much currency as it was body decoration. In my book Ruth and Boaz I do use the term "gerah" to indicate pieces of gold, silver, etc., since it seemed the most convenient to do so. However, in this book, I decided that simply saying "piece" gave more of the flavor of the times.

Power--Just as today, power in Bible times brought responsibility. Much power in the Bible had its origin in influence, and influence was based on honor (see above.) In other words, honor brought power. With death and/or disaster able to descend in so many ways, people eagerly sought anything that might protect the family, and power opened up ways to ease the family's position and provide a small cushion between the family and death. Therefore, when an individual acquired honor/power they were compelled by social norms and sheer survival to seek ways to use that power to benefit their family first, then anyone connected with the family. Because power was connected to honor, however, it must be employed very carefully to avoid anything that would detract from honor, and thus lessen the power itself.

Preserving a Name--The most important thing in the culture of the ancient Near East was to preserve a name and/or an inheritance. Many had no belief in an afterlife, such as that held by the Egyptians, or of an immortal soul that lived on after the body died, such as the Greeks developed. (Christians today get the idea of an immortal soul from the Greeks.) The ancient Israelites believed that when you died, you perished. The concept of eternal life was actually one of eternal remembrance. If a person's descendants remembered their name, that's how the person survived death. They lived on in memory, for a person's name was the person. This made having descendants of utmost importance, since who else would remember your name? To die childless was the ultimate death. The chances of having descendants greatly increased if they had land to live on, making the preservation of the family land of paramount importance also.

Shalom--We do not know the "standard greeting" that the ancient Israelites employed, if indeed they had one. But because modern dialog is so used to having a standard greeting, I have picked the word "Shalom" for it, since this word is already closely associated with Israel.

Teraphim--Teraphim--spirits or gods who protected a house--were part of the Elohim, supernatural beings ranging from spirits and demons on up to the gods. Spirits lurked everywhere and could act for or against humans. It was wise to remain on their good side through offering sacrifices and gifts. Fortunately, all spirits and gods were tied to a geographical location, and their power weakened quickly when outside the geographic area. Crossing a border meant leaving the power of one god and coming under that of another. House gods, teraphim, could only guard a single house, a hill spirit could only operate on that single hill, etc. A god's power was directly tied to the amount of territory he could function in. Thus the more territory a king conquered for his deity, the stronger the god became. That is why war was a sacred activity.

Titles--Hebrew has several titles of respect. I have decided to use them, somewhat arbitrarily, in the following order from least respect to greatest. Geber (sir)--adon (lord)/baal (lord)--sar (prince)--nahsi (governing lord)--nagid (ruling prince)--melek (king). Feminine titles are as follows: Geberet (ma'am)--baalah (lady)--sahrah (princess)--Hassarah (queen.) The Philistines also had sars, but for them, "sar" was the equivalent of the Hebrew "commander" The word they used for "sar" or "prince" was "seren."

In Hebrew, as in many other languages other than English, the title normally follows the name rather than preceding it. But to make it easier for my readers, I have used the English convention, unless the title appears in its most formal sense. Also in Hebrew, it is more courteous to call someone simply by their title. Only intimate family or very close friends would have used the personal names of respected persons. Thus, at first Dahveed refers to Jonathan as "Hassar Jonathan," or "Hassar." For very formal introductions, or when a personage is being called on in their formal capacity, Jonathan's name would be "Jonathan ben Shaul, Hassar Israel," with the title last. It will behoove the reader to pay attention to how people employ the titles in the story!

Transfer of the Throne--The time of Shaul/Dahveed/Solomon was very uncertain politically for the emerging nation of Israel/Judah. Many of the same problems occurred between the tribes as troubled the states here in the U.S.A. under the Articles of Confederation before the adoption of the American Constitution and the inauguration of George Washington as president. Each tribe was independent--indeed each town and clan were autonomous and provincial in outlook. Shaul rose to power on the need for protection from the Philistines, and "ruled" only through his alliances with the elders of towns and tribes who followed him because he was the best one at keeping the Philistines out of the highlands. Dahveed inherited this chiefdom, and gradually moved it toward a monarchy. The old autonomous ways, however, resurfaced after Solomon died, producing the divided kingdom.

As in every political entity, the transfer of power was important, and since Shaul was the first "king," Israelites had no precedent to follow. In the ancient Near East power normally transferred in one of three ways. When the old king died, the throne could pass by inheritance to his son, or return back to the Gebirah (see above) who might or might not be the king's daughter or relative. Her husband, if she had one, became the next king. The throne could also transfer by popular acclaim, the candidate the most people liked getting the position. This method usually disintegrated into civil war with any number of sides until one candidate slaughtered all the rest, or a foreigner with a bigger army invaded and seized the throne. If he married into the previous royal family, he could be accepted. Often, however, the fact of his foreign blood would trigger rebellion against his son or his house--perhaps even generations later.

In the case of Shaul and Dahveed, it is clear that Dahveed rivaled Jonathan in popular acclaim, and married to Michal he became a son of the king. If Michal was named Gebirah, Dahveed would have a very strong claim to the throne no matter which way Shaul chose to pass it on. Hence Shaul's eagerness to remove Dahveed from the picture to assure that Jonathan, the son of his blood, would get to rule.

Units of Measure--I decided to use modern units of measure for terms of length since the flow of the story would not be interrupted while the reader tried to equate ancient ones with their modern counterparts.

A Word About . . .

Geography:

In 1 Samuel 23 when Shaul finds Dahveed at Maon, the geography in the Bible is so confusing that scholars and commentators cannot agree on where the events take place. Therefore, I have ignored the mention of Dahveed in the Arabah, since it is difficult to go "down" to a rock from there, and any mountains would be above the Arabah.

First Samuel 23 has the hill of Hakilah south of Jeshimon, but in 1 Samuel 26 it is "before" Jeshimon. Furthermore, in 1 Samuel 23 Shaul goes to the wilderness of Maon to find Dahveed around the hill of Hakilah, but in 1 Samuel 26, Dahveed retreats to the wilderness of Ziph and camps on the hill of Hakilah. All that is clear is the general area where these places are. I have, therefore, simply picked spots with geography attuned to the needs of the story.

We also struggle with the problem of Dahveed going to the wilderness of Paran (1 Samuel 25:1), which is way down south of the Negev. Most Bibles will note that the word Paran should probably be Maon, as it is in the Septuagint (the ancient Greek translation of the Old Testament). Since, the story is not told chronologically (see below), so we don't exactly know when Shamuel died or when Dahveed moved to Maon. I have chosen to place the latter after his meeting with Nabal.

I also mention the "land stair" to the Shephelah. Remember, Palestine has two rises of land from the coastal plains (Philistia) to the highlands (Israel/Judah). The first rose about 200-300 feet to a plateau with rolling hills called the Shephelah. The next "stair" rose 1200-1500 feet to the central plateau of Canaan and the countries of Judah and Israel. Both rises could be very abrupt because of cliffs and rock ramparts. The rises also gradually smoothed out the farther south you went toward the Negev.

Let's move on to . . .

The way I wrote this book: As with my other books, one of my purposes is to tell these stories in their proper historical and cultural context. This means that I present them from the perspective of the protagonist using the mindset, attitudes, and accepted ways of the world as they were understood back in the late Bronze Age/Early Iron Age when Dahveed lived. Details and comments in the Bible make it clear that Israel and Judah in Shaul and Dahveed's time were very much a part of the Bronze Age culture of the ancient Near East, just as we are part of our culture today. Therefore, to really appreciate much of what these stories have to say, we must forget our own ideas of "the way things should be" and put ourselves in the sandals of the biblical characters, attempting to view their lives and times using the same perspective that they had back then. And speaking of time, let's have a word about . . .

Chronology: As I've discussed in my previous books, historians argue endlessly about chronology. Ancient history has only one generally accepted firm date, and that is 664 B.C. (or B.C.E. if you prefer) and the end of the third intermediate period in Egypt. Every date previous to that one, and many after it, are simply educated guesses. Some guesses are more firm than others, and the further back one goes, the more "guess" enters the picture. The usual estimate for the beginning of Dahveed's reign is around 1000 B.C., give or take 50 years, with Solomon taking the throne around 970 B.C. (with the same margin of error).

The other very important aspect of chronology is that the Bible comes to us from an oral tradition. All the accounts in the Bible were originally told verbally and only written down much later. This means that the stories about Bible characters are presented in thematic sequence, not necessarily in straight chronological sequence. Such a realization is vital for our understanding of them, a fact that should not be surprising. When you are telling someone what happened to you during a period of several days or weeks, you don't relate everything that occurred between the events that you consider relevant. You skip those until you have told the entire connected sequence. Then, if there is some other theme you want to discuss, you go "back in time" and begin another sequence.

The biblical author presents the stories of Dahveed's life in exactly this way. This means, of course, that we don't know how much time may have passed between specific events in a sequence, or even how the sequences actually fit together in straight chronological order. We can only guess. Note, for example, the amount of time I have put between Goliath's death and the covenant between Dahveed and Jonathan.

English readers, however, are used to written history and stories proceeding in straight chronological sequence. Again, to make it easier for my readers, I have given my best "guess" at the chronological sequence of many of the events in Dahveed's life. At times, however, I have followed the thematic sequence, and then "gone back in time" to pick up the narrative in another place. (For those of you who are curious, yes, this thematic sequence is indicated in the Hebrew. It involves the use of the Hebrew letter *vav*, about which Hebrew scholars argue with as much verve as historians do about chronology.) Now, let's move on to a word about . . .

The Ark: The "ark narrative," as scholarly circles call it, is the fragmented account of the whereabouts of the ark of the covenant that interweaves through Scripture from Exodus to Chronicles. Trying to piece the picture together is always iffy. What becomes clear is that the ark was not always lodged within the tabernacle after the Philistines destroyed the tabernacle at Shiloh during Samuel's time. Whither and how far the ark may have wandered after that is unclear in the narrative. We find indications that Shaul had access to the ark during his reign, which would mean it was probably within the tabernacle at Nob. What is very clear, however, is that when Dahveed brought it to Jerusalem, he didn't get it from the tabernacle, which was probably at Gibeon by then. (We know the tabernacle was there because that's where Solomon went after his ascension to the throne to seek God.) Presumably, the ark became separated from the tabernacle at the destruction of Nob.

Where was it during Dahveed's fugitive years? There is a good chance that Dahveed had it with him. Context is clear in the David narrative that the word "ephod," when not modified by "linen," cannot refer to a garment, but to some kind of solid object. In addition, Solomon, when sparing Abiathar's life at the time Adonijah made a bid for the throne, specifically says he is doing so because, "you carried the ark of the Lord God before my father David, and because you shared in all the hardships my father endured" (1 Kings 2:26, NRSV; some other versions use the word "afflicted" instead of "hardships.")

The only time this could have happened was after the destruction of Nob when Abiathar fled to David, and the "ephod came down by his [Abiathar's] hand" (literal translation of 1 Samuel 23:6.) Notice that Abiathar is not the subject/active agent in the Hebrew text. The ephod itself is. Such action would never be attributed to a piece of clothing. But the culture at the time would attribute such actions to the gods through the item they dwelt in. I have, therefore, placed the ark with Dahveed during his wandering years. My apologies if this offends anyone.

Now a word about . . .

Names: Specifically Ahithophel and Mephibosheth. Both names most likely received their present form from scribes editing Samuel's books. At the time of the editing, David was a national hero, and anyone who opposed him was obviously a bad person. Names were then altered to indicate this. We have Mephibosheth's real name,

Meribbaal, which is what I use in the book. But Ahithophel's real name has not survived in the record. However, other name changes indicate that "thophel" was often substituted for "baal," which in David's time simply meant "husband" or "lord" or "owner." Only later did it become the popular name of the Canaanite god. Ahithophel's name could, therefore, have been Ahibaal, and that is what I use. In addition to being a nicer name for the man, it's also shorter. That means less to type. When it comes to typing, I'm lazy.

Now turn the page and enjoy. . .

Tamar bat Dahveed

Welcome back to all of you! I'm glad you came early today, for the next part of my abbi's story is quite long. But it is filled with some of the funniest things that happened, as well as some of the most exciting. Does everyone have some of the bread? Is there olive oil enough?

How kind of you, young geber. That cushion is just what I needed. And here's the harp and signet ring. We'll need that ring this time, for it has another part to play in our story. Now, where were we?

That's right, Dahveed had just married Sahrah Michal. You'll remember what a hard road that was for the young shepherd, called to play for the demon-tormented king. After he saved the kingdom by killing the Philistines' giant champion, he could not swear loyalty to King Shaul and so was enslaved. If Jonathan Hassar hadn't given his friendship to the young man, even though he knew by then that Dahveed would be the next king, I don't know what would have happened.

When Dahveed's military prowess saved the king and kingdom again, Shaul made him general in place of Abner, and Dahveed found himself thrust into an entirely new life. He nearly ran when the hassar let slip that he knew Dahveed was Mashiah, only remaining when Jonathan bowed to him and forced him to claim his true status while making a covenant with him. And with Jonathan's help, Dahveed learned how to act as a sar.

His first war season as general, however, began with the ambush at Zorah when he failed to heed Yah's warnings. Dahveed learned his lesson then, which led to the victory at Lehi and brought an Egyptian follower of Yah named Mahesa into his life.

Back at Gibeah, however, Shaul's increasingly erratic behavior, brought on by the plotting of Balak ben Hod, heralded the return of the demon. This time, Dahveed called on El Shaddai to free the king forever. El Shaddai honored his request, but Shaul feared Dahveed from that day forward, and banished him from his presence, demoting him from general to commander of the second unit, much to Balak's satisfaction.

Yahweh worked that to Dahveed's good, however, when Dahveed trained the second unit into a powerful fighting force, thereby saving Sar Malchi the day the Philistines attacked the Israelite army camp at Birzaith after luring away Abner and most of the army. The second unit became the Sar's Own, and Dahveed returned in triumph, only to find that the praise of the people had turned Shaul against him even more. The king refused to give Merab to him as wife, his promised reward for killing Goliath. Michal rejoiced in this, for as you recall, she wanted to marry Dahveed herself, and now the way was open for her to do so.

Yahweh chose this time to reveal to Jonathan the sin of his abbi against the Gibeonites, but the hassar had to feel the sword of Yahweh at his throat before he would believe. He knew then that he must take the throne, but the thought was so painful for him that he only began to limit his abbi, thinking he could keep Shaul from dishonor to Yah that way. He will learn his mistake, but only after terrible cost.

Advised by Balak, who was working now not just to become honorable, but to become king, Shaul tried again to rid himself of Dahveed by offering Michal for a wife as a reward for killing Philistines. Dahveed found that he wanted Michal and the honor that she would bring him, and in less time than Shaul imagined, Dahveed had collected twice the bride price of Philistine foreskins, binding himself to a young half-blood Philistine named Ittai in the process. When Dahveed presented the bride price, Shaul was pleased and accepted him again, formally sealing the betrothal.

Enraged at Dahveed's success, Balak once again goaded the king into turning against Dahveed. He miscalculated, however, and his own part in the demon attack on Shaul and the Gibeonite killings came to light as Jonathan Hassar raged through town at the treason charge Shaul had leveled at the zammar.

Balak escaped, and the king longed for his zammar again. Jonathan elicited Shaul's oath that Dahveed would not die, and then brought Dahveed to him. And this time, Dahveed received his reward, marrying Michal and becoming Sar.

But now, after only seven months of marriage, another war

season is at hand, and once more Yahweh will use Dahveed to deliver Israel and give Shaul another chance to honor Yah's gift to him as he should. And there is more that Yah must do, for down in Judah lives a very beautiful, intelligent, and troubled woman whose life has just reached the breaking point.

Prologue

Abigail, Gebirah Carmel, sat under the almond tree beside the back wall of her husband's business chamber. The small walled garden had been built for her shortly after she married Nabal, now nagid of her clan. A grape vine grew by the gate, and the almond tree fought for space with the pistachio and olive trees. The tiny pool was supposed to have water plants in it, but it had proved too difficult to keep full during the hot summers, and now only dust coated the rocks littering the bottom.

Shifting on the wooden bench, she leaned back, staring at the dry depression in the ground. She knew that if the pool had dried up before harvest, it meant that there had not been enough rain for the crops. But that didn't matter this year, for the locust had descended in their swarms, leaving nothing in their wake.

Now her people needed her. In spite of the seclusion that Nabal had encouraged, she had seen the desperation in their eyes and overheard enough to know that many clans faced famine. And she was useless to them. As she had always been. As her abbi had been.

Her hands trembled a little as they smoothed the black meil she was embroidering. How she had loved and idolized her abbi. He had taken her everywhere after her immi died, because she was the Gebirah. She owned and embodied the land, he had explained, and had the best warriors, and the richest fields, and the most influence and honor of anyone ever in the history of the clans. And whomever she married would rule all that she owned, just as he ruled because he had married her immi, and as her daughter's husband would rule after her.

He had painted a wonderful picture, and for years she had accepted the expensive clothes and jewelry, the handmaids, and the honor without thought, for she was the kingdom! But her world had crashed around her the day that she didn't call for a handmaid the moment she woke up, and so overheard their conversation.

"I wouldn't be her for anything," Matred had said. "My brothers say the nagid is so indebted that all his income for years wouldn't repay everything!"

"I don't know about that," Namea had answered. "Abbi said that if he was careful, he could repay the creditors in three or four years, but he can't resist getting things for the Gebirah."

"My brothers say it's a disgrace the way things are going. They say we need a real leader as nagid."

"What do they mean by that? My abbi said this nagid has done better than anyone at keeping the adons from quarreling, and Immi says that's good!" Namea declared.

"Well, that can't last because of all the nagid's debts. The Gebirah will have to marry whoever can pay the most instead of someone who can really rule," Matred added.

"Makes her sound like a slave sold off to the highest bidder," Tirzah had giggled. "I'd hate having to marry someone like that. I know my abbi and immi will be sure that I like whomever they pick. They've already asked me about a couple young men!"

"Really?" Matred had exclaimed. "My parents haven't said a thing yet. Who have they asked you about?"

Talk had turned to suitors, and Abigail had been careful to give no indication that she had heard anything when she called them later, but she had been furious. Vowing to prove that her abbi would never do what they had suggested, she had looked forward to disproving her handmaids with the truth.

Now an ironic smile touched her lips as she traced the swirling line of red thread on the black cloth with her finger. The truth had been far worse than the gossip. Once she had learned the reality of her life, such as how much land her abbi had sold already, she stopped asking for things and declined his offers to buy her gifts. But no matter what she did, the debts piled higher.

In another year, when her exceptional beauty became apparent, her abbi had welcomed the rivalry among the adons, selling her face again and again for rich gifts from families trying to influence his decision about her marriage. She had come to hate the way that she looked, all the while knowing that men twice her age would become stuttering fools after one glance at her. Within months her abbi had paid off most of his debts.

Then a wealthy Calebite from much further south in Edom had arrived, offering more on behalf of his son than any of the others. The nagid had strung the man along until he'd visited three or four times, bringing more expensive gifts every time. Abigail had known by then that her duty was to welcome the highest bidder, so she was prepared when her abbi announced that he'd selected Nabal to be her husband.

Her finger switched to a blue thread edged with a silver one. It was the last incomplete line on the garment, and her finger paused above it. Although Nabal had been a disappointment in looks, with his pointed chin and receding forehead, his reverential treatment of her made up for that. True, he had never excited her in bed the way she'd overheard would happen when she married, but she was Gebirah, and her function was to produce at least one daughter and some sons. It was another duty, the one that she'd failed first.

But Nabal hadn't complained, for as the next nagid, he spent all his time with her abbi, learning how to rule, while she set up the household. Then Abbi died. Nabal had been precise in following the path laid out for him, but if something happened for which her abbi hadn't given detailed instructions, he didn't know what to do. The difficulties began then. She had been unable to help much, for she knew little of the people or situations involved. A couple years after that, King Shaul from Israel had come through Carmel after his victory over the Amalekites, and Hezro had arrived, and Nabal's love for riches had appeared along with Tokhath, the scribe from beyond the Euphrates River.

Taking her thread, she worked her way along that last line, following the silver thread which edged it. Tonight, she would give the meil to Tirzah, uncaring what happened to it. Her handmaid would give her another to work on, and Abigail would find some solace from her life again.

The door in the room on the other side of the wall slammed shut. The Gebirah raised her head. This was why she had waited so quietly.

"Well, Tokhath?" Nabal's nasal tone drifted down to her.

"It can be done, Nagid. There is grain, and you should be able to acquire it."

"Excellent, excellent," her husband replied, and Abigail knew that he was rubbing his hands together as he always did when he was pleased.

She remained motionless. Not long after the Israelite king had left, a squirrel had dug a home in the mud brick wall up by the protruding beam over her head. The creature had made a large hole with an opening above the chair that Nabal always sat in. The day she discovered she could hear what went on in the room was the day that she had barred everyone else from her garden. She'd made certain the chamber hangings shadowed the hole, and the things she overheard allowed her to accept her husband's more unpleasant decisions and increasingly greedy business deals with a calmness that had now become legendary.

"We must begin buying," Nabal spoke again. "We'll need a lot of grain. Go to the merchants first."

"Won't merchants charge a lot?" the scribe questioned. "What if you went to Sar Dahveed first since he is from the south. If he has nothing, he should be able to direct you to sympathetic sellers with lower prices."

"Yes, try that first. Arrange for transport, also. If we store the grain, we will only need one or two caravans to bring it south."

"Have you considered transporting the grain in small lots?" Tokhath asked. "If people think there isn't much available, they will pay more."

"Yes, they will. Do this," Nabal commanded, his voice pleased.

"Yes, Nagid. Shall we begin selling with the head elder of Debir? I could open his ear about the small amount you have found for purchase, and do the same in Adoraim. There are also several adons and land-owners near Eshtemoa who could pay a good price, and of course, there is always Jezreel."

"Good. We will wait to fill our own granaries until the second or third trip. I'll know more about the prices then since we will be charging our people the same as we do everyone else."

The scribe said nothing for a time. "The people will be unable to buy much, Nagid," he ventured finally. "Might it be better to--"

"Do you dare question my decision?" the nagid snapped.

"No, of course no," Tokhath quickly responded.

Abigail looked down at her clenched hands. She couldn't be certain exactly what Nabal was planning, but it would be profitable whatever it was. And the nagid's affinity for wealth had produced increasingly richer gifts for his wife. What would he buy for her this time?

¥ ¥ ¥ ¥ ¥ ¥

Harvest was nearly upon us the day I looked out over my courtyard from the roof of my business chamber, smiling at the sight of Josheb hauling water from the cistern as slowly as possible so he could have a few moments longer to talk to Keturah. He still wooed the Gibeonite woman, who showed herself surprisingly resistant to him.

Ahiam was now married to Jemima, Palti of Gallim's sister. Thinking of her made me chuckle. I would never forget the dazed look on Palti's face the day he stumbled from my gate, trying to comprehend how he had just been convinced to marry his sister to a Habiru! Jemima and Ahiam now had the room on the south wall that Ornan and Atarah had vacated. The two Jebusites had acquired a house near the old market by the north gate.

Jamin had also moved, locating a place outside the walls close to the eastern height, conducting Ethan's business from there. Keturah and Naharai, the Gibeonites from Beeroth, occupied the second room on the south wall, Shagay and Josheb the third, and I used the one nearest the gate as my business chamber.

As I watched, Shagay returned from his visit to Bethlehem, looking troubled.

"What is it?" I asked after we greeted each other.

"Locust took all the crops from Bethlehem to Beersheba. With the poor harvests the past four years, there are no reserves, so when last year's grain gives out, there will be nothing to eat."

"Bethlehem, too?"

Shagay looked at me sidewise. "Bethlehem has sufficient for food and seed next year, even though locust ate the fields down to dust, because of your brother Nethanel," my retainer said. "Last year, he stubbornly refused to sell a single grain of your abbi's crops, storing it instead, and then buying enough from Moab to fill the granaries to the top."

"What made him do that?"

"When Hassarah Ruth talked with him that last time, she told him that when the fourth year of bad harvests came, he was to fill the storehouses full, and get the town to do the same. Once he mentioned her name in connection with his actions, everyone followed suit, even though they teased him about being Bethlehem's Joseph. They are thanking him now."

"Things are that bad?" I said soberly.

"They are, adoni," my first retainer replied. "The Habiru down there have nothing at all. Several bands look to Ethan, and he's trying to find ways they can feed themselves. The men can join the army, but that doesn't help the women and children. Or provide seed for next fall."

I fretted over the situation, knowing this meant homes and inheritances lost, many times never to be regained, and starving people roaming the land looking for any way to survive.

Jonathan and Gibeah

CHAPTER 1

Wheat harvest was nearly finished and the clear sky arched over me as I climbed the streets of the town from the west gate. The second unit had just distinguished itself in the spring mock battle, and the men of the Sar's Own were justly proud of themselves. For the first time ever, the second unit had more men left standing on the field than any other unit when the battle was called.

It was close to dusk when I walked through my gate to find Ethan pacing in front of my business chamber. "Shalom! What brings you here?" I greeted him, hurrying over.

"Investigating some very nasty rumors," he answered grimly, his eyes flashing in a way I hadn't seen in years. "Did you deal with Nabal of Carmel?"

"Not that I know of."

"You haven't sold any grain?"

"No. The yield from the two estates Shaul gave Michal only produced enough to fill our granaries and supply our contribution to the town."

"No one came to you for grain?"

"A scribe named Tokhath came just before harvest began. But he wanted grain in quantity, so I sent him to Sar Ishvi."

"That's all you did? You didn't have any part in the deal yourself?" Ethan swung around to face me.

"No. Ethan, what is this about?" His sharp questions left me bewildered.

"That scribe worked for Nabal of Carmel. He bought grain, from Sar Ishvi among others, at 10 silver pieces per ephah, five times the going price, " Ethan said, his voice deadly as he paced some more. "He hired four bands of Habiru to guard his shipments and kept them busy transporting it south as it was harvested instead of waiting until the harvest was complete and taking it then."

"Why?" From what little I'd heard of Nabal, he didn't spend silver uselessly.

"The price, Dahveed! Since the grain arrived in small lots, the buyers thought they were getting the tail end of what he had, and he made four to five times what he paid for it!"

I gasped. "That's nearly two month's wages--one gold piece--of profit per ephah!"

"And that means only the very wealthy got any of it," Ethan added. "Nabal had promised the Habiru he'd pay in grain, enough to last the summer for their families. He also assured the bands that you had arranged this deal, which is why they waited until the last shipment was delivered before asking for their pay.

"When they arrived to collect their grain, they received only three ephahs per man. That's all, Dahveed, for two months of hard work, and that won't last more than six weeks! When the men demanded silver to make up the rest of the payment, Nabal said the contract called for grain, and there the grain was. He had armed guards waiting to handle any trouble.

"They took it and left. Then they came to me, demanding retribution from you."

Trying to comprehend everything he'd just told me, I stared at him.

Ethan paused to look across my courtyard. "They trusted your name so much the bands depleted what stores they had, thinking a large payment of grain was on the way. Now the men will turn to robbery before they let their families starve. Everything we've built up will be lost," he finished heavily. "You were my last hope. I hated the thought that you might have enriched yourself like this, but if you had, I planned on having the gold."

His admission that he would even contemplate such a thing told me how desperate he was. I didn't blame him. The more I thought about the situation, the angrier I became. "Wait for me in my business chamber, Ethan. I'm going to see Sar Ishvi," I said, swinging around and stalking out the gate.

Dusk had fully come when I arrived at the sar's business compound. Nearly everyone had gone, and I walked into his upper chamber unannounced.

He looked up from his seat at the wooden table. "Ah, Dahveed, I've been meaning to discuss something with you," he greeted me. "I'm nearly finished if you can wait a moment."

Realizing that someone else was in the dark room, I nodded.

A scribe waited with his cloak already on as the sar stamped a last clay tablet and handed it to him.

"That is all for today," he said.

The man bowed to Ishvi, then to me, and silently left.

"There is something for which I must ask your pardon, Dahveed," Shaul's second son began, startling me. "Did you know that I spent some time in the south?"

"I wasn't aware that you'd traveled," I replied carefully, deciding I should wait before demanding explanations from my brother-in-law.

"Abbi sent me to Pharaoh's representative in Beersheba with token tribute and a letter informing him of how desperately we are trying to fulfill his wishes," Ishvi said with a wry smile over the diplomatic lie. "I hired a Habiru guide to take me through the hills in order to see how southerners lived."

I studied the papyrus lying on the table top. "What did you find?"

"Things that I never would have believed until I saw them for myself. I thought the time of the judges was past, but it's not down there. How have your people survived, Dahveed?" he asked softly.

"Many of them don't."

"I learned that," he said bitterly, making me jerk my head up to see his face in the lamplight.

"Not far south of Hebron, we stopped at the house of a man named Ezra. There were several men at the door, for we had interrupted a dispute over who should get Ezra's widow. Her husband died last year fighting for Shaul in the north. The men kindly directed us to the nearby spring for water, and it was the widow herself who managed to warn us that a leopard regularly watched the spring, terrorizing the people. Her oldest son had tried to kill it and had been killed instead. His name was Jonathan." The sar paused a moment, his hands clenching.

"That woman had nothing, for the neighbors had already taken her land, and she had no way of supporting her second son, Ishvi, and his little sister Merab. I gave her what supplies I could spare and a few pieces of silver. She begged me to take her and her family with us, but I didn't want the burden on the trip south, so I told her either to go north to Keilah and Joel's Habiru, or eastward to Bethlehem and Ethan's band. She was very grateful."

He stopped again, his jaw muscles working.

I remained silent, the unfolding story a familiar one to me. A man died, or a fire came, or the crops failed at the wrong time, and what had been a thriving farmstead crumbled to ruins, leaving the survivors to wander the hills until they found help or died.

"I couldn't forget them, so we stopped on our way back," Sar Ishvi continued. "The farmstead was burned to the ground. Apparently the neighbors wanted what little I had given the widow, and when she refused to surrender it, they killed her and little Merab. Ishvi eluded them for three days. Then my sentry caught him trying to steal some food."

He leaned on his fists on the table. "It's been a long time since I got that angry, Dahveed. My Habiru guide tracked the attackers to the caves they lived in, but they had even less than Ezra's family. The men had run from us of course, and even in my rage, I couldn't deprive the women and children of the pitiful bit they had.

"What do you do in cases like that?" he burst out, staring at me. "Killing the men would only mean the women and children starve. But they murdered that family."

I didn't have an answer. "And the boy?" I asked.

"I brought him back with me. It was the least I could do after abandoning them the first time," my brother-in-law replied, bitterness again dripping from his tone. "He is determined to avenge his family. The lad told me the names of the men who killed them, and I have published them so that they can be punished and Yahweh will not hold the land responsible for the innocent blood of Ezra's family. I just wish I had the answer for how the criminals' families will live."

"Only Yah has that answer," I said quietly. With the accusation against them sent out on the trails, everyone would know they were under Yahweh's curse for murder.

Sar Ishvi turned to me, bowing slightly. "I hope you will also grant me pardon for the words I spoke to you the day you ordered me to go south and drive the Philistines from the hills. I did not know whereof I spoke, and Yahweh has stripped my arrogance from me."

I bent my head in acknowledgment. "Yahweh has the habit of stripping arrogance from us all, Sar, so pardon is freely given. Young Ishvi is fortunate that he has found you as a friend."

"He would have been fortunate had I taken the family with me. But I never dreamed--" the sar broke off, turning away.

"At least you did what you could after that," I reminded him softly.

"It is little enough," the man sighed. "I will do anything I can, for those people are my people now, and maybe my personal harvest will keep a few families alive. Thank you for sending Tokhath. He seemed so anxious for grain. My steward settled on four silver pieces per ephah, and I very nearly sent him away for charging it. I have the impression that most southerners will find that price quite high, especially now."

I prayed that the dim light would hide my face. *Four* pieces? Ethan said Tokhath had paid *ten*. Everything about this deal stank. I asked more questions, gleaning as much information as I could without revealing what Ethan had told me, for I'd decided not to burden the sar by revealing that his second attempt to help the people in the south had been as marred as his first.

The next evening, sitting at the small table in my business chamber, Ethan and I discussed the food shortage in detail. "The only grain I've got is in my own granaries," I sighed. "I can give you what means I have to buy, but it won't be enough, will it?"

My former teacher shook his head. "No, but I'll take anything I can find right now. I haven't got much to buy with at the moment. Word came today that harvests from Mari eastward were poor also, so we're competing against the rich merchants north of Damascus, and prices are the highest I've ever seen."

My heart sank even further.

"How is your band?" I asked.

"We followed Nethanel's lead last year, just as the town did. I'll take your grandmother's word on anything, no matter how long she's been dead. Jesse gave me everything he could, but with prices so high, what would normally be enough won't begin to touch the need now."

Ethan and I explored the problem from every angle that we could think of, but always came back to the same conclusion. The price of grain was too high wherever it was close enough to be delivered when needed, and any affordable grain was too far away to be transported here in time.

The lamp had been refilled, and we started over the hopeless situation again when, hearing a familiar step outside the door, I opened it.

Jonathan ducked his head to enter, and Ethan rose, bowing. "Shalom, Hassar."

"This is a surprise," Jonathan said, smiling. "Shalom, Ethan. How is your band?"

"Faring well, adon."

"And the harvests this year?"

"We have enough."

The hassar glanced at me. "Then why does Ishvi have the

impression that the Habiru in the south need grain?"

I stared at him in amazement.

Jonathan's eyes twinkled. "My brother has developed the habit of discussing things with his chief scribe, Elihu ben Obed, who has a talent for putting together fragmentary evidence that no one else can interpret. What is the situation down there?"

Ethan explained again for the hassar, including the use that Nabal had made of the grain he bought and his treatment of the Habiru.

Although Jonathan's fists clenched as he listened, he said nothing until Ethan finished.

"Have you sold your harvest yet, Hassar?" I asked.

"No. My overseer has sent several impatient messages asking for my reply on several offers, but I haven't had the time to respond."

Rising, Ethan turned his back toward us.

"What kind of price?" I continued.

"The latest figure he sent me was 20 silver per ephah."

I winced.

"Hassar, would you accept something other than silver in payment for your grain?" Ethan inquired in a strange voice as he looked back over his shoulder.

"I might. What else are you offering?"

"You have asked for my services on more than one occasion, Hassar." The Habiru leader straightened his shoulders and faced him. "Would you accept them for the usual six years in exchange for the harvest?"

Jonathan turned to stone. "You would enslave yourself to me?"

"Yes, Hassar. My people will starve, or they will die while trying to steal food just to keep alive. I will do whatever I can to save them from that. Too much will be lost for me to quibble about a little time."

The silence stretched, and I could barely breathe. Knowing how hard it had been for Ethan to stay with me last winter, I couldn't imagine what he would go through placing himself in such a position for six years, even to someone as understanding as the hassar.

"No, Ethan," Jonathan replied at last. "I cannot accept your offer."

The Habiru's shoulders slumped a little, and he looked down, swallowing. "Hassar, would you reconsider? I will serve longer if necessary."

The hassar's eyes flashed dangerously. "Absolutely not, Ethan."

"My people will starve, Hassar--"

"Only if you refuse my offer," Jonathan cut him off.

Ethan looked up.

"I will sell you the harvest from all the crown's lands at last year's prices. I'll throw my personal harvest in also. Malchi may wish to add his, but I'll have to ask."

Swaying a little, Ethan put his hand on the table to steady himself. "Last year's prices were quite low, adon."

"I remember."

"Why would you give us this hesed?" the warrior said finally, tears unheeded in his eyes. "Hardly anyone in the south acknowledges Shaul as king, and most of those you help will be Habiru, or people too needy to support Israel's throne."

"That doesn't mean I don't see them as my people. Should I enrich myself at the cost of their lives? What kind of honor do you think I have?"

"The kind I could willingly swear to were I able. What do you want of me? Surely there is something I can do."

"Just keep finding things for me, such as that Steward of Tahat," Jonathan replied with a smile. "Now, let us settle the details of the sale."

The oddest expression crossed the man's face. "Yes, Hassar."

I sat back while the two discussed what had to be done. Jonathan sent one of his bodyguards to Sar Eshbaal to find out how much grain the crown's lands had yielded this year, and whether or not the third sar wanted to add his harvest to the deal. Once they knew how much grain was available, they discussed payment. Ethan's tone grew very reserved during the negotiations.

"Remember, I'm adding in for the purchase," I interjected.

When Ethan learned how much I could contribute, he relaxed a little.

After they had figured up the final price, the hassar frowned. "That can't be right," he muttered. He went to the door, sending his guard to Eshbaal once more.

Ethan looked puzzled, and while we waited, I knew he was reviewing everything in his mind, double checking the figures.

The guard returned and handed Jonathan a clay tablet. He ran his finger down it. "I thought so," he said. "The price per ephah is incorrect. It should be less, since the price last year was in coppers. I remember Eshbaal gloating over the deal he had found."

The Habiru chieftain frowned.

Jonathan raised his eyes apologetically. "Much as it embarrasses me, I'm afraid I'll have to ask you to re-figure the price using 15 coppers per ephah."

"No one sold grain that low last year," Ethan blurted out.

The hassar raised his eyebrows, his finger tapping the tablet in annoyance. "Are you questioning my word, Habiru? Because if you are, I'll withdraw this offer immediately."

Although he did not answer, Ethan's eyes glazed slightly as he calculated. I leaned forward enough to get a look at the tablet under that tapping finger. From what I could see, Jonathan had been very creative with his estimate of how many coppers made up one silver piece.

Ethan brought his gaze back to the hassar. "I am not such a fool as to question your honor, Hassar. You are an adon, so what else can I do but accept your word? However, please grant me the indulgence to question your addition," he finished wryly.

Jonathan smiled. "The price is agreed?"

"Yes, Hassar, and it is a stiff one, for you have taken every ounce of pride I have in this exchange."

"Maybe I'm not taking yours so much as regaining mine."

The warrior jerked his head up in time to see that crooked smile. "There was not so much at stake when I guided you in the hills, adon."

"Don't be so certain of that," Shaul's oldest son said. "Had you not guided me, I might not have been here to sell you grain. Yahweh has His own ways of granting hesed to His people. He uses whom He wills. I will not turn away from any task given to me."

Coming around the table, Ethan knelt, touching his forehead to the ground as he had to King Shaul. "I can only say thank you. But even so, I do not count the honor debt abandoned. Whatever my band or myself can do for you is yours, Hassar."

"You are more useful to me now than I can make you understand. What little comes to me through Nimshi is more valuable than gold to the kingdom."

The hassar's comment sent a shiver through me, and I felt the touch of Yah's gift in my veins. I cocked my head. "Make Your wishes plain, Yah," I silently requested.

"Surely you have better information sources than myself, adon," Ethan remonstrated as he stood.

"That depends on what I need to know," the hassar replied. "You don't bring me much news about Egypt's court, but learning of the death of an Egyptian courier, and receiving the tablets that you sent proved more valuable than I dare tell you even now."

As Jonathan finished speaking, the thought of how soon Ethan might have learned of the Gibeonite deaths flashed across my mind. How many of those innocent people might still be alive if the hassar had known about the conspiracy soon after it began?

Would it be possible for the focus of Ethan's efforts to change from protecting me to serving the hassar? Even as the idea came, the certainty settled on me that Jonathan needed the information that the Habiru chieftain alone could provide, and I could clearly see the longing in him to repay Jonathan somehow. But for this to happen, Ethan would have to know the true relationship between Jonathan and me.

"If you had no conflicts, would you be willing to serve the hassar?" I asked slowly, looking at him.

"After all that he has done for us, Dahveed, the only honorable return is my allegiance to him. Since Habiru have no honor, I will do anything else I can."

"You have more honor than many other men I know, Ethan. Yahweh does not personally vouch for someone very often," Jonathan put in.

Lowering his head, the warrior flushed at the praise.

I turned to Shaul's son. "You would accept him as an honorable man?"

"I would, and count myself honored to have him."

Holding Ethan's gaze, I rose and put my hand on Jonathan's shoulder, then reached down and stripped both the king's signet ring and Jonathan's own from his unresisting hand. As soon as I put them on, Shaul's son stood and removed his sar's meil, handing it to me. I put it on and sat down, leaving Jonathan standing behind me.

The stunned expression on Ethan's face made both of us smile.

"Jonathan places Yahweh's will above all else," I said.

"Then he does indeed have the kind of honor I could swear to," the Habiru leader replied, turning to the hassar.

There were some grapes and a piece of bread on the table, and Jonathan used that for the rite as Ethan formally swore allegiance to Jonathan ben Shaul. I remained seated until they were finished and then returned the meil and signets.

After settling the last few details of transporting the grain, the hassar stretched. "Shalom, Dahveed, Ethan. It has been a profitable evening."

"Certainly an educational one," the Habiru said with a straight face. "I've learned more than I thought I would about the price of grain. You'd best take that tablet with you, adoni, before I manage to read what it really says."

"Now that I hold your oath, Ethan, you can't do anything about what you might find," Jonathan chuckled. But he picked up the tablet and tucked it into his girdle before he bowed to me and left.

CHAPTER 2

After glancing at the sun, I scanned the Shephelah. The war season had begun and had quickly intensified. Every day saw some skirmish, brought new wounded, and sometimes added to the death toll. The militia drilled grimly when they weren't on patrol. The Philistines had sent units up and down the Shephelah from south of Lachish and Hebron nearly to Taanach west of the Jezreel valley.

General Abner and Sar Malchi reserved two units near Aijalon, gave six units to Ishvi for the north, and six to me for the south, along with instructions to keep the Philistines from penetrating into the hills.

Then a week ago the raiding stopped. The men were grateful for the rest, but once more, I couldn't rid myself of the feeling that something would happen. Again I scanned the lower hills, searching for any movement and finding none. Shifting restlessly, I rubbed the back of my neck. With the army strung for a hundred miles along the border, if a single thrust penetrated, the Philistines could pillage for miles before enough men could assemble to stop them. I watched the sun set from my vantage point near Socoh west of Adullam, my gift now a constant buzz in the back of my mind.

Late that night the call to meet with Yah drove me from my bedroll, and I slipped out of camp to wander under the elms, oaks, and the occasional pine. As the silence gathered around me, I slowed my steps, finally kneeling beside a young myrtle bush, the white flowers ghostly gray blobs in the darkness.

"I have answered your call, Adonai. Give me wisdom now. I can feel the danger to Your people. Tell Your servant, where should I go?"

Zorah.

"How many units shall I take with me?"

All. Tonight.

"I will do as You command."

In less than two days all six of my units had gathered on the eastern overlook across from Zorah. The units farthest south, around Cabbon, were exhausted and needed a day of rest. I prayed they would get it, but before dawn a messenger arrived at my tent.

"Sar Dahveed, Sar Malchi wishes to see you."

Hastily throwing on a kilt, I strapped on my sword and splashed water on my face. The messenger led me a mile north to Malchi's tent, pitched in the center of the second unit.

"Shalom, Sar," he greeted me, looking as if he'd had a good night's sleep. "Your message was quite brief. What information did you receive? Abner is furious." He added that last sentence more as a curiosity than a concern.

"I have little more to tell you," I replied. "I just know I'm to be here."

"Sar, the lookout says you should come," a sentry called, hurrying over.

Malchi raised his eyebrows. "Perhaps now we'll know why."

I followed him to an overlook, and as the light gradually grew, we saw unit after unit of Philistines already climbing the last step of the Shephelah.

"They marched at night!" Sar Malchi exclaimed. Then he thought a moment. "They'll be a bit tired then."

"So are we," I said. "Especially the units that came from around Lachish."

"Well, we'll just have to stop them however we can. Spread out on the roads and trails and fight them wherever you find them. How many do you count?"

"About 12 units so far."

"Yahweh, fight for us," Malchi muttered.

I barely had time to call the commanders together and give orders before lookouts arrived reporting the advance. As the commanders scattered, rousing the men, Dahveed Jeshua appeared beside me. "Where will we be most effective, Sar?" he asked.

"Send your men to keep track of where they climb the hills. Then inform the nearest commander."

"As you wish, Sar." He bowed before hurrying away.

Ram's unit met the advance first, and the men around me strained to hear the faint shouts that heralded the arrival of the Philistine forces. The battle moved steadily in our direction, and a column of invaders appeared over the rise. An Israelite unit attacked, and about a third of the Philistine line turned to engage us. The rest continued forward even as another unit appeared behind them, pushing further east past the men already fighting. They were like an army of ants, constantly renewed from behind as the forerunners stepped aside to fight, or pushed forward until we attacked them.

Beside me, Josheb's eyes scanned the small clearing I had chosen because of the view to the west. Taking his long infantry spear, he stationed himself, his spear barring the way, in the middle of the road where it narrowed at an outcropping of rock.

"Archers will get him," Ahiam worried.

"Maybe not," I said. "There isn't much room on this stretch, and their column is long and narrow. Arrows would be just as likely to get one of their own as him."

Just as the first of the column reached Josheb, I raised my hand and the trumpeter beside me blew a blast. The unit across from us rushed from the trees. Some of the Philistines turned to fight and the cries and shouts of battle rose around me. I stayed back, watching. The Philistines who engaged us first were professionals, while the militia in the unit continued down the road. Their job seemed to be to advance as far as they could, then hold steady until the next unit with professionals could come up from behind.

"Here they come, adoni," Ahiam shouted, and on my other side Shagay blocked a soldier who had swung his sword at me. My belt knife found its mark, and the man fell, to be replaced by another, making me duck back. The unexpected retreat caused my attacker to over-balance, and I helped him to the ground as Ahiam stabbed him.

Hearing more and more confusion on my right, I glanced in that direction. Josheb danced and swayed at the outcropping, his spear flashing forward and back, keeping the Philistines from reaching him with their swords even as he killed another man. Most of the ones he faced were militia, and by himself, he had almost completely blocked the road.

Another shout from Ahiam took my attention, and I drove forward, flipping the sword from the hand of the man attacking me. He backed away, only to fall screaming from a side stroke by Shagay. But as hard as we fought, the line kept pressing forward.

A group of men, led by one of Jeshua's Habiru, rushed by, headed south of us, and to my right, Josheb had filled the road with bodies, choking the flow of Philistines trying to get past. But my men were tiring, and I shouted encouragement as I joined the fight again.

A cheer reached my ears, and I glimpsed Philistines running past

Josheb while he fought off four professionals, his back to the outcropping, his flashing spear striking like a snake. A stone from my sling felled one Philistine as two Israelites ran to help my retainer, but the enemy militia had enough time to clear a narrow way, and a steady stream of men stumbled by.

Faintly, I heard the battle east of us, and I prayed that Dishon and Pasach would hinder the advance even more than we had. Calling encouragement again, I swung my sword at one invader after another, until finally the stream of Philistines ceased. Panting, I glanced at the sun and reached for the cruse tied to my girdle. To my amazement, less than an hour had passed.

Looking around for men to send after the enemy, I quickly saw that none of us had the strength to do so. Cries of the wounded rose around me, and most of the men had already dropped their weapons to tend their fallen comrades. After cleaning my sword in the ground, I picked my way across the battleground to Josheb.

Breathing hard and holding his side, he leaned on his spear.

"Are you wounded?" I asked.

Stiffly he turned toward me. "Not much more than scratches," he panted. "They got by, didn't they?"

"A great many of them didn't," I replied, scanning the ground from here to the road. "I didn't realize you could handle a spear like that."

"You don't get to be a bodyguard for the hassar without some skill," he said with a faint smile. Then he tried to straighten up, looking beyond my shoulder.

Sar Malchi approached, one hand stroking his beard. "I don't recall your being able to handle a spear this well," he said to me as I bent my head in greeting.

"I can't. But Josheb can."

"I see. Any idea how many are dead?"

"No."

After we counted, my third brother-in-law shook his head. "And I thought Eleazar was good. But there are nearly three times as many bodies here! Ishvi will have a much easier time than I thought, thanks to this."

"He's here?" I asked, looking around.

"Farther east. I sent for him as soon as your message reached me, so there's another ambush waiting for the Philistines. Only now, there are a lot less professionals." The sar smiled. "This should settle them for the year!"

Michal tried to retain her dignity and walk calmly to the anteroom, but she could hardly keep from running. Dahveed was returning, and from the reports that Malchi and Abner had sent, the army had completely routed an invading force of 18 units! This on top of all the other victories in the past five years surely meant an early end to the war season.

As she climbed the anteroom stairs, the sahrah nearly hugged herself. She'd missed Dahveed more than she had expected to. Since Jonathan was on his mule at the gate, she would wait with Abbi, for Immi was at Meholath with Merab. The birth of Merab's second child had gone well, but the baby was sickly, and Immi knew what to do.

The throne room was deserted, the door to the west wall standing open. Her abbi stood by the battlements, the other officials at a respectful distance. She heard the faint cheers and looked across the town into the valley.

The army was almost swallowed by the crowd following along. A line of people streamed from the town gates to meet it, leaving the hassar and Sar Eshbaal with only their attendants. She'd never seen anything like this! Faintly, the shouts of the crowd began to reach the fortress battlements.

"Sar Israel! *Dahveed! Dahveed Israel!* The Sars! Sons of Shaul!" Then the chant began. "Shaul has slain thousands! And Dahveed his 10 thousands!" the crowd roared.

"It is as I thought. Balak was right," she heard the king say in an expressionless tone. "He has supplanted Jonathan now. They run after him and abandon Jonathan, after all my son did for them."

The sahrah looked at her abbi's tense back.

"Well, they will have Jonathan for a king. I will see to that." Then he sighed. "But he is my zammar. He brings light whenever he comes to me, and Jonathan loves him."

"Shaul has slain thousands, and Dahveed his 10 thousands," rose clearly from the road below.

Michal watched her abbi's hands slowly curl into fists. "He is not the zammar," he added in that dead voice. "He is the Dahveed, and he has taken my son's place. I will have to be careful, or Jonathan will be grieved." The king turned away from her, and she shivered from the intensity of his anger as he strode past.

But when the crowd approached the town gates, the king returned to the battlements, a smile on his face. "Come, daughter, let us give the army glad welcome, for they have served well this year."

"Of course, adoni," she said, hiding her surprise. Only when she stood close to him could she feel his rage, and her stomach twisted into a knot. Her concern turned to fright as the king listened calmly to all the cheering and shouts of praise as the army paraded up the west road, dividing at the tamarisk by the fortress turn off. And when Dahveed bowed to the king in the throne room, she barely managed to smile.

"You have served us well, Sar Dahveed," King Shaul said, holding out his hand. Michal watched anxiously as her husband stepped forward to kneel and take the king's hand, a barely discernable shiver passing over him as he released it.

"Jonathan, I must speak with you," she said as she walked from the throne room after court was dismissed.

"Can you tell me now?"

"Watch Abbi. He wasn't pleased with the welcome the Dahveed got."

"He seemed happy to me, but I'll pay attention," her oldest brother promised, hurrying away.

"You didn't hear him on the battlements," Michal said to herself, trembling. Down in the courtyard, Rizpah already had the cooking fires started for the family feast they always had when the war season ended. "Good, Rizpah," she said in relief, thankful the concubine from Jabesh was so competent. Her abbi's anger had driven everything else from her mind.

"Shall we bake the fish that came this morning?" the secondary wife asked.

"Yes, the king likes those, and let's serve the last of the sweet Tekoa figs, too," she decided recklessly, hoping that food might mellow her abbi so that he would forget his anger. But later, as she hurried home to change her clothes, she saw an armed man loitering against a neighboring compound wall. There was another past the gate, and a third lounging on an overlooking rock. Not liking the look of any of them, she resolved to tell Dahveed of Abbi's reaction as soon as she saw him.

But her husband arrived for the feast with her brothers, and she didn't have the chance to speak with him alone. He had on the red robe he'd worn at their wedding, and in spite of her agitation, she noted that the green commander's mantle was the wrong shade for that robe. Why hadn't she thought to lay out his brown one? At least he'd worn a silver headband and earrings, which looked good with either color. And thank Yahweh, Jonathan had that twisted brass earring that never matched anything either of them wore!

Shaul emerged from the lower passage, followed by his new personal attendant. "Dahveed, my son, you looked pleased to be back."

"I am, adoni. I will give thanks next Shabbat for Yahweh's hesed to us again this year."

"Come," her abbi continued, taking the Dahveed's arm. "You must sit with me and tell me all about this Josheb and his demon spear."

"As you wish, adoni." He started the tale as the king led the way up the stairs to the upper room. Dahveed sat with Abner and Jonathan at the king's table, and Michal found herself beside Malchi.

"The war season is over, Michal," her third brother said, touching her hand halfway through the feast.

She jumped. "I know. I'm just a little tense, I guess. This is the first time I've had to do the feasts," she replied, giving the first excuse that came to mind to explain her anxiety.

Malchi looked thoughtful, but said nothing more.

As the evening progressed, she tried to ignore the increasingly distant tone of her abbi's voice.

"Michal, you're going to tear the fringe off your robe if you don't stop twisting it like that! What's bothering you?" Malchi asked in a low voice.

She couldn't resist a glance at Shaul. "I, well, something's not right with Abbi," she confessed.

"He seems fine to me."

"That's what's wrong. He's too upset to be so-so like himself."

Her brother gave her an odd look. "He's upset?"

She nodded. "Up on the battlements, he was angry."

"Why?"

Michal never got to answer because Shaul called for music right then, and Dahveed reached for his harp. She tried to stay still and forget the sound of the king's voice as her husband played, but even his music couldn't soothe her tonight.

The meal ended quite late, and Jonathan stopped by her briefly on his way out the door. "Abbi seems fine to me," he said. "Dahveed has pleased him again."

"But--"

The hassar turned away, walking out with the purposeful stride that indicated he was going somewhere. Michal bit her lip, knowing that he would spend the night at Atarah's house and would brook no interruptions. Ishvi and Malchi left together, both of them tired and eager to rest.

"Shall I wait for you?" Dahveed asked beside her, causing her to jump.

"No!" she answered quickly. "Go to the house. Please. I'll come as soon as I can."

He took her cold hands in his warm ones, raising them to his lips to kiss them. "You can tell me what's wrong when you get there," he whispered.

Michal helped Rizpah clear away the burnished brown dishes while the king and Abner finished up a last cup of wine. Shaul's personal attendant returned, but as he picked up an empty stone bowl, she saw him slip a scrap of papyrus under the king's hand.

She paused on her way into the north ell and looked over her shoulder. Shaul glanced at the scrap, tucking it into his girdle as he turned to his cousin.

"My messengers are still in place?" he asked casually.

"They are ready, adoni," Abner replied.

"They can deliver my message to Dahveed early tomorrow."

The sound of Shaul's voice set her heart pounding. What messengers? And why would they need to wait until tomorrow morning? Unless--those men! Her hands suddenly shook so badly that she nearly dropped the bowl. If those men were the king's agents, the only message they could carry was death!

She took a couple of deep breaths and straightened. After all, she was a sahrah. Her legs were shaking too much to go down the ladder, so she picked up a stack of plates and walked back through the west ell. Leaving the dishes by one of the smoldering cooking fires in the private court, she departed the fortress, turning immediately down the steep path on the east. Once down on the rutted street, she pulled up her robe, heedless of propriety, and ran, trying to stay on her feet and plan at the same time.

Should they cross the Jordan? Head for the private estates, hoping the hassar could talk sense to the king in the morning? Go to Meholeth or Jabesh and Immi's clan? She slowed before she got to the first watcher. Nothing must seem unusual.

The compound gate was locked, and she rattled it quietly. "Open the gate!" she commanded. At last someone swung it open, and she crossed the courtyard, climbing up the stairs, mindful that at least three pairs of eyes watched.

Dahveed looked up from the wooden table as she shut the door. "Michal, what is it? You're pale!"

"He's going to kill you, Dahveed," she panted. "I heard him. We've got to leave tonight, or he'll kill you in the morning before Jonathan comes!"

He stood and wrapped his arms around her. "Calm down a little, and tell me just what you heard."

"It was on the battlements," she said, steadying her voice, "When he saw everyone run to meet you and he heard what the people were chanting, he was very angry. He said you had taken Jonathan's place. And he's going to kill you tomorrow. That's what the men outside the house are for. Where can we go?"

"Was he talking to someone?" Dahveed asked, his body suddenly hard against hers.

"Just himself. He had his back turned to me and didn't know I was there. I've been so worried, wondering what he's planning. But I heard him speak to Abner after you left the house."

"I wondered about the men, but I didn't think things were this serious," he admitted quietly.

"They are! And I tried to tell Jonathan, but he won't believe me," she added, starting to cry. "He thinks the king is pleased with you. But you felt it, didn't you?"

Dahveed hugged her tightly. "When I took his hand on the dais this afternoon, Yah gave me a warning, but that could be because another demon is attacking. Are you sure of what he said, Michal? He was pleased at the feast and asked for all his favorite songs."

"What else would he do with Jonathan right there? But his voice didn't sound right! Dahveed, we have to go now!"

Her husband hesitated. "If his illness is back, I shouldn't go."

Tears of frustration fell from Michal's eyes. "Dahveed, listen to me! Abbi is fully in his right mind, *and he wants to kill you!* If you don't believe me, at least trust Yah!"

"Adoni?" Ahiam said, his voice coming from the ladder hole.

"Yes?"

"Shagay says there are four armed men out there."

Although Dahveed didn't answer for a moment, his shoulders slumped a little. "Maybe you're right, Michal. If I'm gone for a few days, Shaul will have time to think about it, and Jonathan can speak with him."

Shaking with relief, Michal pulled herself away. "Where shall we go? Will Zelah be far enough?" she asked as her husband turned back to her.

"We?" he said. "Just let *me* go, Michal. If you came, Shaul might really get angry and send soldiers after me, and you could be disgraced or die because of me."

"But how will I join you?"

"You shouldn't need to--I won't be gone that long."

As he spoke he stripped off his wedding robe. Slipping on a heavy shirt and a war kilt, he checked for his belt knife.

"Dahveed, I--"

"Michal, I'm not going to cause your death if I can help it!"

She watched without moving, knowing that she would not be able to convince him of the real danger, and knowing as well that her life was tearing apart.

After tying on his heavy campaign sandals, he cupped her face in his hands. "Don't worry, Michal, I'll be back soon." His lips full of longing, he kissed her.

Pulling him to her, she returned his kiss with all the fervor she had.

She wiped the tears from her eyes as he pulled away. "Go out the window so those men won't see you."

He hesitated again.

"Please, Dahveed. Do it for my sake, and avoid the possible trouble."

Bringing a rope from the storeroom below, he showed her how to hold it so that it wouldn't slip. Then he crawled out the window, and she braced herself against his weight, the rope swaying a little, making it difficult to hold, but she refused to let go. Then, after one tug, he was gone.

CHAPTER 3

Slowly, Michal pulled the rope up, staring at the tangled coils at her feet, then around the room. There, in front of her beside his everyday girdle, Dahveed's sword leaned against the wall. He was wearing Jonathan's girdle! Anyone who saw it would know him, and without his sword-- She grabbed the weapon and rushed to the window, ready to call his name, but stopped herself in time. The sentry on the wall would surely hear, spoiling Dahveed's chance to leave without anyone knowing. Putting the sword back, she folded the girdle and set it on the table.

She had never considered that her husband wouldn't let her come with him; she wasn't sure what to do now. With Dahveed out of immediate danger, did she need to do anything else? What would happen in the morning when those men came to deliver their "message?" What should she do--and what of the rest of the household?

As the lamp burned lower, she sat on a stool, planning the next 12 hours of her life. She refused to consider that they might be the last hours, for she had violated family loyalty already by siding with her husband rather than her abbi and king. To keep her chin from trembling she pressed her lips together. She owed highest loyalty to those with highest honor, and Dahveed was the Mashiah. And since Jonathan was her brother, he came next. And Shaul had turned against Yahweh. Besides, she had already committed herself. Dahveed was gone.

By the time she blew out the lamp, she knew exactly what she wished to accomplish. Sooner or later, she would have to face her abbi, but the longer she could delay that, the better. Delay would also serve Dahveed best, giving him time to get well away. And the rest of the household must leave.

First, she should speak to Ahiam. It might take a while to convince him of the danger. Staying in the shadows as well as she could, she crossed the courtyard to the room by the east wall that Dahveed's retainer shared with his wife Jemima. To her surprise, the door opened before she could knock. Jemima uncovered a small lamp when the door shut again.

"You know what has happened?" she asked, looking at the two of them.

"Yes, Sahrah," Jemima said, her face a little pale. "I was in the storeroom, and I heard most of what you told Sar Dahveed."

"I passed the word to Naharai and Shagay," Ahiam told her. "We'll be ready to leave in another couple hours."

Michal nearly collapsed in her relief. "That's good to know," she said, leaning against the door. "If what I plan works out, you will be able to leave after I send the messengers away. They'll be back, I'm afraid, so you should all be gone by then."

"Should one of us stay with you, Sahrah?" Ahiam asked.

"No. I can handle my abbi, and Dahveed will need you."

"As you wish, Sahrah," the Habiru bowed.

Outside again in the dark, Michal considered the best way to carry out the next step in her plan. If she said Dahveed was sick, Abbi might wait a day or two. She must remember to send out for medicine and Atarah in the morning, but right now, she needed something in Dahveed's bed, and those teraphim in the back corner of the storeroom would do just fine, especially the large one with the big round knob at one end.

It took two stealthy trips from the ground floor animal shelter to the storeroom to get the teraphim, and she'd bruised her shins and arms finding them in the dark. Not daring to use the outside stairs, she lugged them up the ladder in the storage room one at a time. They weren't so much heavy as awkward, and the largest one nearly slipped from her grasp. Spreading out a bedroll, she placed the wooden post with the round knob first. Using the blankets from another bedroll, she wrapped the posts, padding them and holding them together. When she covered it over, it did look like a person, except that the head needed hair. The shaggy goatskin from the cupboard where Dahveed kept his harp supplied that lack. It wouldn't fool anyone in broad daylight, so she'd have to keep the windows covered, but she was pleased with it otherwise.

Then she sat down again. The sentry on the wall walked by, and she looked toward the window. "Yahweh, protect Your Mashiah," she whispered to the night, easing back against the wall, tired from her exertions. But she couldn't rest yet. She still had one more hurdle to deal with.

What would she tell the king? She didn't think she dared try to outright lie by saying he'd been gone when she got home, but what else could she do? Her last hurried conversation with Dahveed ran through her mind again and again. Gradually it became clear what she could say. It was the truth, and her abbi could make of it what he would. With a sigh, she leaned her head back.

Michal jerked awake at first light when someone banged on the gate, and she heard it open. Rubbing her eyes, she straightened up on the stool before she remembered why she was on it, and what she had to do today. To her surprise, Shagay climbed up the ladder from the storeroom, carrying a burning lamp and nodding respectfully to her. When he saw Dahveed's bedroll, he stopped short, then flipped back the blanket to inspect what was in it. He lifted the goatskin and after a moment of complete stillness, he gravely tucked everything back in. When he set the lamp on the table, his eyes laughed at her.

For some reason, his amusement heartened her enormously. She smiled back, suddenly ready to play the part she had set for herself, for she didn't owe the truth to the men coming up the stairs, and she didn't intend to tell it, either.

A knock sounded, and Michal opened the door to find four strange men on the balcony with Ahiam standing in back of them, and Josheb lounging against the low parapet, leaning on his spear. Obviously, Dahveed's retainers meant to be certain the king's messengers left as planned.

"Did you bring the medicine?" she suddenly demanded.

"Medicine?" the first man said, taken aback.

"Yes, I asked that it be sent quickly. If you don't have it, what are you doing here?" she asked in a hushed voice.

"The king sent us," he started to bluster, and Josheb straightened up a little, the tip of his spear wandering in the direction of the men. "He, um, he wants to see the Dahveed," the man finished lamely, looking to his companions for help.

"Dahveed can't go!" Michal gasped. "When I got home, he was burning up with fever. A wound taken bad. He's very ill. I sent for herbs long ago!"

"You couldn't have," the second one gasped. "We've been--"

He never finished for Ahiam chose that moment to pull out his sword and inspect the blade, running a small whetstone down it.

"We have to take Dahveed to the king," the first man said, edging toward the door a little.

"You can't possibly disturb him when he's this ill!" she exclaimed, stepping back to allow the man to enter.

As he crossed the threshold he saw Shagay's large form rise from the shadows.

Michal noticed the way the man's eyes riveted on the sword leaning against the wall, then on the robe and girdle still on the table.

"We'll, uh, we'll tell the king that he's sick," he said, bowing out. The four men then hastily left.

As soon as they were out of sight, Ahiam turned to her. "Should we remain, Sahrah?"

"No," she replied firmly. "By the time someone else comes, it will be broad daylight, and they dare do nothing but take me to Abbi. This is your chance to leave."

The three retainers bowed. "Yahweh go with you, Sahrah," Josheb said.

She watched out the window as the three of them left the compound and disappeared into the streets. Taking Dahveed's sword, she put it in the cupboard with the harp. Then she sat down to wait.

¥ ¥ ¥ ¥ ¥ ¥

"What were we supposed to do?" the first of Shaul's messengers pleaded from his knees, looking from the raging king to the hard eyes of General Abner. "She is the sahrah! We cannot lay hands on her, his retainers were there, and I saw him in the bed myself, his sword leaning against the wall and robe on the table."

"I said he was to die at first light!" the king snapped. "What is so hard to understand about that?"

"Adoni, would you have had us kill him before the sahrah?" the man gasped.

Shaul's eyes glittered. "Just go back there and bring him to me, bed and all, so I can kill him myself! Abner, take somebody and go with them! I want him before me now!"

"Yes, adoni," the king's cousin said, driving the trembling men in front of him to the door to the anteroom roof. "Doeg, attend me," he added curtly as they walked out.

¥ ¥ ¥ ¥ ¥ ¥

The gate slammed open, and Michal jumped, rushing to the window. The four men had returned, accompanied by General Abner and Commander Doeg. She closed her eyes a moment. Somewhere in her mind she had always hoped that she had been wrong.

She opened the door calmly when they arrived, stepping aside without being asked. The men crowded in, Abner staying beside her.

The Edomite grabbed the top blanket and yanked it.

Michal looked down, controlling her face. She had tucked that blanket under the teraphim very well, and when the commander yanked it toward him, it raised the heavy wood with it, which then slid off and dropped on the man's toes. With a curse he kicked the blanket aside, revealing the contents of the bedroll.

For a long moment, no one moved.

"What is your will, General?" Doeg finally said, eyeing Michal.

"The king said bring him the bed, so we bring him the bed, and whatever is in it! Just do it *now*." Abner grabbed Michal's arm so hard that she nearly cried out as he rushed her down the stairs. He kept his grip along the street and around the north side of town, glancing often at the swiftly rising sun, and hurrying so fast the sahrah could hardly keep up.

You had better hurry, Michal thought. If Jonathan catches you at this, he'll hack you to pieces.

Panting hard from the fast pace, the guards took the bedroll up the outside stairs to the throne room, and Abner marched her in right after it, passing Sheva who guarded the door. The men dropped their burden on the floor before the dais and hastily backed away. One look at her abbi's face made Michal extremely thankful that Dahveed was outside the town walls.

The king's eyes glittered as he reached down and flipped back the blanket, then tore off the rest of the coverings, revealing the wooden teraphim and the goat skin.

"*How dare you!*" he roared, turning to Abner.

"We didn't dare. Your daughter did," the general said tightly, shoving Michal forward.

Shaul turned on her. "*You* deceived me, Michal? You helped my enemy escape?"

"Do you think I had a choice?" she asked calmly. "You know Dahveed. Am *I* supposed to stand against him? When he said, 'Let me go. Why should I cause your death?' what else could I do?"

As his eyes bored into hers, she was very glad that she hadn't tried to lie--much.

"He threatened you?" General Abner asked skeptically.

"I certainly didn't *want* him to kill me," Michal replied, giving the king's cousin a brief glance. "Did you?"

She saw the quick smile that crossed her abbi's face and walked forward. "Please forgive me, Abbi, for doing this, but I didn't know what else to do!"

"He is gone, then?" Shaul asked.

"I think so. But who can tell?"

"And he may come back. Abner, get a guard together and take my daughter to my estate. She must be kept safe until we find Dahveed."

He wasn't entirely convinced. Michal thought swiftly. "Abbi, that's the first place he would look," she said, allowing some of the strain to show on her face.

Surprised, he turned to her. "What did you say?"

"If the Dahveed looks for me, he'll try your estate the first thing, and Jonathan's next." She hugged herself a little. "May I go to the house you gave me in Zelah instead? He shouldn't know about that one."

"You want to leave?"

Michal looked around the throne room, then down at the bedroll, and suddenly she wanted with all her heart to get away from this place, from the darkness that brooded over it, and from the memories that she would encounter everywhere she turned. She didn't even want to see Jonathan! "Yes, I want to leave!" she cried. "Please, Abbi, get me away from here before anything else happens and Jonathan comes. Just get me away!"

The king took her in his arms. "Hush, Michal, you can go now," he said soothingly. "And you're right, the little house in Zelah will be just the place. You can go there." He hugged her close, and she knew she had convinced him of her innocence. Now she understood Jonathan's distress every time he deceived his abbi regarding Dahveed. Gripping her abbi's robe as if she were a child, she burst into tears.

¥ ¥ ¥ ¥ ¥ ¥

"What do you mean gone?" Jonathan asked, standing half dressed in the doorway of Atarah's healer shop, looking at Malchi.

"Dahveed's house is empty. The servants at least packed a few things, but that's all. Michal's missing, too. She's not there, she's not at the fortress, and Achsah says she didn't come to the residence after she left the feast last night."

Malchi shifted restlessly in the late morning sunlight. "Something was worrying her last night, Jonathan. She startled like a deer every time I touched her. If I didn't know her, I'd have thought she was terrified. I was going to check back with her this morning, but I was called to the barracks about an hour after dawn. Commander Doeg had 'disciplined' four new men of his unit, and one died. I just got back from delivering that Edomite to Nob and arranging for Ahimelech to hold him under Yahweh's restraint until I can sort out the mess. I went to Dahveed's compound as soon as I got back."

"She tried to tell me something, too, but I didn't take time to listen," the hassar said bitterly. "No one has seen her? What could she be frightened of?"

"I think it was something to do with Dahveed."

"She was scared of Dahveed?"

"No," Malchi said, frowning. "More as if she was scared *for* him."

Jonathan went pale.

"The king wouldn't try to kill him, would he?" the sar asked, his voice low.

"Yes," Jonathan admitted just as quietly. "He's tried once before. But Dahveed wouldn't let me do anything about it."

"Well, if anything happened in the fortress last night, Sheva will know. Or Abner."

"Who will never tell," Jonathan grimaced. "Sheva we can deal with. I'll meet you in his chamber."

The quietness of noonday reigned when Jonathan climbed the stairs to the southeast battlements. For a few moments he touched the stone where he had stood with Michal so often. What had happened? Where was she? Had a demon taken their abbi again, killing them both?

Sheva's look of despair when Jonathan walked into the commander's chamber didn't help any. "Are they dead?" he demanded immediately.

"Sheva says not," Malchi replied.

Jonathan drew in a deep breath. "What happened?"

"Michal must have been right about Abbi," his brother began. "He and Abner were in the throne room before first light, and four men reported to them. Abner left with them, taking Doeg along. Sheva assumed his place at the upper door when he saw them leave. They returned shortly with a bedroll and our sister."

The hassar turned his gaze on the trembling commander. "Where is she?"

"King Shaul told Abner to take her to her house in Zelah. That's why the general is gone also. Sahrah Michal is a most unusual woman, Hassar." He told all he had seen and heard in the throne room.

"Teraphim!" Malchi exclaimed. "I wouldn't have thought Dahveed had any!"

"When I saw them, they looked as if they had just been unearthed from somewhere," Sheva said. "Covered with dust and cobwebs. She stood up to the king, faced down Abner, told her abbi I don't know what about Dahveed, then finished them off by bursting into tears."

"That sounds like Michal," Jonathan said, smiling grimly. "Do you think she's in any danger?"

"Not from the king," the commander answered. "I wouldn't want to say when it comes to the general."

"I feel like going on a journey," Malchi announced. "I'll even ride a mule for this trip. But we haven't got much time. We've got to be back for the feast for the honored men tonight."

"We come back when we find Michal," the hassar said, his voice smooth.

When the sars arrived at the house in Zelah, their sister was not there, and inquiries garnered the information that she had never been there.

"Sheva did say Zelah," Malchi commented as they left town.

The hassar nodded. "But wasn't the first place mentioned Abbi's estate?"

"Yes."

By the time they left Shaul's personal estate without finding Michal or news of her, Jonathan's light gray mule danced under him, obviously ready for battle.

"It seems our abbi's esteemed cousin needs to be brought to heel," Malchi said, reining in his brown mule which was responding to Jonathan's mount. "Do we visit him?"

"That does seem indicated," the hassar replied.

When they came in sight of Abner's personal estate, they pulled up short. "The place looks like a fortress!" Malchi exclaimed. "There's Libni, so the tenth unit must be here, and at least one other. What are they doing here?"

"Let's go find out."

"Are you going to knock at the gate?" Malchi asked as they rode up to it and his brother gave no indication of stopping.

"Do you feel like being polite?"

"Not after this long of a ride."

But the gate opened for them. "Shalom, Sar," Sithri said, bowing to Malchi. "We were hoping you'd come. And it's so kind of you to bring the hassar along. He is most welcome."

"Were you welcome?" Malchi asked, sliding off his mule.

"We were, shall we say, unexpected? I believe General Abner thought the eighth unit had accompanied him and the tenth, but he must have been mistaken in his hurry."

Jonathan's lips twitched. "And where is Dishon's unit?"

"Resting peacefully in their barracks, I should hope," Sithri replied. "When Naharai spoke of the trouble that had come to Sahrah

Michal, we could hardly abandon her, could we?"

"I like your unit, Malchi. They are very considerate men."

"Yes, I'm rather attached to them myself," Malchi drawled.

Jonathan rode his mule up to the stairs of Abner's house before he dismounted. Malchi strolled over, positioning himself with enough care that everyone in the compound gathered around to watch.

As Jonathan Hassar reached the top of the stairs, the house door opened. "I'm here to speak with Michal," he announced.

"King Shaul has ordered that she be kept safe," Abner replied, stepping out of the house while still blocking the doorway.

"From me?" Jonathan asked, his voice suddenly smooth again.

Abner hesitated a moment, then reluctantly stepped aside.

The hassar strode past the man, only to emerge from the house a moment later with Michal on his arm.

He took Abner's arm as he walked by, and the general couldn't help wincing as he found himself marched down the stairs. At the bottom, the hassar let go, then placed Michal to one side and folded his arms. "Michal Sahrah Israel?" he said, his voice raised so that all could hear.

His sister straightened up. "Yes, Jonathan Hassar Israel?" she replied clearly.

"Did King Shaul give you into the care of General Abner ben Ner this morning?"

"Yes, Hassar."

"For what reason?"

"He was to take me to my house in Zelah."

"Did you ask him to do otherwise?"

The sahrah drew herself up. "I did not."

The watching crowd got very quiet after her response.

"The king commanded me to keep her safe, and the house in Zelah cannot be adequately defended," Abner declared.

Sar Malchi turned his gaze on the king's cousin. "Are you accusing the king of neglecting the safety of his daughter, impugning the abilities of the units you chose to protect the sahrah, or setting yourself above the king?" he asked.

Abner's face turned red, but he remained silent.

"You have, then, disobeyed a direct order of the king," Jonathan declared. "Malchi Sar Israel, this man is under your command, and has been judged guilty."

"Yes, Nahsi." The sar's fist traveled the short distance to Abner's ribs quite casually, but the power of the blow staggered the man, doubling him over. The crowd in the courtyard watched in total stillness as Malchi delivered a thorough beating that left the general gasping on his knees.

"You dare to treat faithful servants of the king like this?" Abner struggled to get out, lifting his battered face, already swelling from Malchi's blows.

"Was my sentence unjust?" Jonathan asked, his voice smooth again. "Did you, or did you not, carry out the king's orders?"

"Was I, or was I not, given the chance to speak in my own defense?" Abner retorted.

Malchi regarded the kneeling man coldly. "Since there seems to be a difference of opinion, may I make a suggestion, Hassar Israel?"

"Certainly, Malchi Sar."

"Let us give the general the benefit of the doubt and take him to Adon Ner. Surely he cannot object to his own abbi reviewing this case. Would you be willing to submit your decision to the adon's review?"

"I would not want any of the king's kin to feel that I would treat them unfairly. I will submit my decision to Adon Ner and accept his judgment on it if General Abner wishes it."

The blood drained from Abner's face, and he bent his head again. "I--that is, I will accept the judgment," he said, his fists clenched tightly.

"Then you did disobey the king?" Jonathan demanded.

"I did, but only thinking to serve the king as best I could."

"Your wish to serve is commendable, Abner ben Ner, but take care that you do not bring Yahweh's wrath down on the king in so doing. Yahweh will not condone shedding innocent blood, and *neither will I.*"

"My first duty is to the king," Abner said in a low, savage voice.

"As you wish. Amen," Jonathan said, giving the formal covenant word of agreement as he turned away.

"Amen," the crowd around them responded, concluding the judgment.

CHAPTER 4

It was close to noon the next day when Jonathan strode down the north side of town toward Atarah's house, trailed by an escort of three guards. He hadn't been certain he could come here today because the feast last night had ended extremely late. The king had seemed determined to show that the zammar was not necessary to the celebration, and thus not missed.

The hassar had been surprised, then, when the message arrived that Shaul would not hold court today. But the hiatus gave Jonathan a chance to think, and once his abbi was well rested, he might be able to talk the king out of his anger at Dahveed. In the meantime, he wanted Atarah.

Leaving the escort in the street, he entered the small courtyard of the house, and Keturah met him. He was glad to know that at least two of Dahveed's dependants were all right.

"Shalom, geberet," he greeted her. "Is Atarah here?"

"Yes, Hassar. But she was up all night assisting at a birthing. She returned at dawn and is sleeping."

Jonathan hesitated. "I'll wait a while," he decided. "Who are the two men in the corner on the straw?"

"Roeh Shamuel sent them yesterday from Navyoth. They are traveling beggars, I think. The disfigured one has an infected wound, and I started treatment yesterday. But Atarah needs to look at him when she wakes up. Your pardon, Hassar," she added as a woman walked into the courtyard, and the Gibeonite went to see what she wanted.

The hassar stroked his beard in thought. Why would Roeh Shamuel be sending beggars to Atarah? Perhaps he should speak with them. As travelers, they would have news, and if nothing else, it would help to pass the time while he waited. He walked to the corner.

The younger man rose to his knees when it was clear that Jonathan intended to approach them. The older one turned, and the sight of the hideous half-face stopped the hassar in his tracks. The man's nose had been sliced off at an angle, taking most of his left cheek with it. A deep scar ran from his chin to his left ear, and another one from the right corner of his mouth just to the side of that eye. He looked up blankly, and as Jonathan stepped closer, he held up his arms defensively, covering his face, revealing more scars on their underside and his palms.

"Someone really didn't like you," the hassar commented. "Most people who want someone dead don't bother attacking the face. I see you fended him off enough to save your life." He indicated the scars on his arms.

The beggar lowered them, and his brown eyes now watched Jonathan with a shrewd, intelligent light. "No, he didn't like me," he said, his voice raspy, and the hassar noticed the scar across his throat.

Spotting a stool nearby, Jonathan sat on it, flipping his bound hair over his shoulders before motioning to the kneeling man. "Sit down," he directed and turned back to the beggar. "Curved or straight sword?"

"Curved," the man replied.

"You're lucky to be alive."

"That can be a matter of opinion, Sar."

Jonathan's lips twitched. "I suppose it can. Keturah tells me you are travelers. Have you found all you need here?"

"Yes, Sar," the younger one replied after a quick assessment of his clothing. "Much kindness has been shown to us, and we are grateful."

"Where have you traveled from?"

"Navyoth by Ramah most recently," the beggar said, hitching himself up on the straw. His companion helped him sit, and when he folded his hands in his lap, Jonathan's eye was caught by the cross-hatch pattern the man's fingers formed. He'd never seen anyone fold their hands that way and--his thoughts stopped. Underneath the man's hand was a blue tassel with silver threads that could only have come from the girdle he had given to Dahveed!

Jonathan's gaze darted back to the beggar's eyes. "A reminder of your travels?" he asked casually, indicating the tassel.

"You might say so. It came to us from one who saved us from injury and possibly death."

"He was not hurt in the process, I hope?"

"No, Sar. He assured us he was well and comfortable when we left."

The hassar looked away a moment, feeling the tension drain out of his shoulders. Dahveed must have placed himself under Shamuel's protection, the best place he could have gone. His lips curved into a relieved smile. "That sounds like quite a story."

"I will tell it, if you think it will amuse you," the beggar offered.

A bit surprised, Jonathan replied, "I'd like to hear it."

"We arrived in Ramah three days ago," the man began. "A farmer in the market allowed us to sit by his stall, and the people there were generous with us until a man named Bichri entered the market."

The name jarred Jonathan, and the beggar paused. "A rather tall man, walks like he owns the earth, and has a sarcastic way of speaking?" Jonathan asked.

"You know him," the beggar said drily.

The hassar snorted in reply. Bichri was a cousin of his, related by his immi to the Gera clan. He was another family member quietly barred from Gibeah by Shaul.

"He was offended by us," the beggar went on, "and used his sword to drive us from the town. As we left, a man named Gad, servant of Yahweh's prophet, found us. He brought a message from Roeh Shamuel saying we could find rest and help in Navyoth under Yahweh's wings. Taking us to a house there, he told us that the roeh would come the next day to see us."

"Bichri had wounded you, then?" Jonathan asked when the beggar paused again.

The man shrugged, but Jonathan caught the flash of anger in the other man's eyes.

"The next morning Ziba settled me in a convenient place near the house and then went to the market. Shortly after, Ben-geber came by. He spoke frankly to me, and gave me a silver piece so that Ziba and I could eat well that day. He hadn't left yet when Bichri dragged Ziba into the alley, threatening us because he had ordered us to stay out of his sight, and we had not done so.

"A man from the town and a neighbor woman were also there, and they protested, telling Bichri that Roeh Shamuel had given us shelter under Yahweh. He wouldn't listen, threatening us with his sword and claiming kinship with Hassar Israel as his authority to cast us out again."

"He dared to do that? The fool!" Jonathan exclaimed.

"That is when something changed," the beggar said softly. "When Bichri spurned Yahweh's word, Ben-geber became a warrior in an instant, although he had no sword. Something," the beggar paused, "or maybe someone," he amended, "came on him. His eyes turned golden as a lion's eyes, and power surrounded him. He challenged Bichri directly, and when Bichri thrust his sword at him, he grabbed that wrist, jerked him forward, and beat the breath from him with his other fist too quickly for Bichri to even respond. Then he held him on his knees in the dust.

"I don't know what would have happened if the roeh hadn't arrived. He called to Ben-geber, getting him to release Bichri. I don't think he was pleased with what had happened."

"Probably not!" Jonathan said, just imagining what the roeh had thought of Dahveed's behavior when he was supposed to be hiding from Shaul!

"A few other people had gathered by then, and they were afraid that the hassar would be offended because his kinsman had been beaten. The roeh was hesitant about what to do, and Ben-geber commanded that Bichri, with the townsman and the neighbor woman as witnesses, should be sent to an Adon Ner for judgment.

"The roeh agreed, and ordered that Ziba and I be taken to his house. He sent me here late yesterday."

Jonathan's smile had turned cold by the time the beggar had finished his tale. "They sent Bichri to Ner of Zelah?"

"Yes, Sar," the younger man replied. "The roeh ordered him bound also."

"Then Dodi Ner will make Bichri wish he had never picked up a sword in his life," the hassar commented grimly.

Just then Keturah appeared. "Geber, Atarah can see you now. Come into the house."

"The healer's name is Atarah?" the younger man asked, jerking his head up.

"Yes," the Gibeonite woman answered.

"Abbi--" he started to say, but the older man cut him off with a gesture.

As the man struggled to his feet, Jonathan noticed one leg was shorter than the other, and he leaned heavily on his son to walk.

Once the beggar was settled in the house, the younger man retreated to a corner while Keturah brought a lamp, and Jonathan settled himself on another stool.

"Good, Keturah," Atarah said as she entered the room. "I need the light. You must tell me if anything hurts," she added to the man as she inspected the wound. He kept his face turned away, or covered with his right hand, but his eyes kept returning to Atarah, and tears squeezed out of them when he blinked.

"I don't think we should sew it yet," Atarah decided, standing. "It should drain more, and we need to cleanse it often, but we should keep it lightly covered." As the healer unrolled the cloths she had brought, the door opened, and her younger brother Ornan entered. The Jebusite halted when he saw all of them.

"What is it, Ornan?" Atarah asked.

"Nothing special. I'll come back later," he replied, turning to go. His eye caught the beggar's folded hands. "Abbi?" he asked, his voice puzzled.

Atarah whirled around, seeing the cross-hatch of the beggar's fingers before he pulled them apart to cover his face. "Abbi!" she whispered, then drew in a breath to scream.

Jonathan jumped up, turned her to him, muffling her cry in his chest.

Ornan was on his knees, his hands pulling at the beggar's. "Abbi! Abbi! Let me see you!" he pleaded in a low voice.

"No," the beggar said, shaking his head. "I see what I look like in other people's faces."

"I don't care," Ornan insisted. "Abbi, please!"

Jonathan held Atarah tightly, one hand rubbing down her back. "Hush, now," he murmured in her ear. "It's all right. Hush."

She twisted her hands in the fringes of his robe while she tried to stop sobbing.

Looking over her shoulder, he asked, "You would be Tanhum, former treasurer of Jebus?"

"Yes," the man admitted as he finally let Ornan drag his hands away from his face. The young man couldn't suppress a shudder, but he curled up as close to Tanhum as he could get, wrapping his arms around him.

Pulling away from Jonathan, Atarah turned to her abbi, kneeling on his other side. She reached up and traced the scars on his face with her finger, and then smiled. "Your eyes are still the same," she said, and wrapped her arms around him also. Then she looked up. "Abbi, Ziba was with you. Did they kill Ziba?"

"No." Tanhum nodded his head to his right, and Atarah saw the other man for the first time. Without a word, she launched herself at him, and he caught her, holding her close, hiding her face also to quiet her sobs.

Jonathan felt himself tighten up inside. Who was this man? Would he have to give Atarah up to him? Then he remembered that Ziba had called Tanhum "abbi." He would be the healer's brother then. The relief he felt told him exactly how much Atarah had come to mean to him.

Keturah caught his eye, nodding to the door, and they stepped outside to give the family some time alone.

Once outside, the hassar started to pace. If Debir, the current araunah of Jebus, ever discovered that this survivor of his coup was sheltered in Gibeah, he might be angry enough to abandon his neutral position regarding Israel, making it impossible for Shaul to continue ruling. On the other hand, Atarah and Ornan had lived here for some time without detection, and just the thought of the benefits that Tanhum could bring to Israel made Jonathan dizzy with possibilities. And

Eshbaal had more than he could handle now with court records. There had to be some way the man could stay without causing a lot of talk.

Before long, he had an idea of what he could do, if he could just convince Tanhum to let him do it. The thought made the hassar stop in his tracks. Why did he feel he had to *persuade* Tanhum to *allow* him to do things? At what point during their contact had that man wormed into the superior place?! And how much information had he himself inadvertently revealed during the course of their conversation?

Starting to pace again, Jonathan realized that he should have been on his guard the moment that man *offered* to tell his story. Remembering how the former treasurer had skillfully paused at the right moments, and the way he himself had responded made him shake his head in disgust. He was out of his depth with this man, and unless he could find some way of setting Tanhum back on his heels, he would never hold his respect. And without that, the Jebusite would never turn his whole mind to what Jonathan wanted him to do.

But how could he put the man off balance? If Dahveed were here, he'd have no worries, for the very presence of the Mashiah seemed to. . . his thinking paused as did his pacing, and a glint appeared in his eyes. "Thank you, Dahveed," he murmured, his eyes dancing. "Every once in a while we northerners can learn with reasonable speed!"

Atarah came to the door, motioning him to return.

Tanhum met his eyes when he entered. "My daughter has told me of your care and hesed to her. Your god will bless you for it."

Jonathan smiled. "As your younger son so aptly reminded me one time, I probably owe her my life. She means much to me, and I would repay what I can of that debt. Now that you have found your family again, what do you plan to do, Tanhum?"

As Jonathan suspected, the directness of the question floored the man. He probably hadn't heard anything like it in years. And the longer the silence stretched, the greater the hassar's satisfaction grew.

"I should not stay. I frighten people, and they talk," the man finally replied.

"If that is your only concern, consider my suggestion. My brother has more than he can handle with fortress records, the treasury, and the private estates. He could use your skills. You could work from a private house, with a couple of scribes to deal with the public and carry out your orders. Whatever else you may want or need, we can arrange. Would you be willing? And what about Ziba? Is he trained as you?"

"Yes," Tanhum replied, shifting uncomfortably at the continued directness of the inquiries, but unable to refuse answers.

"Then Eshbaal can probably use you both. May he interview you tomorrow?"

"Yes, Hassar." Tanhum bowed his head briefly.

Sometime later, as the hassar prepared to leave Atarah's room, he caught the sound of voices from the outer room and paused.

"What of this position he offers?" he heard Ziba ask.

"Of course we will accept. We can hardly do anything else, as he well knows. But it is an offer honorably made, and we will serve loyally and well. There will be many ways we can help Ornan and Atarah also. El Elyon is showing us much hesed. Be grateful. Bichri would have killed us."

"A man saved us from Bichri."

"A man possessed by a god, as evidenced by what poured out of him there in the street," Tanhum rebuked his son. "Do not be deceived by his rough clothing, Ziba. That man holds high enough status that Roeh Shamuel bowed to his wishes, and the royal house of Gibeah accepts his discipline of their kin. Do not cross him, or the hassar."

"Yes, Abbi."

¥ ¥ ¥ ¥ ¥ ¥

"Gebirah, Nabal wishes to know if you will come to him," Tirzah said from the doorway.

Abigail laid aside the green meil she was embroidering and stood. "Tirzah, I expect my handmaids to show proper respect for my husband."

The handmaid bowed briefly. "My apologies, Gebirah. Nagid Nabal wishes to know if you will come to him."

As Abigail left the room, she relaxed her face into a calm mask. Lately, as the food shortage grew worse, family after family had come for aid, only to find Nabal demanding impossible prices for the grain. More than one householder had looked to her as if expecting help. Her inability to respond drove her uselessness deeper into her heart each time. She could only watch as Nabal took advantage of the situation to strip the countryside, seizing the private fields, the animals, and then the people themselves.

Just yesterday the last family from Maon had come requesting to speak to the nagid. Nabal had kept the head of the house waiting for hours, and then Abigail had sat in the garden, listening to the man plead for half an hour to be allowed to enslave himself and his family in exchange for food. Her stomach had become so knotted that she couldn't eat for the rest of the day.

Walking from the house, she paused a moment to let her eyes adjust to the sunlight. She wished she knew how far Nabal's reach extended. Her traditional lands spread from Maon and Carmel westward and northward toward Jezreel, but she didn't know how much of that her abbi had sold off. Dare she ask Hezro about it?

She waited a moment longer. Hezro, the Israelite commander of the guard, had arrived in Carmel with King Shaul. Before his rescue by Shaul's army, the Amalekites had captured him in battle and enslaved him for two years, and he had been too weak and ill to continue north. Nabal had hired him after deciding he needed a household guard. The man wisely kept his entire devotion to the Gebirah from all eyes, but Abigail had sensed it and occasionally asked something of him.

Her stomach already knotted with dread, she wished that she could retreat to her garden and let the intricacies of the embroidery drive the pain away for a while. Hezro opened the chamber door without a word when she approached, and she entered, ignoring Tokhath at the scribe's side table. The man rarely looked at her, and when he did, she always felt defiled somehow. "Tirzah said you wished to see me."

"I do," Nabal replied in a satisfied tone. "We must celebrate!" he said, touching the records stacked on the top of his table beside two silver goblets. "Just yesterday the last of the land and people came to me. I have recovered all the land your abbi sold, just as he instructed, and much more besides. I own *all* of Maon. Just like Pharaoh."

Abigail smiled slightly. "Oh?"

Her husband nodded, his eyes studying her eagerly. "Tokhath admitted that not even Shaul of Israel thought to do this. Joseph's plan worked just as well for me. He controlled the food, and when he was done, all the land in Egypt belonged personally to Pharaoh, and the people were all his slaves. And now it's the same here in Maon and half of Carmel as well! By next harvest, I should have even more. Come, we must celebrate!" Picking up one of the goblets, he held it out to her.

"It was good of you to recover the lands that Abbi had to sell," she heard herself say as she took the goblet.

"They never should have been sold! It was a dishonor to you, Gebirah. But I have rectified it, and brought you more honor besides." He drank several swallows of wine.

The goblet paused on the way to Abigail's lips. Nabal had never criticized her abbi before. "All my lands are recovered, you say?" she asked, taking a sip.

"Including the pastures to the west, and the farms bordering the Jezreel clan. I have even acquired some of Nagid Jezreel's fields."

The wine left a bitter taste in her mouth and upset her already troubled stomach. "You took land from the Jezreel clan?" she asked faintly. The one thing her abbi *had* insisted that she learn was the knowledge of the clans, their adons and nagids, and the structure of the alliances that held them together. A dozen questions flew through her mind, beginning with which householders had lost the lands, which adons they had pledged to, and how the balance of alliances would change. Some of the most influential adons in Jezreel owned land that bordered hers. Her abbi would never have condoned such a thing! Had Tokhath suggested it?

An ache pounded in her head. She tried another sip of wine and instantly regretted it. Forcing herself to remain calm, she set the wine goblet on the table. "You have indeed done much."

Nabal took another swallow. "And I shall do more. You are Gebirah! You must have honor, and I shall acquire it for you!" His face was flushed, and he stared into the wine cup. "This is very good wine, Tokhath. Where did you get it?"

"It was an older jar, Nagid. I feared it would not be suitable for this occasion, so I added some, er, spices to it. It pleases you?"

"Very much. Here, take this reward for pleasing me!" After fishing around in his girdle, he pulled out three coppers.

In spite of her own discomfort, Abigail glanced at her husband, puzzled. She had never seen him like this before.

The scribe bowed as he accepted the gift. "Your generosity is most gracious, Nagid. Truly you are most honorable among men!"

Her husband drank the last of the wine. "As husband to the Gebirah, it is my duty to give rewards. Show the Gebirah the robes we have for the New Moon feast. No one in Hebron will have anything like my gifts! Ahlai of Jezreel will be nothing compared to me!"

"Yes, you picked well, Nagid. Such garments are not seen every day!" Tokhath agreed, unwrapping a bundle set to one side, then holding up one of the robes.

Abigail forgot her disgust at the scribe's flattery as a magnificent blue robe unfolded, covered with colorful embroidery and hung with long fringe. "That is the best one, surely?" she gasped, walking forward to finger the thick wool. Anyone wearing it would suffocate unless it was the dead of winter.

"All 10 are like this," Nabal said proudly.

The Gebirah stilled. How had Nabal managed to acquire *10* northern banquet robes for kings? The fringe alone precluded anyone else wearing them. "Where did you find them?" she had to ask.

"Eliphelet ben Ahasbai. He always has top quality, and even better prices. His scribe said these were rejected because the colors weren't what was wanted, and the tailor sold them off cheaply. I got all 10 for the price normally paid for one!"

Abigail clenched her teeth. The robes must have been stolen. How could she face the nagids at the New Moon feast if Nabal handed out such inappropriate *stolen* items as gifts? "Is this all you have?" she asked desperately.

"Show her the linen ones," Nabal commanded.

Tokhath opened another bundle. "They aren't nearly as bright," he said with a glance at the nagid.

She fingered the good-quality linen. Each robe was dyed a single color and had a girdle to go with it. "These are nice, Nabal. Give these."

"But they are not as magnificent," her husband protested. "Our honor demands that we give the best."

Abigail closed her eyes briefly, casting about for some way to convince her husband to be reasonable while Tokhath laid out more robes. "How many--with this many you could give one to each adon," she amended hurriedly. "And if you give them the first day, they can be worn for the next two. I'm sure Ahlai won't have anything like that planned," she added hesitantly. "And if you mix up the girdles, that will add some color. It was fortunate you thought to get matching girdles," she finished, watching for his reaction.

"But what of the others?" he asked doubtfully.

"Why don't you keep those for a while?" she suggested. "They are suitable for a melek, which means a nagid could wear them."

"Keep them?" Nabal looked startled. "Yes, *I* might find them useful," he added quickly.

"I'm sure you will, Nagid," Tokhath put in.

Abigail relaxed in relief.

"Now come and see what I have for you," Nabal announced. Offering his hand, he escorted her outside. "Now when I travel, you will be able to accompany me in a manner fitting for a Gebirah." Her husband gestured to a woman's litter sitting outside the door.

Accompany him? She had managed to get herself through this summer only because he traveled frequently. "I didn't realize you wished it," she managed to say.

"I do. Our alliances require constant attention, and you must be lonely when I am gone."

"I am honored you think of me so much," she replied dully.

"Hezro, see to the bearers," her husband directed, and she noticed the four slaves kneeling to one side for the first time. "The Gebirah will want to see your faces," he added to the kneeling men.

The first slave raised his head instantly, but his gaze remained down. His face suggested he might be from Edom, and from his manner had probably been a slave all his life. The second and third glanced at her, their eyes widening, and one flushed, looking down again quickly.

The fourth raised his head last, staring directly at her. She stilled a moment. Parai, son of the Hebron tanner. Two years ago, the tanner had angered Nabal over the quality of some leather, and Nabal had vowed to bring the man to his knees for daring to disagree with him. Her heart sank, although she allowed not a flicker of emotion to cross her features. Apparently time did not cool her husband's anger.

"I carefully selected each one," Nabal announced. "They are perfectly matched in stride and gait. You will have a smooth ride."

"You do me too much honor," she said, struggling to comprehend the consequences to the clan alliances with this purchase. Taking outlying fields from Jezreel was bad enough, but to acquire such a hold over a family in Hebron was on another level entirely. As she watched Hezro take the bearers to their quarters, her stomach knotted so tightly that she knew she wouldn't be able to eat again tonight.

Nabal still watched her, so she fingered the brown curtains of the litter, finding them of the heaviest wool, along with the coverings of the cushioned box inside. They were capable of blocking out the cold from the top of Mount Hermon. The thought made her pause and close her eyes again.

"The quality is very good," she said slowly, turning to Nabal. "Did you get this from Eliphelet ben Ahasbai also?"

"Of course! He assured me it was just what every Gebirah needed."

And which princess of Assyria would not get her litter, Abigail wondered. Then, feeling the stifling air still spilling from the enclosed space, she wondered how she herself would survive riding in it.

"Do you like it?" Nabal asked wistfully

She glanced up. His eyes had lost the hard calculating look, and for a moment, he resembled a child hoping his immi approved of him.

"I'll have a very comfortable seat," she said gently.

Satisfied, he turned away.

Hezro appeared beside her. "Shall I have the men take it out to the pasture for the goat kids to play in?" he asked with a straight face.

After an instant of surprise, Abigail felt her face relax into a smile, which she quickly banished. "No, Hezro, find a place in a shed, and be sure it's covered so it won't get dirty."

"Yes, Gebirah."

She walked to the house, where Nabal waited to escort her inside.

"What did he say to you?" he asked suspiciously.

She looked at him in amazement. "He wanted to know where to put it, of course."

Nabal reddened and retreated.

CHAPTER 5

I opened my eyes, then blinked in the early morning sun. When I'd left my house in Gibeah, I'd gone to a nook made by a courtyard wall as it went around a large tree on the hillside. Wrapped in my gray cloak and sitting absolutely still, I was unnoticeable. To pass the time, I'd started composing. The verses I'd come up with then, and here in Navyoth since, ran through my mind.

"My strength, let me watch for You because God is my refuge.

God of divine loyalty, He will be in front of me. God will make me look triumphantly on my enemies.

Because of the sin of their mouth, the word of their lips, they will be captured in their arrogance, and because of a curse and a lie which they repeat.

Destroy in anger. Destroy, and they are not there. And they will know that God is the one who rules in Jacob to the ends of the earth.

And they will return at evening and they will howl like dogs and go around the city.

They themselves will roam about for food. If they are not sated, then they remain all night.

But I, I sing of Your strength, and I shout with joy in the morning of Your divine loyalty. For You are a refuge to me and a place of escape in a day of adversity for me.

O my strength, let me sing praises to You for God is my refuge, the God of divine loyalty to me."[1]

It felt more like the middle and end of a song rather than a beginning. My hands flexed in frustration, aching to hold the harp. But it was back in Gibeah, along with my sword. The one thing I *had* brought was the one thing I shouldn't have, Jonathan's girdle!

Frowning, I turned over in the bedroll. The New Year's new moon festival was the day after tomorrow. I had been here nearly a month and still had no idea whether the king's heart had softened toward me or not.

What was I going to do? This new moon, all those sworn to King Shaul renewed their vows of allegiance. While I could not formally swear to the king since Yah had rejected him, as his son-in-law, I would offer him great public insult if I did not come to the table.

On the other hand, showing up if the king was determined to kill me didn't seem very wise. But how could he still be against me with Balak no longer here to feed his anger? Then again, I had run and not returned, and that in itself might anger him . . . The same round of thoughts raced through my mind dozens of times a day as I worried over the trouble I would bring on myself if I didn't return for the feast, to say nothing of what might happen if I did! If I knew for certain what the king thought, I would have peace, and I longed to go to Gibeah and find out. Shamuel, however, was immovable. I was not to leave Navyoth.

Rising, I descended to the courtyard to wash and eat some parched grain and a few figs.

When the roeh appeared to break his fast, I bowed respectfully.

"Shalom, Dahveed," he greeted me. "Yah will make His will plain to you today."

Greatly relieved, I accompanied him to the altar on the west side of the small group of houses. The seer slit the throat of the morning sacrificial lamb, and the musicians started a morning blessing. I joined in, using a harp that someone had loaned me. It had the requisite number of strings, which was about all I could say for it.

No one expected the sudden appearance of five soldiers. Seeing

---

[1] Psalms 59

the roeh offering a sacrifice, they hesitated, standing a little aside, scanning the crowd. The way they fingered their swords made me nervous, and I kept my face turned away, gratefully bowing when Shamuel called for a prayer.

The prophet raised his hands upward. "Yahweh, send your Spirit upon us today, that every ear should hear of Your power, and that those who come against You may be rebuked."

What could the roeh mean by those words, I wondered. Then Yahweh's presence rushed on us, bursting in my mind. I bowed to the ground again, hearing the cries and shouts of the men around me as they responded to the coming of our God.

The roeh's powerful deep voice rolled over us as he chanted praises, and I raised my head, striving to banish the worries from my heart and open myself fully to the One who had chosen me.

The five soldiers had fallen to the ground, two weeping, and another shouting "Hallelu Yah! Hallelu Yah!" The fourth sang in a tuneless voice, his hand beating the shoulder of his companion who sat perfectly still, his eyes glazed over while he stared at nothing. The praises lasted for some time, and then Yah's presence ebbed away, leaving us quiet and meditative. The soldiers rose, took their weapons, and headed south.

"Who were they?" I asked Shamuel as they disappeared.

"Soldiers from the king, Dahveed. He sent them for you."

"How did he know I was here?"

"A servant from the fortress saw you two days ago, and he told Shaul."

"Should I go with them, then?"

"No, for Yahweh's Spirit fell on them to protect you. Had they not wished you harm, they would not have been overcome. As it is, when they arrive in Gibeah, they will remember nothing."

I sighed. It seemed that Michal had been more right about the king than I realized. "Shaul is still set against me?"

"Yes, Dahveed, but Yahweh strives with him even yet to show him his error."

To distract my mind, I stayed close to the prophet all morning, listening as he explained to a new group of students how to offer various sacrifices.

After the noon meal, as I helped Gad tend a sheep with a bruised shoulder, I straightened enough to see over the low courtyard wall. Another detail of soldiers stood in the street, and a farmer driving his ox cart was pointing to Shamuel's house. He must be from much further north, for no one here in town would have spoken to them.

As they started forward, I recognized two as being from Natan's fifth unit.

"Go into the storeroom, Dahveed," Gad said quietly without looking around.

Since it was the only place I could go without showing myself, I obeyed.

The men walked into the tiny courtyard, and Gad went to meet them. If they insisted on searching, they would surely find me. Should I let myself be taken? I had no weapon except my belt knife and sling. Feeling more helpless than I ever had before, I edged to the side of the door, wanting to hear what was said.

"May Yahweh's grace fall on you, gebers," Gad greeted them politely.

I strained to hear a response, and when none came, I peeked out the door.

The detail was marching through the gate, and as they did, each one began to sing and shout praises to Yahweh. As they went along, children appeared around them, escorting them though the town. I found myself standing in the courtyard looking after them, my hands shaking so badly that I had to clench them into fists and fold my arms. The singing continued until the men left the cluster of houses, but not one of them turned back as they headed south to Gibeah.

I retreated to the house. I was used to Yahweh rousing my gift so that I could defend myself when it was necessary, but protection without any effort on my part had never happened before. What was I to make of it? Did Yahweh mean for me to stay here the rest of my days? Surely He had more important things to do than make soldiers into prophets.

When the roeh returned in the afternoon, I asked to speak with him. "What am I to do, now that the king knows I'm here?" I asked, pacing restlessly in the small room.

"When it is time, you will leave," Shamuel replied calmly. "But there is more to come." He looked at me with those seer's eyes and sighed gently. "I had hoped you would be able to learn what Yahweh wishes you to know while you stayed here, Dahveed. But I see that you have not. I fear the lesson will be a hard one now. Whatever happens, remember that Yahweh holds you in His hands."

Ceasing my pacing, I bowed my head, discouraged. What was I

supposed to have learned?

" 'Bijah! 'Bijah, come quick," a child shrilled outside. "There are more soldiers coming. Let's go watch them prophesy!"

Covering my face with my hands, I groaned. "He will keep sending them and sending them and sending them!"

"Yes, Shaul has refused Yah's will again. Come. It is time for the evening sacrifice."

This detail headed for the altar as if it was water in the desert. They stopped beside it, staring to the front, waiting. The roeh went about the sacrifice as if nothing was unusual, and when he finished and raised his hands to the sky, the soldiers dropped to their knees, calling on Yahweh while they wept.

Once the blessing had been given, they picked up their weapons and walked away.

Shamuel turned to me. "You will need a good night's sleep, Dahveed. Cease your worrying. All is well with those you love."

The next morning, just after sunrise, Gad woke me. "Dahveed, the roeh wishes you to meet him at the altar."

I had my cloak on me, and I threw it over my shoulders as I hurried down the stairs to the courtyard. Fall was nearly here, and the cool nights showed it.

When I got to the altar, the roeh nodded at me. "Good, you have your cloak. You will not need to go back for anything." He turned his attention to the road from Ramah.

A tall man approached, his familiar voice raised in song, punctuated by shouts of "Hallelu Yah!"

Anguish filled my heart as the king approached, meaningless praises spilling from his lips. He stopped in front of the roeh. "Shamuel, I have come--. There is one here who will praise Yahweh with his life, and bring glory on all sides in the courts of the God of Israel, whose hand will lead all those he chooses, may His name be always remembered above all other gods! His will is majestic in the mountains, and there will be peace from the highest to the lowest in ages to come before his land shall cease, and all his enemies be cut off!"

I couldn't bear to look at the king's blank eyes, and I would have knelt but the roeh's hand stopped me.

"It is not for you to kneel, Dahveed," he said softly.

Shaul's fingers plucked at the fastenings of his cloak. "Let all the earth know of Yahweh's greatness!" he shouted as he flung the cloak aside. Underneath it, he wore a cuirass and kilt, his jeweled war dagger and sword at his waist.

Again I looked away, the irony of him coming against me dressed for battle shredding my heart. I had no weapon with me and could only run from his anger.

"There will be nothing which can be accordingly," Shaul said, dropping his dagger and sword on the ground. "All shall go straight as the mountain washes to the sea, sending the wheat as the greatness of Yahweh will be vindicated."

Singing again, he untied the cuirass, throwing it aside, then stripped off the kilt, and pulled off his undergarment.

Trembling, I looked at the roeh. "Let me go, please," I pleaded. But his hand held me still, and I had to remain where I was.

"Shamuel!" the king called.

"I am here, Shaul," the roeh answered.

"Shamuel, where is--and on the wind he will ride like fish from boats and deserts of seasons as he wills." Bending down, Shaul took off his sandals, talking all the time. He raised his arms, shouting, "Hallelu Yah!", and then pulled at his loincloth, letting it fall to the ground. "Yah is my shobeh!" he cried, laying down in the dust by the altar, his head swiveling from side to side, complete gibberish coming from his lips.

The roeh turned to me, and his voice deepened. "Know this, Dahveed Israel, as Shaul has stripped himself of clothing, so Yahweh has stripped him of the kingdom. Yahweh is about to give His nagid, Shaul ben Kish, into your hand to do with as you will."

"Hallelu Yah, amen." the crowd which had gathered responded. Each one knelt briefly and then quietly went away.

Not knowing what to say, I turned to the prophet.

"Now you may go," he said. "Shaul will be held here all of today and tonight. Perhaps he will listen to Israel's God now. In the meantime, you must make your escape."

"Where shall I go?" I asked, my eyes again on the king.

"Go first where your heart sends you. Then ask of Yahweh what He would have you do."

I knelt to him, and he put his hand on my head. "There is much trouble before you, son of Jesse. I see darkness trying to reach you. Remember what the Hassarah said to you. Remember what Ethan said to you. Above all, remember that Yahweh has given you great honor. You do not need to seek it yourself."

With a last glance at the king, I left, going where my heart sent me, trying to flee the memory of Shaul lying in the dust and to outrun the tormenting thoughts crowding into my mind. What had I done to make the king think he must pursue me armed? Surely there had to be something I'd said, or he thought I'd said. Was there some part of court etiquette I'd missed, that had angered him? Did he expect more of me, and I hadn't done it? There must be something--anything! Anything to indicate that he didn't hate me without reason, that he wasn't seeking my life because he had nothing else to do.

In less than half an hour, I jogged through the old north market of Gibeah, crossing the steep ravine that ran at the foot of the fortress hill and striding up the switchbacks to the fortress itself.

My face was wet with tears, and I was dusty and unfit for the throne room, and I didn't care. At the anteroom door, the sentry's mouth dropped open when I pushed through the crowd and walked in without pausing. I had to know, and Jonathan could tell me, and then I could make it right with the king.

The scribe at the curtains glanced up, raising a hand in protest as I started up the stairs. The guard at the landing knew me, and since my cloak was back and he could see I was unarmed, he opened the door. I stepped over the threshold, stopping in the middle of the room, blinking the tears from my eyes.

"*Dahveed!*" Jonathan exclaimed, pushing himself up from the throne.

I got to him just as he stepped from the dais. Dropping down in front of him, I twisted my hands in the waist of his robe. "What have I done?" I asked. "Is there some crime I've committed? How have I wronged your abbi so deeply that he's trying to take my life? Adoni, please, tell me! *I don't understand!*"

Shocked, the hassar put his hands on my shoulders. "Yahweh forbid, Dahveed! You're not going to die! Did Abner find you and try to take you?"

"Abner?" I exclaimed. "Adoni, the king himself came for me!"

The body under the robe I gripped turned to stone. "Eshbaal, clear the throne room," he said, his voice suddenly smooth.

I couldn't suppress a shudder at the sound of it.

The court scribes and waiting messengers quickly left, followed by the sar.

Jonathan looked down at me. "Dahveed, you know Shaul is

determined that I will rule after him rather than you. Since you've been gone, he doesn't do anything at all without consulting me, whether it's how to negotiate with the next ambassador or what time court will begin in the morning. He opens my ear about everything. He could not hide any wish for your death from me!"

I closed my eyes, squeezing my hands tighter in his robe. He really thought he knew everything the king did! "Yahweh above, Jonathan! Your abbi knows very well how much you love me. And he's kept his actions from you, knowing how upset you'd be over what he's doing! As surely as you and Yahweh live, Jonathan, there is only a step between me and death now, just as there was the day Shaul tried to kill me here in this room! The king sent *15* of Natan's unit for me, and Yahweh covered me from them. Your ab--"

"Dahveed, this cannot be," the hassar said, soothingly. "The king spoke to me before he went to Zelah about how much he missed your music. He may soon be ready to bring you back!"

I looked up at him in desperation. How could I make him understand that the king wanted me dead? "Then where is the fifth unit, Hassar? Where are the king's cuirass and battle sword and dagger? I tell you, Jonathan, King Shaul came for me today dressed for war, and Yahweh holds him yet before Roeh Shamuel at Navyoth so that I could escape!"

Jonathan's eyes flashed as he roughly pulled away from me. Going to the door that opened on the anteroom roof, he yanked it open. "Dara!" he roared.

I stayed right where I was, not daring to move as I heard the shield-bearer's footsteps hurry up the stairs and Jonathan's curt command to bring the king's battle sword and dagger. He waited at the door until Dara returned. Even at the other side of the room, I felt the change in him when the soldier reported.

Shutting the door, the hassar leaned against it, looking suddenly old. Then crossing the room, he stopped beside me. "Forgive me, Mashiah. I will do whatever you tell me to."

I didn't know what to reply. "Shaul said he missed my music?" I asked in the silence, trying to sort out all the contradictory pieces in my mind.

"Yes, just the day before yesterday."

"And Shamuel said Yah was striving with him, too," I muttered.

"And he does miss you, Dahveed. If you came to the feast tomorrow, he would accept you again."

"Are you certain?"

The hassar paused, then sighed. "Not any more, Mashiah."

"Maybe we can find out if the king listened to Yah during my absence," I said. "If he doesn't remember going to Navyoth, will he expect me to be at the feast?"

"I think he does," Jonathan replied slowly.

"All right. Let me stay in hiding for the first two days. If your abbi asks about me, tell him my brother commanded me to come to Bethlehem and take the annual sacrifice there, and I begged permission to do it. If he says 'All right,' I'm safe, and I can come to the last day of the feast. But if he gets angry, we'll know that he hasn't bowed to Yah's will and is determined to harm me."

"It's risky, Mashiah. The king barred you from Bethlehem," Jonathan murmured as he considered. "On the other hand, I'm wearing his signet ring,"

The words had scarcely left his mouth when the enormity of what I had just asked descended on me. In my own haste and impatience to know Shaul's mind, I, *as Mashiah*, had asked the hassar to deliberately lie to his abbi and king! How could I have said such a thing? And force Jonathan to abandon his allegiance and loyalty to his own abbi? Horrified, I jerked my head up to take back my hasty words.

"I will do as you command, Mashiah," Jonathan Hassar said, a hardness on his face I had never seen before.

I could have sunk right through the floor. He had agreed? What had I done? Then fear struck. I could never expect that he would commit such treason! By asking too much, I had surely turned him against me.

The hassar tried to get me to rise, but I resisted, shaking with the thought of how I had ruined everything. Jonathan now had no choice but to give me to Shaul so that I could be killed. And I deserved death, for in asking him to commit treason, I had done so myself, even if that was the farthest thing from my mind. I would never have been this afraid when I first came, or even two or three years ago. But I knew now the extent of the king's reach, the resources he could call on, the power he wielded, and I knew the hassar matched that reach and power. And I was just a southern shepherd from the Judean hills, who had no real claim to anyone's consideration. I only had one recourse. "I would beg one thing more of you, Hassar."

"What is it?"

Bowing my head, I gripped him hard. "You know King Shaul

enslaved me, but even so, you cut a covenant with me, placing Yahweh's hesed between us forever."

"Yes," he said gravely.

"When you speak to the king, if he tells you of anything I've done that's wronged him, or-or if I'm guilty of anything against him," I forced myself to say, "give me the hesed you promised, and kill me yourself. Please, don't give me to your abbi," I begged. "Who knows what he might do to me!"

"Yahweh forbid, Dahveed!" Jonathan exclaimed, his voice rough. "How can you think I'd deliver you to the king? If I had any indication at all that my abbi was going to harm you, much less kill you, don't you think I'd tell you?"

Slowly I looked up at him. The hardness had vanished from his face, planting a tendril of hope in my heart. "I am only the king's slave, Hassar, and he is your abbi and the king. And I just foolishly asked you to lie to him for me. Why should you tell me if your abbi answers harshly against me? Grant me your pardon, Hassar, and ignore my words. I should not have said them!"

Jonathan searched my face, then placed his hands on my shoulders, squeezing gently until I stopped shivering. "Come," he said softly, pulling me up. "Let's go out to the field."

The crowd outside lapsed into silence as we descended the outside stairs and walked out the gate, then a buzz of conversation broke out behind us. He turned west at the tamarisk tree, his stride lengthening, and I matched his pace.

Murmurs again followed us through the west market. Beyond the local gardens and grain fields he turned up a path into the forest across the Jebus highway. He stopped in a tiny open space, with a little bit of grass not quite dried by the sun.

"Give me your belt knife," he commanded, facing me.

I handed it to him, hilt first.

Kneeling, he set it on the ground, point toward himself. "May Yahweh, the God of Israel, be witness to what I say," he began. "I will surely sound out abbi by this time tomorrow or the day after. If he is pleased with you and thinks well of you, I will surely send and tell you."

Pausing, Hassar Jonathan held my gaze. "But if I find that abbi is determined to harm you, may Yahweh cut me in pieces as a covenantal sacrifice if I do not open your ear and send you away in peace." He took a deep breath and added, "And may Yahweh be with you, as He used to be with abbi." Then he touched his forehead to the ground, and waited.

The first thing that raced through my mind was to wonder why he had called Shaul "abbi" and nothing else. The second was that he had not vowed to lie to him. Relief flooded through me, to be abruptly checked by a third thought. He had said that he would send me away in peace. This was a formal vow, so his words had their formal meaning. He had just promised to give back my freedom.

I took a step toward the man who bowed before me, only to pause as I realized that setting me free required that he claim the king's authority. No, I amended, it indicated that he had *already* done so, which was also why he had called Shaul "abbi" in a formal vow, and why he had acknowledged that Yahweh was no longer with him. Furthermore, it explained why he had agreed to my plan to begin with. With Shaul rejected by Yah for treason, it was the hassar's duty to see that no further violation was done to Yah's will. I should have known that he would not agree to anything dishonorable.

"Get up, Jonathan," I said, my voice unsteady.

He straightened up on his knees. "Give me hesed, adoni."

"What hesed do you want?" I asked, my stomach in knots.

"If I'm still alive when Yahweh gives you Israel's throne, swear you'll grant me Yahweh's hesed so that I will not die."

"Yahweh forbid it, Jonathan," I exclaimed, reaching for him.

His eyes full of the knowledge of how things could change, of what might happen between us in the future, he took my hands. "Swear to me that you will forever show your hesed not just to me, but to my house, even after Yahweh has completely cut your enemies from the earth! Swear it to me, Mashiah!"

Holding his gaze, I put my hands around his. "As Yahweh is my witness, may He cut me in pieces like a covenant sacrifice if I do not show you and your house Yahweh's hesed as long as I live."

Slowly his hands took mine. "Swear again, Dahveed. Swear by your love for me this time."

I took a deep breath. Doubling meant the thing was absolutely sure, and he was asking me to swear not as Mashiah but as friend this time. "By my love for you, Jonathan, may Yahweh cut me in pieces if I do not show you and your house Yahweh's hesed as long as I live."

"Thank you, Dahveed." He bowed to me again, then said, "Remember, Mashiah, you do not have to fear that Shaul's power and authority will succeed against you. Yahweh has placed you above him."

I helped him stand. "When I have an older brother like you or an *abbi* like you, how can I forget it?" The startled expression on his face made me smile a little. "You had to think of me as your son to plead for my life as you did last year," I explained.

"You are." Suddenly he pulled me into an embrace. "You are my friend, my little brother, and my son. You are Mashiah and Yahweh's king. I will do whatever it takes to serve my God and my king."

Could I ever repay such loyalty? Who was I that he should do so much? We drew apart at last, and he moved a little stiffly. I shied away from the thought of how many years he carried, at least 45 now.

He gave me a wry smile. "Now, about tomorrow. Was Shaul prophesying when you left Navyoth?"

"Yes."

"Then I think we can count on his not remembering anything, which will mean he'll ask about your empty seat, and I'll have the chance to see what he's thinking. Meet me three days from now--that will be the second feast day, at the same place you hid before by the little waterfall, or wait by the Ezel stone. I'll bring my arrow boy with me for some target practice. If I tell him the arrow is to one side and to bring it to me, as Yahweh lives, it will be safe for you to come back," he said formally, bowing again slightly. "But if I say the arrow is beyond him, there is danger, and Yahweh has sent you away."

"Thank--" I started, and his eyebrows went up. "You have," I hesitated unable to get the word "served" out of my mouth. "You've given me more than I deserve, Jonathan."

"Then remember our covenant, Dahveed. No matter what happens, when Yahweh has fulfilled His promise for you, don't forget me, for Yahweh is a witness between us forever."

¥ ¥ ¥ ¥ ¥ ¥

Late that afternoon Jonathan and Ishvi, accompanied by Commander Zorath and three of his men, rode by the town cisterns with a cart full of straw. While they traveled north to Ramah at the slow pace of the cart animal, Jonathan told his brother what he'd learned from Dahveed.

"Did anyone ask for the king yesterday or the day before?" Ishvi inquired when they were half way there.

"Not that I know of. Why?"

"Just wondering how Shaul knew where Dahveed was. Who is

that?" Ishvi interrupted himself, peering ahead. The low sunlight made it hard to see ahead of them. "Rides like a woman, and there are three escorts."

"It's Michal!" Jonathan exclaimed, urging his mount into a trot toward her. "I thought she was at Zelah now with Immi and Merab."

"Jonathan, have you seen Abbi?" she called when she saw them approaching. "He must have left Zelah, because someone brought his mule back. They said they found it on the Jebus highway north of Gibeah, so I went looking. But we haven't found him, and I was coming to tell you."

"We're on our way to get him," Jonathan replied. "He's at Navyoth. Apparently he's been there since this morning. Dahveed brought the word."

Michal turned to him so swiftly that she nearly overbalanced on her mount.

"He's fine, Michal. The king learned he was with the roeh and went after him. Dahveed got away and came to me."

"Is he home? Will it be all right now?"

"We won't know until I find out what's on the king's mind. Dahveed's hiding somewhere." The others had caught up, and Jonathan started forward again.

The sun had nearly set when they passed Ramah, following the dirt path around the hill the short distance to the group of buildings housing the school of the prophets. A little smoke still ascended from the altar, and they halted the mules when Roeh Shamuel rose from his place beside it. One of the prophets lay on the ground nearby, and the hassar politely kept his eyes away from the naked man.

"Is it you, Jonathan ben Shaul?" the roeh's deep voice inquired.

The hassar slid off his mule and walked forward, touching his knee to the ground. "Yes, Roeh. I have heard that my abbi is here, held by Yahweh."

"He is." Shamuel nodded his head, indicating the man that Jonathan had ignored. The last of the sun's rays glinted on the gold and jewels of the war sword and dagger and off the bronze of the cuirass.

Jonathan bowed to the ground. "Roeh, does he live?"

"He is unharmed. But he may not leave until the dawn. All that he will remember is only that Yah is displeased with him, and why."

"Thank you, Roeh. May we cover your servant?"

"Yes."

Rising, Jonathan unfastened his cloak and spread it over his abbi's body. He glimpsed the shocked look on Michal's face when she realized the man was the king.

"Is there a place in Ramah where we can stay?" the hassar asked.

"My house here is prepared for you, and Gad has a meal waiting."

"May I return and stay with the king during the night?"

"No, for he has displeased Yahweh and must remain alone."

The hassar bowed again and stood, leading his mule as they followed one of the prophets to a house near the edge of the settlement.

Later, a frozen, shocked look still on her face, Michal hardly touched her food.

Jonathan finally sat by her, putting his arm around her while she cried quietly. "That was truly Abbi there?"

He nodded.

"How long was he there?"

"All day."

She shuddered. "With anyone able to come along and see him? People gawking as they pass along the road? Jonathan, he's the king!"

"He's a man who came here thinking to harm the Dahveed," her brother said sadly. "And Yahweh will not permit anyone to defy Him."

"It's so terrible! Abbi lying there that way, with that old man sitting beside him."

He touched her lips with his finger. "That old man, as you call him, is Yahweh's roeh, and his presence would have kept people at a respectful distance. Do not scorn Yahweh's hesed, Michal."

"It's still terrible," she said, crying once more. Once she was asleep, Jonathan went outside. While he couldn't sit with his abbi, he could refuse to sleep under a roof. Easing down by the doorstep, he leaned against the wall. It would be cold without his cloak.

When the roeh arrived at dawn he was still there.

"You have a good heart, Jonathan Hassar," the old prophet said. "Yahweh will fulfill all His word to you. His hesed will remain with you. He will establish the covenant you have made in His name, and your name will never be forgotten among men."

Stiff from the cold night, Jonathan made his obeisance to the roeh. "May Yahweh's hesed cover us all," he responded. Then he went inside to get his brother and sister to take their abbi home.

CHAPTER 6

Abigail stood calmly in the house in Hebron that Nabal had rented for their use during the New Year's new moon feast. The first day of the feast was warm, and the nagid was sweating already in the heavy brown wool of a king's banqueting robe that he'd decided to wear despite her careful cautions. He hadn't told her his intention, coming in to surprise her with his finery just minutes ago.

She had tried to get across the idea that not only would he be miserable in that thing, but also that it was inappropriate. But he'd made up his mind. Furthermore, he'd also brought along several gold rings and three bracelets that he wanted her to put on along with the silver earrings, headband, and bracelets that she already wore with her pale green linen robe. The familiar knot began twisting her stomach, and she knew if this scene went on any longer, she would be unable to eat.

"We must uphold our status, Abigail. Your abbi was clear to me on this. Honor holds the clans together, and we cannot be slack in our duty."

"I know, Nabal, but these will not add--"

"Of course they will. You only have on silver, and these are all gold!"

Silently, she slipped on three of the rings, and a gold bracelet. Nabal left the room, and as she followed him, she removed the rings and handed them to Namea who tossed them onto the bedroll and hastily followed the Gebirah out into the courtyard.

They had spent the morning distributing the linen garments and girdles to the adons who normally allied with Carmel. Everyone had been pleased and flattered by the gift, giving Abigail hope that the feast would go well.

Then Nagid Hebron had invited them to the feast given at his house, pleasing Nabal and putting him in a good mood. Abigail, however, wondered why Dathan would honor them after Nabal had taken Parai. Or was it possible the clan ruler wasn't yet aware that her husband had purchased the tanner's son? Did he know the man had to sell one of his sons? The questions made her head ache.

When Abigail emerged from the house, her litter waited in the courtyard. Dathan's house was only two compounds away, but obviously Nabal planned on making a grand entrance. She seated herself, catching a glimpse of Parai's face as she did. Her stomach tightened again. If Dathan had been unaware of the fate of Parai, he would learn it tonight.

Hezro closed the curtains so that she didn't have to watch Nabal clamber up on the mule dressed in that heavy robe. The litter rose from the ground and steadied as the men carried her out the gate. Very soon another gate opened, spilling out the sounds of people waiting to celebrate. As the litter advanced into the courtyard, silence replaced the murmur of voices.

For the first time she wanted to stay in the litter. Then Hezro pulled the curtains apart, and the calm mask covered her face as he gave her his hand to help her out. The guests in the courtyard watched wide-eyed as she stepped out, and then every eye turned to Nabal.

Hezro took the bridle of her husband's mule. To her horror, she saw Parai down on his hands and knees so that her husband could dismount using his back as a step. Her stomach clenched harder, and she swayed a little. Namea quickly gripped her arm in support.

Once on the ground, Nabal approached her with mincing steps. The robe had been made for a larger man, and it hung from his shoulders, not quite dragging the ground. He held out his hand to her, and she had to give him hers. Her heart pounded so hard that she wondered why no one heard it in the deathly silence. The walk across the courtyard was the longest that she'd ever taken, made more so by Nabal's insistence that they go slowly so that everyone could get a good look at them.

A faint rustle stirred the crowd behind them as they passed, and she heard the gate close again. Dathan waited at the head table in the courtyard, his face impassive. "Welcome, Nagid," he said when they at last stopped in front of him. "You honor us with your presence."

"We were happy to do so," Nabal replied, sweat streaming down his neck. "It is our duty to appear at such functions."

Abigail felt her face drain of any color.

"This way," Dathan said, ushering them himself to two places at one of the head tables, facing the courtyard. Tirzah and Namea took their places behind her as she sat down. Nabal spent considerable time settling himself, and then a servant offered a bowl of bread.

"Welcome, Gebirah," the woman across from her said in a gentle voice. "It does me honor to be able to sit with you."

Abigail raised her eyes, meeting the understanding in the other's face. "You are very kind," she said quietly.

Conversation gradually resumed around her, and food appeared.

She managed to eat a little of the fruit until she happened to glance across the courtyard. The litter sat in the light of some torches by the wall, all four bearers kneeling around it, Parai forced to wait there during the hours of the feast. Her stomach twisted so painfully that she had to sit back and close her eyes.

The endless hours passed, and Nabal grew louder and more pompous the more he drank. No one said a word about what the nagid wore, but the raised eyebrows, tones of voice, and sly comments circulating around the courtyard were almost more than she could bear.

When she could stand no more, she rose.

Nabal looked up at her, his eyes bleary from wine.

"It is late, and I am tired, Nabal," she said quietly. She turned to Dathan as her husband unsteadily climbed to his feet. "Yahweh's blessings on you and your house."

"Yahweh's blessings on you, also," the Hebron nagid replied, bending his head respectfully.

Once Nabal was on his feet, she turned and started across the courtyard.

"Yahweh's blessings on you, Gebirah," someone murmured.

"Shalom to you, Gebirah," another said.

She returned the wishes with what dignity she could, and by the time she reached the litter, one of their guards had Nabal's mule ready for him.

"Hezro, make certain he gets on the mule the first try," she said softly.

"Yes, Gebirah."

Parai provided his back again, moving so stiffly that Abigail knew his knees and legs must be aching from the hard stone of the courtyard. Hezro and another guard managed to get Nabal onto the mule, and once Parai was back at his place, the guard captain handed her into the litter.

Abigail was unable to sleep that night. While Nabal snored beside her on a bedroll, she lay stiffly, staring at the awning over them, her mind frozen in the instant when she had stepped from the litter and all the guests had turned to see Nabal get off his mule.

The sounds coming from the gate seemed loud in her ears. Pulling one of the blankets around her, she went to the head of the stairs and sat on the parapet in the shadows. Tirzah and Namea slept in the room below, and she listened as stealthy footsteps crept across the court and up the stairs.

They paused close to the top, and then a figure stole onto the roof top, the faint light gleaming off the blade in his hand.

"Killing him would only make you a murderer, Parai," she said in a barely audible voice.

The slave whirled, his eyes searching for her in the darkness.

She remained silent and motionless.

"He deserves to die for what he did to me and my house," he said at last.

"Yes. But if you kill him without condemnation being given, you will only bring more dishonor on your house."

"You would defend him then?" the man asked bitterly.

"No. But do not break your abbi's heart more by committing blood-guilt."

Parai started to shake. "He saw me," he said in a hoarse voice. "The gate was still open when Nabal dismounted, and Abbi came by, and he saw me. Abbi's heart hasn't been strong, and he was stricken right there in the street. I just came from my family. We can't get a healer because we have nothing to pay with. The nagid made sure of that. If Abbi dies, I will hold the nagid responsible. Do you hear me, Gebirah? And I will provide my own recompense and kill you both, for you have stood aside and let the nagid do whatever he wishes."

"I can do nothing, Parai."

He laughed bitterly. "You can do whatever you want, Gebirah, and you can make any man obey your whims. He gave us to you, and you could have at least ordered that we take the litter some place where we could rest. Instead, you let us kneel there for hours."

The rage in his voice squeezed the knot in her stomach into agony, and she slumped over a little, gripping herself.

Abruptly Parai turned and retreated down the stairs as quietly as he had come.

Abigail watched him go, dizzy with his accusation. Carefully, she slid off the parapet, sitting down on the roof. Years of memories flooded her mind, and suddenly she recognized the pain for what it was. Never in her life had she been so filled with shame.

¥ ¥ ¥ ¥ ¥ ¥

Dressed in the newest sar's meil that Michal had gotten him, Jonathan fitted his belt knife into his girdle. He didn't normally like black, but he had to admit this meil was worth wearing with his gray robe. Smoothing the garment, he idly traced a swirling red line and wondered briefly who had the time and patience to do such intricate embroidery.

It was a pity that Michal wasn't here to see him in it. But finding Abbi lying naked by the altar had upset her so much that he had sent her back to Zelah to stay with Immi and Merab. Rizpah had organized the feasts for the New Year's celebration both yesterday and again today.

The hassar sighed. He hadn't had the chance to ask about Dahveed yesterday since he had been standing to serve the king. Shaul had given the empty place at the table a puzzled glance or two, but said nothing. If Abbi did the same thing today, he himself would have to broach the subject somehow, and he wasn't looking forward to asking, since he had been unable to come up with a better way to determine the king's attitude other than the lie Dahveed had suggested. "Yahweh, may your hesed stay with me today, that I may know what to tell your servant, Dahveed," he muttered as he left his chamber.

Out in the private court, Abner waited for the king. He bowed slightly to the hassar. "Shalom."

"Shalom, General. Is all well with your house?"

"Yes, Hassar. And yours?"

"Satisfactory, General."

The king appeared and took Jonathan's arm this afternoon. He had taken Abner's the day before. "You look tired, my son. You must rest more."

"I'll try, adoni. When the feast is over, work will usually begin to slow down."

They went up the stairs to the throne room, and Jonathan seated the king and placed the spear of office in its stand. Guests streamed in, and once the food had been served, Shaul glanced again at Dahveed's empty place, frowning.

Jonathan ate little, hardly hearing the talk flowing around him, his mind absorbed with wondering when he would have the time to learn all that he needed to know, and how he would manage to keep his actions from the king's eyes. As a result he almost missed his abbi's question.

"Jonathan, why hasn't the Dahveed come to the feast yesterday or today? Surely he is no longer ceremonially unclean."

The hassar glanced up. "He begged permission to observe the feast with his clan in Bethlehem, adoni. He said Jesse's bekor had ordered him to come. I gave him leave to go."

"*You* gave him leave to go?" The king's eyes started to glitter, and he placed his hands on the table, pushing himself up. "He was here, and you gave him leave to *go*, you son of perverse rebellion?"

His hands clenched on either side of his plate, Jonathan turned white.

"Do you think I'm blind?" the king's voice rose to a roar, "That I don't know you have sided with the son of Jesse to your own shame and the disgrace of the woman who bore you?"

The hassar gritted his teeth, every muscle tense with rage at the attack on his immi.

"As long as that son of Jesse lives, neither you, nor your kingdom, will be safe! Send for him, and bring him to me for *he will become a son of death!*" As the king's shout died away, the room fell silent. No one dared to move, staring at the enraged king towering over the hassar.

Getting a strangle hold on his temper, Jonathan met his abbi's glare with one of his own. "Why should he die?" he asked between clenched teeth. "What has he done? There is no wrong found in him, yet you would kill him?"

Shaul whirled, grabbing his spear from the stand, and hurled it at his son. A horrified cry rose from the guests, but Jonathan had thrown himself to the side, and the spear vibrated in the floor beyond him.

Slowly the hassar stood, stepping back from the table and straightening to his full height, staring at his abbi, his face blank. "You hate Dahveed enough to shed your own blood now?" he asked, his voice a purr. "You *live* because of Dahveed's hesed." Turning to the spear, he yanked it from the floor, rotating it in his hands.

The king watched as if in a trance. The guests sat like stone. Staring straight at the king, Shaul's oldest son raised the spear in both hands and drove it into the floor, bringing from it an explosive crack! "Know this, adoni," he purred, "you have already brought Yahweh's curse down on us! But by Yahweh's life, *our house shall shed no more innocent blood!*" Whirling, he strode out the door, leaving the spear upright behind him.

Still trembling, he headed straight to his chamber, knowing that he dared not go anywhere else for fear of what his temper might do. He barred the door after him, then grabbed the hem of his robe and ripped it apart to his waist. Pacing like a caged lion, his heart burned with fury for the public insult to his immi, and the dishonor brought on Dahveed and himself. Once he had calmed enough to sit, he smeared ashes on his forehead and hands and fasted the rest of the day, sick at heart at what he must tell Dahveed.

It was long past dark when someone knocked. "Jonathan Hassar?" Ishvi's voice asked.

Instead of replying, Jonathan unbarred the door, standing back so that his brother could enter. Then he slammed it shut again.

Ishvi took his right hand and touched his knee to the floor.

Jonathan let out an explosive sigh, sitting down on the clothes chest beside him. "You always were balm to my rages, Ishvi."

"I wish I could find one for mine," the sar replied, getting up. "And the only reason Malchi hasn't spread general slaughter was the look on Abner's face when he went to get the king's spear and the handle came off in his hand. Did you know you broke it?"

Jonathan nodded.

Glancing around the room, Ishvi commented, "You didn't break anything here."

"Too afraid to start."

"Abbi was shaken by what you did, Jonathan."

"Pray Yahweh that he never learns how close I came to killing him," the hassar said savagely. "I don't know what held me back, not after he named Immi 'Perverse Rebellion!'"

"He will sue for peace sometime."

"I don't know that there can be peace between us."

Ishvi leaned against the door. "Will you leave?"

"And give the king free rein to hunt down the Dahveed? Absolutely not!"

His brother sighed in relief. "Good, because I didn't think I'd be able to stop him!"

Early the next morning, Jonathan dressed for hunting. He had wrestled for long hours that night with very bitter thoughts, the worst being that, at present, he was incapable of protecting Dahveed. But he'd been so certain that Shaul would again forget his anger and take the zammar back as always. It wasn't until he had sat there, almost too stunned to move, with King Shaul's spear vibrating in the floor in back of him, that he had truly believed that his abbi meant to kill Dahveed.

His own arrogance had nearly cost Dahveed's life. And he could thank Yahweh that Michal had been married to the zammar and not

Merab, for the bekorah would never have been able to save Dahveed and herself as his little sister had.

Letting himself out of the private courtyard, he walked to the armory. As always, Dara heard his steps and opened the door to the room he stayed in. "Hassar?"

"I'm going hunting. Have my new arrow boy get ready."

"Yes, Hassar."

The boy's solemn eyes and anxious glance made Jonathan smile as they walked down the road through town. This lad was so different from Ethan's son, Nimshi, who never had shown proper respect, but who was always right where he should be. The Habiru lad was 13 now, nearly as good as Dara at repairing armor, and his shield-bearer said that he would soon be able to make armor as well. Jonathan still preferred him to anyone else as an attendant when he left town, but today, he needed someone innocent and too small to ask questions.

The bow on his back was the composite one Dahveed had given him. Having tried it several times, he was amazed at the power and range of the weapon. It gave him an odd feeling whenever he held it, almost as if someone's large, powerful hands covered his. He kept it in a loose leather sheath that Dara had made. The shape of the bow couldn't be disguised, but the maker and the ivory and silver could.

The boy looked around at the forest as they walked, and Jonathan remembered the feel of Dahveed's hands on his wrists that night in the anteroom, and again when he was sick. He smiled briefly at the memory of the zammar's questions, his hesitancy, his efforts to learn and become whatever he was asked to know and be. And through it all, he'd felt the stirring of something more, something greater, growing and developing under the surface. Jonathan wished he might see that some day. Catch a glimpse of the king Yahweh had chosen for Himself, be able to rejoice in the results of his loyalty and labors.

Ezel. "The stone of departure." He knew his heart would break.

¥ ¥ ¥ ¥ ¥ ¥

Afraid to think of what might have happened yesterday or the day before, I waited. I'd used my time alone to compose the rest of the song I'd begun in Navyoth, ignoring my frustration that I couldn't play it. As I ran over the words of the verses again, I thought of all that had happened the day before I left Shamuel. Too distraught to even hunt for my lunch, I paced back and forth, singing the verses again and again, until I could finally concentrate enough to think of more. I rearranged their order a little, and then reviewed the entire song.

"Deliver me from my enemies, O God. From the ones who rise up against me, You will set me on high.

Deliver me from the ones who do deceit, and from men of blood save me.

For, behold, they lie in ambush for my soul. The fierce ones assemble against me, not for my rebellion and not for my sin, O Yahweh.

Without culpability, they run and establish themselves. Rouse Yourself to meet me and see!

Even You, Yahweh God of armies, God of Israel. Awake to take account of all the peoples. Do not be gracious to all the faithless ones of deceit.

They will return at evening. They will howl as dogs, and they will go round the city.

Behold, they belch from their mouth swords from their lips. For who is listening?

But You, Yahweh, You will laugh at them. You will deride all the nations.

My strength, let me watch for You because God is my refuge.

God of divine loyalty, He will be in front of me. God will make me look triumphantly on my enemies.

Do not kill them, lest my people forget. Shake them with your power and bring them down, our Shield, my Lord."

Now I should insert the first verses I'd composed. As I'd suspected, they fit best at the end.

"Because of the sin of their mouth, the word of their lips, they will be captured in their arrogance, and because of a curse and a lie which they repeat.

Destroy in anger! Destroy, and they are not there. And they will know that God is the one who rules in Jacob to the ends of the earth.

And they will return at evening and they will howl like dogs and go around the city.

They themselves will roam about for food. If they are not sated, then they remain all night.

But I, I sing of Your strength, and I shout with joy in the morning of Your divine loyalty. For You are a refuge to me and a place of escape in a day of adversity for me.

O my strength, let me sing praises to You for God is my refuge, the God of divine loyalty to me." [2]

Once I had finished the song, my mind inevitably reverted to worry over the fact that Jonathan still hadn't come. What if he was unable to leave? Had the king killed him in a rage because of what I'd asked him to say? I paced under the oaks on the south side of the huge upthrust of rock called the Ezel stone. Across the meadow I could see the waterfall, now dry, that marked the tiny cup valley where Jeshua's band trained. Where I had first fought the hassar, and beaten him. And where he had first bowed to me, forcing me to acknowledge the honor Yahweh had given me. "Yah, why hasn't he come?" I pleaded in the morning sunlight, resolving that if he didn't arrive by noon, I was going to Gibeah and find out why.

Just then I heard Jonathan's voice. I nearly collapsed in relief, then scrambled to the edge of the forest where I could watch. He stood in the middle of the meadow and took his time getting set, giving instructions to the small boy that accompanied him. I watched with a smile as he strained to string his weapon. Maybe the fact that he'd brought Boaz's bow meant he had good news.

"Run now, and find the arrows I shoot," the hassar's rich voice directed.

The arrow whined through the air, and I shuddered. I'd not want to get hit with one of those. It could be driven right through a man. The boy ran forward as Jonathan shot again, and then again. Holding my breath, I leaned forward. Could I return?

"Isn't that one beyond you?" the hassar called, his voice a bit unsteady as the lad ran for the last arrow.

I hit the oak beside me with my hand. "Yahweh, please, no!" I whispered.

"Hurry, now," he added. "Don't linger. Go as quickly as you can."

My heart leaden in my chest, I slumped down. The king must have been furious for the hassar to add such urgency to his message. There would be no more days in court, visits with Jonathan, and nights with Michal.

But where could I go? I dared not remain in the heart of Shaul's

---

[2] Psalm 59

tribal territory. I knew no one in the north and had few connections there. While I might stay with a band of Habiru allied with Ethan, I would be a constant danger to them.

I could only go south, in direct disobedience to the king's command, and that would fire his anger still more. Finally, I turned, my body shaking, to get one last glimpse of Jonathan Hassar before he left. Watching his arrow boy walk from the clearing carrying the bow and quiver, he stood alone.

At least I could say good-by. I stepped out of the trees with everything this man had ever done for me rising in my memory. What would I do without the hassar's protection? How could I live? When he caught sight of me, I dropped, my face to the ground. What could I say to him?

Then I started forward again, seeing the tears on his face as I approached, and again I knelt, bowing a second time, knowing nothing that I could do would really tell him what I felt, hoping my body would indicate what my words could not. He held out his hand, and I knelt the third time at his feet, the dry grass prickling my forehead as I dug my fingers into it.

"Dahveed."

"Yes, Nahsi?" I replied, raising my head.

His hand helped me up, and once again I felt the strength of his embrace. I clung to him, my shoulders shaking with every breath. Tears flowed from his eyes, and he wept with me.

"Nahsi, no."

"He is determined, Dahveed. You have to go. I cannot protect you. Abner does the king's bidding, and they will kill you if you stay. I could not bear to know that my house had taken your life. Please, Dahveed, you must go!"

"Yahweh, I cannot!" I cried in my heart, clinging to the man who had become the rock of my life, unable to silence my weeping. I knew what it was to live without the comforting presence of someone who cared about me, not just as a clan member or a servant, but as a beloved brother, friend, and son. Now I couldn't bear the thought of going back to that loneliness and insecurity.

His arms tightened around me until I could feel the beat of his heart against my chest while I trembled with grief and fear, tears streaming from my eyes. At last his hold loosened, and he stepped back a little.

"Dahveed, there is no alternative. When I asked what you had done to wrong the king, he threw his spear at me. You must do this. Please, go."

I looked into his black eyes, and read there a pain greater than my own. Not only was he torn by our separation, but by his abbi's opposition to Yahweh and by the slow disintegration that was ripping his family apart. What he had said was true. If Shaul succeeded in killing me, he would die from the shame and grief.

But I could save him from that. There was something I *could* do for him, the one who had done so much for me. I pulled myself away. "I will go, Jonathan." A final time I knelt to him, my hands gripping his. "*Thank you, Nahsi.*"

He didn't correct me, just managed a smile and gripped my hands so hard that they hurt. "You have served the king faithfully. Now, go from here in peace, Dahveed."

Jonathan had fulfilled his promise to give back my freedom! I bent my head, my heart breaking.

"And remember, Yahweh Himself will remain between us and our descendants forever." Pulling me to my feet, he kissed my forehead as the roeh had the evening that he anointed me.

Unable to speak, I tore myself away, walking swiftly from the clearing.

¥ ¥ ¥ ¥ ¥ ¥

Jonathan watched Dahveed disappear into the trees. Could he have prevented this if he had listened to Michal? If he had watched his abbi more carefully? If, if, if . . . Slowly, he headed toward the trees that Dahveed had hidden behind, putting his hand on the upthrust of the Ezel stone. He leaned against it, his pain too great for tears. "Who will be my friend now?" he whispered.

Tamar bat Dahveed

It is time for Dahveed to go, and Yahweh has seen to it. Perhaps nothing less than immediate threat to his life would have sent the Mashiah away from the one he clung to so fiercely. But Dahveed has gained what he needed to know of the court and the king's power and ways. Now it is time for him to learn other things, and as the roeh feared, the lessons will be long and hard.

The Evil One was not pleased that his plan against Yahweh failed, and he has sent his darkness a second time after his enemy's chosen one. Indeed, that darkness already overshadows Dahveed, blinding him to the point that he has placed himself where the Evil One can do with him as he wills. The risk is great, for Yahweh cannot interfere unless Dahveed turns to Him.

Ittai and Gath

CHAPTER 7

Following the bend of the hill south, I wiped the tears from my eyes as I fled from Jonathan and the Ezel stone. The shamed defeat in Jonathan's eyes when he had told me he could no longer protect me had thrust a deeper agony into me than the wounds of the lioness.

The gully I followed suddenly deepened, and I angled east out of it, laboring up the hill crowned by an oak grove. The leaves underfoot rustled briefly as I passed, the mature trees blocking much of the sun, leaving the ground beneath clear of brush.

As I crossed the hilltop, the training Ethan gave me asserted itself, and my mind pulled away from my grief, knowing that I must think carefully now if I was to escape the reach of the king. I was Sar Dahveed no longer, and the sooner I got used to living like a fugitive the longer I'd survive. Speed was my best weapon now, and very nearly my only weapon. I glanced at the sun. Jonathan had come to Ezel quite early, and it was not yet noon. It might be best to find Hakkohen Haggadol Ahimelech before the end of the noon rest, because the tabernacle would be busy with people and sacrifices during this festival. With about three and a half more miles to go, I should make it in time.

I entered Nob using the Habiru's back door, the local garbage ravine. Walking through the town, I avoided the few people on the streets and hoped the stench from the ravine hadn't clung to me. Where would I find the Hakkohen Haggadol? Normally, he would be sitting at the door of the tabernacle, but I dared not approach him publicly. Might he be taking the noon rest near the tabernacle? "Lead me, Yah," I whispered. Dust puffed under my sandals as I left the town and traveled up the well-used road across the hill. One or two Gibeonites were about, but they paid no attention to me. At the top, I spotted the Hakkohen Haggadol resting under the sprawled branches of a terebinth tree. Relieved to have found him so quickly, I hurried over.

"Adoni?" I said softly from several feet away, not wanting to startle him from his rest.

The elderly man opened his eyes and glanced around. He stared when he saw me, recognition flaring to alarm in his eyes and staying the words on my tongue. What was wrong?

Climbing to his feet, he approached, trembling. "You're alone, Dahveed. Why is this?" he asked, clasping his hands to keep them still. "Where are the men that usually come with you? They don't need to wait so far away. This isn't holy ground, you know."

I eyed Ahimelech in amazement. This was nothing like the usual greeting he gave me. He still trembled so the bells on his garment tinkled, and he shifted a little, making the sound more distinct.

Movement caught the corner of my eye, and the realization washed over me that someone else was present. A flash of fear made me close my eyes an instant, sick with my carelessness. I hadn't given a single thought to my surroundings, something that told me eloquently how out-of-practice I was at living as a Habiru.

A nearly imperceptible movement of the Hakkohen's head indicated where I should look, and I pushed back my cloak, turning slightly to see. To my horror, Doeg, the Edomite, lay on the ground just a few feet away, watching us sleepily.

Of all the men who could have been here, Doeg was the worst possible one! Since he had been awarded the Hittite military title "Chief of the Shepherds," he spent his off-duty time either making trouble, or currying favor with King Shaul. What was he doing here, dressed like a servant?

"Surely your escort knows they are welcome here?" the Hakkohen said, his eyes steady on mine as I turned back to him.

"The king sent me on some urgent business that he wants kept private, so I told the others to meet me outside of town. I stopped off to see if you have any food I could take with me. A few loaves of bread, or anything you have readily available would save me some time."

The words came out of my mouth without thought, reminding me of how hungry I actually was, and I hoped Ahimelech would see fit to actually give me some food if he could. But my heart sank at his reply.

"We don't have any regular bread here," he said slowly, "just the old loaves of consecrated bread from the tabernacle that were replaced today. I suppose I could give you that if the men with you have not slept with any women lately."

Doeg yawned and sat up, looking interested at the mention of women.

"My escorts are always consecrated before a journey with me, Hakkohen, even on ordinary errands for the king. I made sure of it this time since the king's business was so important," I played along, having recovered my presence of mind.

"You can take the old bread, then," Ahimelech decided. "It should be around here somewhere. I don't think it's been taken away yet."

"It's right here, Hakkohen," Doeg spoke up, pointing to a nearby sack. "I brought it with me to take back to town after the noon rest."

"Very good, Doeg," Ahimelech replied. "Bring it here."

The Edomite did as requested, studying me while he handed the sack over.

I knew I had several details to account for, not the least of which was my lack of weapons. I turned back to Ahimelech. "I know this is an unusual request, but do you have a sword or even a spear around somewhere? Since I had to leave so quickly I didn't have time to get my own."

The Hakkohen looked perfectly composed now, his earlier agitation gone, as he frowned in thought. "All we have is Goliath's sword. It's been here since you killed him at the Valley of Elah. We keep it wrapped in a cloth behind the ark[3]. If you want to use it, you can. It's the only weapon around here that I know of."

"I'll be delighted to have it," I answered eagerly. "I don't think there's another one like it anywhere."

Ahimelech led the way to the tabernacle, and I felt Doeg's sharp eyes on me every step of the way. He watched while the Hakkohen Haggadol entered the tabernacle and retrieved the sword.

"Yahweh will be with you, Dahveed," the elderly priest said as he handed it to me. "Go quickly!" he added in a whisper.

"Thank you, Hakkohen," I replied, bowing my head before walking rapidly toward the path that would take me to the Jebus-Jericho road. Although I didn't intend to go that way, with Doeg watching, I couldn't disappear into the Kidron Valley to the south. How long would I have before the Edomite told King Shaul what he had seen? Then I frowned in puzzlement. Why was Ahimelech treating the commander as if he were a Gibeonite servant?

As I passed a tree, I acquired a companion.

"Shalom, Dahveed," he said softly. "Since Doeg is likely

---

[3] Contextual clues in 1 and 2 Samuel strongly indicate that the word "ephod," when NOT modified by the word "linen," refers to the ark of the covenant. This change makes more sense of several incidents in the story. I have, therefore, used it. See also A Word About . . . The Ark.

watching, we'll give him something to see."

"Who are you?" I asked through tight lips, continuing down the road.

Dressed similarly to an escort, he wore a sword and carried a bow and quiver with arrows in it. "One who wishes you well, as all here do. More will join us soon. After a suitable time, Doeg will see a group hurrying down the road to Jebus. By that time, he won't be able to distinguish one from another, so you can be well away. In the meantime, there is one who would speak with you."

I said nothing, knowing that I dare not act as if anything was unusual so long as Doeg could see. At the first clump of trees, my companion turned aside, and I reluctantly followed, wanting more and more to be away from here. Six other men waited, dressed as the first. As I entered the shade, a seventh man, wearing a white kilt, met me, bowing.

"Mahesa!" I gasped in astonishment, looking from the ancient gold collar that circled his neck to his dark blue eyes and the piercing glance that seemed to stare right through me. I had last seen him after Shaul had made me general, and he had been forced to accompany the Philistine army into the hills with his unit of archers and his young charge. Against Jonathan's wishes, I had spared his life after he fought us in the battle, letting him continue his interrupted journey escorting a young noble. What on earth was he doing here? Then, in spite of my surprise, I had to shift my gaze from his eyes.

The tall man lowered them in deference to my discomfort. "I beg your indulgence, adoni. If you would give this man your cloak?"

My mind abruptly returned to my present situation, and I turned to see a man who closely resembled my height and build. Stripping off the cloak, I handed it to him. He flipped it over his shoulders as I had been wearing it. Mahesa took the sack of bread from my hands, pulled out three of the loaves, and gave the sack to the man. Holding it where it could be seen, he stepped out of the clump of trees, followed by his escort. They headed swiftly down the road.

"How do you come to be here? Did your charge safely reach his destination?" I asked curiously, studying the man before me, noticing scars on his back and shoulders.

A quick look of pain crossed his face. "Yes, Debeset reached Mari and Babylon, then returned home in safety," he replied, staring into the distance a moment. "Although it might have been better if he had not. I am not skilled in court politics, adoni, and I did not know that Debeset's father was out of favor with the Pharaoh as I suspected myself to be. There were assassins hired to strike us on the Way of the Sea near Mount Carmel. Pharaoh thought to punish us both in one blow."

I chuckled softly. "Instead, we escorted you to Dan, avoiding the ambush!"

Mahesa nodded. "But just after we crossed the border into the Black Land, an old retainer of mine found us and told me the true situation. Debeset's father had already been executed and my son sold, I do not know where." He paused a minute to steady his voice. "I sent the escort of archers away and took Debeset myself to find his mother and helped them flee by ship. Then I returned to my home, hoping to learn more about my son, but Pharaoh found me there, and I was brought to him for trial." His face became very still, and I looked away in sympathy.

"I was condemned and severely beaten, then taken to Egypt's border and cast from my homeland. My retainer followed after me with the collar, staying with me until a family of wanderers came by. He paid them to take me to Beersheba. They took me most of the way, then grew afraid that I would die and they would somehow be blamed. When I woke up one morning, they were gone."

"What did you do?" I asked, as he turned away, leaning against the sycamore fig tree we stood under.

"I had heard that El Shaddai sometimes accepted foreigners as servants in His tabernacle, and I had nothing left in my homeland. Somehow I managed to get here. I don't remember much about the trip," he finished wryly, turning back to me.

"It's a wonder you survived!" I exclaimed, stunned at the mass of scars I'd seen on the man's back.

The Egyptian smiled a little. "Hakkohen Abiathar tells me that I very nearly didn't! I have been here since, serving El Shaddai." He paused a moment before turning toward the tabernacle on the hill above us. "It has always fascinated me, ever since I first heard tales of the temple that moved, and the riches that followed wherever it went. I have learned everything I could about it." Then he met my gaze briefly. "El Shaddai has been gracious to me, and I am content to live in the Great One's land and serve here until I die. Abiathar has promised that I will be buried here at Nob.

"But we have spoken enough, for there is not much time left to you, adoni. The king will declare you outlawed, and you must be out of Israel when that happens."

"Outlawed!" I gasped. "But I have done nothing to deserve that!"

The Egyptian looked at me with grim patience. "You have not died, Dahveed. And you were supposed to, several times over. There will be no pretense any more. Shaul will hunt you."

"How do you know this?" I asked, bewildered at the certainty in his voice and stunned by the revelation that the king I loved as abbi would treat me as a criminal who would bring wrath and justice down on anyone who aided me, or even neglected to report me. My stomach knotted with fear. I could survive as an outcast, but never as an outlaw!

Mahesa faced me. "Yahweh spoke to the Hakkohen Haggadol in a dream last night, revealing the king's mind. The word of your outlawing will go out tomorrow, after the feast has ended. The Hakkohen expected that you would come to the tabernacle later this afternoon. The only danger to you here was Doeg, and he would have been back in Nob by then and would never have seen you."

"But I came early," I groaned. "No wonder Ahimelech was so agitated. Why is Doeg here?"

"He is detained here under El Shaddai while Sar Malchi investigates a possible charge of murder against him. While he is here, he makes himself useful."

"I can't imagine he likes that," I commented wryly.

Mahesa raised his eyes to mine. "Doeg has not been a problem," he said calmly.

Sweat breaking out on my forehead, I looked away. "I can see why not. But he will tell the king what he has seen."

"Only if it will bring advantage to him," Mahesa reminded me. "In some ways, this is a very closed place, adoni. One such as Doeg will only hear what the Hakkohen Haggadol wants him to hear. The Gibeonites do not speak to him and would tell him nothing in any case. They know well who stopped their slaughter, adoni. Their gratitude runs deep. So the king will learn nothing from Doeg for a long while yet."

I shifted uneasily. "Watch him, Mahesa. I don't trust him. He should not be in Israel."

He glanced at me in surprise. "Do not worry about him, adoni. It is not Yahweh's will that he cross your path, but mine."

The certainty in the answer sent a chill through me.

The Egyptian eyed the sun. "Doeg will be in Nob now. It is time for you to go." He held out another cloak to replace the one I had given away.

As we stepped into the sunlight, Mahesa's hair blazed momentarily with red, the highlights testifying to his descent from Jacob's beloved son. "You have amply repaid your debt, Mahesa," I said as I prepared to leave.

"I serve El Shaddai," he replied. "Shalom."

Looking across the Jebus-Bethlehem road, I took a loaf of the consecrated bread from my girdle and tried to eat, but it was too hard to bite. Finally I took out my belt knife and chipped off little pieces to hold in my mouth until they softened enough to chew. Since I had been unable to inquire through the Hakkohen Haggadol, I wasn't certain what I should do next. As an outlaw, I would put anyone who helped me in danger of their life, and sooner or later, someone would betray me. Which meant that I must leave Israel, and given how angry Shaul evidently was, I doubted I'd find much safety in Judah either.

Chipping off another piece of bread, I put it in my mouth. After my dealings with Balak, Moab did not appeal to me, and while King Nahash of Ammon would likely welcome me, going to Shaul's first enemy would only fan the fires of his anger. Giving up on eating more of the bread, I tucked it away. The sun had nearly set, and the road was empty. Slipping across it, I pushed through the brush into the forest beyond and started the two-mile run to the road leading to Timnah. I couldn't go north, east, or south. That left west to Philistia, and limited time to traverse the 23 miles ahead of me before dawn.

Bitterness welled up in me as I fled across the highland plateau. The king had not only stripped me of honor, but of family, inheritance, and place under Yahweh's hand, leaving me where I had begun my life 23 years ago, belonging to no one and with nothing.

The growing darkness under the pines, terebinths, and oaks of the plateau sheltered me as well as forced me to slow my pace. My stomach growled again, and I decided I would stop at the hidden seep near Timnah and soak enough bread to stay my hunger. Ethan had always said that adequate rest served better than speed most of the time. Another shaft of pain went through me. What would Ethan think of Yahweh's Mashiah as an outlaw?

Cresting a rise, I ducked a pine branch, my steps muffled by the thick carpet of pine needles. The wind brought the faint scent of the great sea as it whispered through the branches above. Once on the road, I set my pace to a slow jog, harboring my strength until I reached the seep.

Once there, the rock-like bread resisted softening, but eventually I ate an entire loaf, then half of the second one. I drank deeply, nearly emptying the small basin. It would be another day before it was full again. Leaning back, I looked up at the stars which peeked through the dying leaves. I must be out of my senses to consider the Philistines, but I had one chance in the land of Dagon, and none here.

There, I could sell my fighting abilities. The cities in Philistia with the greatest need for mercenaries would be Ekron or Gath, and I could reach either one before dawn. But the danger made my stomach harden. If anyone recognized me, I would get less mercy than Samson found 40 years ago. Torture and disfigurement were the least I could expect, and more than likely, my body would decorate the wall of the city until the birds had stripped my bones of my flesh.

Shuddering at the thought, I rose and went back to the road, for the stars told me the night was half over. The road wound through a valley north of Elah, and when it climbed up the ridge, I paused in indecision. Gath or Ekron? But Ekron meant Seren Manani, and if I ever fell under Manani's power, only Yahweh Himself could rescue me. The cruel seren would delight in dangling me in front of the hassar, torturing him again as he had done through Nemuel all those years ago. To say nothing of the political uses he would garner with me in his grasp. And given the reciprocal hatred between him and Jonathan, going there seemed completely insane instead of just mildly mad.

Still hesitating, I questioned again whether or not I should continue with my plan. But I couldn't see any way I could survive under Shaul. I had to get away, and that meant out of Israel, and the most salable market for my fighting skills was Philistia.

At last, I turned south, heading for Gath. I followed the watershed for nearly a mile and a half as it dropped 800 feet into the Elah, which twisted and turned, descending the first giant land stair to the Shephelah. I came out opposite the point of a broad triangle of flat plain that pointed to Socoh. Beyond that, at the final drop to the coastal plain, the Elah narrowed again.

When I got to the junction of roads near Socoh, I rested, rubbing my trembling legs. They had to last another hour or more, and the muscles under the lion scars on my right thigh were cramping with fatigue.

The eastern sky had just begun to lighten when I looked down the last step to the coastal plain. Two hundred feet down and five miles straight west stood the walls of Gath. Knowing that I must find some place to hide, I searched for a small cave or nook in the rock for nearly an hour before I noticed a hole just big enough for me to crawl in. I drew Goliath's sword and poked the blade inside. I didn't want any unpleasant surprises when I crawled into my bed for the day.

The hole opened out into a tiny, low room. Setting the sword to one side, I stretched out on my cloak to watch the plain lighten as the sun's rays broke over the hills behind me. Against the sky, I saw the smudge of smoke that marked Gath.

Weariness and discouragement washed over me. "What have I done, Yahweh, that I should find myself here, about to trust myself to my deadly enemies?" I whispered. Rolling onto my back, I pillowed my head on my hands and stared dismally at the gloom of the ceiling of the cave.

When I opened my eyes again, it took several moments to remember where I was. I tried to move and gasped, my muscles telling me plainly what they thought of yesterday's activities. But I forced myself to move and stretch, well aware of the dangers I might meet once I left this place, and I must be ready if I wanted to survive.

It was late afternoon when I checked outside. My disgrace would be broadcast from Hebron to Shechem by now, and would reach Beersheba and Dan tomorrow. I just hoped I could slip safely into Philistia before word reached any of the cities here.

After crawling out of my cave, I did the best I could to straighten my clothes and hair, and then faced west again. For a long minute I stared in wonder. I'd never been this close to the coastal plain before and I'd never seen land so wide and flat. The line toward which the sun sank was perfectly straight and blue. No wonder the Philistines didn't like the hills. I could see now how a horde of chariots could be devastating to an army down here. There was simply nowhere to hide in all that flatness.

Taking a deep breath, I stepped away from the cave, then halted again. I couldn't walk into Gath carrying Goliath's sword! I might as well hire runners and criers to announce my name to the entire city if I did. No, I was going to have to walk into the stronghold of my worst enemies with only my belt knife and my sling. "Yahweh, I'm a fool," I muttered, taking the sword from my back and shoving it back into the cave.

Keeping cover under the trees, I descended the sloping hills, leaving the pines behind, and walking now under cypress, oak, and tamarisk. Increasingly, more paths crossed my way, and I moved with even more caution, listening closely to hear any sound that might indicate the presence of another human nearby.

The sun sank still lower, and I stopped at the end of the forest, scanning the almond grove between me and Gath. I edged forward. The trees were well-kept and had produced a good crop this year. I wondered who owned it. Slowing my steps still more, I squinted in the sun's rays, nearly horizontal between the rows of trees. The youth watching me in the next row stood so still that I had walked into plain view before catching sight of him.

CHAPTER 8

Standing there in the almond grove, assessing the outline of the youth down the row of trees, I cursed myself again. He watched silently, standing with the confidence that came with high status, as I debated what to do. Deciding boldness was the best choice, I approached him, trying to see more of his face. After deliberately turning his head, he then stepped toward me. I heard the faint sounds of others in the direction he had looked. In the rapidly waning light I still couldn't see him clearly, so when he knelt, it caught me completely off guard. Instantly I halted, my ears alert for any sound, trying to understand why he would act this way.

Glancing around, I verified that we were still alone and out of sight. I closed the gap between us, halting a prudent distance away.

"I bid you shalom, adoni," he said. "How may I serve you?"

I began to wonder if I'd fallen asleep in that cave and was dreaming. "Who are you?" I couldn't resist asking, thickening my southern accent.

"Have you forgotten so soon one you took as son, adoni?"

"Ittai!" I exclaimed, remembering the wild storm that had swept through our war camp the evening this youth had outrageously bargained for the rite of circumcision to save his life, in the process binding and subordinating his house to me as I became his covenantal abbi. I smiled a little. "You will have to admit, Ittai, that our previous meeting was brief, eventful, and rather chaotic. I have yet to get a good look at your face today, so come here and let me see you."

Rising with a grace that was inbred, he approached me, turning in the light so I could study him. He had grown considerably since I'd seen him more than a year ago, but the watchfulness in the back of his brown eyes remained the same, as did that steady direct gaze that had fastened on me in my war tent that evening.

"Would there be a place I could stay the night?" I asked.

"Yes, adoni. My house can shelter you. But it is within the walls of Gath, and you will have to go through the gate." He stopped, staring past me, his eyes blank.

"Strangers cannot walk through your gates?"

"Your pardon, adoni, but you are so obviously Israelite, it would cause comment."

I remained silent as he continued to think, his hand reaching up to touch his chin.

"Follow our group. I will get you through the gate. Once inside, go straight across the market to the first alley by the palace. Wait there for a few minutes, then knock on the third door on the right."

I nodded just as a woman called, "Ittai? Where are you?"

"I must go. She worries since last year." He hurried away. "Just over here, Immi," he called as he went.

The words brought to mind my own immi, and my mouth tightened. Keeping track of the group ahead of me by their voices, I glimpsed the road and hurried to it so that it would appear as if I'd been on it when they emerged from the grove.

Ittai walked with his immi, accompanied by four guards and two serving women, and I noted how often she turned to him or touched him while talking the whole time. His abbi may have been an Israelite slave, but obviously Ittai's immi loved her son anyway.

The guard at the gate stiffened to attention as I approached. Ittai spoke briefly, and the man stepped back, satisfied, motioning me in. Ignoring the others, I crossed the square, noting the arrangements of the buildings and shops and where the stairs to the wall were. The palace on my right was two stories with windows only on the second story. It sprawled along the entire length of the market. I turned down the first alley beyond it as directed, and once in the shadows, looked back. No one appeared to have noticed me. The shop keepers were busy closing, and the guard at the gate was changing. Ittai and his party had already left the square, and I waited until the gates had shut and most of the activity in the square had died down before heading down the alley in the near darkness and knocking on the third door.

I knocked again before it opened, and Ittai held a lamp up for me to see my way into the house.

"This way, adoni," he said, leading me down a passage with rooms on both sides. We turned a corner, and as we passed a room with a light in it, a man's voice called, "Ittai, is that you?"

Raising his hand for silence, the youth opened the door a little. "Yes, dodi. I was just going to my chambers."

"Along with that stranger you got through the gates, I suppose?" the voice continued in exasperation.

Cocking my head, I looked at Ittai. He had his bottom lip between his teeth, and the lamp in his hand shook a bit.

"Please wait, adoni," he murmured, and then went all the way into the room, shutting the door behind him without latching it. Making certain that I moved silently, I stationed myself where I could hear what went on.

"Your immi is neither deaf nor blind, Ittai," the man said. "She heard you tell the guard the man behind was a messenger for the palace. Furthermore, she knew the only time you could have spoken to that man was in the almond grove. Who are you trying to bring down upon us this time? Need I remind you what happened a year ago? Your foolishness nearly got you killed."

When Ittai replied his voice was steady. "I learned my lesson last year, dodi. I will never bring someone I don't know into this house again. The man with me tonight is my abbi."

"Your abbi died before you were born," the older man snapped.

"Was executed, you mean," the youth said calmly.

"Where did you hear that?"

"I know the whole story, dodi. The soldiers still talk about it, and I listen. Someday, I'll get Immi to tell me her side. She has never forgiven grandfather for what he did, you know."

"Your immi could hardly know what happened. She wasn't herself."

The man's tone carried a hint of bluster, and my lips twitched.

"Immi knew exactly what happened and why. She loved Ribai, and he loved her."

"He was a slave--and an Israelite!" his uncle snorted contemptuously.

I tensed at his tone. My welcome here seemed shakier by the moment.

"Which makes me half Israelite, doesn't it, dodi? Should I be executed, too?"

There was no answer, and the silence stretched out. "Ribai was a good man," the man in the room finally admitted quietly. "He made your immi very happy, and if it's any comfort, I didn't agree with your grandfather's decision. But none of this is explaining why you called the man you let in the gate your abbi."

"Immi must never learn what I need to tell you," Ittai said, his voice suddenly decisive.

"Why not?"

"She is frightened enough already. I didn't tell everything that happened last year. I've never told anyone."

Another silence stretched in the room, and when Ittai's dodi spoke, his voice had subtly changed. He was no longer a dodi talking to a nephew about a small transgression.

"Tell me now, then."

"After the magician lured me out into the fields, and I saw the soldiers from Ekron, I didn't manage to get away and hide until the next morning like I told Immi. They took me, and there were 10 of them, not five."

I could tell the man in the room was listening quite attentively now.

"Go on."

"They bound me, and took me straight into the hills, past the Shephelah, up into the highlands in spite of the storm sweeping in from the sea. The soldiers had been hired to take me to Manani, dodi."

The sharp intake of breath from the other occupant told me that he fully appreciated the peril his nephew had escaped.

"I was desperate, dodi. I knew what would happen if Seren Manani got me. So when I saw a warrior standing above the trail in the forest, I fell on my knees and silently begged him with my eyes to help me."

The Philistine youth went on to tell the whole story of the fight, and how he had tried to flee, only to be brought back to me.

"Was it one of the Israelite commanders?" Ittai's dodi asked, his voice hard. "Had some of them remained so long after we left?"

"There was only one unit there that entire season. They kept all of our units at bay. It was Dahveed Israel himself."

"Dahveed?! The one who killed Goliath? He had you?"

"Yes, Dodi. He and his unit were the ones who rescued me from Manani's hirelings."

"Why would he do such a thing?" the man gasped.

"I told you, I asked him to."

"How is it that you still live? Surely he had no reason to keep you alive."

"I made a covenant with him."

"You *what*?"

"He was collecting foreskins as a bride price, and only needed one more. I gave him mine in exchange for my life and a covenant of peace between him and my house."

"He cut you? He used your flesh to buy his bride?" The voice from Ittai's dodi raised the hair on my neck. Flattening against the wall, I mentally retraced my way through the house to the door and the city gates. But I waited, suspecting by now that Ittai was headed toward a definite goal, and that habit of curiosity I had acquired from Ethan kicked in, keeping me rooted to the spot.

"No, he didn't, Dodi. I bargained for, and received, the rite of circumcision. Yahweh's hand was on him that evening, and even his own men could hardly remain in his presence. He asked his god what he should do, and Yahweh answered by sending down a bolt of his sacred fire. The Dahveed used the flames from that fire to purify the knife, and after the rite was done, he burned my flesh as an offering in the sacred flames. I saw him do it myself. He took me as a son, and I, *and my house*, must count him my abbi."

"You cannot make such covenants, Ittai," his dodi said angrily. "Our house is not subordinate to anyone!"

"Then you will have to argue with the Dahveed's god," the youth said, still in that calm voice. "That night, Yahweh came to me in a dream. He confirmed the covenant I had made, and as a sign of His approval, He touched me, dodi, taking away the pain. He told me where to go so I would be found by you, and when I woke from the dream, I walked from the tent and made my way to that place. You found me there the next morning. I have worshipped no other god since that day."

The man in the room wasn't the only one stunned by what Ittai had just said.

"How do I know what you say is true?" he asked, clearly shaken.

"Look for yourself, dodi. The rite has been performed, and you know well that to walk away afterward as I did, is not possible."

The rustle of movement came from the room, while I struggled to assimilate all this might mean.

"I don't know what to say, Ittai. Clearly the gods are in this. But if I understand you correctly, you are saying that Dahveed Israel is in Gath?"

"He's in the passage, dodi."

"Bring him in," the man commanded.

The Philistine youth opened the door, and I stepped into the room, eager to see Ittai's dodi. The resemblance between them was immediately clear. Both had the same brown eyes, direct gaze, and facial shape. But Ittai's body build was slimmer, and he'd be taller one day than the thickset man who rose from his three-legged chair to study me as intently as I did him.

"I suppose you listened to every word?" he asked bluntly, raising his hand to his chin.

"With the door unlatched, it would have been difficult not to."

"He told the truth? His circumcision was a sacred rite with your god's fire?"

"It was. And the covenant was sealed with the blood and burning of sacrifice. I am bound to him, and bound to peace between myself and his house as well."

The man looked me up and down, irritation boiling just beneath the surface of his mind. "In that case, we seem to be stuck with each other, Israelite. I don't suppose Ittai bothered to mention what house he bound to you?"

Raising my eyebrows, I looked meaningfully at the young man standing so quietly between us. "Not yet."

He bowed slightly. "Adoni, may I present my dodi, Akish, Seren of Gath."

At the stunned disbelief on my face, the man burst out laughing. "You don't know how it comforts me to find that my sister's son can stymie someone else besides me!" he said, still chuckling with amusement. "Sit down, Israelite. I think you and I need to discuss a few things, not the least of which is what you were doing in my almond grove in the first place." He motioned to a stool with his thick hand, and I warily sat down. "Go bring us something to refresh ourselves with, Ittai," he continued, seating himself again.

As the young man hesitated, Akish waved a hand at him in exasperation. "He'll be fine with me. I'm not going to kill him the moment you walk out the door!"

The young man cast a glance at me also. I smiled grimly. "With your flesh between us, Ittai, your dodi need have no fear unless he attacks me."

Akish snorted. "And what chance would you have unarmed as you are?"

I automatically flexed my right hand, feeling the sling wrapped around it. "I believe that's what Goliath was thinking just moments before he died," I said mildly. "Go on, Ittai. Your dodi and I can manage to stay from each other's throats until you get back." Out of the corner of my eye, I noticed Akish's face redden with anger, and with one last doubtful look at the two of us, Ittai left.

Once he had gone, neither of us knew what to say. Asking after each other's families seemed ridiculous, and I decided silence was my best option. The political implications of my covenant with Ittai were taking dim shape in my mind, and I knew that the seren across from me had grown up maneuvering in the ever-shifting political arena of the Five Cities, and would be far ahead of me in this situation, as his nephew had been a year ago.

I'd been inexcusably careless by not asking the name of Ittai's house. Once he'd told me his abbi was an Israelite slave, I'd assumed he was from a low status family and thus could see no harm in taking him as a covenantal son. At least I'd had the sense to ask Yah what I should do. But what if I forgot to do that next time? I clenched my teeth in disgust at myself.

"Uneasy thoughts, Israelite?" Akish's comment broke into my reverie.

I glanced at him, noting his carefully blank face. I would be foolish to try to spar words with this man. "Yes, Seren."

His eyes widened in surprise although his facial expression didn't alter. Silence descended again. We both turned to the door at the sound of quick footsteps in the hall which didn't even pause as the door burst open.

One hand holding my belt knife, the other in my shepherd's bag closed over a stone with the sling ready for use, I whirled off the stool and back into the shadows. The door banged against the wall, leaving Akish staring at the place I'd been as my cloak settled around me and a rather pretty woman stepped into the room. She was about Sarah Michal's size and her clothes trailed behind her impetuous entrance.

"Well? You must have found out about that stranger by now. I'm sure Ittai tried to bring him into the palace like I said. Tell me who he was and what he wanted with him. He probably tried to lure him away again. That boy is so trusting! He'd cheerfully walk out the gates with anyone that caught his fancy--like that magician." The woman waved her hand in disgust. "I saw him a moment ago, so you must have done something. " She shifted on her feet impatiently. "Don't sit there like a lump! I was right, that awful man wanted him for something. Since you asked him why, you can tell me now. What I'll do with him after this, I don't know, but be assured the situation will be firmly dealt with."

The rapid barrage of words set a bemused look on my face, and made me ease the belt knife back into its hidden sheath.

Akish had his head in his hands. "Who let you in, Hazzel?" he sighed.

"Who *let* me in? I have to be *let* in like a goat into the stable? That's the way you see me, is it?" she asked, throwing her hands up in disgust. "Well, I'll have you know, this goat, who, by the way, happens to be a *nanny* goat, is very worried about her little buckling, as should be obvious from what just happened this evening when that magician showed up again. I expect you to handle these things, Akish, since my poor boy has no abbi to stand up for him like you did tonight. And may Baal, Dagon, and the gods of the Five Cities curse the one who did that!"

While I tried to decide if Hazzel had just cursed her brother or not, Akish tried to stem the flow of his sister's words since she looked ready to burst out again.

"I didn't mean that at all," he said. "I don't think you're a goat. I meant no one was supposed to--er, I meant that I didn't expect to see you here just now."

Hazzel shook her finger at him. "You meant you told those loutish guards not to let me in! I already know that. As if they could keep me out when Ittai's future is at stake. You still haven't told me who that man was. Surely you took steps to see that it doesn't happen again to poor Ittai. Where is he, by the way?" She swung around to scan the room behind her.

"Ittai?" Akish asked patiently.

"Why would I want to know about Ittai? We're discussing the man who tried to make off with him. Do keep track of the conversation, Akish. And why would you want to keep me away from you tonight?"

"Because I'm meeting with someone," he replied in despair.

"How can you be meeting with someone when you're alone?" she demanded, staring around again. "Who would you be meeting with?"

"The man Ittai let into the gate."

"Well, if you're meeting with him, where is he?"

Taking pity on Akish, I stepped from the shadows. "I am here, Sahrah."

She threw a brief glance my way. "So you are. So you were meeting with someone after all, Akish. I supposed I interrupted, but when it comes to Ittai I don't take any chances, as you know. Now, if he's the man who tried to take Ittai away, how's he called?"

Akish turned to me, a slightly malicious smile on his face. "Why don't you ask him?"

"All right," Sahrah Hazzel said, stepping toward me. "Who are you?"

Since Akish had neatly thrown the dilemma of what to tell Ittai's immi into my lap, I decided to make him sorry he had. "I am the Dahveed Israel," I replied, nodding politely.

For the first time since entering the room, Sahrah Hazzel became still. "The one who killed Goliath, saved Ittai's life, and circumcised him?"

The sudden sharp attention in her tone stopped me a second. "I believe so, Sahrah."

"You know about that?" Akish asked in amazement.

"Well, of course, I know," she replied crossly. "Ittai's my son. You don't think I've been this worried about him just because someone played a prank, did you?" She turned back to me. "You're bigger than I was told."

"I've grown since the battle in Elah."

The sahrah glanced at Akish. "Well? Have you gotten down on your knees and thanked him yet? The only good things which come to us always come from Israel. Ittai is content and steady since his circumcision, and you yourself know that if Goliath hadn't died, Manani would have slaughtered our entire family or worse. And why you don't banish the other four fools in that family, I don't know. I'll leave you now since you have so much to talk about." She departed the room as quickly as she had entered.

"We certainly have a lot more to talk about now than before," Akish said sourly, glaring at his sister's retreating back. "Sit down, Israelite. You seem to have turned my house on its ear by your very presence. Should I expect this often now that you're connected to us?"

A smile twitching my lips, I took a seat. "I believe Hassar Israel mentioned sending me to Pharaoh on one occasion."

Akish gave a short bark of a laugh. "I never thought I'd have anything in common with that fiend."

I tightened my right hand again, then relaxed it. "He doesn't hate all Philistines, you know, just one. But he will defend his people."

"We know," the seren replied shortly.

The door opened again, much more decorously this time, and Ittai entered with a tray holding wine, bread, and fruit. The youth set some of each in front of us both, and then occupied a stool to one side, watching silently.

I waited until Akish, as host, reluctantly motioned me to eat. I'd taken several bites of an early apple before he joined me, clearly not enthusiastic about the situation. He was even less so when I nonchalantly produced a belt knife from nowhere, cut a piece from the apple, and held it out to Ittai. The fact that Ittai took it without the slightest hesitation irritated him even more. By that simple act of sharing and accepting food, I had again claimed Ittai as son, and he had acknowledged me as abbi.

"You've made your point, Israelite," he said testily, as I gave another piece to Ittai.

"Then remember this, Akish, as long as Ittai lives, he stands before me as my son, and I do not make war on my own. Yahweh directed the making of this covenant, and I do not go against my God. If your house dies, it will not be by my hand."

"No, it will be by the hand of the serens of the other four cities for treachery against the confederacy. Sheltering Dahveed Israel is not something that can be explained, Israelite."

"You have foreign mercenaries in your permanent army, do you not? What's one more?" I shrugged.

The ruler of Gath eyed me. "You would enter my service as a common soldier?" Then his face cleared a little. "Shaul has finally turned against you, has he? So neither of us can afford to have this covenant made public."

"I would prefer it that way," I said, picking up the wine cup. "But let us be clear about our understanding of what is between us. I will not attack my own, but if attacked, I will fight, and any Philistine, whether from Gath or elsewhere, crossing the Shephelah into the highlands does so at their own risk."

His eyes measuring me shrewdly, Akish picked up his own wine cup. "What you're telling me is that I don't have to worry about my back courtyard."

"Not as long as I'm the one in it."

"What if my house should find itself threatened by enemies?"

"The Five Cities have little need for outside aid, Akish."

"And if the other four turn against Gath?"

"I'd take serious offense at such an attempt to harm a son of mine--or his house."

The seren's eyes blanked out a moment, and he turned the wine cup absently in his hand, the other hand reaching up to touch his beard. "Perhaps the gods are in this indeed," he murmured, bringing his gaze back to me. "I believe we've reached an understanding, Israelite," he said, his eyes meeting mine directly over our wine. "To Ittai."

"To Ittai," I repeated, thankful that I had found a safe refuge. We drank.

¥ ¥ ¥ ¥ ¥ ¥

The sun was low in the west when the litter stopped, settling on the ground. Gebirah Abigail parted the curtains an inch and glanced out. Nabal had stopped by the standing stone of Shaul's monument just outside of Carmel. The ink on the plaster covering one side of the large stone was faded, but still readable.

She leaned back, knowing that he'd be here a while, staring at the stone even though he could not read. The day that Shaul of Israel had come was the day Nabal changed. Seeing the parade of guards preceding the king and his three sons, the lines of animals packed with spoils, and most of all the Amalekite Agag,[4] cringing before his captors, had awakened a thirst in her husband for honor that never seemed slaked.

Nabal had quickly extended an invitation to the king and sars to dine at his house that night. She would never forget the rush to have something suitable prepared before the guests arrived. Nor would the image ever fade in her memory of the tall king and his sons striding into the courtyard gate, the last of the sunlight flashing off the gold jewelry they wore, or the rich colors of their mantles and embroidery on their meils.

The feast had lasted until late. She had dressed in her best, so nervous about having royalty to dine that she hardly noticed the reactions of the four men to her beauty until the king had turned to Nabal and said, "Yahweh has blessed you indeed with a wife fit for a palace, adon."

"Thank you for your kind compliment to our poor house," her husband had answered, practically scraping his nose on the table as he

---

[4] As with many other identifiers of kings in the Bible, Agag appears to be a title, not necessarily a personal name. I have used it as such here.

bowed from his seat. She had seen no evidence of the king's illness that night, but she had noticed that the hassar kept close track of his abbi even while he enthralled everyone around him with his conversation. Sar Malchi had obviously liked the food, and Sar Ishvi had listened with flattering attention to the stilted attempts of the other invited elders to talk to him. By the end of the meal, the second sar had put everyone around him at ease.

Now she sighed quietly. Everything had gone fine until the king was leaving. Nabal had drunk quite a lot of wine that night, and he piled flattery on flattery as he bid the king farewell until she had to bite her tongue. That was the first time her stomach had turned into a twisted knot. Once the guests had escaped Nabal, she had met them at the gate.

"We were honored to have you here," she had said quietly. "Please overlook my husband's nervousness."

Sar Ishvi had spoken for them all. "Think no more of it, Gebirah, for we will not."

"Thank you for your kindness," she had replied.

Now she looked down at her hands. How many meils had she embroidered since then? Scores?

Once in the house at Carmel, the nagid requested her presence in his business chamber. She ate and drank a little while Tirzah and Namea brushed out her hair and got a different robe for her to wear since the one she'd been in was soaked with perspiration from the heat of the litter.

When she entered the door to the business chamber, her husband paced back and forth in excitement, wearing the kingly banqueting robe again. "Did you see them?" he asked. "Did you see the way they all stared when we arrived that first day?"

"Yes, Nabal."

"They saw what I am then," he went on in satisfaction. "No one dared to speak. That's as it should be. I am Nagid Carmel, after all."

Abigail sat down on a stool.

"And the next morning, we had three more invitations to feasts! That robe woke them up, and they are beginning to show proper respect."

She felt her stomach tighten again. The feasts they'd attended on the second and third days of the festival had been torture for her. People had crammed into the courtyards to gawk at Nabal and his garish robe, hiding their scorn until they were safely away. And how Ahlai of Jezreel had managed to contain his mirth at that third feast was more than Abigail could understand.

"Did you see?" Nabal asked again. "They treated me just like I was Shaul! And they should, for I'm nagid, and that's all he is!"

Somehow she refrained from reminding him that being Nagid Israel was much different than being nagid of a small clan in the poor south, to say nothing of the military victories and governance that Shaul's house provided the tribes.

"Things are moving as I planned," Nabal continued. "The wealth and the clothes are in my grasp. I'm acquiring more territory all the time. It won't be long before I'll have all of Carmel. Then Hebron is next." He paused his pacing, glancing at her. "And with you at my side, I'll have even more honor than Shaul or his sons! You're Gebirah." Admiringly, he looked at her again. "You deserve more honor. Shaul said that you would grace a palace. There must be a palace with stone walls and framed windows!"

"Nabal, a palace requires support from the countryside," she observed. "We hardly have enough to be thinking of that."

"That's because we don't have the Shephelah," he said absently, still pacing, kicking the robe with his toes at every step to keep from stumbling over it. "With Hebron, we can look to the Shephelah. That's where the real riches are."

"The Shephelah means the Philistines," she reminded him.

"What are they? Shaul beats them every year. I am nagid. The Philistines won't be a problem."

For a long time she listened as he revealed more of his mind to her than ever before. She couldn't eat all the next day.

CHAPTER 9

Malchi waved his hand in annoyance as Jonathan walked into the upstairs room of the third sar's house. "You let in another fly, Jonathan," he complained. "I have the windows covered for a reason."

"How you ever manage to live through a single war season in a tent is beyond me," his brother said, exasperated.

"There are other things to think about during war season," Malchi replied with a shrug.

"Don't the two of you get started until after we've eaten," Ishvi interrupted, entering behind the hassar. "I, for one, am hungry. What about you, Eshbaal?"

The youngest sar nodded in reply, and the four brothers ate the noon meal quickly.

After Malchi dismissed the servers, Ishvi leaned back against the wall. "What's on your mind, brother?" he asked Jonathan.

"Abbi, and his erratic behavior."

"Is the demon returning?" Eshbaal asked in alarm.

"I don't think it's that simple. Not after what happened at the new moon feast," Ishvi said.

"What could Abbi have been thinking?" the youngest sar asked, bewildered.

"He wasn't. Balak did his thinking for him," Jonathan answered in disgust. "I think Abbi made it plain he intends to kill Dahveed. Are we agreed on that?"

"I think so," Ishvi replied for them all.

Rising and lifting the cloth that covered one window, the hassar stared out it. "That being the case, I wanted to ask you all one question. Are we also agreed that this should not happen?"

There was no sound in the room for several moments.

Then Ishvi spoke again for his brothers. "I believe we all agree that innocent blood should not be shed. Do you have a way to keep this from happening?"

Jonathan turned back to them, letting the cloth fall over the window again. He caught the quick shift of Ishvi's eyes toward their youngest brother, and glanced at Eshbaal, noting the discomfort on the sar's face.

"I might. Now that Abbi has shifted most of the responsibilities of rulership onto me, it's harder to know what's on his mind regarding other things. But if I could know his mind soon enough, I should be able to keep him from dishonoring our house." He paused, casting a quick glance at Eshbaal. His youngest brother looked thoughtful now, not uncomfortable.

"You need to know everything he does," Malchi said bluntly.

"Which is why I need your help." Jonathan nodded at all of them.

"What would we have to do?" the fourth sar asked, frowning.

"I need you to instruct your scribes and their assistants to notify their superior of any unusual request by the king. That message is to be sent first, then they are to attend to the king's request."

"The same instructions to Tanhum and Ziba?"

"Yes. And once the message gets back to you, you tell me, and I will speak to Abbi."

Satisfied, Eshbaal nodded. Then he looked up. "While I'm thinking of it, Hassar, Tanhum has sent in several requests for information. I can answer some of his questions, but not all. He's asked everything from how much rain Shechem got this year, to what Pharaoh's road taxes are, to the price of wool in Moab. What should I do with all that?"

"Give it to me. I've got someone who can find out those sorts of things."

"I assume I tell my scribes the same thing?" Ishvi asked.

"Yes, and in addition, have them notify you of any unusual draws on supplies from any of the royal lands, any changes in workers, scribes, or messengers and such." Jonathan turned to Malchi. "You'll need to find out which commanders will cooperate with this effort, and if some are reluctant, place assistant commanders who will. Can you do that?"

The third sar considered. "Depends on two commanders. One is Doeg, who's still at Nob. No decent man wants to work with him. Abner isn't happy about losing that good of a fighter, but with a murder charge, he can't do much."

"And your second problem?"

"Abner."

Jonathan stroked his beard. "Yes, he was quite plain at his estate that he'll do whatever the king tells him to. We'd probably have to kill him to stop him."

"Surely there is no need for that!" Eshbaal exclaimed, alarmed.

"Not if we build a good enough fence around him," Jonathan replied quickly. "We need to know everything he does, just as with the king."

The youngest brother looked relieved.

"Anything else?" Ishvi asked. "I must get back to the compound."

"Why don't we plan on meeting twice a week?" the hassar suggested. "That will let us know if what we're doing is effective or not."

As the four brothers left the upper room, Ishvi turned to Jonathan. "Elihu remembered something more about the House of Tahat. When its agent contacted him about working for them, he had the impression that he was to work in Dan for a while before moving on to Damascus if he proved satisfactory."

"It must be based up north, then. Eshbaal, remind me to follow up on this. Anything else, Ishvi?"

"Not now."

Malchi lagged behind as they left the house compound, signaling the hassar to do the same.

"What is it?" Jonathan asked when Ishvi and Eshbaal were out of earshot.

"There won't be any way to do what you're planning unless we have Commander Sheva helping us."

"I thought of that. Any ideas?"

"This business with Doeg might be useful. The Edomite is under Sheva's command, so Sheva is responsible for restraining him, which he has not done."

"Giving us grounds for his dismissal," Jonathan added.

"Yes. On the other hand, Sheva is an honorable man, and I think his loyalty to Abbi is tempered by his fear of Yahweh."

"Shall we visit the Commander of the Guard, Malchi?"

"I was hoping you'd suggest it."

The noon rest was not yet over when the two brothers climbed the stairs to the east wall of the fortress and Sheva's chamber.

"Sars, how may I serve you?" the commander asked when they entered.

"What tribe are you from, Sheva?" Jonathan inquired.

"Asher, Hassar."

"You have been a faithful servant of the king, Commander, and I would let you choose what you will do. If you wish, you can choose now to return home."

The man stilled, a bewildered expression crossing his face. "Have I been found lacking in some duty?"

"No, for you have served *the king* very well, and I'm sure *he* has no complaints."

"And if *you* do, would it be connected to the day Abner took Sahrah Michal?" Sheva asked, studying the hassar.

"It could. But there is more concern about the actions of Doeg the Edomite at the moment. Malchi's investigation indicates that you have not restrained the man as much as you should have."

The commander of the guard sighed. "I have done the best I know how, given how much the king favors him."

"I am aware of that," Jonathan replied softly. "That is why nothing will be said against you, *if* you choose to leave."

"And if I choose to stay?" the Asherite responded slowly.

"I will not tolerate shedding innocent blood. Nor will I tolerate anyone willing to do it."

"As with the Gibeonites?" Sheva looked from one brother to the other. "It sickened me, but I didn't know what to do."

"Yes, that, and other things that may arise in the future."

The military officer studied the opposite wall for some time, then he knelt. "Hassar, if it is your intent to guard the king in these matters, then I will do anything I can to help. What is your command?"

"You will continue your duties, as always, and carry out the king's commands, but you will inform me of anything he asks beyond the routine."

"I will do so, Hassar."

¥ ¥ ¥ ¥ ¥ ¥

I soon learned that half of Akish's professional force were mercenaries from all over, and they only cared whether or not I could fight. Giving my name as Ben-geber, I had carefully restrained myself when it came to training, and my unit commander, Shemel, thought I was adequate, but nothing special.

The half who were Philistine were curt in their speech and left me alone. But I was drained and discouraged from three weeks of constant watchfulness, for when I decided to flee to Gath, I had forgotten one critical fact about the city. And when Sahrah Hazzel had mentioned it to her brother, I hadn't paid attention. Four men of Goliath's family still lived here. Saph, Lahmi, Ishvi-benob, and a much younger brother of theirs whose name I never did learn, hated all Israelites, and were unrestrained about showing it.

The three older ones were as big as Goliath had been, and the youngest soon would be. Consequently, the brothers did anything they pleased. I could understand why the unit commanders ignored the situation, any of the three could kill them easily. But I couldn't grasp why Akish allowed them to continue their rule by fear over the entire town. I had asked one of the other mercenaries about it, and he looked at me grimly. "Their clan is related to Seren Manani in Ekron."

Any shred of peace I'd hoped to find vanished with that statement. By asking a couple of questions and listening in the market, I soon realized that Akish ruled by sufferance of Manani. He was surrounded by the Ekron seren's agents, of which Goliath's family were only a part.

His willingness to honor Ittai's covenant now made much sense, for I couldn't imagine that he intended to remain under Manani's sway if he could help it. And due to the consistent defeats from Israel, Manani's position with the serens of the Five Cities was declining, giving Akish an advantage.

Now, I sat in the late afternoon sun with my back against a vineyard wall outside of town, daring to relax for a moment or two. Trying to drive out my disquieting thoughts and get some rest, I eased my back a little. I was sore from blows delivered from behind during training, and twice, someone had nearly managed to stab me in my bed in the barracks. I couldn't even trust my food. Four days after I joined the force, I'd had something added to my wine that sent me running to the latrines the entire afternoon and gave me terrible stomach cramps.

Realizing that I dared not draw attention to myself, I had ignored the harassment, but my restraint only fueled my adversaries' rage, and for the past three days I'd been followed everywhere I went. I'd overheard some conversation about it, deliberately said when I could hear, and learned the brothers wanted a reason to accuse me before Akish. Once I was thrown out of the army, they planned on taking me to Ekron and Manani. I had immediately limited my conversation to "Yes, commander," and "No, commander."

Never before had I felt so trapped. If I went back to Israel, and Shaul found me, Jonathan would die along with me. But just the thought of what the Ekron seren might do with me made my mouth dry and my skin crawl.

Closing my eyes, I let the warmth of the sun soak into my skin. There was absolutely no warning when Ishvi-benob's weight landed on me, and my ears caught the word, "Ekron." I reacted with all the terror I'd suppressed. Rolling with the huge man's weight, I jerked my knee as hard as I could into his groin, leaving him doubled over as I lunged to my feet, only to meet Lahmi jumping for me. Bending my knees, I rolled backward, desperately jamming my feet into him, flipping him over my head. He slammed on the ground hard enough to drive the air from his chest, and I drove my fist into his face as hard as I could.

Twisting to the side, I sprang up, facing Saph. He was nearly on me with sword drawn, and I dodged, grabbing his sword wrist with my right hand and driving my left fist upward into the back of his elbow, breaking the joint and appropriating his sword at the same time. A fourth man, a member of my own unit, stared at me in disbelief as I crouched slightly in front of him, waiting. His face turned white. "It's you!" he choked out, backing away, then running.

Whirling, I drove the sword through Lahmi's shirt, pinning him to the ground, and then I jumped the vineyard wall and hurried back to the barracks. I didn't want to be found anywhere near that fight. Because of the brothers' relationship to Manani, there would be a demand for recompense, and Akish would have no choice but to turn me over to them.

Back at the barracks, I went to my bedroll, worried about what my unit mate might say and to whom. Just before the call for the evening meal, my assistant commander walked in. "Ben-geber, you're wanted in Commander Shemel's chamber."

My stomach tight, I headed for the door. Something fell on my head.

When I came to, I was lying on some filthy straw, bound hand and foot, the back of my head feeling like an anvil with a hammer slamming down with each heartbeat. I stirred groggily, trying to figure out what had happened.

"I tell you, he's Dahveed Israel. Give him to us!" someone said not far away. It was the man who had seen me fight.

"He goes nowhere until I'm convinced! Tell me again how you know this," my commander said roughly.

"I remembered his stance from the Elah battle. He chased me after Goliath died, had me pinned against an embankment. But I managed to scramble up it and get away."

My mind slowly formed the memory of Jonathan on his mule, pointing his sword at a trembling Philistine soldier he was shielding from me and ordering the man to run.

I had been so deep in Yahweh's gift that I had tried to attack Jonathan himself before he was able to bring me out of it. My blood ran cold. *My gift!* I hadn't felt it once since leaving the Ezel stone! What had happened? Why hadn't it roused when I was attacked, or warned me of the dangers to me here?

Biting my lip, I hunched against the fear that invaded my mind, driving out the pounding of my head. Without Yahweh's protection, I had no chance to live! How had I offended Him to the extent that He would abandon me now? I gasped, twisting in the straw, the agony of terror rolling through me. *What had I done?*

The voices on the other side of the door faded into silence as I cried in my mind to Yah, begging Him to keep me under the shelter of

His wings, for I had nothing else left to me now. The darkness in the cell deepened, and I shivered as the faint sound of that howling nothingness I had encountered in the anteroom with Jonathan swirled in my memory, driving the cold it brought deep into my heart.

"El Shaddai, what have I done?" I begged.

I don't know how long I lay there, my head thundering with pain, my heart hammering with an even deeper fear, with the ravenous darkness waiting in the corners of the cell, held at bay only because I whispered El Shaddai's name again and again. Finally, I blacked out once more, waking sometime later, trembling from a nightmare of abandonment by my God. "El Shaddai, don't leave me!" I sobbed. Finally the fear in me lessened a little, and I strained against the cords that bound me, trying desperately to remember what I could have done to offend my God.

The thought that entered my mind made me turn my face to the stinking straw, tears streaming from my eyes. I had disobeyed the roeh's command to ask Yah's guidance! But when I left Nob, I had gone my own way, ignoring the one I had yielded to when He claimed me as His Mashiah.

"Yah, forgive Your slave," I begged. "I have forgotten that You are the shepherd who should lead my life. Like that lamb that the bear nearly took, I have wandered from Your path. Deliver me from those who have watched my steps. Let me continue to walk before You in the light of the living. Please, Yah, do not leave me to die in Manani's hands!"

Slowly, the twisting, threatening darkness in the corners of my mind faded away. Despite the fact that I deserved to be left to my fate, Yah's sheltering presence surrounded me as it had in the past, and I confessed my foolishness again, entreating Him to remain with me, and vowing to sacrifice a thank offering as soon as I had one. I fought sleep as I did in the barracks until the irony of the situation slipped into my mind. I could sleep safer in this cell than I had for the past three weeks. "Thank You, Yah," I said.

I woke just as the cell began to lighten with dawn. The thread of a melody drifted through my mind as I idly watched an insect labor through the twisted pieces of straw I had broken and scattered in my distress last night.

"Be gracious to me, O God, because men have hounded me. Doing battle all the day, he oppressed me."

I fit the line to the melody in my head, and thought back through the recent past.

"My enemies hounded me all the day because many are the ones who battle against me on high."

My fingers brushed against my face, and I realized that my hands had come untied sometime last night, a fact I'd never noticed in my struggle. I could almost feel Grandmother's harp in them, and I closed my eyes, imagining myself plucking the strings.

"In the day I myself am afraid, in You I will trust. In God, I will praise His word, In God, I trusted. I shall not fear. What can flesh do to me?"

Humming the tune now, I shifted to a higher note.

"All the day my words they twist against me. All their thoughts are for evil. They gather together, they hide. They watch my footprints as they wait eagerly for my soul. Because of iniquity bring them forth. In anger bring down the nations, O God."

Sitting up, I untied my feet. Then pacing the small space of the cell, head to one side, I went over the song again. It needed something more. Up another note? No, I decided, back down to the original scale.

"My wanderings, You counted them. You put my tears in Your skin bottle. Are they not in Your heavenly book? Then my enemies will turn back in the day I call. This I know, that God is for me."

Now it should step up again.

"In God, I will praise His word. In Yahweh, I will praise His word. In God I trusted. I will not fear. What can flesh do to me?"

Raise it again, I decided, playing the song in my mind. That will finish it off with the last verse.

"O God, Your vows are binding on me. I will repay thank-offerings to You. For You snatched my life from death. Did You not keep my feet from stumbling? For they walk constantly before God in the light of the living." [5]

I was standing there, humming through the song for the third time, when they came to take me to Akish.

¥ ¥ ¥ ¥ ¥ ¥

Sahrah Hazzel hurried forward, her irritation at her foolish handmaid lending speed to her feet. The elderly woman hadn't told her that Akish had been summoned to the throne room until after doing her hair, and now it might be too late to find out what was happening.

---

[5] Psalms 56

Turning down the dark back passage that only the servants used, she paused at a door, listening closely. Cautiously, she eased it open and stepped through, moving to the shadow of the pillar directly in front of her, keeping behind the brightly colored curtain hanging from it. People shifted about the room, waiting for something, and one guard was stationed at the large door at the end of the room to her left. Her brother sat on the silver-inlaid throne just to the right and ahead of her, the annoyed but patient look on his face signaling that Manani's agent had been at it again.

What could that snake have demanded this time? she wondered, relieved that she had arrived in time to find out. Her baby brother might be Seren of Gath, but there were times when he was blind to his own best interests. So she kept track of them for him, reminding him often of what he should be doing. If Akish would just *listen* every once in a while! She had, after all, warned him not to make that snake his chief advisor, but just because she couldn't tell him exactly why, he'd done it anyway, and then discovered too late the man was Manani's.

When she had reminded him that she'd told him not to, he had protested that she hadn't explained that the man was Manani's agent. Well, she hadn't known that herself, so how was she supposed to have told him? The man was a snake! What other reason did Akish need to throw him out? She chewed her lip in frustration. And now she had to spend half her time finding out what that disgusting wretch was planning next, and there was always something! Maybe she would uncover the latest plot today.

¥ ¥ ¥ ¥ ¥ ¥

I arrived in the throne room surrounded by spear men and followed by most of the commanders, with the soldiers outside craning their necks to catch a glimpse of me just in case I might really be Dahveed Israel. As I walked into the room, one look told me Seren Akish was not pleased about what was happening.

He sat on a silver-inlaid chair on a dais as Shaul had. The hangings and furniture were much more expensive than those in Gibeah, but without Sahrah Michal's sense of color and taste, too many things clashed with each other to make the room comfortable. A man, standing where Hassar Jonathan would have in Shaul's throne room, was speaking to Akish in a low voice as I was marched forward. From the way Akish looked at him, I gathered the ruler of Gath didn't like his chief advisor.

My unit mate was brought forward, and stumbled once more through his story of recognizing me as Dahveed Israel after seeing me in the Elah Valley, and then recognizing my fighting style here in Gath.

I said nothing, letting my appearance speak for itself. After my night of wrestling with Yah in the filthy cell, I looked and smelled more like the beggar from the town dung heap than a military warrior.

"What if this is the Dahveed?" the seren's advisor asked. "You know how much he has done against the Five Cities! How many defeats have we taken at his hands? And we've all heard the song they sing when this man returns from spilling Philistine blood. 'Shaul has slain his thousands, *and Dahveed his 10 thousands.*'"

A soft growl from the crowd in the room made the hair on the back of my neck rise. Most likely every person here had lost family to the wars with Israel, and in the past few years, there had been no return for that spilled blood. The tide of bitter feeling rising around me revealed the demand for vengeance the seren would have to answer. My mind raced. Akish was now trapped between his duty as seren of Gath and the covenant he had made with me.

"He doesn't look like that much of a fighter," Akish said, turning to the soldier. "What was Dahveed Israel wearing when he chased you?"

"Well, sereni, he had on what soldiers normally wear," the man said, shifting uneasily. "And a great long sword in his hand."

"Curved, or straight?"

"I-I don't really, um, curved, curved," he repeated, catching sight of a unit commander signaling to him.

"What does that matter?" the advisor broke in hastily. "This is Dahveed Israel, the one who has slain so many of our people. He should die, Sereni. We've lost enough lives. Payment is demanded."

"And we'll have stopped that chant! It shames us all!" someone else added.

"I wouldn't kill him," someone behind me muttered. "I'd send him to Seren Manani in Ekron!"

Those words went through me like an icy sword. I stiffened, praying no one would put that thought into Akish's mind. It would be the perfect solution to his present dilemma, and I couldn't see any reason for him not to do it!

"What more do you need to condemn this man, sereni?" the advisor urged.

The commanders edged toward me, ready to kill me, and my stomach knotted. But it was the thought of what Seren Manani would have in store for me that flooded me with such dread that I could hardly move. I stood rigid as I fought the terror that clawed at me, but no matter what I did, it only increased, locking my jaws together until they ached. "Yahweh, let me die here rather than go there!" I silently pleaded.

The ruler of Gath stroked his beard. "It would be helpful if his accusers were here, since this witness needs others to tell him his words and cannot remember that Dahveed Israel wore nothing but a shepherd's robe on that accursed day," he said in distaste. "I'm inclined to doubt whether this man actually saw Dahveed then, or now. By the way, why *isn't* the clan of Goliath here?" Akish turned an inquiring look toward the advisor, who flushed a little.

"Their wounds prevent them, sereni."

Akish's eyebrows rose questioningly. "Would you have me believe that when the undeserved ill-feeling of this Israelite overflowed, *all three* of the Rephite giants were unable to adequately defend themselves? I find that very odd. Perhaps we should wait until the accusers can appear. You don't want us to bring down the wrath of the gods by spilling innocent blood, do you?"

"No Israelite has innocent blood," the man retorted, and the crowd murmured in approval.

"Then will you and your house accept responsibility for this man's death if he's not Dahveed?" Akish asked, pinning the advisor with his gaze.

The Philistine opened his mouth, closed it again, and looked away, shuffling his feet.

"You are very free with *my* standing before the gods. And right now, your witness acts as half-witted as the accused looks!" the seren ended bitingly.

All eyes turned to me. I realized I'd been staring fixedly, but when I tried to move, I was so stiff that I could only twitch. Someone near me edged away, looking down uncomfortably. I struggled to make sense of what was happening, reaching for Yah's presence and finding it in my mind. Why, then, was I so afraid?

I tried to turn my head, my eyes rolling instead, and the guard closest to me shuffled away as the court gradually quieted. Suddenly the memory of how people reacted to King Shaul when his illness overtook him burst on my mind. I stopped trying to control my body, and let the trembling I'd been suppressing take over. I parted my lips a little, and the saliva I couldn't swallow leaked down my beard. Rolling my eyes upward, I started humming, getting louder and louder, swaying stiffly from side to side.

The court had quieted completely, and the guards around me openly backed away. I looked at the ceiling, remembering how Shaul had acted, and then looked back, clamping my teeth together several times and making more drool run down my beard.

"Yahweh, cover me!" I silently begged. Then, jerking myself around, I advanced in stiff, long strides toward the side of the room. Every person in my path scrambled away. I stopped suddenly and addressed a richly dressed man. "Do you know what happens to me?" I demanded, my voice coming out in a squeak.

"N-No," the courtier stuttered, glancing desperately around.

"The gods take me. They give me messages. They have one for you."

"That's--uh--nice for you," the man said, retreating.

"No, it's not!" I shrilled angrily. "Are you saying it is?"

"No, no, of course not," he hastened to say, raising his hands placatingly and continuing to back away.

Lifting a shaking hand, I pointed at him. "Did you know that you should never eat the left side of your pigs?"

The courtier shook his head and pressed against the pillar behind him.

It was working. My voice steadied a little. "No, never the left side. That's the side that faces the sea, the side the gods see when they come into the land at night, the side touched by the moon when it's dark and doesn't shine."

I swayed forward. "Want to be like me? I ate the left side of a pig once. I thought, what's the harm? Either side is left depending on where you stand." Turning away, I forced a wild laugh from my lips.

A woman, half hidden by the hanging near a pillar, peeked out at me, her face puzzled as I ground my teeth several times, then let more drool spill down my beard. "Don't move!" I suddenly shrieked, pointing at the scribe's table near the throne. "It's there, behind you!"

Akish's scribe jerked back from his stool, overturning it as he scrambled away, and I lumbered over to him, passing the woman on my way. I focused on the scribe, ignoring the stone-like figure of Akish on the throne, and Ittai standing just behind it, watching me with huge eyes.

Snatching the brush pen and ink box from the three-legged table, I stared just past the scribe's shoulder. "Try to steal things here, and you get caught," I announced, holding them against my chest. Then I looked directly at the scribe. "You have to watch them all the time. That one almost had your writing materials. Let me show you how to keep them safe."

Whirling around, I marched toward the door, risking one glance around as I did. The entire court looked ready to flee at a moment's notice, except that woman by the pillar. She had a hand over her mouth, her eyes dancing with laughter as she watched. I prayed that she would hold her tongue long enough for me to get to the doors at least!

Suddenly I took a detour, stopping before one of the pillars and gravely complimenting it on the fine linen robe it had worn to court today. Then I politely excused myself, and continued down the room to the large doors at the end.

Dipping the pen in the ink, I drew on the door post, lifting the brush dramatically after each stroke. "This should do it. Just add a bit here and there, and that will make sure the left sides of their pigs never stay the same. Wait! It needs to be engraved deeply." I clawed at the door panels, laughing wildly again. "It'll confuse the gods, too! They'll see the wrong side! But what about the moon?" I ended in frustration.

Then after carefully setting the brush and ink on the floor, I nearly tore the tunic off my back, whirling around and hurling it down the room. "No one better touch that garment, and when that gazelle finally comes to get it, I'll kill it!" I yelled, glaring around, noting that nearly everyone except that advisor by the throne would bless the gods if I walked out the door.

Scribbling with the brush again, I added a little dance to my humming, my kilt barely held up by my girdle.

The seren's voice broke the silence. "And *this* is the man you want me to believe flattened all three of Goliath's kin, let alone be Dahveed Israel? Do I need to point out his insanity, or can you see it for yourselves? Just exactly why did you bring him here?" he asked sarcastically.

Turning, he stared directly at his chief advisor. "Did you feel that I don't already have enough madmen in my court, and so you bring me another one? You would tempt me to anger the gods and burden me with this idiot in my own house?" he went on. Then he slammed his fist down on the throne. "*Get him out of here!*" he roared, making everyone jump. "And you had better follow him. Throw them both out!"

Just the sound of his voice told me Akish had waited a long time to take down that advisor, and I hoped he'd have enough goodwill to spare my life. As the man hastily backed away, bowing, I saw a quick look pass between him and a guard, then the slight nod toward my covenant son, who stared at me as if he'd never seen me before. The spear men sprang forward, opening the doors and herding me out. Dropping my brush and ink, I walked through with great dignity, bowing to the people on either side as if accepting their applause, and lengthening my stride to waste no time getting to the city gates.

¥ ¥ ¥ ¥ ¥ ¥

Shaking her head at the amazing performance she had just witnessed, Sahrah Hazzel watched the Dahveed as he headed for the gates, then turned back to the door the advisor had gone out of. She'd seen him nod at Ittai. Unable to make Akish look the fool, he now sought to get revenge through her precious buckling! Biting her lip, her mind scrambled frantically for some way to remove Ittai from that man's reach, knowing in her heart that Manani would stop at nothing to get her son. Glancing out the doors, the occasional dance step the Dahveed put into his march toward the city gate caught her eye. Seeing that final finish to the act instantly made up her mind. Anyone who could get out of danger with that much imagination, who could, with deliberate, studied intent, convince an entire court that he was insane, was just the person to protect Ittai, for absolutely no one would dream that she would give her son into a madman's care. It was perfect! And it would break her heart.

She looked up at the ceiling as Akish stormed out of the room. "Yahweh, You watch over my son!" she commanded softly.

CHAPTER 10

As the spear men cleared the way, I walked straight for the city gate, keeping my gaze blank. As I passed out of the walls, I heard Ishvi-benob say, "You die today, Ben-geber!" My hands tingled, and I increased my pace, knowing that I dared not turn back, and yet afraid that I would be pursued.

As I started to run, a stone hit me. Abandoning the road, I headed toward the hills, praying my leg wouldn't cramp up until I was in their relative safety.

But I wasn't going to get the chance to make it there. Injured though they might be, Goliath's kin pursued me through the maze of walls and fields outside of the city. Unfamiliar with the twists and turns of the paths, I could only scramble over a wall, or backtrack when one of them cut me off as I tried to reach the open country and forests beyond.

Another stone slammed into my shoulder. "Yah, please aid me," I cried. Then I spotted an opening between two orchard walls, leading to the open fields beyond, and I darted toward it, knowing it was my last chance to escape. When I neared the opening, I saw Ishvi-benob waiting there, feet planted solidly although he couldn't quite stand straight, as he sighted down an arrow at my heart.

The instant before he released it, the wind suddenly swirled dust and sand into the man's face. The arrow flew wide as he covered his eyes and stumbled backward. The howl of defeat that rose behind me as I dashed into the open told me that I had a clear run before me.

And at the moment I gave a cry of thanks to Yah, my right leg cramped. The slashing pain from each stride slowed me so that Lahmi, who ran with one hand clutching his side, gained ground behind me. Ishvi-benob kept up a hobbled pace not far behind. The wind blew against my back, pushing me along with each painful movement of my legs. The light suddenly dimmed, and I glanced upward to see the black, angry clouds rising from the sea. Seconds later, when I looked again, the clouds had piled still higher, and the wind now roared.

The Rephites redoubled their efforts. Lost in a timeless dread, knowing only that my muscles took me one more stride toward the safety of the hills, I drove myself onward.

A crash of thunder shook the ground, followed by a second and third, rolling over the land almost as one. I risked another glance upward. I'd never seen such boiling, black clouds! A blinding flash of Yahweh's fire shattered the air overhead.

Lahmi had cut toward me from the side, his arm raised to throw a javelin. Then the dazzling white of Yahweh's fire blocked my view of him as a bolt of Yah's fire hurled to the ground between us, throwing me flat on my face, a searing pain blazing on my arm. My heart seized in my chest for an eternity, only to pound raggedly as I gasped for breath, staggered upright, and ran again with the road rising under my feet. Thunder exploded around me, and the blinding light of sacred fire flared time and again. On a small rise, I turned back once, holding my burnt arm, the wind nearly blowing me off my feet. The sight froze me in my tracks. A massive bolt from Yahweh's hand hurled directly onto Gath, throwing debris high into the air, and the resulting thunder smashed me to the ground.

Scrambling to my feet, I turned my back on the storm and ran. Long before I reached the hills, the rain came, a blinding deluge that made it nearly impossible for me to breathe as I pushed through it. The heavy pounding continued even under the trees in the forest before the climb to the Shephelah. It cooled the pain in my arm even as it set me to shivering.

The ground couldn't soak up the water fast enough, and soon little rivulets spread everywhere, producing a treacherous mat of slippery mud. I pushed on until I was so tired I could hardly make my legs move another stride. I had no idea when I passed Socoh in the lower Elah valley, but I was suddenly faced with the huge second stair from the Shephelah to the highlands. As I entered the upper Elah valley I nearly collapsed from relief. Recklessly, I scrambled up the steep incline on the south side, wanting to be out of the lowlands at any cost. As I pulled myself over the top of the last rise, my right leg gave out, and I came down hard on my left knee.

Moaning from the pain of the cramp in my leg, I rolled over and tried to stand, only to nearly scream. My left knee refused to straighten, and I rocked back and forth, clutching it. As I stared up at the sky, the cold rain still pouring over my half-naked body, one arm aching, my right leg cramped into spasms, my left now completely immobile, I knew I was in the worst trouble of my life.

¥ ¥ ¥ ¥ ¥ ¥

"Have you ever seen anything like this?" Ishvi asked in awe as Shaul's four sons stood in the upper room of Ishvi's Gibeah house while the earth shook under them with another ear-splitting crack of thunder. The wind roared around the house as if trying to tear it apart, driving rain horizontally through the small windows. Water seeped down the walls from the roof, and the wind blew out the one lamp as another blast of thunder seemed to rock the foundations of the town. A dazzling bolt of Yahweh's fire blinded the brothers, making them all retreat to the far wall.

"Yahweh must be raging over something," the hassar observed.

"Pray it's not us," Malchi nearly whispered.

More than an hour passed before the brothers dared to sit at the table and the wind had died enough so that they could light lamps. Young Ishvi soon appeared with three braziers and some wood to begin drying things out.

The noon meal followed, and after eating, Jonathan turned to them. "What progress has been made, Ishvi?"

"All my scribes know to report any unusual requests from the fortress to my assistant scribes, who will tell me. Ziba will also. Incidentally, he and Tanhum are very grateful for the hesed that Dahveed showed Atarah and Ornan. I believe both of them would defy Shaul if necessary."

Eshbaal nodded in agreement. "Tanhum would, without a second thought. None of the fortress scribes seemed at all reluctant to do as we've asked."

"Malchi?" Jonathan said, turning to his second brother.

"The armor-bearer who took Shaul's armor and weapons for Abner has been dismissed," Malchi began. "I interviewed the fifth unit myself. A courier met them on the road as they were returning from patrol on the Shephelah, and led them to a valley just south of Ramah where Abbi was waiting. The next day, he sent men to Navyoth, and the day after, he went himself. When he didn't return that night, Natan brought what was left of his unit back to Gibeah. The men who went to Navyoth have no memory of it. The last they remember, they were on their way to Gibeah from the Shephelah."

The third sar looked at his oldest brother. "The men don't like what happened, so I haven't had much opposition to asking that odd requests be told to me," he continued. "Of the 14 commanders, five would quietly ignore an order from abbi if I asked them to. Four still back Abner, but I have assistant commanders in those units who will report to me. The rest will send messages, do what Abbi or Abner asks, and wait to see what happens."

"What about you, Jonathan?" Ishvi inquired.

The hassar sighed. "I've had to dismiss three scribes, and find excuses to send two fortress sentries home. Michal found one servant whom we can't trust, and is fairly certain there's another. But I think we've brought things under control. Abbi shouldn't be able to do much, now, that we don't hear about. You're looking thoughtful, Ishvi. What's on your mind?"

"We still need to know how Abbi heard where Dahveed was."

Someone rapped on the door, and Ishvi opened it. "This message just came," he said, handing it to Sar Malchi.

"Our plan seems to be working," Malchi said wryly after reading it. "Shaul just decided to send me south with three units to hunt Dahveed!"

¥ ¥ ¥ ¥ ¥ ¥

Exhausted, I had fallen asleep in spite of the rain, and I woke up hours later to cold and clammy clothing and a deep ache in my left knee, which was swollen to nearly twice its size. I also hesitated to use my left arm, for the burn on it ached also.

Wincing at the pain when I moved, I cautiously stretched the right leg and found the cramp nearly gone. I sat up, flexing the leg repeatedly. It warmed me somewhat but increased the ache of the burn. I looked around for something to use as a crutch. After several minutes of study, I admitted that anything I could reach was useless. Reluctantly, I worked off my kilt, used my belt knife to cut it into strips, and wrapped my knee as tightly as I could stand. The skin wasn't broken, and what little I could feel through the swelling didn't seem to be out of place.

Again I fell asleep, waking to sunshine and a raging thirst. Dragging myself to the nearest tree, I managed to get upright. The weight of my left leg pulled it straighter, and the pain made me queasy. I stayed still, waiting for the faintness to pass. Then I started forward. Barely able to put weight on the left knee, I inched along, using anything that came within reach for balance and support. I'd hitched myself past two more trees before I found a dead branch on the ground sturdy enough to be a staff. With that in my left hand, I shuffled a little faster.

I started south, knowing Adullam was that way, but a steep 50-foot descent blocked my way. I frowned in puzzlement. The drop off continued to both sides as far as I could see. Checking the sun again, I determined that I was indeed facing south. Reluctantly, I retraced my steps, but I hadn't gone even 100 feet when I encountered the 200-foot descent I'd scrambled up yesterday. Resting against a tree, I looked around. This was not the Elah valley! I had no idea where I was.

Remembering the twists and turns that I'd taken while in the fields around Gath, I realized I had no sense of which direction I'd been headed when I made it to the open country. If the wind hadn't blown me east, I might have run myself right into the Great Sea. I had no way of knowing whether Adullam was north or south.

I would have to turn east toward the central plateau and King Shaul. Sooner or later, I would come to a road since they all fanned out from Jebus like the fingers of a hand. Once there I could determine where I was. If I was lucky, I'd be south of Elah and Adullam.

Not knowing where I was also meant I didn't know where to find water. Pushing myself off the tree, I started down the long finger of the ridge. As hard as it had rained, I'd find water somewhere, if only a little pool in the hollow of a rock.

I found two of them in the next hour, both so small that they barely slaked my thirst for a brief time. My knee had become a constant agony of pain, and my right thigh wasn't going to stand the extra strain much longer. Checking the landmarks I'd picked when I started, I calculated I'd come about a quarter of a mile. Then I heard the faint trickle of water.

Hurrying forward as quickly as I could force my leg, I located the small gushing spring just 10 feet over the edge of the drop on the south. It might as well have been a mile. The slant was too steep for me to manage, and I had nothing to reach the water with. When I tried to turn away, I found that I could only stand there and stare at the wonderful wet coolness I couldn't reach.

Easing down, I tried to rest, still staring at the water. I automatically reached to my waist for my water cruse, but it had disappeared before they put me in the cell in Gath. I was lucky they hadn't taken my girdle. They would have found my belt knife and sling that I had hidden in it. My girdle! It was long and made of absorbent cloth.

With trembling fingers, I untied it. Dragging myself as close to the edge as I dared, I let the girdle drop down from my hand. By stretching as far as I could, I got the last two feet of it into the falling water. After a few moments, I pulled up the soaked cloth and wrung it out into my mouth.

Again and again I lowered it until I was no longer thirsty. After resting, I wet it five or six times more, wringing it out over the bandages around my knee. The cold water deadened the ache a little.

Carefully wrapping the girdle around my waist again, I tucked in my belt knife and struggled upright. A couple more hours of daylight remained, and I might make another quarter of a mile if I started now.

For three days I struggled east, managing a mile a day. It rained hard, keeping me constantly cold and wet, but also assuring me that I could find small pools of water when I needed them. I got used to sleeping while I shivered since my loincloth made a very thin blanket, and burrowing under piles of last year's leaves or the pine needles added little warmth, but lots of bugs. I kept the girdle around my waist with my belt knife and two sling stones. The sling was wrapped around my arm again. Eating sour wild apples, dried up berries, and what few grapes clung to the wild vines, I barely kept enough strength in my body to keep moving.

On the fourth day I turned south. I still had to go around most obstacles, my knee refusing to bear my full weight even standing still. At dusk, my heart sinking, I stared at the stretch of road south of Timnah that led toward Gath! I'd passed this very spot less than a month ago. I was in the heart of the country Shaul would probably search first as he tried to find me!

"Yah, where can I shelter from the king?" I whispered. Suddenly, I remembered the cave at the head of the Elah valley that I had stayed in the summer I'd made so many trips to supply my brothers in the army. It was only two miles from here and well concealed with a small spring close by. I'd left a few things there for convenience, including fire-making materials. And, most of all, it would be dry!

Hope gave me strength, and I crossed the road after dark, pushing myself south as far as I could go. At last I stopped for the night. It would take most of two days to reach there at my present pace, a distance I could have covered in less than half an hour a week ago.

The next morning I woke to find the country crawling with soldiers. From the cover of some brush I watched several pass. If they were looking for something, they weren't putting much effort into it. They seemed to be just passing through, not searching. Knowing that if they saw me, I could not get away, I remained in my hiding place until the sky clouded over and rain drenched the land again. I moved now only when it rained, or was dark, ever alert for the sound of another human, hiding before I could see who it was. It might not be Shaul's men, but defenseless as I was, I could easily be enslaved, so I avoided everyone. While I was in hiding, I distracted myself by composing some verses. I didn't have a melody for them yet, but the verses stayed in my mind.

"I sought Yahweh, and He answered me, and from all of my horrors He delivered me.

This afflicted one called, and Yahweh heard. And from all his distress He saved him.

The messenger of Yahweh encamps around about the ones who fear Him, and He will deliver them.

They cried to Yahweh. He heard, and from all their distresses He rescued them."

Early in the morning of the eighth day since I'd fled Gath, I looked across the last ravine to the bench of land that fronted the cave. In spite of my eagerness to get there, I took my time going down, more than once inching down on my behind, using the staff to steady and control my descent. I'd done this so often that my loincloth was wearing out, and when that happened I'd have nothing to wear at all. I hadn't seen another human today, and I hoped I'd gone unnoticed.

Once across the ravine, the climb out was easier, and I reached the small bench with a sense of relief. Hobbling across it, I had one last climb to make, the 15 feet up the steep hillside to the ledge that concealed the cave entrance.

Before tackling that, I drank deeply from the spring against the hillside. Anxious to be out of sight, I crawled, pulled, and maneuvered myself up the last climb, and rolled onto the ledge protruding from the low opening to the cave.

It slanted back into the first chamber, and there was at least one more beyond. I eased down inside, the hard stone softened by the debris washed into the place. Tomorrow I'd scrape some of it together for a fire, but now, I was simply too exhausted. Dry, and fairly warm for once, I quickly fell asleep, listening to the downpour that, for the first time in days, wasn't soaking me along with everything else.

I woke up close to dusk, rousing from a dream of Immi's cooking, the smell of stew lingering in my nose. I swallowed, my stomach so empty I couldn't remember what it felt like full. Then my eyes flew open as I realized that I wasn't asleep but still smelled stew and smoke. Sitting up, my heart pounding, I half crawled, half dragged myself up the small rise of the ledge and peeked over. Directly below me, not 15 feet away, stretched beside a warm fire and casually eating the bread he dipped in a bowl of hot stew, lay Sar Malchi. Beyond him on the bench camped at least three units of King Shaul's army. I was trapped!

After the initial shock of finding myself in the midst of the army, I studied the camp. Unhurt, I wouldn't have worried, knowing I could have passed through the entire three units in the dark without anyone knowing. But now I couldn't even move around the cave without risk of being heard by the sar directly below. My only hope was that they would leave in the morning. But this camp had all the earmarks of an extended stay. When the sar's attendant started stacking fire wood beside the tent, I knew the situation couldn't be worse.

By now I was thirsty again, but there was no way to get to the spring. I'd just have to wait. I stayed on the ledge as the sun sank and dusk blanketed the land. The attendant built up the sar's fire, and soon the three unit commanders had gathered for a conference. In the quiet of the night I heard every word.

"Anything today, Libni?" Sar Malchi asked when everyone had seated themselves around the fire.

"No, Sar," the commander of the tenth unit sighed. "I think we looked into every bit of brush, possible cave, and gully in the entire land. Not a single sign of him."

The wind brushed by, and distant thunder rumbled faintly. Malchi looked up at the sky in disgust. "Not that we'd find anything in this constant rain. You nearly got lost this afternoon, didn't you, Pasach?"

The commander of the eleventh unit nodded as the others chuckled. "It was raining so hard that we didn't see the path turn down the hill. If your Habiru guide hadn't caught up to us, we'd likely still be headed west, trying to catch up to you."

The mention of a Habiru guide made me sit back in dismay. Now I knew I dared not budge. Clumsy as I was, any Habiru could read the signs of my passing at a dead run. I wondered who Malchi had with him.

"How do we even know Dahveed is anywhere around here?" Natan of the fifth unit asked.

"We don't," Libni replied sourly.

Another man stepped into the fire light, his mismatched dress and excellent weapons proclaiming him Habiru.

"What have you heard, Zeri?" Sar Malchi asked.

"From whom?"

"Did you get anything from around Timnah?"

"Most of the rumors there agree that Dahveed passed by riding the wind before the king's proclamation ever reached the market. They disagree on the direction in which the wind was blowing. Reports there have placed him anywhere from Dan to Jebus. Incidentally, if he's in Jebus, he will be taking over the city by palace coup and sending bands of soldiers to sack any city that has offended him in the past."

"Who starts these stories?" Malchi fumed. "Anyone who's ever met Dahveed knows the ridiculousness of that one!"

"There are others, worse than that," Zeri said, squatting down by the fire. "But there are people who say he's in Shechem, or possibly Taanach. Ramah is always a good choice, because the roeh can blind the eyes of any who try to seek him there, so he can live openly, and no one will ever know."

"That one at least has a faint hope of being true," Pasach said, tossing a small stick into the fire.

"Anything worth listening to?" Malchi interrupted.

"Depends," the Habiru replied. "Ethan isn't searching."

I pulled back a little. That my old mentor would search for me was the one fact I'd taken for granted. To hear that he wasn't left me feeling as if the world had come to a sudden halt.

"Why wouldn't he? Do you think he knows where Dahveed is?"

Zeri didn't reply for several seconds. "Ethan isn't considered the best dahveed among us for nothing, Sar. He knows Jesse's son better than anyone, I think. He and his band know something about the zammar which they do not speak of. If Ethan will not search, there is a compelling reason."

"What could that be?" Libni questioned.

"I think Ethan knows Yahweh is hiding him, and we will never find him unless it suits Yahweh for us to do so." The guide stood and looked at Malchi. "I will take you where you wish to go, Sar, but I will not help search for Dahveed Israel."

Total silence greeted the man's statement.

"Fair enough, Zeri," Sar Malchi said. "Are you willing to tell me why?"

"I think the Dahveed has been chosen by our God. I do not relish standing in the way of El Shaddai." Zeri walked away, and the silence continued until the commanders left one after the other.

I didn't know what to think as I eased back. Somewhere in the back of my mind had been the certainty that Ethan would find me, and everything would be all right again. Now that hope had vanished. I'd never felt so alone. I stared bitterly at the opening to the cave. How could this situation get any worse? Easily. That night it turned cold.

Three days later I was at the end of my strength. The first day it had rained three times, and I was able to soak my girdle in the run-off and wring out enough to keep thirst at bay. But yesterday, and again today, the clouds had passed over without dropping any rain, and my lips were cracked and my mouth sandy with thirst. The cold continued, and I shivered almost constantly.

Perversely, the enforced rest had benefitted my knee. It was still swollen, but it would bend and support most of my weight. Now, however, I was too weak from hunger and thirst to go anywhere.

Below me, the camp was never deserted. Men came and left unpredictably as they scoured the country within miles, looking for me as I died above them. Twice a day, the smells of cooking food tormented me, and now I was so light-headed and famished that I could only lie back on the hard stone and let the tears of weakness and defeat soak into my tangled, filthy hair.

Hardly knowing the difference between faint and sleep, I roused from one such to find myself staring at the stars. I was out on the ledge, without strength to go back into the cave, and too cold to shiver anymore.

I was going to die. There was no escape this time. Jonathan would mourn if I never returned, but he would go on to be a better king than I could have been, and Yahweh would rule His people just fine without me.

I wasn't necessary for anything. How could I have possibly believed that Yahweh needed me? I was certainly no help to Him. I couldn't even manage to keep myself warm, let alone do anything for Him.

The stars whirled dizzily above me, and when I tried to raise my hand to my face, my arm only flopped across my chest. I was useless and defenseless, able only to lie here and slowly die, a failure before I had even begun. How could any person care about me, let alone Yahweh? No, I was just an unwanted man, as I had been an unwanted boy.

I'd been given a chance, but was now cast off when I had shown that I couldn't manage to do what was asked of me. In spite of all the Hassar had tried to teach me, Eliab was right. I caused nothing but trouble, leaving behind problems that others had to clean up. Just think how many times the Hassar had had to do that! It would be a relief to him not to have to do it again.

The lights in the dark sky blurred, and shimmered, seeming to draw closer. Somehow I didn't feel so cold anymore. I smiled a little, realizing that I had at least been able to crawl into a hole to die alone and save everyone the trouble of burial, for who would want to remember my name?

In the black sky the stars twinkled in the cold. I knew the stars. I'd watched them often. They had spoken to me once or twice, and I'd written a song about it. I could feel the Hassarah's harp in my hands. How did it go?

"The heavens proclaim the glory of El;
And the firmament announces the work of His hands.
Day to day they pour out speech;
Night to night they announce knowledge.
There is no voice, there is no speaking
Without their voice being heard.
Their voice goes forth in all the earth,
And at the end of the land is their word." [6]

They were so close. If I could have moved, I could have touched one. "What knowledge do you have for me now?" I asked, "or am I too low-born for your notice?"

"But surely He had no reason to keep you alive! Why would He do such a thing?"

"I told you. Because I asked Him."

Why was I hearing Akish and Ittai? I opened my eyes. The dark sky still stretched above me, the stars watching. "What did you say?" I asked them.

"Ask Him to," the stars responded.

"Why should He care? I have failed."

"Because I decided to," the Hassar's voice rang in my mind. "Put it down to the incomprehensible foibles of the royal family, since it seems you are unable to believe anything else." The vision of the twisted brass earring Jonathan had given me that day, to remind me of his regard for me, rose in my mind.

"If Jonathan Hassar can grant you such honor because he decided to, dare you to think that Yahweh will do any less when He has decided to? Do you question Yahweh's honor now?"

"I-I should not come to Him with my small troubles," I twisted my head away from the stars.

"If Yahweh cared enough to protect and shelter a young Moabitess who didn't even know His right name, He will care for you. Do sheep fend for themselves when they are under the care of a shepherd? Is it

---

[6] Psalms 19

their responsibility to find pastures, take their lambs to pools of water, or fight off wolves?"

"No," I admitted, not daring to look into the face of the sky. "But I am not a sheep. I am a man. Surely there is something I'm supposed to do!"

"What are sheep supposed to do?"

I chewed on my lip, cracked and sore though it was. "Follow," I said. I took a breath of the cold air, and weak as my body was, my mind seemed strangely clear. "They are to follow, and not worry about anything else. But sometimes they remind the shepherd they are hungry, or want to drink, and sometimes, some of them even fight bears when the shepherd is with them."

The shimmer of the stars seemed to laugh. "And is the shepherd offended or angry when the sheep do this?"

"No. He usually laughs as you do now, and tells the sheep to be patient a little longer."

"When does trouble come, then?"

"When the sheep try to go without the shepherd. Then the sheep feel the shepherd's rod. I'm certainly feeling it quite clearly now," I said, resignedly.

For a moment, I thought the stars would break into audible laughter. "Why would that be?"

"I tried to go on without the shepherd, and I have tried to provide for myself what I should ask and receive from his hand." The sympathy of the stars had made me bold, and I added, "But why should He care whether I have more than a ragged loincloth to cover myself?"

"As your place is higher than a sheep, so is His will higher for you than for them. He will provide all you need. But sometimes in order for Him to help, you must ask. So, troubled one, we have come full circle, as you always will with the stars. Why would He do such a thing? Because you asked."

I closed my eyes as the stars retreated to their places in the night sky. I was to ask, and apparently not just about the big things, but the little things such as having more to wear than rags, and keeping my feet under me when I ran down a muddy path. It didn't seem possible that He would really care, but I seemed to feel the weight of the earring on my chest, even though I knew it hung on the gold chain around Jonathan's neck.

I smiled with memory. "I do not question Your honor, Yahweh," I whispered. Then I told Him everything that I needed. I reminded Him that I would die here unless He provided for me somehow, and I told Him the change in my heart. Not only had I learned that Yahweh expected to provide all I needed, but I also realized that He was the only one who could do so.

This was the lesson Roeh Shamuel had tried to teach me in Navyoth. I could not depend on Jesse, or Ethan, or Jonathan Hassar, for protection or for my needs. No matter how much these people loved me, they were sheep, just as I, and sheep were unable to protect each other from predators. Only the shepherd could do that. Only Yahweh El Shaddai could be my refuge, the one who could shelter me in any situation. He might choose to use others as He willed, but the responsibility was His.

I had rested that way in Yah as a child, and I knew when I had first gone to the court of Shaul, I had depended only on Yah. But somehow during those years I had come to trust in Shamuel, Jonathan, Michal, and others to shield me from any who wished me harm. But I would never forget this month and the knowledge it brought of my place--and Yahweh's place--in the world.

The cold was still as biting, I was just as hungry and as near to death as before, but I went to sleep without fear.

¥ ¥ ¥ ¥ ¥ ¥

"Gebirah, come quickly," Namea gasped, rushing into the chamber where Abigail was collecting her embroidery basket to go to the garden. "It's Parai! He'll kill him!"

Her face pale, Abigail rushed from the room and across the private courtyard, remembering too well the slave's threats that night on the roof. But when she got to the street, Nabal stood over the tanner's son who lay on the ground, coughing and holding his side.

"You are mine," her husband snarled, "you and your house with you! And unless I tell you to move, you stay still. All those who dare despise my honor will be as you." The nagid smoothed his hair back from his forehead and stroked his pointed chin, stepping back as Parai struggled to breathe.

Abigail stared at her husband, sudden anger pouring through her. As she suspected, Nabal hadn't bought that litter as a present for her so much as a way to torment Parai and his house. "Your slave, Nabal? When did you withdraw your gift to me?"

Quickly he looked around. "Gebirah, you should not be out in the street for anyone to see!" he exclaimed.

"No more should you be conducting business such as this in the street," she said, her voice clipped with anger. "Bring him inside." She turned back into the courtyard, and Hezro helped Parai stand, easing him to the ground in the courtyard.

Nabal followed.

Once the gate was closed again, Abigail turned to her husband. "Have you withdrawn your gift?"

"Why, no, Gebirah."

"Then Parai belongs to me?"

"Well, I suppose you could say that."

"I do say that. Therefore, any discipline he deserves comes from me. What has he done?"

"I caught him sneaking around town, Gebirah. When I demanded to know what he was doing and where he had been, he refused to answer!" Her husband's lips tightened as he glared at the tanner's son.

"Beating him in the street is unworthy of a nagid," Abigail told him, her eyes flashing. "Hezro, take Parai to his place and confine him there. I will deal with him later." She turned her back to Nabal and went into the house. Tirzah and Matred left her chamber when she entered, and she paced the floor, wondering at her loss of self-control. It had been years since she'd spoken out like that. In the past she'd done it all the time, and her abbi had been concerned, talking to her about the problems that could arise if she was not careful of her tongue and actions.

Clenching her fists, she strove to banish the anger at Nabal surging through her. After a while, she picked up her silver mirror and looked at her face. Her features were still the same, thick eyelashes, smooth cheekbones, unblemished ivory skin, a face that made people stare. A face to grace a king's palace.

An ironic smile tugged at her lips. Age hadn't touched her yet. She'd had an easy life, always plenty to eat, servants to do the work, time to care for her hair and skin, the only mar on her the needle pricks on her fingers from her embroidery. And what had she really done to help her people? The look on her husband's face when she had come into the house had been one of dismay, if not fear. Could Parai have been correct? What would have happened if she had stood in Nabal's way more often instead of retreating to her chamber and her garden?

Standing, she went to the window. The day all those years ago when Abbi had visited her immi's clan had been hot and dusty like this one, and the streets of Bethlehem radiated the heat as they had walked down them to pay their respects to Hassarah Ruth. The tall woman had fascinated her, the calm commanding demeanor impressing her greatly. Somehow she knew that the Hassarah rarely raised her voice or spoke without thought. Since then she had striven to pattern her behavior after Ruth's, gradually acquiring a commanding self-control that rarely failed her.

She had also heard the Hassarah sing and play her harp. Closing her eyes, she remembered the beauty of the voice and the sound of the instrument. Later Abigail had held it herself, running her fingers down the lines of inlay on the smooth wood and softly plucking a string or two before giving it to the boy who came to take it away. Now she wondered what had happened to it when Ruth died. As always, thinking of that day and the music calmed her. After lifting her chin as she had seen Ruth do, she summoned up her usual mask. Once she had tended to Parai, she'd go to the garden.

Picking up her embroidery basket, she walked out the door. "Come, Namea," she said to her handmaid waiting in the outer room. As she left the house, she saw Nabal hovering indecisively in the private courtyard. She didn't look at him.

Hezro approached her when she started for the servants' quarters.

"I will see Parai, now," she said to him.

He bowed and led the way.

The slaves' quarters were in a separate compound, and Abigail noticed immediately that the place needed cleaning. Parai lay on a pile of straw, securely bound.

"I will talk with him alone," she said.

"Keep your distance, Gebirah," Hezro said quietly as he left.

Abigail waited until the guard commander and her handmaid had gone and then she sat down on the one stool, putting her basket beside her. The silence stretched, but she knew Parai was awake because his hands kept flexing in the ropes that tied him.

"I have thought much on the words you spoke on the roof, Parai," she said at last. "I don't know if they are true, or if there is any way I can restrain the nagid. In any case, I wondered if there was anything I could do for you and your family."

The man didn't reply.

"As you wish," she said, standing up and brushing off her robe. Taking the basket, she started for the door.

"Your concern is just a little late, Gebirah. Abbi died last night."

She stopped. "I see."

"No, I don't think you do," the slave's bitter voice said. "My brother can't run the tannery. He doesn't know enough. Immi's clan is from Carmel, and there's not a person in it who dares to help her for fear of what the nagid will do. My family fled immediately after the burial this morning. I would have been with them, but I came back to recompense you as I promised I would. It was my misfortune to run into Hezro just inside the town gate."

Abigail clenched her fist and pressed her hand against her side, hoping to ease the familiar pain.

"I doubt my Immi, sisters, and brother will survive very long alone, so I now have my entire family to avenge, and now that everyone is gone, I have lots of time. Don't sleep too soundly."

Wondering why she didn't feel frightened at the certainty in the man's voice, Abigail looked down. Then she spoke without turning around. "Now you're the one who's just a little late, Parai. I haven't been able to sleep soundly for years."

As she stepped into the sunshine, a courier ran by on the road. She'd have to hurry if she wanted to hear what had happened. At the garden entrance she dismissed Namea and settled on the bench, getting her breath back and taking out the embroidery just as the chamber door behind her opened.

"Did the message come?" Nabal's thin voice inquired.

"Yes, Nagid," Tokhath replied. "Your source in Bethlehem says Elhanan the innkeeper has found a buyer for his inn. Buying up his debts and demanding immediate payment have forced him to sell."

The innkeeper? Abigail frowned. Then she recalled her husband's anger when he'd come back from his trip to Jericho while looking for more grain at the end of harvest. The innkeeper hadn't treated him as he had wished. She seemed to remember that the man's son was very ill, and the innkeeper had left Nabal in the care of his assistant while he stayed with his boy. Nabal had taken insult.

"That was quicker than I expected, but he'll get a good price for it," she heard her husband say. "We must get someone there quickly. Whom can we contact this soon?"

The scribe gave some names, none of them familiar to Abigail, so they must not be from the Carmel region.

Nabal hesitated over the names.

"If you hire the Habiru, Nagid, they can travel quickly. Because there is a band around Bethlehem, they are less likely to be noticed.

Just give them strict instructions that nothing is to be done until the sale is complete, then they should bring the man to you alive," Tokhath advised.

"Yes, and after I've defended my honor to him, he'll be begging me to take the purchase price of the inn, and once I have that, they can kill him. No one impugns my honor. I am Nagid Carmel, equal to Shaul, and you know how closely the hassar guards his honor."

"Yes, Nagid, your honor must be avenged so that all will acknowledge it," the scribe said, his voice steady.

Abigail's hands still rested in her lap. Dizzy, she suddenly realized that she had been holding her breath. Carefully, she inhaled, laying down the embroidery needle and folding her hands, struggling to make herself believe what she'd just heard. Her husband was planning to commit murder because a man chose to stay with his sick child. This, on top of Parai, was too much. She lowered her head. Something had to be done, and what little honor remained in her house demanded that she do it. But how?

CHAPTER 11

When I woke up, I was covered with a cloak, and Ittai's face looked anxiously into mine.

"I was afraid you'd never wake up," the young man said softly. "Here," he held a water skin up to my lips. "Drink some more."

I obeyed, and the fact that it soon satisfied my thirst told me I must have drunk much more previously.

"What are you doing here, Ittai?" I asked, bewildered.

"Immi sent me. She told me to find you and stay with you."

I shook my head. I had to be dreaming. "How did your units get here without running into Sar Malchi?"

"I came alone."

"Ittai, your immi is very, um, protective of you. I can hardly believe that she would send you to the land of your enemies alone."

"I'm half Israelite and circumcised to prove it. When Immi decided it would be safer for me here with you rather than back there in Gath with Seren Manani's agents, there was no convincing her otherwise."

I could only stare at him. "Seren Akish must have been desperate about you, or moon-touched!" I finally said.

Ittai's face reddened, and I groaned.

"He doesn't know where you are, does he?"

The youth shook his head. "No, adoni. Immi isn't going to tell him, at least not right away. All he knows is that Manani's agents don't know where I am either."

"If he finds out you're here, he'll kill me."

"I doubt it. Not after that bolt of sacred fire hit the palace. It blasted all the way though into the throne room and blackened the floor where Dodi's advisor had been standing. When I left, the entire town was offering sacrifices and pleading with Baal not to harm them for the way they treated you, since you obviously must be innocent. Dodi took the opportunity to charge several of Manani's agents--of whom that advisor was one--with treason against him by trying to bring Baal's wrath down on him. He killed four, and most of the rest fled."

I shook my head in wonder.

"I found some cast off clothes once the army units left," Ittai continued. "And there is food and water." He indicated some items on the floor near us.

I glanced around the cave. "How did you know I was here?"

"Immi told me that Yahweh would lead me to you. You were headed in the general direction of the Elah valley when you ran, so I came here. I've been helping around the camp in the fifth unit, and I overheard one of the soldiers mention someone on the ledge above the Sar's tent. His sentry post was above you on the top of the hill. You can look right down on the ledge, and once I realized you were there, I stayed up there a lot, and eventually they moved the sentry post. I didn't realize you were wounded and couldn't leave the cave until I came to you after the sar left."

Easing back down, I sighed. I'd forgotten something as simple as looking up, in more ways than one. "I won't forget it again," I murmured.

"Adoni?" he asked, puzzled.

"Never mind. How come the sar didn't check up here when he heard the sentry's report?"

Ittai smiled. "There's another ledge just below where they moved the sentry post, and no one ever saw anyone there, so no one believed the man. He finally quit talking about it."

As I struggled to sit up, he hastened to help me. My head felt clearer than I'd expected, and I noticed that my knee was nearly back to its normal size.

"Why did the units leave?" I asked, deciding I must have eaten in the recent past also.

"They got a report that you were at Gedor, so the sar packed up and went there in spite of the rain."

With Ittai to help, I descended from the cave and washed thoroughly in the spring, dressing in the clothes he had found. While I worked the tangles and filth from my hair, I realized that I had begun humming, and my fingers twitched. How I wanted to feel the Hassarah's harp again! Since I couldn't do that, I sang softly instead, my weak voice cracking at times.

While my covenant son prepared some food, I considered my next move. The easiest way to Adullam took me perilously close to Malchi at Gedor, but I would be more than 1,200 feet lower, on the upper edge of the Shephelah.

After we settled down in the cave for the night, I began humming again, the melody intriguing me. I worked it over a little, then searched for some words. *"In this way I walk, they hide a trap for me. My refuge was lost to me. No one inquires about my soul."*

That went well. *"You are my refuge, Listen carefully to my shout, for I am brought very low."*

Now, something about my persecutors. I stared up at the shadows in the roof of the cave for a while. This song was coming in pieces, not all at once as the one in Gath had.

"Look to the right and see, for there is no one who shows consideration for me." I smiled sadly. Only Jonathan had ever stood on the right for me, the position of a protector, acting as my elder brother should have.

"Bring my soul out of captivity" [7]

Or would something else go better? Nothing more occurred to me, and I settled down to sleep after thanking Yah for the gifts that this day had brought me.

We left just at sunrise. My pace was still slow, and the easiest route added another two miles to our six-mile journey, since the swells at the very foot of the highlands were gentler than the ones farther west. We would probably arrive at Adullam sometime tomorrow.

Ittai helped me wrap my knee, and I wore the old shepherd's bag I had left here long ago. I put in three good-sized stones the first thing. Locating the trail at the head of the Elah valley, I led the way south and down. By mid-morning, we were traveling under the steep-rising ridges

---

[7] Psalms 142

to the highlands.

We made better progress than I expected, since the clouds above simply floated by without drenching the land again. Once we were directly below Gedor, Ittai unexpectedly stopped.

"Adoni, these are fresh lion tracks, are they not?" he asked.

I limped up, looking where he indicated on the path. "Very. They could have been made just moments ago," I replied, looking around. "Two of them jumped from that rock." I pointed. "They've gone ahead of us, and they are after something. Look how even the stride is."

"Lions don't usually hunt by day, do they?"

"No, but with this constant rain, they may not have found any prey for some time, and will take the risk of daylight."

I did not want to meet a hungry lion. As we continued down the trail, I brushed my hand across my thigh, bringing the loops of the sling up to my first finger joints, then made certain I could get my hand around one of the stones in my bag unhindered.

A gap in the trees opened to the right, and I looked down toward the west. Another storm was on the way, thunder rumbling faintly over the sea. My eye caught a glimpse of a tawny coat flashing behind some brush. Not far away another prowled. Ittai pointed ahead, and less than a quarter of a mile down the trail, a third lioness dropped down from the hills, crossed the trail, and angled toward the other two. All three were fixed on something specific. They had located prey. We scanned the country to see what they were after.

"There," my companion indicated. Half a mile away, and 180 feet below, a man rode a mule toward a hillock. He was probably hunting, for he carried bow and quiver and had two javelins beside him on the harness. "They want that mule!" I exclaimed, watching him. "I hope he has sense enough to let them have it. Find a place to shout from! We have to warn him."

Something about the countryside tugged at my memory as we moved farther down the trail, turning into a path to the west. I limped along as fast as I could until the man was almost directly below us with the lions closing the distance rapidly. He turned the mule up the hill, headed into a notch above him.

As the rider reached the top of the rise, I remembered why the area seemed familiar. I'd spent a day up in that notch not long after I'd killed Goliath. "I know this place," I said to Ittai, pushing myself faster along the trail. "Four hills crowd together, and the ravines between them make a cross in the middle. Just beyond that notch is a natural pit more

100 feet across where the ground just drops 15 feet straight down. Without a rope, there's only one way out on the east side, but it's not easy to find. If he doesn't know about that pit, the lions will have them both!"

We could see the predators rapidly climbing the hill. "Shout to warn him, Ittai," I said as a roll of thunder reached our ears.

"Geber! Get off the mule!" my covenant son yelled.

The man's head swung around, and he paused, turning back.

It was Sar Malchi! I nearly fell, my heart skipping a beat. What was he doing down here?

"Yahweh, no! Save him," I cried. In a rush the sounds around me faded, and the colors of the trees and bushes made my eyes ache with their brilliance. I was running, gaining the natural bench, seeing the lions as they charged from three directions, hearing the terrified bray of the mule as it bolted with Malchi clinging to its back.

My feet hardly seemed to touch the ground, and I heard Malchi's shout as he threw himself backward, trying to save the mule from the fall as a lioness prepared to leap. All three vanished.

I got to the edge in time to see the mule's hind legs kicking frantically, front legs undoubtedly shattered from the drop, and the lioness just hesitating at the lip. She launched herself at the sar scrambling to his feet about 10 feet away from the mule. He came up with a javelin in his hand, shoving the weapon into the lion's chest from below, arcing the animal over his head. Malchi then landed on his knees, facing the opposite way, his neck reddening and his robe torn on the shoulder where the lioness's paw had connected, but the sar had his sword out and ready.

Everything about me slowed down. There was a stone in my sling, and I whirled it around, shouting my warning as the second lioness hurled itself from the edge of the pit the same moment that I jumped. I launched the stone before hitting the ground, rolling with the jar of my landing. The projectile hit her solidly in the side, and she seemed to fall in slow motion as she smashed her shoulder into the ground, tumbling over twice. The third lion landed in the pit, then retreated toward the opposite wall, ears flat, snarling in defiance.

I had the second javelin in my hand, my sling hanging from the loops on my fingers. On the edge opposite me, a fourth lioness paced back and forth, growling, eyes on the groaning mule. As I swayed slightly, I heard the grass crush beneath the sar's sandals as he backed toward me. The lion that he had speared was dead, but the one I'd hit with a stone tried to get up, only to collapse when nothing on her right side would move.

"You arrived at a very opportune time," Sar Malchi said quietly, never taking his eyes from the lions. "To whom do I owe my rescue?"

He'd asked a question. I should answer. No, I shouldn't. The mule started thrashing again, and the fourth lion jumped down, ears flattened, growling and advancing toward us.

As I stepped forward I felt the rise of Yahweh's gift again. Looking the beast in the eye, I forced it to retreat up against the wall of the pit.

Moving my left hand slowly, I gestured the sar toward a boulder on the east side. As he backed toward it, I went with him, always facing the lions, keeping them pinned against the wall with my gaze.

Once close to the boulder, I heard the sar's sword slide into its sheath, and he scrambled up.

"Give me your hand, friend," he said in a low voice.

Turning slightly, I held up my left hand, and he grasped my wrist, his powerful arms and shoulders lifting me to his side. We pushed our way through the brush in the crack of the hillside, and my enhanced hearing told me that the lions had killed the mule the instant we had disappeared from sight. Thunder rumbled again, the sound so loud to me that I cringed a little.

"And Jonathan's going to kill me, too," the sar muttered. "We just bought that mule, and he said Shammah worked extra with it just for me." He raised his hand to his neck, wiping at the blood seeping from the deep scratches there. "At least I've got something to show for it. Maybe knowing that I'm already bleeding will soften him up a bit. Do you have an older brother?" he asked, pausing to work his way around a protruding rock in the crevice.

I didn't answer, the gift still holding me so strongly that I couldn't talk.

"He couldn't possibly be as over-bearing and pig-headed as mine! And Michal will take strips from my skin for ruining another robe." As he raised his hands to his eyes, I decided that his grumbling was a way of coping with his brush with death.

I could feel the gift seeping away as he talked, and as my mind connected with other aspects of reality than just lions in a pit, it occurred to me that it might be wise to conceal my identity from the sar. Thunder rolled over us, and I pulled up the hood of my cloak, hoping it would start to rain soon.

"Finally!" the sar said triumphantly as he led the way onto the hillside. As he helped me scramble out after him, I felt the gift lessen still more. It would be gone soon, and I needed to be away from the sar when that happened.

"As I said before, your coming was very welcome, friend," he said, facing me once we were out in the open forest.

Keeping my head down and wondering if my voice would work yet, I shrugged. "I-I'm pleased to be of service," I managed to croak hoarsely. "Where were you headed, adon?"

"They're waiting for me at Gedor. If you could point the way back there?"

I turned and started for the top of the eastern hill. I could still walk normally, but as the gift faded, that would change. I wondered how much damage I'd done to my knee by jumping into the pit like that. Likely I'd find out tomorrow. Then that habit of curiosity from Ethan kicked in, and I asked, "How did you get here from Gedor, adon?"

"Following someone I should better have beaten," he said in disgust. "We've been up there for three days now, and a man showed up about noon while I was resting. Said he could show me where the Dahveed was, but that I should come alone since bringing any more would warn him of our presence. He took me down the ridge and pointed out those hills I was headed for. Said Dahveed was camped in the middle of them. Then he demanded payment. I pulled out my purse, and he tried to take it!"

"Did he get it?" I couldn't help asking.

"He got a foot in his chest, and a near trampling by my mule. The man disappeared after that."

We were almost to the top of the hill, and I wouldn't be able to go on much beyond that.

"If you see him, he has a scar on his cheek just under his left eye that looks like an arrowhead pointed down, and a face that could be Ammonite," the sar added.

"Why did you keep going?" I inquired as we topped the rise.

"Just because he was a thief didn't mean he was a liar."

"See the ridge on the right side of the deep ravine in front of us? Gedor sits at the top. Just follow it up."

"You have my gratitude, geber," Malchi said. "Is there something I can do for you?"

I could feel the last of the gift draining away. "No, adon. Shalom."

"Shalom, friend." He started down the hill.

Feeling the sudden collapse of my body as the world returned to normal, I backed away. Quietly, I tried to suck in as much air as I could while wondering where I could go to be out of the sar's sight and yet allow Ittai to find me. But after only three steps I folded up in the middle, unable to stand any longer. Resting on my hands and knees, I panted for breath, the usual terrible thirst drying my mouth. Then my arms gave out, and I rolled half onto my side. Maybe Ittai would find me right away, or the rain would begin.

Someone shouted, and footsteps ran toward me. I tried to push myself away and failed. The gift had drained me so much that I was unable to move even a finger. Someone's hands gripped my shoulders and rolled me onto my back. The hood from my cloak fell from my face.

"Yahweh above! *Dahveed!*"

I looked into his face, and my lips twitched a little. "Yes, Sar," I whispered before I lost even the power to speak.

¥ ¥ ¥ ¥ ¥ ¥

From his seat on his abbi's throne, Jonathan Hassar lifted his head, listening. Shouts of greeting rose faintly from the road to Jebus. Shaul was in Zelah, spending as much time as possible with his grandsons before Sahrah Merab left for Meholath again. Besides, the only things that still engaged the king's attention were plans for the war season, visiting emissaries, and possible news of Dahveed.

Jonathan frowned, wondering why he couldn't talk his abbi out of killing the zammar.

More cheers and greetings drifted up the hill. The door opened and a guard stepped in, bowing. "Hassar, Sar Malchi is returning."

"What's left, Eshbaal?" Jonathan asked, glancing at his brother who sat nearby.

"Three reports for review about the olive harvest from crown estates north of Bethel."

"Close court, then."

"Do you think he found Dahveed?" Eshbaal asked in his quiet way.

The hassar refrained from voicing the devout hope that his brother had not. "We'll have to go see," he said instead, rising from the throne and acknowledging the bows of the scribes. Out in the courtyard, he faced the huge cypress wood gates and waited for Sar Malchi to arrive.

It took longer than expected for the units to negotiate the steep hair-pin turns outside the gate, and he shifted restlessly.

The limping, exhausted, dirty band of men that straggled in little resembled the three, fresh, well-equipped units who had left almost six weeks ago. Jonathan eyed the men as they shuffled into some semblance of three separate units. Malchi brought up the rear, riding a stiff-gaited, bony-looking mule that obviously hated him as much as his brother hated it. Behind him trooped the second unit, alive with curiosity, and the rest of the crowd soon filled the fortress courtyard.

One look at the frozen rage on his brother's face was enough to make Jonathan, older though he was, hesitate. A stirring at the gate and a few shouts opened the way for Sar Ishvi, who took his time dismounting as he eyed the returning units, then walked over to stand by Jonathan.

"What's happened?" he nearly whispered.

"I don't know that I dare ask. What do you think?"

"Correct me if I'm wrong," Ishvi muttered, studying his brother's mount, "but wasn't Malchi riding one of Shammah ben Jesse's mules when he left?"

"As far as I know, he was. Did you see the way that thing moves? What do you think our brother's backside feels like about now?"

Ishvi pursed his lips a little. "It's probably as sore as his temper."

"Maybe you should be the one to speak to him, Ishvi."

"Only if the king commands it, Hassar, and the king isn't here! You do it."

The door to the guard commander's chamber on the east wall opened, and General Abner appeared, followed by Sheva. King Shaul's cousin descended the steps, his face frowning with disapproval as he looked over the returning men. They shuffled uncomfortably under his gaze.

Sar Malchi ignored the general, sliding stiffly off the mule, which one of the stable hands immediately led away.

Jonathan got the distinct impression that only the presence of half the town kept his younger brother from kicking the animal.

The sar took several painful steps toward Jonathan before Abner spoke. "Well?" he barked impatiently. "Did you find him?"

Malchi halted, shoving his fists against his hips as he slowly faced the general. "Does it look as if we found him? Do you see him here?"

"You've been down there for more than a month, and you couldn't find a simple zammar?"

"That simple zammar was trained by the Habiru, General, and if you'll recall, Jonathan Hassar needs half the army to find him when he's here in Gibeah! Did you expect me to do any better when he's down in that wilderness below Jebus? It's like nothing you've ever seen. There's another cave, niche, or hole in the ground every step you take. And the forest is so dense that sunlight never reaches the ground. This entire town could disappear there, let alone a simple zammar!"

The crowd murmured as Malchi turned toward Jonathan again, and Abner snorted in disgust. "Come to the armory later and give me a proper report. The king will want to know why you've come back empty-handed."

Jonathan fought not to say anything. Since the beating that Malchi had given him, Abner had taken to disdaining the sar's honor at every opportunity.

When Malchi spoke, his voice was full of that icy wrath that chilled both his brothers when it was roused. "A proper report, Abner? All right, I'll give you one." He gestured toward his bedraggled men. "You want to know what we found down there? We found rain. Every day. We found reports of Dahveed. Every day. He was in Lehi, or was it Zorah? The wind carried him by Timnah one night, but in which direction no one seemed to know. Of course, we could have found him in Jebus, after the palace coup he staged before taking over the entire land."

Folding his arms across his chest, Malchi stared at his abbi's cousin. "Then there was the report that he was in Ramah, hidden by Roeh Shamuel from profane eyes. He must not have stayed there long, because he was in Dan shortly after that, and the wind must have been busy, because someone else swore to me the Dahveed was traveling the road to Kabzeel and Beersheba. 'Only last night, Sar!'"

His face hardening, Abner turned away.

"Don't go yet, General," Malchi said in a deadly voice. "All those reports might have been wrong, you know. He was really staying in a cave above my tent in the Elah valley, listening to every word of the commander's meetings. I suppose we had him properly trapped there, if anyone had bothered to notice his presence. But then, as I recall, Dahveed's been known to disappear between here and Sheva's chamber on the wall."

Abner stood stiffly, his face flaming, as snickers spread through the crowd, and even the exhausted soldiers had to hide their grins.

"When we got tired of the Elah valley, and learned that Dahveed had actually been staying in Gedor in a nice dry house while we camped in the rain, we moved, in the rain, to Gedor. Gedor has more nooks and crannies than this town, and more ways in and out, too. The fifth unit knows all about them, since they spent two days searching every inch of the place, while Pasach and Libni and I dispatched men in every direction, hunting for a piece of the wind.

"Of course, unbeknownst to us, Dahveed was really making his stately way right past us, just 1,200 feet down on the Shephelah. I know he was there. Someone told me so, and pointed out the exact spot where he was camped."

Ishvi moved restlessly beside Jonathan. "You don't think Malchi is angry enough to lie to Abner, and in public, do you?" he whispered as their younger brother paused again, his unrelenting gaze fastened on the general.

"Not wanting to be counted slack in my duties," the third sar continued, "I actually took it upon myself to go to the supposed camp. Naturally, Dahveed was not there. But I suppose I can't report that, can I? That would be such a disappointment to you, and might possibly make the king think I was remiss in my duty to him. How about lions? Would you be happy if I found lions? Shall we say four of them? That should be enough to keep even me busy."

Suppressed laughter from the crowd swept around the courtyard, and Abner, clearly furious again, started to leave.

"Abner ben Ner!" Malchi's voice rooted every person in the court. "Your sar is not through yet."

Jonathan's eyes widened, and beside him, Ishvi froze.

Bitter rage glowed in his brother's eyes, and Jonathan knew that if Abner didn't turn back, the general would die.

But the king's cousin, his back straight, angrily faced Malchi.

"It would be extremely discourteous of you to leave before my report is done, General," the sar reminded him. "I suppose my mule might have been able to outrun the beasts, but it fell in a big hole. They have them down there, you know. Big enough for several houses! The lions followed, naturally. I got one with a javelin; I hadn't noticed the others yet. But that wind must have been feeling generous, because who did it drop into that hole with me but Dahveed, sling and all! He held off the maddened things with his eyes alone until we could escape, so the lions only got to eat the mule instead of me. And lest you think I was wasteful of the mule, let me inform you that both forelegs were broken from the unexpected drop."

"Look, he's been wounded, Ishvi! He must be telling the truth!" the hassar whispered fiercely, studying Malchi's shoulder.

"In all the excitement, I'd lost track of where I was," Malchi continued, "and Dahveed kindly pointed the way back to Gedor when I asked. Then again, it couldn't have been Dahveed, since when I got back to Gedor, I met a man who stated positively that Dahveed was busy in Gath rousing the Philistines against us."

The sar took a step or two toward the general, who remained frozen in place, eyes burning furiously. "This report said Dahveed was so angry when the Philistines refused to fight us in the rain that he'd nearly emasculated one, pinned another to the ground with a sword, and broke the arm of a third. Then he walked out of town, leaving Akish raving like a madman. And to really show his feelings, he brought down bolts of Yahweh's fire on the palace.

"So, no Abner, we didn't find Dahveed. No one finds Dahveed! *He finds you!*"

Turning on his heel, Sar Malchi strode toward the private residence, passing Jonathan as he did.

"How many lions did he hold off?" the hassar asked as his brother walked past.

"Two," Malchi grunted, then disappeared into the house.

Hours later, the three brothers sat in the upper room of Ishvi's house on the north side of Gibeah. They had eaten and dismissed the servants. Once Ishvi had checked that everyone had gone, the two older brothers looked at Malchi.

"Talk," Jonathan ordered.

Malchi gave a more detailed account this time, shorn of the distracting elements in his report to Abner.

"You're certain he wasn't hurt?" Jonathan asked, his lips tight when Malchi told about Dahveed's collapse on the hilltop.

"Not a scratch, Jonathan. But only half of him was there. He looked almost as bad as he was when you stayed with him in Bethlehem after that lion nearly killed him. And he'd been hurt, too. I don't know how. His left knee was wrapped up, and he had the oddest scar on one arm, as if he'd been burned in some way. You owe him my life three times, now? Or is it four?"

"Who's counting?" the hassar said softly. "We already owe him more than we can hope to repay. What happened next?"

"I figured out that he was exhausted from his gift, and I tried to do the best I could for him. I had water, at least, and some raisins and figs in my girdle. Everything else was still on the mule, and I wasn't going back there to get it.

"But I was in a real quandary. Dahveed needed help, and I knew that if I took him to Gedor, I'd have to bring him here. After what he'd done, I wasn't about to hand him over to Abbi to be executed. I won't hunt him again, not even if *you* command it, adoni." He looked at Jonathan defiantly.

"I wouldn't name you brother if you made any other choice," the hassar said evenly. "You give me hope there's still some honor left in this family. Go on."

Malchi eased back on the cushions. "That's when the Habiru showed up. I didn't know if they were safe for Dahveed, or just an ordinary band of robbers. So I greeted them with my sword. Dahveed was so weak, he couldn't talk, let alone move. I don't know if he even knew anyone else was there.

"One of them recognized Dahveed, and I nearly got killed again, Jonathan. Those Habiru have given their lives and honor to him, and all they saw was a son of Shaul standing over him with a drawn sword. I threw your name at them a few times, but they still might have attacked me if that young man hadn't arrived. His accent was Philistine, but he looked Israelite. I didn't care where he was from after he backed up my story about the lions.

"They took Dahveed, and one of them kindly escorted me back up the hill to Gedor. He made it very plain that I'd die if I turned around."

"He's safe, then," Jonathan said, rising and turning away.

"I'd say so. My guess is that Ethan has him now."

Hassar Jonathan leaned against the wall, his broad shoulders trembling beneath the load of grief and shame that his abbi and king would betray the loyalty of the one who had brought light and laughter back to a house imprisoned by darkness and fear. "Yahweh, grant us hesed," he whispered.

Tamar bat Dahveed

See, Dahveed has learned his lesson. He is ready for the next step in his life, for if Yah's champion is to lead men, he must turn his whole mind to the learning. And without the security of Yah's protecting care, he would be too distracted by other events to find his new place in Yah's plans.

And what of Gebirah Abigail down in Maon? Can't you just feel her desperation? She, too, has no preparation for the task she must accomplish. And although she does not call on Yah with the intimacy that Dahveed does, her resolution to right the wrongs of her husband will summon forth Yah's surest answers and tenderest help for her bruised heart.

Jesse and Moab

CHAPTER 12

I sat on a hillside, my back against the large trunk of a sycamore fig tree, screened from sight by the oleander bushes growing between me and the trail below. It had been two weeks since Sar Malchi and I had fought the lions, and I was enjoying the warmth of the sun. After the constant rain, it was nice to have a little dry spell.

Easing my left knee down, I rubbed the now healing burn mark on my arm. I still tired quickly, and it was sometimes hard to get enough to satisfy my ravenous hunger and feed Ittai also. We lived in a cave on the hillside south and west of Adullam, which gave us a good view toward the highlands. Out on the brow of the hill we could see the lower Shephelah just as well, and on a clear day could pick out the rising smoke of Gath. We had one neighbor in a cave a little lower down. He was an older man than I, and had been living there for some time. We avoided each other, while at the same time keeping watch on each other.

I found myself humming the song I'd begun in the cave above Elah, and automatically reached for the harp, then sighed again at the frustration of not having it. *"I cry to Yahweh. I declare my trouble before Him."* The words ran through my mind. *"When my spirit was overwhelmed, You knew my path."*

Continuing the melody, I recalled the phrases I'd already worked with, adding in a reference to the despair of that night in the cave. *"I pour out my complaint before Him. I make supplication to God."* I closed my eyes, listening to my heart as the melody flowed through my mind. An hour later, after revising nearly the entire thing, I had the song. It was in a sad mode, and instead of ascending, it descended until the final two lines. Since my voice had regained its resonance and timbre, I took in a deep breath and sang.

"With my voice to Yahweh I will cry out. With my voice to Yahweh I will plead for pity.

I will pour out before Him my complaint. My distress before Him I will announce.

When faintness is on my spirit, then You Yourself knew my path. In this way I walk, they hide a trap for me.

Look to the right and see that there is no one who shows consideration for me. My refuge was lost to me. There is no one who inquires about my soul.

I cried out to You Yahweh. I said, 'You are my refuge, my portion in the land of the living.'

Listen carefully to my shout for I am very low. Snatch me from the ones who pursue me for they are stronger than me.

Bring out from the dungeon my soul to praise Your name. The righteous surround me for You render good upon me."[8]

Satisfied with my effort, I glanced at the sun. It was time to check my snares. Between Ittai's harvest of what wild plants we could find and my hunting, we usually had something to eat. In addition, Hanan, a young Habiru who sometimes scavenged for us, had shown up this morning with a small pestle and mortar. After the noon rest, Ittai had gone to Adullam to buy barley, and both of us anticipated bread tonight.

Alert for any movement, I slipped silently through the hillside forest. It wouldn't be much longer before I was back to my full strength, and I must find some way to support myself and my covenant son. I knew that Joel, dahveed of the Keilah band, would welcome me, but I hesitated to go for fear of bringing the king's wrath down on him.

A flash of movement on the opposite slope caught my eye, and I froze instantly. Two strange Habiru with bows at ready made their way down the slope, spreading apart as they did, intent on something below.

Scanning the bottom of the little valley between us, I watched a man in a bright town robe break cover and run toward the next copse of brush. But he'd only gone a step or two when he stumbled, rolling over on the ground. He scrambled up, only to collapse, clutching his ankle. With one look behind him, he half crawled back into the brush. The man had no weapons.

I debated what to do. This had all the earmarks of a manhunt, and I had no desire for an unarmed man's blood to bring Yah's curse down on the land that I had to live in. But if I moved, the two hunters would surely see me, and an arrow could kill me just as well as that man in the valley. My hand flexed in frustration.

My sling! Getting one of the small stones I had for slinging at

---

8 Psalms 142

conies, I put it in the sling pan and waited. When some brush shielded me from the Habiru, I set the sling in motion, aiming for the opposite hillside just past the copse the injured man had hidden in.

I let the stone fly, praying the men were too far away to hear its faint whir through the air. It hit the hillside, then fell into the streambed with a faint rattle. In moments, the strange Habiru came into sight, intent on what might be down the gully. Cautiously they advanced down the watercourse and out of sight.

As swiftly and silently as I could, I descended the hill to the copse and crept in the back side. The man had his back to a tree, his attention on the streambed beyond him. "They're gone, friend," I spoke softly.

Whirling around, a belt knife in his hand, he lunged toward me, and he would have had that knife in my leg if he hadn't had an injured ankle! As it was, I barely caught his wrist, twisting him to his back on the ground.

We stared at each other, then both spoke at the same instant.

"Elhanan?"

"Ben-geber?"

"What are you doing here?"

"You show up at the oddest moments!"

Again our questions rushed over each other.

I grinned. "Let me get you back to my cave, and we'll see about that ankle!"

It was late afternoon before he was settled in and I'd returned from checking my snares. As I tended his ankle, I found the sprain so bad that he could hardly bear to put weight on that foot. Ittai had not returned yet, and once the meat was in the pot, we studied each other from opposite sides of the fire. I was eager for news from home, but Elhanan hadn't seemed willing to talk much, so I'd restrained my questions.

"How is everyone?" I finally asked.

He looked at me. "Your family is still all right, as far as I know."

"What about you? How is your wife, Jerioth, and that boy of yours?"

"They're gone, Dahveed," he said heavily. "Both of them."

"I'm sorry, Elhanan. What happened?"

"Fever took Jerioth. She caught something from a guest, I think. The healers did everything they could, but she slipped away after two weeks. She was bearing our child, too."

"And your son?"

The man looked down. "He cut his foot, and the wound turned bad. He was afraid to die, Ben-geber." My old friend's face crumpled into tears. "He clung to me so, and I couldn't do anything for him. I'm glad I was there when he died, even if it did cost me the inn!"

After stirring the meat in the pot, I shoved the sticks of the fire closer together. "You lost the inn?" I prompted.

"With some help from Nabal of Carmel!"

I glanced up in amazement. "How could he take the inn?"

His lips tightened and his shoulders tensed. "He was there the afternoon before my son died. He was so demanding that I left my son for a little while to attend to him myself. But that evening, I turned him over to my assistants. When he left the next morning, he promised me that he'd see that I never ran an inn again. I didn't pay any attention to him. My boy had died, and I didn't care about anything else."

He glanced away. "I suppose I should have cared," he continued bitterly. "I'd just finished expanding the inn, and I owed several people. When the third bill came in for immediate payment, I found out the nagid had bought up all my debts. I held on until I found a decent buyer, then used everything I had to pay the debts. The afternoon I sold out, I left town immediately. Someone had been watching the inn since I'd first contacted the buyer. Once I got to Immi's people here in Gedor, I thought I was out of trouble, but after this afternoon, I'm not sure what to think."

The stew was boiling, and I dished it up, leaving some for Ittai when he returned. We ate in silence, using our belt knives to spear the pieces of meat and drinking the broth from the pots. When we finished, Elhanan set the bowl down. "It fills you up, but that's about all I can say for it."

I smiled ruefully. "Times like this, I miss Ahiam."

"He's not here?" Elhanan asked curiously.

"No. Why would you think he was?"

"Everyone knows the Habiru are sworn to Boaz's blood, Ben-geber. That includes you!"

"I've been declared outlaw by the king, Elhanan. Anyone who associates with me is asking for trouble, and the Habiru don't need more of that."

He cocked his head at me. "Somehow, I don't think that will make much difference to them. You and Jesse and Hassarah Ruth gave them hope and dignity, and more than that, a place in society. Boaz named them Yahweh's Arrows, and it will take more than a king's decree to divide them from the blood that placed them directly in Yahweh's hands. Don't think they've forgotten, Ben-geber."

I shifted uncomfortably on the cave floor. "You must have been outside of Gedor for those Habiru to pick up your trail," I commented, changing the subject.

Elhanan nodded. "I was delivering a message to Timnah for my cousin. He'll worry when I don't come back. Can you return it to him tomorrow?"

"We have to get you back up there tomorrow, so you can do it yourself. I'm outlawed, remember, and just sitting here could get you killed."

It took both Ittai and me most of the day to assist Elhanan up the steep ridge to Gedor. His cousin was very relieved to see him, and since the message was an important one, I ran it the five miles to Timnah. By the time I returned with the reply, Elhanan's cousin asked if Ittai could stay and tend to the innkeeper while he was recovering. My covenant son was willing, so I arranged it.

It was fortunate I did, for just three days later, Joel's Hanan met me on the trail. "There's someone looking for you, geber," he announced. "I left him where you can get a look at him."

Puzzled, I followed the young Habiru to where a man paced in a small clearing. The wind blew his robes around him briefly, and I glanced at the sky. It was clouding up to rain again. He turned toward me.

"It's one of my brothers, Hanan," I said. "You did well to bring him to me."

The youth nodded and disappeared into the trees.

"Abinadab?" I called, stepping into the clearing.

At the sound of my voice he whirled around.

As I hurried to him, he dropped to his knees, and his hands gripped my girdle. "Mashiah!" he whispered. "Thank Yahweh we found you!"

"Abinadab, what's wrong?" I asked, alarmed.

"The king sent troops to Bethlehem, adoni. Ethan warned us. Abbi knew that if we stayed, we'd bring trouble to the whole town. Shammah's Jonathan went to the Habiru encampment, and they told us you were here. We came as fast as we could."

My hands tightened on his. I'd feared that Shaul would do something like this. "Who came?"

"All of us, Dahveed. Abbi, and your immi, and everyone. Only

Zelek stayed. He thought he could risk it since the hassar will want mules. We had to leave so quickly, I couldn't think of anywhere else to go. It's taken so long, and we had to avoid the roads, and with the cart for Abbi and all, it was--"

"Abbi needs a cart? Is he all right?" I demanded, pulling my second oldest brother to his feet.

"He's not sick, he's just old, Dahveed," Abinadab hastened to assure me. "Your immi is fine, too. But this on top of everything else--I didn't know where else to come," he repeated.

"Where are they?" I asked eagerly. My immi was here!

"We were just coming down the last of the hills to the Shephelah, adoni, when that young Habiru met us and brought me to you."

I looked around, and Hanan waited at the edge of the clearing. Taking Abinadab's arm, I started in that direction, my brother stumbling along beside me. As Hanan led the way, I nearly walked on his heels in my impatience, and he increased his pace until we were nearly running.

"Dahveed, slow down," Abinadab gasped behind me. "I'm not used to this!"

I did, until I glimpsed the group of people across a valley. My eyes found her unerringly where she stood beside the cart pulled by two donkeys. "Immi!" I shouted.

Even though she hadn't heard my voice in years, she whipped around instantly. Then I was beside her. Tears so blurred my eyes that I couldn't see her face, but I knew it was my own immi I held in my arms. She hugged me so hard that her fingers left prints in my skin. We cried over each other for a long time, and when I finally stepped back and looked around, everyone was there. Shammah, with his wife Keziah on a donkey, and their two boys, Jonathan, 10, and Jonadab, 7.

Nethanel stood beside the cart, looking more like Jesse every day, his wife beside him appearing less tired than her husband despite her advanced pregnancy. Raddai and Ozem, the twins, stood together as they always did, comical in their differences, Raddai as short and solid as ever, and Ozem with a dignity to his tall frame that I didn't remember seeing before. Finally I spotted Eliab. The bekor waited behind the cart, looking uncomfortable, as he always did now in my presence.

Last, I looked into the cart for Abbi. Nethanel helped him down so that I could put my arms around him. He seemed thin, and the lines in his face were deeper, his hair almost completely white. But there was still enough strength in his arms to nearly crush me.

"Not too hard, Abbi," I gasped.

"You're too thin," Immi said worriedly, taking my hand again. "Haven't you been eating?"

"As best I can, Immi," I laughed. "But I'm not a very good cook, and sometimes it takes a lot of energy to catch my lunch. How did you all get here?"

"You didn't think we'd leave your blood to the tender mercies of King Shaul, did you?" Shagay asked indignantly.

Now that I'd taken in my immediate family, I noticed everyone else. Shagay with his family grinned at me from beside Ahiam and Jemima, who looked surprisingly contented with her exile. Eliab's family stood with Abinadab's, and two strangers I had to stare hard at to recognize.

"Abishai?" I exclaimed, astonished at how he had changed and grown. "And that's Asahel with you? I'd never have known you two!" Abishai had filled out into a solid young man, with eyes too old for his face. Asahel had an irrepressible grin hovering on his lips, and his long lean frame outstripped his oldest brother by inches. I could well imagine that he deserved his reputation as a racer.

"Where's Joab? And Zeruiah?" I asked, looking further.

Immi's hand tightened on mine. "Zeruiah died two months ago, Dahveed. It was more of a blessing than anything else. You know the kind of life Joab led her."

I nodded. "And Joab?"

Abbi's face hardened. "He is not welcome."

"What has he done?" I asked, my arm tightening around Immi's shoulders.

Jesse remained silent, and I glanced at Abinadab.

"He killed an Egyptian courier," Abinadab explained.

"An *Egyptian*? Was he out of his mind?"

"Unfortunately, no." Eliab took up the tale. "Turned out this wasn't the first time he'd killed. The decree came shortly after Zeruiah died. They want him however they can get him. He disappeared the next day, and no one's seen him since."

Now I understood Abinadab's comment. My outlawing was nothing compared to Joab's. I could at least hope to find safety outside of Shaul's kingdom, but Joab would be wanted no matter where he went from here to Mari. He was just fortunate that Pharaoh had more on his mind than troubles in the highlands of Canaan. Many of the kings in the area had shorted or delayed their required taxes, or like Shaul, had stopped paying them altogether.

"What about Abigail?" I asked. Zeruiah's full-sister had been one of the mainstays of my childhood, and I missed her almost as much as I did Immi.

"Last we heard, she was doing fine," Abinadab answered, "and Amasa is growing too fast to keep up with. Jether's business has expanded, and he's running three caravans now in addition to those he still operates with his uncle. He remains closer to Rabbah Ammon, so they don't travel so much. It's easier on Abigail with Amasa, but she doesn't like staying around the royal city much. Ala's there, though, and King Nahash took a liking to her, so she may get another husband yet."

I hugged Immi once more, and we started for Adullam. While I talked with everyone, the back of my mind worked on the problem of where to put 30 some people for the night, and how to feed them all.

Ahiam eased my mind on one score. "We brought food," he said when he had the chance to talk to me alone a moment. "Jamin probably has more on the way by now. He said he'd tend to that."

"What's the situation, really?" I asked quietly.

My retainer looked thoughtful. "We didn't have time to do much more than pack the most necessary items and get everyone out of town, but I don't think it would be wise for your family to return any time soon."

The supplies from Jamin arrived the morning of the second day. When I saw the extent of them, I knew the news would be bad.

"They searched the town and then stationed soldiers in your compound, geber," Caleb, one of Ethan's band, told Jesse. "The commander in charge said scribes from the king would arrive soon."

Jesse bowed his head, knowing that Shaul would seize our land for the crown.

"But we will lose everything!" Keziah gasped. "How will we live?"

Abinadab turned to me. "Might the hassar be any help to us?"

"That depends on what you mean by help," I said. "He will not want to lose his source for mules, or the wines that Raddai and Lahab supply him with, so he will probably keep the land rather than sell it. In the future, he may be able to hire us back to work it."

"But he's the hassar!" Keziah protested again.

"He's not the king," I reminded her. "But I also think you will all keep your lives, particularly if I'm not with you."

Immi slipped closer to me, and I put my arm around her.

"The king is that hostile toward you, Dahveed?" Jesse asked.

"The king wants me dead," I replied bluntly.

"We will have to consider this," abbi said, his hand touching the bump showing under his robe on his chest.

I looked at it curiously. Whatever made that bump had come from Grandmother Ruth, for she wore it all her life, only taking it off when she gave it to Jesse just before she died.

Jesse glanced at my immi. "What do you say, Keren? It will be hardest on you and the other women and children."

She returned his look. "It's time, Jesse. The Hassarah knew we would need her gift, and this is the time."

My abbi nodded. "All right. We will go to Moab."

"Moab!" Eliab gasped. "Why would we go there?"

Jesse smiled a little. "We may have more welcome there than you expect, Eliab."

I'd never traveled with the Habiru when they moved before, and I watched closely as Shagay and Ahiam organized our little group. Because we had three carts and wanted to avoid the roads during the 10 miles south to Adoraim, Ahiam and Caleb spent most of the first day scouting ahead. Before long, I slipped into the role of second-in-command to Shagay. Abishai became my chief aide, as Shagay's son Jonathan was his. A real friendship had sprung up between the two young men, and I was glad to see another member of my family learning true appreciation for the Habiru and their talents and skills.

That first day was a hard one, with the carts needing constant pushes or shifting of some sort because of the softened ground from the rains. The 1,600-foot climb to the highlands was the worst. In two spots, we had to unload some of the baggage and hitch all four donkeys to one cart to get it up the trail.

"And I thought harvest was hard work," Nethanel groaned as he gingerly sat down for a moment when the last cart crested the top.

"Maybe this is why Habiru rarely use carts," I said, easing down by him.

He nodded. "Donkey packs make a lot more sense now."

Shagay had deliberately brought us up from the Shephelah south of Adoraim, so that it would appear that we'd come from that direction. We stayed there the night, and with Abbi's decision to go to Moab, we headed back north on the road to Hebron early the next day.

Outside of Hebron, Shagay split our caravan up, sending most of us through the forest to the north and south. Each cart rolled past Hebron separately, with only one or two people with it. Once east of the city, we joined up again.

As we waited for the last cart to catch up, I noticed Eliab standing apart, a frown on his face. He'd been very quiet today, and I remembered that expression well. He was debating some course of action. I wasn't surprised when he called Abinadab over, and they discussed something. What did surprise me was Abinadab motioning me to join them.

"Eliab has an idea, Dahveed," Abinadab said. "I want to know if you think it's worth considering."

Wondering when I'd become essential to the decision-making processes of my older brothers, I asked, "What's the idea?"

"Eliab wants to go back to Bethlehem. Maybe not openly, but he thinks one of Jesse's sons should stay there, and he insists it be him."

The tone of Abinadab's voice suggested that he expected me to disagree. But the look in Eliab's eye stopped me. He'd always been a stubborn man, but there was more than that in his expression now.

"Why?" I asked.

"The Hassarah."

His answer rocked me back on my heels. Our grandmother's last words to him had been that someday Jesse's inheritance would depend on Eliab's care.

"Do you think this is the time?"

"Yes."

"Then I'd agree. You should go to Bethlehem."

"Are you out of your mind, Dahveed?" Abinadab said, glancing around to be certain no one else was listening. Not getting any response from me, he turned in exasperation to Eliab. "What makes you think you can do anything?"

"The fact that we're Boaz's blood. You know how the town feels, Abinadab. Shaul isn't strong enough to strip Boaz's inheritance from us without the consent of the elders. He's angry with Dahveed, but it's no secret that I haven't liked Dahveed either, and the way I acted before, alienating the whole family, will just further the impression. The king's representative might find a family quarrel useful."

My second oldest brother looked taken aback, and I smiled a little. "He's got a point, Abinadab."

"Besides, if the hassar tries to save what he can for you, Dahveed, having someone of Jesse's house there might help him, too."

"It's worth a try," I agreed.

"But Eliab could get killed!" Abinadab protested. "We don't have any idea who is there, or how many soldiers, or what their orders are, or anything!"

Jesse's bekor looked down. "I'm already under a death sentence, aren't I?" he nearly whispered.

Neither Abinadab nor I replied.

"I could go as a beggar, or something, to begin with."

"You'd be recognized!" Abinadab nearly shouted, then looked around again hastily to see if anyone had noticed. "You've lived with those people all your life, Eliab!"

"Who in that town is going to betray Boaz's blood, particularly to Shaul?" Eliab persisted.

"You're both crazy! It's out of the question!"

"Let him go," I said, knowing that since Abinadab held the order for Eliab's execution, he could refuse.

"Dahveed, I will not--"

"Abinadab, let him go," I commanded.

Eliab stared at me in amazement, which only grew as his brother didn't react to my blatant disrespect.

"He might die," Abinadab protested desperately.

I softened my tone. "If he's willing to let that be in the hands of Yahweh, we shouldn't stop him."

"As you wish, Dahveed."

Glancing from Abinadab to me and back, Eliab didn't know what to think.

"You two should sit down and talk sometime," I said.

Not long afterwards, Caleb and Eliab left for the 13-mile trek across the highlands for home. I prayed Yah's blessing would be on them. Our road gradually turned southward into the heart of the southern highlands, and the country became wilder and more untamed with every mile. The thick forests of Ziph crowded around us, making Immi nervous, and I stayed close to the cart.

"Where did Eliab go?" Abbi asked.

"Bethlehem. He wants to see if there might be something he can do to keep our inheritance. He had some persuasive arguments in favor of his idea, including the Hassarah. It seems that she saw more things than we knew."

The children were tired after the additional seven miles to Carmel, but Jesse passed word down that we'd go the extra mile to Maon before we stopped. Maon soon came into view, and although the fields and houses looked respectable, the place had a subdued atmosphere to it that made me want to keep a sharp lookout behind me. I glanced at Shagay. His teeth were gritted together, and he moved his shoulders uneasily.

We turned left off the highway and climbed up the hill. Maon was small, and people watched us with wary eyes. Not even the children ran out to ask the usual questions about who we were and where we were going.

I raised my eyebrows in query.

"You'll find much different, here, Dahveed," Ahiam said quietly. "Since Nabal has seized power, nearly all the people have been enslaved. Most of this land used to be held by farmers and townspeople just as around Bethlehem. Now Nabal owns it all."

We stopped at the inn, and Abbi inquired about lodging.

"I don't know, geber," the innkeeper replied, wringing his hands. "I will have to inquire of the nagid."

"Are there other guests here?" Abbi asked calmly.

"No, geber, but I will have to ask the nagid," the man repeated, glancing around helplessly.

"Have these people asked for lodging?" a calm voice broke in.

When I turned to look I froze, unable to breathe. Nothing in my life had prepared me for the woman standing there, and I could only stare. She was stunningly beautiful in the way you'd expect a goddess to be, with perfect eyebrows arching over her long-lashed eyes. Flawless skin smoothed over her cheekbones down to a mouth that looked painted, but wasn't. Her firm figure turned gracefully as she held out her hand to the innkeeper, who dropped to his knees and bowed over it. My own knees nearly gave way.

Ahiam stepped on my toe, hard, and I wasn't quick enough to suppress my yelp. I was still bent over, nursing my painful foot, when the woman turned to Abbi, so I had no idea if she had seen my stare.

Shagay's hand was rough on my arm. "Gebirah Abigail is Nabal of Carmel's *wife*, Dahveed, and you are a married man!" he hissed at me. The pain from his fingers brought me back to reality with a thud, and I kept my face down until my heart quit pounding, and I was no longer flushed.

"Yes, Gebirah," the innkeeper was saying. "They asked to stay, and the nagid is not here to say what should be done." He twisted his hands again and watched us from the corner of his eye.

"We shall, of course, extend hospitality," Abigail announced.

"Gebirah?" the man gasped. "But the nagid has not said if--"

"No, *I* have said," she interrupted, her voice serene. "Find out how many will sleep here and how much food to prepare."

I cocked my head, my zammar's ear picking up something odd about her voice. I looked at her sharply. Her calmness had something disturbing about it, but I couldn't place what it was.

Thinking I was staring again, Ahiam jabbed his elbow into my ribs so hard that I nearly grunted. I stepped away to protect the rest of my body from his attacks, but he stepped after me, and rather than make a dance of it, I held still and studied the dried mud clinging to the cart wheels.

The innkeeper stared. "But, Gebirah, there are so many. What will the nagid say when he sees--"

"Not all of us will be at the inn," Abbi hastened to say. "Our escorts will camp in a field if there is a fallow one we may use?"

"Hezro, would you show these people to an appropriate place?" Abigail asked, turning to one of the two armed escorts attending her.

He bowed. "Of course, Gebirah."

"Would there be food our escorts could purchase?" Abbi asked next.

Abigail glanced at the trembling innkeeper, who kept his head down.

"I'm sure some of the townspeople might have some to sell if the inn's provisions are not adequate," Hezro replied.

"Then have the people bring what is available here," the Gebirah directed.

I risked another glance at her. Had that been relief in her voice? Had she not been certain how to answer my abbi's query? Things were certainly strange here.

Seeing that the innkeeper was too upset to be helpful, Immi tactfully received permission to inspect the inn's supplies, and by the time a few women hesitantly approached with bread, dried fruit, and some nuts, she knew what we'd need to purchase from them.

With many glances at the Gebirah, the village women accepted the coppers that Jesse gave them, saying hardly a word before hurrying away, the bits of metal clutched in their hands like expensive pearls.

Once everything was settled, the Gebirah bid us farewell. I

surreptitiously watched her leave, and as she walked away, a couple women hesitantly approached and spoke to her. The Gebirah answered without a flicker of emotion breaking the calm of her face.

She looked back once, and I'd have sworn something flashed in her eyes when she glanced briefly at me, but, given my reaction to her, that had to be my own wishful thinking.

Well, as Shagay had said, she was someone else's wife, and I was a married man. I turned my thoughts to the process of getting Abbi and Immi settled in the inn, and then setting up camp in the field.

CHAPTER 13

Jonathan paced the floor of the throne room, barely restraining himself from kicking the dais. The Egyptians had lost another courier, which was enough bad news to spoil the week, since the death of a second messenger might prompt Pharaoh to serious investigation. But the messages in the pouch, which had arrived via Ethan three days ago, raised the possibility that Pharaoh might authorize the Philistines to collect Israelite taxes.

If that happened, the Philistines would start raiding at any time, not just during war season, and he didn't want to think what that would mean for the people of Israel, particularly since Dahveed wasn't here. His lips tightened. He would wager Manani had been the one to suggest this, and the Ekron seren would dance with delight if the Egyptians granted support for Philistine invasions into the highlands.

That bad news had so absorbed his attention that he'd completely missed what Shaul and Abner had done, only learning of it less than an hour ago. Malchi's quick footsteps sounded on the stairs, and Jonathan looked up as the sar pushed the door open. "Well?"

"He didn't send the army," Malchi replied. "Every commander is accounted for, with all their men."

"Then who did Abbi dispatch to Bethlehem? What exactly did your source say?"

Malchi thought a moment. "He used the word 'soldiers.'"

Jonathan sighed. "That could mean armed men of any kind!"

The door to the stairs opened, and both brothers turned impatiently.

The guard looked apologetic. "Your indulgence, Hassar. Commander Sheva insists on seeing you now."

"Send him in," Jonathan said.

The commander of the king's guard bowed to both sars.

"What is it, Sheva?" Jonathan asked.

"The usual men didn't show up for their rotation as fortress guards an hour ago. I inquired, and one of my assistants informed me that General Abner sent Doeg and eight fortress guards to Bethlehem three days ago."

"Doeg is under restraint at Nob," Malchi interjected.

"My assistant also confessed that he'd been sent to Nob four days ago with a message from King Shaul freeing Doeg."

Jonathan stared hard at the commander.

Sheva bowed. "The man is no longer my assistant, Hassar."

"You've done well, Sheva. Let me know if you learn anything more."

With a bow the officer left.

"How dare Abner!" Malchi exploded when the door closed.

"You'll notice that he didn't," Jonathan replied. "He had to get Abbi to order Doeg's release, so we've limited what he can do some, anyway."

"But to send Doeg down there? Does he want to start a war?"

"I wouldn't put it past him. We've *got* to bring him to heel!" Jonathan rubbed his eyes tiredly. It felt as though he were trying to hold onto a wet fish. Every time he thought he had closed any avenue that Abbi could use to strike at Dahveed, something like this happened. He sighed. "We must do something about this immediately. Who knows what could have happened down there in three days!"

"When do you leave?" his younger brother asked.

"I can't go. It would raise too many eyebrows."

"Who else is there to handle this?" Malchi asked, frustrated. "And don't send me! I still haven't recovered from my last trip south."

Footsteps sounded on the stairs, and Sar Ishvi stepped into the room, looking from his older brother to his younger brother. "Am I late?"

Jonathan smiled. "No, brother. You walked in at the perfect moment!"

¥ ¥ ¥ ¥ ¥ ¥

Sar Ishvi and his entourage left Gibeah shortly after dawn. The breath from his mule hung in the chilly air as he rode down the hill and turned south toward Jebus. How much of a mess would he find in Bethlehem, he wondered.

Riding south in full court dress brought back memories of the time he, Jonathan, and Malchi had attended the celebratory feast for Dahveed's recovery from the lion attack, and he chuckled quietly, remembering Malchi, overwhelmed for a second time by those twin girls of the Habiru. Caleb, their abbi's name was. They had brought their friends that time, and Malchi's normally immaculate court dress had become a disaster as he had surrendered to the inevitable and played donkey with the children.

Thinking of why he was headed to Bethlehem this time, his hands crushed the reins in his grip, and his mule pranced restlessly. How could Abbi possibly believe that Dahveed was disloyal when the zammar so obviously loved the king that Shaul had called him son? What could be driving his abbi's animosity, he wondered for the hundredth time. Shaul missed Dahveed, for Ishvi had seen the wistfulness in his eyes when he spoke of his zammar.

The sar shifted impatiently on his mount. How had Shaul sent that message to Nob, releasing Doeg? Absentmindedly he touched his girdle in which he had a copy of the orders that Doeg carried. Eshbaal had found it in the fortress records room. But how had it gotten there? Was it even supposed to have been there? He rather thought not. Someone had made a mistake. But who? He wished his older brother would pay some attention to these questions.

He pushed the pace of his mount, and soon the Jebus battlements appeared on the left, towering over the Kidron valley. His foster son rode behind him on another mule, back straight and head up. It would be the first time the young man had been south since the sar had taken him in.

As he rode toward Bethlehem Ishvi wondered what the townspeople would think of his arrival. With Doeg involved, there was no telling what sort of situation he might run into, and two full units followed the sar in addition to the scribes and messengers with gear and supplies enough for an extended stay. Libni's unit had accompanied them, with its commander primed to be General Abner's eyes and ears, and he had chosen Zorath's third unit. The commander had southern militia with him every season and got along well with them.

Stopping outside of town, Ishvi took two scribes, young Ishvi, and Zorath's unit with him to Bethlehem, leaving everyone else to set up a camp. When Shaul's second son rode through Bethlehem's gate, it looked as if the entire town had gathered, but not to greet him. Standing around seven men in the middle of the square were Doeg and his guards. The men in the center had been stripped to their undergarments, and Doeg stood over the one that he had apparently just beaten. It was Zemirah, the town's head elder. The old man's white hair was matted with damp mud and his face was bloody and swollen.

As Ishvi halted his mule, the animal bowed its head, bunching its haunches as it did when he rode into battle. The complete silence and nearly unbearable tension seeped into the sar's mind, making him feel as if he stood between two lions arguing about a pride. Unless he was badly mistaken, had his arrival been delayed by only a moment or two, he would have ridden into a battle. Stomach tight, he swiftly assessed the situation. The townspeople stood around the market, their deceptively slouched postures indicating hidden weapons.

Instantly he realized that the slightest misstep on his part would plunge the place into blood and death, and the hassar had sent him specifically because he could keep his head and do the right thing.

"Yahweh, direct me!" he appealed silently.

His son's posture on the mule caught his eye. Young Ishvi had relaxed, sitting a little slouched, his legs dangling. Was formality equated here with hauteur, not respect? How could he know? Did he dare dismount? It was worth a try.

"Zorath, come hold my mule." His voice sounded distant and haughty to himself, and several faces in the crowd hardened more as his ears caught a muttered comment about arrogant northern adons. A feeling of almost hatred rose from the crowd. His stomach tightened again. This wasn't going well.

The commander took his mule's bridle while he dismounted. "Spread your men out a little and tell them to stand as if they've been on boring guard duty for several hours," the sar said in an undertone. "Be easy and slow. We've stepped into something ugly."

Zorath led the mule away, spreading the word to his men while Sar Ishvi walked slowly toward the central figures and paused, trying not to stand as if he was in Egypt's court as he scanned the area again. A man with watchful eyes stood by the leather stall, and a beggar lay against the wall of a produce stall.

Commander Doeg smiled maliciously. "These men may be ready to answer the king's questions, now, Sar," he declared.

Ishvi closed his eyes briefly. Doeg had done this in the *king's* name? Suppressing the surge of anger that rolled through him, he clenched his teeth until his jaw ached. He recognized several faces from the feast for Dahveed, but every one was hard and closed against him. Near despair filled him. How could he wrest a chance to be heard from these people? Order the immediate release of the seven men?

But Doeg had invoked the king's authority. Arbitrarily overruling that might seem an easy way out now, but the consequences might be enormous back in Gibeah. Somehow he had to reestablish himself again as a friend to these people! "Yahweh, help me!" he pleaded silently again.

Then he caught sight of two light-brown heads nearly hidden in the folds of a woman's skirt. Likely their immi hadn't known of the situation when she came to town, and Caleb's little twins, Rachel and Leah, peeked at him with anxious faces and frightened, tear-filled eyes. Something inside him turned over, and he swallowed the bitter taste that flooded his mouth with something far beyond mere rage at what Doeg had done.

In an instant, he realized that if he had any chance to be heard, it was through those two little girls. Every eye in the square followed him as he walked toward the twins, and he knew that if he looked in the least threatening, the place would explode.

They looked up into his face as he stopped about six feet away. Remembering how Dahveed always lowered himself when talking to the children, he squatted down, shifting his sword with one hand, one knee touching the ground. The silence strained around him, and the twins peeked at him from behind their immi.

"Sahrah Rachel, Sahrah Leah, Dodi Sar couldn't come with me on this visit," he began gravely, using the name the twins had for his brother Malchi. "But I know he will ask me how you are when I get back." He waited to see if they would respond, and was relieved when one of them sniffed a little. "What shall I tell him?"

"Dodi Sar?" the one who sniffed asked in a small voice.

Ishvi nodded. "You remember him, don't you?"

Both little heads nodded this time.

"I know he would want to hear that you are well, but right now I don't think that's true. Why are you frightened?"

"Because the soldiers are here," one said.

The head of the other one bobbed in agreement. "And the man said that when soldiers come, they kill everyone, and then burn everything all up. You're not going to let them, are you?" she finished anxiously.

"Well, little sahrahs, I can assure you that burning the town was not on my mind when I came here today," Ishvi replied.

"Are you sure?" one asked, looking at him doubtfully.

"Rachel!" her immi gasped.

Ishvi held up his hand to stop the woman's comment. "I'm very sure, Sahrah Rachel. You have my word as Sar Israel on that."

A ripple of reaction ran through the men standing around him, and he smiled.

"Then why did the man say you would?" Leah demanded.

"Maybe he got that idea from someone who didn't know what he was talking about." The sar took a deep breath. "Do you think I would?"

They hesitated. "Nooo," Rachel said at last, looking around the men at the soldiers waiting in the square. "But your soldiers might. Is that why you have them?"

"No. Hassar Israel sent them because there are lots of wild animals here, and sometimes robbers or thieves, and he wanted me to be safe."

The twins both leaned around their immi to look into the square at Zorath's unit. "There aren't very many of them for that," Leah stated.

"I have more where we pitched my tent," he said casually, noting the reaction of the surrounding men to that bit of news. "But I still need to know what to tell Dodi Sar about you."

"Tell him we'll be all right if no one burns our town," Rachel said promptly.

Her immi hissed at her again, and Ishvi hid his smile. "What about you, Sahrah Leah?"

"I want to know why those men are standing in the middle of the market without their clothes."

The air around him crackled with tension again.

"I was wondering exactly the same thing," Ishvi responded. "Have I your leave to go and ask them?"

The little girl straightened up, eyes wide. "May I come with you?"

Ishvi blinked. "I don't know," he managed to say. "You'll have to ask your immi. It would be all right with me," he decided suddenly.

Both twins urgently demanded permission to go with Dodi Sar's brother.

"Why do you want to?" the woman asked finally, her refusals met with renewed demands from the girls.

"The boy on the mule has been watching us," Leah said.

"And he might give us a ride," Rachel added. "We've never been on a mule before!"

The sar looked at the girls' immi. "He's my son," he said quietly.

Above him, heads swivelled to look again, and for the first time he got the impression that his peaceable intentions might be believed. He looked back at the twin's immi. "You can come also, if you wish."

The woman looked around the square again. "We will do as you wish, Sar," she decided. "Maybe there will be no blood shed today after all. Come, girls."

As the four of them walked out into the square, the man by the leather shop stepped out, also. Ishvi recognized him now. Caleb, the girls' abbi.

"Ishvi," the sar said to his son, "these are the little sahrahs, Leah and Rachel. They have never been on a mule before, and they thought you might be willing to give them a ride. If you are willing, you could go outside the walls. Caleb will pick two of the townsmen to accompany you to reassure the town that I have no wish to burn it around their heads."

His foster son hesitated only a moment. "All right, Abbi." Sliding off the mule, he turned to the twins. "Which one is which?" he asked.

"I'm Leah and that's Rachel," Leah said.

"Can we really ride your mule?" her sister added, touching the animal's leg. The mule twitched the skin around where she touched, and she giggled, touching it again. The mule turned to see what was there, and then curiously snuffled the girl's head, making her hair fly around her face. She laughed with glee.

Sar Ishvi picked her up and put her on the mule. Caleb added Leah, and young Ishvi took the reins and led the mule toward the gate.

"He will be safe, Sar, never fear," Caleb promised, following his family. He searched the crowd, choosing two mature men to accompany him. As the significance of his action sank into the assembled crowd, a murmur of amazement broke the stubborn silence and shattered the thick tension hovering over the place.

"Yahweh, I will give You a thank offering for this," Sar Ishvi vowed. He faced the assembled men, knowing that he now held everyone's attention. Walking to a place in front of the seven prisoners, he dropped his casual pose to one fitting for a king's representative. "Zorath, bring seven stools, and send my head scribe to me."

The commander of the third unit passed the orders along, and Ishvi waited motionless while his scribe set up his low table and seated himself on a cushion on the ground next to it.

"I am ready, adoni."

"Very good, Elihu. We will begin then."

Sar Ishvi controlled his face as he approached the men. His naming of his scribe had drawn attention to the man, and three or four of them stared at Elihu wide-eyed. The youngest son of Jesse and Miriam was taking in his surroundings quite well. His quick gaze paused only once, in the direction of the produce stall. The sar wondered what had caught the man's attention to that extent.

As soon as the stools arrived, Ishvi turned to the elders. "Please be seated," he directed. While they complied, Ishvi went himself to help Zemirah off the ground.

One of the other men knelt by the elder also. "He should be taken home and seen to, adon," the man said, his voice angry.

"Yes, he should," Ishvi replied. "See that it is done."

While the man called for help, Ishvi wet one end of his girdle with water from his cruse and gently cleaned the blood and dirt from Zemirah's face.

As the head elder was led away, the sar turned to the man who had spoken to him. "How are you called?"

"Telah."

"Send for your clothes."

When the garments arrived, Ishvi took them and proceeded to dress Telah himself, helping the man into his robe, and tying the girdle around him. Without a word, he dressed each of the other men also. As he tied the girdle of the last, an individual younger than himself whom he was certain he should know, the man asked in an undertone, "If I may, adon, why are you doing this?"

The directness of the question reminded him sharply of Dahveed. "Because the honor unjustly stripped from you by one of my house should be restored," Ishvi replied, stepping back and gesturing to the stool.

Once all six remaining men were seated like a tribunal facing the guards that had surrounded them, Sar Ishvi moved to their left and turned around. Of the nine men who had come to Bethlehem three days ago, only Doeg still remained standing. The others knelt on the ground, their faces clearly indicating their fear.

"The king will hear of this," Doeg said, glaring at Sar Ishvi. "You have interrupted an inquiry sanctioned by his authority."

To one side, Ishvi heard the swift scratching of the stiff brush pen on papyrus as Elihu took down the words.

"Your orders were to come to Bethlehem and notify Jesse ben

Boaz that his lands were forfeit to the crown because of the actions by his house against the crown. Which of these men is a member of Jesse's house?"

Doeg reddened. "I couldn't find any of Jesse's house, so I inquired."

Sar Ishvi folded his arms, staring at the commander of the guard. "If none of Jesse's considerable household were here, that makes securing their land a simple task for you and your men. Again, what do the men in front of you have to do with this?"

"I was to do more than secure the lands," the Edomite said angrily. "General Abner wished to know if anyone here knew where Dahveed was hiding, and to impress on the population that they should notify the king immediately if they heard anything."

Ishvi thought swiftly. With Abner apparently adding orders to the king's, the waters had been muddied considerably. "Are you intending to imply that General Abner's authority exceeds the king's?"

Two of the kneeling guards bent down even farther, moaning softly.

Doeg's red face slowly turned white. "No, adoni sar."

Ishvi turned to the elders. "These men stand before you for judgment for laying hands unjustly on residents of this town. What is your will concerning them?"

Telah rose from his seat. "We have forgotten ourselves, and I ask your pardon, adon," he said, gesturing to the unused stool. "Please, seat yourself, adon. And where is our guest's son? It would not be right for us to continue until all has been restored."

In a very few minutes young Ishvi came across the square, accompanied by one of the townsmen and Caleb. His face was composed, but he went immediately to the sar and his hand was shaking when he gripped his foster abbi's.

"All is well," the sar assured him. "This is likely to last a while longer. Do you want to go back with the sahrahs or stay here?"

"Go, if I may." A shy smile broke over his face. "The twins are so funny!"

"Be ready when I come."

The boy nodded, and Sar Ishvi jerked his chin after him to Caleb. The Habiru followed the boy, and Ishvi noted that one of Zorath's men trailed after them this time.

The crowd turned their attention back to the guards while the elders conferred. Ishvi remained apart, signaling that this judgment was entirely the town's. Other men from the crowd were called up, and 12 judges faced the guards by the time they had reached a decision.

"Hear our decision," Telah began. "For the pain and dishonor done to the head elder of this town, we require payment for Zemirah's loss of time from the man who beat him. The rest of us require nothing for ourselves, since the House of Shaul has today restored the honor taken from us, and granted us more besides. Amen," the elder ended.

"Amen," the crowd echoed.

Ishvi rose. "Zorath, disarm the guards with Doeg. They shall return to Gibeah bound and shall not be allowed in the king's presence until their next rotation as guards."

The men of the third unit came forward to collect the guards' weapons and escort the men from the square.

"As for Doeg, strip him to his loincloth, bind his hands behind him, and find a suitable pack animal whose tail he shall follow back to Gibeah. Pending further investigation, final judgment will be given there."

Then Ishvi turned back to the elders. "There is one other item of business to be taken care of, but perhaps you wish to attend to that after some rest and refreshment."

"Your consideration of us is appreciated, adon," Telah said. "We will meet again after the noon rest. Lahab, see if anything needs to be done for the adon's comfort."

As the people left the market, the younger man that Ishvi had robed came forward. "What do you require, adoni?" he asked.

"Some of your excellent wine would be a treat for me," Ishvi said, recognizing the man's name. "I have everything else I need at my tent."

"I'll send some immediately."

Sar Ishvi took his time returning to the market after the noon rest, finding himself oddly loathe to leave for Gibeah. Well, he had plenty of men and supplies, and it seemed a pity to return without experiencing some of the wildness that Malchi had talked about. And hadn't Jonathan wondered more than once what was down here below Jebus? Maybe he should wander around a little and find out.

Besides, if he trailed his robes around Dahveed's front yard long enough, he was sure to attract attention. And if he'd guessed correctly about the extra pack hurriedly added to his personal things this morning, Michal might be hoping the same thing. It looked about the right size to contain a certain harp case, as well as other items of a personal nature. If nothing else, he could try to get it to one of Ethan's band.

Why not just send Elihu back tomorrow with the disgraced guards and half of Libni's unit to report to Jonathan? The scribe could easily handle the king's business, better than he himself could, for the man reveled in knotty problems--like the one facing him now.

As soon as Sar Ishvi took his place in the market square, people began drifting over. The overt animosity against him was gone, but most faces were wary, wondering what he would do about Jesse's lands. He sighed. He wished he knew that himself.

He'd had time to think through the implications of the town's action this morning. Clearly, it would be impossible to attach Jesse's lands to the crown without the cooperation of the elders, for after he left, the town would simply ignore his decision. That would be a blow to the king's authority. But given the injustice of the procedure to begin with, the king's authority had already taken a blow. It seemed no matter which way he turned, he was caught, but he could see no other alternatives. Finally he decided that going through the forfeiture would bring the least dishonor to his house.

The beggar sat by the gate now, and as Elihu took his place at his scribes' table, the sar caught the quick glance that passed between them. It didn't take Ishvi much study before he decided the beggar was another of Jesse's sons. And one who might come in very useful, he thought as an idea flashed into his mind. Perhaps he could salvage some honor from this situation after all.

The elders arrived in a group, likely having conferred during the noon rest. Zemirah was not with them, so Telah spoke for the rest. "What business do you have at our gate, adon?"

Ishvi rose from the stone bench he had sat on. "The order has gone out that the lands of Jesse ben Boaz of Bethlehem in Judah are forfeit to the crown because of actions against the crown by one Dahveed ben Jesse. I have come to see to the forfeiture and take an inventory of all that the crown will now own. I request what aid the town elders can give in this proceeding."

Telah regarded him thoughtfully, not missing the out he had thrown them. They could claim to have no aid to give. "We will hear what you have to say, adon."

Relaxing a little, Ishvi knew that his actions earlier had garnered him this much grace at least. "I have a list of the lands owned by Jesse and his house which indicates his house is involved in some joint ventures with other houses. I request that representatives of those houses be present during this proceeding."

At Telah's nod, Lahab stepped forward. "Jesse's house has a joint venture in wines with my house. I am here to represent it at your request."

Another man stepped forward, with a distinct Ammonite cast about him. "I work with Shammah ben Jesse raising mules, adon. I am called Zelek."

Ishvi controlled his expression. Given Abbi's hatred of Nahash, the Ammonite king, he'd better mention Zelek in his report to Jonathan.

When no one else stepped forward, Ishvi nodded to Elihu. "Read the summary of land."

While Jesse's seventh son complied, Ishvi assessed the crowd again. Many people were displeased, but all of them watched the elders, who kept a carefully neutral demeanor.

When Elihu finished reading, he turned to the sar. "Since the vineyards and mules are joint ventures, I beg your leave to begin with them. I have prepared contracts that only require reading by the parties involved before they are sealed."

The sar heard the slight change in his scribe's even tones. Elihu had prepared contracts in advance? Just what might be in them? Ishvi hesitated only a moment before deciding to trust that Dahveed's brother had found a way to honor the king and preserve justice. Whatever was in those contracts shouldn't interfere with what he himself had decided to do. "Continue, then," he directed.

"Lahab ben Bukki, since you are currently working with the vineyards in partnership with Jesse's house, you are asked to review this contract and see if it is acceptable to you." Elihu handed Lahab a clay tablet.

"Zelek of Bethlehem, if you would review this contract regarding the disposition of the mules?"

The man read the document swiftly, giving Elihu just one glance, and without a word, he sealed the contract.

Ishvi turned to watch Lahab, who listened while the contract was read to him in a low voice by another man. The wine-maker's face grew more and more amazed, and when the reader finished, Lahab stared at Elihu, who remained impassive.

Curiosity got the better of the sar. "Something is not to your liking?"

Lahab seemed to wake up. "Uh, no, adon." he said hastily. "Not at all. This is fine with me."

"Your face did not agree, geber. Do you feel the contract is unjust, or detrimental to you?"

"Not at all. I can seal it immediately." He reached for his seal, but Ishvi rose.

"Let me read it," he demanded, holding out his hand, and noticing the tension that now gripped his chief scribe.

Reluctantly, the man who had read the contract brought it to him, and Ishvi scanned it swiftly. By the time he got to the end of it, he could hardly control his expression. The contract stated the above listed vineyards would continue to be administered by Lahab for the good of the partnership, and the other vineyards owned by Jesse's house were placed under Lahab's care as steward for the family until such time as charges against Dahveed ben Jesse were investigated and proven. At that time, final disposition of the vineyards would be decided upon.

Struggling to keep his face as passive as possible, the sar turned to Lahab. "I see nothing to object to in this contract."

"As I said, I can seal it now, adon," Lahab stated, his voice shaky.

Returning to his seat, Ishvi stayed there while the other portions of Jesse's lands were signed away. He noted that Telah got the grain fields, with the olives and nut groves and pastures all going to various others of the elders. The curiosity of the crowd grew as all the men sealing them reacted one way or the other.

The sar watched, his face expressionless, thanking Yahweh that he had decided to bring Elihu even though the land involved belonged to his family. When the only remaining properties were the houses of the brothers, and the compound in town, Ishvi rose again. It was time to carry out his idea.

"People of Bethlehem, hear now my words," he began. "King Shaul is very displeased with what the house of Jesse has done, and he wishes his displeasure to be made known to all. Therefore, the houses and compound belonging to Jesse and his clan will be given to someone of low status to emphasize the disgrace brought on the house by displeasing the king. The king will expect that whomever is chosen to oversee these properties for him will be elevated to similar status as Jesse for as long as he shall hold the houses and compound. All those who are accepting distribution of Jesse's land will submit a report to the steward of the houses as well as reports to the crown."

He looked around, catching the hesitation in Elihu's smooth movements.

"Bring the beggar by the gate to me," Ishvi commanded.

A town sentry brought the man, and when every elder's face either turned away or became completely bland, Ishvi knew he'd guessed the man's connection to Jesse correctly.

Elihu's brother bowed. "What is your will, adon?" he asked sullenly.

"How are you called?"

"Eliab ben Salmon."

The bekor! Hastily Ishvi suppressed his smile, wondering how many generations back the man had gone for Salmon's name.

"All right. Eliab ben Salmon, my scribe will write up a contract making you the overseer of the houses of Jesse's clan. Once you understand it, seal it with the hem of your garment."

"Yes, adon."

Once that was done, Ishvi stood again. "Has everything been settled to your satisfaction, Elihu?"

For the first time, he got a reaction from the man, one swift startled glance.

"Yes, adoni."

"Then I believe my business at Bethlehem's gate is concluded." He nodded to the elders as he left.

CHAPTER 14

"Gebirah, I've remembered."

Abigail paused her supervision of the cleaning of the last storeroom in the slaves' compound, turning her emotionless face to the guard commander. Ever since she had overheard Nabal plotting the death of the Bethlehem innkeeper, the pain of shame in her stomach ate at her constantly. The reaction of the Maon innkeeper to the travelers the day before yesterday had only emphasized the state her people had been driven into by her husband's increasing unreasonableness. Yet in spite of her conviction that something must be done, she had no idea what. That and her frustration only grew as, for the first time in years, she walked around Maon.

The filthy state of the slave compound had revolted her, and when she asked Namea why no one had said anything, her handmaid had looked surprised, telling her the nagid had forbidden anyone to bother her with such common, unimportant details.

As soon as Nabal had left for Carmel this morning, she had

ordered a thorough cleaning, then discovered that unless she herself was present, no one dared actually to do the job. She refused to think of what might happen if Nabal returned and demanded an explanation.

"You have seen the man before?" she asked Hezro now, remembering the awestruck stare the stranger had given her before someone stepped on his toe.

"Yes, Gebirah. I got a good look at him when I took them to the field. It was Dahveed Israel. I'd seen him when I was in Shaul's army. I'd guess the people with him were his family. They must be fleeing from King Shaul."

Her heart beat a little faster, and she took care to keep her voice even. "Do I remember correctly that he is from Bethlehem and of Boaz's clan?"

"Yes, Gebirah. He is a direct descendant of Hassarah Ruth and Adon Boaz."

She thought a moment. "Isn't Bethlehem north of us, not west?"

"Yes. But they had Habiru guiding them, and with Habiru, you never know."

His wry tone relaxed her a little, and she almost smiled. "I see. Do you think anyone else would recognize him?"

"Tokhath would."

Abigail hesitated. If Nabal knew of the family's passing, he might decide to curry favor with King Shaul by informing the ruler. But how much could she ask of the commander? "I don't see any need to mention them to the nagid," she commented carefully.

"Then I'll be certain not to bother him with such a mundane detail," Hezro said, his face carefully neutral.

"An excellent decision, Commander. You did well to inform me," she said, surprised at the relief that went through her.

The man bowed slightly and circulated around the compound, checking on the guard for Parai and the work being done.

Abigail sighed. Parai had not caused trouble since his return, but even though she had said nothing to Hezro about the slave's threats, the tanner's son was always closely guarded. He submitted to Nabal's commands when he had to, but the air of waiting that surrounded him set everyone on edge.

A couple times Abigail had wondered what she would do if she woke one night to find the slave bending over her with a knife, but somehow she couldn't make herself care very much. That frightened her a little.

Late that afternoon, she opened the gate to the garden and settled on the bench. She hadn't had time to come here much in the past couple days, and she welcomed the quiet, taking out the meil she was working on, thankful that she had made it back to the house before Nabal returned.

Her needle had pierced the fine red wool only a few times when she heard the nagid enter the compound. Not long after, the door to the business chamber opened, and Nabal stomped across the floor.

"There is something more you wish me to do?" Tokhath asked.

"How did it happen that Elhanan ben Dodo did not die?" her husband replied coldly.

"As the Habiru explained, they lost his trail down in--"

"I know what they said!" Nabal shouted, his thin voice almost shrill. "What I want to know is how they managed to fail? This man refused me the courtesy and honor due me! Shall he live?"

"Perhaps if you had given them a second chance, instead of driving them from Carmel, they could have--"

"And do you now question a decision of mine?" The nagid's voice was frigid.

Tokhath hesitated before replying. "No, Nagid. Whatever you decide is, of course, the best decision. Forgive my presumption in suggesting otherwise. We must find someone more competent to fulfill your wishes."

"See that you remember I always deserve the best," Nabal said witheringly.

"Of course, Nagid. I beg again from my knees your pardon in this matter. I shall inquire immediately who is best for this task."

"Do not fail me again."

"I shall not, Nagid. Will you take some wine to refresh yourself? If it is pleasing to you, I can prepare it with the same spices as I did before."

"Yes, bring some," Nabal commanded.

Abigail chose another color, threading the needle and working steadily while Tokhath went after the wine.

"This has a distinct taste of cinnamon to it," Nabal said. "But there is a bitter bite also. What do you put in it?"

"You have penetrated my secret, Nagid. The bitter comes from an herb obtained at the other end of the Great Sea, and is a variety of wormwood. It is reserved only for the greatest of those who dwell in the land where it grows, and is said to enhance the great qualities of those who are fit to rule."

"Yes, I can understand," Nabal said, his voice a bit odd. "You have pleased me again, Tokhath. Perhaps you shall keep your life after all. But I shall require more of this wine. It brings out the best in me."

"It shall be as you wish, Nagid. It is the joy of my life to be able to serve you, and I give you a multitude of thanks for your graciousness to me."

"I am gracious. It is a required quality of those fit to rule," Nabal replied, and Abigail heard wine pour into a goblet again.

A shudder went up her spine as the scribe piled flattery on flattery, his voice humble and adoring, and at the same time, nearly making her ill.

At last, they left the chamber, her husband's steps a bit unsteady. The light was beginning to fade, and she wouldn't be able to work much longer. As the needle slid in and out of the cloth, her mind replayed all that she had heard today. At least the innkeeper had escaped for now. She had tried to moderate Nabal's reactions to the man more than once to no avail. Her husband seemed determined to play the fool, insisting on his rights and honor regardless of anything else. If he didn't stop soon, he would be . . . Her needle slowed, then stopped altogether.

Bits and pieces of memories, comments, and experiences swirled around in her mind. She smoothed the red cloth. "One thing at a time," she whispered, a finger tracing a single strand of gold thread as it interwove through the colors of her pattern. As she stared at it, her mind recaptured the thought that had briefly surfaced moments before.

Mundane details. No one had bothered her with mundane details, and she had lost touch with what was actually happening around her. Just overhearing some of the comments while she cleaned the slaves' compound had revealed several other things that she should look into.

Carefully, she fit the pattern together, while her fingers traced line after line of color on the meil. It would be risky at first, for feeding Nabal's sense of honor might rebound in ways she didn't want, giving Tokhath more chances to influence her husband. And the man's shrewd advice was rapidly increasing Nabal's riches and power. Therefore, she would need a scribe completely loyal to her. A pity her abbi hadn't seen the ability to read and write as essential to a gebirah. But with a good scribe, she could destroy everything that her husband had done. It would take years, but the wrongs done by her house would be recompensed, and some day her house might have respect again. But where would she find a scribe?

As she closed the gate on her way back to the house, the intense look that Dahveed Israel had given her as she left the inn day before yesterday came to her mind. She didn't think he'd been staring at her beauty that time. What had he seen?

¥ ¥ ¥ ¥ ¥ ¥

It took two days after we left Maon to reach the Salt Sea plain and descend into its heat. We started early this morning, but even though the road was flat, it was hot, and the sun's glare on the pale landscape of the Arabah hurt our eyes. At least we weren't making this trip in the summer when it would have been much worse.

Ethan had caught up to us last night, and we walked with Abbi.

"It's a comfort to have you here, Ethan, but I didn't expect you," Abbi said with a smile.

"I'm filling in for Caleb since you sent him back to Bethlehem, geber. How did you know Eliab needed to be there?"

"We didn't," Abbi said slowly. "The Hassarah knew."

"She would. Well, geber, between Miriam and your oldest and youngest, you have your land back again."

"What happened?" Abbi asked, surprised.

In a few sentences Ethan sketched the events in the market. "The town is divided on whether or not the sar knew what he was doing. My silver is on the sar," he finished.

"So would mine be," I agreed. "Sar Ishvi is the most cautious of them. He'd have every move calculated before he made it."

In spite of the heat a spirit of rejoicing spread among us as the word of what had happened in Bethlehem passed down the line. I was glad for something to hearten my family, for the journey had been hard, and they were not used to it, and we must travel through the noon heat today to cover the 20 miles to Zoar.

Asahel had joined us, and he turned to Ethan. "Tell us something about the Hassarah."

"What about her?"

"Anything you remember," my nephew shrugged. "Who first called her the Hassarah?"

The expression of pain that Ethan always got when he thought of his abbi crossed his face. "Shoher did. I guess I've never told that story, have I?"

"Tell it now," I urged, knowing that it would help distract the children from the heat and their fatigue.

"It starts with Boaz, I guess," Ethan mused. "He was much older than Ruth, you remember, in his 40's when he married her. She gave him new life with Obed, and he was still strong and vigorous 20 years later. By then, the Philistines had become much more of a problem, raiding deep into the hills every year. There had been skirmishes between us and them on occasion, but usually miles from Bethlehem."

The children gathered close to hear, and we took some bundles out of the carts so the littlest could ride and listen at the same time.

"Once the Philistines started the policy of killing or capturing all the metalsmiths in the land, the clash with the Habiru was inevitable. When Boaz was about 64, the coastal people figured out all those defeats they'd suffered back in the hills weren't just chance, and they came looking for the army that opposed them.

"Patah had most of the responsibility of running the band by then, and he'd consulted with Geberet Ruth, who, as you know, had the uncanny knack of seeing around corners. He'd been training the townsmen to fight for more than a year, so when the Philistines arrived, we were ready." Ethan paused, and Shammah's little Jonadab hopped into the cart so he could hear better.

"From the very first the battle didn't go like the Philistines had planned. Patah had erected a barricade across the road a few miles south of Bethlehem, with men behind it primed to make a quick defense, and then run. Just around the curve in the road, the hills narrowed down, and the rest of them waited for the Philistines to come running. It worked. The fighting turned fierce after the initial surprise. The Philistines just couldn't believe that hill people could fight like this, and they had two well-trained and experienced units.

"They pressed the Habiru back, and the line nearly broke. Patah was thinking that he should make this a running battle when Boaz took a hand. He wasn't supposed to be there, everyone had insisted he was too old to fight. His hair was heavily streaked with white by then, and you know how much of it he had. But just when the battle was almost lost, he strode from the trees and strung that bow."

I remembered the feel of his bow, the power in it, and the beauty of it, and I could just imagine that big man, hair blowing in the wind, standing like the doom of Yah in the road.

"That bow makes arrows sing like no other," Ethan went on, "and Boaz shot so swiftly it seemed as if one arrow had hardly left the bow before another was in the air. Patah said more Philistines died in those short minutes than in all the fighting previously. When his quiver was empty, he swung the bow onto his back, took out his sword, and simply walked in. The Habiru gathered around him, and he spearheaded the drive to push the invaders back.

"Patah said he simply wouldn't give ground. He just plowed forward, cutting down anything in his path. They drove the Philistines clear back to the barricade and killed any who couldn't get away there. According to Patah, only three or four of that force made it out alive, and the Habiru heard stories of the white-haired devil with a god's bow for years afterward. It was there at the barricade that they discovered Boaz was wounded."

"Did he die?" Jonadab asked anxiously, his eyes wide.

"No, not then," the Habiru replied. "But he was very badly hurt. He had to be carried back to the town, and it wasn't until they returned that they discovered his bow was missing. Patah says they searched for days, but could never find it."

"Didn't they ever find it? Not ever?" Shammah's Jonathan pressed.

"No," Ethan said, with a sidewise glance at me. "Boaz lived for two years after that battle. But he was never really strong again. He just sort of tired out and died. Geberet Ruth never left him the last days of his life. Boaz wasn't strong enough then to even talk, and they just sat there together. She was holding his hand when he died. My abbi was a boy at the time.

"After the burial, they thought Geberet Ruth would die, also. She went to the forest house and shut the door. No one saw her for 10 days. The only way they knew she was alive was because they could hear the harp every once in a while."

"What was she doing in there?" someone asked.

"Mourning," Ethan said, his voice catching. "She took her pain and grief to Yah, and mourned for 10 days. When she came out after so long in the arms of her God, no one could look into her face. Shoher ran to her anyway, and wrapped his arms around her legs. 'I'm so glad you're alive, Hassarah,' he said. And they called her Hassarah ever after."

"That's a good story, but I still wish they'd found the bow," Shammah's Jonathan sighed.

I raised my eyebrows at Shagay and glanced at Ethan. My retainer shook his head, so Ethan didn't know that I'd given Boaz's bow to Hassar Jonathan. Now that I'd heard the story, I was more glad than ever that I'd done so. I felt certain that the bow had been made for him as well as Boaz.

Another question from one of the children started Ethan telling what he knew of Grandmother Ruth's life in Heshbon in Moab, and how a man named Abiaz had tried to bring her harm.

"What happened to him?" my brother Shammah inquired.

"He tried to play Kemosh-dan off against Amarel of Dibon, and found himself enmeshed in the struggle between them. The overlord caught up to him first, and if the stories are correct, Abiaz was glad to die. His family managed to flee across the Jordan, and stayed first at Jericho before moving on to Jebus, and then Bethlehem."

We were so engrossed in our stories that none of us noticed when we crossed into the land of Moab.

That night we stayed at Zoar, and the next day made the difficult trek to Horonaim which ended with the nearly 5,000 foot climb up a finger of land to the Moab plateau. No one had the energy to do more than to prepare a meal and collapse into bed, so I was surprised when Abbi sent for me.

"Are you all right?" I asked, finding him waiting inside the inn.

"I'm fine, Dahveed. I want to talk to you alone. Let's go outside. There is more you need to know about your Grandmother Ruth."

Abbi and I went outside, walking nearly to the inn yard gate. When abbi was certain we were alone, he pressed something that felt like a signet ring into my hand.

"The day before the Hassarah died, she talked with me a long time. Do you remember?" Abbi asked.

"Yes."

"She told me about her ancestry. I'd known some, and as I found out, the Habiru have always known the full truth of who she was. Because of the unsettled political situation in Moab at the time she left, her ancestry was kept secret, although Pashur, and later Patah, kept close track of the political changes for her at all times."

"Who was she, Abbi?"

"The last surviving daughter of Sar Mesha, son of King Eglon. When she was born, Eglon's grandson, Kemosh-dan, held the throne. Her immi was Mesha's youngest wife, and when Kemosh-dan, tired of his uncle's constant plots to take the throne, slaughtered the entire house, she fled, taking Moab's royal signet with her," Abbi said, touching my hand.

I shivered in the night air, wishing I'd put on my cloak, and glancing around again to be certain we were alone. The stars overhead gleamed with a chill white light.

"Although wounded, Ruth's immi made it to Heshbon before labor overtook her. She gave birth in the house of another woman, also in labor, and died immediately thereafter. The other woman's child died, and the mid-wife gave the live baby to the live mother. And Ruth grew up as the second daughter of Ithmah, a palace scribe, and Shimrith, his temple-singer wife."

"Did they know who she was?"

"Yes, the mid-wife's assistant had found the signet ring. They carefully protected Ruth, for after finishing off his uncle's house, Kemosh-dan decided to kill the entire bloodline, and nearly wiped out all of Eglon's descendants except his own. Then a man named Amarel of Dibon decided he wanted to be over-lord of Moab."

I sucked in my breath. King Yira, the present ruler of Moab, was a descendant of Amarel of Dibon. Abbi pulled his cloak more securely against him, and I closed my hand tighter around the signet.

"Amarel knew he could legitimatize his over-lordship if he could marry into Eglon's blood. He began an intensive search for anyone that Kemosh-dan might have missed. His agents had traced Ruth's immi as far as Heshbon when they came to Ruth's attention. She knew what would happen if Kemosh-dan heard of her, so when her mother-in-law, Naomi, decided to return to Bethlehem after the death of her sons, Ruth had two reasons to accompany her back."

"What of Amarel of Dibon?"

"He married a distant relation of Kemosh-natan, Kemosh-dan's abbi. There was just enough of Eglon's blood there for people to accept. Once on the throne, he killed all Kemosh-dan's descendants."

The ring felt icy in my hand. "What does all this mean, Abbi?"

"It means that if holding Moab's throne is dependent on Eglon's blood, I, or any of my sons, have more right to it than anyone alive."

The night suddenly felt much colder than before. "Why would we come here, then?"

"Because we are also kin. And if we, carrying as much of Eglon's blood as we do, acknowledge Yira as king, his hold on the throne will be greatly strengthened."

"But he has to believe that we have truly ceded our right," I said slowly. "Otherwise we are a threat."

"Yes."

"Isn't this something Abinadab should do? He's older than me."

"He doesn't bear the mark of Eglon like you do." Abbi reached for my free hand and his finger pressed into the increased webbing between my second and third fingers. "Only you and Abigail of my children carry Eglon's mark, as I do. That along with Moab's signet should be enough to convince anyone of who we are."

I shivered again and couldn't seem to stop. Abbi took off his cloak and threw it over my shoulders. The warmth from his body still clinging to it eased my shaking. "I don't know if I can do this, Abbi."

"You must, Dahveed. I am too old for Yira to believe that I would threaten him now. Your brothers have houses, land, and businesses waiting for them back in Bethlehem. None of my sons have the type of training necessary to compete with someone such as Yira, except for you. We will not be safe here unless you convince him that you have no desire for his throne."

"What if I cannot?"

Abbi was silent a minute. "Then we will have to return to Judah. There is always Nabal of Carmel."

"What does he have to do with this?"

"We are kin. Our clans descend from the same son of Tamar and Judah, and there has been intermarriage several times. He will be obligated to aid us in some way, especially as long as I can make it well worth his while to do so."

Thinking of my family dependent on the hesed of Nabal made me shudder again.

"I'll do my best with Yira," I said.

I left early for Kir-hareseth[9] 12 miles north, reaching the crossroads to the king's city in less than two hours. Lush pastures and grain fields surrounded me with a sea of green, and every house I saw had vineyards and fruit trees. It was like traveling through a perpetual garden. I wondered if they ever had drought here.

The road west to the city climbed a little, and in another half hour I saw the walls of the fortress, standing on a steep hill with sides that

---

[9] The Bible states that David took his parents to Mizpah of Moab to the king there. (1 Samuel 22:3.) The location of this city has never been determined. However, Kir-hareseth was the capital of Moab during the united monarchy in Israel. And since Mizpah means "watchtower" and Kir-hareseth stands high on the cliffs of eastern Moab, I have equated the two.

plunged into the Karak canyon which tore through the land and dropped to the plain of the Salt Sea. The only approach, from the south, was hardly less steep.

I had changed from my travel clothes to a plain brown town robe, worn, but of good-quality wool. The girdle was sand-colored, and the light cloak was green. As I climbed the switchbacks, I wondered how soon I could get in to see the king. I had the means to stay several days if necessary, but I prayed that I wouldn't have to wait that long. The inn we had stopped at was expensive.

The road was busy, although not crowded. A well-dressed woman carefully picked her way down the steep incline, the little smile on her face making me wonder what secret she kept. Farther up, a donkey half hidden by a large load of sticks waited patiently for the cart ahead of it, full of pithoi and drawn by oxen, to negotiate the sharp turn of the road.

I paused also, looking back the way I had come, wondering how to convince Yira that my family did not threaten him. My hand strayed to the lump in my girdle. Abbi and I had decided I should not take the actual signet with me, and I carried a clay impression of it. I was glad not to have the responsibility, for it was carved from ivory and surrounded by rubies.

An ox bawled and frantic shouts of alarm made me turn. Hurling straight down toward me rolled one of the pithoi from the cart, headed directly for the well-dressed woman! It bounced upward, and I lunged forward, gripping her waist, whirling us both to the side, yanking her down to her knees and pressing us against the hillside.

The pithos flew over our heads, skimming the top of the embankment we crouched against which set it spinning frantically before it smashed itself to pieces as it collided with the road a little farther down. Grain of some sort erupted from it, spraying everything for yards around.

"Geber! Geberet! Are you all right?" another traveler cried, rushing toward us, his face white.

"I think so," I said, standing up. "It didn't hit us."

"Only because you moved so fast! Thank Kemosh you did! Geberet?" he asked, helping the dazed woman to her feet.

"What happened?" She looked around at the rapidly growing crowd. A dozen voices answered her, and she turned to see the smashed pithos below. "I owe you thanks," she said, holding her hand out.

I touched it briefly and bowed. "It was my pleasure." While the people began to chatter again, I extricated myself, continuing up the road. The cart driver anxiously inquired if I was unhurt when I got up to him, and I assured him that I was fine.

"I will thank Kemosh you were there for that woman," he added, shuddering at what could have happened. "Is there something I can do for you?"

"Yes, if you would be so kind," I replied. "I'm a stranger here, and looking for the palace. Where in the city would I find it, and which scribe would I go to with a petition for the king?"

He readily answered my questions, sending me on my way with his well-wishes. As I entered the gates, I automatically noted the position and numbers of the guards, and with a couple glances around the market square, had located the guard towers and stairs. I had to smile at myself. Ethan's training ran deep.

At the palace I waited in line to see the scribe, and when my turn came I requested that my name be put down to see the king. "Is your petition urgent?" he asked in a bored voice.

I hesitated. "No, geber, I wouldn't call it urgent. But I think it is something the king would want to know."

That caught the man's attention, and he put a mark beside my name. "King Yira is quite busy today, so I will have you see his chief counselor right after the noon meal."

"You're very kind, geber. I'll be here then," I said, bowing and giving my place to the next man.

With several hours to wait, I wandered around the town, comparing it to Bethlehem, Gibeah, and Jebus. In the markets I bought bread, sour cheese, and Jericho dates. I didn't try to barter the prices down too much, knowing that as a foreigner, I would be expected to pay more, but I wasn't going to be robbed blind either.

I stayed in a shady seat near one of the town wells during the noon rest, and was back in front of the palace in good time. The building was larger than Akish's in Gath, and had wooden framed windows on both floors. The stir in the crowd announced the arrival of Yira, and I edged to where I could see my distant kinsman. Nothing about him reminded me of my grandmother until he turned his head, and I saw the line of his jaw. It could have been the side of Abbi's face, and that meant Nethanel's too.

Even from here, I could tell that the quality of his clothes equaled the hassar's very best, and I wondered what the man would wear to a really formal occasion. Gold embroidery flashed from his girdle, and the circlet on his head was studded with jewels. Undoubtedly, the throne room here was more magnificent than Akish of Gath's, not that I'd been in any condition to appreciate that room when I was in it.

Not long after the king entered, the scribes opened the doors and called several names, mine among them. Nervously, I walked forward, my mind still blank on how to secure safety for my family.

"The chief counselor will see you now," the scribe said when I entered the palace. Thankful that I had a hearing so quickly, I hurried after the man to a room about the same size as Shaul's throne room. The usual guards stood around, and three scribes had tables at various places. I passed a couple courtiers in attendance also.

The scribe announced me. "Dahveed ben Jesse of Judah, adoni."

"Yahweh, give me words," I prayed. Keeping my eyes lowered, I walked forward and bowed deeply, waiting for the adon to speak first.

"It has been a long time, Dahveed. What could you possibly wish from me?"

The sound of his voice whipped through my mind, and I looked up, my eyes meeting the malicious gaze of Balak ben Hod!

CHAPTER 15

As I stared into my old enemy's face, any hope that my family would find welcome and safety here shattered. Indeed, they'd be fortunate to escape with their lives. Certainly I would. All I could do now was keep the presence of my family a secret, and trust Yahweh to get word to them somehow so that Ethan, Shagay, and Ahiam could slip them away.

"You know, Dahveed, when my scribe brought your name to me, there was only one reason I could think of to explain your presence here, given the fact that Shaul has declared you an outlaw. Where did you leave your family?" Balak asked.

I swallowed the gall in my throat. "At the edge of the plateau, adon."

"Dare I think that you stand before me to petition for safe haven for that family?"

I couldn't bring myself to reply.

Balak laughed a little. "As always, you crawl back to the Hassarah, don't you?"

I remained silent.

"What? Has that zammar's tongue failed you in your hour of need,

Dahveed? That is unfortunate, because maybe, just maybe, if you ask humbly enough, I'll say yes."

I looked down, the empty feeling in the pit of my stomach growing with every moment. "Yahweh, what should I do?" my heart cried out. How could I leave my family here, under Balak's power? But was Nagid Nabal any better? In addition, if my family returned to Judah, there was always the possibility they would be recognized and betrayed to Shaul. Neither alternative offered safety, just the chance to choose where we would die. I never should have agreed to see anyone but Yira himself.

I caught my breath. Was there any way that I still could see the king? How much authority did Balak actually have? There was only one way to find out. I knelt, bowing my head.

"Just what is it you are about to beg from me, Ben-geber?" his hard voice asked.

Every muscle I had went rigid. Only the thought of what might happen to my immi if I failed here held me still. "I appeal to King Yira," I said evenly.

"I am the king's chief counselor, Ben-geber, which means I carry the same influence and power the hassar does in Israel. Do you imagine there is a single situation that would provide you with safety in Israel if the hassar did not wish it?"

I raised my head. "I can think of one, adon."

"Then it is a pity you are not in Israel, for there is no safety here without my consent!" he said savagely.

Out of the corner of my eye, I saw one of the courtiers leave. I chose my next words carefully, knowing that I spoke more to the others in the room than to Balak. "*If* that is true, then I will have to beg that consent from you, for it appears that I am under your hand."

"A fact you should keep firmly in mind."

"I will do so, adon, for I see you have gained much honor here."

Balak smiled. "And you have less honor now than ever before. You should have stayed in the sheep pastures, Ben-geber."

A door beyond Balak's chair and to the right opened silently, and the man who stepped over the threshold could only be Yira.

I bowed again, bracing myself to get the words past my teeth. "I beg you, again, adon, reconsider my appeal to the king."

"You will not see Yira's face, for I will not consent."

"Grant hesed, adon, more for your sake than for mine," I said quietly. "My petition touches very near to your adon, who rules all of

Eglon's blood, and I beg to appeal to the adon of that blood."

The mention of Moab's past overlord riveted Yira's attention.

"Your appeal is denied," Balak said. "I am very much afraid that the politic thing to do is to bind you and send you to Shaul with Yira's compliments. Unless you would rather that I decide how you will die, and then kill you myself?"

"You take too much on yourself, ben Hod," the king's cold voice interrupted. "No one has the authority to deny my right to hear a petition!"

The counselor hastily stood before touching his knee to the floor. "I would never think of it unless the circumstances were extreme, adoni. I know this man and his treachery. This is Dahveed Israel, son of Jesse, the man Shaul recently outlawed for treason. His presence can only mean danger."

I remained motionless.

"Have you been outlawed by Shaul?" King Yira asked.

"Yes, adon."

"Why?"

"I would guess I killed too many Philistines," I said wryly.

Someone behind me choked a laugh into a cough, and Yira regarded me with some amusement. "What is your petition to the adon of Eglon's blood?"

I reached into my girdle and took out the piece of clay wrapped in a cloth, holding it toward him.

One of the guards took it from me and gave it to the king, who flipped open the cloth, got one glance at what was in his hand, and covered it again. "Bring him," he said shortly to a guard, who pulled me to my feet and marched me toward the door that Yira had entered by. As I walked by, Yira turned on Balak, his eyes flashing with anger.

"Do not *ever* refuse someone who appeals to me," he exploded as the door closed behind me.

I waited for some time in a small room down a passage, getting more nervous the longer I stayed. Balak would be thirsty for my blood after I caused him to be publicly rebuked in such a manner, and I had no idea what he might tell Yira about me.

When the king finally entered, I was quick to kneel.

"Should I call for more guards?" Yira asked. "My counselor just advised me that when you are on your knees, you are the most dangerous. From what I observed in the other chamber, I believe him."

"I have begun badly, then, adon. I had no wish to disgrace your official so publicly. I hope I have not caused a lack in your court."

Yira snorted. "Balak knows his position is secure enough, as he is the one man who surrounds me who is not a fool! But he needs a strong hand!"

I smiled a little. "He would."

"And since he is not a fool, I will also believe him when he says you are always armed. Lay down your weapons."

I looked up in surprise.

"I believe slings are considered weapons, even where you come from," he said in disgust.

Reddening, I unwound the sling from my right arm and placed it on the floor. A guard picked it up.

"Is that all?" he asked.

"Yes, adon."

Yira folded his arms like the hassar, and with exactly the same exasperation on his face. "So far, Balak has proved true on every point, including this one. Will you now tell me that you have actually forgotten what you carry in your girdle?"

I could have sunk right through the floor. "I did, adon," I confessed. "I suppose he also mentioned how irritated Hassar Israel was the first time this happened with him."

"No. What did Shaul's son do about it?"

"He gave me permission to wear it in his presence, adon."

When the king said nothing else, I glanced at him, flipping my belt knife free. "Rather than have the guard take this, would you hold it?" I drove the point into the wooden three-legged table and backed away, bowing.

The flash of surprise in his eyes told me I'd finally done something other than what Balak said I would.

"Please, adon?" I added, holding my left hand out in appeal, spreading my fingers slightly.

Yira turned to the guard. "Wait outside." When the door closed, he turned to me. "You dare hand me a weapon, and then show me Eglon's mark?"

"Why should I not trust myself to the adon of that blood?" I asked.

"You recognize me as such?"

"Yes." I bowed again.

He went to the table, pulling the knife from the wood, dropping it immediately with an exclamation. "What is this knife?" he asked, gingerly picking it up again.

"It was made for my great-grandfather, to protect his family and clan."

"And who was your great-grandfather?"

"Adon Boaz of Bethlehem, who married Ruth of Heshbon, granddaughter of Eglon of Moab, through Sar Mesha."

Yira thought for a little, driving the knife blade into the table again, and letting go as if the touch of it hurt. "So that dog Abiaz told the truth after all," he finally commented. "No one believed Mesha had a surviving daughter. What happened to the traitor's family? I've never been able to find out."

I looked at him in surprise. "They escaped to Jericho and then Jebus, adon."

"And do they still live there?"

"Some of them."

"Why do I get the feeling you are not telling me all you know?" His eyes bore into mine.

"I find myself in an awkward situation, adon."

"It can get even more awkward, ben Jesse!"

I looked down. "One branch of the family moved to Bethlehem in Judah. I grew up with Balak. There has been animosity between us from the first. Had you not come, he would have tried to kill me."

Once again, I had the overlord's entire attention, and he kept me answering questions about Balak and his family for some time.

Once he was satisfied, he asked, "And why does Eglon's blood come to me?"

"King Shaul's anger had extended to my family, adon, and we came seeking shelter under your wings. My abbi is old, and my brothers and their families are grieved at leaving their homes and businesses."

I paused a moment, wondering how I could make him understand. "For myself, adon, I carry Eglon's blood, but I am not of Moab. My god is not Kemosh, but Yahweh, and He has taken me for His. I am bound to the land west of the Salt Sea with ties I cannot break, and I must return there."

Yira studied the clay impression that he still held.

"Bring your family to me, Dahveed, and I will find a place for them." He gingerly pulled my belt knife from the wood and tossed it to me. I flipped it into the sheath.

"And Balak?" I asked.

"I believe I am capable of handling my own counselor," he replied drily.

"Forgive me, adon," I said, flushing again. "Your kindness is great."

"My kindness is very self-centered, ben Jesse. I would have Eglon's blood where I can find it if I should want it."

My relief at gaining his permission was so great that I could hardly walk straight as I opened the door to leave.

"How many men would it take to capture my gates, Dahveed?"

"Twenty, and two Habiru, one of whom was inside," I responded without thinking. Then I froze, before turning back to face whatever Yira might decide to do after that gaffe.

"You are indeed a dangerous man, Dahveed. Maybe as dangerous as Balak. You will leave Kir-hareseth immediately after your family's audience with me day after tomorrow."

"As you command, adon."

At the appointed time my abbi and brothers accompanied me to the palace. The scribe sent a message when we arrived, and King Yira interrupted the court to receive us.

We entered the room and all of us bowed before the throne. I had prepared them for the sight of Balak, standing to the right of Yira, his face unreadable.

"What is your petition?" King Yira asked formally.

Abbi wanted me to speak for the family, and I had carefully thought out the wording of my petition to emphasize not only their position, but my own. "Please let my parents remain with you until I know what Yahweh will do for me," I explained.

"Are these all your sons, Jesse ben Boaz?" the overlord asked, inspecting us carefully.

Abbi had everyone dressed in plain, good-quality clothes suited to townspeople. Only I wore the traveling clothes of the Habiru. "No, adon. Two of my sons remain in Judah, doing what they can for me there. We would return as soon as we may."

"Your petition is granted. Let everyone know that I, personally, have taken the clan of Jesse ben Boaz under my wings to shelter them. Anyone who touches them, touches me."

I bowed my head in relief. Such a public commitment of protection would prevent Balak from harassing my family. Yahweh had provided for us again.

"Your kindness is great, adon," Jesse said. "In return, may I offer a small gift to you?"

He handed me the signet of Moab, and I took it to the throne, presenting it to the overlord. He fingered it briefly in surprise, then closed his hand over it. "Your family is singularly unambitious, Dahveed," he said quietly.

"Yahweh is our God now," I replied.

Satisfied, he sat back. "Your gift is unique, and I will treasure it. Go now, and see to your families."

We had said our farewells already, so by the time Abbi and the others reached the bottom of the hill, I had slipped away, taking a trail Ethan had told me of that dropped into the Karak canyon, and by dark, I had descended the steep defile to the Salt Sea.

¥ ¥ ¥ ¥ ¥ ¥

"Have you found out anything about Parai's family?" Gebirah Abigail asked Hezro as she walked up the road to Carmel with her oldest handmaid, Matred, and three guards.

"No. But I have only limited places where I can ask."

"Keep trying."

"Yes, Gebirah."

During the short trip she stopped twice, both times to inspect fields near the road. The workers were hesitant in her presence, but responded courteously to her greetings and questions, although she could tell they were puzzled as to why she would ask. More frustrated than ever with her own ignorance, she realized how badly she needed a scribe and someone to teach her.

Abigail pushed those thoughts aside when they arrived in Carmel. Commander Hezro brought her to a compound close by the city gate with a large two-story house facing a row of storerooms. It had a grape arbor, a cistern in one corner, and an almond tree.

"Why are they selling?" she asked Hezro as they stood in the courtyard looking around.

"The widow can't keep up the land."

"When did her husband die?"

The guard commander cast a quick glance at her. "He met with an accident last year."

Something about his tone made her curious. "What kind of an accident?"

The commander shrugged.

The way he avoided her gaze made that knot appear in her

stomach. She faced him. "Hezro, tell me what happened."

Her tone of command startled him.

Remembering the expression that she'd once seen the Hassarah give one of the servants, she raised her chin, staring directly into his eyes.

To her surprise, sweat appeared on his forehead, and he dropped his gaze. "Gebirah, please, don't ask. The nagid has said--"

"I no longer care what the nagid said. You will tell me now."

Hezro still hesitated, and she let the silence stretch.

"The man was on a trip to Hebron and was robbed. He died of his wounds before anyone found him."

"And you suspect Nabal arranged his death, or do you have proof?"

"Please don't speak so loudly," Hezro cautioned, trembling. "Someone might hear."

"Then tell me what I want to know quickly."

"I have no proof."

"Now, take me into the house. Where is the family?"

"I don't know. The innkeeper is taking messages for them."

She looked over the upper room. It was large enough for what she wanted with the addition of a few more niches in the walls for lamps, and a dais at the far end. "Send for the widow. And see if you can find someone who will give me an honest estimate of what this compound is worth."

While she waited, she and Matred looked over the house thoroughly and then the storerooms and sheds on the opposite wall. When she emerged, the Carmel innkeeper waited in the courtyard.

The man bowed. "Gebirah, you are interested in this house?"

"Yes. What is the price?"

He hesitated a little. "One hundred fifty silver, Gebirah."

"Innkeeper, I am not the nagid. What is the price?"

After studying her for several moments, he said, "I beg your indulgence, Gebirah, but the nagid has shown some interest in this place, and he will not wish to pay more than he must."

Abigail's stomach knotted again, and she tried to ignore it. "I will handle the nagid," she heard herself say. "What is the price?"

"Three hundred silver."

"That's still below what you told me a week ago," a hard voice declared from behind them.

Abigail turned to see a plain woman about her height staring at the innkeeper.

"Geberet Jotbah, I didn't know you were there," he said, embarrassed.

"Obviously." She bowed to Abigail. "Gebirah."

"What price did he tell you the compound was worth?" Abigail asked in a neutral tone as Hezro took his place beside her.

"Four hundred and five silver."

"Does that sound reasonable, Commander?" Abigail asked.

"Yes."

"Then I will buy at that price. Come to Maon tomorrow, and I will have the price for you."

"I will be there."

Afterward Abigail accompanied the woman to the gate. "I am sorry to hear of your husband's death."

Jotbah looked up. "My abbi," she corrected. "Immi left me here to settle things since I was scribe for him."

A scribe? Abigail thought a moment. She liked the woman's directness and her unflinching attitude. "I need a scribe, someone who will do what *I* say." She emphasized the pronoun slightly.

Jotbah looked her in the eye. "Why should I work for the house that destroyed mine?"

Abigail looked right back. "To help me destroy the nagid."

The woman held her gaze for several moments. "I'll bring my things when I come for payment tomorrow."

"I'll be expecting you."

The woman bowed and left.

The Gebirah returned to the waiting innkeeper. "I believe you sent a message that the caravan representative had come?"

"Yes. He's at the inn now."

Once at the inn, however, she had to wait, for the nagid had summoned the man. She and Matred sat on a stone bench to one side, watching the street through the open gate. The sounds from the town were subdued, and there were few people in the streets.

After almost an hour, a man strode through the gate, his face dark with anger.

"Did the nagid like your wares?" the innkeeper asked without really looking at him.

"He had the gall to tell me I was charging two and three times more than I should for the inferior goods I brought him!" the trader exploded.

As he spoke, another man led three donkeys through the gate, the packs so hurriedly fastened that one almost fell off as the animal stopped.

"You don't know how to talk to the nagid, Hadar," another man said, lounging at the door of the inn. "Gold speaks so loudly with him, he hears nothing else."

"If he deals with you, Samlah, it must," Hadar said in contempt. "You'd better watch your steps. The caravans know you and that thief, Eliphelet, who feeds your greed."

"Come, Hadar, be reasonable. It's not *my* greed," the other said, his voice amused. "Our goods are equal to yours, and if we can bring the blessing of the gods to those who trade with us, why should you care? Or is Jether the Ishmaelite still convinced Eliphelet is responsible for his, uh, misfortune a few years back?"

Hadar's eyes glittered, and Abigail saw him reach to his girdle. "Take care, Samlah. One day that thief will steal from the wrong man and find himself snared like a fly in a web. Without him to supply you, you will be begging for bread--or mayhap your life."

Chuckling, the man disappeared into the inn.

Hadar turned to the man with the donkeys. "We will not come here again," he said to his companion. "I'll have nothing to do with any who deal with the likes of Samlah, to say nothing of Eliphelet ben Ahasbai."

"Yes, geber," the other replied.

Hadar went into the inn, and Abigail followed, trailed by Matred and Hezro.

"Geber Hadar, I would speak with you a moment," she said.

He turned in irritation, then stopped, his mouth dropping open as he saw her. Recovering, he bowed. "How may I serve you, Baalah?" he asked, struggling to keep from staring at her.

She smiled and gestured to a bench by the wall. "Do sit down, geber. I would know from you the kinds of goods your caravans can supply."

Looking dazed, the caravaneer sat down, crowding into the corner when he realized she would join him. He was sweating and couldn't keep his eyes from her face. "What goods did you want?" he asked automatically.

"I'm planning a little surprise for my husband, and I wanted to be certain I got the best," she said, smiling again.

"Yes, Baalah," the man replied, looking up at Hezro, who stared back, his eyes hard.

It was almost noon when she finished talking to Hadar, telling him what she wanted, and getting prices. She promised that she'd let him know in the morning how much she would order now, if he would be so kind as to stay until then.

"I will be here, Baalah," he said quickly.

They arrived back at Maon just before the noon meal. Abigail spent a few moments in her chamber to organize her thoughts and take some deep breaths. If she had guessed incorrectly about the wooden key her promises to both Jotbah and Hadar would be worthless.

While her handmaids prepared some food, she went to her husband's business chamber, closing the door. She searched hurriedly under some old blankets near the back wall, then under a cloth once used to cover the nagid's table. She had heard Nabal get the treasure room key several times, and it had sounded as if he was moving something made of fabric each time. At last she found the large, toothed, boomerang-shaped key hidden in the pillow her husband sat on.

Turning to the treasure room door, she inserted the toothed arm of the key through the circular hole in the door. The teeth fit into the slots on the inside, allowing her to lift the latch holding the great bar into place, but she wasn't strong enough to raise the bar itself.

Abigail chewed her lip a moment. Now what? That bar was heavy, to fit the massive door and the thick walls of the room. She didn't think that she'd be able to get it up even if Namea helped. No, she needed Hezro.

A few moments later she left the chamber carrying the key between the old blankets and the table covering. They needed washing, which would give Tirzah something to do this afternoon besides sit around and talk to the gate guards.

Once Abigail was certain her maids were asleep after the meal, she had the gate guard send Hezro to her at the business chamber. Leading the sleepy commander inside, Abigail handed him the key and pointed to the treasury door.

Instantly Hezro woke up. "Gebirah, if I open that door for you, I could lose my life," he gasped.

"Something must be done about Nabal," she replied. "I am responsible for the people in my clans. They have suffered enough because I was unwilling to face the conflict of restraining the nagid."

The soldier stood rigid. "Will you protect my life?" he asked at last.

Trying to stave off the familiar tightening in her middle, she took a deep breath. "I will do my best."

To her surprise, the commander fell to his knees, and then bowed to the floor. "Swear to me, Gebirah. Swear that you will shelter me. And if that is not enough, swear you will kill me yourself!"

At that Abigail almost panicked. She trusted Hezro's judgment, and if he was asking this, the risk must be much more than she imagined. What should she do? Her mind scrambled frantically for answers. What would Hassarah Ruth have done?

Abigail steadied herself. Ruth would have given her hand and sworn. And she would have carried out her oath. Trying to make sure her hand wasn't shaking, Abigail held it out.

Hezro took it.

"As Yahweh lives, Hezro, if you will do as I command, I will do all in my power to shelter your life. And if necessary, I will take it myself rather than let another do so."

"Thank you, Gebirah," he said, touching her hand to his lips. "I will do whatever you ask of me."

"Open the door."

When they left the business chamber, she carried enough gold pieces to pay for the compound in Carmel. That afternoon Namea took the key to a carpenter, bringing it back by sunset.

Carrying the now washed blankets, Abigail returned to the chamber, slipping the key back into its place in the cushion before she put the blankets back.

"I didn't know you came here when the nagid wasn't here," Tokhath's voice said.

Abigail whirled around. Had the scribe seen what she'd just done? Surely he hadn't been in here when she came in. "You startled me," she said. "Has the nagid returned?"

"Yes. He'll be coming in a moment."

Tokhath walked to his table, bringing him closer to her, and Abigail suppressed the urge to edge away. She picked up the blankets and returned them to the chest they had been sitting on.

"The servants can't return blankets?" he asked.

"The servants don't enter the business chamber unsupervised," she replied drily. "How is it you are here?"

"I work here," he retorted.

"When Nabal is not present?" She raised her eyebrows, trying not to shiver with the feeling that his stare gave her.

"You dared to be alone with my wife? No one toys with my honor this way!" Nabal shouted from the doorway. "Hezro!"

The commander rushed in, followed by three of his guards.

"Take this man into the courtyard and kill him!" Nabal shouted, pointing to Tokhath. "He thought to have the Gebirah! Take him and kill him! Kill him now!"

Tokhath sat motionless, sweat running down his face, after giving Abigail one glance of appeal.

"Control yourself, Nagid," Abigail said calmly. "Such passion is most unseemly and unnecessary."

"But he was about to lay hands on you!"

"Enough of this shouting," Abigail said coldly. "You are Nagid Carmel, Nabal. Can you imagine Hassar Israel losing his dignity so, let alone Shaul?"

Her husband clenched his fists and closed his mouth, straightening up.

"Now, do you dare to suggest that I would consent to be in the presence of a man who would dishonor you?"

Her husband's mouth nearly dropped open. "Of course not, Gebirah!"

"Then just what were you suggesting? Tokhath simply arrived to begin his work with you."

"I-I thought only of you, Gebirah," Nabal said, looking around a bit dazed.

"As you should," she replied. "But in thinking of me, be aware that I might have something to say. I will expect you to remember my honor that way in the future."

"Of course, Gebirah," he said, practically bowing.

She turned to the commander. "Hezro, return your men to their posts. Tokhath, I believe the nagid would enjoy some of that special wine you prepare. Mix some at once!"

"As you command, Gebirah," the scribe said without looking at her. Pulling a small vial from his girdle, he added a little to a goblet, and then filled it from the jar behind his table. When he brought it forward, Abigail reached for it, noting that his hands were shaking when she took it from him.

Taking a small sip, she passed it to her husband. He drank some also.

"You are dismissed, Tokhath," she announced.

The scribe bowed deeply and left.

The Gebirah turned back to her husband. "As nagid, you must be circumspect with your words. It is time now for the evening meal, Nabal. Let us partake."

She held out her hand, and he took it, escorting her to the house.

Shaul and Judah

CHAPTER 16

I came up into the highlands from the En-gedi springs. The days with my family had allowed me to regain my full strength, and I took to the Habiru trails again, traveling swiftly into the heart of the southern wilderness. While on my way across the Arabah, I had decided I would return to Adullam. The cave there was comfortable, and poised on the Shephelah between Israel and Philistia, I could seek refuge in the highlands or on the coastal plain should either be necessary.

Now that I was back in the highlands, however, my lack of any real weapons pressed on me. I could always make a bow and some arrows, but they would be suitable only for killing my lunch. While I had my sling, I needed a battle dagger at least, and preferably a sword.

Down in the lowlands battles might normally be won by archers, but here in the forests, too many things could get in the way of an arrow's flight. Close-range weapons such as swords and javelins were more useful.

Crossing what passed for a road down here, I stopped. Sometime in the not too distant past a considerable force had come along it. That curiosity habit from Ethan took over, and I studied the trail closely, noting the signs where a cart had caused problems, and I wondered when they would be sensible and load the stuff on donkeys for transport.

Farther on, small parties had gone into the forest and then returned, for seemingly no reason. Indeed, the caravan itself didn't seem to be headed anywhere. I found where they had camped in the early afternoon. The remains of several fires told me that it equaled about two units of men. Someone of high status was with them since one tent had been larger than the others and had been surrounded by the others. I also found the cart, hidden in the brush.

Hoof prints revealed two mules. As soon as I saw them, I looked over the campsite again, detecting the layout of units in the professional force. Shaul? More likely someone he'd sent. But if they were searching for me, they were doing it in the oddest way that I'd ever seen.

The wind blew, and I wrapped the light cloak around me, trying not to shiver. As puzzled and curious as I was, I was ill-equipped to spend time in the highland winter. I had to get to Adullam, where it was lower and warmer and I might have a chance of making some coppers as a courier.

Reluctantly, I left the caravan's trail, picking up a fast jog west to make up for lost time and keep warm. It was nearly dusk, and I'd come a dozen miles when I topped a rise in the trail and saw a group of five men just ahead of me!

Instantly, I swerved, ducking behind the nearest large tree, trying not to pant too loudly.

"What was that?" a voice asked.

"Where?"

"In back of us. I thought I saw something just at the rise."

"Another lion?" a third voice said, amused. "You're as jumpy as a cricket!"

"I saw a leopard, not a lion! And something has been following us!" the first voice insisted.

"So you've been saying for three days! And when Libni sent us out to look, did we find anything?"

I eased my belt knife out. *Commander Libni?* How many units were down here? Or was this the same one I'd already tracked? But they'd been headed south. Of course, the way that trail had wandered, they could be anywhere by now.

"Well, there's nothing there now, and I've got better things to do than backtrack looking for phantoms. I'm hungry, and the scribe is halfway back to camp by now. And if anything happens to him, we'll catch the sharp side of Libni's tongue."

Scribes? What was going on? I waited until full darkness before I continued down the trail, finding the camp less than a mile away.

I circled the place cautiously, but the sentries stayed close in, and I identified Zorath's third unit at full strength, but only half of Libni's tenth. Torches and firelight lit up the central part of camp, where three scribes worked by the large tent. Before long, Sar Ishvi stepped into the light, accompanied by his foster son. He questioned each scribe, and when the reports were finished, they were placed in a king's messenger pouch.

That pouch still lay on the low three-legged table outside the sar's tent when the place quieted for the night. I kept staring at it. Slipping into the camp was foolhardy. It was an unnecessary risk that could get me captured and maybe killed. In fact, the very presence of those reports informed me that whatever the sar was doing, he wasn't looking for me, and I should not intrude on him. But I couldn't rid myself of the urge to read the things!

About midnight, I gave up trying to convince myself that going into the camp was a bad idea, and I circled it again, finding a convenient entry point between two guards who were more asleep than not.

Remaining in the deep shadows of the trees, I crept between them and then picked my way silently through the third unit to the sar's tent. All was still, and I studied the positions of the tents in case I had to make a quick exit. Sticks were stacked conveniently by the fire, and I threw two or three on the coals, then picked up the message pouch. Drawing out the reports, I unfolded them carefully to make as little noise as possible.

Crouching down, I angled the top one toward the low flames. It was addressed to the hassar, and was a summary of the resources found on a certain parcel of ground. Estimates of the numbers of oak and pine were listed, along with the type of soil on the hillside, and what was likely to grow there if the forest was cleared. The scribes had estimated the value of the timber available now, and then given a rough evaluation of how much the land might produce if it was farmed, or planted to fruit, nut trees, olives, or as a vineyard. My eyes widened at the totals at the bottom.

Taking up the next one, I read the same sort of report, this one mentioning the presence of springs on the hillside, along with an estimate of whether or not they would run year-round and thus serve as a source of water for irrigation, or if they were seasonal only. The summary at the bottom was dual, giving expected yields of the land if the springs were seasonal, then if they were permanent.

After the third one, I just scanned the final summaries at the bottom, growing more and more amazed. Returning them to the pouch, I stood and stared into the night, doing some calculations. According to these reports, this land was capable of producing sizeable riches. The thought of what this could mean to my people took my breath away. I'd never considered having someone look at the land from this perspective. I hadn't even known anyone could make these kinds of estimations. Could Elihu do this?

I would bet that he could, and knowing Elihu, his estimates would be reliable. My people didn't need to struggle to barely survive. They could have nice homes, adequate food, and the comforts of life.

An awareness that I was watched tingled through me. After bending down and putting a couple more sticks on the fire, I glanced around as if checking on things, and then walked on like a sentry who had varied his beat. But once in the shadows, I headed swiftly to the edge of the camp and departed, knowing the sentries wouldn't be worried about anyone leaving.

I got little sleep that night. As usual, Jonathan was looking far ahead, and he was getting a good idea of how valuable the south could be. I ached to talk it over with him, and the bitterness of not being able to see him made me grit my teeth.

Homesickness swept over me. Not for Bethlehem this time, but for Gibeah, and that cold stone fortress with the rain beating down on the stones of the common court and the warmth of the braziers, and the sight of Jonathan's black eyes as he quizzed me about everything I'd seen and done on my latest errand for him. Then I'd go to my compound by the wall, and Michal would welcome me home, the tone of her voice telling me if she had a hard day or not. We would sit in the upper room, eating, while she told me everything that had occurred in the throne room that afternoon, and then asked about what had happened to me on the training ground.

"Yahweh, grant them your hesed," I pleaded. "Keep them under your wings. They have given me so much!"

Early the next morning, I lingered at the edges of the camp as it woke. As he always did in war camp, the sar left his tent before he ate for a little time alone. What he did during this time, no one knew. But every day that he was in camp, he invariably did it.

Shortly afterward, young Ishvi also left, heading out into the forest. Silently, I tagged along, discovering that the young man had set snares the night before, and was checking them. He took a bird from one. But since he left the snares in place, I concluded that the sar didn't plan to move today.

Ishvi met him coming back. They stood close to each other, the young lad staring off into the forest. "Abbi, I think I need to tell you something," he broke the silence. "I can't figure out if it's important or not. Nothing was taken, so I don't know."

I pricked up my ears.

So did the sar. "Tell me about it."

"Last night after midnight, I woke up and had to go out of the tent. I was quiet, because I didn't want to wake you. When I looked out, I saw a man standing by our fire, just putting the message pouch back on the table."

"What did he do?"

"He just stood there. Then he threw some more sticks on the fire, checked the area, and walked away. I can't decide if he was a guard or not. He acted like one, but something wasn't right about him."

"The scribes didn't say anything was wrong with the pouch this morning," Ishvi said thoughtfully. "Did he take out the reports?"

"I don't know. I just saw him laying the pouch down. I wish I could think of why he looked wrong."

Vexed, I bit my lip. Well, that was the sort of thing that made invading someone's camp dangerous. You never knew when chance would take a hand. I was lucky the youth had not raised an alarm.

"Did he have a cloak?" the sar asked.

"Yes, it flapped around him when he moved. But he didn't have a spear!" the boy said excitedly. "That's what was wrong. The sentries all carry spears! Who could it have been?"

"We'll probably never know," the sar replied. "It might have been someone just curious about our camp."

"I suppose one of the Habiru might check us out," young Ishvi said slowly. "Or maybe one of those others."

"You still think someone was following us?"

"I know there was, abbi."

Thinking deeply, I withdrew. That one of Libni's men would imagine he was followed here in the southern wilderness didn't surprise me. But for a young man born and bred here to feel the same was altogether different. Still, I hesitated. The wind was chill this morning, and the clouds scuttling across the sky promised more cold to come. And I'd barely stayed warm last night. I should get to Adullam as soon as I could and earn enough coppers for some leggings at least! To say nothing of assuring my covenant son that I hadn't permanently abandoned him to Elhanan.

I was still telling myself this later as I backtracked the sar to his previous camp about six miles southeast. There was too much coming and going at his present one for me safely to do a thorough check of the surrounding country. I started with the location of the sar's tent, then found the animal runs where young Ishvi had set snares. On my second circle around the area, I found what I was looking for, and I almost missed it.

The trail was faint, made by one man who was used to forest travel, and he had completely circled the sar's camp at least once. I soon determined that he wasn't Habiru, for while he didn't leave much sign on the ground, he left plenty elsewhere, picking the bark off trees, pulling dead leaves and crushing them, and breaking little twigs off anything in reach. He also seemed unable to stand still for long.

I located his camp before noon. Two men had slept here, one who never got far from the fire, and the one I followed. Even here, he left tracks everywhere, scuffing the ground and slashing at shrubs with what was probably a sword. The bones of their supper were scattered by the fire, and they hadn't eaten nearly as well as the sar did.

But why would they be trailing the sar, I wondered. Sighing, I pulled the thin cloak around me. I had yet to eat today, and after that I'd head back to Ishvi's present camp to see if I could learn anything more. Likely I'd get nothing but another chilly night for my pains.

At dusk I waited until the smells from the sar's camp assured me the men were preparing their evening meal before I started circling the camp. One of young Ishvi's snares caught my eye just as I heard the young man approaching on the trail in front of me. The sar's foster son walked into view, going directly to the snare, which was empty. He shifted it to another place on the animal run, and moved on to his next one.

I waited until he was around the bend in the trail before following. As he bent over the second snare, a man grabbed him, dragging him back in to the trees, stifling his cries with a hand over his mouth. It happened so quickly that I was caught unaware, wasting precious moments convincing myself that someone had actually dared to snatch a member of the royal family!

Then I sprang forward, but by the time I got to the snare, the man was out of sight in the near dark. The sounds of young Ishvi's struggles caught my ear, and I ran that way, glimpsing a roughly-dressed man hauling his captive into a gully. I saw enough to know he was from the north somewhere as I slid to the bottom. Firelight gleamed from a blade, and the man cried out hoarsely as his captive raked his leg with a belt knife. The angle was awkward, so it wasn't enough to really cripple, but sufficient to make him lose his hold.

The boy streaked toward me, his now enraged attacker right after him.

I had time to whirl the sling twice before letting fly with a small stone that hit the northerner's thigh, making him stumble, and giving the youth a couple more moments' lead. He flashed past me, and as his attacker lunged after, I threw my right fist across my body, connecting with the man's chin like a club. I followed my arm's motion with my shoulder, slamming into him at nearly the same moment my fist landed. Flying through the air, he collided with the side of the gully before he fell, lying motionless.

Young Ishvi glanced back frantically as he scrambled to the top of the watercourse, and I met his eyes. "Run!" I ordered.

As he vanished, I turned back, swaying slightly, my gift roused by the chase and the danger to the boy.

A second man stared at me from beside the tiny fire, his face white and shocked. "Is he dead?" he nearly whispered in an accent that I'd never heard before.

It took a moment to find my voice. "Probably not. His kind don't die easily."

"Are you going to kill him?"

"Why should I bother? If the sar finds him, I won't need to, and if the sar doesn't find him, I doubt he'd recognize me again, or want to meet me if he did." I shoved my belt knife into my girdle, having no memory of taking it out, and turned to go.

"You're leaving?" The stranger's voice sounded panicked.

Puzzled, I hesitated long enough to reply. "Geber, it won't be long before this place is crawling with two units of soldiers and one very irritated sar. I intend to be as far away as I can get." Again I started to go.

"Take me with you."

I caught my breath. What had he just said?

"Please," he added. "If I stay with him, he will either get me killed, or kill me himself. You are my chance to escape from him. I will be your servant, your slave, anything you want, but do not leave me with him."

Once more I halted.

The firelight flickered on his white face, which was battered and swollen. He favored one side as if it hurt also.

"I am Habiru. Your lot will not improve with me."

"I didn't think you could be anything else," he said, starting to shake. "But you told that boy to run, and you haven't killed Hiddai, or me. I would rather die with you than live with him!"

"You don't need me. Just walk away."

"Don't leave me," the man behind me pleaded. "I have no skills in the forests. I cannot keep myself alive alone, and he knows it, geber. He could force me to do anything, like he did today. He wanted the sar to pay to get his son back, and he beat me so I would make a convincing messenger to ask for the ransom. Take me with you!"

Feeling trapped, I searched desperately for a way to refuse him. "You would be useless to me, and there is no room for uselessness in the wilderness."

"Please, geber. I will do whatever you tell me. There must be something I can learn which will be valuable to you!"

I seethed with frustration. Why did this always happen to me? "Yah, what shall I do now?" I demanded in my mind. On the run as I was, I needed to be free to move and react at a moment's notice, something that I couldn't do with an inept companion. But his assessment of Hiddai matched what little I knew. The northern Israelite probably would murder him one night.

I wasn't the least bit happy about this, but I dared not stay around any longer, for I could hear the soldiers approaching.

"How are you called?"

"Igal, geber."

"You will do exactly as I say."

"Yes, geber."

Igal and I barely made it out of the area ahead of the search party, and only because they made so much noise did we get away at all. Igal sounded like an entire army behind me, and as I bedded down for the night, I wondered what possible use this foreigner would ever be to me!

About dawn, I rose and drank at the small seep not far from my camp, studying the tracks to see what had come there during the night. I hunted for my breakfast, bringing down two birds with my sling rather than running them down as they were usually taken.

Igal slept all during the time I prepared breakfast, and I ate, leaving one bird roasting over the fire for him when he woke. I wanted to check on the sar's camp.

The sar was gone by the time I arrived, leaving the camp deserted except for one donkey, which brayed periodically, and was loosely tied where the sar's tent had been. I scratched my head over this. Ishvi was not one to leave fully packed donkeys behind. Further scouting assured me that everyone had gone, so I went to the animal, talking softly to it. Its ears swivelled to hear me, and then it reached to snuffle my hands.

The pack caught my eye. The coverings on it looked familiar, so did the knots tying it. My hands shook as I yanked them apart. One touch, and I identified the long object on the top as my sword! I tried to pull it out, but it was caught in the cuirass and wrapped in the hassar's girdle, which I had left at Navyoth! Stunned, I reached farther into the pack with shaking hands. My campaign cloak! More clothes, and then the unmistakable feel of the harp case in the bottom.

As I leaned against the donkey, I wondered what had been risked to get these things back to me. Once again the royal family left me with no way to repay the hesed they showered on me. Wiping my eyes, I looked up. "Yahweh, who am I to take what has been given to their house? Your gift is more than I can bear!"

I strapped on the sword immediately, settling it at my side. The cloak hid leg wraps, and I put them on before fastening on the cloak itself. My heaviest sandals were there, too, so I changed into them also. I left the cuirass and Jonathan's girdle in the pack, but strapped on the harp case. I wasn't certain how to fit the harp case over the cuirass, and if push came to shove, I'd leave the cuirass off. Never again would I be without Grandmother's harp.

Feeling like a new man, I returned to my camp. The donkey gave every indication of being Habiru trained, and after untying it, I walked away. It tossed its head a little, then followed along after me, keeping about four feet behind me no matter what pace I set. My sense of well-being vanished as I got within smelling range of camp. The scent of charred meat drifted by, and I hurried forward, wondering what had happened.

Staring, I halted at the edge of camp. Igal had built up the fire into a blaze that was consuming the breakfast I'd left for him. He sat so close to the flames that I wondered that he hadn't scorched his cloak. His head was buried in his knees which he hugged tight to his chest, visibly shaking.

"That's your share of the meat you're burning up," I said, walking forward.

When he raised his face, I stopped at the sight of the tears streaking it. He stared at me as if I was a ghost. "You came back?"

"You didn't expect me to?"

He gulped a little. "I didn't know. There wasn't anything left here of yours, and . . ." His voice trailed off as his face drained of color. "What's that?" he asked, pointing a shaking finger at something behind me.

I threw a glance over my shoulder. "It's a donkey, Igal."

He lowered his head and didn't look up again, so I pulled the fire apart to let it die down, and cleaned up around the camp. The bird I'd left was inedible, so I threw it into the fire. "Have you filled your water cruse?" I asked.

"No, geber."

"There's a seep down there." I pointed. "Fill it now."

He unwound and limped in the direction I pointed.

I sighed. It was going to be a long day, and I wanted to catch up to Ishvi again. I'd just remembered that I had some news important enough to risk my neck over.

Early the next morning, I waited outside the sar's camp. Yesterday in between irritations at Igal, I'd decided that the best time to contact Sar Ishvi was during his morning time alone before he ate.

True to his routine, he started out of camp after dressing. I'd guessed correctly the direction he would go, and was able to parallel his progress. Once out of sight of the camp, he stopped, folded his arms, and stood, watching the sunlight filter through the trees. After several minutes, he bowed his head.

He was at worship. The presence of Yah gradually rose around me, and I bowed my head also, knowing that no matter how urgent my errand, it could wait until the sar had finished. Soon he straightened, took one last look around, and then started toward to his tent.

I stepped toward him. "Don't turn around," I said.

Ishvi halted. "Is there something I can do for you, friend?"

"No, sar. You have already done more than I can repay," I responded quietly.

He moved.

"Do not turn." I commanded.

Slowly he spread his hands a little from his sides. "Then what do you want with me?"

"To ask that you carry two messages."

"If I can."

My voice shook when I spoke. "Please tell the king that Balak ben

Hod is now chief counselor to Yira of Moab. And if you would tell--tell Hassar Jonathan and Sahrah Michal that their thoughtfulness will always be remembered."

"You have recovered?" the sar asked. When I didn't answer, he added, "They will want to know."

"I am well, sar." I couldn't stop myself, and I knelt in the leaves behind him. "Take my love to them both, and my obeisance." I bowed.

"The hassar will rage at that," Ishvi said, his voice a little unsteady.

"It'll be good for him," I said, smiling. "Shalom, adoni sar."

CHAPTER 17

"Are you going to town tonight?" King Shaul asked Jonathan once court had dismissed for the day.

"I had planned to," the hassar replied. "Did you need me, abbi?"

"No, but you go many nights. You have found someone who pleases you?"

Jonathan felt his face redden slightly. "I have, adoni."

"Hmm." Shaul said nothing more.

Later, as Jonathan walked to Atarah's house, he wondered why abbi had asked where he was going. When he arrived, Keturah let him in, looking flushed, and there was a sparkle about the shy woman that he hadn't seen before.

"Come in, adoni," she said, standing aside. "I'll tell the geberet you're here. She has someone with her now."

Before long, Atarah entered. She was in his favorite green, and the perfume she wore blended with the aroma of the herbs she used. He needed her tonight, and her eyes promised that she would be there for him, but when he tried to go to the back room, her hand stopped him.

"There is someone you need to see," she said quietly, and took him to her consulting room.

Resigned, the hassar stole a quick kiss before opening the door. "Ishvi!" he said in surprise. "I didn't know you were back!"

"I just got here," his brother replied.

Jonathan closed the door. "If you've come to me this quickly, more must have happened down there than the survey reports you sent!"

"Yes. I'm afraid I lost a donkey."

The hassar's eyebrows rose. "Oh?"

"I know it was careless of me. Lost the pack on it, too. As near as we can tell, some Habiru ran off with it. I'll be reporting to Eshbaal tomorrow that it is missing."

"I must say, that was careless of you, Ishvi. You didn't happen to see who took it, did you?"

"No."

"Be more careful next time. What else?"

"I have two messages to convey. Incidentally, the people down there are extraordinarily shy, Jonathan. The man who gave me these messages didn't even want me to look at him. I respected his wishes of course, but it was rather odd."

Jonathan clenched his hands. "What are the messages?"

"The first is for the king. Balak ben Hod is chief counselor to Yira of Moab."

The hassar looked grim. "I'll have Ethan check that out. I want that news confirmed. And the next message?"

Ishvi knelt and bowed his head. "With the thanks of one who is well," he said.

The hassar stared a moment, then whirled around, slamming both palms into the wall. "How dared he!" he said in a choked voice, leaning on his hands.

Behind him, Ishvi rose and chuckled. "I mentioned that you'd rage. Those southerners are not just shy, but impertinent, too. That one had the gall to say this would be good for you."

Jonathan reached up to the twisted brass earring. "I'll make him pay for this!" he vowed. "Someway, I'll get this thing back down to him! And he better wear it!" He paused a moment. "Is he well?"

"He sounded fine. But he would not let me see him. Deliberately, I think."

"He would. That way if Abner or the king asked if you'd seen him, you could say no."

"I think he read some of the reports I sent you, Jonathan. Young Ishvi saw someone standing by our tent one night, just putting the message pouch back."

"Good. Those reports were a revelation to me. I hope they plant a few seeds in his mind, too. The south could be prosperous."

They stood in silence for a time, and then Ishvi broke it. "I stand with Malchi, Jonathan. I'll not hunt him. He saved my son out there, and risked being seen to tell us of Balak."

"I'll never ask you to search for him. He is in Yahweh's hands, and

I will never seek to take him out."

¥ ¥ ¥ ¥ ¥ ¥

How I ever made it back to Adullam with Igal in one piece I've never been able to determine. I'd never seen anyone so inept and helpless in my life. The man didn't even know the difference between dry wood suitable to burn and green wood that did nothing but make smoke and sizzle.

Eager to be back, I had increased my pace, Igal puffing at my heels, stumbling over every rock on the ground, and yelping whenever a branch whipped back into his face. When I had suggested that he follow a bit farther behind me, so that the branches bent in my passing wouldn't hit him, his eyes widened and he glanced at the donkey following him before agreeing. Two minutes later, he was back at my heels. I suppose I should have realized sooner than I did that he was terrified of everything around him, which fact explained his attachment to the fire once it was built, and most of his other irritating habits.

At noon I saw the blood on his leg wraps and discovered that his feet were a mass of blisters. We stopped at a stream so he could tend to them. He looked blank when I told him to take off his sandals and soak his feet. I came back sometime later to find he'd simply dunked his feet into the water, sandals, leg wraps, and all. Knowing what would happen to the leather if it didn't get oiled and dried immediately, I exploded.

"What are you doing, Igal?" I nearly yelled. "Get those sandals out of the water now!"

He jerked his feet out, and I grabbed an ankle, yanking his leg up, tumbling him on his back while I inspected the footwear. Fortunately, the leather had been well-cared for in the past so that not as much water had soaked in as I feared.

"Take the sandals and the leg wraps *off*, Igal. Then soak your feet, not your clothes!"

Turning a deep shade of red, he muttered, "Yes, geber," and started to tug at the sandal straps.

Igal limped back to the fire when I called him later, carrying the sandals and leg wraps.

"Why did you walk back here in your bare feet?" I demanded. "Now you've got sand and dirt on those blisters, and unless you wash it all off again, you're going to be even more uncomfortable! Go wash off, put on the sandals, and come back!"

As he looked down his face assumed that deep shade of red once more. "I don't know how," he muttered. "I've never had to do this before."

I'd never been so flabbergasted in my life. "You've never taken off your own sandals before?"

Miserably, he shook his head, holding them up. The straps were still tied. He had shoved them down his leg someway and pulled the sandals off.

"Where do you come from?" I asked in bewilderment.

"I lived in a city, with lots of servants," he said, his face going white and his hands shaking.

It was on the tip of my tongue to ask more, but the agony in his eyes stopped me. "Go back to the stream," I said instead, too dazed to think yet.

I spent the rest of the day finding out that Igal had told me the straight truth. He didn't know how to do the simplest things about anything, even caring for himself. Wondering where he really was from, I resigned myself to supervising someone who, for all practical purposes, was little more than an infant. We started with the basics, dressing. Once he got over thinking I was going to hit him for every mistake he made, he learned fast enough. But he was very clumsy. I made him uncomfortable, staring as I did, but I couldn't believe that someone could reach maturity and not know how to tie a sandal. Or put on a loincloth!

What with teaching Igal how to be at least as competent as a child, tending his feet, and slowing my pace to match his painful limp, it took a week to get back to Adullam instead of the two days I'd planned. I might have made it in three if Igal could have ridden our donkey, but he was too frightened of it.

Once back at my cave, he looked around in astonishment.

"You actually live here?"

"As do you," I said with some asperity.

"Yes, geber." His face reddened again. "Which part is mine?"

I pointed to a spot by my fire pit. "Right now, that part, because that's where you're going to be sitting."

He dropped down quickly, and I grabbed the large jug I used for water, heading down to the spring. Movement in the cave below told me I still had a neighbor, and a glimpse of his face said it was the same one. Once the jug was full, I set it aside, taking the time to scout around the area. Aside from animal tracks, including one from a large dog or small wolf, my neighbor and I seemed to be the only ones using it.

When I returned, I noticed the man standing at the mouth of his cave, staring at mine. Then the raised voices drifted down to me, and I wondered what sort of trouble Igal had found now.

"No! He told me to stay here. Ask him yourself when he gets back," he was protesting. "I don't know! He grabbed some big jar thing and went out. I don't know where."

I shifted the jug so that I could launch it off my shoulder if necessary and made certain my sword was loose in the sheath.

As I climbed the path up the hill, I listened with interest to the sounds coming from my cave. Someone was trying to get Igal to move, and the man refused with the obstinance worthy of a mule, or the hassar on occasion. Well, there was one thing I could say for him. He did what I told him to.

Coming into sight of the entrance, I identified Shagay's exasperated voice and noticed his son Jonathan lounging against a rock, watching the show.

"He told me to stay. I stay!" Igal protested again.

"He couldn't have meant right there!" Ahiam said reasonably. "And you still haven't told us who you are, and why you're in this cave. As you can see, someone already lives here."

"He said I did, and he pointed right here when he told me to sit down."

I stepped up behind a fourth person, staring over his shoulder to see my two retainers confronting Igal, who looked as if he'd grabbed onto the earth itself to keep from moving.

Jonathan saw me, his eyes wide with mirth, and a grin spread across his face.

"Move, Abishai, so Dod Dahveed can see," he whispered.

My nephew stepped aside.

Shagay and Ahiam were advancing on Igal, intent on removing him bodily from the cave. But no sooner had they grabbed him, then he jerked, or twisted, or yanked in some way, and they lost their hold. I watched with growing interest as the two Habiru tried again and again to hang onto Igal. He worked up a sweat escaping from their grasp, which only made him harder to hold onto. How did he do it?

I edged closer. Shagay had a good grip on the man's wrist, and I knew how tightly the big man could squeeze. But there was a flash of movement, Shagay's arm twisted in response, and then Igal was clawing his way back to the spot where I'd put him.

"He's worse than a wet fish!" Ahiam panted.

"And I know how to deal with fish," Shagay said, his voice angry. "Spear them!" He pulled his sword.

"That does seem a bit excessive, Shagay," I drawled.

Both retainers froze, and Abishai and Jonathan stifled their laughter.

"How long have you been there?" Ahiam asked sourly.

"Long enough to see that Igal here has some unexpected talents. One of which is that he does what he's told. Sit back there by the wall, Igal," I directed, pointing. "That way Ahiam can use the fire."

Instantly he shifted position.

"See, you just have to know how to talk to him." I put the water jug in its place. "How are Abbi and Immi, and why is Abishai with you?"

"They're well settled and Abishai insisted on coming," Shagay answered. "Don't tell me he's staying, adoni," he added, staring at Igal.

"As you've already learned, once he gets an idea into his head, it won't leave. If you can figure out how to separate him from me, let me know. I haven't found a way yet."

Igal sat like a stone, just his gaze shifting from speaker to speaker.

"Just throw him out!" Shagay said, looking as if he would do just that.

"That would be like throwing a child to the lions," I said resignedly.

"He doesn't seem like a child to me!"

"You have no idea how wrong you are, Shagay."

The next few days must have been a living nightmare for Igal. Shagay refused to notice that he existed, Jonathan had no use for him, and Ahiam treated him like a piece of furniture. I was gone much of the time, scouting the area, checking in with Elhanan and Ittai in Gedor, picking up what news I could, and wondering how I could earn my living. Only Abishai paid him any attention. He became the most adept at finding ways to show him what to do without being obvious about it.

One evening after Ahiam had left and Abishai was off somewhere with Jonathan, Igal spoke to me. "Geber, are they Habiru, also?"

"Ahiam and Shagay? Yes."

"But Abishai?"

"Not really. But he's lived most of his life in a small town, so he's spent considerable time in the fields and forests around it. How are your feet?"

He looked at them. "Mostly healed now, geber. I'll be able to walk soon." Then he began to stir restlessly, the first I'd ever seen him do that. "They call you 'adoni.'"

"Yes. I'm a dahveed to them."

"It's more than that."

I gave him a quick look.

Igal shrugged. "The dahveed is the war leader, right? But you command more than just their fighting skills. It's there, in their voices. And they never say your name, not when I can hear. Just the titles. I don't know what to call you."

"Dahveed will do."

He took a slow breath. "Dahveed, will you send me away when I can walk? To the town down there?"

I leaned back against the water jar. "I can't imagine that you want to stay, Igal. This is not what you're used to."

"No," he said with a half laugh. "But I don't want to go. You've seen me," he said reddening again. "I can't even do the things most children do. The only reason I can do what I can now is because Abishai has shown me so much. But I can learn more, I think." Nervously he rubbed one finger up and down a little trough in the dirt. "I don't have anywhere to go, Dahveed. If you let me stay, maybe I can learn enough to be useful."

His face was white now, like it had been there in the forest. I wondered once more where he had come from and what he *was* used to. Staring at him, I realized that I couldn't send him away any more than I could have a child. "It won't be easy, Igal."

A shrug. "Nothing's easy anymore."

"My life is very uncertain. You could die tomorrow if you remain with me."

"I should have died a long time ago, Dahveed. Death is the one thing that's not new to me."

His matter-of-fact tone sent a momentary chill up my back. "All right, Igal. You stay. I'll tell Ahiam you'll help him for a while."

He had to swallow twice before he could speak. "Thank you, Dahveed."

"Don't thank me yet," I replied gently. "You may have made the worst bargain of your life."

The next day, Elhanan appeared in the valley below the cave, and I went down to him.

"Shalom, Elhanan. What brings you here? Is Ittai all right?"

The former innkeeper grinned. "He's fine. But my cousin is in a ferment of anxiety wondering if you are going to take him away again. That young man has already sold all the wool my cousin has, and it's not even sheared yet! He talked the local scribe into showing him what he knew about cuneiform, saving my cousin the price of paying the scribe. Did you know that he could read and write script?"

"It doesn't surprise me."

"He reviewed every clay tablet and papyrus scrap my cousin had stuffed in that jar he keeps them in, found that four times we'd been shorted on payments, another payment that we only had a week left to make or we'd lose half the grape harvest, and one more contract for leather from the tanner that everyone had forgotten about, including the tanner! And then he went to the people that owed us, and came back with every copper. And how he managed to get our payment from the stingiest man in town, no one can figure out. Although I think he had to go there twice." My old friend eyed me. "You don't seem surprised at any of this."

"Considering my own experiences with Ittai, I don't think anything would surprise me," I replied wryly. "I was fortunate that Yahweh led me to him. Is Ittai content?"

"He told me he enjoyed the work."

"Then you can soothe your cousin's anxiety. Ittai can stay as long as he wishes," I decided. And he'd be safer up there. Neither Gath nor Ekron was that far away from Adullam. "Any other news?"

"Are you still interested in serving as a courier?"

"I'm interested in anything that will keep me fed and supplied with necessities."

My boyhood friend laughed. "Good. My cousin complained that there aren't any reliable messengers in the area, and he's been keeping me busy since I don't mind the travel. A couple neighbors have asked if I'd deliver for them, and that's when Ittai suggested we start a courier service."

"I'm willing. I'll just have to be careful where I go."

"Ittai thought you could operate a route between Adullam to Keilah to Nezib and once a week farther south. And maybe Shagay's Jonathan could run between here and Gedor every day."

"Let's try it. If we charge a copper a message, we should be able to earn our keep."

"I've been considering something, Dahveed," Elhanan said, wiping his hand across his eyes. "I'm alone now. I've been the innkeeper in Bethlehem too long to be accepted as anything else, and I'm an extra in my cousin's household. He'd never turn me out, but I don't really belong. I've only felt once as if I really belonged anyplace."

His words brought to mind my own feelings the night the hassar had wished that I could be in his service, even though he hadn't known who I was.

"Let me swear to you, Dahveed."

My head jerked up.

"Those years in Bethlehem, when you and I were friends, are the only time I've ever felt as if I belonged."

"Elhanan, the king wants to kill me! I live in a cave with barely enough to keep me alive! I may be on the run again before dawn. Who wants to live like that?"

He looked up with a wry smile on his face. "So, what's changed? The enemies are bigger and more dangerous, but we're bigger too. And you still know the back way to anywhere. Let me swear, Dahveed. You're the only link I have left."

How could I refuse? He was more alone than I was. So I'd have four retainers instead of three. I could see in his eyes what it would mean to him.

"All right. Come for the evening meal. In the meantime, pass the word of the service we're starting."

That afternoon Ahiam sent Shagay and Jonathan off to hunt meat for the swearing and set things up out on the ledge in front of the cave, since there wouldn't be enough room inside for everyone.

Igal watched, looking tired from his first day of more strenuous activity, but I was glad to see that Ahiam only asked for things that Igal could do and remained aware of the man's limitations.

"Dahveed?"

"Yes, Igal?"

"If I'm staying on, I might as well swear too, shouldn't I?"

I winced, knowing that I'd lost this argument before it even started. But I tried anyway. "Not necessarily."

"But it's just a formality, right? Just publicly saying what's already happened?"

Knowing it was useless, I gave in without any more protest. "I suppose you can swear also."

"Good," he said with satisfaction, retreating back into the cave.

Ahiam looked at me sidewise and then turned back to the stew he was making.

"What else could I say?" I asked defensively.

"Nothing, adoni."

"I mean, it's only two more, right?"

"Right."

"Just four retainers. That's not a lot."

"Don't forget the hassar's body guard." He stirred the pot again.

"Josheb's not here, and likely won't be, especially if he marries Keturah." I looked at Ahiam for confirmation.

"You never know, adoni," my retainer said with a straight face.

"I know," I said positively. "Just these two. No more."

"Whatever you say, adoni."

Shagay, Jonathan, and Abishai returned with a small deer. Ahiam expertly cut and spitted the pieces, with Igal watching him closely. The smell drifted down into the valley by the time Elhanan and Ittai arrived.

"Shalom, Elhanan!" Jonathan called. "Nice of you to come. We're having a swearing ceremony. Abishai and I get to swear to Dahveed!"

My mouth dropped open.

"Really?" Elhanan said, grinning. "And here I thought I was the one swearing to Dahveed."

Jonathan grinned. "Welcome to the band, Elhanan!"

I looked at Ahiam's expressionless face. "Did you know about this?" I hissed at him.

"Something might have been mentioned in my hearing."

"I can't let them!"

"How can you not, Dahveed?" Ahiam's tone reminded me of when he'd tried to tell me how to act at Chephirah, and it stopped me cold. "What will Jonathan feel, to say nothing of Shagay, if you refuse him? Isn't he worthy to be sworn to you? And what about Abishai? Considering what his brother has done, who else would take him? You're his only hope for any sort of honorable life. Are you going to tell him no?"

"Yah, how do I get into these messes?" I asked under my breath. I'd swear I heard laughter in reply!

Resigned, I went out to the ledge and sat down in the place of the chief. Shagay and Ahiam had places on either side of me, since they were already sworn to me. Ittai sat a little behind and to my right in the place of a son. All four of the others took positions on the other side of the fire, and when Ahiam brought the meat, I took it and stood up. "May Yahweh witness what we do here," I began. Then I sliced a piece of the meat and set it aside for myself, supplying Shagay, Ahiam, and Ittai with some also. Cutting another one, I said, "Abishai ben Jesse, to you does this cut belong. Whose son are you?"

He took the meat from me and knelt. "I am Abishai ben Dahveed, and I accept this token for I am a true son of the Dahveed."

Then I turned to Jonathan with another piece. "Jonathan ben Shammah, to you does this cut belong. Whose son are you?"

"I am Jonathan ben Dahveed," he said, taking the meat from my hand as he too knelt, "and I accept this token for I am a true son to the Dahveed."

Next I faced Elhanan, then Igal, and at last sat down, picking up my own piece. We ate in silence, and then Ahiam brought out the rest of the food. Before long, Elhanan had Abishai, Jonathan, and Ittai laughing so hard at stories about me as a boy, that the three of them couldn't eat.

I looked over the group, and then back at Ahiam. "This is it," I said. "Absolutely no more!"

"Yes, adoni."

Our courier service caught on quickly, keeping both Elhanan and me busy. After the third day, his cousin asked if someone could carry messages in Gedor itself, and I sent Abishai up. He learned the streets and layout of the clan houses quickly, and with his attention to detail and quiet manner, he soon had more than enough to do every day. The three of them came down to Adullam every Shabbat, bringing news from the highlands, and asking about what was happening in the Shephelah and the lowlands. Soon I had to give the Adullam-Nezib route to Jonathan, for there were enough messages to towns such as Beth-Zur, Hebron, and even Jezreel for me to begin a twice a week route for that area.

One Shabbat back at Adullam I wandered down to the spring with Grandmother's harp and tuned the strings. I'd never had the chance to play the song that I'd composed in the cell in Gath, or the one from the cave in Elah, and I had another one flickering in and out of my mind that I wanted to try.

I played softly, working toward the right starting point for the song from Gath, and cocking my head to listen to myself as I sang it for the first time. It sounded almost as I'd expected it would, but I altered the melody in two places before I was satisfied and played it through twice to memorize it.

The silence of the forest around me reminded me of the silence in Akish's throne room when I'd first acted insane. A smile quirked my mouth, as I wondered how many of the courtiers worried about eating the left sides of their pigs every time they had pork. Then I sobered. I was alive because I'd been covered by Yahweh's hand that day. That and Akish's unaccountable actions in not ordering my execution. Was it possible the covenant his nephew had made with me had that much of a hold on him?

Thinking of the verses I'd already composed, I realized each one began with a different letter of the script alphabet. Why not make this one an acrostic by starting each verse with a successive letter? I'd never done that before, and the challenge inspired me.

Remembering the night in the cell, I started with that.

"Guard your tongue from evil and your lips from speaking deceit.

The eyes of Yahweh are toward the righteous and His ears are open to their cry for help.

The face of Yahweh is against doers of evil to eliminate from the earth mention of them."[10]

They were good verses and started with different letters, but they weren't in the correct order. Writing a song this way would take some time.

I looked up to see my neighbor staring at me, the first he'd ever approached me. "Shalom," I greeted warily. He was older than I, stocky in build, and with dark brown hair.

"You are Habiru? The others with you, they are Habiru?"

I smiled slightly. "Yes."

He edged closer. "But they call you adoni. And they swore to you, like honorable men."

"They are honorable men," I said coldly, rising and putting the harp into its case.

"Not many call them so." Reaching back, he rubbed his head. "And that new one, who couldn't move around much. You accept him?"

"Yes." I stepped forward, slinging the case onto my back, and he stood in my way.

"But he's not of Israel."

---

[10] Psalms 34

"How do you know?" I asked, curiosity stirring.

The man snorted. "The accent is too marked to miss. He's from one of the cities in Zobah."

Zobah? The kingdom north and west of Dan was a long way from here. What was Igal doing this far south?

"You accepted him?" my neighbor pushed again.

His own words had an odd twist as if the vowels were longer somehow, and he couldn't quite pronounce some sounds correctly. His demanding questions puzzled me. "Yes."

His dark eyes searching and intent, he studied me. "Then I would swear to you, too. If you will take the man from Zobah, you will take me. I am not of Canaan."

"I'm Habiru," I reminded him. "You will find little honor or place outside of my company."

"I have nothing now, but I know much that would be useful to you. I am trained in war and military organization. I can teach, and some of those with you need instruction!"

That was true, but I didn't want another retainer. I had too many now, and I didn't need the responsibility of one more mouth to feed.

"I don't think it would be a good idea," I said, starting to leave again.

"You must accept me," he insisted.

"Why?" I asked, irritated.

"Because it is in you to take in those who have need. You do not care who they are, or why they have need. You receive them."

Unable to meet his steady stare, I looked down. He'd never even spoken to me before! How could he know this? But he did, and he wouldn't go away, and I was going to accept him, too. I sighed. "If you insist. Just know that your life may be short if it is tied to mine."

"I think that will depend on you, adoni."

The title told me he'd made up his mind. "All right. Where are you from, and how are you called?"

"I'm a Hittite. My name is Uriah."

After the swearing that evening as we all sat around the fire on the ledge, Ahiam gave me another look. I returned it disgustedly. "This is absolutely the last one! There will be no more! The only way I'll accept another retainer is if he falls from the sky!"

Ahiam glanced upward suspiciously. "Whatever you say, adoni."

CHAPTER 18

Shaul leaned away from the low table, one hand stroking his beard. "Things are quiet tonight."

Jonathan pulled his mind away from the report that had come in with another indication that the Steward of Tahat was in the north. "It makes a nice rest before the war season," he answered.

The king chuckled a little. "True, but do you know what we need around here?"

"What?"

"Children. It's too quiet. There should be children running around, getting in the way, like you boys used to, and Merab's sons do."

"Rizpah's two sons spend much time here," Jonathan pointed out.

"Yes," his abbi sounded doubtful. "But it's time you married, Jonathan. I have been remiss in not tending to this sooner."

The hassar froze an instant. What had put this train of thought in his abbi's mind? "I don't mind," he shrugged. "I've been able to concentrate on tending the kingdom."

"And you need an heir to take the kingdom after you."

Jonathan suppressed the pain the words caused. Would Abbi never accept that Yahweh had given away the kingdom?

"I also need to find a suitable husband for Michal. She is pining away into nothing, and I'll have Ahinoam demanding that I do something soon."

"Michal has a husband," Jonathan said quietly.

"He seems to have abandoned her, so we will find someone more worthy. Put this on the agenda of business, Jonathan. Michal needs someone, and I don't want grandchildren who are half Jebusite!"

"Yes, adoni." The hassar fought to keep his face expressionless.

There was only one way Shaul could have discovered that Atarah was a Jebusite, Jonathan thought as he strode out of the fortress gates, followed by two of his guards. He turned down the west road to the barracks where the eight men of his personal guard stayed. Throwing open the door, he stalked in, startling the five men in various stages of undress, and Abiezer was already in bed.

"Get up," he ordered, his voice smooth.

The men scrambled to their feet, watching him with alarm.

"Which one of you talked?"

Six pictures of astonishment greeted his gaze, but as he stared at the men, he felt a subtle chill on his left shoulder and darkness hovered at the edges of his vision. Without a word, he reached around and twisted his hand in the shirt of his escort, dragging the man in front of him.

"Anything you want to tell me, Azmaveth?" he asked quietly.

The man trembled under his hand, and his spear clattered to the floor. "He-he took my son, Pelet, adoni. What else could I do?" he whispered.

"Who?"

"Adon Abner. Last month," he said, sinking to his knees. "Some of the king's soldiers came to my house. They said my wife had requested that my son be sent to Abner's estate. I didn't know what to say, adoni. She may have. She has no love for Dahveed."

Jonathan studied the man's face. "That's right, your wife is close kin to Bichri, of Gera's clan. But if I recall, Roeh Shamuel sent Bichri to Dodi Ner in disgrace. What does that have to do with the Dahveed?"

"Dahveed attacked Bichri, adoni."

"Only after the fool attacked Dahveed first," Jonathan said in disgust. "But knowing that family in the clan, I can't imagine that made any difference."

"No, adoni," Azmaveth agreed miserably. "Hesed, please! Pelet didn't want to go. He looked so frightened when they took him. I could do nothing. They were from the king, adoni!"

As Jonathan looked into the man's pleading eyes, he throttled his rage. There was nothing Azmaveth could have done, but the fact that Abner would resort to such tactics infuriated him.

The other men in the room stood as silent and still as the stones in the walls.

The hassar took a deep breath, his hand twisting tighter in his guard's shirt. "Anyone else want to say anything?"

No one spoke. Slowly he released the man. "All right, Azmaveth. We'll do nothing now. I would not endanger your son. Continue to report to Abner as if nothing has happened. I'll decide what to do with you eventually."

"Thank you, adoni. I will be as blind and deaf as I can. And I will tell you of anything that may involve Dahveed, Hassar. I have a brother in the permanent forces who is alive because of him. We have not forgotten."

"Very well, Azmaveth. Pick up your spear." Doing an abrupt about-face, he exited out the door.

Thankfully, no one was with Atarah when he arrived.

She took one look at his face and held out a hand. "Come in, Jonathan."

He let her lead him through the door, then stopped, catching her hand and pulling her to him.

"What is it?" she asked, her voice muffled by his robe.

"The king has decided that I should marry," he said, tightening his arms around her. But when he tried to continue, he couldn't.

Atarah pushed herself away a little. "He won't accept me as your wife?"

The hassar shook his head silently, blinking back tears.

She remained motionless a moment, then looked up at him. "Kings can be like that, so let us not waste the time we have now."

When Jonathan left her house early the next morning, he hurried directly to Tanhum's house, arriving just as the women were leaving to get water. One of them informed the Jebusite that the hassar had come.

As always, Jonathan braced himself for the sight of the man's face. The disfigurement was so terrible that Tanhum never left the confines of his house and courtyard.

"How may I serve you, Hassar?" he asked in his hoarse voice.

"I need to make arrangements for Atarah," Jonathan said. "The king has decided I should marry, and he will not accept her as my wife."

"A not unexpected development," the man said slowly. "What sort of arrangements?"

"I want to provide for her as a proper wife."

The Jebusite gave him a startled look. "That will take some doing, Hassar. Especially if this is to be done quietly?"

"Very quietly. I believe my richest lands are in the north, around Shechem?"

"Yes."

"Deed enough to her to keep her as I have said. I'm sure you can arrange for the proceeds and reports from the land to pass through your hands every year."

"Easily enough, Hassar. Atarah already uses me in her business."

"Good. Make whatever arrangements you need, Tanhum. Your daughter has been more to me than I can say, and I do not know that I will be able to see her again."

"You have meant much to her, Hassar. She has said so. She, too, knew someday this would happen. I will take care of everything."

"You're a good man, Tanhum. Debir was a fool to waste your

talents." He left.

When Jonathan was gone, the scribe raised a hand to his face, an odd smile on what was left of his mouth. "Not such a fool as you believe, Hassar," he sighed, as his benefactor left the house.

Ziba, his son, immediately entered. "So, he's cast her off," he said tightly.

"Only because he must. And he has dealt very generously with her and us. We have nothing to complain of in his honor."

"He should have at least tried to convince Shaul," Ziba protested.

"He picks his battles wisely," Tanhum replied. "And an open breach with his abbi would weaken the entire kingdom, something he cannot risk now. And to save his people from harm, he will accept personal loss and pain. Do not cross him, Ziba. One day, he will roar, and the land will never be the same."

¥ ¥ ¥ ¥ ¥ ¥

I stretched on the cave's ledge in the early dawn light of Shabbat. Harvest was nearly in, and Shagay's Jonathan said that the Philistines were stirring on the plains. It seemed odd not to be getting ready for war season. I had the feeling that I should be stepping up the last of the training schedules for the second unit, and seeing to the details of a call to arms.

Instead, I was wondering what surprises Uriah would spring on me this week! When he said he was trained in military craft and organization, I'd only half believed him, but I quickly learned that he never exaggerated anything. I'd heard tales of the military might of the Hittite empire which was at its height before the time of the judges, and after watching Uriah this past winter, I could see why. I'd never seen a man so organized and meticulous about his possessions. Ahiam was the first to appreciate what he saw, and my cave took on a distinctly similar look to Uriah's. But he could now pack my essential possessions in just moments.

However, it was Uriah's teaching skill that took us all by surprise. Once things settled into a routine, Shagay had begun regular practices with Ahiam, Jonathan, and me, with Igal hanging on the sidelines and Elhanan, Abishai, and Ittai joining in when they were down from Gedor.

Uriah had observed for a few days, and then taken Igal aside and began working with him. Ahiam had kept an eye on them, and then told me I should watch sometime.

"What is he doing?" I had asked curiously.

"I've only heard of this in stories," Ahiam had said, "but I think Uriah knows the training of the shalishim."

I'd never heard the word before. "Something to do with 'three?'" I asked.

Ahiam nodded. "My grandfather used to speak of it. The shalishim were elite, highly-trained warriors who fought in groups of three. The training was supposed to come from the northwestern lands, perhaps beyond the Great Sea. Grandfather always suspected that it was Hittite since it demanded such a high level of discipline, but he never knew for certain. What he did know was that the Hittites had a highly-trained and disciplined army. The king's body guard was the highest level, then the professional troops, filled out by calls to arms and mercenaries as needed."

As Ahiam had talked, I had studied the way Uriah worked with Igal, patiently instructing him in nearly every move to make. "What makes you think Uriah knows this training?"

"Listen to his explanations. He is preparing Igal to fight with two companions, and he's demanding a very high level of response from him. We Habiru fight mostly as individuals, so such attention to who is beside you is unnecessary. But if three men are to be trained to fight as one, they must always be aware of what the other two in the shalish are doing. Grandfather said a good group of shalishim could routinely rout larger and better equipped forces."

The value of knowing such a form of combat didn't have to be pointed out to me, and I observed closely, more and more intrigued. I soon wondered how I could involve Shagay in this, given the value he placed on Ethan's style of teaching. But I had a feeling that I'd need something more than just Habiru tactics before Yahweh was done with me.

Two months later, I had found a way. One afternoon when I had no messages to deliver, I decided to test Igal's progress. "Spar with me a while," I invited, drawing my sword.

Uriah jerked his chin forward in encouragement, and the northerner put his sword at ready. I circled, studying the way he moved as he turned. Uriah had done a good job, for Igal held his defensive position well. Shifting my sword in a small circle to signal I was going to use it, I struck at him. Although he jumped back, his sword met mine even so.

"Harden up your guard," I said.

The next time I struck, he met my blow firmly. I kept him busy for the next five minutes, finding him about the equivalent of the older boys in Ethan's band. But considering what Uriah had started with, this was indeed progress.

Stepping back, I smiled. "Well done, Igal."

His back straightened, and he flushed with pride.

"I noticed you are teaching him to fight as one of a pair," I said to Uriah. "Show me what he knows that way."

Uriah gave me one of his steady looks, and silently drew his sword, stepping up on Igal's right side. I again circled, studying how they moved as a pair. Without warning, I thrust, and Uriah parried easily, driving my point down. I barely slipped it from under in time to meet the strike from Igal. The fact that I did caused a look of surprise in Uriah's eyes. As my sword danced in front of me, I knew that when Igal improved, I'd need my gift to best the two of them.

Then Ahiam stepped up on my left, and the pace picked up, Uriah sweating as he covered for his weaker partner. Then, without warning, a sword point snaked toward me. My shout of surprise as I jumped back brought Jonathan on the run.

Panting, I stared at Igal. How had that happened? The corners of Uriah's mouth quirked up.

"Do it again," I said, stepping forward and repeating roughly the same moves that had led up to that moment. Even expecting it, that sword came near to touching me as I leaped back the second time.

"Shagay, come here, and tell me how this happens! I can't see it," I called to my retainer, who'd been napping in the shade.

Yawning, Shagay walked over. We began, and once more, I saw Uriah's sword, blocked it, and the next instant had to leap back from the point of Igal's blade. Ahiam continued his thrust toward Igal, and Uriah's sword parried, giving Igal the time he needed to recover.

Shagay stood back. "He'd get killed doing that in a real battle, unless he could be sure someone would cover for him," he commented.

"Take Ahiam's place," I said. "See if you get the same feeling I have. It's like fighting one person with four arms."

Shagay and I made heavy going for the two, but with Igal's very best effort, they held us off.

I stopped the bout and turned to Shagay. "Can you imagine what it will be like when Igal is better?"

The big Habiru nodded. "It was harder to break through than I thought it would be."

"Is there any way we could work some of this into the Habiru style?" I asked. "You know it better than anyone. It would mean some changes, but it might be worth it."

Uriah, thank Yahweh, said not a word, simply waiting for Shagay's opinion.

"We could," he said at last. "But it seems like . . ." his voice trailed off. "Didn't someone used to talk about something like this from the north?" Shagay asked, turning to Ahiam.

"What came to my mind was shalishim," Ahiam replied neutrally.

"If Uriah knows some of that, it would be useful, Dahveed," my first retainer said bluntly. "Your training has turned Shaul's professionals into something worth fighting, and if the king catches up to us, we're going to need all the help we can get." He turned to Uriah. "How much do you know?"

The Hittite's eyes flickered. "Enough to keep people busy for a while," he said without expression.

I had to look away. I'd bet my sword that man knew every bit of shalishim training there was, and I intended to have as much of it out of him as I could get.

As the weeks passed, Uriah and Shagay hammered out a style of fighting that blended the best of the Habiru with the discipline and awareness of the shalishim, producing something that challenged them both and turned us into much better fighters. I was almost sorry there would be no Philistines to fight this year so that I could see how we did in a real battle.

Now, I finished my stretches and wound my sling on my arm. I needed to hunt today. Nine men ate a lot. Thank Yahweh I didn't have any more sworn to me. I knew Uriah wanted additional men to form into proper shalishim, but my mind was made up on that score. Nine of us were too many.

I had a successful hunt, and Elhanan, Ittai, and Abishai brought fresh bread and dried figs with them for our evening meal.

"The call to arms has gone out," Elhanan said after we'd eaten out on the ledge, and I had played a couple songs. "General Abner and Sar Malchi will be leading the army again. And there are rumors that Shaul is looking for a wife for the hassar."

"That is news!" I exclaimed. "I know Jonathan wants a son."

"I thought he had one," Shagay said, looking at me.

"He deserves one of his blood, Shagay."

"Yes, he does," my retainer agreed, his eyes straying to the head of his own Jonathan, who was discussing something with Abishai.

"What else do rumors say?" I asked Elhanan.

My friend looked uncomfortable. "That Jonathan isn't the only one slated to be married. Sahrah Michal might be given in marriage before long also."

I stared into the fire. The king meant for my exile to be permanent, then.

"I'm sorry, Dahveed," he added.

A surprised cry echoed around us, and something slid down the hill, launching itself into the air and landing by the fire, then tumbling into my lap and knocking my harp over on some rocks. I grabbed for it, afraid that it would have another dent, when the pair of astonished eyes staring at me widened as another yell echoed, and the man who'd just fallen down the hill yanked his legs out of the fire, bowling me over backward and sending us both rolling down the hillside behind me.

By the time I stopped my descent, I was angry enough to kill the first thing I could get my hands on, and the shouts of laughter up on the ledge didn't help any. Locating the idiot who had tumbled me down here by the noise he made, I seized his clothes and yanked up. Too wild to speak, I hauled him back up the hill, debating what I'd do to the eight witnesses up there still gasping with mirth.

When I got to the ledge, I threw him into the circle, nearly sprawling him on the fire for the second time. Sputtering with rage, I glared at him, then at my now silent men.

Ahiam sighed. "Well, Dahveed, you did specify that the next one had to fall from the sky. But it might be easier if you'd quit dictating how Yahweh has to send you more men."

The mention of Yahweh replaced my rage with stupefied realization. I looked into Abishai's dancing eyes, and did the only thing I could. "Yahweh, grant me hesed!" I groaned, collapsing on the ground, sitting there until the explosion of laughter around me finally died.

By the time we had collected ourselves enough to think of our unexpected guest, he had pulled himself into a sitting position, nursing various bumps and bruises.

"I beg your hesed, geber," he said sincerely. "It was an accident. I've been looking for Adullam all day, and sat down to rest. The next thing I knew, it was dark. I saw your fire and was trying to come down to it when I slipped, and then I was *in* your fire, and I just tried to get out. Are you hurt?"

"Not much. How about you?"

"Oh, I'll be all right," he assured me. "I grew into clumsy as a boy, and never did grow out, so I'm used to it. It's other people I scare. I'm from Benjamin, Zalmon is my name."

Shagay's sword appeared in his hand, and both Jonathan and Ahiam were on their feet, ready to fight.

I raised my eyebrows. "And after telling me Yahweh has dumped him into my lap, you're ready to kill him? That seems just a little incongruous, doesn't it?"

"He's from Benjamin, and that means Shaul!" Shagay said tightly.

Zalmon looked around, worry creasing his forehead. Then he looked back at me and gasped. "You're the Dahveed! I mean, you're the hassar's Dahveed, not just a regular dahveed, and . . ." He stopped, his mouth open, and glanced around again. "Oh." he said, frightened now.

"And what were you doing this far south?" I asked. "Sit down, Ahiam. You too, Jonathan."

"I was just passing through," the Benjamite said, trying to keep his voice steady. "Headed on further south into the Negev, or maybe Egypt." He cast a look at Shagay still holding his sword. "If you'll just point the way south, I can go right now."

"I'll never get a decent answer from him so long as you loom over him like death, Shagay. Put the sword away," I commanded. "If Yahweh dumped him into my lap, he won't threaten me."

Unwillingly, my retainer shoved the sword back into its sheath.

I turned back to Zalmon. "You were saying?"

"Well, I was, actually, odd as it seems, I was rather meaning to, uh, it's such a coincidence, but I was sort of, uh, looking for you."

"Whatever for?"

"Well, you see, my town is right at the bottom of the drop to the Arabah, and we do a lot of trade with Jericho. And I was in Jericho one day, and got into rather a mess, like just now, and one of the adons there wasn't very understanding, like you're being," he added, looking around timidly. "And he made trouble for me with the elders at home, saying he wouldn't buy any of our products so long as I was around. The other elders overruled my clan and said I'd have to leave. And when I asked where was I supposed to go, someone said if I couldn't think of anything else, I could go find Dahveed. Then I could either get rich by selling him to the king, or he'd kill me. In either case they'd be rid of me.

"And, well, I couldn't think of anything else, so I started south. You weren't in Bethlehem, but I'd heard someone say there were lots of caves at Adullam, and that seemed like a good place to hide, so I've been looking for Adullam."

I shook my head. People like this were frightening. They were as direct as a child, and too often came to better conclusions than other people did. Then again, Yahweh undoubtedly had a hand in this, too.

"Sounds as if the elders were more than ready to throw you out, Zalmon. Is there more to that story?"

"Yes," he admitted. "My clan has had the best deals from the merchants in Jericho for several years."

"And the rest of the town was envious and evened the honor balance by pouncing on you."

"Yes."

I picked up my harp, finding the new dent on the crossbar and sighed. If this kept up, Uriah would have all the men he wanted for shalishim. With the war season about to begin, there would be less opportunity to provide courier service, and we were barely getting along now.

¥ ¥ ¥ ¥ ¥ ¥

Gebirah Abigail looked around the upper room in the compound by Carmel's gate. The dais at the far end had three steps, fringed hangings backed it, and the inlaid three-legged chair was covered with a leopard skin. Carpenters were working on the tables she had ordered, one for a scribe, a small one to go beside the throne, and a large one for the nagid to eat at if he wished, perhaps with a visitor or two. They were all elaborately carved, the one by the throne inlaid on the top.

She was spending freely, but after that look in the treasure room, she knew she could afford to. That was only part of Nabal's wealth, and she would only use about half of what was there by the time she finished with this room. More hangings were ordered for the walls, and there would be rugs on the dais and under the tables.

Hezro came in, looking around in disgust at the clashing colors.

"What do you think, Commander?" Abigail asked.

"Begging your indulgence, Gebirah, it seems a bit garish."

"A very restrained comment. But the nagid will like it."

"Of that I have no doubt."

"Gebirah, Hadar is here," a guard announced.

"Very good. Show him up."

The Ishmaelite trader entered the room, then stopped in amazement, staring around at the use to which his wares had been put. After several moments of silence, he closed his mouth and turned to the Gebirah. "Shalom, Baalah."

"Shalom, Hadar. Do you bring news of the silver lamps?"

"Yes. They are on the way from Gezer and should be here in a day or two."

"What of the other hangings?"

"I have had no word, but they are probably en route from Damascus, so they will take longer to arrive. Please pardon my curiosity, Baalah, but is this for a wedding or special celebration?"

"No," Abigail said serenely. "This will be my husband's business chamber. What do you think of it?"

Hadar looked around again, struggling to find words. "It will be unique, I'm sure. Spoken of by all, no doubt."

"That's what I thought," the Gebirah replied. "Did you receive the latest payment?"

"Yes, Baalah. I have the receipt here, and that settles your account."

"It's been a pleasure doing business with you, Hadar. I will certainly call on you if I want anything else."

The trader bowed. "You are gracious, Baalah." He left, giving one last shudder as he went out the door.

Abigail watched him go. "Do you think others will feel the same as he did?" she asked Hezro.

"May I speak plainly, Gebirah?"

"Please do."

"This room will be ridiculous when it is done. Things like these are meant for the palaces of empires."

"But once he has seen it, do you think Nabal will work here?"

Hezro slowly turned his head to her, dawning understanding in his eyes. "I can't imagine you'd get him out of it. It will be the perfect setting for him. People will take his silver, cater to his wishes, and pay no further attention to him. But what of your people, Gebirah?"

"I will have to learn a great deal in a very little time, commander."

That night after the meal, Nabal sat back from the low table, drinking his fourth cup of unmixed wine. "I got the last of them today," he announced. "Tokhath told me that Ahlai of Jezreel is in debt again, placing him in my power if I bought them all up. They come to quite a sum." He rubbed his hands together, chuckling. "I'm going tomorrow to Jezreel to collect."

"Has Ahlai returned from his business trip?"

"No."

"How can you collect?"

"I probably can't. So his lands will be forfeit. He left some woman in charge of his estate. My informant says the estate is stretched to the limit, having to buy food because of the famine last year and paying off the debts of that youngest son. The woman doesn't know about the debts I've bought up! You will accompany me, of course."

Abigail looked into the wine goblet she held. Now that the business chamber was completed, she would have to convince the nagid to travel less.

"Wouldn't it be better to let the man come to you?" she asked carefully. "You are Nagid Carmel, after all."

"Not this time, Gebirah. I wish to appear before the elders. They will grant me the land since the debts cannot be paid."

"If you're sure. It seems beneath you to run across the country after someone like this."

Her husband set his goblet down too hard. "Of course it is beneath me! Most of what I do is beneath me, but I'll have those lands!" His eyes flashed with anger.

She raised an eyebrow and calmly tasted her wine again. Without the additive, the wine made Nabal belligerent before he got sleepy. But she had planted a seed, which would sprout, especially after the trip to Jezreel. Nabal might find it harder than he expected to take all the lands of a Jezreel adon.

They left early in the morning with 10 guards.

"I didn't know the roads were this dangerous," Abigail said to Hezro as he handed her into the litter.

"They aren't," he said, his face tight. "We're along because Tokhath told Nabal that he should have enough men with him to teach the elders of Jezreel proper respect if they don't want to hand over the land."

As the brown curtains closed around her, Abigail chewed her lip. What could she do if the debts could not be paid? Such an incident as this would have repercussions throughout the Calebite clans, none of them good. In order for Tokhath to have advised this, he must not understand the structure of the clan alliances, or else didn't care.

They arrived in Jezreel in the late afternoon, staying at a house outside of town whose owner owed silver to Nabal. Abigail had deliberately not reminded him of the obligation to bring a gift, and the householder was hard put not to take offense, especially when Nabal got drunk on his best wine that night and kept the household awake expounding on everything he would do in the morning.

He was too sick to do anything in the morning, however, and it was not until after the noon rest that they left for Jezreel. Nabal's head still ached from the wine, and he didn't notice the looks of contempt that followed him out the gate.

When the litter stopped, and Hezro parted the curtains, Abigail stepped down to find the nagid sitting on his mule, which now had a bloody mouth, staring at the elders in the town market. "I have come to collect the debt owed to me by Ahlai," he announced. "I require payment of the entire amount immediately. Bring Ahlai to me at once."

"Adon Ahlai is traveling," a courteous female voice answered, and Abigail turned to see a young woman emerge from the crowd. "I am overseeing his house until he returns. How much is the debt he owes to you?"

"Ten gold pieces."

"Will you accept partial payment now?"

"No. The entire amount must be paid, or I shall be forced to take his land as forfeiture for the amount owed."

"Ten gold pieces will acquit the entire amount?"

Nabal looked down his nose at her. "I have said so."

"And we are witnesses," the town's head elder said.

"And if paid that amount you will have no claim on Adon Ahlai's lands?"

Abigail glanced at the woman again. Why would she specify all these details?

"*If* payment is made, which he cannot do, I will have no claim," her husband answered impatiently.

"We are witnesses," the elder spoke again.

Calmly, the young woman walked to the nagid and held up a pouch.

"You would approach me?" Nabal said, his voice angry.

"It is the only way I know to give you your payment," she said blandly, still holding up the purse.

Nabal stared at her. "Payment?"

"Yes."

"You cannot!" the nagid shouted. "Ahlai has no gold! His lands are mine!"

"Ahlai of Jezreel is not destitute! Here is your gold."

"This is a trick of some kind to rob me," he sputtered, yanking the reins of the mule, which humped its back and crow-hopped in protest. Nabal quelled it savagely.

Tired of holding the pouch, the young woman tossed it to the ground in front of Nabal and walked away.

While the Gebirah did not blame her for her act of contempt, she realized the nagid was capable of ordering Hezro to sack the town for it, and she did not want a public scene. Seeing her husband was too stunned to respond, Abigail seized the opportunity. "Nagid, it is hot," she said. "I require rest and refreshment. We will leave now. Hezro, send a guard to take our payment."

Returning to the litter, she seated herself and gestured for the bearers to move on. The litter lifted and Abigail clasped her hands tightly together, hoping no one could see how she was trembling. Her eyes closed in relief as the nagid nudged his mule after her.

CHAPTER 19

I should have remembered what Grandmother Ruth had said many times, I thought as I climbed the land stair on my way to Beth-Zur. Yah knows what we need and sees that we get it. With the beginning of war season, we actually had more messages to deliver than ever, and Shagay was taking supply caravans north to the army for the people in Gedor and the surrounding towns. I sent Zalmon, who had also sworn to me by now, with him, for the man was good with animals, and when they arrived at the war camp, the Benjamite passed through the lines without a question being asked.

Topping the ridge, I paused to look over the country and catch my breath before the quick two and a half miles to Beth-Zur. I delivered three dispatches there, then set a jog trot on the Hebron highway south for the eight and a half miles to Jezreel. I hoped the army would stay in the north this year. I didn't want to have to dodge Shaul's soldiers while I tried to deliver messages.

I reached my destination not long after the noon rest. At the town cistern I refilled my water cruse and took a long drink. A man on a mule escorted by several soldiers entered the square. I gave the brown litter that followed a curious glance, but didn't have time to stay in the market to see what was happening.

Familiar with the town by now, I went directly to a compound and knocked at the gate.

"Enter." The man working in the shade of a fig tree glanced up, recognizing me with a smile.

I delivered the message, then waited while the geber wrote his reply. By the time I left I decided to get some bread in the market when I passed through. But when I reached it, the market stalls were deserted, for everyone had crowded around the elders, listening intently. That curiosity habit reared its head, and I wandered over.

"After what she did, you tell us there is nothing?" the chief elder's voice rose clearly. "We were promised surety for our loan, and she has angered him even more!"

I edged closer. "How could you not know your own immi's dowry was missing? She deliberately deceived us! Adon Ahlai owes us five gold pieces in addition to the other debts."

"Adons, gebers, there was no way my sister could have known the jewelry from the dowry was missing! You know that when Adon Ahlai returns he will repay every copper, and--"

"No, we don't know that," the chief elder's cold voice rose again. "The adon does not have to deal with the stings of that scorpion Nabal, and he has cared nothing when *our* lands disappear. We will have surety, and of the best, for this loan."

I heard the sound of a body falling, and managed to approach close enough to see two town sentries lifting an unconscious man into a donkey cart.

"You, messenger, you are Habiru?" the elder called, looking directly at me.

"Yes, gebers," I replied, puzzled.

The rest of the elders glanced at each other. "We have a commission for you. It will pay well."

Yah's gift whispered in my mind, and I straightened, shrugging my shoulders a little. "How well?"

"Ten silver."

What did they want me to do for 10 days' wages, I wondered. "I can use 10 silver," I said cautiously.

"Take this man with you. We will tell you when to bring him to us again."

The whisper of Yah's gift grew, and I flexed my hands.

"What am I to do with him?"

"He is to be kept out of sight until he is redeemed. That means we need him alive," the elder said drily.

My gift intensifying, I stirred restlessly. I wanted out of this situation. "I know you are honorable men," I said, "but I am a poor one. You must pay in advance."

They hesitated, as I knew they would, and I turned away in relief.

"Wait!" the elder commanded. "Ten silver in advance."

A bit dazed, I collected the silver and, nearly driven by my gift, urged the donkey out of the town as fast as I could make it go. I had plenty of time to think about what had happened on the way home. None of it added up to anything good, and the mention of Nabal's name made me even more wary.

Before I reached the crossroads to Hebron, I drove the donkey off the road, hid the cart, and loaded the still-unconscious man on the donkey's back. Avoiding even the Habiru trails, I worked my way down the land-stair to the Shephelah, and then back to Adullam, arriving long after dark and nearly starved, for I hadn't had the chance to buy any bread in Jezreel's market.

Shagay found me by the spring early the next morning where I'd gone with my harp. On the way home yesterday, more verses for my acrostic song had come to mind, prompted by my hunger.

"Taste that Yahweh is good. Those who fear Him have no want. Young lions suffer hunger, but those who fear . . ."

I stopped. No, it didn't sound right. The cadence was off.

"Adoni, why is Zabad ben Ahlai in our cave?"

"I'm keeping him for the Jezreel elders until--What did you say his name was?" I ended quickly, jerking around.

"That man is Adon Ahlai's oldest son. He is also the best warrior in the clan. Why do we have him?"

"How do you know him?" I asked, bewildered.

"I know all the good fighters in the south, Dahveed."

"That's what they meant about surety!" I exclaimed, telling Shagay everything that happened. "I didn't question it when Yah's gift came on me, I just got out of town as fast as I could. I hope I didn't misinterpret what happened. Should I have refused to take him?"

"That may be the least of our worries, Dahveed," my retainer said soberly. "He still hasn't wakened. Ahiam checked him over, and whoever clubbed his head did a good job. Ahiam isn't certain he'll live."

I didn't want to even imagine what might develop if the son of a Cabelite adon died under my hand! "Well, all we can do is leave it in Yah's will and wait to see what happens," I sighed.

Shagay shook his head. "Rest assured, Dahveed, something will happen!"

It did, two days later, on Shabbat. By then I had one worry off my mind, for Zabad had wakened that morning, drank nearly a cruse full of water, and then fell into a natural sleep. He'd have a bad headache for a while, but he'd live.

We were just rousing from our noon rest when Jonathan entered the cave.

"Adoni, there's a woman down there. She's pretty, and she's alone."

"She can't be alone," I said reasonably, sitting up.

He stiffened. "I checked, adoni."

"I meant no disparagement of your skills, Jonathan," I apologized, rubbing the sleep from my face. I settled my clothes and walked to the entrance of the cave. Through the trees I could see a young woman, standing by the little stream that ran from the spring while a donkey drank from it. She was pretty.

"Wake up your abbi," I told Jonathan. "You two go out and make sure no one's hanging way back behind her. Out there in the open, she can be seen for at least a mile."

I waited until they had time to get well beyond the cave before starting down the slope.

She had taken a drink also and was resting on a rock when I stepped out of the trees.

"May I help you, geberet?"

She looked up quickly. "I hope you can. I'm looking for the Habiru courier who goes to Jezreel twice a week."

"May I ask why you wish to see him?"

She wore good-quality clothes, which were durable and would travel well. The donkey had been sensibly packed, and I noticed that her water cruse was still dripping. She must have filled it before drinking.

"My brother was with him when he left town. I understand he was ill. I've come to see about him."

I smiled, and she unaccountably blushed, looking down. "He'll be glad to see you," I said. "But he didn't wake until this morning. Whoever hit him nearly killed him."

She paled. "He was struck?"

"On the head. Are the town elders ready for him to be returned?"

"They, well, they might wait a day or two yet. I was only told he was ill. What happened?"

I checked the valley beyond her, thinking rapidly. She was fishing for information, so the elders hadn't told her much. However, she looked enough like the man in the cave to be his sister, and she'd risked coming alone to look for him, finding her way here somehow. I decided to be frank, so I told her what had happened at the gate as far as I knew it.

She was trembling by the time I'd finished. "Immi's jewelry gone? How can that be? I thought Zabad-- But that means--" Then her cheeks flushed. "Abbi took them!" she whispered. She looked at me. "If Zabad can travel, I'll take him back with me. I brought some gifts for your trouble. I hope they are enough," she gestured to the donkey.

Before I could answer, Jonathan burst from the trees at a run. "Cavalcade. Ten guards with adons, and they've got Abishai!"

"Ahiam! Uriah!" I shouted.

"Yes, adoni?" both answered.

"An armed group took Abishai. They're coming. Spread out!"

I turned to Jonathan. "Is Abishai all right?"

"He looked like it. He was out hunting, and they must have stumbled on him."

I jerked my chin toward the cave, and he disappeared. Uriah and Zalmon crossed the valley at a run to vanish in the trees on the far side, both carrying bows.

That left Ahiam, Igal, and Jonathan on this side with Elhanan and Ittai in the cave. Shagay would be behind the group, and I would be in front.

"If anything happens, you drop to the ground," I instructed the woman.

The group appeared in the trees, two adons on mules, three attendants on foot, and an escort of 10 armed men. I flexed my hand around the sling and brushed the loops to my first finger joints. I had four stones in my pouch always attached to my girdle. My sword was in the cave, and I vowed that I'd never walk outside without it again. Noticing the bows the soldiers carried, I decided the cuirass would be a good idea too. Living as I did now, I couldn't count on honor to cover me, so I'd better make use of what I had.

Abishai walked just behind the two adons, clearly unhappy with the situation. They came up to us and stopped. The armed men were not used to dealing with Habiru. They had looked around, seen only me, and relaxed. The attendants simply waited, and I guessed none of them would be very skilled at fighting.

The taller of the two adons glanced at the woman and his face darkened. "What are you doing here alone with this man, Ahinoam?"

"Shalom, Abbi," she replied, her voice remarkably cool. "I am here looking for your son, whom the town elders apparently took as surety for repayment of the gold they paid to keep Nabal of Carmel from taking your inheritance."

The man snorted. "Nabal! When I'm done with him he'll never trail his robes around Jezreel again. I've already settled with the elders, fools that they are! How was it that they dared do this?" he asked accusingly.

"What else could they do when Nabal bought up all your debts and demanded either payment or your land? Since we have no gold in our coffers, the elders paid to keep Nagid Carmel from taking any more from our clans!"

"No gold? I left you with plenty to live on while I was gone!"

"It would have been, except for the debts Lael forgot to mention, the ones he has accumulated since, and the bad harvest which necessitated the purchase of food to keep our dependents alive."

"Why didn't you notify me things were in this state?" the man said angrily.

Ahinoam turned white. "I see you didn't bother to read my messages."

Ahlai's mule shifted under him, and the man reined it in impatiently. Looking at that mule, I got an odd feeling. A mule's attention is indicated by its ears. Wherever the ears are pointing, that's what's on the mule's mind. The second adon's mule had its ears turned back toward its rider, as any well-trained mule would.

But Ahlai's mule had his ears pointed at Abishai. Instead of settling down, the animal bunched its haunches and lowered its head, mouthing the bit that the adon had unwisely let it bite down on.

"Well, get your brother so we can leave. I haven't been home yet."

"You will have to ask this man where he is," Ahinoam said, gesturing to me.

Ahlai turned a sour face to me. "Get him at once!"

The adon's voice must have been loud enough to be heard in the cave, for when I looked in that direction, Ittai was just coming from the trees, supporting Zabad, who clearly had a bad headache from the blow on his head.

Ahlai's mule shook its head, dancing a little. The Jezreel adon yanked its nose to the side, turning the animal in a tight circle. When he settled his mount, he saw Ittai just arriving.

"That's not Lael" he said, his voice threatening. "The message said the elders took my son!"

Zabad raised his head, squinting in the sun. "Abbi? They said Ahinoam came." He tried to look around.

"I came all the way out here for *you*?" the adon nearly shouted, then turned on the woman. "Ahinoam, how dare you lie to me!"

"I said I was looking for your son. And I was. You have two of them as I recall."

"He is no son of mine!"

"Abbi?" the man gasped, looking up. "Abbi, what--"

"Don't ever call me 'abbi' again," Ahlai cut him off. He turned blazing eyes to me. "The elders gave him to you, he belongs to you now. Do whatever you wish with him. He is no longer mine."

Zabad's knees gave out, and landing on them made him cry out in pain and clutch his head. "Abbi, no!"

His abbi yanked his mule around. "Let's go," he said angrily.

"Adon, there is still an item of business between us," I said, trying to keep my voice even after the way the Jezreel adon had just disowned his son.

Ahlai looked back impatiently. "What is it, Habiru?"

I pointed to Abishai. "I see you found something of mine. Accept my gratitude for returning him safely."

The adon glanced around, seeing only Ittai and myself. "You took something of mine, Habiru, I take something of yours. And take whatever my shameless daughter brought on that donkey if you wish." Then he urged the mule forward.

"I think not," I said.

Abishai spoke, and that mule exploded, lashing backward with its hind legs, rearing and bucking, throwing the unprepared Ahlai to the ground, and then twisting around among the retainers and men, who scattered out of its way.

"Abishai! Hold your hand!" I commanded, catching sight of my nephew's white face as he held his belt knife against Adon Ahlai's throat.

The second adon remained perfectly still, his mule as motionless as a rock.

"What is your connection to him?" I asked, indicating Ahlai.

"I was on my way home and asked to ride in the company of his guards. He said he was headed to Gedor. This detour was unexpected."

"If you would wait to the side," I said.

As he turned his animal, for the first time I noticed the youth, just becoming a man, sitting like a statue behind him. He watched me with wide eyes, his head barely turning as the mule walked away.

"Let him up, Abishai," I ordered, my attention once more on him.

"The guards will attack."

"Scattered as they are? They're perfect targets for my men." To prove my point, an arrow whistled by, making everyone in the open freeze instantly.

Reluctantly, Abishai rose, stepping back, the expression on his face one that I'd never seen before.

Adon Ahlai shoved himself up, rubbing his throat and cursing the mule.

I glanced at one of the guards. "Get his mule, and that donkey."

While Ahlai and the mule decided whether or not the man would ride, I again turned to Abishai. "What did you say to that mule?" I asked, amused.

"It was one of Dodi Shammah's. It wasn't quite good enough as a war mule for the royal family, but it had all the training. It's one that Dodi Eliab sold off, I believe."

"How did you fall in with them?" I asked.

"They said they needed a guide, but after they took my weapons, I didn't trust them. I knew I could get away if I could get the mule to buck at the right time. I was almost ready to run when I saw Jonathan in the trees, and I decided to bring them past our cave and see what happened."

"Good thinking on your part, Abishai. But you are very quick to take offense. There was no need to kill the man. You of all people should know the trouble that can get you into."

He looked down. "Yes, dodi."

The cavalcade re-formed, the guards looking uneasily at the trees, and Ahinoam had charge of the donkey again.

When their adon was mounted, I spoke. "You are not welcome here. I would advise you to remember you owe your life to your daughter's courtesy. Now go, and take your son with you," I pointed to

Zabad, still kneeling on the ground.

Ahlai spat once and rode away. Ahinoam gave one glance back, her face white and strained. Then, stumbling, she started to leave.

"Who are you?" I asked the other adon.

"I'm from Giloh. I'm called Ahibaal." He said the name as if I should know it.

Glancing at the sun, I saw there was just enough time to get to Giloh before dusk. "The easiest trail up the heights is this way, adon. But you and your son might have to walk part way. I'll be back in a moment." At the cave I donned the cuirass and strapped on my sword.

During the climb up the land stair, I kept the pace suitable for Ahibaal and his son. The boy asked me question after question on the way. His abbi didn't say much, and I could tell he wasn't too happy with the way the lad talked to me, but he didn't silence him.

"I am grateful for your guidance," Ahibaal told me when we arrived at the top.

I shrugged. "It's no trouble. Your son is a credit to you. He behaved perfectly down there."

The man smiled. "Yes. Eliam is a good son."

I ran before the mule to Giloh, and the way the animal acted made me wonder if it wasn't used to this. I left them once we were in sight of the town, to the adon's approval. I also refused the silver he tried to give me.

The next day, I checked on Zabad. He tried to sit up when he saw me, but I motioned for him not to. "Don't move around until your head is better," I told him. "You're welcome here as long as you wish to stay. Uriah is always looking for another fighter, and since Ahlai expects me to make use of you, I'm willing to, but it is your choice."

"I don't understand, geber. He gave me to you."

"I find friends more reliable than slaves, Zabad. Think about it for a couple days if you want. We don't have much here, and we may have to leave at any time. But since Ahlai can't appreciate the honor he's thrown away, I would use it if I could."

"Honor?" His amazement made me smile.

"You got into this mess because you were trying to save your abbi's lands. I can't imagine his reaction to you yesterday was that much of a surprise, was it?"

He turned his face away. "No, geber."

"But you were trying to save his inheritance just the same. I know honor when I see it." I walked out, leaving him staring after me.

Zabad ben Ahlai decided to stay. Uriah's eyes lit up when he watched the man spar the first time, and soon we all knew why. Zabad deserved his reputation as his clan's best warrior. About a week after he'd sworn to me, I sent Zalmon to Ahinoam with the message that her brother was fine and asking how she was. The message back satisfied Zabad that their abbi wasn't being any more difficult than normal, which relieved his mind.

The war season passed while we delivered messages, trained, and kept out of Shaul's sight. The Philistines must have had enough to keep them busy up north, for none of them raided anywhere around us.

Occasionally we got news from Moab. Abbi and my brothers were doing well, although all of them were chafing under the charity of King Yira. They were living like adons, but having been busy with lands and businesses all their lives, having nothing to do was a greater trial than they expected.

And Elhanan brought news that the Bethlehem elders appointed as stewards were working closely with Lahab, Zelek, and Eliab to preserve Boaz's inheritance. I'd have to find some way to properly thank Sar Ishvi for his hesed.

CHAPTER 20

The hassar found Michal on the southeast battlements, staring at the tiny light that shone from Jebus nearly every night at this hour. Since it was late, very likely the light came from a prostitute's window, but neither of them ever said that aloud. The light was a dream that would never come true for either of them. It was from the south, from Dahveed's country, and as long as it glimmered, maybe there was hope in their own darkness now.

"I'm sorry, Michal," he said, standing behind her and putting his arms around her.

"When do I leave?" she asked, her body hard with tension.

"Tomorrow."

"No feast, no farewells, no celebration?"

"Not here. But I'm sure Palti will have something at his house, although by the king's command, it must be private."

"That's hardly the way a king's daughter should be married."

Jonathan took a deep breath. "You can say no, Michal."

"Would you back me up?" she asked bitterly.

"Yes."

She stiffened even more in his arms. "Really?"

He turned her around, looking down into her face. "I couldn't bear to condemn Merab to a life of torment. Knowing how much you mean to me, do you think I could do the same to you?"

Michal threw herself into his arms, silent sobs shaking her body.

He held her against him, muffling what cries she made against his chest, his own heart breaking with hers.

"Until now, I always had the hope that Abbi would relent, and Dahveed could come back," she said at last.

"I don't think Abbi ever will," her brother said softly. "I wish I knew why."

"Because of you, Jonathan. He's determined that you will rule. And haven't you noticed that he talks about the zammar and the Dahveed as if they were two different people? He would welcome the zammar back with open arms, but he'll kill Dahveed to keep him from being in your way."

"Maybe you're right, Michal," the hassar said slowly. "But tonight I need to know what you would have me do for you."

"Let it go, Jonathan. Abbi will never rest until he thinks your throne is secure, and that can't happen if I'm married to Dahveed."

"I could insist that he wait the required two years before he gives you away."

"That would just put off the inevitable. I like Palti, and he'll be good to me. And he lives close, just over in Gallim. Besides, I might hear some news. His sister Jemima married Ahiam, you remember."

"You're not just saying this to make me feel better?" Jonathan asked doubtfully, gently tightening his arms, conscious of how thin his sister had become.

"No, I'm saying it to make myself feel better, too," she admitted. "But it's all true, Jonathan, and I'll be all right. What about you? Have you been able to see Atarah?"

"No. Abner has people watching her house."

"Can't you do anything about him?"

"At the moment, I can only hedge him in a little more, and I do. Malchi is a great help there. Abner hasn't realized yet that he's lost Malchi's loyalty."

"How can he not know that?" she asked in disbelief.

"Maybe he never realized the three sars have grown up."

They stood in silence for a while until Michal stirred again. "You got some good news today. What was it?"

"Another indication about the House of Tahat. From Hazor north of Chinnereth this time. Our man there thinks he's identified a regular carrier for the House. I'm eager to hear more."

They watched the light in Jebus until it winked out.

¥ ¥ ¥ ¥ ¥ ¥

The war season passed, and just days after Shagay's son reported that the Philistines had gone home, the news flashed across the land that King Shaul had chosen a wife for the hassar, and the wedding would be in just three weeks.

"Everyone's talking about it," Elhanan reported, having come down to our cave for Shabbat. "I can't make out exactly who he's supposed to be marrying--the rumors have three or four names attached to his--but I'll let you know as soon as I can pin anything down."

"I'll be grateful, Elhanan," I said, getting up and leaving the cave. Alone under the trees, I turned and stared north. "Yah, You told me once that You would give Jonathan Hassar his heart's desires. Of all the people in this land, surely he deserves Your consideration and blessing the most. Fulfill Your promise to him. Grant him a son of his blood, an heir to carry on his name. Give him Your hesed, for his hesed to me has no boundaries."

I bowed my head in worship, and as I stood there, remembering all that Jonathan had done and risked for me, the determination grew that, outlawed or not, this was one wedding I wasn't going to miss!

¥ ¥ ¥ ¥ ¥ ¥

It was late in the day when Abigail returned to the house barely ahead of Nabal. She grabbed her embroidery basket and hurried to the garden, her head full of Nabal's demands to the farmers for crops that he could sell rather than ones that would sustain the populace. Much extra work must be done to circumvent his orders regarding not only what was grown, but where.

She was trying to remember what one farmer had said about the differences in barley and wheat depending on which field they were planted in when she heard the door to the room behind her slam against the wall.

"That cannot possibly be true!" Nabal said coldly. "If Dathan of Hebron got one, I surely must have. I am Nagid Carmel!"

"I can't imagine how you were overlooked," Tokhath said, his voice puzzled. "You are of higher status than Dathan."

"It is an insult of the highest order! I must answer it somehow!"

Abigail's needle paused.

"But it is Shaul himself, Nagid. We will have to be careful."

Hastily, the Gebirah stuffed the meil and thread into the basket, easing open the gate without making any noise. Leaving the basket by it, she nearly ran to the door of the business chamber, pausing only a moment to straighten her dress.

Opening the door, she stepped over the threshold. "Why Nabal, what has upset you so?" she asked, her chin held high as she approached the nagid's table. At the same time she noted the wine cup in his hand.

"I have not received an invitation to the hassar's wedding!"

"That is a serious offense," she said gravely. "How did you discover this?"

Nabal gulped some of the wine, making a slight face at the bitter taste. "Tokhath learned that other nagids have had invitations for days, but none has come here! And I am the principal nagid of the Calebite clans!"

"Clearly, such an insult must be answered, Nagid," she stated. "But by some means which will show how much greater you are than is expected."

At the side table Tokhath was already mixing a second cup of the wine.

"Greater? How greater?" her husband asked, subsiding a little as he drank more.

Abigail thought frantically. "Since Hassar Israel has offered you insult, you should reply the same way. Have your own feast! Invite those who are loyal to you. Make it a greater feast than any that could be seen in Gibeah. The adons of the clan will come to you, and marvel at the way you reply to slights to your honor."

"Yes, yes, they will." His eyes glinted. "They will see how much greater I am! I will do this. Let there be a great feast prepared. Let it be on the same night as Hassar Israel's wedding, and we shall see who has the most guests!" He swallowed the last of the wine, and Tokhath handed him the other cup.

"Surely the evening meal is prepared," Nabal said. "We must eat, and then plan. This feast will be long remembered, Gebirah," he promised as he escorted her to the house.

¥ ¥ ¥ ¥ ¥ ¥

I sat conspicuously by Zalmon on the cart of supplies while we waited for the carts ahead of us to pass through the fortress gates in Gibeah. The hassar's wedding was in three days, and his clan in Benjamin was sending enough food and delicacies to make it a feast long remembered in the land.

I wore old robes too big for me, making me look much thinner than I was. I didn't have a girdle on, and I kept one hand twisted in Zalmon's robe, the other occasionally touching the strip of cloth bound firmly over my eyes. That cloth had gone on yesterday afternoon, and the hours spent unable to see had already given me the hesitant movements of the blind.

The cart moved unexpectedly, and I clutched at the edge of it to keep from falling off.

"And you are?"

"Zalmon from the Ahoah clans around Adummim. I've hired on to help out."

"What's in the cart?"

"Wheat, I think; Jericho dates; two jars of Tekoa figs; and I don't know what else."

"They'll want the grain over in the northeast corner. Take the cart there. Unload quickly. We've got chaos in here now!"

We jerked forward into a bewildering array of sounds. I tried to sort out what I couldn't see. A donkey's bray, a mule's snort, the sounds of creaking cart wheels much too close on my right for comfort, a woman's voice raised in protest, and then Rizpah's calm tones, straightening out whatever had happened. Suddenly Abner's voice rose over the din, shouting at the gate guards to check the carts before allowing them in.

The oxen pulling us lurched forward in stages, rocking my head on my neck. I could smell the smoke of fires and hear the crackle of flames.

"Wheat?" a man asked.

"Some," Zalmon replied.

"The whole country from Dan to Beersheba must be coming!" the man complained. "And the food being prepared here is just for the family feast! What's the town like?"

"It took more than an hour to get here from the gate," Zalmon responded. He started to get down, and I clung to him, nearly tumbling on my side.

"Oh, I forgot," he said, sliding back and giving me time to maneuver to his side of the cart and get down after him.

"Who's he?" the man asked.

"I don't know," Zalmon replied. "I found him by the road yesterday in the Arabah. He didn't have much on and just sat there, calling out something. I think it's a name. I have no idea how he got there, but he can't see anything, and I don't think he understands a word I say. I gave him something to drink, and he grabbed onto my robe. He won't let go. I couldn't just leave him, so here we are."

"Well, see if you can get him to sit down somewhere, and we can get this cart unloaded. Baalah Rizpah wants the animals and carts out of the courtyard as soon as possible. There's barely enough room as it is."

"All right, but I haven't been able to move without him hanging on to me."

To emphasize Zalmon's words, I refused to let go of him for nearly half an hour, stumbling along behind him as he tried his best to help the man unload our cart.

At last, a woman said. "Do let the man sit down!"

"He won't, geberet," Zalmon replied.

"You just don't know how," she said. Her voice was familiar, and I listened intently. Yes, it was Judith, Shaul's kinswoman, and Balak's wife. "Bring him over here."

Zalmon led me somewhere, and Judith took my free hand, guiding it to a stool set against what must be one of the walls of the storerooms in this corner of the fortress. Then she gently pushed me downward.

I felt the stool again, then eased onto it, transferring my grip from Zalmon to her.

"If he'll stay with you that would be a help, geberet," Zalmon said. "I'll come back and check on him when I'm done."

"We'll manage," she said as he left.

I waited a few moments, and then said loudly, "Igal?" When there was no response, I tried again. "Igal?" Judith patted my hand, and I tried to stand.

"No," she said firmly, pushing me back down. "Sit."

Three or four more times in the next few minutes I repeated the same behavior, and by then, Judith realized that when no one spoke to me for several minutes, I'd get restless. Since she liked to talk, she started commenting to me about everything she saw. It was hard to listen without giving indications that I understood what she said, but her words painted for my mind's eye a picture of the crowded courtyard, hot fires, and the coming and going of carts. Gradually I relaxed against the wall and listened. Eventually, Judith needed someone to hold something, and she put it into my hands, pressing them firmly around the large bowl. And at the approval in her voice when I held onto it, I smiled just a little.

Soon several other women gathered around, all of them grinding wheat for flour and talking among themselves.

"Well, I never thought this day would come," one said. "After all these years. You'd think the king would have done this sooner."

"It's Merab's sons that have done it," another said. "They say the king dotes on them, and she's going to have another child soon."

"After so long for her, I do hope none of hers die. There can't be much time left for her. She's in her 40's you know," a third woman added, from my left.

"It's a shame she had to wait so long," the first voice replied. "And now the hassar. I hope his wife gives him a son first thing."

"Well, Taphath should do that. Although, I will say I wouldn't have picked her for the hassar. She seems too quiet and faded, somehow."

"Maybe that's just what he wants after dealing with Sahrah Michal all the time!" the second woman said, and everyone laughed. I struggled to keep my face straight.

"Where's she from? I've heard four different towns now."

"Taphath's from Jabesh, in Gilead," the first woman said positively. "With his wife and concubine coming from there, where else would he go to find a faithful wife for his son?"

"Judith, who's your helper?" someone asked, and I heard my "story" repeated, slightly embellished with the telling. By mid-afternoon everyone in the fortress had heard how I'd been found nearly dead by the road, blind and helpless like a babe, and how whatever had happened had addled my wits so that I didn't remember anything, couldn't speak, and wasn't aware of much that happened around me, except to call out for someone. As a consequence, I was petted, tended to, fed, and fussed over. A rivalry soon developed among the women to see who could get me to give that half smile the most often.

"This the blind man?" General Abner's rough voice said from the other side of the fire.

"Yes, General," Judith answered, while I forced myself to stay relaxed, carefully holding the bowl someone had handed me.

"Who brought him in?"

I turned toward his voice. "Igal?"

"What's that he said?" Abner demanded, his voice getting nearer.

"We think it's a name. Zalmon the Ahohite brought him in his cart."

I could feel Abner's stare, and I rocked my torso back and forth nervously as I'd seen a blind man do once. "Igal?" I asked plaintively.

"Has he said anything else?" the general demanded, getting closer, and I rocked faster.

"You're upsetting him, General," Judith scolded. "He's blind, and can't understand a word we say! What you're fussing about, I don't know. You act as if you expect Seren Manani of Ekron to invade during the wedding! Now go away, and let us get back to work."

Muttering, Abner retreated, and when Zalmon stopped by again to bathe my eyes, (something only he or I could do, since one sight of my distinctive eyes would reveal my identity instantly), he entertained the women with a rendition of the grilling he got from Abner.

When the Benjamite came to the fortress toward dusk, bemoaning the fact that he couldn't find any place to spend the night, and preparing to take me out into the fields somewhere to sleep, a general uprising stopped him, and the women bedded us down right by the storeroom where we could be by the fire and stay warm. They provided me with plenty of bedding so the stones of the courtyard wouldn't be hard to sleep on.

We were up early the next morning, and I had a chance to look around as I washed my face in the water that Zalmon had brought.

"Will you be all right today, adoni?" he asked very quietly.

"I should be. Have you heard anything?"

"Yes, someone named Nimshi came to me with a message. He said Ethan hasn't made contact because General Abner is watching him and his band. I'd never seen the young man before. How could he know I'm with you?"

I smiled. "Origins, names, and descriptions of anyone who swears to me will reach Ethan. Nimshi is his son, and also on the hassar's personal staff."

"The Habiru seem more unusual than I expected," Zalmon commented.

"Ethan and all his men are far from usual," I agreed. "They take their position as Yahweh's Arrows very seriously, and will do whatever they feel is necessary to safeguard what is in their care. But if Abner is watching Ethan's band, I hope Igal is able to get here tomorrow with my wedding present," I ended worriedly.

Ethan had gotten essential messages through to me, and one, brought by the messenger from my family in Moab, had informed me that the promised case for Boaz's bow had been finished by the bow maker and had been brought to the Forest House. I'd arranged for Jamin to deliver it to Igal who was waiting in Jericho. But with Abner watching, things might be delayed.

"Someone's coming, adoni," Zalmon said, and I shut my eyes, letting the Benjamite tie on the blindfold again and lead me to the stool.

Today was much like yesterday. I remained by the fire, holding things for whoever happened to be working there, listening to the talk, and giving out smiles. Some of the frank comments about the royal family enlightened me considerably.

Shaul was respected, but many of the people were reserved now, because of actions of people like Doeg who used the king's name to enrich themselves. Everyone loved the hassar, and the unspoken thought that he should be king hung in the air. No one was too happy about Shaul giving Michal away, particularly since he hadn't waited the required two years to fulfill the charge of abandonment that he'd leveled at me. And everyone mourned the fact that I was no longer here to play the harp.

Toward mid-morning the sounds around me lulled me into a half doze, and a melody formed in my mind. I hummed a little, then straightened on the stool, cocking my head as I listened intently to everything around me, the story of a wedding feast unfolding with the melody in my mind.

"That's a nice tune," Judith said, touching my hand. I jumped, truly startled, and raised my head. "Igal?" I asked, pronouncing the name as he had drilled me. He had worked on several phrases with me, and I'd used two or three. The words were related to Canaanite, but different enough that they couldn't be understood.

"No," she said. "It's Judith, remember?"

I fumbled for her robe, grabbing onto it in response.

"You do remember. Good. Then you remember how to hold the bowls for me," and she put another one onto my lap.

The next day, everyone was up before dawn, for all the raised bread for the feast must be made today, and most of the meat would be roasted as well. There wasn't much conversation, just hurried inquiries and quick responses. I kept my feet out of everyone's way, and didn't make any trouble.

But as the sun rose higher, I grew more worried. Where was Igal? Close to noon, I'd almost given up, and was trying to decide how I'd get my gift to Jonathan when I thought I heard my northern retainer's voice coming from the direction of the gate. My head jerked up, and I nearly spilled the bowl in my lap, making the women around the fire cry out in alarm.

His drawling voice came to me clearly, and I jumped up, unheeding of the bowl that someone managed to rescue before it hit the ground. "Igal! Igal!" I shouted, not having to falsify any of the relief in my hoarse voice. I started forward, blundering into the fire, causing three of the women to come to my aid, all trying to get me to sit back down.

I kept shouting, adding the phrases Igal had taught me, while attempting to go around the fire to get to him. The commotion we raised caught the attention of everyone in the fortress.

"Where's Zalmon?" someone asked. "Maybe he can calm him down! What's he yelling about?"

Abner's voice bellowed for quiet, and I heard Igal clearly. "If you would just let me get to him--"

"Igal!" I yelled again.

His voice raised to a shout. "Elyaton! Elyaton!" He said something else, and then added in Canaanite, "Just give me a minute. I'm coming."

But I started forward anyway, and Judith sprang to my side, trying to steer me around obstacles, until I let her guide me. Then Igal's voice spoke from in front of me. "Elyaton," and followed it with something else.

I reached for him, grabbing onto his robe.

"Not there," he said, trying to loosen my hand, finally convincing me to shift my hold to the side of his robe, not the front.

"I do apologize for him," he said, a tinge of embarrassment coloring his heavily accented words. "He hasn't been any trouble, has he?"

"He's actually been a help," Judith said pleasantly. "Until you came, he would sit very quietly and hold whatever we gave him."

"I see," Igal said, with some disapproval. "Hardly the place his position should demand, but I supposed there was no way you could know."

"None at all," Judith said, her voice cool. "He was brought in by a clansman who knew nothing more than that he was found by the road, helpless and alone." Her tones carried accusation. By now, I was sure, everyone around strained to hear the conversation.

Igal stiffened. "You don't need to champion my brother. We were separated. He was hit by El's fire some time ago and nearly died. Since then he's been blinded, and in the simple state you see now." Shoving the sleeve of my robe up, he revealed the scar made by Yahweh's fire on the road from Gath.

"Let me see that," Abner said, coming from behind me. His rough hands grabbed my sleeve, and I crowded close to Igal while he inspected the burn.

"If you please!" Igal said indignantly. "I could get the idea you think I'm lying!"

"And you may be," Abner retorted. "How did you lose him?"

"We were attacked by bandits, or some of those Habiru you have down here, while we were in the Arabah on the road to Jericho. He was carried off. They probably left him behind when they saw he was useless. I've been looking for him since, and finally traced him here," he finished with dignity.

"Then he is fortunate to have such a devoted brother," Judith replied, relenting.

"What has happened, General?" the hassar's rich voice asked.

Involuntarily, my hold on Igal tightened, and I felt the blood drain from my face as I struggled to stand still and give no indication that I understood.

Judith explained the situation.

"Something like this hardly seems worthy of your time, General," Jonathan said.

Snorting, Abner walked away.

"You've met with misfortune," the hassar continued. "Where are you from, and how may we be of service?"

"To whom am I speaking?" Igal asked.

There was an amazed pause.

"My abbi is Shaul, King of Israel. I am Jonathan, Hassar Israel."

"Oh yes, the lad giving the Philistines such a time," Igal said. "I am a nagid Zobah, envoy to Geshur, Ammon, Moab, and Egypt. I apologize for my rough attire. Most of our things were stolen, due to the carelessness of the guards."

His voice hardened, and he'd turned away from me when he spoke his last phrase.

"We will do all we can to recover them, Nagid," I heard Uriah say humbly.

"I should think so," Igal replied.

"We will do our best to accommodate you," Jonathan said courteously, but I heard the anger underlying his tone. "We are preparing for a wedding feast tonight, but we'll find a place for you to stay outside of town where it will be more comfortable for you."

"A wedding? How quaint! The doings of you hill people always amuse the court, so of course I shall wish to attend. I'm sure you can arrange something for me to wear."

The silence was longer and quieter this time. "We would be honored," Jonathan said at last, his voice nearly purring. "I'll see that something is arranged for you immediately."

I found myself trembling, whether from shock at my retainer's effrontery, or reaction to the hassar's anger, I couldn't tell.

"Oh, and I will require someone to tend Elyaton during the feast," Igal added. "As you can see, he needs someone to hang on to. Such a change from what he used to be."

"I can arrange something for him, adoni," Judith spoke up. "He'll be out of the way, and can still be close to his brother."

"See to it, then, Judith. Sahrah Michal?"

"Yes?" Michal replied, and I heard her steps coming closer, increasing my shaking.

"Nagid Zobah does us the honor of attending the wedding tonight. Unfortunately, bandits have stolen his clothes, and he needs something suitable to wear. Would you see what we have that might satisfy him?"

"Of course, Jonathan. I'm sure we have something to fit a little man like him around here somewhere."

I nearly shouted with laughter. Trust Michal to pick up on her brother's rage.

"You are too kind," Igal replied. "I can hardly wait to see what sort of costume is required here."

He turned away, taking me with him. "Where has my brother been sitting?" he asked.

"This way," Judith replied, her voice almost cold.

Igal put me back on the stool, talked to me for a while, telling me I don't know what, and then left with Uriah. When he didn't return, I received even more attention and sympathy, and as the afternoon wore on, I didn't have to sham any restlessness. I wanted to know if Igal had managed to get the bow case or not.

Zalmon came twice to bathe my eyes, and I took the time to look around when he did. I saw Michal directing preparations with Rizpah, helped by Rizpah's boys, grown so much that I nearly didn't recognize them. Michal was thin, and her eyes were shadowed, but she seemed well otherwise.

Finally Igal stopped by before he went to dress, but I didn't have the chance to speak to him. Not long after he left, Judith returned. "You others go on, now," she said, dismissing the women. "We can't do anything more, and it's time to dress."

"I found a girdle for you to wear," she said. "Stand up, so I can put it on."

Without thinking, I stood.

"So it is you, Dahveed," she said softly.

I stiffened.

"I'm not going to say anything," she added. "I recognized you yesterday. You were leaning forward with your head cocked, composing that song. Be careful you don't do it again, or everyone here will know who you are."

"To what do I owe your kindness, Judith?" I asked gently.

"To the hassar, of course. When Balak left, he protected me and the child that I carried. I would not bring pain to him. But I would know something from you."

She nudged my arms out, and I held them up so that she could put the girdle around my waist.

"Whatever I can do for you, I will," I said.

She knotted the girdle and smoothed it down. "The news came that Balak is counselor to Yira. Is that true?"

Remembering to keep my head looking over hers instead of down at her, I lowered my arms. "Yes, geberet."

"Sit down."

I felt behind me for the stool and sat. She stood in front of me, shielding me from view. "Tell me."

"I went to King Yira looking for a place of safety for my family. Your husband was there as chief advisor." I hesitated a little. "I spoke with him briefly."

"Did he mention me?"

"No, geberet."

"Was there anything of Israel at all that he talked about?"

I reached up and fumbled for her hands, finding them clenched in front of her. "No. He is where he wishes to be, and he will not return here. My family mentioned that they have learned Balak has a wife there."

Her hands tightened under mine. "He will not return, or send for me?"

"No, Judith."

"Thank you, Dahveed."

I held her hands a moment longer, then let go, and we sat in silence.

Zalmon returned when it was time for the ceremony to begin. When Shaul and Ahinoam arrived, Jonathan went to the entrance to the residence to escort his wife as I had Michal. The vows, bride price, and dowry, would have been exchanged at the betrothal ceremony.

Taphath came out, and Jonathan welcomed her with a smile and took her hand. He led the way across the private court and through the gate, passing very close to Zalmon and me in the shadows. I had adjusted the cloth over my eyes so that I could peek out a little to see the hassar and his bride as they went by. Then Zalmon tightened it again before Judith came to give us our place in the line of guests going into the throne room.

"Where's Igal?" I whispered to Zalmon.

"He's in front of us. They've given him to Sar Ishvi!"

"What Ishvi doesn't suffer for his brother."

We didn't say anything more, and I could follow our progress up the familiar stairs and into the throne room. It was odd to be here again, unable to see anything, but able to imagine it all in every detail. Judith took us to the right from the stair door and around the corner into the smaller west ell.

"He can sit right here. It's in the shadows, and you can bring him something to eat in a little while."

"I'll do that, geberet," Zalmon promised.

Smiling a little, I settled back on the familiar zammar's stool, sitting where I was most comfortable, listening to the conversations and laughter as the hassar celebrated his marriage.

CHAPTER 21

Hassar Jonathan toyed with the wine cup. The wine had been some of Lahab's best. The food was perfectly prepared and served with the special touches that only Michal and Rizpah could manage for so many. He glanced to his left where Ishvi kept that arrogant envoy from Zobah plied with wine and Tekoa figs. Somehow he'd have to think of a way to repay his brother for this. Lowering his gaze, he caught a glimpse of his bride's eyes. She had hardly looked at him yet, and he wondered what she was like, and how they would suit each other as husband and wife.

Someone said something to him, and he turned the other way, his eye catching the figure on the zammar's stool in the shadows. For an instant, his heart stopped, and then he looked away. It should have been Dahveed there, ready to play at his wedding, instead of the poor blind man who would have to endure that envoy's degrading comments the rest of his days.

"Preoccupied, Jonathan?" his sister asked, as she set another bowl in front of him.

"You should be sitting and enjoying the food, Michal," he said in surprise.

"I tried," she answered ruefully. "But I'm too restless. Rizpah's been dealing with this for the past week, so I took over for tonight. She was so grateful."

Seeing the figure on the stool, she froze for an instant.

"You, too?" Jonathan asked.

She nodded. "I can't get over the feeling that he's here. I swear I felt his eyes on me this afternoon. I always could tell when he was watching me."

"He couldn't be here, Michal. Abner's had this place under armed guard all day, and everyone who entered the gates had to be known personally in the clan."

"I know. Yet I can't shake the feeling. But don't mind me, brother. You have a good time."

As she hurried off in response to a frantic wave by a server, Jonathan glanced around again. Ethan pushed his way through the crowd, and the hassar smiled warmly.

"May Yahweh bless you abundantly, adoni," the Habiru said with a bow.

"He has already. But Taphath will be the best blessing yet." He noted her blush of pleasure even though she didn't seem to be listening. "How did you manage to get in? You're not a clan member."

"No, but your personal guard is well acquainted with your reactions if my messages are delayed," Ethan said with a wicked smile. "I simply reminded them of that, and one of them escorted me in."

Jonathan chuckled. "I see Nimshi comes by his ways naturally."

"I also came to bring you my apologies, hassar," Ethan went on. "General Abner has been difficult lately, and I was unable to bring your wedding gift here, so it will be at your private estate later."

"I should be apologizing, Ethan. I will do what I can to limit the general."

"Don't trouble yourself too much. I'm traveling again, so it will not be a problem. If you don't mind my asking, how is the adon from Zobah getting along?"

"He seems to like the wine," the hassar commented wryly. "Ever seen him before?"

"No, but adons from Zobah are much alike and can't be mistaken for anything else. How many times have you thought of strangling him?"

The hassar, nearly choking on his wine, looked in Ethan's dancing eyes. "Somewhere around four or five."

"He must be in an unusually good mood. Likely the next one won't be so easy to get along with."

Jonathan bit his lips to keep from laughing. "Thank you for the warning. I had wondered if it was me or possibly the kingdom."

"No, it's simply that you are not of Zobah. I've heard that they can manage to be in Pharaoh's presence for an hour or more without giving offense, but no one else I've met believes that."

"You relieve my mind, Ethan. How may I reward you?"

"Let me give you my congratulations and at least get a look at the bride."

Taphath's head came up, and she blushed again at the smile that Ethan gave her, although her brown eyes widened a little at the sight of an armed man in a black shirt and cloak.

"Ah, a smile. I am amply rewarded, Sahrah." He turned back to the hassar. "Before I leave, are there any instructions?"

"Just the usual, Ethan, and anything you learn of the House of Tahat."

The Habiru leader gave him the odd smile, and bowed again. "In that case, I'll take my leave, adoni."

"Good journey, Ethan."

"Was that the Habiru?" Taphath asked, watching with a slightly puzzled expression.

"Yes." The hassar concealed his surprise. Her question indicated that his new wife had heard of Ethan before.

"But he looked respectable and was well-spoken."

"Ethan is both," her husband replied, his heart sinking. If someone had spoken to Taphath about Ethan, what else might she have been told? He'd have to be careful until he knew.

That, he realized, had been the restful thing about Atarah; he didn't have to be constantly watching his every move and word. With her he didn't have a list of subjects he couldn't talk about, or wonder if something he did would rebound at him later. He'd hoped he could find the same thing with the wife his abbi had picked for him, but now it didn't seem as if he would.

The feast went on, and Jonathan was glad to see Abbi and Immi enjoying themselves so much. Ishvi appeared to be faring better than expected with the envoy, and Malchi would have left hours ago if he could have. The hassar smiled. He knew why Malchi had insisted on the second unit as the escort for him back to his private estate. His younger brother wanted to get out of town as soon as he could.

Just then the envoy from Zobah stood up, swaying a bit unsteadily as he did. "Hassar!"

Jonathan turned to him politely.

"I have brought a wedding gift," he announced a bit loudly.

"Under the circumstances, that wasn't necessary. Your presence here is honor enough," the hassar said, wondering that the words didn't stick in his throat.

"No," the man said, swaying again. "No, when a Nagid Zobah goes to a wedding, he brings a gift."

The envoy's brother had his head turned this way. He'd been very quiet the entire evening. But then he didn't understand the language, and Jonathan hoped the poor man hadn't been bored. Surely his brother should have more consideration for him.

"A gift," the envoy repeated, his words a bit slurred as well as accented. "I found something suitable. My guards have managed to recover two donkeys with their packs, an' so I have a gift."

The envoy's body guard, who looked Hittite, handed over a long slim box. "This is the gift," Igal announced. "It will bring much honor to this house, since it was originally intended for the Pharaoh. But, unfortunately, the contents were stolen because of the carelessness of my guards, as I mentioned before."

The Hittite reddened and lowered his head. "They will keep their miserable lives because I have found a use for the case, even though the bow itself is gone. However, I have not yet found a replacement gift for the Pharaoh. But that need not worry you," he said generously.

"How kind of you," Jonathan said, clenching his teeth.

The envoy shoved the case back at the Hittite, who brought it to the Hassar and laid the hide-covered box in front of him.

Jonathan looked at it without touching it.

"It's a case for a composite bow," the envoy said helpfully. "I'm sure you can fit one of your little hunting bows into it."

The hassar nearly left his seat.

"How nice of you to think of that," Ishvi's voice cut in, and the look Jonathan got from his brother held him still. "Look it over, brother. We've never seen one before, have we?"

Making sure his hands weren't shaking, Jonathan felt the hide, then lifted it a little to see under it. Silver and ivory gleamed faintly, and curious in spite of himself, he pulled the hide back more. Five symbols were inlaid with ivory in the ebony wood of the case. A 24-string harp, a sheaf of wheat, a fringed adon's robe, and a Habiru kilt. Under them, closest to the latch of the case, was a royal scepter.

In disbelief, Jonathan opened it. One look at the carefully crafted, cloth-padded nest for the bow, and he knew his would fit perfectly. Hanging down the back as he lifted the top was a blue and silver tassel from the girdle he'd given the Dahveed. Shock held him motionless. His eyes went automatically to the stool in the shadows. It was empty.

The blind man was walking forward, hands outstretched, accompanied by someone.

"Igal?"

Carefully Jonathan closed the case, his face a mask.

Ishvi stared at him.

The nagid looked at the attendant. "What?"

"I think he needs to go outside, adon," the man said. "I couldn't keep him on the stool any longer."

"Well, it is time to go." He turned back to Jonathan. "I have enjoyed your feast," he said condescendingly. "Eshpecially the wine. Perhaps I shall speak to you about buying shome. But you have not thanked me for the gift."

"Igal!"

"I hardly know what to say," Jonathan said, truthfully. "It was very much a surprise, and I will treasure it, I assure you. Such an honor you've done me. I might even have a bow that will fit in it."

The envoy beamed. "I shall report to my court that the hillmen in Moab--"

"Israel." Sar Ishvi said quietly, his now puzzled eyes still measuring the hassar.

"--Israel know how to be properly grateful. You have pleashed me, Hassar."

"*Igal*!" The blind man's hoarse voice was loud now.

"I bid you a good night." Turning grandly, Igal walked around the table, took possession of his brother, and progressed out of the side door, much to the guard's surprise.

As he watched the man leave, Jonathan was suddenly sick of the feast, the incessant congratulations, and pretending that he was enjoying himself when every thought in his head turned to the Dahveed and the injustice that had barred him from attending tonight.

Malchi stood at his side, eyes watching the retreating back of the envoy. "Shall I slit his throat now or later?"

"Make it later. This *is* my wedding," Jonathan replied wryly. "Malchi, do we have enough mules to mount the second unit?"

"Yes, but I think only half of them can really ride."

"Mount up the ones who can. Put them outside the fortress gates, and bring the mules for me and Taphath to the private court."

"Yes, Hassar."

When Malchi left, Jonathan turned to Taphath. "Sahrah?"

"Yes?" she answered a little timidly.

"Are you ready to leave?"

"I suppose," she hesitated. "I can stay longer if you wish it, though."

"I'm ready to go."

"Then so am I," she said, relief in her voice.

He rose and turned to his abbi. "Adoni?"

Shaul looked up. "Yes, Hassar?"

"With your permission, my bride and I will leave now."

"Certainly, Jonathan," his abbi said, looking at Ahinoam with a smile.

¥ ¥ ¥ ¥ ¥ ¥

As soon as we were away from the feast and no one could hear, I turned to Igal. "What were you thinking to insult the hassar that way? And at his wedding!"

"I'm supposed to be a nagid of Zobah, adoni," he said reasonably. "That's what we do."

I hardly knew what to say to that as we hurried out the fortress gates and down the road to the house where Igal was staying.

Once inside, I took off the blindfold to wash my eyes the first thing. I'd managed a peek at the hassar's face when he'd opened his present, and I was still chuckling over that when I lay down to sleep.

It seemed only moments later that Zalmon burst in. "Dahveed! He's leaving now! Jonathan's got the second unit mounted on mules, and they're leaving!"

"Where are they headed?" I asked, scrambling after my clothes.

"I think his private estate, but I don't know for certain."

"You're certain it's the second unit?"

"That I know for sure."

Someone banged on the door, and I whirled around as Zalmon opened it. "It's Nimshi. I've got Dahveed's mule here!"

I threw on the last of my clothes, Uriah fastening on the cuirass as fast as he could. Then, as I buckled on my sword, I said, "Nimshi, can you guide Zalmon and the others to the private estate? They need to be there by dawn."

"Of course, dodi. Half the second unit is on foot anyway, so we'll go with them. Lotan is the commander now. He won't say anything, but you'd better get going. My geber is in a big hurry. Ahiam and Shagay will be running alongside. The hassar can't go too fast as his bride can't ride that well yet. About all she can manage is a slow canter."

"Thank Yahweh for that," I said, making sure I had everything.

"Here." Igal held out the harp case.

I strapped it on. Outside the gate, my brown mule waited, nickering a greeting. I spoke to him, and he caught my urgency as soon as I'd mounted. Once out on the road headed west, I gave him his head, and he sprang into a gallop. I could smell the dust from the hassar's escort and knew they weren't that far ahead. Within a mile, I could see them moving in and out of the shadows of the moonlight, and in another half mile, I was cantering with the last of the escort in line. Keeping my pace just a little faster than the others, I inched my way forward, noticing at least two of the hassar's personal guard with the second unit, one of whom was Abiezer. Soon I rode right behind the hassar and his bride. Even in the dark, I could tell that she was making hard work of the ride.

Easing my mule beside hers, I matched her pace. The moon was out, and I glanced over to see Malchi on the other side of Jonathan.

"You got it?" the hassar asked.

"For the third time, yes, Jonathan! It's coming with us. What's so important about the envoy's gift?"

"I'm not certain that I believe what I saw in there, so I want time to look at it in private."

I smiled, enjoying myself very much.

Tapheth wasn't, however.

"Sahrah?" I said quietly.

"Yes?" she said, trying to look my way.

"Sit down on the mule and then lean back just a bit, and let the mule rock you."

She tried it. "Oh, that's better. I wasn't expecting to have to ride much."

"I doubt you will after this," I replied. "The hassar is in a hurry tonight."

"Do you know where we're going?" she asked timidly.

"To his private estate, I'd imagine. Didn't he tell you?"

"No. He just put me up here, and we left."

I chuckled. "Don't let him do that, Sahrah. Make him tell you next time. Just ask until he answers. He forgets his manners on occasion."

"He won't mind?"

"Oh, he might fuss a little, but he gets over it if you remind him not to be mulish."

"You tell him he's mulish?" she gasped.

"Yes, Sahrah. But only when he gets to the point where he stops telling people things they should know. You have to be direct with him when he gets that way, but he prefers people to be honest."

"Oh." Her voice was thoughtful.

I pulled back a little, and not long afterward she edged her mule closer to Jonathan's.

"Adoni, could we rest a little? Or go slower for a while?"

"Certainly," Jonathan said, pulling his mount up to a walk. "Are you tired?"

"I-I don't ride much, adoni, and I'm not used to this. It shouldn't take long for me to learn, though," she ended bravely.

"I should have thought to ask," the hassar said immediately. "Are you used to mules?"

"Not much," she confessed. "But this one is more comfortable than a donkey now that he's walking."

I pulled farther back, and the rest of the escort slowed also, giving the two some privacy. Before long, Malchi's mule paced mine.

The forest closed in, and Shagay silently joined up in the back of the mules, followed closely by Ahiam. The pace slowed still more, as the hassar and his bride fell deeper into conversation. They paused once or twice, and we waited patiently for them to start forward again.

Malchi kept his mule even with mine, but on the other side of the road.

"Sar," someone behind me said, "the rest of the unit is coming."

In just moments, the men on foot trotted up. And not long after that, a couple more arrived, someone joined up from the side, and another rose from the ground after the group had passed.

"How many more of your men should I expect, Dahveed?" Malchi asked finally.

I chuckled. "I haven't seen Nimshi, yet, but I think most of them are here." We were silent a while and then I asked, "How did you know it was me?"

"I finally figured out what you've got on your back. You're the only person I know who would wear a harp case over a cuirass!"

"Ahiam fitted it so I can wear it that way. How's your neck?"

He shrugged. "I've got a little scarring, but that's all."

"I will have to admit, I never saw anyone kill a lion that way before," I commented.

"I'd rather not do it again if I can help it," he shuddered. "You going to tell my brother you're here?"

"That wouldn't be very fair to his bride. I thought I'd wait until he spends some time with her. Nimshi said Lotan was commanding the second unit. How'd you convince him to take that?"

"I told him that as commander of the Sar's Own, he'd get first chance at any of the bronze we captured in battle. He jumped at it." I could see his grin in the moonlight.

We spent the rest of the trip discussing the war season just past, and from the quiet murmurs behind us, the men with me now were getting acquainted with the first group I'd trained.

¥ ¥ ¥ ¥ ¥ ¥

"You're sure you don't mind coming here tonight," Jonathan asked as he led Taphath up the stairs to the second floor of his private residence.

"It was actually a relief," she confessed. "I'm not used to lots of people, and it's nice to be quiet. May we come here often?"

"You can come as often as you wish," he replied. "I have to spend most of my time in Gibeah, but that doesn't mean you have to."

Someone had left a lamp burning on the middle of the three-legged table, and there was water, wine, bread, and fruit waiting for them.

"How nice," Taphath said. "I was getting thirsty." She looked around. "Are you very wealthy, Jonathan?"

He grinned. "Depends on to whom you compare me. Compared to the kings in the kingdoms around us, no. But compared to the people you know around Jabesh, yes."

"Do you mind my asking questions?" she said, looking down again.

"No," he said gravely. "We are married and need to be acquainted. That's the best way I know."

"Well, if I asked you something right out, would you get angry?"

"I shouldn't think so," he said, startled.

"Do you get mulish sometimes?"

Jonathan stared at her, his mouth slightly open. Then he couldn't keep back a smile. "I've been told so. Who's been talking to you, anyway? Ishvi, or Malchi?"

"Neither. So he was right? You do get mulish?"

"I'll have to confess that on occasion, I do. But only when it's warranted!"

"May I see the brass earring?"

Wondering very much why that would interest her, he pulled it out from under his robe, slipping the chain over his hair, and held it out to her.

She fingered it curiously, then sat down. "That was really Ethan the Habiru who spoke to you at the wedding?"

"Yes. But Taphath, why all these questions?"

"I'm trying to sort things out," she said slowly. "He said you liked people to be honest, and that sometimes you forgot your manners. And you did forget your manners earlier, so I decided to see if he was right about you liking people to be honest, and you do. What I don't see is how Abner could have gotten so much wrong."

The hassar sat down also, knowing he needed to be very careful how he reacted to this. "Did he talk to you?"

Taphath nodded. "He was the one who came with your offer of marriage. He spoke with me a long time before he'd let me make a decision. I didn't say very much. I never have, I guess. But he didn't sound right when he was talking, and I wondered if it was because you had some kind of illness like the king did. He said you were touchy about some subjects, and I'd have to be careful how I found out about them, otherwise you'd get angry and then I'd never have any chance of pleasing you. He said I should come and ask him about anything if I had questions.

"Then when I met you at the betrothal, I knew you weren't ill at all, so I've been thinking about it ever since."

"Can you tell me what some of the subjects were?"

"He told me about a brass earring that you sometimes wore, and about a Habiru named Ethan, and about someone named Atarah who had some kind of hold over you. But then, Ethan came, and he wasn't anything like Abner said he'd be."

"I don't think Abner has ever met Ethan," Jonathan said, swallowing his anger.

"It did seem odd that the general would get so much wrong about him. Then tonight, everything the escort guard said was true, and you're not what Abner told me to expect you to be." She gave the earring back, her brown eyes troubled. "Why would Abner tell me those things?"

Jonathan stood, leaning on his hands on the table, jaw clenched as he debated what to do. How honest should he be with Taphath? She was a nice, sweet young woman from Jabesh who had no experience with all the intrigues of power and was already bewildered by the atmosphere of the court. Yet, she was his wife, and simply because she was, people would try to influence and use her, and if she was unprepared for that, disaster might result.

"Probably he was hoping you would come to him for advice. And then he could . . . talk to you," he said at last.

"Why would he want to do that?"

"It would provide an opportunity to ask what had happened with me lately."

"If he wanted to know that, why wouldn't he ask you?"

He turned to face his new wife. "Because I am the hassar, Taphath, and there might be some things I wouldn't tell him."

The frown on her forehead gradually cleared, replaced by tentative understanding. "I would be almost a spy for him?"

"Essentially."

"But what could he possibly want to know that you wouldn't tell him?"

"Shall we begin with anything I might learn about Dahveed? Can you tell me exactly what Abner said?"

When his new bride finished, Jonathan sighed. "I'm sorry, Taphath. You shouldn't have to deal with things like this."

Her eyes were very direct when she looked at him. "Am I correct in thinking that because I married you, I *will* have to deal with such things?"

"I'm afraid so. I will do my best to keep it to as little as possible, though."

"Well, my immi told me before I left that our clan was greatly honored by this marriage and that I could uphold that honor best by being a loyal wife. I'm going to be." There was a quiet determination in her tone, and her eyes flashed.

"Then I am very blessed, indeed," Jonathan said, reaching up and stroking her face. "Come here, Taphath. We've talked about other people long enough."

She looked down, blushing.

Pulling her close to him, he buried his hand in her hair, gently covering her lips with his.

Hours later, Jonathan rolled over in the bedroll, pleasantly rested, listening to the song drifting into the windows. The tale of a wedding unfolded in his sleepy mind, and he smiled. Dahveed must have used several incidents from yesterday in this song, including the cries of the blind man, and the snooty tones of the Zobah adon. He'd even gotten Abner in there, disguised as an over-fussy guard.

Dahveed?! Throwing off the blankets, the hassar yanked on some clothes, awake enough now to realize from the laughter that the singing must have been going on for some time.

Taphath opened her eyes. "What is it?"

"I'm going to look," he answered. "And if it's really him, I'm going to strangle him! I'll shake his teeth out. And when I catch up to that insolent Habiru again, I'll turn him inside out! Telling me his gift was here at the estate! The gall of the two of them!"

He brushed his hair back, throwing on an old robe hanging on the wall. Then he nearly tore the door off the wall. "Dahveed!" he roared as he came out onto his balcony.

The singing stopped. "Yes, Nahsi?"

Jonathan glared down at the assembled men, all staring up expectantly, the one standing in front with the harp looking hopelessly innocent.

"You're late!" he accused. "I got married yesterday."

"What makes you think I missed that?" Dahveed asked. "I've just played the song I wrote about all the things that happened at your wedding, including the spat Rizpah settled and that disgusting adon from Zobah. Incidentally, how did you like his gift?"

"How did you learn about all that so soon? You weren't there!"

"You wound me, Jonathan! I sat right there on my stool during the entire feast, and you have the nerve to say I wasn't there?"

Jonathan gaped. "*You?* You were that poor blind man who arrived days before--" he sputtered to a halt, speechless. Wordlessly, he marched down the stairs, striding over to him.

Dahveed put the harp down before he got there. Tears glistened in his eyes when he dropped to his knees. "Nahsi!" he said, his hands gripping Jonathan's.

"Zammar!" the hassar answered, pulling him to his feet and into his fierce embrace.

¥ ¥ ¥ ¥ ¥ ¥

When I opened my eyes, tear-blurred as they were, I could see someone standing behind us, waiting. I pushed away, and Jonathan stepped back, also. Wiping my eyes, I touched one knee to the ground. "You're even more beautiful now than in the moonlight, Sahrah. May Yahweh grant you His richest blessings."

Jonathan turned around in surprise. "Taphath!" he exclaimed.

She ignored him. "He forgets his manners more often than you led me to believe," she said to me.

"My humblest apologies, Sahrah."

"Do you know him?" her husband managed to ask.

"He's the escort guard who told me last night you could be mulish. Are you going to introduce us now?"

"You rode with me here?" Jonathan whirled around, advancing on me.

I scrambled back. "Hesed, Nahsi! Hesed!"

The hassar stopped, his hands on his hips. He looked into Malchi's wicked grin and sputtered, "Did you know about this?"

"Why, brother, how you could have missed the man in the cuirass with a harp case strapped on his back is beyond me. And we kept gaining more men as we went along. The second unit must grow on trees out in that forest," Malchi drawled, regarding his brother in perfect puzzlement.

The hassar growled.

Taphath quietly cleared her throat.

Jonathan turned to her. "Sahrah, may I present the most exasperating example of southern hill men in the kingdom. If he didn't have a voice that can summon the gods, and the skill to flatten anyone in battle, there wouldn't be a useful bone in his body!"

"Oh. You must be Dahveed," Taphath said.

"I am, Sahrah," I said, unable to keep from glancing at Jonathan.

He didn't seem interested, but he watched Taphath closely.

She studied me for a few moments. "I don't see why you're making such a fuss, Jonathan," she said at last. "He's sweet, and I want to hear him sing that song about our wedding." Going to where Jonathan stood in stunned silence, she took his hand. "Pick up your harp and sing for us, zammar."

I grinned and bowed. "Whatever you command, Sahrah."

We talked the day away, Peleth quietly directing the house staff to serve food and drink to all of us wherever we sat. Jonathan laughed until his sides ached as I told the tale of my three days in the fortress.

"So while Abner has his men guarding all the nooks and crannies he can find, you're standing in the middle of the courtyard yelling," he gasped. "I assume that nasty adon from Zobah was part of this?"

I called Igal over, and he was so appropriately apologetic that Jonathan readily forgave him. We had a feast that night, and I sang and played until late. As I put the harp back in its case, I realized it had been sitting in a puddle of wine, staining the bottom. I did what I could to clean it up before falling into a bedroll. Fortunately, no one stirred until noon the next day, but then our visit ended abruptly.

Jonathan, followed by Taphath, had just come from the house when Abiezer, his most trusted body guard, hurried over.

"Yes?" the hassar questioned.

"Adoni, Azmaveth is not here this morning."

Jonathan looked up in alarm. "How long has he been gone?"

"He was here when we went to bed, adoni, but no one has seen him since."

Jonathan's jaw clenched, and then he turned to me. "Abner is holding Azmaveth's son, Pelet."

I understood immediately. "Shagay!" I called.

He trotted over.

"We are leaving immediately. Abner has been told we are here."

"I doubt that, adoni," Shagay said with a smile. "Abner and four units are halfway down to the Arabah combing the Kidron valley for Ethan. When Ethan left the wedding, he had several donkeys packed with what obviously could only be supplies for you!"

The hassar smiled grimly. "I owe the Habiru yet again, it seems. You'll have a bit of time, Dahveed, but not much. Abner won't be fooled for long."

"What have I done to set the king against me this way?" I once again asked.

"It's not you, Dahveed," Jonathan answered, just as frustrated as I. "But he must be implacable now to have Abner coercing members of our own clan."

"Would this Azmaveth be of Bahurim?" Taphath asked Jonathan, her eyes wide.

"Yes."

"Are you saying that Abner has taken *my* cousin's boy, Pelet, hostage?"

"It would seem that way," the hassar replied, looking at his bride in surprise.

"Abner should not have done that," she said softly.

CHAPTER 22

The six of us headed south from Zelah, but as soon as the forests closed around the road, we turned off. Knowing that Abner would expect me to head for the safety of the southern highlands, I had no intention of going there. We cut east over to Ramah, arriving by mid-afternoon. Leaving the others in the forest, Shagay and I made our way to the alley behind the vineyard wall.

While we checked the streets, clouds moved in from the sea.

"This is a bad time to be traveling, Dahveed," Shagay said in disgust. "We'll be wet most of the time." Thunder rumbled in the distance when we went over the wall into the roeh's courtyard.

I knocked on the door.

Gad, the roeh's servant, opened it. "Come in, Son of Jesse."

"Does he always know when you come?" Shagay asked in an undertone as we stepped into the hall.

"Nothing is hidden from Yahweh," I reminded him.

My retainer settled down close to the door, and I followed Gad into the inner room where the roeh had his place. As always, the smell of incense greeted me, and the roeh's knowing eyes watched me bow.

"Much has happened since I saw you last, Dahveed. I see you have learned the lesson of trust in Yahweh."

"I have, Roeh," I said, sitting down where he indicated, and noticing that his bound hair was almost completely white. "It was hard, and I nearly learned it too late."

"Tell me," he said in his deep voice.

I reported all that had happened since I left Navyoth. When I finished telling how Ishvi left my things for me, he was nodding in approval. "Yahweh works quietly," he commented. "But He has bound the king's children to you. There is a time coming when they will be His instruments. It is pleasing that so many of them have chosen to let Yahweh use them so." His eyes rested on me a moment. "But now we come to what is troubling you. Speak to me plainly, son of Jesse."

"I am finding myself more and more entangled in the lives of others," I began. "I have tried to remain free, so that I can move and respond to whatever Yahweh wishes, but whether I would or not, others have come to me."

The roeh smiled. "And how many have sworn to you now, Dahveed?"

"Ten," I said mournfully.

Yahweh's seer laughed aloud. "Ten! Dahveed, you will need many more than 10 before Yahweh is through with you! How can you learn to lead men without men to lead? And I would guess that not one of them is from the same place, either!"

"No, I guess they're not," I said, surprised.

"Do not hesitate to accept such individuals. They are Yahweh's way of spreading your connections over the land. When Yahweh directs your attention to someone, listen to His prompting."

"But Roeh, they are not important or influential people. Some of them do not worship Yahweh or observe His commands."

"Would you have believed that Yahweh would tie the royal family to a mere shepherd boy, Dahveed? Did it matter to Him that your

Grandmother Ruth didn't even know His name? Yahweh uses whomever He wills. It is not even necessary for a person to be honorable or good as we view them. Yahweh may send you runaways, thieves, debtors, disgraced adons, or murderers, perchance. While they are with you, you should command them as best you can, and show them the way of our God, but remember that they are with you for a purpose. It is not even necessary that you like them. But each one will be there to be used of Yahweh. Respect them as Yahweh's tools, even as you are."

"I will try," I said, thinking hard. "Thank you for your patience and words to me, Roeh. I have much to learn."

"Yes, and there is much for you to do. You still do not desire Shaul's throne?"

"No. The hassar is dearer to me than ever, and I cannot contemplate taking his place."

"This is well, since you have far to go yet, son of Jesse. Now, you and those with you must leave as soon as you return to them. Abner has turned back from the Kidron, and his anger will be hot against you when he learns what you have done."

"Roeh, was it foolish of me to visit the hassar?"

"The impulse was born of the love of a generous heart, Dahveed. The evil one will bring trouble from this, yes, but Yahweh is working to bring His will from it, too. Before long, Jonathan Hassar will face a terrible choice, and your gesture will help to sustain him. And I think you have done more than you know by being there to speak to Taphath."

I bowed my head. "I did not think of Yahweh's will when I came," I confessed. "I thought only to bring Jonathan happiness."

"And what is wrong with that? Do you think Yahweh must tell you the smallest move to make in order for you to remain in His will? If you are puzzled, ask. But if you know something is good, do not hesitate. Yahweh will accept what you have done as He accepts gifts upon His altar. Both bring honor to Him."

I sighed. "I am worried, I guess, that someone will be hurt because I may have angered the king."

"The evil one will always bring pain from the best of gifts, even as Yahweh can bring good from the worst. That is the way of things until Abraham's seed comes. You must always remember this, Dahveed. Despite our will and intentions, the accuser can bring evil from what we do. When that happens, do all you can to help those harmed, and leave the rest to Yahweh, for He will repay." He hesitated a moment, his eyes suddenly unfocused, and I felt the presence of Yahweh drawing very close.

Covering my face, I bowed to the floor.

The roeh sighed after a time, and spoke. "You must go now, Dahveed. Do not stop for anything, but hasten to the north. It will not be safe for you to get supplies until you reach Beth-Shean!"

When dawn streaked the sky, we had left the smaller hills of Benjamin behind, crossed the higher, rolling hills of Ephraim, and traveled 30 miles to the border of Manasseh on Mount Gerizim. We'd stopped twice during the night for Igal and Zalmon's sake, but only briefly each time, for the rain seemed to chase us north, always at our heels but never quite catching up.

Before dark, I pushed on again, knowing that we could stay at an inn in Rehob down in the Arabah, 22 miles away. I gave the men one day of rest while I purchased supplies in Beth-shean, only three miles north of the inn. Jonathan Hassar had given me a purse heavy with gold and silver, and I'd taken the gold out to keep in my girdle, substituting a small sling stone instead. The heavy-looking purse reassured the merchants that I could pay for what I ordered, and my trip to the market went smoothly.

At dawn, after our fourth night of travel, we slept in the lowlands of Geshur east of the Sea of Chinnereth, and I had acquired two more men, Elika and Shammah, from the En-harod springs at the foot of Mount Gilboa. I'd run into them at the market in Beth-Shean. They were Manassah clansmen, both forced into debt by the Egyptian governor's steward, who had then stripped them of their land. I had also run into the headmaster of the scribal school in town, who mistook me for Elihu.

He had been eager to hear of his star pupil, and I told him everything that I safely could. That evening he took me with him to dine with the Egyptian governor. It seemed that Elihu had served the man with distinction on more than one occasion and was a favorite of his. When I left, I had an invitation to return as well as a mental map of the layout of the governor's palace.

Now that we were out of Israel, the need to push the pace disappeared. We made the steep climb to the Geshur tableland at an almost leisurely pace, ignoring the road and following one of the Habiru paths. The country was new to me, and I stopped often to look around.

Toward dusk, we saw the fortified walls of Laruba, the principal city of Geshur, and Igal volunteered to go into the market and buy some bread. When he returned, he passed out the bread and his news. "King Talmai is in town," he said, taking a bite. "He's supposed to announce the betrothal of his oldest daughter, and the town is expecting a wedding in a couple more months. How long are we staying?" He turned to me hopefully.

"A day or two is all. We need the rest. Does Ethan have any connections here?" I asked, turning to Ahiam.

"Ethan has connections nearly everywhere. I'll see what I can find out."

¥ ¥ ¥ ¥ ¥ ¥

"Any word?" Gebirah Abigail asked Hezro.

"No. Parai's family seems to have disappeared. No one knows anything."

"Keep trying. Sooner or later something must turn up. Do you think he's heard anything?"

The guard commander frowned. "I don't know, Gebirah. He's changed in the past couple weeks, even though he still watches you."

She smiled. "But he's puzzled now."

"Maybe that's it."

"Gebirah, I've finished the inventory of the treasure room. There is a considerable sum there."

"Good, Jotbah. Let us inspect the fields now."

That evening Abigail waited in the upper room of the house for Nabal to arrive for the evening meal. News had spread rapidly among the farmers of her willingness to circumvent Nabal's orders about their land. Jotbah and Hezro had helped her sort out what could be done to provide the crops that the nagid wanted and still grow enough other things to support the people themselves.

Once she returned from her inspection tour, Oholah, a second scribe Jotbah had recommended she hire, had records for her to review. Abigail could recognize all the letters now and tell when they were used as numerals, as well as read the names of crops, flocks, and produce. A couple of the reports she had read herself, and Oholah told her she had understood them correctly.

It made her feel more able to fulfill her place as gebirah. But bitterness touched her. For all his talk of her position, her abbi had done very little to prepare her to be a true gebirah. He had simply encouraged her to be a wealthy man's wife, who spent her time buying things in the market and embroidering meils. The thought made her glance at her basket. She hadn't been to the garden in a week.

"There seems to be a lot of activity here lately," Nabal said, looking around as he walked into the upper room for the evening meal.

"Yes, I believe the overseer is keeping the workers busy," Abigail said absently.

"Overseer?"

"Of course, Nagid. We must have one since it would be highly improper for you to be concerned with such common concerns. Jalam has done a commendable job. Now, how did the interview go with the Edomite adon?"

Her husband's face lit up, and he chuckled. "I received him in my business chamber. He was awed, Gebirah, completely speechless, and he stared and stared. Twice he bowed, and I had to encourage him to speak. That chamber is truly a fitting background for me. He had heard it discussed after the feast I gave.

"That feast was a grand success," he added, and Abigail settled back for another meal listening as he again described how the guests had stared open-mouthed at the business chamber where he received them. The most favored ate there, the others in the courtyard below.

"I'm sure the man was properly impressed," Abigail said when her husband finished. "What gifts did he bring?"

"Gifts?"

"If he came before you, he should have brought a gift of some sort. You are Nagid Carmel."

Nabal's face darkened. "He brought nothing. I gave him some incense. Your Abbi said that was appropriate."

"Yes. But then, Abbi always got gifts in return. You know how important the interchange is. Being in the favor of Nagid Carmel can be very advantageous to an adon. We must plan carefully how you will distribute your favor. It wouldn't be honorable to distribute largess where the adon has no respect for you."

"And he had none. He appeared without any gift at all. I should not have given him anything," Nabal said angrily.

The Gebirah settled into silence. The power of a clan nagid lay in his alliances, and alliances were made from the exchange of gifts and military might. King Shaul held nearly all the clan alliances in the north because he provided military protection. Her abbi had maintained his alliances through distribution of wealth and hiring warriors to protect Carmel during the war season. It had been several years since a raid, however, therefore Nabal must depend on distribution of wealth to maintain his power. It was proving very easy to encourage him to keep his wealth instead of sharing it.

In addition, Hezro had reported that the fear which Nabal had once commanded was fading rapidly to contempt for his foolishness, and the balance of power was shifting toward Dathan in Hebron with Ahlai in Jezreel as his principle rival, even though he was still only an adon. She would have to keep a sharp watch on the political situation as it developed.

¥ ¥ ¥ ¥ ¥ ¥

My men and I drifted into Laruba, Talmai's capital in Geshur, two at a time. I found Uriah's company much different from what I was used to. He treated me as more of an equal than anything else. Although he didn't say much, nothing got by his keen gaze and sharp ears.

The market was crowded, and I soon lost track of the others. I fingered the hassar's purse, which I had tied to my girdle.

"Make way! Make way for the king!" Runners entered the market, clearing a path for the king's chariot. He was a tall man, with dark hair and silver flashing from nearly every part of his body. The ruler had on a silver head band, breast piece, and armbands for both upper and lower arms, besides earrings and finger rings. His robe was blue, with darker fringe to match his mantle. With his stern expression and thick black eyebrows drawn together, he looked majestic, and the crowd bowed when his chariot stopped in the middle of the square.

A herald stepped to the front, and the crowd pressed close to hear.

I had to listen closely since the words were accented to such an extent that they were nearly unintelligible to me. Uriah seemed to follow them easier, and I turned to him.

"It's the announcement of his daughter's betrothal," he said in an undertone while standing at my left shoulder. "Malcath is to be given to a prince of Hamath in two months. There will be a great betrothal feast at that time."

By the time the herald finished, my zammar's ear had begun picking up on the accents in the words.

The crowd cheered, shouting their good wishes, as the king's runners cleared the way in front of him out of the square. A richly dressed adon with a loose striped robe crowded close to me, and as he turned to go he bumped against me.

A quick apology on my lips, I backed up. "I beg for your pardon, adon."

"Please excuse my clumsiness!" he said at the same time, then hurried away.

Uriah stared after him in puzzlement.

"What's the matter?" I asked.

"Why would he apologize?" the Hittite said slowly. "You are not of his status."

The fact that I hadn't thought of that startled me. The adon should have simply accepted my apology. As I wondered why the man would make a mistake like that, the slight tug I'd felt at my girdle registered in my mind, and I whipped my hand down. Neatly sliced thongs were all that remained of the hassar's purse.

Lips tight, I scanned the crowd. But the man had disappeared.

"What is it?" Uriah asked, curious.

"He stole my purse," I said softly between clenched teeth, feeling the perfect fool. I should have had that purse tucked into my girdle. Thank Yahweh I'd taken out the gold! "Let's call the sentry."

Uriah put a restraining hand on my arm. "By the time we get someone to listen to us, he'll have thrown your purse away. But if we don't say anything, he will assume the theft hasn't been discovered, and he's likely to continue working. He might change his robe, but I'll recognize his walk."

"And I'll know his voice," I said, feeling my anger settle into a slow heat. "Let's wander the market, Uriah." Once in my sight, that man wasn't going to slip away again. And I'd know that purse anywhere by the knot I had tied it with.

However, try as we might, we couldn't spot the thief. Finally I stood on an old stump beside a stall, carefully surveying the area spread out before me. The usual assortment of people milled around the stalls, the only difference from Bethlehem that of the quality of most people's clothes and the size of the market. Nearly everyone wore jewelry, and one woman I'd seen several times had four attendants with her. The shine to her black hair reminded me of my sister Abigail, and the longing to see her swept over me.

Then I smiled. There wasn't any reason I couldn't go south to

Rabbah in Ammon for a visit! The thought cheered me in spite of my angry disgust at being robbed.

"Adoni, that's the third merchant a messenger has taken down that alley," Uriah said, indicating an opening between the stalls to our left.

If merchants were leaving their stalls when the market was this busy, there had to be the possibility of significant gain. I stepped down from the stump, and Uriah pushed himself off the wall he had been leaning against.

As we came upon the corner to the alley, we saw a pavilion set up just down it, with an empty chair on a dais. Our thief was standing just to the side of it, studying the wares of four or five merchants, talking to them in a foreign language.

"Those cloaks are Babylonian, and they'd probably cost a month's wages each, and the boxes are alabaster," Uriah said softly.

"What language is he using?"

"Akkadian dialect, probably from south of Babylon itself from the sound of it."

I cast a quick glance at my retainer. I hadn't expected him to actually know the answer to my question. Not for the first time, I wondered about his past.

"He doesn't seem to be very protective of my purse," I commented, studying the way he let it swing freely from his girdle. "If I could get close to him, I could probably get it back."

"That would take some doing, adoni, dressed as you are now."

I settled myself to watch while I tried to decide what to do. The young woman I'd noticed earlier wandered from place to place, looking at wares, with her attendants and a bored guard trailing along behind. A slight breeze drifted by, bringing the scent of sandalwood and myrrh from the stall beyond me, and I saw a young boy expertly snatch an apple on his way past a fruit seller, hiding it in the rags he wore.

Shagay drifted over. "Talmai is entertaining an envoy from Babylon who is passing through to Egypt," he said quietly.

I turned back to the dais thoughtfully. This man was certainly taking advantage of circumstances. The merchants probably thought they were dealing with the envoy's man, and the presence of that chair and dais would reinforce the assumption. Since the merchants here must be used to dealing with people from all sorts of different countries, this thief must have the clothes, the language, and the manner of exactly what he claimed to be.

How was I going to get my purse back from him? I was just a strange Habiru who had wandered into town and didn't want to attract attention. Likely the thief himself wanted to avoid too much attention, one reason he might be in this alley instead of out in the market itself.

The "envoy's man" must have placed some large orders, for the merchants bowed repeatedly as they gathered up their wares, promising to deliver his goods within the hour. The man unbent enough to accompany them the few steps to the square itself, and as he did, the perfect way to expose him hit my mind.

I turned my back a moment, and then just as the merchants finished speaking to him, I whirled around and stepped forward, staring at him with my mouth open. "Why, whatever are you doing here and dressed like that?" I asked cheerfully, looking him up and down. "You have certainly come up in the world! The last time I saw you, you were carrying a purse with rocks in it, and hurrying off to avoid getting caught!"

Everyone within hearing turned to stare.

The thief drew himself up haughtily. "How dare you speak to me in such a manner?"

Laughing, I walked up to him and threw my left arm over his shoulders before he could react. "I dare anything after that last job we were both part of! You've got very nice clothes now, so who are you being today? An envoy or something?"

"How dare you approach me, you disrespectful, impudent liar!" the man sputtered, shoving me away roughly. "You'll pay blood for this outrage!"

He was actually shaking, and he looked the picture of affronted dignity until he saw what I now held in my left hand.

"You stole my purse!" he blurted out in amazement. Then he pointed at me. "Thief!" he yelled. "Sentry! Thief in the market!"

One or two men started for me, and I slipped Boaz's blade into my hand again, while raising the purse high over my head. Seeing the knife, the would-be attackers stopped, and no one knew what to do as I calmly stood there, ignoring the sound of running footsteps as two sentries hurried our way.

"Are you actually going to accuse me of stealing *this* purse?" I asked the thief. "It's just got a rock in it. Something that I'll bet the merchants didn't know, did they? How much did you order this time?"

"How dare you do this to me!" he said, his voice angry, but frustration blazing from his eyes. "Do you have any idea who I am?"

I cocked my head. Those sounded like the first sincere words I'd heard from his mouth, unless it was his surprised reaction to my having the purse. "I know exactly who you are," I replied cheerfully again, and in that instant, that man went from angry to terrified.

Realizing that I had just touched on something, and having no idea what, I hastily suppressed what I had been intending to say next.

"What's the commotion about?" an official-sounding voice demanded, and I looked around to find a sentry and his commander shoving their way through the crowd. That young woman with the black hair stood by also, her eyes sparkling with amusement.

"This--this disreputable lying Habiru has taken my purse," my accuser said bitterly.

The commander turned to me, obviously puzzled as to why I was standing there, holding the purse over my head.

"Shalom, Commander," I said, smiling. "I am grateful you joined us, because my arm is getting tired. But I think every person here can testify that this purse has been in full view of them all since I acquired it."

"It has, Commander," the young girl said, all of her attendants nodding.

The officer bowed to her slightly.

"That being the case," I went on, "I'm going to give it to you, Commander, and I want you to open it. I think the merchants standing around so attentively will be very interested in what it contains." I tossed the purse.

The commander caught it, fumbled a little with the knot, then spilled the contents into his palm. "Some kind of stone?" he asked, looking up, puzzled.

By now, half the market watched, and every eye looked directly at the man in the striped robe.

"Nothing but rocks!" one merchant gasped, dropping the cloaks he held and starting forward. "You--" Before he got any further, the thief whirled and fled, racing across the dais this time, yanking the chair over and slicing through one of the pavilion guy ropes as he charged by. The resulting chaos delayed any pursuit.

I watched, judging from the way that the man picked up his robes to sprint that he would most likely out-distance any pursuers so long as he knew where he was going. Shagay stepped up beside me. "Do you want him, adoni?" he asked resignedly.

"No, Shagay, this is one chase you don't need to join. Take the men back to camp. I'll be there shortly."

"How did you know?" the commander asked, joining me as my men left.

"It's my purse," I grinned, showing him the sliced thongs still attached to my girdle.

A quiet laugh beside me made me look around. The young woman who'd spoken in my support stood there, her eyes dancing.

When I smiled back a touch of pink reddened her cheeks.

"You must be a sahrah, at least," I said. "I hope you've been entertained by this afternoon's trip to the market!"

She laughed again, her black eyes sparkling. "I have, geber. So much so that I would invite you to come tomorrow to my house, and entertain me there after the noon rest."

"You are very gracious, Sahrah," I said. "But I am unaccustomed to the ways of your country, and I fear to give offense in some way."

"Don't worry, I shall be properly prepared for anything," she said, laughing again. "I shall expect you tomorrow. Just come to the residence by the north gates and ask for Maacah bat Talmai."

I bowed and when she had gone I turned to the commander, collecting my purse. "Was that one of the king's daughters?"

Avoiding my gaze, he nodded. "One of the younger ones, and a great favorite."

"Are such visits as she requested usual?"

"No, geber," he said at last.

"I see. Which way is the palace?"

He pointed down a street, and I bowed and left. When I arrived at the two-story palace in the center of town, I approached the nearest scribe. "Geber, I have a message for the scribe who sets appointments with the king. May I use your pen and a papyrus?"

Although he gave me an odd look, he let me have them. I wrote swiftly, folded the papyrus, and addressed the front, then handed it to the scribe. He called a messenger boy while I waited. Very shortly, a second scribe appeared and took me inside.

We went down a passage, turned a corner, and continued to a room with two doors. "If you would wait here?" he said.

As I entered I smiled to myself. Elihu's explanations about the organization of a palace were coming in useful. Had I asked to see the king, I would have been denied. But unless Elihu was wrong, Talmai himself would come through the other door before very long.

He did, accompanied by two guards. Although he wore much less jewelry now, what he had on was expensive. When I touched my knee to the floor and stood, he looked me over. "Your message said that my daughter Maacah has made a request of you?"

"Yes, adon. Happenstance in the market introduced us, and she was gracious enough to invite me to entertain her tomorrow after the noon rest. I felt I could only accept with your permission."

"Your note said you are a zammar?"

"Yes, adon. If you approve, I will play for your daughter tomorrow."

Not much expression crossed his face, but he seemed thoughtful. "My permission is granted, zammar."

I was outside Laruba and had turned off the road into the forest when the first whisper from Yahweh's gift brushed through me. Slowing to a walk, I checked my surroundings as well as I could. Something moved behind me.

"I knew all I had to do was wait," the thief's voice said.

I started to turn. "Don't bother. My arrow would take you long before you could reach me."

Relaxing, I gave myself to the gift as it welled up inside. When I glanced up again, the forest was a dozen shades of green, and the smells of the still damp leaves, earth, and wind from the Chinnereth nearly overwhelmed my mind.

"Just walk on into your camp," the voice ordered, and I obeyed.

CHAPTER 23

Ahiam looked up from the fire as I arrived. Instantly recognizing that the gift possessed me, he flicked a hand signal to Shagay, who shifted off carelessly to one side. Uriah noticed, and being ever cautious, he shifted off to the other side, although he didn't know why yet.

"You have come, adoni," Ahiam greeted.

"But not alone," the man behind me said, stepping into view. "You ruined more than you know there in the market, and in return, you're going to hand over that purse again, and the cuirass you're wearing, and the sword at your waist, and anything else of value in this camp. You will instruct your men to do just as I say because not one of them is going to move fast enough to beat my arrow. And if I so much as get suspicious, you'll die!"

Keeping my left hand where he could see it, I reached toward my purse, brushing the loops of the sling to my first finger joints as I did. Then untying it, I slipped the sling over my hand so the pan dangled below it, and dropped in the purse, glancing at Ahiam.

His eyes shifted to the man behind me, and I waited. Shammah sat up from a nap and Ahiam flicked his fingers.

Instantly, I whipped the sling, unwinding it as I whirled around and to the side. With only a moment to aim, I dropped to my knee, sending the purse through the air. It hit the man's chest, the impact making him grunt, and he fell as he stumbled backward, his arrow flying harmlessly upward. Holding my belt knife by the blade ready to throw, I waited to see if he would get up.

The thief didn't move.

"Well, now that he's got the purse, it doesn't look as if he wants it," Igal drawled from his spot by the fire.

I struggled to make my voice work. "Bind him," I finally managed to say.

Shagay obeyed, using the man's girdle. "He'll live," he announced, bringing back my purse.

I slipped Boaz's knife back into the sheath, and Ahiam put food into my hands which I started eating even as he helped me back to the fire. When I could talk reasonably again, I told everyone what had happened and about my appointment tomorrow with Maacah. By then, our thief had recovered enough to answer questions, although he walked slightly hunched over from the pain.

"How can you treat me this way? You said you knew who I was!" he accused.

"I do. You are the man who took my purse, and you shouldn't have. Your second mistake was not leaving town immediately, and your third was coming here." I shifted positions and took another drink of water. "It hasn't been a very successful day for you."

"Don't waste my time with insincere sympathy," he snapped. "Just kill me like you Habiru dogs always do. I doubt you're intelligent enough to do anything else!"

I regarded him thoughtfully. He wasn't a fool, given the way he'd been operating in Laruba, and talking as he had had already angered some of my men enough to kill him, so why . . . I turned to Ahiam, deciding to test my guess. "The adon doesn't seem to appreciate our company. Take him back to Laruba and give him to the city magistrate."

Ahiam's lips tightened, but he bowed. "As you wish, adoni." Gripping the thief's arm, he pushed him toward the trail.

The man pulled away. "You can't do that, not after what I just said!" he exclaimed.

"Why not?" I asked, as my men looked on curiously.

"Well, because, I robbed you, cut the purse from your girdle, and accused you before the town! You can't just send me back without answering my insults."

"Let the city have him," I said again, certain that he was trying to force me to kill him.

Ahiam started toward him, and he backed up again. "You don't want to do this, shobeh," he protested. "There should be justice for all the trouble I've caused. Just think of how angry you felt when you discovered your purse was gone."

"I have the purse back again, and nothing was missing," I said, the game Abigail and I used to play coming to mind. "I'm feeling kindly toward you since I met a very pretty woman because of you. Hesed for your plight has filled my heart. Someone as talented as you must be desperate if you have turned to the low life of stealing. Rather than cut short your career, I'm going to send you back with the admonition to repent and mend your ways."

"But, shobeh, you can't!" the man nearly wailed. "Do you know what would happen to me? You have to enslave me at least, and maybe beat me every day and force me to work for you!"

"Going back to Laruba is that bad, is it?"

"You have no idea, shobeh, the things they'll do," he said fervently, shuddering. "Haven't I done enough to at least get me enslaved?"

I considered while he waited. "What do you think?" I asked Ahiam.

"It takes quite a lot for you to enslave someone, adoni."

Regretfully, I shook my head.

"Please, shobeh," he begged. "What do I have to do to stay with you?"

"It helps if you ask," Igal spoke up, his drawl amused. "I can't figure out what he'd want with a thief like you, but then, he couldn't figure out what he'd want with someone like me, and he took me anyway. As far as I know, everyone here tried that, except Zalmon. He just sort of descended on us."

Shagay's shoulders were shaking, and Ahiam had to bite his lip and turn away.

I did my best to keep my own face straight.

Our thief looked around, not certain of his position, but willing to try anything. "I'm asking," he said. "Shobeh, don't send me away. I'll serve you well."

"What is your clan and how are you called?" I asked.

"I am from Abel Beth-Maacah, in Dan, shobeh. My name is Eliphelet ben Ahasbai."

Something about his eyes and the set of his facial features bothered me. "You don't look Danite."

"My family comes from Ur."

"You can stay."

He took a deep breath. "Thank you, adoni. I promise that I won't steal anything from you."

I considered that. "Or anyone else I'm connected with," I added, looking him in the eye.

He gulped. "Or anyone else you're connected with."

"Turn him loose, Ahiam."

The next day, I dressed in the dark brown shirt, kilt, and mantle the Headmaster of Elihu's school had given me for my dinner with the governor. I added the gold headband, earrings, and armbands that came with the clothes. With Ahiam attending me and carrying the harp, I went to the residence by Laruba's north gate. It looked large enough to be a second palace, although only one story, and most likely had been one at some time.

"Maacah bat Talmai requested my services as an entertainer this afternoon," I announced to one of the door guards. "Where should I go?"

"We've been expecting you. Please follow this man."

I bowed slightly and Ahiam and I followed our guide inside, down a passage, then through three rooms to a door that opened into a private courtyard. Sahrah Maacah waited for us with two attendants under the shade of an almond tree. The sky was clouding over, however, and I wondered what we'd do if it began to rain.

"Shalom," she said. "That is the right word, isn't it?"

"Yes, Sahrah," I replied, bowing. "You are kind to a stranger to use it. You are also kind to invite one such as me into your presence."

Her eyes sparkled, and she laughed. "And you are kind to say so. Sit down. Where are you from?"

"Judah, Sahrah."

"That's south, isn't it? Is it as wild as they say?"

"I don't know what they say, but it is much different there than here," I answered, and went on to talk of my home, digging around in my memory to find things I thought would amuse her. She wasn't so much small as not fully grown, and I decided she must be even younger than I'd first thought. I was puzzled as to why Talmai would have allowed such a visit, but was very glad that I'd spoken to him first.

Ahiam didn't hide his feelings that he didn't think much of her, and his opinion made me watch her carefully. She was pretty, and when she was grown, she'd be beautiful. Her laugh was enchanting, but it was the things that she laughed about that finally caught my attention. She enjoyed as much flattery as I wished to give, and was amused by anything that showed how superior she was to anything I knew. A bad combination.

I was talking of living in a cave when the skies opened up and rain poured down without any warning. The two attendants screamed and ran toward an open door. Without thinking, I scooped Maacah in my arms and ran after them, Ahiam following me. "It's much dryer here, Sahrah," I said, setting her back on her feet inside the door.

She looked at me, her black eyes blank. "You picked me up as if I was a child," she said softly.

I had badly offended her. Almost certainly, no one had handled her like that in her life. I met her gaze. "You should not call yourself a child much longer, if even now, Sahrah," I said, bowing. "It was my privilege to serve as a bearer to keep you from the rain."

The sparkle returned to her eyes. "In that case, I forgive the impertinence you had in touching me. But now, what shall we do?"

"Is there someplace we can sit? I brought something with me that might entertain you even yet."

Reluctantly, she led me to a room that probably served as a private audience chamber. I took out the harp while she settled herself on some cushions, her two attendants with her. Two palace guards appeared, and I sensed someone else just outside the door. Tuning the strings, I played a few notes. "Perhaps you would like this song," I said, beginning the Answering song. As the urgings of the young man, and the silly excuses of the young woman unfolded, Maacah's smile grew bigger and bigger until she clapped with delight, laughing at the final squashing of the youth by his baalah.

"Sing another one!" she ordered.

I started the one about the goat kid, judging that she was young enough still to enjoy it. She did, and before I finished that one, several more people had entered the room, including King Talmai, who'd been out in the hall.

"You play very well," he said, startling his daughter when he spoke.

"Thank you, adon," I said, bowing to him. "Your daughter has been an appreciative audience."

"Play something else."

The song about the adon who'd gone hunting and had to surrender to children crossed my mind. "Here's one about a nagid of Zobah who found more than he expected when he went hunting."

As I suspected, Talmai was acquainted with the Zobah nobility. Before the song was half done, he was gasping with mirth and wiping his eyes. "Where did you hear that one?" he asked. "It's priceless!"

I sang several more, but now that other people were present, Maacah had lost much of her interest in me. She kept looking from her abbi to me as if she expected something to happen, and when it didn't she grew very thoughtful.

Finally the king rose from his chair, and everyone else did also. "You have given us a very pleasant afternoon," he said to me.

"Thank you, adon."

"Bid your guest take his leave, Maacah," Talmai said.

The quick glance she cast at her abbi revealed that she hadn't expected him to know she had invited me, but his acknowledgment that she should grant me leave to go flattered her.

She approached me, holding out her hand.

I handed the harp to Ahiam. "I am honored to serve you," I said, touching her hand briefly, and then one knee to the floor briefly as well.

"You have pleased me, zammar. I'm certain my abbi will find some way of repaying you."

"Such generosity is not necessary, Sahrah." I stepped back respectfully, and she swept out of the room.

"Since my daughter has ordered repayment, you will come with me," King Talmai said.

"As you wish, adon."

The two guards fell in behind Ahiam and me as we walked to another room in another part of the residence. "You are a man of many talents, zammar," Talmai said. "Not much goes on in my kingdom but what I don't hear about it sooner or later. I heard that a strange Habiru band had entered my borders. I have enough trouble with Habiru as it is. What would you say to that?"

"I am a zammar, adon. How could I know anything of Habiru and war?"

"Because of that," he said, pointing to my right hand.

My fingers automatically flexed around the sling.

"If I mistake not, I have been entertained by Dahveed Israel this afternoon."

Straightening, I nodded slightly. "You have, adon."

"What is your purpose here?"

"Traveling. I stopped here to rest and came to the market to make a few small purchases." I shrugged.

"And what is to stop me from using you to lure your men into my walls, and then turn you all over to Shaul of Israel?"

I refused to rise to his challenge, but knew that I must reply, and do so without placing myself under this man's hand. Since he had guessed my identity, he had probably also thought out several uses for me. I needed to let him know a blade could also cut the one who held it. "Adon, you would not need to lure my band in. There is a way into every walled fortress or city, and the Habiru know them all. They would come in whether you will or no."

Talmai laughed. "Then why haven't the Habiru taken Jebus?"

"They have no use for it."

He stopped laughing, staring at me.

I smiled a little. "Adon, let there be peace between us. You have nothing to gain and everything to lose. I wish only to find my way back home. I came here at the request of your daughter and entertained you as a zammar should. Let me leave behind only the laughter and joy my songs brought while the rain washed the world."

The king smiled ruefully. "You are as quick with words as your hands, zammar. I have never seen such an expression on Maacah's face as when you scooped her up and ran inside!" He chuckled.

"My apologies, adon. I didn't think," I said, reddening slightly. "I meant no disrespect or offense."

"That is the odd thing about you. I should be angry with you for handling her so, but somehow . . . Oh, go in peace, Dahveed Israel."

"And peace be with you, adon." Bowing again, I quitted the room, and Ahiam and I left as quickly as we could. The rain had stopped, but the low clouds promised more at any time.

"Do we leave tonight?" Ahiam asked.

"No. We need more supplies, which we'll have to get tomorrow."

But Shagay waited for us at the city gate. Uriah had anticipated me and purchased a number of things while we were entertaining. I paid for them, and we continued on our way, glad we'd be able to slip away in the dark.

We were close to the turn off for the trail that led toward our camp when Shagay suddenly paused, hand up, listening.

I caught the same sound, the shuddering breaths of a man in pain. Within moments we'd found him, dumped half naked by the roadside. The man's back was a bloodied mess, the stripes from a whip covering nearly every part of it.

"Bring him into camp," I directed, knowing my plans to leave tonight had just been delayed. If we didn't take him in, he'd be prey for any predator that came along, human or otherwise.

Once in camp, Ahiam heated some water to steep willow bark, and then washed the man's back. When he finished, he came to me. "Adoni, be careful. Whoever beat this man made it look much worse than it is. The stripes are bloody, but not deep."

"All right, Ahiam."

The man roused a little in a short time, and I sat down beside him.

Gasping from the pain, he tried to look up at us. "Are you the dahveed from Judah?" he asked, his accent so thick that I could hardly understand him.

"Yes."

"Someone said there was a man from Zobah with you. I would speak to him."

"As you wish." I found Igal by the other fire. "The injured man asked to speak to you since you're from Zobah."

Igal's face tightened when he saw the man's back, and he knelt down by him. "Geber? Geber, what did you want?"

The man's eyes widened. "Igal?" he gasped.

My retainer bent down to see the man's face. "Jaas? Jaasiel, what are you doing here? What happened?"

The man said something in his native tongue, and Igal reverted to the same speech.

They spoke for some time, and Igal's face hardened, his teeth clenching. He asked a few short questions, and then sat back.

"You know him?" I asked.

My retainer nodded. "Jaasiel is a childhood playmate, I guess you could say. His family got caught in a political battle and lost. They came to Geshur. He has some distant relatives here on his abbi's side. There was enough of a blood tie for them to take his family in. Then he trained as a palace servant and was assigned to Sahrah Maacah's staff when she was old enough to have one of her own."

Igal glanced at me as if he wasn't sure how I'd take what he said next.

"Apparently, Talmai wasn't supposed to know about your visit this afternoon. It seems Malcath, the older sister, has been rubbing in Maacah's secondary status. And Maacah wanted to prove that she could do as she wished. When the sahrah realized her abbi knew of the invitation, she decided that one of her staff had said something. Jaas couldn't account for his time sufficiently, and so she blamed him."

After a pause, Igal added, "Adoni, if he just disappears, it will be assumed Maacah had him killed, but there will be no other reprisals against his family. I have no right to ask anything more of you, but if he is found, the sahrah may do anything at all."

"I can hardly refuse him since I myself told Talmai of my visit," I said softly. "What happened is my responsibility. He will come with us."

"Thank you, adoni," Igal said gratefully. "It will ease his mind to know that his family will be safe."

I wished my mind could be eased. Every mouth that came to me made it harder to feed the ones I already had. And injured men do not travel far and fast. At least we were outside of Israel. I thanked Yahweh for that small favor as I went to sleep.

The attack came without any warning.

One moment I was asleep, and the next I was on my knees, a blade at my throat, a shout of warning from the trees echoing in my ears. One brief glimpse was all I needed. "Hold!" I shouted. "Do not take arms!"

My men froze where they were, Shagay was on his feet, facing three indistinct figures. Ahiam was sitting, and I could tell that he had a sword in the hand still under the blankets which the men standing over him hadn't seen. Uriah had two attackers by him, and surprisingly, Igal was standing also, facing a single man. The injured man and my thief still lay by the fire, also with men standing over them. But where were Elika and Shammah?

As if in answer to my unspoken question, the two men from Manasseh were shoved into camp, Elika with a cut lip. Their captors put them down by the fires and added wood as two more men drifted in from the trees around us.

The darkness receded as the flames danced higher from our three fires, revealing 14 Habiru warriors.

"Tell your men to move to one side," the man holding me said.

"Do what they say," I directed. I was still out of breath from the shock of being suddenly awakened, but my gift hadn't roused so there was no real danger yet.

Reluctantly, my men gathered by Jaas and Eliphelet, both still lying down. I noticed the intent looks they gave the man holding me, and wondered why. He let go, backing away, and I didn't move.

"This was easier than I thought it would be," a deep voice said from the trees. It sent the chill of my gift down my spine. I raised my head slightly, catching the rustle of his footsteps as he walked toward my back. I started to stand.

"Stay down."

Again, his voice intensified my gift until I could barely restrain myself from moving. Whoever this was meant to harm me, and I ached to engage him. The cloth of his kilt swished against his legs, the sound slightly different as it brushed against the sword on his left side.

"You should have stayed west of Jordan."

"We stopped only briefly," I managed to reply.

"Just long enough to settle a commission price with Talmai, curse his black heart."

I fought to be able to speak. "What commission?"

"Do you take me for a fool? Talmai has waited for years to find someone to send against me. And when he sees what is left of you, he will wait years more before he finds another!"

His words set my gift on fire in a way that I'd never felt before, and I abandoned myself to it. He was nearly to my back. I raised my hands, holding them out a little from my sides as the man behind me took one more step.

Spinning my body, my left hand gripped the man's sword hilt, pulling it from the sheath as I lunged backward to my feet, facing him. I stared straight into the middle of his chest. It gave me pause, even this deep in the gift. I raised my eyes, and kept raising them. He stood taller than Shaul, and my eyes widened when I finally looked up into his face.

"If you insist on personal combat, I have no objections," he said. "Even though you have the advantage of holding your sword in your hand already!"

What came from my mouth might have been a laugh. "It's not mine," I managed to say. I drove it into the ground and scooped up my own sword from where it lay.

His hand flashed to his side, and a shout of rage burst from him as he sprang forward, grabbing the hilt. He tried to drive the sword through me, but I wasn't there, and that was the last clumsy move he made. As he whirled after me, I turned his blow. His reach was much longer than mine, but he wasn't nearly as powerful as Malchi, and with the gift burning through me as it was, I had no difficulty repulsing his sword to one side or the other.

"Tiras, Tiras!" his men shouted encouragingly. Smiling again, he thrust toward me, and I slipped my blade by his, twisting it around until his wrist turned, and then flipped the blade from his hand. It landed beside Shagay's foot, and before any of the Geshurites could move, he picked it up and casually tossed it back.

The other dahveed snatched it again, his eyes flashing at the contempt that Shagay's action had shown. I took the fight to him, unable to hold back, knowing only that I must give him a battle he would never forget.

Parrying my thrust, he brought his blade down on me from above. Twisting right, I rammed my shoulder up into him as my left hand helped his downward thrust. Pulling back instantly, I watched as he toppled over backward, his sword jammed again into the forest soil, the firelight flickering off the blade.

"Pick it up," I forced myself to say. What held me was not through with this man yet.

Gathering himself, chest heaving for air, he reached for the sword, and when he walked into me this time, he was cautious. His attacks and circles drove us toward the fires until I stood firm once more. When he tried a straight lunge at me again, I swayed to the right, took a quick step forward on my left foot and swung my right around into the back of his knee, buckling that leg while my left fist smashed into his chest over his heart.

"Adoni!" Ahiam called, and I caught the cruse he tossed, draining it while Tiras knelt there, struggling to breathe once more. His men were silent now, watching me with fearful amazement.

Hatred spilling from him, he staggered to his feet, and the burning fire in me blazed higher, using me as it would as I stood there immovable in front of him, repulsing everything that he tried. Then I drove forward, forcing the pace of strike and parry faster and faster, until I was batting his sword aside and lunging forward so quickly that he had to retreat nearly at a run. My men parted to let us through, and my opponent slammed into a tree, his head cracking against the trunk, leaving him dazed.

A battle cry poured from my lips, and I yanked out my belt knife and drove it through the cloth of his shirt and mantle pinning him to the tree. The blazing firelight beside us reflected off the knife handle, and Tiras stared at it, then into my face, and all the color drained from his. "The Lion of Judah!" he whispered, the sword dropping from his fingers. "Grant hesed! It burns!"

Beside me, the camp erupted in chaos.

"Shalish! Shalish!" Uriah roared as my men charged the attackers, grabbing any weapon they could get their hands on, pairing together and fearlessly throwing themselves into battle. In moments, cries for hesed reached my ears, and the fire within me eased. I shook my head, struggling to remember what the man in front of me had said and to find my way back from the gift.

"Dahveed, what is your will for him?" someone asked.

I took a deep breath, then another, and felt the blood rushing into my arms. Grasping my belt knife, I pulled the blade. It came away bloody. I must have cut him when I drove it through his clothes. He sagged to his knees, one hand at his side.

"Dahveed!"

I shook my head, finding my voice. "Take him to the fire."

He disappeared from my sight, and Ahiam stood beside me, offering a drink. I grabbed for it. I'd never been this thirsty! Sucking in air, I bent forward, then drank again and again, draining the cruse handed me each time, before I could eat the raisins and bread.

When I went back to the fire, Tiras rolled to his knees the moment I looked at him. "You called me the Lion of Judah. Why?"

"We have heard the stories of the dahveed with lion's eyes, who had the power of his god when he fought. I didn't believe them--until now." He looked around at his men, sitting without their weapons in the center of our camp. "Let the blame fall on me alone," he added. "Those with me only did as I bid them. Talmai will be satisfied with me. Let them go, or sell them if you wish, but do not give them to Talmai!"

"Why would I give any of you to Geshur's king?"

My captive smiled bitterly. "I do not believe you are foolish enough to betray the man who pays you."

Shagay caught my eye, directing my attention to one of the captives, who watched Tiras. The man instantly looked away when he realized I was watching.

"Bring him here," I said softly.

The man hesitantly stood, and I watched in amazement as he rose. He topped Tiras, standing as tall as Goliath, if not taller! Every bit of color had drained from Tiras' face again as Shagay brought him forward.

"How are you called?" I asked.

"Uzzia, of Ashterath in Bashan," he said in a toneless voice.

That explained the height of them both, I thought, remembering the stories of the size of men that Joshua found in this area when he came through. Even kneeling, both of them were barely shorter than I. "Younger brother?" I asked after comparing their faces.

The dahveed's eyes closed in defeat. "Hesed, adoni! Do not give him to Talmai," he pleaded.

"I have no dealings with King Talmai, nor am I an assassin!" I said coldly. "Ahiam, can Ethan use caravan guards in Geshur?"

"Yes, adoni. There are only two bands here and in Tob to the east. Both are small."

"You are bound to Ethan the Habiru?" Tiras asked, surprised.

"Yes."

"Adoni, let my men become Yahweh's Arrows! They can serve faithfully and well. Adon Ethan will be pleased with them. Grant them this hesed."

"All right," I agreed. "You will send one of them to Ethan, who will tell you what you are to do."

"At once, adoni. I will send Uzzia tonight."

I smiled grimly. "Your brother will be staying with me, Tiras, as surety for the oath you are about to take."

"I will swear to whatever you require, adoni," the man promised, bowing.

I took his oath, binding him to obey and serve as Ethan directed, on pain of his brother's death.

Then I returned Tiras' sword, and his men retrieved their weapons also. As they left camp, he stopped, looking at Uzzia. "He will be well-treated, adoni?" he couldn't help asking.

"Ask Igal," I replied.

Igal gave the tall man a crooked smile. "Since he'll undoubtedly be more useful than I am, he'll be treated as least as well as I am."

"You've improved of late, Igal," I said.

"Thank you, adoni."

As the brothers said farewell, I realized they had probably never been separated in their lives. But I knew there was nothing else I could have done, short of killing Tiras.

We rested the next day, packing and readying for travel as dusk settled down. While the last of the sun's rays reddened the land, we descended into the Yarmuk gorge, crossing nearly two miles before climbing up the other side and joining the road to Ramoth-Gilead. I pushed on all the way to the city, feeling the need to get some distance between me and Talmai. Jaasiel, or Jaas as Igal called him, was nearly dead on his feet by the time we arrived.

CHAPTER 24

Two nights later, we were outside Rabbah Ammon, King Nahash's capital. Jaas was holding up well, but he needed to rest. I supplied Igal with silver so that he and his friend could stay at the inn Ahiam recommended until we decided to leave.

Dawn was breaking by the time we were settled on the east side of town. The seasonal river south of the city had plenty of water from the rains of the past two days, and a caravan had camped close to where we slept. Apparently it was a regular stopping place for them. As I watched, my sister Abigail stepped out of a tent, stretching before picking her way down to the river.

With a grin I cat-footed to the path. When she walked past, I rose from the ground behind her. "Sahrah, you are too beautiful to leave here, so I shall take you with me," I said, grabbing her in my arms, whirling her around and around.

Her first shriek woke the entire encampment, and she kept screaming, only now it was my name. I set her down so that she could turn around, and she threw herself at me. "You terrible, impossible boy!" she cried, "How could you do that to me? Oh, wait until I tell Jether. He'll peel your hide!"

"Only if I can peel you off it first," her husband said in disgust.

I looked up to find half the men in the encampment standing around half-dressed, but all with weapons ready.

"Dahveed, I should nail you to the ground," he went on, as Abigail hugged me again. "But somehow I'm too glad to see you!"

He offered his arm, and our grip became an embrace. When he waved his men away, they turned back, smiling tolerantly at what I'd done.

I sent a message to Ahiam telling him what had happened, and then spent the day with Abigail, meeting little Amasa and hearing all the news. Ala was in town again, married now, and a great favorite at court. Abigail had arranged to visit her the next morning, and she wanted me to go with her so that Ala could see me and they could introduce me to their grandfather, King Nahash. I sent for the clothes the headmaster had given me, and spent the night with Jether's caravan. I'd missed enough sleep that I didn't wake the next morning until after both Abigail and Jether had already gone. He had business in the city for the caravan. It was after the third hour by the time I'd dressed and headed into Rabbah.

Noticing a commotion in the square by the palace, I approached cautiously. As I peered over the heads of those watching the disturbance, I froze in amazement as Commander Libni, and several men of the tenth unit surrounding a woman, marched her toward the palace. General Abner held her arm tightly.

From her disheveled appearance I knew that they had had a hard time capturing her. The angry expressions and mutters of the crowd had the tenth unit worried as they tried to keep people back and follow Abner at the same time. Then I got a glimpse of her face. "Abigail!" I whispered, stunned. Suddenly icy fear invaded my mind.

How had it happened? Shoving my way through the rapidly growing crowd, I watched the palace. Guards barred the way, more coming every second, the commander standing in front of the closed doors. Dodging between people, I glimpsed Ala, her face calm and implacable. She spoke rapidly to a small boy, and he ran off in the direction of the city bazaars. I smiled grimly. Jether would be here soon.

Ala stood to the side, and I crossed the square, heedless of those I shoved out of my way, my clothes and gold jewelry keeping protests to a minimum. Abner had stopped, never loosening his hold on my sister, by the time I worked my way to Abigail's cousin.

"If you won't open the doors, then at least send a message," the general said, his annoyance barely controlled. "My son is before the king now, speaking of this very subject."

"Ala, do you know what's happening?" I asked in a low voice.

Abigail's cousin glanced my way, taking only a moment to

recognize me. "No, but I will soon. She was crossing the square to meet me when the men seized her. You go into the palace. I'll stay here and watch her until Jether comes. Nothing will harm her, Dahveed."

"How can I repay this?"

"I have a long memory, Dahveed." Her tone sent a chill through me, and the expression in her eyes as she watched the tenth unit reminded me of a viper's gaze. I wondered what exactly had happened to her before she had hidden in my brothers' tent in the army camp the night her own brother Zelek had tried to assassinate the hassar.

Signaling one of the guards, she ordered, "Take this man into the throne room."

"Yes, Sahrah."

I followed him inside and up the stairs to Nahash's second floor audience room, and walked into the second shock for the day. Across the anteroom, the eleventh unit surrounded my men, all of whom were bound. Only Igal and Jaas were missing. Elika looked white and sick, Zalmon not much better, and Uriah, Ahiam, and Shagay had obviously put up quite a battle. Shammah appeared unharmed, and Uzzia towered over the others, his face blank. Where was Eliphelet? Then I smiled grimly. Perhaps he'd felt safe enough this far from Geshur to slip away. Ruthlessly stifling my desire to yank my sword from its sheath and attack the entire eleventh unit, I slipped away in rigid acknowledgment that there was nothing I could do now.

"Sahrah Ala sends the adon to the throne room," the sentry said to the guard at the door. The man looked at my sword, but stood aside without question, and I walked in, slipping immediately to one side to stand with some other courtiers. Ala must have a great deal of influence if she could get me into the throne room with my weapons.

I eased my way through the officials and petitioners waiting in the back until I could see and hear the man speaking. It must be Abner's son. Jaasiel ben Abner had the same square chin, rugged features, and brown hair, his abbi just had more gray. He stood a little taller than the general and possessed a certain grace in his movements completely absent in Abner.

Apparently the normal greetings had already been exchanged, and Jaasiel was coming to the point of his request.

"Adon, King Shaul has been troubled lately with a persistent rebel who has been a plague on the land," he said in his pleasant tenor voice. "Since the Philistines have not come to our lands this year, my adon has had the time to turn his attention to this problem. We have found that this man has a sister who married a caravaneer. His caravan rests even now to the east of the city. King Shaul requests his brother king to cooperate with him in returning this woman to Israel, from whence she is."

The doors opened again, and a guard approached Jaasiel, handing him a message. Abner's son read it, turning to King Nahash. "Yahweh has blessed us, adon. The woman has already been found. With your permission, we need only to return to Israel."

Ala appeared from a side door, looking a bit breathless. She approached the throne while Nahash considered the request, his natural suspicion of anything Shaul wanted preventing him from making a quick decision. When she spoke to him briefly, his eye brows went up, and he turned to Jaasiel.

"Bring the woman here."

"As you request, adon," Abner's son said, not completely able to suppress his puzzlement.

Ala had anticipated him, and when the doors at the other end opened, Abner stood ready to enter with Abigail and six men of the tenth unit. My sister stood stiffly in the middle of them, fringe torn from her dress, her hair in disarray, dust on the bottom part of her robe, a red mark on her check, and her arm still in Abner's painful grasp as he marched her up to Jaasiel.

Jether and five of his men walked in behind them, the Ishmaelite's face smooth and blank, but his eyes burned.

King Nahash stared a moment, and then he shifted position on the throne, reminding me of a snake coiling to strike. "This is the woman?" he asked, his voice hard.

"Yes, adon," Abner replied.

"They took her in the middle of the square outside your doors, adoni," Ala said quietly.

Nahash's face turned white, and Jether's men spread out, making Commander Libni glance worriedly at them. The king turned blazing eyes on Abner. "You laid hands on *my granddaughter* in the middle of the public square? You dare to hold her in my very presence?" he roared.

Only the stunned expression on Abner's face prevented Nahash from ordering the general killed where he stood. Abner's hand fell from Abigail's arm, and she stepped away without deigning to look at him.

"What should prevent me from taking all your heads?" Nahash demanded between clenched teeth.

"Our ignorance, adon," Jaasiel said, dropping to his knees, his voice steady. "We have made a terrible mistake. King Shaul would not knowingly offer any insult to his brother king. You yourself know that I was here before you requesting permission to find the woman."

"Then how is it that you seized my granddaughter?" Nahash snapped.

"Through my carelessness, adon," Abner said, joining his son on his knees. "I was eager to fulfill my adon's wishes, and when our informant pointed out a woman and said she was the one we sought, I unwisely ordered my men to take her. I beg your forgiveness, adon. I will send whatever recompense is necessary to restore your granddaughter's honor. It never entered my thoughts that someone would want to cause war between your country and mine!"

In the ensuing silence I watched Nahash. Abner's last sentence had hit home. The genuine surprise of both men, and their instant acknowledgment of guilt had prepared the king's mind for the seed that Abner now planted. Nahash knew well that Yira to the south was always waiting for a chance to push even farther north of the Arnon, and a war between Israel and Ammon would benefit only Yira.

The rest of the tenth unit had dropped to their knees when Abner did, and their strained faces backed up Abner's words. Before Nahash responded, I knew that Shaul's cousin had managed to slip out of death's grip. He and his son made a formidable combination, and I no longer wondered why Hassar Jonathan had so much trouble bringing Abner under control. His cousin was just as astute as he was.

"I can see that undue haste in this matter would not be wise," King Nahash reluctantly admitted. "It is not like Shaul to seek trouble."

"He would not, adon," Jaasiel said. "He knows well that you aid him every year against the Philistines by allowing him to fight them unhindered. It is something he has frequently commented on. Especially since the offense given you by Manani of Ekron, when he murdered your son."

Nahash's eyes glittered, and Ala stepped closer to him.

"We beg your forgiveness again, adon. Name the recompense to be paid."

"I will consider," the king said, looking at Abigail and then at Jether, who nodded reluctantly. The Ishmaelite stepped forward, and Abigail went to him.

I sagged back in relief. Abigail at least was safe. That left my men.

Jaasiel and Abner exchanged a brief look.

"Adon, we would plead for your indulgence a little longer. Because of what has happened here, there is something we should tell you," Abner said. "My adon was hesitant to say anything, since there are only indications as yet of trouble. But because we have given such serious offense, you have a right to know more of why we came. While our men withdraw, I would ask your patience to listen to me a little."

Nahash nodded stiffly. The tenth unit rose and backed away, eager to get out of the throne room and away from the baleful glares of the Ishmaelites surrounding them.

"My adon knows that you and he have common enemies. Seren Manani of Ekron threatens every ruler in the land with his ambitions," Jaasiel began, building on what had already been said. "My adon, King Shaul, sent his request to you because he judged the rebel in his ranks a threat to you also. Indeed he may be in your borders, now, King Nahash. He was treated as a son by my adon, and then turned against his benefactor, plotting to take the throne from him."

"So, this is about Dahveed Israel," Nahash interrupted, looking impatient. "What does he have to do with me?"

Without missing a beat, Abner's son continued. "He may have much to do with you, adon. What you may not know is that Dahveed has an army, men who will do whatever he commands. How much trouble have you had with Habiru lately?"

The unexpectedness of the question caught the king's attention. "Less than usual."

"It is the same with Adoni Shaul, King Talmai of Geshur, and King Yira of Moab. The south of Judah has been quiet also. This is not coincidence, adon. King Shaul has discovered that the Habiru are no longer separate bands, but have allied together under a single leader. This Ethan of Judah has for years worked to gather into his hands the Habiru bands, uniting them under his command. And Ethan bows to one man only--Dahveed ben Jesse of Bethlehem.

"Think of it, adon," Abner's rough voice slipped in, strangely persuasive, "how many Habiru are within your borders? Where are they? If they suddenly attacked your citizens under the direction of one leader, how would you defend yourself? The network this Ethan has formed stretches from the Negev below Judah up both sides of Jordan to the land of Hamath and Damascus."

My stomach so sick that I was dizzy, I nearly doubled over. To hear Ethan's life work blackened in such a way, knowing what could happen to his people if something like this was believed, nearly drove me to my knees with horror. Was there never to be any place for Bodbaal, Geresh, and Caleb's twins? Would Dahveed Joel and Hanan, Zeri, and the rest of Jeshua's small band be hunted and slaughtered because they had finally found a little security in their lives? Even proud Tiras and his men should be allowed some place under Yahweh's hand.

Tears stinging my eyelids, I closed my eyes. If Abner had been looking for my weak points, he had found them. Scores of them. For if Nahash and others believed this story, widespread slaughter would result. And it would be believed, for the truth was in it. "Yah, do not let this happen," I pleaded. "What can I do?"

King Nahash shifted again on the throne. "How do I know what you say is true? You claim that Dahveed is in my borders, and you imply that he will bring about a rebellion against me, but I have no proof of any of this." The king's skeptical tone gave me a single light of hope. Of all the kings to approach with this, Nahash was the one who would be hardest to convince. But then, if he did accept it, the others would fall into line.

Yah, do not let these lies be believed, I begged in my mind.

"With your permission, I will bring proof before you," Abner replied.

"Bring it."

Jaasiel turned to the doors, and the guard opened it. The eleventh unit shoved my men to the center of the room. "These men are some of Dahveed's personal retainers. The blessing of Yahweh led us to them just last night. If these men are here, Dahveed is here, adon. That is why we came with our request. King Shaul asks that his brother king allow him to do what is necessary to find and to bring to justice this rebel who endangers every throne in the land. What other purpose could Dahveed have to collect such men? It is a testament to his powers of persuasion that one of these men is from King Shaul's own tribe of Benjamin!"

Nahash eyed my men suspiciously. "They look like a rag-tag bunch of Habiru to me," he said drily. "If they are such warriors as you ask me to fear, how is it that you are able to bring them before me? They look well beaten, but I see little evidence that your men have been in a battle."

"Yahweh gave them into our hand," Abner replied.

King Nahash snorted. "More likely, you crept up on their camp in the night and overwhelmed them with numbers. What do you want me to do with them?"

"Release them to us, and we will take them to Israel," the general said.

"Yah, what do I do?" I asked, knowing the fate that would await any of my men in the hands of Abner and Shaul.

"Give yourself into the hand of Abner."

I shivered, my stomach sick again, I couldn't imagine what I would suffer under Abner's hand now. Surely there was some other way. I waited.

"I thought it was Dahveed you wanted," Nahash continued, still suspicious.

"He will follow his men to rescue them. You will not be troubled with him then."

The thought seemed attractive to Nahash. He was probably tired of the situation, ready to get rid of the nuisance as soon as he could.

"If he would do that, he cannot be as treacherous as you imply, Abner," Abigail interrupted. "All he would have to do is abandon these men, and call up others. If you are so certain he will follow them, you must be certain of his loyalty."

"And his information about the Habiru is nonsense, adoni," Jether added. "Ethan the Habiru is well-known on the caravan trails. His men and allies are the best guards for the caravans to be found. As the caravans travel from Damascus, the guards cycle through the Habiru allied to Ethan so that each band escorts the caravan through their territory. Such local knowledge as they have is invaluable to us.

"The House of Tahat will not hire any other guards, or even send their goods where Ethan's guards cannot be found. Half the other caravans on the roads use them, and the other half wish they could. Ethan has not raised an army; he has simply spread the knowledge of which bands are trustworthy. If you interfere with this, adoni, you will lose at least half the trade that comes through Rabbah." He looked Nahash in the eye. "My caravans will not be able to operate, either, adoni. Such a drop in income would not be well-received by my kin. I'm afraid I cannot answer for the ways in which they might decide to make up the loss."

My mouth nearly dropped open. Jether had practically assured Nahash of war with the desert raiders on his unprotected eastern boundary if he took any action against the Habiru!

"Such possible consequences do not seem to be worth the risk, envoy," Nahash observed. "If you had not assured me otherwise, I would suspect your adon of troubling my land."

"You have taught me that I must look to my information sources closely, adon," Jaasiel said humbly.

I sent silent, fervent thanks to Yah in relief. With the caravaneers themselves backing the Habiru, rumors of the sort Abner had brought would get nowhere.

"I need only to know your will for these men, adon," Jaasiel went on, bowing from his knees.

"Take them," the king said, waving his hand impatiently. "I care not."

"Do not leave me, Yahweh," I pleaded. "Give me Your presence."

As Jaasiel and Abner rose and the guards turned to my men, I emerged from the assembled courtiers and officials.

"I do care," I said. "Let them go, and I will return with you."

"Dahveed, no!" Abigail cried.

"You know my weakness well," I went on, looking at Abner.

He smiled grimly. "Bind him."

I held up my hand, and the man who had started forward stopped. "I said I would return with you when my men are free--or do you wish the alternative, Abner?"

The general reluctantly nodded to a soldier, who jumped to Shagay, quickly slicing through the bonds that tied his hands.

I watched until my men were all free, then jerked my chin at the door opposite the one they had come in. "Go."

Shagay looked at Ahiam, and they shrugged. He turned to the others. "Go."

No one moved.

"Take them out, Shagay," I commanded.

"I cannot, adoni, since I'm not going," he replied calmly.

"This is not the time for this, Shagay. You gave your oath. Take them and go," I said savagely.

He came and stood behind my right side. "Then I am foresworn."

Ahiam bowed. "Your pardon, adoni, but I believe I will foreswear also," and he took a position on my other side.

I looked at Uzzia. He was the one who might tip the balance and get the others to leave. I knew it was useless to argue with Shagay and Ahiam.

"You have one who loves you waiting," I said. "I am sending you out in peace as of now. Return to your home."

"I am no longer bound to you?" he asked, his dark eyes watching me seriously.

"Correct."

"Tiras will be glad to know that. I'll tell him if I get the chance," and he walked over to stand beside me. The rest of them spread out around me.

"You do what you wish, Dahveed," Shagay said. "We'll follow along to be certain you get to Israel--and the hassar."

At the mention of the hassar, the men of the unit edged back a little, beginning to think of what might happen when they returned, and Abner's face hardened.

"Jether?" I unbuckled my sword and held it out to him.

He accepted it. "You will really go?" he asked in an undertone.

"I must. Yah will go with me." I pulled the belt knife and sheath from my girdle, then unwound the sling from my hand and wrist.

After he took them he stepped back, and I heard Abigail's quiet sobs in the background.

Taking a deep breath, I left my men and knelt in front of the general. "I am in your hand, Abner."

"But you are in my court, Dahveed," Nahash broke the silence. "Ala tells me that you held her as captive. Perhaps I wish to deal with you myself."

It was an out, and I knew it. But Yahweh had been clear. Still, I had to force myself to reply. "Speak to General Abner of that, adon."

A murmur went through the crowd.

Abner snatched the gold headband from my head, taking some of my hair with it, and then took the gold arm bands as well. I didn't resist, and his grip on my shoulder forced me farther down while he bound my hands himself. Then he jerked me to my feet, and I steeled myself, knowing this was just the beginning.

"We bid you shalom, adon, and give you the assurance that our adon, King Shaul, will not forget how you have aided him this day," Jaasiel said. "We have trespassed on your time long enough."

Abner spun me around, and the group started to withdraw.

"General Abner, I believe there is still some business to discuss," Nahash said, adjusting himself on the throne.

Abner turned back. "Yes, adon?"

"There is the matter of your recompense for the dishonor you showed my granddaughter earlier today."

"Of course, adon," Abner bowed. "What do you require?"

"I believe I'll take Dahveed. Somehow, the thought of you having to explain to King Shaul how you had Dahveed bound in your hands, but still weren't able to deliver him, soothes me for the outrage you did to Abigail."

Abner looked at Nahash in disbelief, his face matching the feeling going through me. His face gradually turned red, and his hand tightened on my arm.

"I trust you're not contemplating a refusal, General. There is always your son, and the priest of Milcom has been talking to me of sacrifice again."

Abner swallowed, and the look he gave me was one of hatred. "He is yours, of course," he said, managing to keep his voice under control. "Your generosity in laying on us such a light recompense for the offense will long be remembered."

The king stared at Abner, and the general knelt again. "Please, take him," he urged, placing the headband and armbands at my feet.

Nahash flicked his hand, and one of the guards by the throne took me and the jewelry to one side.

"You are dismissed, Abner. Jether, may I impose on you for some men to escort the general and all his to the Jordan River? With all the rains we've had lately, they should cross it as soon as possible. Otherwise, they might be trapped on this side of it, and that would be a great misfortune."

"I will be happy to accommodate you, adoni," Jether answered, his smile as chill as a desert night.

When Abner had gone, I knelt in front of the throne. "What is your will for me, adon?"

"I am simply repaying a debt, Dahveed," he said while Ala and Abigail both came to untie me. "Ala has told me of your kindness to her and her brother. You are free to go, but I hope you will accept my invitation to share the evening meal." When he stood, I saw with surprise that he was not much taller than Abigail.

"I will be honored, adon. You have my gratitude."

"I will expect you then." He left the room.

I turned to Ala. "I owe you much."

Her dark eyes looked at me. "I told you, I have a long memory, Dahveed."

I glanced at Abigail's tear-streaked face, so like Ala's except for her lighter skin. "So do I, Ala," I promised.

I could barely get my sister to let go of me, but I had to return to our camp, if only to see what we needed to replace after the capture of my men. In addition, I must check on Igal and Jaas. Eliphelet was probably miles away by now, and I dismissed him from my mind.

But when the eight of us returned to camp, we found it in good order, with a fire burning, by which Igal lounged as usual.

"You're back sooner than we expected, adoni," he said. "Eliphelet said that it might take you a while to rescue the others. Jaas," he called, "where did our personal thief go?"

"He said something about bringing the rest of the items he found," Jaas replied, stepping into view, being careful how he moved his back.

I stared around the camp. The first thing that caught my eye was my harp which someone had taken out of its case and broken part of a tuning peg off. "And may I never find out who in the eleventh unit did that!" I fumed, inspecting the damage. After putting the instrument away, I noticed the neat stack of swords near a fire, another of war daggers, and a pile of bows with quivers, probably comprising enough weapons to equip two entire units! And stuck in the ground to one side stood a single blade.

I walked over to it. It was familiar, and I stood a minute, thinking back. "Eliphelet!" I roared, "come here this instant!"

He appeared after a couple moments. "Yes, adoni?"

"Why am I holding General Abner's personal sword? What did you do? Rob the Israelite army?"

"I couldn't have robbed them, adoni. In order to rob, the owners must be present. We simply picked up a lot of things that were left lying around outside the palace doors in the care of a very beauteous woman named Ala." He kissed his fingers in appreciation. "She was most dainty and obliging, adoni. Far too delicate to be saddled with such clumsy things as these," he gestured toward the piles. "She was very grateful when we offered to take them off her hands."

I glared at him, beginning to sense the amount of trouble he might cause in the future, let alone at this moment. How was I going to manage to return the general's sword this time?

Once I decided to keep the weapons, my men looked them over, laughing over the tale of how Eliphelet had slipped away during the night attack and notified Igal and Jaas what had happened. The three of them had seen the Israelite units enter the palace and decided that no matter what happened, being deprived of weapons would make things harder for Abner and his men.

That night, Jether gave me clothing fit to wear before Nahash, and Jether, Abigail, Ala, her husband, and I sat on cushioned chairs around the table with King Nahash, talking and laughing. I had brought my harp, and Abigail and Ala both urged me to play. I treasured the time I had, knowing it would be a long time before I saw Abigail again. When I left, Nahash presented me with a purse of small gold ingots, waving away my thanks.

"Ala has brought me much pleasure, and I would not have her if it weren't for you."

"In Yahweh's name, I will always remember your kindness, adon," I said. "Not only did you save me, but you protected Abigail also. She is very dear to me."

"Then let there be peace between us forever."

I bowed. "Forever," I agreed.

"Amen," we both ended.

We left the next morning, headed south for Moab. Before crossing the border, I requested permission of Yira to see my family, and when he summoned me, I once again forgot to remove my belt knife. I think his amusement at my embarrassed discomfort prompted him to grant me three days to visit. He also invited me for an evening meal, at which I played at his request. While I entertained him, he relaxed in my presence for the first time.

When I left for Judah, Abbi urged me to take Asahel with me. Zeruiah's youngest missed Abishai terribly, and he was becoming a problem with the local young women, his easy laugh and amusing ways charming them all too easily. Abbi didn't want the slightest chance of offense to Yira, so Asahel returned with us.

After four days of travel in the constant rain, we descended into the valley leading to Adullam. The thought occurred to me that we'd need to find another cave, for the one I'd left Zabad in would hardly hold the 12 men with me now. In addition, after being gone three weeks longer than expected, I hoped it wouldn't be difficult to start running messages again. My men must have something to do, and it was too late to plant grain. Maybe we could hire out as guards for travelers or as day laborers in the fields. I'd have to consult with Elhanan.

Zabad wasn't at our cave, however. Zelek was.

"Shalom, Dahveed," he said.

"What are you doing here? Is everything all right in Bethlehem?" I asked, alarmed.

"As far as I know, it is," my half-cousin assured me. "But it seemed best for me to leave. I think my family connection to you has come into the open."

"It has. I saw Ala. She is well and happy."

"Good. I hope you don't mind, but we've added two more men here. They showed up two weeks ago. Their names are Gareb and Ira. And they've been delivering messages, along with Jonathan and Abishai. Elhanan was grateful to have them when you didn't return as planned."

I sighed. With Ittai, that brought the total up to 19. I watched as the men crowded in, finding places to put their wet things and sit down to rest. How was I going to feed, clothe, and employ 19 men?

Tamar bat Dahveed

Did you see how Yah is teaching both Dahveed and Gebirah Abigail what they need to know? Look how Dahveed's trust that Yah would protect him led to the saving of all his men! And Abigail can now truly be Gebirah to her people.

Even though there is much neither of them understands, they will see later how Yah was building for the future, bringing the pieces together now that they will need many years ahead. That is something it is well for all of us to remember. You may not understand now, young geber, why you must study so hard, but Yah wastes nothing, and what you learn He will use for your good. There, you've distracted me again.

Now, let us turn back time once more and go to Gibeah for much is happening there. As Dahveed has seen, Abner has more power than the hassar guessed, and Jonathan has missed a very important piece of that power, Abner's son, Jaasiel. So, while Jonathan's attention is on the king and the kingdom, Yahweh is working on the sidelines to separate Abner and his son, and bring about the transfer of that kingdom.

I know, most people think Shaul reigned until his death, but we must not forget the word of Yahweh, that the kingdom would be torn from Shaul, not just his house. And so it will be, for Yahweh's word always comes to pass. But the tearing will rend the hearts of the royal family with bitterness and sorrow, creating a division among them that will never be bridged.

Jonathan Hassar's greatest test is upon him, and he will need every bit of strength Yahweh has given him to withstand the blow. His family will aid him, and one man, nurtured in a faraway land and carefully placed by Yahweh, will turn the tide when the hassar needs help the most.

CHAPTER 25

Doeg. Jonathan stood to the side of the stair door to the throne room, watching the Edomite leave by the far door after Abbi had spoken to him. The king shoved a papyrus into his girdle, and the hassar knew that no messages like that had come through his hands. He sighed silently. Doeg would have to be shuffled aside somehow, and he knew there would be a fight with Abbi over it, to say nothing of what Abner would say to the dismissal of as good a fighter as the Edomite.

More and more he hated the way that he had to constantly watch his abbi, gradually hemming him in, always alert for the slightest hint that someone had slipped through his guard to endanger Dahveed. When he entered the throne room, the king greeted him with a slightly bland expression. Jonathan's stomach sank. He'd seen that look a lot lately. How much more had he missed?

Later that afternoon, the scribe at the door reported that General Abner had returned and was waiting to report.

"Show him in," Shaul said quickly.

As his abbi's cousin walked in, the first thing that Jonathan noticed was the empty sword sheath, the next that the general was very angry, then that he was also worried.

"Did you enjoy your visit with family?" the king politely asked.

Jonathan kept his face straight. He hadn't even known that Abner had left. Why hadn't Malchi reported it?

The general shrugged. "Our brother wasn't in too good a mood."

A shadow crossed Shaul's face. "I'm sorry to hear that. Tell me about it later. You must be eager to get back to work, so I won't keep you."

"Yes, adoni."

After court was dismissed, Eshbaal approached Jonathan when they were alone. "I know you didn't want me to say anything about this, hassar, but this re-equipping of the tenth and eleventh units seems odd."

"What re-equipping?"

His youngest brother handed him a list, and he scanned it quickly. Malchi's seal was at the bottom. "It was good you noticed this, Eshbaal. I'll check with Malchi." Eshbaal left, and Jonathan slowly sat down on the bench of the long table. Was it possible his brother had teamed up with Abner? Clearly in his mind he saw Malchi's eyes and heard his voice when he spoke of what Abner had done to Dahveed.

"Yah, this doesn't make sense," he said aloud. There had been no change in Malchi's manner, no avoidance in his eyes, no indication at all that he had switched sides. The hassar smiled bitterly. Families weren't supposed to have sides. But he could see them becoming more definite with each passing day, and he wondered again who would join whose side when the chasm finally opened.

Sighing once more, he picked up the list and put it in his girdle. He'd ask Malchi about it after the evening meal.

"Is there something wrong, Jonathan?" Malchi asked, ushering him through the door to the upper room.

The hassar handed him the list without a word.

"So the re-equipping you ordered went through?"

Jonathan froze. "That's your seal, Malchi. And why didn't you tell me that Abner left to visit family?"

"Why should I tell you? You ordered me to let him go!"

The hassar stared at him. "*I* ordered you?"

"The message had your signet."

"Mine, or the king's?" he asked, his mouth dry.

His brother thought for a moment. "Your personal seal."

"Did you seal that list, Malchi? Do you remember actually pressing your seal on it?"

"No, I don't."

Fists clenched, swearing under his breath, Jonathan turned away. Someone had to be secretly running messages for the king! He should have paid more attention to Ishvi's concern about how the king knew so much!

"Can I take that to mean you didn't send any messages such as I described?" Malchi asked, his voice dry.

"You can, brother."

Malchi put on his cloak. "Shall we see what Ishvi's doing tonight?"

As they walked down the dark streets, Malchi commented, "This could have looked as if I had joined up with Abner."

"I know. Maybe it was meant to. I didn't know what to think when I first saw it, especially after finding out that Abner had been gone only after he got back."

Malchi stopped. "If you have any question about my loyalty, Jonathan Hassar, I--"

Jonathan reached up and touched his brother's lips, silencing him. "I have no questions, Malchi-shua, Sar Israel. I think more of your honor than that!"

Ishvi greeted them sleepily, but the expressions on their faces quickly woke him up. He pulled on a robe. "What's happened?"

"Have you gotten any messages from me telling you not to question something I've done which you'd normally take care of?" Jonathan asked.

"No."

"You're certain?"

"As certain as I can be. Nothing has come to me personally, and I haven't had anything like that handed to me by Elihu."

"Elihu sees all your correspondence before you do?"

"Yes."

Jonathan and Malchi glanced at each other. "If our lines of communication are destroyed, we lose the war," the third sar drawled.

"Get Eshbaal up, Malchi, and have him go through all the court correspondence for the past three months," Jonathan ordered. "Anything that strikes you as odd, as something you should have done, but didn't, bring it to Ishvi's business chambers by the west gate. Ishvi, send for Elihu. We'll meet him down there."

Ishvi had a lamp lit in his business chamber when Elihu arrived, looking as if he had risen for the day, instead of been summoned in the middle of the night.

When Jonathan asked about certain correspondence, the scribe replied, "No, Hassar. Sar Ishvi has not seen anything like that."

"I didn't ask if he'd seen it, Elihu," the hassar said softly. "I asked if anything like that had come."

Elihu remained silent.

"Dahveed is my son, Elihu," Jonathan said roughly. "I cannot protect him if I do not know what is happening around the king."

Dahveed's brother took the hassar's gaze for the first time that Jonathan remembered. His look was as direct as Dahveed's, and just as demanding of truth. "Who holds your loyalty, Hassar?"

Jonathan paused, knowing that if he gave the wrong answer, he would get nothing more from this man. "My first loyalty lies with the one who deserves the most honor, Elihu. Yahweh commands me above all others."

Elihu bowed, giving the hassar the strange feeling that this was the first time the man had ever truly granted him his respect. "Sar Ishvi has received several messages such as you describe in the past couple of months. I set them aside."

"Get them now," Ishvi ordered.

When Malchi and Eshbaal arrived, the four sars looked the documents over.

"Why did you pull these, Elihu?" Ishvi asked.

"The seals are counterfeit."

Jonathan looked up quickly. "How do you know?"

The scribe got some wax and melted it on a papyrus. "Stamp it," he said to Malchi.

The sar pressed his ring into the wax.

Then Elihu handed the re-equip list to Malchi. "Compare them."

After a few seconds, Malchi threw the list down in disgust. "It's smaller, but that's the only difference. How could this happen? This ring never leaves my finger!"

"It didn't have to," Elihu explained. "All that is needed is a good impression of your seal. The impression was coated with olive oil, and then wet clay was pressed into that and taken out, giving a perfect image of your seal. As the clay dries, however, it shrinks a little. You have to know what you're looking for to notice."

Jonathan felt like swearing again. He let Malchi do it this time.

"Those seals could be with anyone, then," Ishvi observed.

"And we can't go around comparing seals and impressions on every message we get," Malchi added in disgust.

The hassar noticed that the scribe had his lips tightly pressed together as if he was holding himself back. "Elihu, I hold your gratitude, do I not?"

"Yes, Hassar."

"In that case, Elihu ben Obed, whenever you have a suggestion regarding the safety of your brother Dahveed, you will tell me as soon as you can. Is my will clear?"

The man bowed slightly. "Yes, Hassar. Rather than compare sizes, you could alter your own seals by a tiny nick which will be noticeable only if looked for. You could identify a false message immediately, and then discover who delivers them to you. The couriers must lead to the source sooner or later."

Jonathan pulled his personal seal off his finger and handed it to Elihu. "Start with mine."

The next day, instead of eating and resting at noon, the hassar dismissed his personal guards, joined Sar Malchi, and went to Quartermaster Nadab's chamber.

"I've got some questions about the re-equipping of the tenth and eleventh units," Jonathan said.

Nadab grunted. "You're not the only one. I want to know how two units come back from Ammon having lost nearly every weapon they took, but somehow survived the experience. To say nothing of all the tents and animals! But since you said not to make a fuss, I didn't," he added, looking at the hassar accusingly.

"The time wasn't right," Jonathan said smoothly. "It is now. They lost *everything*?"

"Almost. I had to drain the armory to re-supply weapons. Bows weren't so bad. We've still got plenty of those. But the battle daggers and swords they lost were the better quality ones, so what they have now is second-rate." He snorted. "Which is what they deserve, I suppose. And the sword Abner has isn't much better. He was furious at losing his blade."

"Abner's personal blade is gone?" Malchi asked incredulously.

"Stolen so they say. But the scuttlebutt among the men is that everything was confiscated by Nahash himself because of some insult. That's more likely to my mind since Abner isn't raging against thieves or complaining about all those animals we lost!"

"You've been helpful, Quartermaster," the hassar said, rising. "Let's go, Malchi. We have more to do."

His brother followed him. "We're going to be hard put to replace that many tents, Jonathan," the younger sar commented angrily.

"I know. And if Nahash really did confiscate them all, Abner must have created a diplomatic mess of leviathan proportions. We need to talk to the commanders immediately!"

"I'll send for Libni, first," Malchi decided.

When Commander Libni entered the throne room and found the sars waiting, he touched his knee to the floor and rose. "You sent for me?"

"Yes, Libni. I'd like a complete report on the trip you took to Ammon." At the commander's puzzled expression, Jonathan went on. "You've already given one?"

"Yes, Hassar. General Abner said he'd be certain that you received it."

"The general has been busy and hasn't gotten it to me yet. Something has come up now, so I need to know what happened and why."

Libni's face paled. "We didn't know she was the king's

granddaughter, Hassar! You must believe that!"

"I'm sure you didn't, commander," Jonathan assured him without missing a beat. "But start at the beginning. You left when?"

Under his adept questioning Jonathan soon had the story.

"What was Jaasiel doing there?" Malchi asked. "He's never strayed far from home most of his life."

"He attended his abbi," Libni said. "He kind of smooths over any feathers that Abner ruffles, if I may say so."

"Then what happened?" Jonathan inquired.

"The king dismissed us, and we got out as quickly as we could. I don't know what happened with the eleventh unit and Dahveed's men. We had to wait in the square. Our weapons were gone by then, and with those Ishmaelites watching us, I wasn't certain we'd make it out alive! And not even Abner dared say anything when we got back to our camp and found everything gone there, too!"

As soon as the door closed after the departing commander, Malchi turned to his oldest brother. "Did you know Dahveed's sister is Nahash's granddaugher?"

"Yes. Her immi was Jesse's second wife, I believe, and died before Dahveed was born, so Dahveed has no actual blood tie to Ammon. Let's get Pasach in here."

The commander of the eleventh unit arrived and bowed. "You wished to see me, adoni?"

"I understand there was some trouble in Nahash's court when you were in Ammon. I'm trying to get as complete a picture as possible, so I'd like you to tell me everything you remember."

The man looked down. "Would that be a command, adoni?"

"If necessary. Have you been told to remain silent?"

"I wouldn't want misfortune to befall me. Or my family, adoni."

Jonathan debated, suppressing his anger. Just what was Abner doing to intimidate one of his own commanders this way? Unfortunately, he had to know what had happened in Rabbah. "What is this on my finger, Commander?" Jonathan asked, holding out his hand.

"The king's seal, adoni."

"Then in the king's name, report!"

The commander talked.

"He actually had Dahveed bound and in his own hands when Nahash took him away?" Jonathan eventually interrupted, not knowing whether to laugh or rage.

"Yes, adoni. And then Abner had to beg Nahash to take him."

Malchi had a crooked grin on his face. "Wish I could have seen that, brother."

"It does strain the mind," the hassar commented. "Continue, Pasach."

When the man finished, Jonathan leaned back in his chair. "What did Abner tell you to reply to any questions?"

"We were instructed to say that thieves took our things, and much as General Abner wants to blame Dahveed, he can't. He and his men were still in the throne room," Pasach added.

"I think this will be all, Commander. Be sure to let me know if there is any trouble over your report."

"Thank you, Hassar."

"What do you think?" Malchi asked as the man headed down the stairs to the anteroom.

Jonathan chuckled. "I think this will have settled Abbi and Abner for some time! It will take a while to recover from a defeat like this."

Over the course of the next three weeks the network serving the king began to emerge, involving everyone from fortress servants to individual soldiers in the units to beggars in the streets.

"Leave this to Elihu and me," Ishvi said the day the extent of the problem became clear. "Malchi has the army, and you have to handle Abbi himself, as well as run the kingdom. You simply can't keep aware of everything, Jonathan."

"I know, Ishvi," he sighed. "But let me know of any major developments."

Late that afternoon, as the last of the scribes were leaving the anteroom, the hassar jerked his head up at the eruption of shouts from the other side of the courtyard.

"Close the gates!" Commander Sheva roared. "Get them shut now! He's got to be in here somewhere, and I want him in front of me or know the reason why! You two, search the armory rooms under the wall. West sentries, to the king! North wall sentries, check the king's residence and the store rooms. The rest of you search the walls and courtyard."

By the time Sheva finished his instructions, guards stood outside of the throne room, spears at ready, but clearly confused about what they were guarding against.

"Go see what has happened, Jonathan," King Shaul said.

The hassar walked into the courtyard, two sentries with him, and mounted the stairs to the eastern wall where Sheva stood outside his commander's room, sputtering with rage.

"The king wishes to know the situation," the hassar told him.

"Look inside," Sheva replied, barely getting the words out.

Jonathan took one look and jerked back. Then he looked again, and faced Sheva.

"I stepped outside no longer than half a moment, Hassar, and when I returned, that's what I saw!"

Just then Jonathan caught sight of Nimshi who was watching wide-eyed. "Get the king," he said to his youngest armor bearer.

The young Habiru ran off, and soon King Shaul himself climbed the stairs to the commander's chamber.

The hassar pushed the door opened and stepped inside, holding it for the king to enter and indicating the commander's table with a nod of his head. There, with the point buried in the wood, stood General Abner's personal sword.

Shaul's mouth twitched, and a wicked gleam appeared in his eyes. "Send for Abner."

While they waited, Jonathan approached the table, examining the sword. He brushed away a couple of splinters. The sword had been cleaned, oiled, and sharpened like a razor. The worn leather on the hilt that he remembered Abner complaining about had been replaced, and he examined the workmanship. Casually, he reached up and ran his fingers across it, removing the single dark blue thread twined with silver which hung from it. He would wager his supper tonight that this thread would exactly match the ones in the tassel hanging on the back of his bow case. But he forced himself to keep his face impassive.

Malchi appeared with Abner in the courtyard below, their mules both heaving from the climb to the fortress. Abner raced up the stairs. "What is it, Sheva? Why were the gates closed? Is the king well?"

"I'm fine," Shaul replied. "But Sheva was quite upset to leave his chamber for a few moments and then find this when he returned."

Abner stepped inside, followed by Malchi. The look on the general's face when he recognized his sword strained Jonathan's self-control to the limits.

"It would seem that King Nahash repented of his confiscation of your sword, Abner," Shaul said seriously. "Such generosity seems strange for him. Should I send a letter acknowledging this?"

His face flaming, Abner gulped. "I don't think that will be necessary, adoni." He gripped the blade and pulled it from the table, testing the edge. "Someone knows how to sharpen a sword," he exclaimed in spite of himself. Then he took out the one he'd been using and sheathed his own, walking out of the door.

The others left in silence, Nimshi following Jonathan down the stairs. Once the rest were well away, the hassar looked down at Ethan's youngest son. "How do you like your new duties as my armor bearer instead of arrow boy?"

"There's a lot more to do, geber," the youth replied seriously. "But Dara is a good teacher."

"Learn all you can from him. And Nimshi, if you have to return the general's sword again, do it a little less dramatically, would you?"

Laughter flashed from the Habiru lad's eyes. "I'll try, geber!"

The winter passed, days of cold wind punctuated by drizzly rain and blending into the warmer rains before harvest which gradually cleared in time for the grain to dry in the sun.

"What do you think, Taphath?" Jonathan asked, pulling his bride to him after they finished the evening meal. They sat on the rooftop of his private estate, enjoying the warmer weather.

"I'd like to go. It's been six months since we were married, and I know my family in Jabesh will be eager to have more than messages from me. I don't mind staying there while you go up to Dan. You're excited about the latest news, aren't you?"

The hassar smiled. "This is the best indication we've had yet that the Steward of Tahat is known there. It's odd that it comes from a scribe. Apparently nothing can be found out in the markets or on the trails. But this indicates that the Steward should be around Dan."

"And you think that by going there, you can pull him from the shadows?"

Jonathan chuckled. "Something like that, I guess."

"I think you just want to get away from Gibeah. You miss going to war."

"Whatever gave you that idea?"

"The way you keep looking wistfully at Sar Malchi when he talks about where they'll go this season. Sometimes you're as obvious as a thunderstorm, Hassar!"

With a laugh he caressed her. "That's settled. We'll go at the end of harvest. Court business is light then. Ishvi can help Eshbaal with Abbi if necessary, and Malchi and Abner will be busy with the Philistines. We shouldn't be gone more than three or four weeks, anyway, including travel time. You do realize, Taphath, that when you sit in that spot this close to me, you make your husband very uncomfortable."

"Oh? I'm comfortable. Surely there's some way you can get comfortable!"

"Well, since you suggested it . . ." he said, leaving the sentence unfinished and tightening his arms around his wife.

¥ ¥ ¥ ¥ ¥ ¥

"It's done," Taphath told her mother-in-law the next day. "We'll be leaving before threshing."

"Excellent, Taphath," Hassarah Ahinoam said. "It's been impossible to get Jonathan out of that fortress for the past couple years. He needs the rest, and with him gone, I might find out who's taken a hand behind the scenes with the king and Abner. Now, Michal's been listening to good purpose, and she heard a name that I hadn't thought of. What do you know about Abner's son, Jaasiel?"

"Well, he's the youngest, I think. Immi didn't keep up well with Ner's kin. There didn't seem much reason."

"There wasn't, back then," Ahinoam said thoughtfully. "Two of your cousins married into Benjamin, right?"

"Immi's cousins," Taphath corrected. "One to the king's uncle, and the other in Bahurim. You know, I wonder if Azmaveth would know about Jaasiel. Seems like I remember stories about them from Immi."

"Azmaveth of Jonathan's personal guard?"

Taphath nodded. "I haven't told you about this, because I didn't know if Jonathan wanted me to, but Abner is holding Azmaveth's son hostage."

"Abner or Jaasiel?" Ahinoam wondered. "And that explains why Abner and the king always know what Jonathan is doing."

"Yes. Jonathan has known for a long time, but what can he do? He doesn't want to endanger the boy."

"Effectively tying his hands and keeping them informed at the same time," Ahinoam declared in disgust. "We need to know more about Jaasiel." The hassarah paused. "Perhaps it might be well for you to have a small guard while you're traveling, Taphath, and since Azmaveth is related, he would be a natural choice."

Taphath's eyes sparkled, and she smiled without saying a word.

CHAPTER 26

"If I may speak to you, adoni?" Doeg requested as the king left for the noon meal and rest.

King Shaul frowned. "Talk to Jonathan," he said dismissively.

"The hassar left three days ago, adoni," the Edomite reminded him. "And what I have to say would not be welcome to his ears in any case. I would open your ear alone, adoni."

"Attend me, then," Shaul said, leaving the tamarisk tree on the hill and taking the road to the fortress. Several years ago, Jonathan had suggested holding court here on hot days since the daily wind across Gibeah's hill blew freely, which it could not do in the rooms of the fortress.

The king waved his guard ahead so that he walked alone with Doeg. "What is it?"

"I investigated some of the stories of Dahveed attending the hassar's wedding," he began.

Shaul snorted. "Lies! He could not have been there."

"They are not lies," Doeg said softly. "He did attend. The blind beggar supposedly found on the road in the Arabah was actually Dahveed. The man who brought him, and the adon of Zobah who took him away are members of the band of Habiru that he has assembled. Dahveed feasted all the next day while Abner was distracted by the Habiru trader he thought was supplying Dahveed."

"How do you know this is true?" the king demanded, his anger rising.

"I have talked to men who know. Abner's agent with the hassar reported Dahveed's presence to Abner, and the general spent much time and men barring the way south from the estates in Zelah while Dahveed and those with him headed north. By the time Abner picked up the trail again, they were past Shechem, and even his swiftest runners could not catch them. Then some days later, his servant Ahiam was seen entering an inn in Ramoth Gilead."

"So that is why Abner suggested his visit to Rabbah," Shaul muttered. "He would not tell why he thought it would be useful. But he will not withhold such information from me again," he added, his eyes flashing. "But where is Dahveed now? How can we find him?"

"Word is that he is living in the caves near Adullam. He and his men act as couriers for the surrounding towns, and hire out as guards to protect the flocks. They also work as laborers. It is said the landowners pay good wages to them."

Shaul's face darkened. "And after defying me to such an extent, he lives openly? Send messengers, Doeg. Find out exactly where Dahveed is located. The units need some exercise before the season begins. Instead of a mock battle this year, perhaps we will have a real one!"

"You have pleased me greatly, Doeg."

"Thank you, adoni."

¥ ¥ ¥ ¥ ¥ ¥

The roeh's servant, Gad, held the next petitioners back while the presence of Yahweh pressed close on his geber. It was noon, but the people had been waiting for some time and looked worried. He knew Shamuel would want to see them in spite of how tired he was. Gad sighed. The roeh's health was failing, but he could not get his geber to rest.

"Gad!"

The urgency in Shamuel's voice surprised him. "Yes, Roeh?" He hurried into the inner room.

"You must leave instantly. Take your cloak and the riding mule we bought last week, and this food," he gestured to the meal prepared for himself. "Go to Adullam. Do not stop for anything at all! In the market place at the well you will find a young man named Asahel. Take him aside and tell him that his dodi has been discovered and must flee immediately to the forest of Hereth in Judah. He will deliver the message. Then you will leave the market and climb to Gedor, where you will see the lad again, talking to a man. Follow that man and serve him.

"You will need this, also." The roeh held out a purse, and Gad took it, surprised at how heavy it was.

Roeh Shamuel smiled sadly. "You will need it all, my son, for you will not be returning to me. I have taught you all that you need to know to be a prophet of Yahweh. Serve your new geber well for he is Yahweh's Mashiah."

Gad paused in amazement. He had long suspected that the roeh had anointed another king, and he had his own suspicions about who it might be, but the aging prophet had never mentioned the subject, and he knew better than to bring it up.

"Do not linger. Go immediately, and as fast as you can!" Shamuel said sharply. "I will send a change of clothes and the materials for the chronicle you are keeping in a day or two."

The servant bowed automatically. "Yes, adoni!"

White lather dripped from the mule's heaving sides when Gad at last sighted Adullam's walls. He slowed his mount a little. The animal had withstood the grueling 26-mile run better than Gad had expected. While he had paused occasionally to allow the mule to drink, the fast pace in the heat of the day had drained the animal. Gad glanced at the sun. It was after the tenth hour, but urgency still pushed him onward.

When he rode through the gates, the mule had recovered enough that Gad knew he could drink the cool well-water without injury. He dismounted by the water trough and reached for the bucket to fill it. A couple young women watched, water jars full, and a dark-haired slim young man lingered with them. Then he approached the servant.

"That's a fine mule, geber, and you both look as if you've had a hard run. Let me draw the water."

"That's kind of you," Gad replied. "Whose house do you belong to?"

"I am Asahel, the messenger, geber. My house is not far from here."

Gad waited until the youth poured the water into the trough. "I have a message for you to run, Asahel. Tell your dodi that he has been discovered and must flee to the Forest of Hereth immediately."

The young man looked up quickly, wariness in his eyes. "How am I to know this is true?"

"I am Gad, servant of the roeh. You will see me again, but go warn your dodi. There is no time." He held out a copper piece.

The youth took it. "I will deliver your message right now, geber," he said loudly enough for the women to hear. With a smile, he trotted off. Gad watched while the mule drank the trough dry and snuffled for more. Glancing through the city gate, he saw the lad leave the road for a path into the forest, and when he glimpsed him next, the youth's long legs were carrying him swiftly over the ground.

After the mule had drunk more, Gad tested the straps on the pack behind his seat, then mounted and rode out of the gate, turning off the road at the same place the youth had, but continuing up toward the steep rise of the highlands. He had an idea that he didn't have much time to get to Gedor. That young man could run!

¥ ¥ ¥ ¥ ¥ ¥

I took off my sandals, having just returned from carrying a message to Keilah. The leather was wearing thin, and I'd need to replace them soon. There wasn't much to spare for the heavy traveling sandals I'd need, but I couldn't put off buying another pair any longer. Threshing had begun, and there were many landowners with grain to sell to the grain merchants who came to the Shephelah every year. Odd, how often the grain we grew here ended up feeding our enemies on the coast, while we used the silver they paid to buy the weapons to fight them.

"Adoni," Zabad called, running up to the cave entrance. "Something has happened. Asahel is running!"

"That's his usual pace."

"Not like this, adoni. He is heading here as fast as he can."

A tingle of apprehension ran up my spine. I'd been restless lately, unable to forget the roeh's comment that trouble would result from my trip north.

Reaching for the sandals again, I tied them on. By the time I finished, Asahel was in sight, and as Zabad had said, he was racing flat out, long legs flashing in the elegant stride that carried him to victory in countless races. I went to meet him, Ahiam following me out.

"Dodi!" my nephew gasped, "Man on a lathered mule. Said he was from Roeh Shamuel. Named Gad. You are discovered. Go to Forest of Hereth." Panting, he bent over.

The afternoon suddenly seemed cold, and everything got very still. "He said his name was Gad?"

Asahel nodded. "The mule could have come from Ramah. It had been ridden a long way, fast."

"Did he say anything else?"

"He said there was no time!"

Ahiam ran back to the cave, yanking the pot of water from the fire and dumping it. Igal looked up in surprise, jumping to his feet as my retainer snapped orders. Word spread, and the men who were here hastily grabbed up their possessions, stuffing them into packs. I sent Zabad to warn the others who were living in caves farther on, and minutes later Uriah arrived, returning from a hunt.

"What is it?" he asked.

"Shaul has located us," I said, trying to picture the best way to get from here to Hereth. The roeh was sending me to the thick, wild forest south of Gedor and east of the road from Hebron to Timnah[11]. The only people in the area stayed close to Giloh, nearer the drop to the Shephelah and Keilah.

"Ahiam, what's the best way--" I started to ask.

"Let us worry about that, adoni. Shagay knows the best routes to the top. Uriah and I can get the men moved. You need to get into the highlands now. Elhanan must be warned, and he may know the best ways into Hereth. We'll wait south of Gedor for you to meet us there and show the way."

Zabad approached with a donkey, and while I told Uriah which of my men had gone where for the day, Ahiam packed the animal with my things. I was halfway up to the highlands before I realized that Ahiam had sent me out of harm's way first, and I had gone like a lamb.

While I nearly turned around and went back, I realized that there was merit in the plan, and the roeh had said there was no time. Now that I was climbing the steep hill, all the things I should have done, the messages that I should have sent, plans made to warn the others, all ran through my head. "Be with me, Yah," I whispered. "This was so sudden."

But I knew things would always be that way from now on, and I must be able to respond instantly. I didn't have time to berate myself, however. I had much to do in Gedor.

Once in the settlement, I went to the stall in the market where Elhanan stayed. He was the central point for our courier service.

"What is it, Dahveed?" he asked when he saw me.

"Shaul has found us," I said quietly. "Roeh Shamuel sent warning, and we are to go to Hereth. I've come to warn you, and to ask what are the best routes for us to go east."

Elhanan looked around. "What of our service?"

"I don't know," I said to my old friend. "We may be still able to deliver some messages, using men that Shaul doesn't know, but it will be difficult."

"It will be impossible," Elhanan admitted with a shrug. "I'll tell my relatives that I must go. If I remember correctly, my cousin mentioned a long ridge in Hereth about a mile back from the road. It might be a good place. He said it was easy to get to from the south."

---

[11] The exact location of the Forest of Hereth is not known, but it must have been in this general area in order for Dahveed to be close enough to rescue Keilah from the Philistines' attacks.

"Good. The others plan to wait on that side of town when they come up the land stair."

Elhanan closed up the stall and left. Watching the busyness of the market around me and trying to still the butterflies in my stomach, I waited for a while. I must plan the next move for my men. Looking down, I caught sight of my worn sandals. I still had the gold pieces the hassar had given me, and the purse of ingots from Nahash, but the time might come when that gold would be needed to save lives instead of my feet. I could make sandals if I had to. It was one of the first things the Habiru had taught me.

Then I looked up at the blue sky overhead. Yah had granted us a winter of rest with time to sort ourselves out and train with Uriah. Our occupation as messengers kept us on the edges of honorable society. But with this move, we became Habiru and nothing else.

Like that dragonfly so long ago, I had stayed close to the place from whence I came, testing my wings. But now I had to go, as that little insect had suddenly turned and flown into the reeds, disappearing from sight.

"Yahweh, I am afraid," I admitted softly as the sounds of the market eased, and the sun lowered in the sky. "I don't know what to do, or how to guide those with me. There is no hassar to turn to, no quartermaster to supply what we lack, no fortress to protect us from those who wish us harm. Truly, Adonai, you will have to gather us into Your hands if we are to survive the wrath of the king."

The merchants closed the stalls around me, and my donkey dozed patiently to one side, occasionally shifting its feet. Asahel trotted through the gate, looking tired for the first time since he'd been with me. Catching sight of me, he hurried over. "Dodi, the men are at the top of the land stair. Shagay and his son stayed behind to keep watch. Ahiam said to tell you that most everything came with us, but some of the men may be a bit more organized after this."

I had to smile, betting that anything left behind had been personal items. I had no worries about our extra weapons. Uriah had charge of those, and I knew they would have been packed to go before anything else. Uriah was a soldier from first to last.

"All right, Asahel. Tell Ahiam I'm waiting on Elhanan, but that we should be there soon. You can walk the message if you want," I added.

His quick grin flashed across his face. "I think I can manage more than a walk, Dodi. But not if I have to come back!" he admitted.

I chuckled, watching a hard-ridden mule pass through the gates, the rider dismounting and glancing around.

Asahel straightened up. "Dodi, that's the man!" he said suddenly. "He gave me the message in Adullam. I remember now that he said I'd see him again."

"Very good, Asahel. I'll keep an eye on him."

My nephew trotted out of the market and through the gate. The mule's rider watched him, and then led the exhausted animal over to the well, drawing water for it. Elhanan appeared beside me, a packed donkey trailing behind. "Are the others here?" he asked.

"Yes," I said, rising. Elhanan fell in beside me. As I'd half expected, the man with the mule let us get to the gate, and then led his animal after us.

"As tired as that mule is, you'd think he'd be staying in Gedor," Elhanan commented after it was clear the rider wasn't going to remain in town.

"I suspect he wants to talk to me," I said. We slowed our pace, but the rider didn't try to catch up until we had turned off the road on a path into the trees.

"Adon, I would speak with you," he called.

I turned back.

He came closer, his expression one of curiosity as he looked at me. "Dahveed ben Jesse!" he exclaimed, surprise flickering across his face.

"Yes, Gad?"

He looked tired, and more than that, lost somehow.

"What has happened?" I prompted.

To my surprise, he dropped to his knees. "Roeh Shamuel has sent me to follow and to serve Yahweh's Mashiah," he said, bowing to the ground.

Elhanan's mouth dropped open.

I froze a moment, but I couldn't make the remark go away, anymore than I could make his obeisance disappear. "Get up, Gad."

He rose to his knees again, and I gave him my hand which he briefly touched to his lips.

"The roeh does me more honor than I deserve. You have been his right hand for many years. He will miss you, I know. And you him."

Gad looked down, blinking at the tears in his eyes. "Yes, adoni."

"Come, then. If the roeh has sent you to me, he knows I will need you. There are others waiting. Let us go."

We started down the path.

"Dahveed, he called you 'Mashiah'," Elhanan said hesitantly.

I glanced at my oldest friend. "Still want to stay with me? The king will stop at very little in his search to find me for he is determined that Jonathan shall rule after him."

"What of the hassar?"

"He grants highest honor to Yahweh."

"And what of me?" he asked, his face pale as the implication of his knowledge sank into his mind.

"You are my oldest companion, and as long as there are bullies in the streets, I'll be looking for you beside me," I said with a grin.

He grinned back. "I'll be there, Dahveed."

¥ ¥ ¥ ¥ ¥ ¥

Abigail sat on her folded cloak in the tiny garden, enjoying the warmth of the sun while she worked on the meil. It was almost done. Much had happened this past winter, and she was glad it was over. Her plans had worked well. Nabal spent all his time in Carmel sitting in his business chamber summoning people to see him and scheming to acquire more control over Hebron.

As she had hoped, rumors of his behavior had spread during the winter, and several adons were planning to visit during the summer. If all went well, Nabal would have lost even more ground by the New Year's feast. She would have to find some way to keep him from attending it. Her needle flashed in and out, drawing the red thread after it. She had some decisions to make and wasn't certain what to do.

First, she must decide if she should actively interfere with Nabal's treatment of the local people, or continue working behind the scenes to ease the trouble after he caused it. At least now, she knew everything the nagid planned. Tokhath had proven surprisingly willing to talk to Tirzah, and Abigail suspected her handmaid repaid the man with her favors. That was apparently enough for him to continue, since he had to know that Tirzah told her everything. Why would the shrewd scribe do this when he was often at cross purposes with her trying to influence Nabal?

The Gebirah glanced around uneasily. She had never been alone with Tokhath since that day in the business chamber, and the man hardly noticed her when Nabal was present, but she still felt defiled when he was around.

The one disappointment of the winter was her continued failure to discover anything about Parai's family. Thinking of disappointments brought the latest news to mind, and she had to smile. It hadn't taken long for the story of Abner's encounter with Dahveed Israel in Rabbah Ammon to fly from one end of the land to the other. She didn't know how the north reacted, but the south rocked with laughter, raining blessings down on Dahveed's head for the way he had yielded himself for his followers. What sort of a man would do that? She wished she could see him again, have some time to study him a little. His eyes on her that last time had summoned a flash of something that she'd never felt before. What had Dahveed Israel seen when he looked at her?

Nabal, of course, had been delighted at the news, gloating over the dishonor to General Abner, and through him, Shaul's house. "They are beginning to fall," he'd said last night, after his second cup of mixed wine. "And when Shaul's house is destroyed, there will be a need for a strong, capable leader, one fit to rule, to step into his place. I must be ready."

That remark had increased her determination to know everything the nagid planned, for his normal avenue to what he wanted involved violence, and any such attempt against the house of Shaul would bring about the destruction of her own. And that would spoil all that she was working toward.

The gate opened, and she looked up in surprise as Parai entered. She froze, that calm mask settling immediately on her face, and raised her chin, fighting to keep her gaze steady. "What did you want with me, Parai?" she asked, surprised that her voice sounded so cool.

"A few words, Gebirah." He shifted uneasily on his feet, his glance looking everywhere but at her.

She stuck the needle in the meil and folded her hands. Their trembling would be less obvious that way. "I'm listening."

"I've watched you," he began uncomfortably. "What you're doing, I mean. I didn't understand at first. It seemed crazy, as if it would make things worse. But then I overheard the talk at the feast Nabal gave, and I've thought much since then. You're destroying him, Gebirah."

"Yes."

He glanced at her. "Why? His fall will be the fall of your house and honor."

She picked up the meil, taking the needle in her fingers again. "What honor, Parai? For all the wealth that Nabal has at his fingertips, we have nothing. You taught me that on the roof the night of the New

Moon feast. My actions, or lack of them, stripped my house of that which had most value. It is my responsibility to restore that treasure, or make it possible to regain it in the future."

"But why?" he pressed again, approaching closer.

She sighed. "Because I am Gebirah, Parai. These people are mine, and I failed them. I owe them recompense."

"You care, then, about what has happened to us? You would give recompense to me?"

"I believe that you have already planned your recompense," she replied, looking him in the eye.

Parai stepped back, then slowly left the garden, forgetting to close the gate behind him.

CHAPTER 27

Jonathan checked the pack again. The case with his composite bow was in it, and he wanted to be certain it was secure. He had stayed with Taphath's family longer than expected, waiting for information regarding the Steward. When he finally left, he set a fast pace north, wanting as much time as possible in Dan since the trail to the Steward had nearly dried up again. The hassar frowned in irritation. How could the man be so elusive? His agent here had reported that no one knew anything about a House of Tahat, and yet Pasach had said Jether's comment in Nahash's throne room had carried a lot of weight with the king of Ammon.

But Jether was gone again, and Jonathan wasn't going to poke around in Ammon searching for Abigail after the way Abner had enraged her grandfather, which left him grasping at straws in the markets and hanging on the words of scribes. He was no longer certain that he'd find the steward anywhere! Why would a merchant be so secretive?

He looked around at his guards under the command of Abiezer. They were dressed plainly, as he himself was, and they resembled a messenger party rather than that of a sar and his retinue. The seven of them rode Shammah ben Jesse's mules, with Nimshi up behind Dara. They had come up the Arabah from Jabesh, and finding the Yarmuk fords there overcrowded, Nimshi guided them east up into the tableland, then down to the ford for the Laruba road into Geshur. They had crossed there after only eight hours of waiting.

Now they were camped in a small clearing on the highland not far from Talmai's capital. Nimshi appeared beside him. "The roads are crowded this year, geber," he said. "But with the mules, we can take the north trail by the Chinnereth Sea to the Hula Valley. A trail there runs up the east side of the valley all the way to Dan. It's about 40 miles."

"What do you think, Dara?" Jonathan asked, knowing his shield bearer would balance his desire to push on at all costs.

Dara looked at the mules thoughtfully. "We could do it in a day, depending on what that northern trail is like. But we might strain the mules. I think we should stop in the Hula."

"All right," Jonathan agreed.

Ethan's son stood. "We are watched, geber," he said without seeming to speak.

"How many?" the hassar asked without looking up.

"Probably only one or two. But many of the Habiru here are not allied to Abbi. We should be cautious."

The next morning, they left before the sun had peeked over the horizon, passing Laruba before its gates opened. The trail north turned into the forest from the road 10 miles farther along, and was clearly made for donkeys. But so long as they watched for overhead branches, travel was smooth.

Close to noon, they emerged in a small clearing with a tree in the middle, and Jonathan signaled a halt. They had made good time, and if the trail remained passable, they would reach the Hula well before dark. He shared some parched grain and dates with Dara and Nimshi, and then dozed a while.

The other five guards lay spread out in a loose circle, the mules standing under the shade of the tree also.

The next thing Jonathan knew, his mule snorted, and Nimshi rolled to his feet, yanking out his belt knife just as the mule brayed, pulling back so suddenly that the tether broke. The animal reared and whirled, jumping away from the tree, bucking and kicking.

Once on his feet, Jonathan glanced around. His entire guard fanned around him, weapons ready, watching the only mule in sight--his, and it was still bucking. The pack split, spewing his possessions on either side of the animal, which finally subsided to merely dancing around, snorting and facing the tree.

"Today just gets more interesting as it passes."

At the sound of the ironic comment, everyone whirled around. Standing behind them, sword in hand, was a dark-haired man, taller than Shaul. The hassar's hand went instinctively to his own sword hilt, then stopped. Ten men, armed with bows had appeared around them.

"What do you want with simple travelers like us?" Dara asked.

The man smiled. "Now that's a good question. You might indeed be simple travelers, in which case I don't want much of anything. But you're not like the usual parties who use this trail. There aren't any trade goods, so you're not merchants. You haven't got women or children, so you're not a Habiru band moving through."

He edged around them a little, and Jonathan kept him in sight.

"You're not from Tob east of us because you came up from the Yarmuk. And you're not dressed like cocks impressing the hens, so you can't be useless nobility from Zobah. On the other hand, your clothes are all very good-quality. And I haven't seen such a group of mules in my life. And that one at least," he pointed to the light gray still staring at them, ears flattened, "is trained for war."

His eyes missing nothing, he walked a few steps farther. "And from the way everyone came off the ground, you've all fought before."

A movement beyond him made the hassar flick a glance that way. Two more men tried to herd the mule back, succeeding to a limited extent. He clenched his teeth. So far the only thing that had gone right was the uneventful trip to Jabesh. And being robbed by Habiru in broad daylight was something he'd never live down! Everything not actually with his men had already disappeared, including the mules. While he could afford to replace the animals and the top-quality bows his men personally owned, the arms they carried were forged by Lotan and practically irreplaceable. And the composite bow was another story all together. He couldn't afford to lose that on more than one account. The question was whether he should fight for it now, or go after it later.

The Habiru dahveed continued studying them. "Now why would eight such well-disciplined soldiers be quietly slipping through Geshur? I don't suppose you'd just tell me what you're doing here?"

"Traveling through," Dara replied.

The man's eyes wandered over them, finally settling on Nimshi. "And this would be the Habiru guide. Quite young, too."

"We found nothing, Tiras," one of the man's warriors said, emerging from the trees. "They're all stripped down to essentials only."

Jonathan noticed that his guards had widened the circle they were in, giving themselves more room to fight, despite the close watch kept on them by the Habiru archers. Abiezer had shifted to stand nearly in front of him on his right, leaving Dara on his left in battle position.

How could he really repay men such as these?

"Collect what that mule spread all over the clearing then. Maybe there's something there. There's got to be a reason for their presence here. And this is just the sort of thing that interests my adon most," the tall dahveed directed.

While two men obeyed him, three more led the other mules back into the clearing. Each one still had its pack.

Jonathan exchanged a glance with Abiezer. Were their things going to be returned?

"Tiras!" one of the men in the clearing called excitedly. "We've found a bow case!"

The dahveed looked around in surprise as his man hurried forward, handing him the slim box. Unfastening the rawhide cover, he pulled it off, revealing the five symbols inlaid on the top. "Yahweh's Bow!" he gasped, dropping the case as if it had exploded into flames and backing away from it. When he looked up at the group again, his face was pale. "What does the Lion of Judah want with us? We have served as he directed."

The archers guarding them looked around nervously. "Do not anger him, Tiras!" one of them pleaded.

The Habiru dahveed checked the bow case again, then approached closer, studying each of them with care. "The Lion of Judah is not with you. How is it you have this bow?"

"Who is this Lion of Judah?" Abiezer asked, voicing the very question in Jonathan's thoughts.

"He is Yahweh's warrior, and he has the eyes of the lion when he fights and the power of Yahweh comes on him."

Dahveed! The thought stirred Jonathan's memory. Something the zammar had said when he received the bow, about what he should say if anyone asked how he came to have it.

"We carry it because it belongs to us," Dara said.

Tiras' face darkened. "If you claim it, you have stolen it! And Yah's judgment will fall on you all!" he said, his voice suddenly hard.

"It was not stolen," Jonathan spoke for the first time, stepping forward. "It was entrusted to my care."

Tiras held his gaze for a long moment, then bowed his head and knelt. "We are Yahweh's Arrows, and you carry Yahweh's Bow. What is your will, Nahsi?"

Hearing that title from other lips than Dahveed's confirmed Jonathan's suspicions that Dahveed had guessed something like this might happen some day and hadn't given him any warning. When he saw that exasperating hill man again, he would--he would--he'd think of something!

"Get your mules," he said to his guards. They broke the circle around him and collected the animals, Nimshi going after Jonathan's light gray.

"You have allied with Ethan of Judah?" the hassar asked.

"Yes, Nahsi."

"Why did you stop us?"

"We meant only to search your packs to see who you were. Then your mule took exception to the proceedings. Things ran awry from there," Tiras said in disgust.

Jonathan had to smile. Then the implications of Tiras' statement came to his mind.

"If you're Yahweh's Arrows, do you protect the caravan routes?"

"Yes, adoni."

"Have you heard of the Steward of the House of Tahat?"

"Of course, adoni. How could I not?" the Habiru replied, surprised.

Suddenly Jonathan felt very kindly toward the tall Habiru kneeling in front of him. "Tiras, take me to the House of Tahat, and I will give you whatever you request, if I can."

The man didn't move. "Anything, Nahsi?" he asked in a shaking voice.

"If I can."

"Do you know the Lion of Judah? "

"Yes."

"Will you speak to him of my brother? I attacked him when he was here, and he took Uzzia as hostage. I do not ask for my brother back, I know that cannot be, but I beg you to request that he be well treated, and if I might hear of him from time to time . . ." His voice trailed off.

"Dahveed is not a cruel man, Tiras. Uzzia will be fine."

"You have not seen his eyes, adoni, how they burned in mine!"

"Yes, I have, Uzzia. And I have felt his anger, and I have seen the power of Yahweh on him. Your brother will be safe, unless he tries to kill Dahveed."

"He will never do that, adoni. You will speak to the Lion of Judah of this?"

"I will communicate with him of it," the hassar promised.

"Thank you, adoni."

"Then, shall we go, Tiras?"

Two days later, just after the noon rest, Jonathan followed Dahveed Tiras through the gates of Dan. Carrying the bow case, which Nimshi seemed to assume would come along, Nimshi and Dara followed him as they crossed the market by the gate and entered the narrow streets. There was nothing special about the door Tiras stopped at, and when they stepped inside, several other people were waiting. A scribe sat at the end of the room, and Tiras murmured something in his ear.

The scribe indicated a guarded door to the side, and wrote something on a scrap of papyrus that a waiting messenger boy disappeared with.

Jonathan looked around. The place was neat, and there were bowls of fruit and small jugs of wine for everyone to take from as they wished. The atmosphere was subdued and business-like. He approved. This was just the kind of place he'd been hoping to find.

"Yahweh blessed us, adoni. The steward is here. You are to wait in the next room," Tiras said, indicating the guarded door. "I will be here when you return," he added, bowing.

A servant appeared as soon as they entered and lit three more lamps. The hassar glanced around in amazement. The room was lined with cedar, two ebony tables held silver bowls with sweet Tekoa figs and Jericho dates, and when the servant poured wine into a silver goblet, Jonathan accepted the cup, tasting it.

He nearly choked, making Dara look at him oddly. He tried it again. Without a doubt, this was some of Lahab's pressing, the excellent one from last year, of which he had several jars in the fortress. A three-legged chair sat on a slightly raised dais, and he wandered over to inspect the fine sheepskin thrown over the back, finding the long, thick wool of the Yidla-Dibon cross-breeding.

Dara stood in the middle of the room, by a larger table with two chairs opposite each other, looking as if he didn't dare touch anything. But Nimshi had already found a comfortable cushion in the corner and was snuggled into it. The hangings on the wall were embroidered with vines and flowers and gleamed with silver and gold threads.

If the Steward of Tahat was doing this well with products from Judah, Jonathan wanted to talk to him more than ever. But he hadn't expected anything of this level of wealth, and he instantly realized that the approach he'd planned to use would be useless. Obviously, the House of Tahat needed no help from him. Glancing at what he wore, his heart sank. It was very out-of-place in this room. He admitted to himself that he'd never felt so overawed.

How was he going to convince the agent that it would be profitable for him to combine with a tiny, shaky kingdom like Israel? He would be a fool to think that he could offer anything they didn't already have. And coming to them as a petitioner with nothing to offer would be presumptuous and a waste of time, something the Steward wouldn't appreciate. The temptation to leave nearly overpowered him. But the sight of Nimshi, nearly asleep on the cushion by the wall, was oddly comforting, and he sighed. He'd have to think of something. Maybe he could offer escorts through Israel that might provide swifter travel from Judah to Dan.

Dara still stood stiffly where he'd stopped.

"You don't have to stay in the center of the room, Dara," Jonathan said. "Over there by Nimshi will be fine. And you can put the bow case on that table by you."

"Yes, adoni," the shield bearer said, looking around wide-eyed before deciding to do as told.

Jonathan noticed the dispatch pouch on the three-legged table by the far door, sealed and ready to be sent out, as footsteps sounded from the far side of the door. Taking a deep breath, he faced it, standing by the large table near him.

The door opened a little. "He is in here, Nagid," a scribe's voice said, and the door opened farther.

"Be sure to send the message carrier as soon as he arrives," another voice answered, and the Steward stepped into the room, turning to face the hassar. His eye caught sight of the bow case on the table. "Is everything all right with it, Dahveed?" the Steward asked, looking up.

Jonathan Hassar stopped breathing, thunderstruck, the wine glass hovering just above the table where he'd been about to set it. Frozen in place, and staring back at him with speechless amazement, was Ethan ben Shoher! He wore dark gray robes, the silver embroidery on them flashing in the light whenever he moved. On his head he had a worked silver headband, and on one hand a single ring with the largest ruby the hassar had ever seen.

"I'm glad you're here, Abbi," Nimshi said with a yawn, climbing to his feet. "I was afraid we'd get all the way up here, and you'd be gone." Jonathan watched as the young Habiru walked over and put his arms around his abbi. Ethan hugged Nimshi automatically, then looked down at him.

"Why didn't you tell me?" Jonathan and Ethan both said in the same outraged voice.

Nimshi looked at them in surprise. "How could I? You both said I couldn't say anything to anyone."

When neither of them got a word out in response, he went back to the cushion and snuggled into it again.

Jonathan couldn't stop staring at Ethan, and before either could collect their wits, the door opened again.

"The scribe said you had dispatches ready for me, Nagid," the man said hesitantly.

Ethan gestured. "They should be delivered as soon as possible," he managed to say, unable to take his eyes from the hassar.

The messenger picked up the pouch and read the name on the front. He looked up in bewilderment. "You want me to deliver them?"

Ethan nodded.

Appearing as if he thought everyone in the world had gone crazy, the courier took the pouch, walked across the room, and handed it to Jonathan. "Will there be anything else, Nagid?"

"No."

Giving the two men another puzzled look, the messenger left.

Jonathan managed to glance at the dispatch pouch in his hands. It was stamped with Ethan's seal and was clearly addressed to him.

The Habiru took a deep breath. "Since I can't imagine my time with you will be short, adoni, I will attend to my other customers first and return as soon as I can. Please make yourself comfortable. If there is anything you want, just speak to the servant outside the door." He bowed and escaped, closing the door behind him.

The hassar stared at it, still wondering if he'd seen what he thought he'd seen. "Dara?" he asked.

"Yes, adoni," his shield-bearer answered.

"Dara, was that Ethan? The Habiru Ethan? The one who finds things for me, and who taught Dahveed how to fight, and who lives down near Bethlehem?"

"Yes, adoni."

The hassar found himself sitting on the floor, still clutching the dispatch pouch. He looked over at his young armor bearer, now sleeping on the cushion. "I'll-I'll shake him until his bones fall apart! He's as bad as Dahveed! No, he's worse! I'll-I'll condemn them to live with each other for the rest of their days! They *deserve* each other!"

Climbing to his feet, the hassar put his hand on his forehead, trying to see if he could still think. At last he sank down in one of the chairs. "After this, I don't think anything can surprise me again," he sighed. "No wonder Ethan gave me that strange look when I asked him to find the Steward of Tahat!"

"You asked *Ethan* to find the Steward?" his shield-bearer repeated.

The hassar nodded.

Dara gulped, and then folded up with silent laughter.

Jonathan put his head in his hands, but the humor in the situation just wouldn't go away. "Don't ever tell anyone about this, Dara," he gasped when he could speak. "Do you know what Malchi will do if he hears of it?"

"Might be entertaining to find out," the man replied with a sly glance.

"You're my shield-bearer. You're supposed to protect me, Dara!"

"From the Philistines, adoni. Last I knew, Sar Malchi was Israelite--and related."

"I can see I'll be in your power for the rest of my life," Jonathan groaned. He leaned back on the chair and picked up the cup, taking another taste of the wine. "I could get used to this very quickly," he said, looking around once more. "So could Malchi! How on earth did it come about?"

"Why don't you read your messages?" Dara suggested.

"I will, if you'll make yourself comfortable. Sit down, Dara. I don't think anyone is going to attack us today."

When his man eased down on another cushion against the wall, Jonathan broke the seal on the pouch and was soon lost in the dispatches. His hand was fishing in the bowl, trying to find another date, when the door opened again. He glanced up. Ethan stood by the table in his usual black kilt and mantle, his hand smoothing the wood of the bow case.

"Just give me a moment, Ethan," Jonathan said, his mind still on what he was reading.

"As you wish, adoni."

When he looked up later, having finished the last dispatch, Ethan still stood waiting for him. Jonathan rose hurriedly from the chair. "Do you stand for me in your own house, Ethan?"

"You are my adon," the man replied.

"I'm not so certain of that. From what I see here, your status is higher than my own, Nagid."

"We are stewards, adoni, not owners. There is a difference."

The wistful tone tugged at Jonathan's heart. "You still see yourself as outside the covenant, don't you, Ethan?"

"My people still are, adoni."

The hassar looked around. "Not for much longer, I would think. As steward, you must hold these things in trust for someone. Who is it?"

Ethan looked up. "For the Mashiah, of course."

"Does he know?"

"No. And he will not know until I die, adoni. If I may ask a question?"

"Certainly."

"How did you find me? I know it was not through the markets and caravan trails."

Jonathan smiled. "No. It was through a comment that Elihu made, and my other agents found a couple of other scribes who seemed to know something."

"I plugged that leak too late, then."

"Not entirely. By the time I left Jabesh, I was uncertain of finding you. I probably would not have if not for this." He touched the bow case. "Tiras knew, and when I asked, he answered."

"For which I cannot fault him," Ethan said ironically. "When his messenger came to me saying that Dahveed swore them as Yahweh's Arrows, I impressed on him that he should give any aid requested to the adon of that bow, should he ever appear. That is why I assumed it must be Dahveed here, although I couldn't imagine why. Nor did I know that Dahveed had given Boaz's bow to you, and he will answer for that oversight, believe me!"

Jonathan chuckled. "Sit down, Ethan." He indicated the chair on the raised dais.

The man shook his head. "The steward's chair belongs to another now." Instead, he took the chair across the table.

"You have a great deal to tell me," Jonathan declared, sitting also. "Where does it all begin?"

Ethan smiled and touched the bow case. "It begins with this bow, adoni, and a promise made to Yahweh when death nearly came to all my people. It begins with food, with Dahveed's harp, with elders at the gate, and with warriors. And it will end with a king," he continued, touching each of the symbols. "It begins when my ancestor looked into the eyes of a 7-year-old boy and saw the life of our people in them. Meshullam had led his band to the hills east of Bethlehem and . . . "

And the hassar sat in silence as the story unfolded, with each passing chapter growing more awed at what Yahweh had done. When Ethan finally fell silent, Jonathan shook his head. "Yahweh's Arrows doesn't begin to describe you and your band, Ethan. You are much more than that. You have been Yahweh's very hands, working to bring into being His will. Boaz was right. You stand higher in the covenant than I." He rose, and Ethan did also. "Ethan ben Shoher, as of now, you are released from your oath to me, for I have no right to hold it. Go in peace, for you belong to Yahweh and His Mashiah. But if I may, I will ask of you the same thing I did of the Mashiah. Will you grant me your friendship?"

The Habiru gripped the offered forearm. "With all my heart, Hassar."

The two sat down again, and Jonathan again looked around. "So this is what has grown from the businesses that Boaz began and Hassarah Ruth extended. Why did you decide to gather the interests she sold off before she died?"

"My abbi had suggested something like it to Patah more than once. Then when Shaul began acquiring land for the crown, and bred sons who could protect it, I knew Israel would become a settled nation. Trade seemed the best way to bring my people to a settled life also, and Patah and I formally combined everything into the House of Tahat before he died," Ethan finished.

"Does Jesse know of this?"

"He knows of the House and that it has grown considerably, but he does not ask questions. He is content for it to go to Dahveed when the time comes."

"It has not always been easy, has it?"

"No, Hassar. Your generosity just a couple years ago saved us from ruin. It was a terrible time, knowing that there was not enough in the House's coffers to feed my people even though in a few months' time there would be, but by then that it would be too late. What you did"--he stopped, averting his face. "If you would take my oath again, I would give it again, Hassar."

"I will not take it, Ethan, any more than I would have taken your freedom then. What all this means, however, is that the foundation of my dream for Israel is already in place, and has been growing for generations."

"Yes, Hassar. Yahweh has a way of anticipating us, I've found."

"But if I understood you correctly, you are no longer steward, Ethan. Who is?"

"My brother Jamin. I turned the seals over to him before I came in here to you." He looked sheepishly at the hassar. "I had no idea what state your anger would be in, only that it would be burning, and I wanted to be free to fulfill my oath, however you demanded that I do it."

The hassar eyed the Habiru for a while. "You look very satisfied with your loss. Would I be correct in thinking that it is more of a relief than anything else?"

A crooked smile crossed Ethan's mouth. "I guess there is more of my abbi in me than I thought," he admitted. "I find the life of the trails to be my life, and Jamin was already doing most of the business of the House anyway. Now he can do it without having messengers chasing all over the land looking for me."

The hassar leaned back in the chair. "I think I only have one more question, Ethan. Why did you hide from me?"

"At first because what I hold in trust is for the Mashiah, adon, and may not be yoked to anyone else. Then I learned your dedication to Yahweh's will regarding Dahveed. Before I had time to tell you after that, Nimshi sent word that Abner had found some way to know all your doings." The steward looked Jonathan straight in the eye. "And no Steward of Tahat will allow the House to fall in the hands of the one rejected by Yahweh. We will destroy it first."

A shaft of pain went through Jonathan's heart. Why couldn't his abbi see the blessings, the prosperity, the joy for the entire land, waiting to be poured out by Yahweh's hand if only he would submit to Yahweh's will? "Do you doubt that I share your dedication, Ethan?"

"No, Hassar, which is why Jamin has cleared the entire day tomorrow to talk to you about the ways that we can combine the House of Tahat and your dream. We have taken the liberty of dismissing Tiras and would request that you spend the night here."

"And the message that I am doing so has already gone to my men, right?" Jonathan asked, his eyes twinkling.

Ethan grinned. "Tiras needed something to do after sitting in one place for so long."

Tamar bat Dahveed

So another of Jonathan's heart's desires is met. He has found the Steward, and has begun to make his dream for Israel come true.

But the Evil One has not rested, and much has happened in the past few months which is coming to fruition now. As Roeh Shamuel told Dahveed, his trip to the Hassar's wedding will bring trouble as well as happiness. For the Evil One has his agents and his means, and after whispers of Dahveed's presence at the wedding fell on Doeg's waiting ears, he continued to listen and question and search, patiently sifting through everything that came to his notice. Dahveed has eluded the Edomite once, adding to the man's anger, but now Doeg has learned what truly happened at Nob, and his rage waits now for a time to strike.

But Yahweh knows human hearts, and He has already prepared for what will come.

CHAPTER 28

Doeg cursed to himself, annoyed that he had to get up this early for another message that told him once again that Dahveed still could not be located. How had the zammar been warned at Adullam? He himself had spoken only to the king, and immediately after the noon rest, he'd contacted his drinking companions who liked the silver he gave them. They had been riding mules south by the seventh hour, reaching Adullam before dusk, only to find Dahveed already gone.

His face hardened with frustration. After Abner's aborted attempt to bring Dahveed in, the king had been more than furious. With court business slow, Shaul had plenty of time to brood about the disappearance of his enemy and the fact that Doeg had failed to produce him. The commander hardly dared to show his face.

The only comfort he had was the absence of the hassar. With Sar Ishvi attending to the threshing at the private estates, Sar Eshbaal buried in court records with the scribes, and Sar Malchi in charge of the training of the permanent forces, Doeg had had free rein the past two weeks to use whatever resources he could to locate the Dahveed.

And while he hadn't found him, he had learned some things that made his heart burn with anger. For instance, when Dahveed had come to Nob, the sar hadn't been on any errand for the king! He'd been fleeing from Shaul, and the Hakkohen Haggadol must have known about it. The thought of how the two had misled him made his anger flare afresh. Sooner or later, he would get the chance to even the score with both of them. Now he dressed carefully. Today his unit guarded the king, and he wanted to be certain to avoid anything that might annoy Shaul in the slightest.

The day promised heat, and Shaul sat outside under the tamarisk. Doeg stayed toward the back, out of the king's sight while still being certain that his men performed their duties. Court business concluded quickly, but instead of dismissing everyone, Shaul sat silent, his face showing his anger at something.

Finally, he looked around at the courtiers. "Are you not all my kin," he asked, "from my own tribe and clan?"

Eshbaal looked up, puzzled, but recorded his abbi's words.

"So how is it," the king went on, "that you look to the son of Jesse and not to me? Will he give you fields and vineyards? Or make you commanders of units or squads? Does Dahveed have the wealth or power to do such things?"

No one replied, the scribes keeping their eyes on their tables, the guards looking straight ahead, and the courtiers finding something absorbing about their clothes or the ground.

Angry contempt rose in Doeg. Didn't anyone dare to speak against the Dahveed? After all, he was outlawed, cowering in some cave down in the southern wilderness! Surely that man hadn't stolen every heart in Israel just because he could sing a little!

"Shall I take this to mean that all of you *have* conspired against me?" Shaul said, anger rising in his voice. "Why didn't any of you bother to tell me when my son cut a covenant with the son of Jesse? Weren't you concerned enough to open my ear when my son encouraged my slave to turn against me and try to kill me as he's doing now?"

Doeg held his breath in disbelief. Sar Eshbaal's pen had stilled as he stared at his abbi. The king had openly, *in court*, accused Jonathan Hassar of treason! No one moved, too stunned to respond.

The king looked around, then shifted uneasily on the three-legged chair, a slight breeze ruffling the robes of the statues staring at him with blatant disbelief on every face. "Well, when my son sneaks away the night of his marriage to feast with the son of Jesse, what am I to think?" he went on, but his eyes were uncertain.

The chance was too perfect to pass up. If Shaul was ready to accuse the hassar, he would see treason in anything and be enraged that the priests had helped Dahveed with food and a weapon. Then, too, everyone knew that Dahveed often inquired of Yah at Nob, so maybe he could add that in. Sort of a subtle reminder to Shaul that Yahweh had left him, which would just feed into a fear of rebellion. Smiling inwardly, Doeg stepped forward. He'd be in the king's favor for as long as he wished after this.

"Adoni, while I was detained at Nob, the son of Jesse came there on the last day of the New Year's feast. He talked to Ahimelech the son of Ahitub," he said, deliberately omitting the priest's title.

Shaul turned to him. "You saw him that day? The day he fled from me? What did he say to the hakkohen? What did they do?"

"The hakkohen inquired of Yahweh for him, gave him food for his flight, and supplied him with Goliath's sword when he asked for a weapon."

"So, it is the priests!" the king muttered. "Bring them here! I want them all before me! You," he pointed to one of the court messengers, "go to Nob and bring the priests of Yahweh to me!"

"Yes, adoni," the man said, bowing nearly to the ground before he ran down the steep path on the south side of the fortress, clearly determined to do his adon's bidding as fast as possible.

Without another word, Shaul rose and started up the road to the fortress. Doeg nodded to his guard, and they followed, the courtiers trailing along behind, uncertain what they should do. They didn't want to continue, but the king had not yet dismissed them.

Once in the fortress, Shaul entered the throne room, his face like a mask, and seated himself on the throne. The guards took their places, and Sar Eshbaal went to his table, his hands unsteady as he readied his materials again. Doeg stationed himself next to the king, where the hassar usually stood. The court officials and others waited uncomfortably in the back of the room, bunched like sheep, the Edomite thought with contempt.

The wait dragged on through the noon hour and into the noon rest, with the king's anger growing the longer that he had to wait. At last, one of the guards stationed outside reported that the priests had arrived.

The silence in the throne room was such that everyone heard the murmur of the priests announcing their presence to the scribe below, and then their footsteps on the stairs as they climbed to the second story and came through the door.

The Hakkohen Haggadol's resplendent robes outshone the king's and the bells on his garment tinkled. Doeg remembered the sound from the day that Dahveed came, and he smiled. This much revenge was worth the wait.

Shaul didn't wait for a greeting. "Son of Ahitub, you will listen to me!" he snarled.

The Hakkohen's eyes sharpened at the absence of his personal name, and the other priests glanced at each other because of the king's rudeness. "I am here, adon."

"How was it that you committed treason against me with that son of Jesse? You gave him bread, armed him, and inquired of Yahweh for him so that he could escape when he rebelled! He waits to kill me even now!"

The priests stirred with surprise and fear at the charge hurled by the king, but Ahimelech hardly blinked. "Adon, who has been more loyal to you than the Dahveed?" the Hakkohen Haggadol asked, his voice carefully steady. "He is not only your son-in-law, but he protected you as commander of your guard, and was honored in your house. He would not now think to take your life!"

Doeg smiled a little, noting how the Hakkohen avoided the issue of the aid that he had given Dahveed.

"He is son-in-law to me no longer," Shaul retorted, his fists clenching. "And he fled from my house after all I had done for him, so do not tell me he is honored! You aided him! Inquired of Yahweh for him!"

"Dahveed has indeed come often to consult with Yahweh, adon, but I did not consult for him this time," Ahimelech said firmly. "We are *your* servants, King Shaul, serving you faithfully, and we know nothing about any rebellion. Do not accuse me or any of my abbi's house, for we know nothing about any such affair!"

"And I say you lie, son of Ahitub! You aided the one I outlawed, sent him on his way in peace! You will die, Ahimelech, you and all your house!" Shaul shouted, rising from the throne and turning to the guards. "Kill them! Kill them all," he ordered. "They knew Dahveed was fleeing from me, yet refused to tell me. They have joined with him to seek my life!"

The officials in the room turned as pale as the priests at the suggestion of such sacrilege. The guards stared at the king, and one of them stepped back, shaking his head, his eyes filled with horror. "No, adoni! They are the anointed priests of Yahweh!"

"You will kill them!" Shaul shouted, looking at another guard.

The man's spear clattered to the floor as he dropped to his knees. "I dare not, adoni! They are holy to Yahweh!"

The king's glance raked across the others, seeing the same refusal in each one, until Doeg met his eyes squarely. "*You* kill them," he ordered the Edomite.

Doeg pulled his sword from its sheath and stepped quickly to the Hakkohen Haggadol, smiling triumphantly as he pierced the old priest's heart. Before anyone could react, he turned on the others, slashing and stabbing, the sons of Aaron too shocked to run or defend themselves. He had slain the last one when the other officials recovered enough to make their escape, stumbling from the room, fleeing from the fortress.

"Kill them, kill them all," Shaul repeated, his face a mask of rage as he looked over the bodies of Yahweh's priests.

Smiling slightly to himself, Doeg decided that he would take the king at his word. Sheathing his sword without cleaning it, he left the fortress, stopping at the king's stables to order several riding mules made ready. Then he went to the wine shop where he knew his friends would be.

As he walked in, he saw only one of them there.

"You look like there's silver to be made, Doeg," the man said.

"There is, if you don't mind a little fighting."

"Not at all. Where are we headed?"

"Nob."

The man froze. "Nob?"

"By order of the king," Doeg added. "Just think of what must be in the tabernacle coffers, my friend."

"I am," the man said. "I'm also thinking of my body scattered across the field for the dogs to eat."

"Who's to know, if there's no one left to tell? And the priests are already dead, lying in the throne room as we speak."

The man hesitated.

"It'll be gold this time," the Edomite added. "Lots of it, for the taking."

The man swallowed. "Just you and me?"

Doeg smiled again. "Two or three others should be sufficient."

The little group of men soon left Gibeah, urging their mules toward the southwest.

"Give no warning," Doeg said as they rode. "The king said to kill them all, so we'll put the ban on them."

"That means anything that lives, dies," one of the men said uneasily.

"Yes, and if everything doesn't die, our lives won't be worth a river pebble."

"All right," the man said. But he looked pale.

It was nearing the ninth hour, time for the evening sacrifice, when they neared the gates. Doeg noticed that one priest had stayed behind and was preparing to offer the lamb. The Edomite looked from the tabernacle to the town. He'd leave the tabernacle for last. If he attacked there first, someone in the town might notice and decide to resist.

"The town first," he directed. "The tabernacle can wait."

The men rode into the market and spread out, then pulled their swords and simply started to kill. In moments, screams and cries filled the air as people fled, racing from the market down the narrow streets.

Knocking aside one sentry's spear, Doeg killed the man, then threw coals from a cooking fire into the straw of a market stall. Soon the place was ablaze. His men followed suit, and fires sprang up quickly. While the others chased through the streets, Doeg rode his mule to the gate at the far side of town. When the sentries ran to him, asking what had happened, his reply was his sword, and soon he stood in the shadows as the terrified families of the priests ran toward him. He thought he heard someone shouting orders, and some of the people turned aside, but he paid no attention. The fires had spread quickly, and the entire west end of the town was ablaze.

As he waited he vowed that he would repay each and every priest for all the orders that he had had to follow, the menial chores he'd had to do, and the humiliation he'd endured during his weeks in this place. And when he was done here, he'd find that cursed Egyptian slave up at the tabernacle, and there would be nothing left of those blue eyes by the time he finished. The defenseless inhabitants ran toward him, and he stepped from the shadows, sword raised.

It was a long time before he lowered it again.

The choking smoke from the fires that had reached the edge of the square drove him out through the gate. Circling the town, he went back into the smouldering remains of the west market. The mules were tied just outside the gate, and he looked around for the men who had come with him. They were nowhere to be seen.

Uneasy, he ignored the destruction around him, picking his way down a couple streets, but finding nothing living. They had done a good job. Remembering the pale face of one of the men, he snorted. Most likely they had all finally lost their stomachs and run like cowards. Well, that left more for him.

It was hard to see, and he looked up, surprised to see that it was dusk. The east end of town would take a while to burn down, and then cool, so he retraced his way back out the gate, looking up the hill toward the tabernacle.

It was gone.

He paused, staring, stepping forward again as he peered through the drifting smoke.

The tabernacle was not there.

"Forgot about that, didn't you, Doeg?"a voice said in the dimness around him. "Every piece of it can be taken apart and carried away. So now it is gone, and you will never hold one piece of the gold in it, or the treasure for the service of Yahweh."

Rage filling him, Doeg advanced in the direction of the voice. "You!" he said. "You with your Horus eyes! They will see nothing more after this day! You should have run, slave, before I came out of the gate."

"No, you should have run, Doeg."

Mahesa emerged from the dimness, dressed in Egyptian warrior's linen, a gold collar flashing around his neck, holding a long spear.

Surprised, the Edomite retreated a step. The man held that spear as if he was used to it.

His blue eyes fastening on the Edomite, Mahesa smiled. "There is indeed much about me you do not know, Doeg," he said. "I am much more than just an Egyptian slave brought to this place to serve out my life. I am nobility, trained in the methods of war. My family is descended from Lord Paanekh, whom you would know as Joseph, son of Jacob. And though you will see his golden collar around my neck, you will never touch it, for you have done despite to El Shaddai, slaying his priests before King Shaul and destroying those whom He chose to serve him. My family has honored El Shaddai for generations, and we do His bidding. He bids you die, Doeg."

As he advanced toward Doeg, the Edomite raised his sword, surprised to see how it shook in his hand. Those blue eyes pierced his soul, and he backed away, trying to summon up his courage, to shout for his friends to come.

"They would not answer," the implacable voice said to his unspoken thought. "Only one was wise enough to flee when he could."

The Edomite backed away again, noticing for the first time the stains on the spear pointed at him. He shook his head. But from nowhere, a dry desert wind seemed to blow around him, and he was standing on sand, not soil, and the figure in front of him was surrounded by a light that seared his eyes. And then he was stumbling away, his hands empty, running from the footsteps that always followed behind him, and he knew he was dead before he felt the blow between his shoulder blades that sent him face down on the bare ground where the altar of sacrifice had stood not long before.

¥ ¥ ¥ ¥ ¥ ¥

"What is it, Eshbaal?" Sar Ishvi asked anxiously, leaving his sweat-lathered mule with a fortress guard. "What is this about Abbi? Is he ill?"

"No," his brother said, his pale face. "It's not Abbi. No, Abbi is sleeping."

"Then what is it?"

Tears trickled down his brother's face. "Just come," he said, taking

Ishvi out into the darkness. The lamp shook in his brother's hand, and Ishvi almost took it from him. The common court seemed eerie as Eshbaal produced the large wooden boomerang-shaped key that opened the door to the anteroom. Trembling, he couldn't fit the toothed arm through the hole in the door.

Ishvi did it, fitting the teeth into their places inside the door and twisting to release the latch. Once inside, Eshbaal barred the door again and picked up the key to the throne room itself, starting up the stairs, hardly able to walk on his shaking legs. At the door, he handed the key to Ishvi. The sar unbarred this door also. His youngest brother handed him the lamp.

"Abbi--" he began, and then stopped. "Abbi ordered it," he finally said.

His stomach tight with apprehension, Ishvi slowly opened the door and held up the lamp. At first the shadows on the floor didn't mean anything, but as he stepped forward, he realized the area closest to the dais was covered with dead bodies. With a soft exclamation, he hurried forward. One of them was clothed in the garments of a priest, he realized, and so was another. But it wasn't until he touched the shoulder of the richest dressed one and heard the tinkle of the bells as he eased the body over that he realized he looked into the face of the Hakkohen Haggadol, that every dead man in the room was a priest, that there were enough of them here to account for all of them in Nob.

He couldn't comprehend it. All the priests dead? In the throne room? What had Eshbaal meant when he said that Abbi ordered it? Blindly, he made his way back to the door where his brother waited, sitting on the stairs. Ishvi sat down beside him.

"Tell me," he whispered.

In a toneless voice Eshbaal recited what had happened that day. The records he had written were on the scribe's table in the anteroom, and the two of them went down there so Sar Ishvi could read them over. Eshbaal had managed to record everything said until Doeg began the slaughter.

When the sar finished, he turned to Eshbaal. "Can you do something for me?"

"I'll try."

"Get Malchi. Tell him to bring Zorath and the third unit. You know the way?" Ishvi asked, concerned about the glassy stare in his brother's eyes.

"I'll make it," Sar Eshbaal managed to answer.

"Where are the sentries who refused the king's orders?"

"In seclusion in the armory."

"Do the sentries on duty now know what is in here?"

"They know that blood was shed in the throne room, but not whose."

"You've done very well, Eshbaal. Get Malchi."

As his youngest brother left, Ishvi crossed the court to the armory. One of the storerooms had been hastily emptied, and Commander Sheva guarded the door. Inside, Ishvi could hear the sounds of grief.

"I just intended to stay here until someone else could come, Sar," Sheva explained. "But when I heard the men talking inside, I thought it would be best if I remained. Sar, is it true? The king ordered the killing of the priests?"

"Yes."

"Who did it?"

"Doeg."

"He shall become a son of death!" the guard commander vowed.

"First, we have to find him, commander. Open the door."

When Ishvi entered, the faces of the guards turned to him with fear, and in the light of the single lamp, he saw the same glassy stare as that on Eshbaal's face. Sheva brought a stool, and the sar sat down, his quiet manner slightly easing the tension in the room.

"I have seen the throne room," he said softly. "I must know what happened. The records say that all of you refused to touch Yahweh's priests, and for this you are to be commended. But apparently your refusal was not enough to change the king's orders. Tell me what happened."

The stories were fragmented and nearly incoherent, but with a quiet question here and there, and by waiting patiently for a man to find the words to describe what he had seen, Sar Ishvi acquired a comprehensive picture of the event. When the men fell silent, he stared at the floor for a long time, his face reflecting his struggle to control his emotions. There could be no doubt. These men agreed completely with the records he'd read, and what Eshbaal had told him. Abbi was guilty of the slaughter of the priests of Nob. All of them.

At last he rose from the stool. "You have done well to tell me this. You will remain here for now."

"Yes, Sar," they said, settling down again.

As he walked from the room, Sheva closed the door.

"I will have some of the third unit escort them to my private estate later," Ishvi told the commander. "Until then, no one sees them."

"Yes, adoni."

Outside in the courtyard the gates opened, admitting Malchi with Zorath and the third unit.

"What is this about?" Malchi asked as Ishvi met them. "Eshbaal couldn't tell me. Has Abbi done something?"

"He brought all the priests of Nob before him, and then ordered their deaths. Commander Doeg carried out the order."

Malchi stared at him in disbelief, then glanced toward the throne room. "In there?"

"Yes. We must remove the bodies and clean the room. Abbi's sentries refused to touch the priests, and they must be escorted to my estate. Then we must return the bodies to Nob for burial to avoid any further sacrilege from non-burial."

"Not to Nob," a voice said.

Ishvi looked around, startled to see what could only be an Egyptian standing in the light of the torches by the gate.

"Doeg the Edomite came to Nob after he killed the priests of Yahweh," the man continued. "He brought the ban with him, and there are none left alive in the town."

A gasp ran through those of Zorath's men who could hear.

"Nob is destroyed?" Ishvi asked in disbelief.

"Yes, Sar. It burns even now."

"What of the tabernacle?" Malchi asked, his voice hoarse.

"It is gone. I am called Mahesa, and I serve El Shaddai and His tabernacle." He bowed. "I have come for the breast plate and ephod of the Hakkohen Haggadol. It must be taken where it belongs."

"What will we do if Nob is destroyed?" Ishvi asked, glancing toward the throne room.

"Take them to Anathoth," Malchi said. "I think Ahimelech's family is from there. But now that Eli's line is gone, who will be priests for us?"

"The Levites should know where other lines of Aaron are living," Ishvi replied. Then an odd expression crossed his face.

"What is it?" Malchi asked.

"Shamuel's prophecy said one man would escape." Although he glanced at Mahesa, the Egyptian remained silent.

"May Yahweh cover him," the sar said.

It was late the next day when everything was finally done. While Malchi supervised the cleansing of the throne room, Ishvi wrote messages and talked to the courtiers and officials who had been with the king the day before. Shaul slept until nearly noon, and Ishvi ordered that no one was to disturb him until he woke on his own.

It was late afternoon before Sar Ishvi sent off the message he'd been dreading. And when it finally came down to it, he couldn't find the words to put on the papyrus, so he simply told Jonathan that a dire emergency had occurred and the king required his presence at once. Dispatching the message, he wondered how long it would be before the hassar got it. Then he steeled himself to face his abbi, knowing that he dared not leave the king alone again until the hassar returned.

CHAPTER 29

Hassarah Ahinoam looked up from sorting the lentils for the noon meal as a courier approached her in the private court of the fortress residence, holding out a message. When she took the sealed papyrus, the man left without waiting to see if there was a reply. She didn't blame him. Since the murder of the priests four days ago, a pall hung over the fortress, as though the bodies still lay sprawled in the throne room.

Shaul seemed the only one who didn't notice the atmosphere, going about his business as if nothing had happened. But the townswomen no longer vied with each other to work in the fortress, and the servants who had to remain were silent and fearful. Ishvi's face could have been carved from wood as he attended the king, and only the shell of Eshbaal remained as he automatically kept up the court records.

Abner was closeted with the king every day, carrying military courier pouches and planning the war season, while Malchi stayed at the military training ground, working with the men. She had seen her third son watching Abner once or twice as the general climbed the stairs to the throne room, and the unreadable expression in his eyes made her shiver. It surprised her that Malchi would let Abner have so much time with the king, but her son's purposeful stride when he left the fortress made her wonder if Malchi was busy on his own account while the general left him alone.

Inspecting the seal on the message, she saw it was from Taphath. Ahinoam opened it quickly, hoping all was well. It should be, but with Jonathan, one never knew. She read swiftly.

"Greetings to you, honored mother-in-law.

"We have arrived safely. My clan sends their greetings and gratitude that I was able to come to them. Cousin Barzillai misses Jonathan already. He left two days ago to attend to his business in the north. I expect him back whenever he decides to come. While I wait, the guards the hassar left are a great help to me.

"Azmaveth received a message from his loved one, who enjoys all the activity where he is, especially the messengers and messages coming and going all the time. He did not expect that at such a small estate."

After scanning the rest, Ahinoam carefully folded the papyrus and tucked it into her sash. Very astute of Taphath to find a way to pass along Pelet's whereabouts. Azmaveth's son must have managed a way to contact his abbi. One could not call Abner's estate small, so the boy must be held with Jaasiel, not far from Zelah. It sounded as if messages might be collected there, and then probably transported via military courier to Abner, who had plenty of opportunity to pass the information to the king. Ahinoam sent for a fortress messenger. Michal might have noticed military pouches circulating around.

Two days later, her daughter responded, passing along more than Ahinoam had expected.

"Hassarah, the bundle you sent for is on your bedroll in your room," Basemath informed her.

"Very good, Basemath," Ahinoam replied, hiding her puzzlement. In her room she unbound the bundle and lifted out several old robes suitable for court servants to wear. Then she felt the lump in the middle and caught sight of a leather delivery pouch. Hastily, she put the clothes back.

Hours later, in the privacy of her chamber at Zelah, Ahinoam inspected the pouch. Abner's seal was already broken. She laid aside the messages and read the hurriedly written papyrus from Michal.

"Immi, I'd noticed the military messengers, but never gave them a thought. I believe this is what we're looking for. It comes from Jaasiel's estate. The servants will cooperate. Since last week, things have changed."

Lost in thought, Ahinoam stared at the lamp. Michal was correct. A lot had changed since the destruction of Nob. Shaul had overstepped himself, and many people who would never have thought of going against the king before would do so now, if they concluded that it would help to expiate the guilt the entire nation had incurred when

Shaul slew the priests.

"As the king, so the people," she whispered. The king represented the people to Yahweh, and if the king offended God, then, through him, the entire nation had done so also, and the entire nation would suffer Yahweh's displeasure.

She closed her eyes. In one way, she was glad that Jonathan was not here. The messengers still had not located him. She could only imagine what the knowledge of Shaul's sin would do to her oldest son, and she dreaded facing his pain.

Lips pressed tightly together, she looked at the messages spread out around her. If there was anything at all that she could do to protect her boy from part of the agony that would tear his soul, she would do it. And Sheol take anyone that got in the way.

Ahinoam thought for a little, and then a smile crossed her face. Tomorrow would be a good time to call in the clan women and do some extensive housecleaning.

"Everything needs to be moved, the entire floor swept, and the place thoroughly cleaned," she directed the next day. Leaving the women to get started, she went down to the others waiting near the storerooms.

"Empty them out. Sweep and clean everything," she said again. "Once it's all out, I'll need to go through it. This is the one place Eshbaal never got around to inventorying."

"Yes, Hassarah," they all said.

Soon the courtyard and balcony were littered with all kinds of items. Women from most of the family estates had come, and Ahinoam chatted with them familiarly, sharing news of babies, gardens, and how quickly boys could ruin anything they managed to put on their bodies. She also learned who served at which estate, where their relatives worked, and who might be willing to help her.

At the noon rest Ahinoam approached one woman. "Iscah?"

"Yes, Hassarah?"

"You said that your son works on Jaasiel's estate. I noticed that no one from there is here today."

"Geber Jaasiel has so much to attend to that no one was free to leave. My son has been, concerned, about the situation for some time."

Ahinoam frowned. "That's too bad. I don't want them to feel left out. Perhaps we should send some food there. Would your son be able to distribute anything we sent?"

"Yes, Hassarah," the woman replied, her thoughtful eyes on the queen's.

"And if a small message could be taken there also which might address your son's concerns?"

"He would be most grateful, Hassarah," the woman said with an impassive face.

"Good. We'll do that then."

Just after the noon rest, a donkey cart with the provisions left the gates, Iscah riding along with a message to her son tucked into her sash. She returned some time later.

"My son said to express his gratitude for your kind message and your gracious thoughtfulness to the women at the estate. They were delighted to be remembered, and send their thanks also."

"We did well, then," Ahinoam said with a smile.

"Yes, Hassarah. My son also said he would do his best to repay you as he could."

"He is most courteous. You have done well to raise him so."

The woman blushed. "He is a good son and knows his duty."

The next messenger arrived after dark. Ahinoam asked him to wait while she opened the bundle he brought. The woman's son had indeed repaid her. Opening the case he sent, she stared at the contents. Seals made of clay? Her hands shook when she replaced them after inspecting them. If these seals were used the way she suspected they must be, her sons needed to know about them immediately!

When she reached for a papyrus to send a message, she paused. Just having the seals wasn't enough. She needed more. It was some time later that she handed a message, wrapped and sealed in a skin pouch, to the sleepy courier. "This is to be delivered immediately."

The man bowed. "Yes, Hassarah."

¥ ¥ ¥ ¥ ¥ ¥

"Sar Malchi, there is a message for you."

Dragging himself from the blankets, the sar took it. As his steward left the room, he yawned and sat down at the table by the lamp that had been left for him. He unwrapped the skin and stared at the seal. What on earth?

Breaking it, he read the terse lines, and suddenly, he wasn't sleepy anymore.

"To Malchi-shua ben Shaul, Sar Israel.

"I require Commander Zorath and the entire third unit at the king's private estate by dawn.

"Ahinoam, Hassarah Israel."

Malchi stared at the message. Never in his life had he known his immi to assert her position. What was going on at Zelah? He'd overheard a couple couriers discussing the difficulty they had delivering their dispatches there since so many people were helping Hassarah Ahinoam clean house. But why was Immi cleaning house during threshing, and why would she need an army unit for that? But the command in the message was clear.

Slowly, he pulled a pen and papyrus toward him.

"To Zorath, Commander Israel of the third unit.

"You will report to the private estate of King Shaul in Zelah before dawn. There you will place yourself and your men unreservedly under the command of Ahinoam, Hassarah Israel.

"Malchi-shua ben Shaul, Sar Israel."

Pressing his seal into it, he sent the message off. After blowing out the lamp, he returned to bed, wondering what his immi was up to. Well, if she was taking a hand, there was trouble in it for someone. And he devoutly hoped it was Abner.

For the first time since Ishvi had summoned him to the fortress in the middle of the night, a smile crossed his face.

¥ ¥ ¥ ¥ ¥ ¥

"Good, you have come, Zorath," Hassarah Ahinoam greeted the commander early the next day as she descended the outside stairs into the still-littered courtyard.

"Yes, Hassarah," he said, bowing and trying not to look too bewildered. "Sar Malchi has commanded that I place myself and my men under your orders. What do you wish of us?"

"A little guard duty," she answered. "Until then, please have your men make themselves comfortable outside the courtyard. I will send for you when I need you." She looked around. "Of course, if any of them would like to help us clean--"

"I think they will all be happy to get some more sleep," Zorath said hastily, recognizing the look on the hassarah's face.

Once the women arrived and began work, Ahinoam sent a message to Jaasiel, and awaited developments.

Before long, a courier rushed panting into the gates, obviously having come as fast as he could.

"Hassarah, my geber sends his gratitude that you have found the missing box. He requests that I return with it."

Ahinoam frowned. "Not there," she said to some of the women. "Remember, those need to be set aside until I can make a decision about whether or not to keep them. What did you say?" she asked, turning back to the messenger.

"Hassarah, I am to return with the box you found."

"How did it come to be here?"

"I don't know, Hassarah."

"Well, tell Jaasiel that he needs to get it personally. It looks very valuable, and I'm not even certain it came from his place. It might be from Jonathan's. You could not imagine the stuff we've found. There was an old corroded dagger in one of the clothes chests that I seem to remember Abner missing years and years ago. Likely one of the boys put it there and forgot it.

"Here, bring those back over," she called, looking past the man. "Those came from the third storeroom, right?"

"Yes, Hassarah," a woman said in response.

"Then they need to be put back here with the rest. Keep it all together until I get the chance to look it over." She looked back at the man. "Are you still here? Get Jaasiel. I haven't got time to waste today, and if he doesn't want that box, I'll leave it for Jonathan to look at as soon as he returns."

The messenger gulped, "Yes, Hassarah." He fled out the gate.

When he had left, Ahinoam sent Iscah for Zorath.

"Commander," she said when he appeared, "Jaasiel ben Abner is going to come through my gate before very long. I don't know if he'll have guards with him. I want you and your men to be around, but not obvious. I'll take Jaasiel into the upper room with me, and when I do, you will remove any guards he leaves in the court."

"Would that be quietly remove?"

"Yes, commander. Once you have taken them, if any, I want you, and three of your men, to come into the upper room and detain Jaasiel. You will obey?"

The look in her eyes sent Zorath to his knees. "Yes, Hassarah!"

"Get your men in place now."

It didn't take long for Jaasiel to appear, his steward with him.

"Dodah Ahinoam, you found a box of mine?" he asked anxiously.

The hassarah turned to him. "Oh, here you are. Yes, I think so. I saw it lying around yesterday after we sent some things to your estate. It must have been brought back with the things that returned."

She led the way up the stairs. "I put it in here, but I don't know for certain where it came from. The only other one it might belong to is Jonathan."

"From the description you gave, I'm certain it's mine," Jaasiel said, following quickly after her. "I missed it last evening. You're right, it's valuable, and I was quite worried about it."

Ahinoam opened the door, looking into the room which was still in disarray. "Now, where did I put it?" She searched through things while Jaasiel shifted from foot to foot. "Here it is!" she exclaimed, when she heard footsteps on the stairs. She held it out.

"That's the one," he said in relief. "Thank you, Dodah! I was very worried."

"Well, no need to worry now. As long as you're certain it's yours."

"Yes, it's mine," he said, as the door opened, and Zorath and his men entered. They quickly pinned Jaasiel's arms to his sides, and Ahinoam took the box back.

"Who are you?" Jaasiel asked, bewildered. "What is this about?"

"They are men of the third unit," Ahinoam said. "And they have very strict orders concerning you. This was a very interesting box, Jaasiel. Particularly the contents."

The man's face turned white.

"When Jonathan gets back, I can't imagine he'll be in any mood to grant hesed, considering recent events. So you have one chance to live. Do you want it?"

Disbelief and fear fighting in his eyes, he stared at her. "Dodah, what have I ever done to you?"

"Shall we say that you shouldn't have threatened my son's safety by tampering with his personal guard?"

Slowly he sank to his knees. "What do you want?"

"First, you will send your steward to bring Azmaveth's son, Pelet, here. Some of Zorath's men will accompany him. And if there is any suspicion *at all* that anything is out of the ordinary, you will die, Jaasiel."

"Yes, Dodah," he whispered, looking at her as if he'd never seen her before.

"And when your steward gets back, you will tell him that you must leave on business, and will take Pelet with you, and that he is to carry on as normal. And Jaasiel, when that steward walks from my gate, he had better believe every word you said!"

Some hours later, Ahinoam placed the box with the seals in her private chest. Azmaveth's son was sleeping in the upper room and would remain here under the protection of part of the third unit until his abbi returned. Jaasiel was traveling to Ramah, escorted by the rest of the third unit, where he would be held in Navyoth until she sent for him. As she sat by the table, Ahinoam knew that she had done everything she could for now. Then a thought occurred. No, she hadn't. After reaching for the papyrus, she sent off one more message.

¥ ¥ ¥ ¥ ¥ ¥

King Shaul arrived back at the throne room early after the noon rest. Abner was already there, giving them a few minutes alone before Ishvi showed up.

"What have you learned?" the king asked.

Abner took a dispatch from the pouch he carried. "Dahveed is in Keilah. The Philistines were raiding, and he came down from the hills. The town apparently hired him to guard it."

The king scanned the message. "What took so long for this to get here? Dahveed arrived in Keilah more than a week ago!"

"Bad luck, adoni. One of our messengers somehow lost his pouch, and then Jaasiel was called away on business, so it took a while to straighten that out."

"All is well now though?" Shaul asked anxiously.

"Yes, adoni."

"Good." He smiled, holding up the papyrus. "Dahveed just made his first mistake, and El has given him to me. The gates and bars of that town will be just the trap for him! He never should have left the forests."

The door rattled, and Shaul shoved the papyrus into his girdle.

Sar Ishvi entered the room. "You are starting early, adoni," he commented politely.

"Yes, Ishvi. I'm glad you came now. Abner has just given me a message. The Philistines have shown up again this year." He motioned to the general, who passed a papyrus to the sar. "They've been raiding in Keilah. We were wondering if we should intervene. If the Philistines occupy the town or force it into an alliance of some kind, they'd have a base for raiding. What do you think?"

"I think anytime the Philistines invade the Shephelah, we should worry. Have they shown up anywhere else?"

"Not so far," Abner said gruffly, glancing at the king.

"Maybe they decided to see if we'd respond if they just threaten Judah," Shaul suggested.

"Judah is part of Israel, adoni," Ishvi commented.

"I suppose so, even if there isn't much down there. Put out a call to arms," he declared with sudden decision. "Let's go down to Keilah and teach whoever is there a lesson."

"Yes, adoni," Abner replied.

¥ ¥ ¥ ¥ ¥ ¥

Jonathan Hassar guided the mule around another mud-filled rut in the road. Ahead of him, a large ox cart filled with grain sacks lurched along, the small children giggling with delight as they tumbled from side to side on the sacks. Remembering trips to market with Abbi and Immi when he was that age, he smiled.

He studied the sky. The mud wouldn't last much longer, even this close to the Jordan. Summer's heat was promised in the morning's warmth. The day did turn out as hot as he expected, and he kept the pace down in consideration of the mules. The hassar felt satisfied with this trip, even though the arrangements with the House of Tahat had, instead of just a day, taken more than a week. Still, the time had been worth it.

The House did indeed have the rudiments of the internal trade he envisioned, with a simple method of collecting merchandise. As trade goods became available, they were sent to several centrally located collection points, and once enough had accumulated, a larger caravan left for Dan. Few caravans took the King's Highway to the east, preferring, as he'd suspected, to employ the Arabah or the forest trails. Many of the caravaneers were Habiru, used to such travel, and a steady stream of goods flowed quietly through the land to Dan, where the House marketed them from Egypt to Hattush to Mari and Ur. The only things not in place were the internal lines of supply, and Jonathan had assigned that task to Tanhum. The disfigured scribe was uncannily acquainted with the cities and politics of the land, and the hassar knew it wouldn't be long before such a network would take shape and begin to operate. After that--Jezreel.

The thought that he might live to see Israel control the Jezreel

Valley thrilled through him, and the mule broke into a canter in response. The road was clear ahead, and Jonathan let his mount go, its pace eating up the miles on the last leg to Jabesh. They were almost to the turn-off at just past noon when he slowed the animal to a walk to wend through the knot of people on its way to the city.

"Hassar!"

Uncertain that he had actually heard anything, Jonathan looked around.

"Hassar! Hassar!"

He kneed the mule off the road, his escort following.

A courier fought his way through the crowd toward him. "Thank Yahweh, I found you. Have you received Sar Ishvi's message yet?"

"I haven't received any messages," Jonathan replied. "What's wrong?"

Instead of replying, the man handed up a sealed packet of papyrus.

Jonathan broke it open and scanned it quickly. "When was this sent?" he snapped.

"Nearly two weeks ago now, adoni. We've covered the land looking for you, but no one could tell us where you were. I finally came back here and waited."

"Hassar!"

Turning again, Jonathan saw another messenger approaching. "Hassar, there is an urgent message from Sar Ishvi," the man began, then noticed the open papyrus. "Oh, you have it. Every courier in the land has been told to send you back to Gibeah if we see you."

"Is the king ill?" Jonathan asked, his heart in his mouth.

The messenger looked away. "No, adoni."

"Is there any other information?"

"I have no other instructions, adoni. But a call to arms has gone out."

Dismounting, Jonathan took it, breaking the seal. Proclamation for a call to arms for war against Keilah, giving the towns involved, and listing the muster point--he froze.

Against Keilah? The independent town was a buffer between Israel and Philistia, normally left alone by both because of the rich harvests gathered there. What was Abbi doing? An attack like this would drive the town into the arms of Gath, giving them control of that portion of the Shephelah and providing a base of operations just that much closer to the highlands. In addition, Philistines in Keilah could threaten the major trade road up from Hebron. Abbi knew all this as well as he did. Something was wrong.

With a frown he returned the dispatch and waved the courier on his way. Turning to Nimshi, he asked, "What's down around Keilah?"

"Well, Gedor is at the top of the highlands there. Adullam is a couple miles north, and then the Elah valley. South you won't run into much after Nezib."

Grimly, Jonathan tightened the girth on the mule. "Is Dahveed down there?"

"Yes, geber."

Jonathan leaned against his mule, closing his eyes. Surely Abbi wouldn't start a war, risking the loss of a buffer like Keilah, just as an excuse to send the army south after Dahveed! But in his heart, he knew that his abbi had.

He sprang on the mule. "Nimshi, what's the fastest way to Gibeah?"

"With the mule, take the road down the west side of the Arabah to Jericho. Then up to Jebus. They are the best roads, with less chance that your mount will break a leg."

"I'm coming, adoni," Dara said, stripping off the pack his animal carried.

Jonathan knew better than to argue. "Nimshi, go with the guard to Jabesh. Bring Taphath home as soon as you can."

"Yes, geber."

"Clear the way, Dara," Jonathan said, tightening his legs around the mule. "I'd pull rank on the Egyptian governor for this!"

CHAPTER 30

Head down, the mule trudged up the ascent toward Jebus. Jonathan's eyes felt gritty and dry. They had stopped somewhere on the west side of Jordan last night, but he'd been unable to rest, much less sleep. The only comfort he had was that it would take at least a week to muster the militia, which meant he should be home in time. But could this be the dire emergency that Ishvi had mentioned?

As much as he wanted to believe it was, he couldn't. Ishvi's message had gone out long before the call to arms, and the feeling of it was different. Darkness seemed to shimmer at the side of his vision whenever he re-read it, trying to draw something more from it, no matter how little. He remembered how the courier had avoided his gaze when he asked if he had any more information. Thinking of it now, he realized the man must have known something, but didn't want to speak.

The Jericho-Jebus road was busy, but as the hassar rode, a cold chill went over him. The usual conversations and shouts were missing. Caravans coming down from Jebus traveled silently. What conversation there had been before the ascent began had now faded away. He and Dara exchanged a glance, and he urged the mule to greater effort. Even though the ascent was rather easy, he dismounted, knowing the mule had to have something left for the run from Jebus to Gibeah. The silence seemed to deepen the closer they got to the top, and as the road dipped into the ravine for the two mile stretch just before Nob, the darkness pressed closer. The sun dipped toward the hills, and Jonathan walked faster, chasing the light.

Little puffs of the evening breeze from the sea brushed against his face, and he bowed his head, watching where he put his feet. The stench of death rode the wind. He knew it well, having when younger come on more than one settlement after the Philistines had passed through. And he'd never forgotten the odors of decay, charred flesh, and burned stone.

The smell was stronger now, carried along by the wind, and he looked back at Dara, who nodded. He detected it also. The sun dipped lower, and the hassar pushed ahead, the darkness seeming to gather behind him in the ravine. When at last he emerged from the gully and turned to see Nob, he stopped in his tracks.

Without taking his eyes from it, he pulled the mule forward and mounted, taking the side road that led up the hill to the town. The stench of death grew the closer he got. His heart pounding, he pushed the mule up the steepened trail until he finally faced the gate, the wood blackened with fire. Staring, he slid from the mule.

Dara appeared beside him. "In Yahweh's name, what happened?" he whispered.

Jonathan just shook his head, advancing through the gates and into the market square. It had been a while, his mind told him. This had happened more than a week ago, more likely two. Right when Ishvi had sent that message.

"Yahweh, no!"

The town had burned, starting with the far side of the square, pushed by the breeze which blew on his back even now. Dazed, he walked down the main street to the east square. Everywhere he looked he saw complete destruction.

"The ban," he said. "The ban came to Nob?" It didn't make sense, but all the evidence told him it was so. How had this happened? Unable to stand the sight of more desolation, he looked up at the light of the setting sun, but it brought little comfort, glowing red against the streets and walls, washing them with what looked like blood. Finally, he stumbled back to the west gate.

Dara waited there, his face etched with shock. They went outside, not knowing how to take it all in. The hassar knew before he looked that the hill where the tabernacle stood would be empty, and it was. He landed on his knees. "Who?" he grated out. "Who did this? Jebus? Ammon? Who?"

"Neither of them, adoni," a voice said.

"Who, then? Who is guilty of this desecration? To put the ban on Yahweh's priests?"

"The guilt lies with Shaul, Nagid Israel, and Doeg the Edomite."

The words fell on his ears, but he paid no attention. He was dreaming surely, for that voice said his house had done this.

"No," he protested. "Abbi wouldn't. Who did it?"

"The king ordered the priests killed, and Doeg decided to do a thorough job of obeying him."

In agony Jonathan bent forward. "Abbi wouldn't!" he shouted. *"Who did this?"*

Someone knelt in front of him, forcing him to look into his eyes. Deep blue eyes that bore through the barriers of disbelief and denial building in his mind. "Jonathan Hassar, listen to me. Shaul, Nagid Israel, summoned the priests of Yahweh before him in Gibeah and ordered their death. Doeg slew them there, then brought the ban to Nob that same day."

Jonathan felt the truth drive home, and he looked down, fully expecting to see a sword thrust into his chest. "Abbi ordered it?"

"Yes, Hassar."

"The king turned against Yahweh?"

"Yes."

In horror, he let go of the hands that held his. As the king, so the people. What had Abbi done? The whole land would suffer Yahweh's fury! He felt numb, one part of himself still kneeling in the deserted road, another part watching dispassionately, mercifully detached from the pain that swam in his mind.

As the king, so the people. What could he do to shield the people, save them from the king's sin? But there was no sacrifice for this, and no place to give it. The tabernacle was gone.

"Yahweh's hesed shall be found with you always." How long ago had it been since he'd heard those words from Roeh Shamuel's lips? He needed Yahweh's hesed now. Not for his own house; they would all die, he knew that. No, the people in the land, the ones who had no way to stop the king from his crazed sacrilege, they needed hesed. Taphath and Caleb's twins, Azmaveth in agony over his son, Ethan who was so much more than he seemed, Nimshi who would never call him anything but "geber," and Eleazar who had saved Ishvi's life in the battle. All of them, and more.

Blood for blood. The land must be cleansed and the people covered. Without a word, Jonathan stood and walked up the hill to the place where the tabernacle had rested. He remembered the scene clearly. Dahveed had stood just there, his harp in his hands, watching the Hakkohen Haggadol for the signal to begin the singing. The Levites had raised the curtains of the outer wall so that everyone could see into the court where the sacrifice would be offered, and the altar had stood here. Another memory flashed through his mind. As hassar he had come here with the two bullocks as a sin offering for the slaughtered Gibeonites.

He should have accepted then that Yahweh's covenants meant nothing to his abbi. And this time he had no young bulls. Just himself, and the hope that maybe his blood would bring enough of Yahweh's hesed to the innocent in the land. Kneeling again, right on the now bare spot of the altar, he fumbled for his belt knife. They were useful things, as Dahveed had said. He wouldn't have any trouble finding his heart, the pain pulsing through him with each beat marked it indelibly.

"Yahweh, fulfill your promise," he said, slipping the knife from its sheath.

A hand like bronze closed over his wrist. "No, Hassar."

"It's the only way."

"No."

"You don't understand," Jonathan said savagely. "The whole land will shatter under Yahweh's wrath. Thousands will suffer because of my house! Shall I live when I can give my blood to help them?"

"Your blood is not required."

"Abbi put the ban on Yahweh's chosen priests!"

"No, Hassar. Doeg did that."

Jonathan struggled against the grip, but somehow he had no

strength.

Those blue eyes bored into him again. "Jonathan Hassar, listen to me! There is work for you."

"Let me die! I can serve them better that way." It hurt too much to continue living. Better to die.

"That is not the way."

"It is for me!" He would not live; he must pay for the lives of Yahweh's people.

The voice did not answer, but the hand would not let go. "What about Dahveed?"

"He is Mashiah. Yahweh will preserve him."

"And the evil one seeks him even now, to take his life. Would you leave him without your aid when he needs it most?"

"Don't talk to me of Dahveed." He could feel the detached part of himself pulling away, and he grasped after it desperately. The agony was too much otherwise.

"Remember him, Hassar? The way he can smile and you swear that you'll never be angry with him again? And then two days later, you would gladly choke him to death *if* you could find him? Remember his eyes? The way they look when he sings that song about you?"

Jonathan turned his face away. "Don't remind me," he pleaded. "I mustn't live!"

"Remember how he came to your wedding? He risked everything because he knew how happy you would be if he showed up."

"He shouldn't have come. It was too dangerous," Jonathan muttered, watching the numb part of himself fading away, leaving only the part of him kneeling on the bare ground, rocking back and forth.

"You know that, but he didn't care. He rode with you to the estate, too. What was it he told Taphath about you on the way?"

"He said I acted mulish sometimes," the hassar replied, his voice faintly exasperated. "She never says it, but the way she raises her eyebrows tells me that she's thinking it."

"He's right, Hassar. You do. You're doing it now," the voice went on, those blue eyes holding his against his will as the numbness wore off. "Dahveed needs you. There are things only you can do. He is frightened of the task that Yahweh has said he must perform, for he is not yet ready to step into the honor Yahweh has in store for him. You had many years to learn to rule. He does not. He struggles now to find his way as a leader, and would you leave him with the burden of war also?

"Abner is not yet reined in, and if you are not there, the king will do worse than you see here. Your death will not shield the people, Hassar. It will expose them to even greater danger."

Jonathan swayed on his knees. The numbness had gone. There was nowhere to go. In the last light before full dark, he lay on the ground and wept.

Darkness still closed around him when he woke. He was exhausted and sore, and when memory came crashing back, he twisted on the ground.

"Adoni?" Worry filled Dara's voice.

He sat up, looking overhead at the stars. His head pounded, and he was horribly thirsty. "Is there anything to drink?" he croaked.

"Here." Dara handed him a cruse, and he half drained it.

"I suppose it was too much to ask that I could have died while I slept," he said despondently.

"I think so, adoni."

Jonathan felt at his girdle. Yes, the belt knife was gone, as well as his sword. "And that persistent demon who wouldn't let me die in peace is still determined that I won't, isn't he?"

"Yes, adoni," someone said.

Jonathan thought a minute. "Mahesa?"

"Yes, Hassar."

When he finished drinking the water in the cruse he handed it back to Dara. Then he lay back down. "When may I have my weapons back?"

"When I'm convinced that you won't kill yourself with them."

"You'd better keep them for a while, then." He continued to stare up at the sky, wanting to float up to the stars and wander among them, leaving the hardship and troubles of life behind, but a lump on the ground dug into his back, something was crawling on his leg, and Dara's anxious hovering annoyed his mind.

Brushing the insect off, he sat up again. "Tell me," he sighed, giving up.

Mahesa told everything he knew, then endured the grilling questions Jonathan had for him.

"As far as you know then, the king actually only ordered the killing of the priests in the throne room, and Doeg took it on himself to come to Nob."

"Yes, Hassar."

"That means there might still be some things Abbi won't do. But what about the tabernacle? This grass hasn't been burned. Was it looted? I can't imagine Debir of Jebus passing up that kind of wealth. How was it destroyed?"

"It wasn't."

Jonathan glanced into the darkness where Mahesa sat. "But it's gone."

"It is portable, you know."

The hassar gasped.

"Even in Egypt we'd heard of the Tabernacle of Yahweh, the temple that moved and the wealth it contained," Mahesa went on. "Some didn't believe it. Our temples are of stone. So when I came here, I talked to the Levites, and they told me how the tabernacle should be taken down, how it was transported, everything."

"Mahesa, are you telling me that the tabernacle, and all the furniture for it, the treasure that belongs to it, that all that is safe?"

"Yes, adoni. When Doeg and his men attacked, the Gibeonites fled instantly, leaving the town by any way they could. I didn't know how many had attacked, and I could not defend both the tabernacle and the town. But I knew El Shaddai's house came first. I got some of the Gibeonites to help me, showing them what to do. Abiathar had stayed here to officiate at the evening sacrifice. We hid him in the Kidron, and when I could, I sent others back to the town to see if we could save anyone there. There were a few."

"Abiathar lives?" Jonathan asked in wonder.

"As the prophecy said. We took the tabernacle down and carried it away. The Gibeonites used their own clothing to cover the furniture. The Kidron is a long, dark valley, Hassar, and it will conceal much. By the time I went down to Nob, this hill top was bare."

"Why did you go to Nob? Most everyone must have been dead by then."

"Yes, Hassar. But by then I knew how many I would face, and I am a warrior. The men who had brought death to my God's people were still here. And I went down to them. Only one had the intelligence to flee. The others seemed to think three against one were good odds. It wasn't much of a fight."

"What of Doeg?"

"He came back to loot the tabernacle. He died where the altar had stood."

Jonathan shivered a little at the coldness in the Egyptian's voice.

"Is the tabernacle still in the Kidron?"

"No, hassar. It rests at Gibeon, with the Gibeonites serving it as always, and priests of Aaron's line ready to offer sacrifices for any who come."

"So Abiathar is there?"

"No, adoni. I thought it best that some things should be removed from Shaul, lest the king abuse them. The Habiru took charge of him and what he carried."

"He will be safe with Dahveed," Jonathan observed, lying down again. "I would have killed you, Mahesa, the day of that battle. I knew Dahveed was wrong to let you live. And now, you are the one who gives me back hope for this land and its people."

"I am only returning the hesed given me by you, adoni. Because of you, the young man whose safety had been charged to me still lives, and I have hope that I will see my own son again someday. Sometimes El Shaddai uses us whether we would or no."

"Thank you," Jonathan said humbly.

"Thank you, friend," the Egyptian replied.

"Dara, get the mules ready to travel. Mahesa, will you take me to Gibeon? I know of no other place to go to learn what I am to do."

"As you wish, Hassar."

Jonathan kept the pace slower than normal since Dara's mule was carrying double, but even then, Mahesa switched mules half-way through the seven-mile trip. The hassar was silent the entire time, wondering how he could approach Yahweh. Half of his mind still wanted to die, and the other half trembled with fear that he would.

Dawn had broken when they came into sight of the town, the sun's rays catching the gleaming gold of the tabernacle entrance where it sat on the south end of the hill on which Gibeon stood.

The hassar dismounted, climbing the hill to the tabernacle on foot, staying well back from the entrance. How did one approach an offended God? Very humbly, he decided, and under cover of whatever hesed he could find, such as that of the morning sacrifice. He stripped off his sword sheath, the girdle, and his sandals. After some more thought, he took off the kilt, shirt, and under robe, leaving just his loincloth. His cloak had a hood, and he'd use that to cover his head.

Then he settled down to wait. As the morning progressed, he noticed the gathering of people outside, all of them quiet, and then a priest appeared. He wore only the white linen robes of the lowest order of priest.

"Mahesa, what happened to the breast-plate of the Hakkohen Haggadol?" he asked, speaking for the first time.

"I don't know, adoni. When I went into the throne room to get it, it was gone. Sar Ishvi cannot remember if it was still on Ahimelech's body."

Jonathan fell silent again. When the time for the sacrifice arrived, he put on the cloak, pulling the hood over his head, and walked toward the entrance, surprised at how much his legs were trembling. It wasn't as if he cared whether he lived, did he?

He bowed with the rest when the priest emerged after the slaughtering of the lamb and its burning on the altar, wondering if any blessing given would remain with him. As the people started to disperse, he moved forward, stopping at the entrance. The air seemed to thicken in front of him, and he hesitated to go any farther.

"May I be of assistance?" the priest asked.

"I would approach my God, if He will let me," Jonathan said.

As soon as the priest heard his voice, he stiffened, peering into his face. He looked a little pale when he recognized the hassar. "What do you want here?" he asked in a low voice.

"To present myself before Yahweh and accept His will for me, whatever that may be."

The priest hesitated, and Jonathan bowed his head, not moving. At last the man stepped aside, and the hassar went forward again, staying on the side of the altar with the lavers. If anyone needed washing, it was he and his house. It seemed to get harder to walk the closer he approached the tabernacle itself. His legs dragged, and he labored to breathe. The air shimmered around him, making him dizzy, and he staggered a little. Recovering, he pushed on until he could go no farther. Then he stretched out face down on the ground and waited.

The dizziness stayed with him, and thoughts spun though his mind. The images and memories seemed to have no connection or reason, and he didn't try to understand their meaning. He was here to accept whatever came from the hand of his God. Hunger filled him, and thirst, and fear. Images of Nemuel forced themselves into his mind, and he dug his fingers into the grass, his stomach twisting with the memories of what his friend had endured for him. Then he saw again Dahveed's eyes, almost seeming to glow golden as he faced him in the house, listening to Naharai's story, only this time Dahveed didn't pull back, and Jonathan felt the sword of Yahweh cutting into his neck.

Although he squeezed his eyes shut, the images remained. He was a child again, playing with his Abbi and Abner, riding on Abner's broad back, kicking his small legs to make the donkey go faster and exploding with laughter when the donkey turned stubborn and dumped him off. And then his Abbi was a king, and he was a sar, and his abbi's eyes blazed into his for the honey he'd eaten, and he heard that he was to die. The darkness closed in on him, as it had in the anteroom when Dahveed returned from Chephirah, only this time no one was there to hold onto him, and the light receded away no matter how he fought to follow it. Nob was burning, and he couldn't stop it because he held the torch that had started the fire.

Suddenly, Dahveed stood before him, dressed in far richer robes than any that Jonathan had ever seen. He bowed before him, conscious of the rags he wore, holding a child in his arms. "Covenant? What covenant?" Dahveed said, then sent him away. He heard Abbi laughing, and they were eating the evening meal, and Malchi was just a baby poking his finger into the food, trying to get some to his mouth while Immi laughed too hard to feed him. Faster and faster the images spun until he could endure no more.

"Yahweh, grant me hesed," he whispered. "Torment me no more. If my blood is required, take it." The words sounded familiar, and he remembered them from the throne room before Dahveed had come. The crazy scenes stopped in his mind, and he felt suddenly alone, led to the realm of the Elohim, and abandoned there to die, far from anything that he knew. The feeling of hopelessness grew, building in him until he lay limp, crushed beneath the howling darkness that rushed toward him, triumphant in its victory.

"Yahweh, save me!" he screamed, but no sound came from his mouth.

A huge pillar of flame exploded in front of him, and the darkness recoiled, writhing in fury, the howling growing to a shriek that battered against the wind roaring down with the flames. They grew, burning brighter, flaring around the place where he cowered on the ground. And then everything blacked out.

"Jonathan?"

He stirred. "Yes?"

"What have you come for?"

"To die."

"If you wish to die, why did you fight so hard to live?"

The hassar had to think about that. "Because I wanted my death to do what my life cannot. Someone has to cover the people from the king's sin."

"Yes, someone should. But can you?"

"No," he admitted, closing his eyes in defeat. "But who else is there?"

"Who covered you?"

"Yahweh. But He's the one that Abbi offended."

"And you are Shaul's son. If He would do that for you, tainted as you are with the guilt of your abbi, would He not do the same for the innocent people of His land?"

"But He is angry with us, and they are not threatened by the darkness."

"Are they not? What made the king turn against his God?"

Jonathan bent his head. "The darkness," he said at last.

"And when the king is allied with darkness, what of the people?"

"They suffer."

"Why? What does it mean to say, 'As the king, so the people'?"

"It means that when the king allies with the light, the light can work and has power to bring good, so the people are blessed. But if the king allies with darkness, the opposite comes and the people will suffer."

"So, Jonathan, what have you come for? You already know what you can do for your people."

"It is treason," he whispered.

"Is it treason to deny the darkness the power to harm your people? Whom do you fight, Hassar?"

He bowed his head again, thinking. "I fight the darkness, and only as Abbi clings to it do I fight him," he said in wonder. "But Abbi *has* chosen it, and what I must do will hurt, just as it hurt when Abbi condemned me after Michmash."

"Yes, it will hurt. That is why the decision is yours alone. Only the Evil One forces people against their wishes."

"I am afraid I cannot do it."

"No man can fight the darkness alone and prevail, Jonathan."

"Will Yahweh go with me, even now? As you said, I am tainted with Abbi's sin."

"Did Yahweh stand between you and the darkness, Jonathan? He will always come when one who trusts in Him calls. His hesed will cover them, and His strength goes with every one who wishes to fight against the darkness. Even when they get a little mulish at times."

"Or are, perhaps, the most exasperating hillman in the land?"

"Yes, Hassar, even then." Laughter shimmered around him.

Jonathan smiled a little. Then he returned to the thoughts in his mind and asked himself what he would do in light of what it would mean in his life.

"What is your decision, Jonathan ben Shaul?"

"As the king is, so the people are," he said softly. "With Yahweh to be with me, I will be king so that the darkness may not have power in this land."

"My hesed shall be found with you always, Jonathan Melek Israel. My strength will be with you, and your name will be ever before Me."

The hassar turned his head, feeling the grass prickle his cheek. He had to try twice to raise himself from the ground, surprised to see that it was almost sunset. At last he stood with head bowed, knowing what he had to do. As he walked from the tabernacle, the people gathered around, staring at him in awe. Even the priest bowed.

Conscious of his dress, he walked to the waiting and restless mules.

"Let's go, Dara. Do you have my clothes?"

"Yes, adoni."

"Mahesa, do you need to return to Nob?"

"No. My place is here, now. Your weapons are with your clothes."

"Thank you."

The Egyptian bowed slightly. "Do not thank me, adoni, I but serve El Shaddai."

"Shalom then, Mahesa."

"Shalom, adoni melek."

Jonathan caught up the reins of his mule and led the animal down the hill, followed by Dara. At the bottom, he dressed again, mounting the mule in the fast fading light. "Why was everyone gathered there when I came out?" he asked.

"Because of the evening sacrifice, adoni. The priest had just placed the lamb on the altar, when the fire flared up and smoke poured from the altar of incense, driving out the priest who was there. The incense gathered over the court, hiding it, and remained until just before you walked out. No one could approach, not even the priest! I thought Yahweh had taken your life!"

They rode down the path to the highway.

"Adoni, Mahesa called you 'melek.'"

"Mahesa has eyes that see much."

"Good."

Jonathan smiled briefly at the satisfaction in his shield-bearer's tone, then sobered. The pain of the king's sin still beat in his chest, but he straightened his shoulders. Somehow, knowing that Yahweh stood with him against that which his abbi had chosen, made the burden bearable.

CHAPTER 31

As soon as he arrived at the fortress, he sent for Ishvi and mounted the stairs to the throne room. Now that he had made his decision, he wanted to get it over with as soon as he could. There was hope that the pain would end once it was done.

Ishvi appeared sooner than he expected. His brother was carefully dressed and carried a pouch of records. Commander Sheva attended him.

"We've waited your arrival, brother," Ishvi said.

"I didn't get your message until day before yesterday when I was near Jabesh. I came up the Jericho road." He paused, his lips tightly pressed together.

"I'm sorry, Jonathan," Ishvi nearly whispered. "I couldn't find the words to put on the papyrus."

"I don't think I could have either. I know some of what happened. When did it start, Ishvi?"

While he paced in the long ell of the throne room, Ishvi's quiet voice told him of the unthinkable. Jonathan read the records that Eshbaal had written, and the ones Ishvi had kept since then. Then he turned to Sheva and questioned him closely on what he knew. After he had learned everything he could from the man, he asked the commander to wait in the anteroom below.

Now he just had to figure out a way to tell Ishvi what he meant to do about it all.

"Something has to be done, Hassar," his brother said, standing in front of the dais, staring at the empty throne.

"I know, Ishvi. I've been thinking about it."

"So have I."

Something strange in his brother's voice caused Jonathan to stare at him. "What have you thought?"

"That our house shed sacred blood, and our blood must answer for that if the people are to live. You are the only one who can control

Abbi and Abner. Malchi has the army following him. Eshbaal keeps the court running so you can do your part. Our sisters are out of it and away from here, thank Yahweh." He looked steadily at Jonathan. "That leaves me, Hassar. I should never have gone to Zelah. Eshbaal has never been a warrior, and when violence broke out in the throne room, he was helpless. But I could have done something. Only I was more interested in getting the grain in on time so that we could get a better price this year!" he finished bitterly.

Then he knelt in front of the dais. "Give my blood to Yahweh, Hassar, and maybe He will be appeased for the deaths of His priests."

In the silence Jonathan's footsteps sounded loud as he approached his brother. Sweat shone on Ishvi's face, but he held still. Jonathan took out his belt knife and sat down on the dais, stabbing the knife into the wood between them. "I tried that, Ishvi. Twice. Yahweh said no."

His brother stared at the knife. "No?"

"No. Doeg the Edomite took the ban to Nob, and he died by Mahesa's hand where the altar of sacrifice once stood. The others who attacked the town, but one, were already dead. Mahesa was not willing to let the desecration of El Shaddai's tabernacle go unpunished, so blood has been requited already."

"But if they were all dead, who destroyed the tabernacle?" Ishvi asked, still staring at the knife.

"No one did. As Mahesa reminded me, it was made to be portable."

"He moved it?" his brother questioned, amazed.

"It was the one thing that he could do at the time," Jonathan said with a faint smile. "It stands at Gibeon. I went there last night, half hoping I'd die in Yahweh's presence. He said no."

"Who survived?" Ishvi asked suddenly.

"Abiathar. Mahesa sent him south with the Habiru and some other things from the tabernacle. I wonder what they were. All the furniture was at Gibeon."

"It can't be the breastplate. Abbi has that."

Jonathan's face hardened. "Along with the Urim and Thummin?"

His brother nodded. "He keeps them in his room."

Well, the hassar thought, that answered one of his questions.

Someone knocked at the door. Jonathan stood and Ishvi eased into a sitting position on the dais. "Enter," Jonathan said.

Michal came through the door followed by Basemath. They carried trays of food and set them on the long table. Basemath quickly left, and Michal looked at her older brothers. "I see Jonathan decided not to take your blood, Ishvi." She indicated the belt knife thrust into the wooden dais.

Jonathan hastily pulled it out and sheathed it. "Yahweh had already said no," he explained.

"Twice," Ishvi added, his expression bland.

"Once should have been enough. You shouldn't be so mulish, Jonathan," Michal said tartly.

"I'll try not to be. Yahweh has given me quite a task, and I will need all the help I can find."

"Then I'll send Sheva for the rest of us," Michal announced, heading for the door.

"Who is here?" Jonathan asked in surprise.

"Everyone."

"Merab, too?" the hassar asked Ishvi while his sister went out the door.

"Yes."

Things could move quicker than he'd thought. Maybe this was a sign that Yahweh's hand was indeed with him. He hoped so.

Ishvi lit three of the lamps, setting them around the throne, and then extinguished the torch, which had nearly burned out. When all six of them had gathered, Eshbaal secured the door. "Sheva barred the anteroom, and he's standing guard outside the balcony door," he told Jonathan.

"Good." Now that they were all here, the hassar still had no idea how to present what must be said. Then the flickering light of the lamps aroused a memory.

"I'm sure you remember the last time we gathered here like this," he said softly. "I asked then for your will in the matter of the tax exemption for Dahveed's house. You gave me your support, knowing that it meant going against the king, because it would save the honor of the king and our house." He paused.

No one stirred.

"Since then, all of you have continued your support while I have tried to guard the king from more dishonor. These walls can testify to my failure."

Ishvi moved restlessly, denial on his lips, and Jonathan raised his hand. "It's true, Ishvi. I could have done more, but I held back, hoping that half-way measures would be enough. They were not. If any of our house's honor can be salvaged, and the people protected from the effects of Shaul's sin, I can hold back no longer.

"I must know if I still have your support, even if I must take the throne."

"It's yours for all practical purposes, now." Malchi said, eyeing his older brother.

"Yes, but I have kept myself under the king's command. That would have to change."

"What of Abbi?" Merab whispered, tears trickling down her cheeks.

Jonathan sighed, knowing how much it cost the gentle bekorah to say those words. Of them all, he and Merab shared the most memories of what Shaul had once been.

"If my plans work out, Abbi will become a figurehead, and nothing more. If they don't, there is always seclusion at an estate somewhere. I will not do more unless Yahweh says there is no other way."

"You are asking us to trust your word on that," Eshbaal said, his face strained.

"I am."

"You stated that you came from Gibeon and the tabernacle," Ishvi said. "Did you inquire of Yahweh?"

"The tabernacle wasn't destroyed?" Malchi interrupted.

"No, just moved," Jonathan explained. He told them what he had done and the decision that had come from his experience without saying much of the struggle he had gone through, and nothing of what Dara had told him of what had happened.

When he finished, Merab said, "If you left the tabernacle just at sunset, you left out a lot, Jonathan. One of the couriers was talking of what he'd seen on his way past Gibeon late this afternoon. I didn't know whether or not to believe him, since I thought the tabernacle was destroyed. Yahweh Himself gave you this task, didn't He?"

"Yahweh verified that the only way I could shield the people from Shaul's sin was to take the throne, but He left the decision to me because I must be willing to pay the cost, no matter how high. I decided that I would do the best I could to protect the people of this land. But if He would not use me without my consent in this matter, I have no right to use you unless you are willing."

He paused, then went on. "I'm not asking for formal oaths of allegiance. I want to do anything I can to avoid rebellion and war. But I must know how far you, as my brothers and sisters, will support me in this family matter of Abbi's sin." Observing their faces, he waited.

Michal bit at her lips, her expression troubled.

"What are you thinking, little sister?" Jonathan inquired.

"I think there is one more thing which must be said before anyone decides," she replied. "Everyone should know where your highest loyalty lies."

Jonathan turned away, staring into the shadows behind the throne. Confess his own treason? "You know what you are asking?" he said, his voice tight.

"Yes. But it is time, Jonathan. If we are to serve Yahweh, we must do so knowingly."

He faced her. As usual, Michal had cut to the heart of the matter. The others waited, puzzled and uneasy. She was right. If he was going to ask them to commit treason, they had the right to know that he had already done so.

"Five years ago I cut a covenant binding myself and my house forever to Yahweh's Mashiah. My loyalty to him outranks all else but my loyalty to Yahweh Himself."

The silence settled thickly in the room.

"Roeh Shamuel anointed another nagid for Israel?" Ishvi gasped.

"No. Roeh Shamuel anointed a *melek for Yahweh*."

Malchi jerked his head up.

"Abbi was anointed nagid," Merab said, staring at Jonathan.

"Yes, Bekorah. But Yahweh's Mashiah is to be melek to Him."

The silence stretched out.

"Who holds your covenant, Jonathan Hassar?" Ishvi asked.

"Dahveed Israel of Bethlehem."

"I was right!" Malchi exclaimed softly. "There's always been something about Dahveed, from the day he pulled Abbi from my throat with his music. It spills out of him when he fights. I couldn't imagine what other use Yahweh would have for it."

"Are you still willing to help me, knowing what I have done?" Jonathan continued.

Malchi smiled. "I gave my allegiance to you some time ago, Jonathan. I don't see any reason to change now."

Merab straightened to her full height. "I owe to you and Dahveed a peaceful home and the chance to raise my children without fear. I will do whatever you ask me. Abbi must be stopped for everyone's sake."

"Ishvi?"

"I don't see any other way," the sar replied.

"And you, Michal?"

"You know where my heart lies, Jonathan. This should have been done sooner."

The hassar nodded his head in acknowledgment. "Eshbaal?"

Instead of replying, the youngest sar came and touched his knee to the floor, taking Jonathan's hand. "If you will keep any more blood being shed from this room, I will do whatever you want."

"With Yahweh's help, I will do my best, Eshbaal."

In the shadows cast by the flickering light of the three lamps surrounding the throne, the others came one by one, kneeling briefly, sealing their promises to him. But with each brush of lips on his hand, the hassar's heart weighed heavier with the knowledge of what he took from his abbi. Yet there was no other way, and as Michal had said, it was past time for him to act. If he had done so when he learned about the Gibeonites, perhaps Nob would not lie in ashes, and his house would not bear the burden of the blood of priests.

"Yahweh, be with me," he murmured again.

The silence of the room made the footsteps on the stairs seem loud. Jonathan nodded at the door, and Eshbaal had the bar off before the knock.

"Enter."

Commander Sheva pushed the door open, and Immi walked in. He closed the door behind him as he left.

Ahinoam looked at her children, settling at last on Jonathan. "Come here, son."

The hassar obeyed and touched his knee to the floor.

"What was your decision?"

His heart twisted in him, tears pricking in his eyes. "That Abbi should no longer rule, Immi. What else can we do?"

Ahinoam nodded. "I thought you would decide this way. That's why I sent for Merab. All of you needed to be here." She smoothed back the hair from his forehead. "You have my blessing, and my promise that I will do everything I can to preserve Shaul's house, for in that way I will serve the king the best."

"Thank you, Immi," Jonathan said, burying his hands in her robe as she hugged him.

"Come here," she added to the rest, kissing them one by one, wiping the tears from Merab's face, and giving Eshbaal an encouraging smile. "Now," she said, "you must establish control tonight, to prevent anyone's taking advantage of the king's accusation in court against you.

It was nonsense, of course, but it can still be used."

A sense of irony filled Jonathan. The charge had indeed been nonsense when it was spoken, and yet oddly prophetic. Perhaps some of Yahweh's Spirit still clung to the king even yet.

"Am I right in guessing that if you can muzzle Abner, you can handle the rest?" she asked.

"Yes, Immi," Jonathan replied, starting to pace along the table again. "That's been the foremost thought in my mind. Abner endangered my life some time ago, and I have enough evidence to put him to death, but that could start a clan war. On the other hand, his experience in battle is invaluable, to say nothing of how Abbi depends on him. But I must either control him, or he'll have to die."

Fists clenched, Malchi abruptly turned away.

"If you know anything else I can do, Malchi, I'll jump at it," the hassar added, weariness in his voice.

"I know, Jonathan."

"How about controlling his courier network?" Immi asked.

"If I could be certain of that, I wouldn't need much else. But I'd have to be certain. We just recently got a lesson in how important communications are," he ended wryly.

"Yes, Jaasiel deceived you very well with that one! But since spending several days at Navyoth as my guest, talking to the men of the king's guard who are now there, and visiting Nob, I think he has something to say."

Nonplussed, Jonathan watched as Immi pulled the door open and his cousin Jaasiel entered, holding a box. Seeing all the king's children flanking the hassar, he paled, but came forward, handing Jonathan the box and then dropping to his knees, bowing to the floor.

"Light another lamp," Jonathan ordered.

Eshbaal took one from a niche in the wall, lighting it from one of the lamps on the dais. He put it on the long table by the hassar.

Lifting the lid, Jonathan slowly took out the clay seals nested in the cloth. "Get Elihu," he ordered. The scribe could tell him if these were the seals used, and if only them. While Eshbaal sent Sheva for the scribe, he turned to his cousin, struggling to control the surge of rage that flashed through him. "You are responsible for these, and you sealed messages with them?"

"Yes, Hassar." When no one spoke, Jaasiel straightened. "You know I haven't left Zelah much, and there were a few things that Abbi neglected to tell me when he talked to me. I wouldn't believe Dodah

Ahinoam when she told me what the king had done. But then the fortress guard came to stay at Navyoth, and Commander Zorath took me to Nob." A shudder passed through him. "When Roeh Shamuel said that Yahweh had given the kingdom into your hand because of Shaul's sin, I had to believe."

His anger cooling a little, Jonathan sat down on the bench. "Tell me what you've done."

"Some time ago, Abbi announced that someone local was reading the king's dispatches. I thought of making clay seals and putting them on routine messages that didn't matter so we could trace them and find out who was intercepting them. Abbi was so pleased," he said, tears shining in his eyes. "He said the king wanted to try my idea, but we'd have to work it from my estate to keep anyone from knowing what was happening. Two scribes came to help, and Abbi sent me a new steward. I copied out a lot of the messages, none of which were important, and used the seals. I assumed the other scribes were doing the same. It appears they weren't," he ended.

"No, they weren't." Jonathan's voice was smooth. "Anything else?"

"I didn't know what to do after I got back from Nob," Jaasiel said, shuddering again, "but when the roeh said that Yahweh had given the kingdom to you, I decided I would tell you what had happened and see if there was anything I could do to make up for it. I-I didn't know!"

As usual, Jonathan had a lot of questions, grilling his cousin until someone opened the door in the anteroom, and footsteps sounded on the stairs once more.

Moments later Elihu entered. He glanced quickly around, taking in the scene, before his eyes riveted for a long moment on the empty throne. Then his gaze flew back to the hassar. He knelt where he stood. "My skills are at your command, adoni."

The oddness of the comment piqued Jonathan's curiosity. "Haven't they been before?"

"You held my gratitude before, adoni. From now on, you can command anything you wish of me."

As Jonathan regarded Dahveed's brother, an idea of what that might mean began to form in his mind. "That's quite a statement, Elihu. Why?"

His sweet smile crossed the man's face. "Because the last time I spoke with Hassarah Ruth, she said the night that I saw three lamps surrounding an empty throne, I should not fear to give my talents to the man who held Yahweh's will above all else, for His hand covered the one who would have need of me in Yahweh's time."

Ishvi gasped, staring at the lamps that he himself had placed earlier in the evening.

"It would seem Yahweh's hand is indeed with us," Hassarah Ahinoam said softly.

"We will need it. Elihu, are these the seals used on the messages you've been tracing?"

The scribe inspected them. "Yes."

"Could other seals have been used?"

"Not that I've seen."

The hassar turned back to his cousin. "Jaasiel, is there anything else you can tell me?"

"Not that I can think of."

"All right. Wait in the anteroom. Elihu will be down in a moment."

"Yes, Hassar." Jaasiel got to his feet and Eshbaal closed the door behind him.

Jonathan turned to the scribe. "Shaul just issued a call to arms directed against Keilah, and I suspect he did so because Dahveed is down there. How did he learn that?"

"Not through the network I've been tracing," Elihu replied immediately. "That is a local one only, passing messages between the king, General Abner, commanders, and couriers running errands. But it wouldn't surprise me to learn that King Shaul is getting information from other sources as well."

"Then there is more work for you to do. From the volume of messages that Jaasiel ben Abner just told me about, I'd say there is more happening on his estate than he himself is aware of. You'll have plenty of time to talk to him. I'm turning him over to you. Keep in mind that he is a willing hostage, but a hostage nonetheless. I don't think I need to tell you how important this could be to the safety of the Dahveed."

"No, adoni," Elihu said, his voice hard. "Does Abner know that you have his son?"

Jonathan turned to his immi.

"He thinks Jaasiel is on business at the moment," she explained.

"How free a hand do I have with this situation?" the scribe asked next.

As Jonathan studied Elihu's intent expression, the memory of what the man had accomplished with his abbi's estates rose in him. "You have a very free hand, Elihu. Report to Sar Ishvi. Just be sure whatever you do is quietly done. I don't want a clan war."

"Or a civil war, adoni melek?"

Another silence fell on the room.

"Or a civil war," Jonathan answered, his eyes steady. "I do not intend to see this kingdom torn in two."

Elihu bowed, that smile again crossing his face. "The Hassarah saw much." He left the room.

"And so do you," Jonathan muttered. "Ishvi, how do you work with that man?"

"By staying out of his way. He's like Tanhum. Tell him what you want, and it appears."

Sheva appeared at the door. "Hassar, one of your personal guards is asking to see you."

"Is it Azmaveth?" Immi asked.

"Yes, Hassarah."

"I'll see him. Probably he's looking for Pelet. The boy's sleeping in the residence now, but he's been eager to see his abbi," Ahinoam turned to go.

"Uh, Immi?" Jonathan said, eyeing his mother.

She glanced at him. "Yes?"

"Was there anything else you took from Abner besides his seals, his hostage, and his son? I might need to know," he said apologetically.

Immi raised her eyebrows. "Not this time."

"Would you let me know if that changes?"

"I'll think about it." Again she turned to go.

"Immi?"

"Yes, Malchi?"

"When may I have the third unit back?"

"When the furniture and chests have all been put back. The women helping me clean are getting tired of moving them. Do you have objections?"

"No," Malchi said hastily. "Use them as long as you want."

"I'll see to Azmaveth then." She walked out the door.

Jonathan raised his eyebrows at Malchi.

"When Hassarah Israel demands the third unit, I send it!" the sar explained.

"Tell me about it later," the hassar said, his lips quirking into a smile.

It was early morning, and Jonathan stood alone on the roof of his house on his private estate, absently fingering the twisted brass earring on its gold chain. He'd done everything he could think of to set in motion his coup. Then he'd come here, knowing that if Azmaveth had returned, so had Taphath. She had welcomed him sleepily.

Now he wondered what he should do next. Ishvi had offered to attend the king today so he could rest, but he didn't know how much rest he would get. He still had to warn Dahveed someway, and he must do something about Azmaveth. The man had betrayed him, and while that was understandable, he must still respond. Exile? A post on one of the other estates?

While he debated, Azmaveth strode through the gate. He'd spent the night at the fortress with his son.

Jonathan descended the outside stairs.

"Adoni," the guard said, kneeling to him.

"Azmaveth. Your son is well?"

"Yes, adoni. He is eager to return home. I bade him farewell before I came. What is your will for me, adoni? I know that I cannot remain as your personal guard any longer."

"No, you cannot," the hassar said slowly, trying to think of what he could do. The chain of the earring slipped from his fingers, dangling under his hand. Suddenly he had an idea. "Azmaveth, how willing are you to protect your son?"

"What do you mean, adoni?" the guard asked, bewildered.

"If you are completely out of Abner's reach, he cannot coerce you again, and it will be easier for me to protect your family."

Azmaveth studied the hassar's expression. "Where am I to be exiled?" he asked, his voice shaky.

"Not very far. I want to send you on an errand to someone who just may find you useful."

"I'll go, adoni. I haven't had a peaceful night since all this began. I can stand it no longer!"

"All right. You'll leave now, just as you are." He pulled four silver pieces from his girdle. "Here is some silver so you can eat on the way. Take the most direct route to Keilah. And when you get there, give this to Dahveed," he directed, putting the earring into the guard's hand. "Tell him the king is bringing an army to besiege the town in hopes of capturing him. And Azmaveth, go as fast as you can."

"Yes, adoni," the man said, bowing once and jogging out the gate.

Jonathan watched him leave, wondering what Dahveed had been doing in the past month, and how he'd gotten involved with Keilah.

CHAPTER 32

I was pleased. The ridge in the forest of Hereth that Elhanan remembered was indeed a suitable place to stay. The morning after we arrived, Shagay's Jonathan brought a message from Hanan saying that Hassar Jonathan and his bride had left three days ago to visit her relatives in Jabesh. I was glad to hear it, and the thought occurred to me that Hanan might be an avenue by which I could contact Jonathan Hassar. Right now, however, we needed to set up a camp. The site had a couple small caves, and we had three or four tents, but other than that, we made do with whatever we could construct. Compared to one of Ethan's encampments, it was a sorry-looking place, but it was defensible, and I ordered some trees felled to make it more so.

Now that we had no work at all, I started the men on a training program such as the army used, supplemented by Uriah's knowledge of the shalishim. Most of them also needed to learn many of the skills of the Habiru, so for several weeks there would be much to keep them busy. What I was going to do with such a group of highly trained men in a year or so, I left to the future. But I had learned already that men who are busy are much less quarrelsome. So are men who are well-fed.

Hunting parties went out each day. Knowing that we might need game close to us in the future, I sent them deep into the highlands now. It would be a while before game became wary of us and thus harder to find, so while we had more than we needed, I set the men to smoking and drying the meat.

Threshing passed. Gad took over many of the camp chores that Ahiam had attended to, and he had received two donkey loads of things from the roeh, including scrolls, ink, and pens that he used to begin a chronicle.

With hours of practice each day, my men rapidly increased their fighting skills, and with 18 of us to work with, Uriah often watched us spar, assessing the strong points of each man, and then combining us in various ways to form the shalishim. Many of the men surprised me. Igal was developing into a very good center for a shalish, while Zabad had to struggle to fight in one. Yet if he fought alone, not many in the group cared to come against the Jezreelite. His sister, Ahinoam, crossed my mind once or twice, but I had so much else to worry over that I didn't have time to think of her for long.

Elika and Shammah fought well as a twosome, but put someone with them, and they fell apart. Eliphelet had the fastest hands of any of us, myself included. He could manipulate a dagger in ways that appeared impossible, but he seemed hesitant about fighting. And it wouldn't be long before Ittai would surpass most of my men with a bow, his Benjamite blood coming to the fore.

Abishai and Jonathan soaked everything up, and would one day be formidable with any weapon at all. Asahel practiced and improved, but his heart wasn't in it. My half cousin Zelek, and the two Judahites Ira and Gareb, plus Zalmon, Ahiam, Elhanan, and Igal's friend Jaas were solid men, the kind that make the backbone of any army. Uzzia spent hours unlearning his habit of depending on his height to scare an opponent. I suspected that he'd also been left alone because of his brother, Tiras. Shagay had always been a good fighter, but he was improving more, and regularly forced me into my gift when I sparred with him.

He did it again today. Uriah had formed three shalishim, and the rest of us were to attack, trying to break the threesomes up. I organized the eight men working with me, but we weren't certain of our success. Uriah's training was rapidly hardening the shalishim into single units with six arms, six legs, and one mind. As we sparred, I tried to watch all that went on, but with Shagay as the center to the shalish that I faced, I couldn't do that for long. Soon the sounds around me began to fade as I focused more on the fighter in front of me. My gift came to the fore, and I lost track of everything else.

The knowledge that it was a sparring bout remained in my mind, and my desire was to win, not kill. The man in front of me was fast and could threaten me from either side. I retreated and circled and side-stepped, a subtle rhythm awakening in my body that soon became nearly a dance, and then something changed. The man in front of me switched weapons. He was taller, with a lithe regal grace that flowed from his shoulders through his arms and hips, guiding his spear with lethal quickness. His long cloak swirled around him with each movement, and he picked up the rhythm of the dance as we circled each other.

Every time I attempted to reach him, his spear barred the way, and my blade turned it aside at every strike. Unable to force the spear up or down, I managed to push it aside, but when I lunged toward him, my sword felt only the swirl of the cloak as he spun past, so I spun with him, trading positions. Who was this man? He was the best spearman I'd ever encountered, and as much as I hated spears, I admired his skill with it.

At last we drew apart, panting for breath. I drove my sword point into a log near me, and he reversed the spear, thrusting the metal-covered point on the butt end into the ground. The sounds of the cheers and shouts of approval from the watching men rang in my ears, and I shook my head a little, then accepted the cruse Ahiam handed me.

The opponent waited, his cloak motionless around him now, the thick fine wool dark gray. His high-quality shirt and kilt were lighter gray, and he carried sword and battle dagger at his belt. Everything about him, from his clothes to his elegant grace of movement, shouted of high status.

The world around me came into focus again, and I took another drink while someone supplied our visitor with water also. As I approached him, he watched with a quiet smile, his eyes twinkling at me.

I stopped several feet from him. "Josheb!" I exclaimed. "Josheb ben Zabdiel, what have you grown into?" I asked my third retainer.

His smile widened as he knelt gracefully. "I see from your face that I have indeed changed since you saw me last, adoni Dahveed."

"That you have, and your skill with that spear is even greater, if that is possible!"

"You pushed me to my limits," he admitted. "I've never met someone who fights like you do."

"I'd never have known it. Everything I tried, you had an answer for."

His eyes sparkled, and that smile crossed his face again.

"How did you locate us here?"

"I wouldn't have but for a young Habiru named Hanan who found me wandering around early this morning."

I sighed. The Habiru lad from Joel's band kept a discreet watch on me and my doings. I wasn't certain that I approved, but there was little I could do about it. The youth was like a wisp of mist in the woods. "What news do you bring?"

He sobered instantly. "Nothing good, adoni. I dare not go back, so I am with you to stay, unless you send me elsewhere."

I gave him my hand. "Get up, Josheb, and tell me what has

happened."

"Jonathan Hassar and his bride left to visit her family in Jabesh nearly three weeks ago now. Then the day before yesterday the king accused him of treason in open court because he welcomed you to his private estate after his marriage."

At first, Josheb's quiet words didn't sink into my mind. What he had said couldn't be. "The king accused *Jonathan Hassar*?" I asked just to be sure.

"Yes, adoni. When I heard that accusation, I knew I dared not stay any longer. But I fear even worse has happened." He paused. "After someone spoke to Shaul, he ordered the priests brought to him from Nob. I slipped away from the court at that point, but as I left Gibeah later in the afternoon, I noticed a column of smoke from the southwest. I don't know what it was, adoni, but the king was furious, and the hassar is not there to balance him."

Nob was southwest of Gibeah. But I couldn't fathom the king attacking the tabernacle. On the other hand, I couldn't make sense of him accusing his son of treason, either.

"This is serious news. Come into my tent and tell me everything," I said, catching a glimpse of the white, worried faces of the men around me. Now I understood why Ethan had always received visitors and messengers in private. I shouldn't have invited Josheb to present his news in front of all the men.

Once in the tent, I questioned him closely. He'd been near the tamarisk tree when Shaul had made the accusation, so he'd heard most of that personally. When he quoted what the king had said about the hassar, I felt the blood drain from my face. "He actually used the words, 'cut a covenant'?" My mouth was suddenly dry.

Josheb nodded. "Then, when everyone stared at him, he asked what else he was to think when Jonathan feasted with you after the wedding. I began easing away right then, but I heard the king ordering the priests brought to him before I left the street for that alley."

After a little thought I decided that the king could not possibly know about the existing covenant between the hassar and me. If he had, he would not have sent for the priests. Remembering the way that Hakkohen Haggadol Ahimelech had helped me during my flight from Shaul, I prayed that he was safe, protected by his anointing and dedication to the service of Yahweh. But like Josheb, the fear lurked in my mind that the king had done something terrible.

By the next morning an entirely different atmosphere pervaded the camp. The men were afraid. For the first time they fully realized what running from Shaul could mean. If the king would accuse his son of treason for his friendship with me, he would not hesitate to do anything to find and kill us.

The second morning after Josheb arrived, we had another visitor. Hanan brought him again. "He was wandering around Gedor, looking for you, adon," the youth said. "He's waiting at the bottom of the hill."

I went down to him, first studying him from the safety of the trees before I stepped out. His clothes in disarray, he paced back and forth. He'd come away quickly, and had probably traveled several miles. Then something caught my attention. Those looked like fresh grass stains on his robe, and that meant he could have come from the Shephelah where the vegetation was lush and green.

"You were asking for me?" I asked after I'd emerged from the trees.

He whirled around. "Dahveed Israel?"

"Yes."

Quickly he bowed. "I have been sent from Keilah. The elders of the town beg you to help us fight the Philistines. They are stealing the harvest from the threshing floors."

My face tightened. This looked like a year when the Philistines needed more grain, but didn't want to pay for it. Those years when they didn't need it, they just burned the fields.

"I'll need some time to consider this," I said.

"We will pay, Dahveed."

I was about to indignantly refuse, when I remembered that I wasn't in the Israelite army now, and that I had to support my band by whatever means I could. Instead, I bowed in acknowledgment. "As I would expect. But I will need time to consider this. Hanan?"

The youth appeared from the trees.

"Please stay with this man until I return."

"Yes, adon," he said, settling down.

I walked into the forest. A grove of large oaks not far away reminded me of the hillside near Bethlehem where'd I'd first felt the presence of Yahweh. I went there now, standing in the middle of it with my head bowed.

"Yah, Your servant needs Your guidance. Please listen to my request." While I waited Adonai's answer, I tried to still my mind, letting go of the worries that crowded it, and simply tarry for Yah's coming.

His presence crept softly into the grove, and I bowed to the ground. "Word has come that Keilah is under attack, Adonai. Please tell Your servant what I should do. Shall I attack the Philistines?"

"Yes. Go and deliver Keilah."

"You are gracious to Your servant," I said, remaining on my knees until the presence of Yahweh lifted from the grove. Then I hurried to the encampment. "Shagay, Uriah," I called.

"Yes, adoni?"

"Get the men ready. The Philistines are at Keilah, and the town has asked us to help them fight."

Everybody gathered around.

"You want us to fight?" Eliphelet asked. "Dahveed, are you out of your senses? Shaul is trying to kill us! You want us to go back down to the Shephelah, while he's looking for us? And you expect us to go up against an army? I know that we've trained and can put up a decent fight against each other, and maybe some other Habiru, but Dahveed, the Philistines? They're professionals! They have mercenaries! We'd be slaughtered!"

I looked at the men in surprise. It had never occurred to me that they might hesitate. What had we been training for, if not for combat? And who better to fight than Philistines? I was about to say this, when the look on Ahiam's face stopped me. He nodded his head slightly toward the men, and I took a good look at them. Those used to fighting, such as Shagay, Zabad, and Josheb, waited to see what the orders were. The others, however, were afraid. They had never been in battle without professional backup.

"No, Eliphelet, we won't be slaughtered," I finally replied. "All of you have more training now than the usual soldier gets who answers a call to arms. Alone, the weakest of you is more than equal to the average soldier, and the best of you can outfight most mercenaries. But in the shalishim, you can win against anything I've seen.

"And I've fought with and against the best. You have two of the best here, teaching you every day. In addition, Uriah has given you skills that few others will have." My words made some impression, and Igal, Jaas, Elika, and Shammah looked as if they'd enjoy the challenge of pitting themselves against a real army, if it was a small one!

I went on. "We are Habiru now, remember? But we cannot simply stay in the hills and starve. We have to live, and that means employing the skills we possess. How well we live will depend on how well people value our skills, and this is a good opportunity to show what we can do. We have no stores of food. There are no houses or lands waiting for us when late winter comes and the rains are cold and the hunting is poor. If we must buy food, we must have silver, and that means we must fight now."

I glanced around again. Sober faces looked back. "But there is something else we have," I added. "We have Yahweh's hand to fight with us. When this call for help came, I went to Him, and I asked what we should do. He said we are to save Keilah."

My three first retainers, my nephews, and Jonathan walked away.

"Where are they going?" Igal asked.

"To get their weapons," I explained. "They know that when Yahweh says to fight, I fight, and I will go alone if necessary. I do not ignore my God."

"That's good enough for me. Come on, Jaas. Let's see if we've learned anything in the past few weeks." The two went to obtain their armaments, followed by Ira and Gareb. Elika and Shammah looked at each other and shrugged, joining the Judahites with Zabad trailing thoughtfully behind.

"Adoni?" Zalmon said.

"Yes?"

"Um, I know that you asked Yahweh about this, but for the rest of us, could you ask Him again?"

I went back to the oak grove, kneeling in the same spot. "Adonai, please help Your servant again. Those who are with me who have not felt Your power are afraid of the task You have given us. The king seeks our lives, and the Philistines are great foes in their eyes. They have asked that I come to You again. What answer shall I give them?"

Yahweh's presence enveloped me quickly, and the command sounded clearly in my mind. *"Arise, go down to Keilah, for I have given the Philistines into your hand."*

"I will obey," I said, bowing to the ground.

When I returned, the little group looked at me anxiously. "Yahweh has given us a command. We will go to Keilah." Reluctantly, they turned to get their equipment, Eliphelet the last one to go. He was shaking.

Gad stayed to watch the camp. He had only begun to learn how to handle a weapon and would be more useful here than with us. I left Ittai with him so that the youth wouldn't have to fight his countrymen. In addition, if seen, he might be recognized. When the men were ready, we started down the hill.

The man with Hanan looked relieved to see us. "You will come?"

"We'll come."

"When?"

"Now. Lead the way, geber."

He looked at Hanan, and the Habiru lad rolled to his feet and started down the path toward the road from Hebron.

As we crossed the road, Ahiam caught up to me. "What is our payment?"

I sighed. "I forgot to ask. Do you know what Ethan usually received?"

"Depended on the situation. If we were low on silver, he'd charge that, but if we needed other things, he'd sometimes work for plunder. It's taking a chance, but sometimes paid more than a fee."

"Considering the little we've got, plunder would be a good idea. And it's one the town would readily agree to."

"Yes, but you don't want to get the reputation of working only for plunder, adoni. They should pay something."

While my mind turned over the problem of payment, I listened behind me. The last time the entire group had traveled, it sounded as if an army were thundering along, but now the noise of our passing was much less.

I caught up to the geber from Keilah. "How big a Philistine force is there?" I asked.

"We think about two units, filled out with militia. They can send out several raiding parties at once, which is why the town needs help this year."

I considered. "All right. With that many, there should be enough plunder to cover part of the fee, and I can reduce it for the town because of that. I assume that will be acceptable?"

"It should be."

"Good. My normal charge is a double day's wage per man per day--" The geber turned a little pale and gulped. "--but because the chances of plunder are so good, I'm willing to cut that in half for all the men except my four best. That will add up to 24 silver pieces a day."

"That seems a little high, Dahveed," the geber protested. "Surely a day's wage per man with double for you is sufficient."

"I'm already shaving my price," I reminded him, "and my men are risking their lives. They must be adequately recompensed. Some of them have families."

"Oh, yes, of course. Well, I can ask the elders about this when we get to Keilah."

"As you wish, geber. It's your grain, after all," I said politely.

He frowned, not liking my allusion to the spot they were in, but as determined as I was to attack the Philistines, I must set a precedent now, otherwise things would be worse later.

Once down on the Shephelah, Shagay and Jonathan scouted the country and made certain that the geber found his way back to the town's gates. It was two hours before Jonathan returned. "At least two full units, adoni," he announced. "They've already taken quite a lot of grain."

"Are they settled in one camp, or spread out?"

"They have one camp, on the west side of the town. There's a lot of livestock with them. Mostly donkeys. A couple mules, and they probably stole the local sheep and goats."

"Did you see pack saddles?"

"Yes, and sacks."

"Someone must have decided to refill the city granaries from Keilah, and it's probably Gath," I said in disgust.

Jonathan looked back toward the town. "Adoni, how far do you think a Philistine soldier would be willing to carry one of those sacks of grain?"

I chuckled. "Not far, Jonathan. See if you can find a good place to drive those animals to."

He disappeared, and not long after, Shagay reported in.

"Did the geber make it to town?" I asked.

"Yes, grumbling all the way about the fee you charged. How did you come up with it, anyway?"

"It seemed fair to get at least a day's wage from our work, and then I decided that since we could get killed doing it, we should get double that."

Shagay chuckled. "Most Habiru work for less, but your fees are fine with me."

"Most Habiru don't have the training we have. Between you, Uriah, and Josheb, I'm counting on having the best band of fighters in the land."

Giving me a surprised glance, Shagay flushed a little. "Thank you, adoni. But a word to open your ear. Get paid as soon as we finish the battle. Those elders aren't any too willing to part with their silver."

"I'll keep that in mind."

By that evening everything was settled. The elders had agreed to my fee, including pay for today, but only if we recovered all the grain. Jonathan had come back with word of where we could hide the livestock, and I sat with Josheb, Shagay, and Ahiam, planning the attack.

"We don't have enough men to follow all their raiding parties around," I said, "so we have to attack while they're all in one place. Dawn would be the best time."

"You're thinking one hard blow to drive them from the hills?" Josheb asked.

"Yes. And it needs to be done before they can transport any of that grain. Otherwise we've got to recover it, and I don't want to go down to the coastal plain. That reminds me, we chase them to the last land stair, and that's all. Once they're headed for the plain, we leave them alone."

Josheb gave me a sidewise glance. "That's asking for trouble on another day, adoni."

"We'll have to see. Depends on where these Philistines are from. Do you think we have enough men to split our forces?" I continued. "We need some to collect the livestock, and some for an attack."

"I doubt it," Josheb said. "If the men had several seasons of fighting behind them, you could. But not now."

"I agree, adoni," Ahiam added. "Deal with the livestock first. We'd only need to leave a man or two to hold them, and the rest can attack the camp."

"That only works if we can be quiet with the animals," I commented.

Shagay smiled. "We can manage that."

We left long before dawn the next morning, the pace slower than normal. It was the first time that my men had traveled to a battle in the dark, and I didn't want to lose any of them. Jonathan led us directly to the livestock. The mules stirred restlessly, ears pointed in our direction. The other animals scented us by the time we closed around them. Shagay took the first sentry, and Zabad the other, with barely a sound.

By now, the animals were milling a bit, and Jonathan opened the gate of the pen, then caught the three mules and led them out to the men waiting to take charge of them. The rest of us quietly climbed over the fence and hazed the animals out. The donkeys docilely followed the mules, and with six men on each side, we drove the herd nearly a mile to a fold in the hills where it was easy to keep them bunched.

Eliphelet had eagerly volunteered to stay with the animals, and I chose Zalmon to accompany him.

The rest of us crept back toward the Philistines' camp. The first streaks of dawn were lightening the sky when we gathered before taking attack positions.

"Remember," I said in a low voice. "Any Philistine on the Shephelah is fair game, but once they get to the land stair, break off pursuit." I looked each man in the eye. "I will not tolerate any disobedience of this order from anyone. I don't care if they're carrying your favorite grandson in their arms. You let them go."

Zabad looked at me curiously. "What if they were actually carrying our favorite grandson?"

"Tell me, and I'll deal with it."

"Yes, adoni," he said, looking thoughtfully to the west.

"Take your places, and when Shagay shoots his first arrow, everyone is to charge."

"Can we yell?" Jaas asked. "I'd always heard that Habiru yelled when they attacked."

"Since the goal today is to scare the enemy out of their blankets and back to the plain, yell as much as you want," I said, hiding my smile. "Anything you can think of to help them flee will be useful. Remember, if we meet any resistance, and we will, form into your shalishim, and attack."

That sobered everyone, and they silently took their places. Shagay waited until one or two of the Philistines had emerged from their tents, then he shot his arrow, and my men raised a shout, charging into the camp, Jaas yelling at the top of his voice, slashing tent ropes as he went by.

Elika and Shammah were on my left, screaming "fire" and throwing coals from the fire pits into the tents. Shagay stood back, using his bow to good effect, and I noticed Abishai, Asahel, and Jonathan beating on tents and screaming about hill demons attacking. When the bewildered Philistines burst out, Uzzia rose to his full height, and the terrified enemies fled, dropping whatever they were holding.

In moments the Philistine camp was a mass of confusion, the militia running west as fast as they could go, and only the professionals managing to form into any sort of order.

"Shalish! Shalish!" I shouted, knowing this was the moment of truth for my men. Zabad on my left, and Shagay on my right took up the cry, and to my relief, my men responded.

"Forward!" I yelled, and they charged into the half-formed battle line, crazy with the rush of battle. In the confusion, I could see little, being occupied with driving a few remaining men from the tents we'd left behind. Ahiam and Igal stationed themselves behind me, facing the rear with bows, ready to protect us from anyone who might come from that direction, and I joined up with Uriah at the battle line.

We fought side by side, quickly forcing the men in front of us backward. Glancing to either side, I saw the Philistines falling back, hesitating as they faced our groups of three.

"Forward!" I roared again, and once more the men drove into the enemy line.

"Shalishim! Flee for your lives!" someone yelled--I'd swear it was Zelek--and the line in front of us broke, the Philistines scattering without trying to resist. As my men followed them, I shouted, "Shagay, keep them going!"

He waved a hand, and I turned back to the camp. Ahiam, Igal, and I found several Philistines still there, most of them trapped underneath the tents. None put up a fight, and we had six prisoners and the animals back in their pens by the time the rest of my men returned. They had two more prisoners, and I took a quick report, quieting their shouted celebrations. None were badly hurt though Zabad was the worst off. The man he'd chased down was one of the professionals, and the fight between them had been with fists, not weapons. He'd have a black eye, and he might have a cracked rib from the way he favored his side, but he shrugged it off.

"We celebrate later," I said. "There's too much to do now. First, we must take what we can use from among the camp and the animals. Abishai, I'll need you to aid me. Go through the spoils quickly, before the townspeople arrive," I directed.

While the men dispersed, I turned to our captives. Most were militia, but two were professionals, both wounded. One prisoner was a youth, barely as old as Abishai, shaking so badly that he could hardly tell me he was from Gath. I pulled him to his feet and took him to the edge of camp, then cut his hands loose.

"Do you know your way to the palace in Gath?" I asked.

He nodded stiffly, eyes huge as he watched me sheath my belt knife.

"Go there, and tell Seren Akish that the adon of his sister's house meant what he said."

After repeating my message, he frowned a little. "That doesn't make sense."

"Tell him anyway, word for word. Now go!"

Turning to leave, he was half a mile away before he realized he was free, and then he sped off for the coastal plain.

Back at the row of prisoners, I checked the two professionals. One had a minor wound on his foot, which would heal soon, but until then, he'd have a hard time walking. From the look of his face, this was the man who'd tangled with Zabad.

Blood seeped from the other one's side, and he kept his elbow pressed as tight as he could against it despite the fact that he had his hands bound behind him.

"He looks like more trouble than he's worth. Just kill him?" Abishai asked.

"Are you still so ready to take life, Abishai?"

"He's Philistine. We owe him nothing."

"He is now our slave. What sort of treatment does Yahweh command for slaves?"

My nephew was silent.

"If there was one thing I learned from the hassar, Abishai, it was that hesed should be granted if there is any way it can be. There are times, yes, when hesed cannot be given. This is not one of them."

"Yes, dodi," he said, looking thoughtful. "You want his wound seen to, then?"

"Yes."

"Asahel knows a lot, and there's bound to be some healer supplies here somewhere."

"See if Elika or Shammah have run across any in the tents, and then bring Asahel here."

After he left I asked a couple of questions of the other prisoners. Most were from Gath, two from Ekron.

Eventually Abishai returned with his brother.

"Who's hurt, dodi?" Asahel asked.

I nodded to the prisoner. "You will need to check his wound. Keep in mind that he's a professional soldier, and an enemy."

As Asahel nodded, Abishai drew his sword. But as I untied the man's hands, I got a good look at his face. I froze an instant, and he suddenly looked sick. It was Shemel, my unit commander from Gath.

"Ben-geber," his lips soundlessly formed, and he closed his eyes. Not knowing how he might react to the situation as it now stood, I handled him cautiously, re-binding his hands once they were over his head. He was rigid and bit his lip to suppress the groan when we turned him.

After Asahel cut away the shirt we could see that the wound was fairly deep and had bled significantly. "If it's kept clean, I think he'll live," he said.

When Shemel realized that we were treating the wound, he relaxed a little, and after it was bound up, he watched my face while I tied his hands behind him again. Seeing the question in his eyes, I gave a half smile.

"I was awake enough in that cell to hear you refuse to give me up," I said just loud enough for him to hear. "Hesed has a way of coming back around, commander."

He closed his eyes again.

Asahel treated the other wound, which wasn't much more than a deep scratch. Just as he finished Ahiam returned, announcing that all the spoils we could use had been packed. "You and Zelek take them back to Gad," I directed.

While they left, I set everyone else to loading grain. Elika and Shammah had found some donkey carts, and we filled them. It was past mid-morning when we started back to Keilah. Once it was clear who we were, the gates opened, and people streamed out, shouting and cheering. The men responded well to the reception, keeping their places in line while acknowledging the praise.

Once everything was in the market square and the prisoners handed over, I approached the elders who had stood watching our return. "Adons," I said with a slight bow. "The Philistines are gone, and your grain is returned. As the contract is now fulfilled, all that remains is our payment. Forty-eight silver pieces was the price."

The elders looked over my men. "That was for 20 men, Dahveed. There are only 18 here."

"Two of them have already left for our camp. I am sure you are all honorable men, and would not wish to deprive, or anger, anyone who is fresh from battle on your behalf."

"Certainly not," the head elder assured me cordially. "But we did think that you would wait until after the celebratory feast tonight before you would leave."

"We wouldn't think of refusing such a gracious offer. However, I've always found myself better able to enjoy my pleasures when all my business is taken care of. I'm sure you understand."

"Certainly, certainly," the man agreed again. "Is the purse ready,

Negbi?"

"Yes, Teman."

"Then pay these good men."

Negbi held out a purse.

I looked at it with a slightly puzzled expression. "Surely it should be counted out for the records of the town?"

"Of course, of course," Negbi said a bit too heartily. He counted out the silver pieces, surreptitiously adding back in the three that he had previously removed.

"It has been my pleasure to do business with such honorable men as you," I said, taking the purse and tucking it firmly into my girdle. "Since you have so kindly invited us to a feast tonight, we will go prepare for it."

Teman nodded in dismissal, and we left the square.

When we returned to Keilah that evening, if the elders were a little restrained, at least the townspeople were clearly grateful for what we had done. I wore a good-quality plain brown kilt and shirt that we'd found in the Philistine camp, and Ahiam and Zelek had returned in time for the feast, so we were all here. I sat at the table with Teman and Negbi, who, I discovered, was treasurer for the town.

We had finished eating and more wine had appeared when Teman turned to me with more than just a banal comment. "The elders had a meeting today, Dahveed," he began. "The subject under discussion might interest you."

I turned to him. "Say on, adon."

"First, let me express our pleasure at how efficiently you and your men defended our town. You filled a gap that we have long been aware of. We had thought of hiring some guards on a permanent basis, since we often have trouble in the spring, being so close to the plain as we are."

"I can indeed see where such guards would be welcome here," I replied slowly. "You are right that I may be interested in supplying some. But surely there is no hurry at this time?"

"Certainly not. I realize that such a change for you must be closely considered."

I smiled in spite of his reminder of my current position and status. "Your consideration is appreciated."

"Excellent. Now, we have prepared an old barracks for you and your men for the night. You must spend it with us."

"You are too kind, adon. My men will be pleased with the offer."

As I looked out over the crowd in the market square I felt a little frown forming between my eyes. Torches lit the place, and my men had spread out, talking with the people around them. Habiru didn't normally get this sort of reception. Well, I'd just have to keep my eyes and ears open.

The next morning I awoke to a restlessness that I couldn't explain. At noon, I gathered up some bread and cheese and slung the harp case over my shoulder. With Josheb behind me, I left Keilah and headed toward the deeper forests at the foot of the land stair to the east.

Settling in a comfortable spot against a rock, I played for some time. Hanan appeared, hunching down and listening until I finished the song. Stilling the strings, I regarded the youth. "Do you do anything else besides follow me around?" I asked.

A smiled crossed his face. "No."

"Why?"

He shrugged. "I feel drawn to do so."

Realizing it was just that simple for him, I said nothing more.

"Something comes, adon," he said after a time. "There is power with it." He shifted uneasily. "It arrives from the north, nearer every day. I think it is here now. On the Shephelah."

"Are you frightened?" I asked curiously.

"No."

"Then we will wait."

With a nod he disappeared into the forest.

"Something? Yah, what did he mean?" I wondered. Putting my puzzlement aside, I turned my mind to more verses for the acrostic song[12] I was composing.

"Who is the man who takes pleasure in life? Who loves days to see good things?

Extol Yahweh with me, and let us exalt His name together.

Fear Yahweh, O His holy ones, for there is no lack for the ones who fear Him."

Only those three came to me, so after reviewing what I had, I collected my harp and Josheb and started back to town. A fox barked to my left, and I swung off the road into the trees, startling my retainer with the suddenness of my response to the covert call for help. "What

---

12 Psalms 34

aid can I give?" I asked aloud once I was well into them.

Dahveed Jeshua from Gibeon appeared, looking haggard. "Please come. There is someone you must see."

I followed him back toward the rise to the highlands. Tucked into a fold in the land was a ruined house. The upper story was in shambles, but I noted the careful underpinning of the first story that said the building was actually quite sturdy. For all that the door looked like it might fall from the hinges, it was solid and firmly attached.

Leaving Josheb to wait outside, I stepped into the darker interior.

"Adoni!"

Someone knelt before me, and I waited for my eyes to adjust to the dimness. The man was dark-haired and oddly dressed with mismatched clothing that hardly fit. Noticing that he trembled from weakness, I quickly said, "Sit down. What did you want of me?"

"Sanctuary, Dahveed."

The voice seemed familiar. I stepped closer, straining to see clearly. The Hakkohen Haggadol's son, Abiathar, waited for my answer, his face lined with pain. He could barely sit upright. "Yahweh above! What has happened, Abiathar?"

He averted his face, trying to answer, but unable to find words. "They are all dead," he managed at last. "He killed them all, and then everyone in the town. It was burning, like the sacrifices, and everything was gone. The children, the animals, my sons--all gone."

As he sagged toward me, I caught him, easing down beside him.

It was hours before I got the entire story. I had him repeat it to me more than once, for I couldn't believe what he said was true. Jeshua came in with a kill, and I left Abiathar while I questioned the Habiru dahveed.

"It can't be true?" I asked.

"It is, Dahveed. None of Abiathar's house survived. He is all that is left of Eli's line."

"The tabernacle?" I questioned, my voice suddenly hoarse.

"Gone," he said shortly.

Unable to find words for the horror that filled me, I said nothing more. Once Abiathar wakened, we ate, and I had him tell me once more all that he could remember.

"It was Doeg, then," I concluded.

"I saw him, Dahveed."

"I knew it!" I said, striking the ground with my fist, furious with myself for my lack of care that day. "I knew when I saw him there that he'd tell the king! But I never dreamed this!" I turned to Abiathar. "I've caused the death of your entire family! Shaul couldn't have accused them if I hadn't gone there, or been careful enough to stay out of Doeg's sight!"

The smile he gave me, the one that usually made everyone else smile too, was sad. "It wouldn't have mattered, Dahveed. What Yahweh decrees cannot be stopped. We all knew that we would die someday for Eli's sin. I just never thought I'd be the one left." He stared into the small fire. "I wish I weren't."

Sickness rose in me. I'd have given anything to live that day over again, bearing the pain of leaving Jonathan gladly, if I could bypass Nob. "Yahweh, forgive me," I said, tears trickling down my cheeks.

"You cannot blame yourself, adoni. We were cursed, and Yahweh's curses cannot be turned aside."

Guilt at what I had caused nearly overwhelmed me. I sat in silence. Then the roeh's deep voice whispered in my mind. "Against our will and intentions, the accuser can bring evil from what we do. When that happens, do all you can to help those harmed, and leave the rest to Yahweh, for He will repay."

I trembled under the weight of the evil which had come. But I would have to leave it to Yahweh, for only He could answer what the Evil One had done. The thought helped me pull myself together. "What would you have of me, Abiathar?"

"Sanctuary, adoni," he said again.

"I am not your adon, Abiathar."

"Yahweh told abbi that you are the Mashiah, and I will serve you as my house served Shaul."

"Stay with me then. Since King Shaul wants to kill us both, I will do everything I can to guard your life, even if I have to give my own."

"Yahweh may have something to say about that," the priest replied. "Now, there is something else that you must know."

I followed him out of the door. In a well-concealed shed four men, Gibeonites from the look of them, slept exhausted on the floor. The covered object sitting on the straw by them drew my attention. An eerie silence settled over me, and my scalp prickled. I threw myself on the ground, overwhelmed with something close to terror.

CHAPTER 33

After leaving Abiathar, I spent the rest of the night on Keilah's wall, staring north. I could not rid myself of the guilt and anger at what Doeg had done. At last, I turned to Grandmother's harp, forcing the discipline of composing on my mind. Before dawn, I had completed the song,[13] and I had found relief.

"Why do you boast in evil, O mighty man? The divine loyalty of God is all the day.

Your tongue will devise destruction as a sharpened razor, O worker of treachery.

You loved evil rather than good, falsehood rather than to speak righteousness.

You loved all words that devour, O tongue of deceit.

Yet God will break you down for ever. He will snatch you and will tear you from (your) tent. And he will uproot you from the land of the living.

But the righteous ones will see and they will fear. And at him they will laugh.

'Behold, the strong man who did not make God his stronghold. He trusted in the abundance of his riches. He strengthened himself in his wickedness.'

But I am as a luxuriant olive tree in the house of God. I trusted in the divine loyalty of God forever and always.

I will praise You forever because You have done it. And I will eagerly wait on Your name because it is good to be in the presence of Your faithful ones."

I was still asleep when a message from the elders arrived. They had invited us to stay in the barracks while they discussed whether or not to hire us as guards. I accepted the invitation, much to the men's approval, but I was wary of the situation. However, the townspeople did extend a genuine welcome to us, and many requested escorts when they went to work outside the city walls.

I made certain that the men received a decent fee for their guard duties and let them keep whatever they earned. I also sent Jonathan and

---

[13] Psalms 52

Shagay out scouting.

My first retainer discovered what the elders were doing on his second day out. "The town has a sentry on top of the land stair to the plain. The Philistines are still sitting out there, debating on whether or not they want to come back," he said in disgust.

"And until they make up their mind, the elders of Keilah will also debate on whether or not they want to hire us!" I exclaimed, then had to chuckle. Teman had worked the situation to his advantage in more ways than one. We weren't hired yet, but we were here, which meant the Philistines were less likely to try again. If the invaders did leave, Teman would apologize profusely and say that the town had decided that they couldn't afford us this year, but if the Philistines returned, we were immediately available for its defense.

"What are you going to do?" Shagay asked.

"Nothing. We are earning fees for guard duty from the people, and the town is feeding us free of charge. That evens it out, I believe. How are things on the highlands?"

"Hanan says Gad and Ittai are content to have the place to themselves and the animals."

"Then let's grant the town the protection we give them as long as we can. It may be the last rest we get for a long while."

Emerging from the barracks after I heard Shagay's report, I was nearly run down by Zabad.

"Your pardon, geber," he said hastily, a papyrus clutched in his fist.

"What's wrong?" I asked, seeing his white face.

"It's Abbi-Ahlai," he choked out. "He's going to sell Ahinoam! She thinks it will be tomorrow, in Hebron. She overheard the steward and--" he stopped, tears in his eyes. "She wouldn't have angered him, geber! And she's frightened. She must be. The scribe said he could hardly read the message!

"Please, geber, you must let me go to Hebron. I've got to help her somehow! Please!"

I put my hand on the distraught man's shoulder, making him look at me. "Zabad, a Habiru band is like a clan, only much closer. Your trouble is our trouble. Let me see the message, and you go find out who doesn't have guard duty tomorrow."

Looking bewildered, he obeyed, and I scanned the message. It was indeed hardly readable, but I figured out enough to reach the same conclusions the scribe had. But I also got the idea that Ahinoam was destined for a particular buyer, and if the buyer's name was what I thought it was, she wouldn't be happy with him.

Zabad returned. "Abishai and Josheb are free."

"Find out about Ira and Gareb," I decided. "We'll leave an hour before dark. I want to be on the highlands and on our way to Hebron tonight. We'll go the rest of the way early tomorrow."

"Leave?" he asked, dazed. "You are coming?"

"Along with every other man we can scrape up. This isn't something you can do alone, Zabad."

¥ ¥ ¥ ¥ ¥ ¥

"Matred, have you seen Tirzah?" Gebirah Abigail asked.

"No, Gebirah," her handmaid replied without looking up from the loom where she worked in the courtyard.

Abigail went back inside. "Namea, where's Tirzah?"

"Last time I saw her, she was in the courtyard," she replied, her face slightly flushed as she looked up from the stack of papyri she had just brought to Oholah, who kept the ever increasing amount of records organized and stored.

"She's not there now."

"She'll be here for the evening meal, no doubt," Namea said with a sniff, making an oblique reference to the woman's plump form. "What did you need her for?"

"I finished another meil, and she always takes care of them for me."

"Maybe that's why she left a new one in your chamber."

"Alright. Is there anything else to do today, Jotbah?"

"No, Gebirah. Things are done until the morning."

"Then I'll be in the garden until the evening meal."

She picked up the new meil and made certain her basket was well-supplied with thread. Walking quickly to the garden, she latched the gate behind her and jammed a stone into the catch to keep it down. Ever since Parai had intruded on her, she had locked the gate this way. Then she worked until the light began to fade. Nabal returned from Carmel without Tokhath, and she heard only occasional sounds from the room behind her seat. As she packed the basket, the door to Nabal's business chamber opened.

"What are you doing here?" she heard him ask.

"I have some information you might be interested in, Nagid. An addition to your honor," Tirzah's voice replied.

"Oh?"

His attention was caught, Abigail knew. But what information could the handmaid have?

"There's been talk, Nagid, that with Yahweh blessing your house with such honor, there should be a child to complete your happiness."

"What does that have to do with you?" the nagid asked coldly.

"Nothing, Nagid," Tirzah replied, surprised. "But many speak of this. Why, even the stranger I met on the street today told me he had heard something that might interest you, but he was too afraid of your greatness to come before you, and he asked that I find some way of informing you of his message. He sent this."

Abigail listened closely. This sounded extremely strange.

"An admirable gift," Nabal said. "I will listen to his message."

"He said there was a slave to be sold in Hebron tomorrow that he thought would be worthy to bear a child to you and the Gebirah."

Silence filled the room for some time. "I will consider what you have said," Nabal replied at last.

"Thank you, Nagid." The maid left.

Slowly, Abigail let out her breath. Nabal taking another wife had been one of the risks she ran when she started her plan, and now that the seed of the idea had been planted, she had no doubt that it would grow. Sooner or later, she would have to deal with it.

She thought over Tirzah's comments while she fingered the colored thread in the basket. They were uncharacteristic of the impulsive handmaid, sounding rehearsed, intended to slip around his pride in Abigail's beauty and hook the nagid. From the complete lack of sound in the business chamber, they had done just that. Someone behind the scenes had planned carefully. Probably Tokhath. What should she do? Let him travel to Hebron? What if he came back with someone? Could she discourage him from going?

Finally, she heard wine being poured into a goblet. There went one option. He'd have at least two goblets by the time he came to the house, and without Tokhath here to put in the additive, he'd be too belligerent to discuss anything. Should she send someone tonight to try to find the seller and buy the slave herself? Maybe her best course was to simply let the sale go through and see what happened. Besides, if Nabal was distracted by another woman, would that be so bad?

Rising, she walked slowly to the gate, wrenching out the stone. With the current feeling toward Nabal, she didn't think anyone would be doing this to aid the nagid. She decided to do nothing.

¥ ¥ ¥ ¥ ¥ ¥

We arrived at Hebron in good time after a seven mile run. Sending Abishai to the east side of town, the rest of us distributed ourselves about the market square. I browsed through the leather stalls, looking at sandals and keeping my eye on the gate. Much sooner than I expected, Abishai appeared, signaling that my guess at the buyer's identity had been correct. I returned my attention to the sandals.

By the time my nephew joined me, I was deep in a bargain with the merchant, who gathered that I had silver to spend and wanted as much of it as he could get.

"But the sandals are not made of golden leather, geber," I said. "It takes less than a day to make one pair. One silver piece each is more than adequate to repay you."

"Ordinarily, that would be true, geber," the stall owner replied. "But did you notice the extra stitching on the sandals? This pair is guaranteed to last more than normal even with heavy use. I happen to know that one of Shaul's sons bought a pair of these, and has sent me an order every year since for more."

I very much doubted that, but it made a good story. "Well," I hesitated. "I don't know. A sar doesn't travel like I do. But I'm willing to try. How about a silver piece each for two pair?"

He thought a moment, and then Nagid Nabal rode into the market. "Alright," the man said, eyeing the new arrival, who appeared to be headed his way.

Quickly I gave him the price and handed the sandals to Abishai. "Find out how many guards Nabal brought," I whispered, hoping the nagid didn't have as many as I'd seen in Jezreel when I had acquired Zabad. Not long after Abishai left, a man riding a donkey passed through the gate, Ahinoam walking behind him.

Josheb strolled by, his cloak back over his shoulders as the day warmed up. I'd already told him what I wanted to do if the intended buyer was Nabal, and my retainer moved into place as the merchants all tried to attract him to their wares. Several women in the square watched him, their eyes a bit dreamy. I smiled. Josheb was wrapped up in Keturah, who hadn't yet consented to a marriage.

Zabad disappeared since he dared not let his abbi's overseer see him, and I warned Abishai to stay close to him. I didn't know what he'd do when he realized his abbi not only intended to sell his sister, but to sell her to Nagid Carmel.

The overseer caught sight of Nabal and headed his way, pulling Ahinoam along with him.

I edged closer, while Josheb's attention was caught by something in a stall on the other side of Nabal, and he went to look at it.

"Adon Nabal, I would speak with you a moment," the overseer said.

Perched on the back of his mule, Nabal turned cold eyes on him. "Nagid," he corrected.

The man bowed instantly. "Your pardon, Nagid! Forgive my ignorance."

"What is it?" Nabal demanded.

"I had heard that you are a very discriminating buyer, and I have something that would meet your standards." The overseer yanked Ahinoam closer. "She is skilled in many ways, Nagid."

Nabal looked her over, his eyes showing approval as he studied her face.

Ahinoam clenched her fists and tried to edge away.

"Yes, I'd be very interested," the Carmelite said.

"I wouldn't be," I said a little loudly, butting into the sale. "I'd not give two coppers for her!"

"This doesn't concern you," the overseer growled, glaring at me.

Ignoring him, I stood back and examined Ahinoam, finally shaking my head. "Just consider those eyes. Anyone who bought her would have to watch their backs every moment, to say nothing of other body parts."

"There are ways of getting around that," the overseer retorted, his voice hard.

"Maybe," I shrugged. "But with her good looks, why's she being sold? Before I paid my silver, I'd want to know that much at least."

Our conversation had attracted a small crowd, and Ahinoam stood stiffly in the midst of it, glaring from me to Nabal.

"That seems a fair question, geber," the Carmelite interjected. "Why is she being sold?"

"Her geber is displeased with her," the overseer said, his lips tight.

"I can't imagine why," I said sarcastically. "Did you ever see such fury in your life? I wouldn't waste my silver, Nagid. You might survive for a while, but sooner or later she'd get a chance, and you'd find a knife in your heart."

"Don't you believe it, Nagid," the overseer protested. "She would never do any such thing!"

"I just might," Ahinoam said between clenched teeth.

The overseer swung his hand, making Ahinoam cry out from the blow. "She'll do well enough for you, Nagid," he said.

Nabal considered. Clearly, he liked her.

"Where's she from?" I asked, carefully keeping my voice casual and unconcerned.

"That doesn't matter to you," the overseer snapped, glaring at me furiously.

I looked at him. "Seems to me you're very intent on selling her to the nagid here. Why would that be? Don't you think anyone else has gold to spend? Or did your geber tell you to sell only to him?"

The man reddened a little.

Ahinoam glanced at the overseer, judging her chances of getting hit again if she spoke.

Gareb slipped next to me. "Adoni, the nagid travels with only two guards today."

I turned back to see both the overseer and Nabal watching me. Taking advantage of Gareb's comment, I asked, "Is the man right? Is she from Adon Ahlai's house in Jezreel?"

At the name, Nabal's face settled into a mask.

"I am," Ahinoam said, glaring at the overseer. "And he was instructed to come directly to Nabal!"

The Carmelite narrowed his eyes, one hand stroking his thin beard, his eyes suspicious now.

I chuckled before the overseer could answer. "Sounds as if you almost got properly taken, Nagid! If she's who I think she is, the adon's probably selling her because he didn't like the way she kept his records. He probably discovered that he was considerably poorer than he thought! I'll bet he's eagerly waiting to see if he foisted her off on you and got paid in the bargain!"

Ahinoam was completely white in the face by now, and the crowd murmured a little, smiles crossing several faces, although no one laughed outright with Nabal sitting there on his mule.

The overseer's red face was all that the nagid needed to conclude that his rival had tried to outwit him. He looked at the man with disdain, then rode out of the market.

The overseer looked around, but no one seemed interested in a sale. I let him stew a little, knowing he dared not go home with

Ahinoam and admit to Ahlai that he'd failed. When nearly everyone had wandered away except me, he turned to me again.

"Geber?"

"Like I said, I wouldn't give two coppers for her. But maybe four." I reached into my girdle and started forward.

"That hardly seems a fair bargain," Josheb interjected pleasantly. "Seems to me the woman hasn't been given much of a chance. And she is pretty," he said admiringly, his northern accent pronounced.

The overseer turned to him gratefully. "You have good taste, adon. This lout here wouldn't know a good woman when he saw one. Now, a cultured northern adon like you can properly appreciate what I have here."

"And what about me?" I butted in again.

Josheb turned to me. "It might be best if you would go about your business, geber," he said, his eyes so chilling that I stepped back involuntarily, surprise on my face.

"Do keep going," my retainer added.

"But--"

The tall man took one step in my direction, and I backed away, bowing once before hurrying off, very glad that Josheb was on my side.

Not long after, I watched him leave town with Ahinoam, heading west to the crossroads. The rest of us left by the east road, heading into the forest as soon as we were out of sight of the town.

"He hit her!" Zabad stormed. "Did you see her cheek? And to try to sell her to Nabal! That overseer better pray Yahweh I never find him alone."

We took the forest paths back to the encampment, arriving well before Josheb. It would take them a while. Ahinoam had probably walked at least 10 miles already from Jezreel.

The sun was sinking when they appeared at the bottom of the hill, Ahinoam looking around in puzzlement for the estate which would go with Josheb's obvious wealth.

I stepped out into the open. "You made it."

Josheb gave his slow smile and touched his knee to the ground. "Yes, adoni. But she's a fiery one. She'd have to like the man who gets her!"

Ahinoam recognized me. "He belongs to *you*?" she demanded.

"Yes. When your brother said we needed to do something about your being sold, I agreed," I shrugged, smiling.

Zabad hurried from the trees, and his sister ran to him, wrapping her arms around him, tears of relief on her face.

"How much?" I asked as Josheb and I climbed to our camp.

"He was desperate, adoni, but it took a gold piece." He handed me the other two pieces I'd given him.

When Zabad brought his sister up to the encampment, it looked much different than it had just days ago. The new tents were up, equipment neatly stowed away, and a stew simmered on the fire.

"I cannot repay you for this, adoni," Zabad said, his arm around Ahinoam.

I grinned. "Nabal didn't strike me as the right person for your sister."

"Why didn't you just buy me?" Ahinoam asked, puzzled.

"What story will reach Nabal and your abbi after what happened in the market?"

She smiled. "That some northern adon bought me and took me north with him!"

"And that means both of them will put you out of their minds," her brother added.

"Take her to eat and rest, Zabad," I said next. "We must go back to Keilah tomorrow, and you'll need to find some place there for Ahinoam to stay."

That night long after the others were asleep, I remained awake, the manner in which Yah had arranged things to help Zabad and Ahinoam running through my mind. By the time I went to sleep, I had four more verses[14].

"Let me bless Yahweh at all times. Continually His praise is in my mouth.

In Yahweh my soul will boast. The afflicted will hear and they will rejoice.

They looked to Him and were radiant, so let not their faces be ashamed.

Taste and see how good is Yahweh. Blessed is the man who will take refuge in Him."

Once Zabad had made arrangements for Ahinoam in Keilah, our lives settled into a routine again. The Philistines lingered beneath the Shephelah on the coastal plain, and we became the de facto guards of

---

[14] Psalms 34

Keilah. The town elders still stammered and shifted around whenever the issue of their hiring us came up, pretending that there was some dissent among them, and I didn't push the subject. The town still fed us for free, and the men were still earning silver with guard duty.

I had told no one of Abiathar's arrival, or that he had brought the ark of the covenant with him. They stayed at the Habiru hideout which Josheb and I stocked with supplies. Josheb remained as an additional guard, a position he readily accepted since more than Abiathar and the four ark-bearers had come. Keturah had also made the trip. She and Naharai had been in Nob when the attack came, and I learned from them how the tabernacle had been saved. But the experience had again frightened her so much that she refused to leave her brother, who was one of the ark-bearers. The fugitives were more than happy to stay in one place and rest, and I kept touch with Josheb through Hanan. Thinking of them had produced six more verses for my acrostic song.

"Young lions suffer want and they hunger, but the seekers of Yahweh will not lack any good thing.

Many troubles have the righteous, but from all of them Yahweh will deliver him.

He keeps all his bones. From them not one was broken.

Evil shall slay the wicked, and the ones who hate the righteous will incur guilt.

Yahweh ransoms the life of His servants, and they will not incur guilt, all the ones who seek refuge in Him.

Yahweh is near to the broken of heart, and the crushed of spirit He will save."

I spent the rest of my time making certain the men kept up with their weapons practice and that Eliphelet didn't steal the town blind. I'd already caught him working the market twice, and managed to return what he'd taken without raising an outcry, but if he couldn't curb his urge to steal, there would be much trouble in the future.

It was late one night when Zabad, who was a sentry at the gates tonight, woke me. "Adoni, there is someone here to see you."

I pulled on a shirt and kilt, walking into the light of the torch by the barracks door. A man stood there, nearly falling from fatigue. "Sar Dahveed, I am to give this to you."

The familiar feel of the twisted brass earring set my heart pounding. Grabbing his arm, I hurried him to the center of the deserted market.

"Is the hassar well?" I asked tersely.

"Yes, adoni. He is fine. He also sends a message. The king knows you are in Keilah, and he is gathering an army to besiege the town."

Besiege Keilah? Surely not! This close to Gath, the Philistines would angrily and quickly react to the presence of an entire army. All-out war would result, something far different from the yearly raids and small invasions that normally comprised a war season.

"Who are you?" I asked.

"Azmaveth of Bahurim, adoni."

I froze, my hand tightening on his arm. This was the guard who had betrayed Jonathan. How could I believe him? I forced him to his knees, and he went without resistance. "You betrayed one adon, Azmaveth, why should you stop with him?"

"Hassarah Ahinoam rescued my son, but so long as I am in Abner's reach, not one of us was safe. Rather than sending me into exile, the hassar gave me the brass earring and sent me to you. Please believe me, adon. The muster call went out a week ago. There is not much time."

The earring dug into my clenched fist. Either this man was telling the truth, or Jonathan was dead, and I didn't think something like that could be kept hidden. I let go of him, and he sagged down. "Come," I said.

Wearily he followed me back to the barracks, and I assigned him a place to sleep. Then I woke Ahiam and Shagay.

They swiftly dressed, and Zabad let us out of the pedestrian door by the gates. I set a fast pace back to the forest. That Shaul would start a war just to get to me was hard for me to believe. I needed to know for certain if it was true.

Naharai challenged us when we got close to the ruined house.

"It's Dahveed," I replied. "I must speak with Kohen Abiathar."

Both Ahiam and Shagay checked, glancing at me.

Before long, Abiathar stepped from the house, coming to where I waited in the rising moonlight.

"Bring the ark, hakkohen. I would inquire of it."

"Yes, adoni."

"The *ark*?" Shagay gasped.

"Yes," I said. "Mahesa sent Abiathar and the ark to me, fearing that Shaul would use it against me if it remained in his power." I told them what had happened at Nob. When I finished, they took up positions on either side of the clearing, and I stood alone when Abiathar returned, the four bearers bringing the ark with them.

As he came forward, I knelt.

"What do you wish, adoni?"

"I would inquire of Yahweh, hakkohen."

He waited a minute, then asked in that distant voice, "Why have you come, Dahveed ben Jesse?"

"Yahweh, God of Israel, I know not what to do. Reliable word has come to me that Shaul is coming to Keilah to destroy the town because I am here. I must know if I should leave or remain where we have found welcome and a task to do. Will the men of Keilah surrender me to Shaul's hand? Is Shaul coming here as I have heard? Please, Yahweh, God of Israel, tell Your servant."

"Shaul will indeed come down."

"Will the men of Keilah surrender me to him, or will I be safe here?"

"They will surrender you."

"Thank You, Adonai Yahweh. Be with Your servant always."

I stayed motionless until Abiathar touched my shoulder.

"You have your answer?"

"Yes, hakkohen. We must leave. Be ready in the morning."

"Yes, adoni."

I bowed to him, and then the ark, and left the clearing.

"What is it?" Shagay asked.

"Shaul will besiege Keilah. Yahweh just told me that the elders will surrender us at the king's demand. We leave, now."

As the sun rose over the hills, the last of my men exited the gates of Keilah.

"But Dahveed, the elders will make a decision in just another day or two," Teman protested, standing beside me, his hurriedly donned clothing in disarray. "Surely it is not necessary for you to leave like this! What of the Philistines? There must be a reason for you to go so suddenly."

I glanced at the town's head elder. "Teman, I will open your ear on this. Word reached me last night that King Shaul is raising an army to besiege your town in an attempt to capture me. If we stay, we bring war."

The elder stiffened. "The rumors that you were outlawed, not just outcast, were true, then."

"Yes. If he comes, do whatever you must to save yourselves. But the best thing you can do is let it be known that we've left."

"And what if the Philistines return when they hear that?"

"I'll tell Dahveed Joel to keep an eye on things. If the Philistines appear again, you can request his help. Pay him the same way you paid me."

"But--"

"You would prefer Shaul?"

"No," he sighed. "Your God go with you, Dahveed."

"We are grateful for your welcome and kindness, Teman. Shalom."

The men waited in the clearing by the ruined house, Naharai and Josheb standing guard in front of it. Clearly the others didn't know who or what was there. I studied the group.

Twenty of us had come to Keilah, leaving Gad and Ittai at the encampment. With Abiathar, the four ark-bearers, Azmaveth and Keturah, that made 29. I had half a small town looking to me for their livelihoods. Walking into the clearing, I looked around for Hanan, intending to send him to notify Dahveed Joel that we were leaving. For once, the youth didn't appear when I wanted him. Then Joel himself stepped from the forest.

He pulled at his beard a little once I'd told him of our departure. "I'm glad I came then. I've been meaning to speak to you about Hanan."

"I don't mind him," I replied.

"Whether you did or not wouldn't make much difference," the dahveed chuckled. "But I'm glad to hear you say so. Despite his youth, he's already a warrior to be reckoned with. He can go anywhere in the forests, for the animals seem to accept him as one of their own. Take him as yours, Dahveed."

"If he came with me, he'd be leaving his family and band, Joel."

"He has no tie to us. We found his immi, Maacah, ill in the forest years ago. We took her in, and after she recovered, we found she was carrying a child. She never spoke of why or how, and she stayed with us until she died when Hanan was 7 or 8. He took to the forests afterward. I've tried to be an abbi to him, but he needed little from me. Then you came, and he was drawn to you as he has been to no one else."

"I'll welcome him then, Joel," I assured him.

The dahveed relaxed. "Shall I keep an eye on Gath now that you're gone?"

"If you would. I told Teman he could request your help, and that he was to pay you what he did me."

A slow smile crossed Joel's face. "That much?"

"You are Yahweh's Arrows, Joel, allied with Ethan. Just make certain you earn your pay."

"Yes, Dahveed. Yahweh go with you."

"Shalom, Joel." I turned to Shagay. "Divide the men up," I directed. "I want 10 in front, and 10 behind as escort."

"Yes, adoni. But you'd better tell the men what we are escorting, and why we had to leave. They are not happy about going."

When they gathered around, I gave them a brief summary of the situation. The news of the death of the priests naturally upset them, although they'd had some warning of that when Josheb arrived. But the destruction of Nob shocked them.

"What happened to the tabernacle?" Zalmon asked.

"It was saved, dismantled and hidden in the Kidron. I assume it has been taken elsewhere now, but I don't know where. The ark left, however, along with Abiathar ben Ahimelech. He had stayed in Nob to officiate at the evening sacrifice."

One or two of the men glanced at Naharai and Josheb, and then back to me.

"Where did the ark go, adoni?" Igal asked.

"To us."

"The ark--the sacred ark--is here?" Elika gasped.

"Yes, so Yahweh goes with us, which is a good thing, for the king is raising an army against us. The call to arms went out a week ago. Shaul intended to besiege Keilah, trapping us there. When the news reached me last night, I inquired of Yahweh, and He said the town would surrender us to save themselves. That's why we are leaving."

"How did you learn of the muster?" my half-cousin Zelek asked.

"I brought the message," Azmaveth explained. "I am of the hassar's personal guard. I trained at the same time Josheb did."

The men turned to my retainer.

"He speaks truth," he confirmed.

"The ark," Eliphelet said in wonder. "I'm going to be escorting the ark!"

"Just don't try to steal it," I said drily.

Even with the ark, we made the trip to our encampment before noon. The men were a little surprised to see Keturah, but she stayed close to the ark, and the men assumed she was to serve it in some way. I did nothing to dismiss that assumption, knowing it would prevent trouble. Besides, with Naharai and Josheb to protect her, only an idiot would bother her.

Gad and Ittai were even more surprised when they saw what accompanied us. Knowing the prophet was more used to sacred things than anyone else, I assigned him to work with Abiathar in deciding how the ark would be handled. When I asked the Gibeonite bearers if they needed to return to Israel, I found that Mahesa had anticipated me and made sure the bearers could follow me wherever I might have to go.

Much of the spoil we had taken from the Philistines was now a liability, and I insisted that essential items such as the tents and extra weapons be packed on the donkeys. The men would have to carry whatever spoils they wished to take with them and hide the rest. Several of them grumbled, but I knew that would stop after the first three days of travel.

It wasn't until just after dawn the next morning that I realized I had two women on my hands, not just one.

"Zabad!" I growled when he walked by.

"Yes, geber?"

"What is your sister doing here? We settled her in Keilah."

"Where else would she be?" he asked, puzzled. "We both belong to you, geber."

I sighed in exasperation. "You are not my slave, Zabad."

"My abbi said I was," he retorted, "and you bought Ahinoam. I don't know how much you paid; Josheb won't tell me. So we're yours. Will there be anything else, geber?"

"No." I accepted defeat. "But two gold pieces will rid me of the burden of you both!"

He grinned a little. "Yes, geber."

By the time the sun's rays reached us, the 30 of us were on our way east. I remembered well the dark wildness of Ziph south and east of Carmel. If the king was determined to follow me, I'd take him into a wilderness such as he'd never dreamed of, where the last thing he'd have to worry about was me.

Tamar bat Dahveed

Dahveed's trials are about to come upon him, and how well he has learned the lesson of complete dependence on Yah will dictate how well he and those with him will live.

And through his pain, Jonathan has found the determination to do Yah's will to the uttermost. But the bitterness of not obeying Yah's clear direction the first time will stay with him the rest of his life. Even so, he still could be used of Yah to cover the people of Israel from the sins of Shaul, but only if he can accept what comes of Yah's hand and learn to follow where Yah leads. It remains to be seen if his abbi will learn the same lesson or not.

CHAPTER 34

Walking down the passage of the fortress residence, Jonathan steeled himself for another day in the throne room. Every time he looked into his abbi's eyes, he saw a blankness that chilled him, reminding him of the blackened houses and the stench of death at Nob. It was all he could do to continue with the normal order of business. Eshbaal had recovered his composure, and his youngest brother was better able to work with the king than he was.

In addition, the press of court business left little time for him to plan the next steps he must take to extricate the kingdom from Shaul's hand. While he could not yet move forward, he needed to know exactly what to do when the time came.

He shuddered as he glanced through the door to his abbi's chamber. The breastplate of the Hakkohen Haggadol sat on a chest in the room, the cloth stiff and brown with the blood of Ahimelech. The Urim and Thummim sat on top of it, proof that his abbi had tried to use them to discover where Dahveed had gone after he vanished into the uplands. The Keilah elders had been cooperative, but obviously had no idea where Dahveed had disappeared to.

It was certain now also that the Philistines were not mustering an army. The attack on Keilah had probably been from Gath alone. Oddly, Abner had advised that the militia be sent home, leaving the professional units to patrol the Shephelah during the summer. When Shaul readily agreed, Jonathan had realized that the army was now available to hunt Dahveed, hardening his determination to make certain that it didn't.

The scribe greeted him respectfully when he entered the anteroom, and he nodded in reply, walking through the doors at the far end and up the stairs to the throne room. Eshbaal was already there, two other scribes setting up their tables to aid him.

"You look tired, Hassar," Eshbaal said.

"I am," he replied. "There is too much to do, and I have no time."

The voice of the anteroom scribe greeted the king, and Jonathan faced the door, taking a deep breath. He had to get through another day somehow.

King Shaul entered, the purple mantle hanging from his shoulders, and the open-worked gold of the formal royal headband flashing on his forehead matched by the armband on his right arm. Jonathan bowed, avoiding his abbi's eyes. General Abner accompanied the king, wearing the dark blue general's mantle. The hassar's eyes flicked back to the king. Why such formal dress for a day of routine business?

Shaul took the throne and nodded to Jonathan to open the court. Abner had the first presentation.

"Adoni, the report I have today concerns some carelessness in regard to your security," he began.

Puzzled, Jonathan looked up, having heard of no threat to the king. He glanced at Eshbaal, who shook his head slightly.

"What has happened?" Shaul asked, showing no surprise at the announcement.

"As you know, when word came that Dahveed's sister was with a caravan in Ammon, we sent messengers there, asking for her to be given to us so that Dahveed could be brought under your hand, adoni."

"I remember."

"It was at that time we learned that Abigail bat Jesse was actually a blood relative, a granddaughter, to King Nahash. This came as a surprise to us, but I have since learned that it was no surprise to Hassar Jonathan."

Jonathan's stomach tightened up as Shaul turned to him, raising his eyebrows. "The general is correct, adoni," he said, bowing his head briefly. "I knew that Abigail bat Jesse had a blood connection to Ammon. Dahveed himself, however, did not. Given how faithfully and well the zammar served you, I saw no threat."

"Perhaps a slight misjudgment on your part, Hassar," Abner said thoughtfully. "Nahash seemed very willing to protect him. Indeed, he took him directly from our hands. It would appear, then, that Ammon values Dahveed more than you thought, which brings into question how much loyalty Dahveed may owe to your abbi's greatest enemy."

"Let us not forget that the circumstances whereby Nahash protected Dahveed were forced on him by some miscalculations on your part, Abner. If the situation were reversed, I would expect us to do the same as Nahash did," Jonathan replied.

"Possibly," the general acknowledged. "But the question of Dahveed's loyalty still stands. Dahveed has served well against the Philistines, of that there is no doubt. But his loyalty has never been tested against our enemies in the east. Perhaps he would not do so well in battle then."

"Since Dahveed is no longer here, that may not matter, General." Behind the calm mask on his face, Jonathan's mind raced. What did Abner hope to gain by this? How would it affect Dahveed?

"One regrettable instance might have been chance," Abner went on, "but two of the same type seems too much to tolerate, especially when the king's life might be at stake."

"Another one?" Shaul asked. "Explain yourself, Abner."

"It seems the Dahveed has a connection to royal families other than Nahash, adoni," the general said. "When Dahveed's family fled Bethlehem, they went to Moab, where King Yira welcomed them like long lost clansmen, which, as it turns out, they were."

"Surely you didn't know this, Jonathan?" his abbi asked.

"Certainly I knew it, adoni. Dahveed was open with me about his ancestry from the very first. If you would like to go further, Hassarah Ruth's husband, Boaz is descended from Jericho, and I suppose that would give Dahveed a connection there. But Dahveed strove only to serve you as best he could. I saw no threat in that."

"Times change, Hassar," Abner said softly. "Dahveed now has a band of warriors, and has rebelled against the king. His connections to Moab, Ammon, and yes, Jericho, are in a rather different light now. How is it that you didn't inform the king of these things as soon as Dahveed fled?"

Forcing himself to remain calm, Jonathan turned from Abner to Shaul. "Because in my judgment, Dahveed will never bring harm to the king."

"Or maybe, in your judgment, Dahveed's well-being was more important than the king's," Abner added softly.

The hassar could almost feel the jaws of the trap snapping shut around him. There was nothing he could say to that, because it was truer than even Abner knew. His heart sinking, Jonathan waited as his abbi stared at him. He endured the dark blankness in those eyes until he had to avert his face, sick with the shame of what his abbi had done just weeks before.

"I should have executed you after Michmash," Shaul said, his voice cold. "It seems my hesed at that time has been poorly repaid. When you put the life of a slave over that of your king, I can no longer place my trust or confidence in you."

The throne room was deathly silent.

"Yes, adoni," Jonathan said.

The king held out his hand. "You will return my seal ring."

The hassar slipped it from his finger and knelt, placing the ring in his abbi's hand.

Shaul put it on. "You are over-tired from too much work,

Jonathan. You will return to your estate to rest until I summon you."

His face drained of color, the hassar bowed on his knees. "As you command, adoni."

"You are dismissed, Jonathan."

Silently, he rose and backed a few steps before turning and walking to the stair door.

"The next item in the report is the possible location of Dahveed," Abner said. "Our scouts have located what is probably his last encampment in the Forest of Hereth."

Jonathan stopped in his tracks, standing with his eyes closed as he fought the urge to send his belt knife spinning into the general's back.

"Was there something else, Jonathan?" Shaul asked coldly.

Slowly, the hassar turned back. "No, adoni," he purred, and disappeared through the door.

Seething, Jonathan strode into the passage of the fortress residence. To be sent away like a child. Told to rest! In public. In *court*! Rage choked him. After all he'd done for Abbi. All those years. Then to be told he should have been executed after Michmash! Clenching his fists, he slammed the door to his chamber against the wall. And in front of Abner!

Without doubt the general had arranged this. Such a blow to his honor would only come from the king's cousin. How he'd convinced Abbi to go along was the mystery. Stripping off the court robe, he flung it onto the floor and threw a kilt around his waist. His eye caught the chest where he kept the records that detailed the attempt on his life. As he stared at it, he wondered what would happen if he went back into the throne room and presented Abbi with the evidence. But with the influence Abner had now, it might not do any good.

Stuffing the records into a travel pouch, he slung them over his shoulder and snatched the campaign cloak from the peg on the wall. Dara stood in the open doorway, holding out the sword that Lotan had forged for him. He buckled it on and pushed past his shield-bearer into the passage.

Immi watched him, her eyes calm and direct. "While you're in Zelah, send us some meat for the king's table."

The hassar gritted his teeth. "Do I still rate a mule, or must I walk?"

His immi's lips tightened. "Check and see whether Nimshi has your mule here yet. Then decide."

He stormed down the passage again, rage making it hard for him to see. Nimshi held the mount, and Jonathan leaped on.

"Your guard is coming, Hassar," the Habiru lad said.

"What for? I may not even be hassar by the time Abner is done!" Digging his heels savagely into the sides of the animal, he sent it careening unevenly across the private court, nearly coming to grief at the gate into the common courtyard. Yanking the animal's head around, he directed it across the courtyard and out the fortress gates, almost standing it on its hind legs to make the turn in the road just outside. The ride down the steep hill cleared his head a little, and he maintained a somewhat sane pace through the streets of the town. But once out of town, he kicked the mule into a gallop, crouching down, trying to outrun his fury.

Jonathan hadn't managed it before he reached Zelah. By the time he rode through the gate of his estate, his anger had settled on Immi. Asking for meat! He'd just been completely disgraced *in public* for no reason, and she wanted meat for the table! Probably she planned a feast with the rest of the family because he was gone! All right, she wanted meat, he'd give her meat. Enough so that every one of them choked on it!

Dismounting and leaving the mule to stand and drip lather on its own, he flung himself up the stairs, brushing rudely by the person standing at the top of them. Yanking open the door to the upper room, he snatched up the first bow case and quiver that came to hand. Then, leaving the door swinging, he charged back down the stairs, ignoring the silent astonishment of the people in the courtyard, and slammed out of the gate, heading across the fields for the forest.

Someone called to him, but he kept going, too angry to even see straight. Strangely, two of those people in the courtyard had looked exactly alike. He headed west for the deeper forest that barred the way to the Shephelah. Meat! Maybe he'd just drag a live bear into the fortress by the tail, and let them kill it themselves. It would be fresher that way! The trees closed around him.

Hours later, tired and drained, the hassar stopped by a small spring and drank, then sat back on his heels and looked around. He was lost. The reddening sky told him which way was west, and he picked up the bow case, heading uphill. He and Nemuel had hunted all over this forest, and if he could get a good view of it before dark, he could probably locate himself.

The sun had nearly vanished when he crested the hill, but there was enough light for him to decide he'd come more than halfway to Zorah, and that there should be a path in the next valley that would take him toward home. Not far to his right, a huge old terebinth stretched its low massive limbs upward nearly from the ground.

Settling himself under it, he stared down the slope in front of him. What was he going to do? A tall pine stabbed the sky, and he put the quiver on the ground, opening the bow case. To his surprise, he pulled out the composite bow. Jonathan sighed. He was an idiot to be out here alone in the first place, without carrying a kingdom's ransom around with him. Standing, he strung the bow and then sat again. Holding it horizontally, he fitted an arrow and let fly at the pine. It thunked into the trunk, vibrating a moment as it did. After sending a second after the first, he then put another between the two, lining them up vertically.

Dusk closed down in the valleys, climbing the slope toward him, and he sighted for a wild olive beyond the pine. The arrow sped true. Carefully he laid the bow down. There was no doubt of it, other hands than his always accompanied his use of this bow. He could feel them even though he knew they never touched his skin.

Picking up the bow again, he studied it. "Yahweh's bow," that Habiru had called it. Could it be Yahweh's hands guiding his? He shied from the thought. The night brought the sound of crickets and insects, droning around him, and he eased down on the duff under the terebinth, placing the bow against his side.

The stars were brilliant overhead when he woke up, surprisingly rested. Their positions in the sky announced that dawn wasn't that far away, and he sat up, taking the bow again. The sense of another presence came with it.

"Yah, let someone else do this, would You?" he asked. "I thought I was ready for whatever would happen, but to have Abbi wish that he had executed me was more than I expected. How am I to do what I must when I've been disgraced by the king? What chance do I have to command others when my own abbi has declared me too honor-poor to remain in his presence? Let Ishvi do this, or Malchi. I've been slapped aside like a bothersome child."

A bitter laugh escaped his lips. "Abbi was right about one thing, Yahweh. I am tired. Too tired to fight this battle. I don't even want to. I just want to rest, and have Abbi pleased with me, and Abner too caught up with the war season to care about disgracing me. Most of all, I want to hear Dahveed playing that harp in the evenings after our meal. Why does that have to be too much to ask of my life?"

The other presence settled around him a bit more, and he relaxed against the tree.

"Do you know what I did?" he asked. "I threw the biggest temper tantrum of my life. I can just imagine what Abbi thought at the way I left. I couldn't have done anything more to show him he was right." Another sigh. "Well, I've got all kinds of time now. Eshbaal can handle the routine of the court, and with war season here and the Philistines staying home, things should be quiet for the summer. But that leaves Abbi free to chase Dahveed, and that's what worries me, Yah. If he were alone, I wouldn't have a single doubt. But he's not, and he's inexperienced at leading men, and Mahesa said he was frightened."

Pausing in his thoughts, he brushed his hair back. "We're quite a pair, aren't we, Yah? One of us frightened of having to govern this land, the other one furious because he may not! Why do You even bother?"

In the silence the hassar's memory roamed back through the years, thinking of Nemuel and the price that he had paid for friendship. Jonathan remembered asking for Dahveed's friendship and smiled at the blank astonishment his request engendered. He'd had no idea how difficult it would be for the young zammar to believe him and come to trust him. They'd almost lost that hard-won trust after Merab's marriage.

"I couldn't believe he wasn't offended," the hassar said aloud. "But he just shrugged it aside."

Again he fell silent. Maybe there were some things Dahveed could teach *him*. Such as realizing that living without honor might not be so hard. Or that perhaps, if he bent himself to the king's will as Dahveed had, there might be even more honor given to him so that he could still protect the people of this land.

"And what of Ethan?" he spoke. "If there is one man in this land whom You have honored, Yahweh, it is him. He has more wealth than Abbi, and yet he stands ready to give it to the one for whom it is intended. Ethan would have fulfilled his oath to me even if it meant death. And he chooses to travel this land as one despised because in that way he can serve his people best, content with the honor You have given him. Stacked up next to that, I come up rather short, don't I?"

Rising to his feet, he slipped the quiver over his shoulder. "Too bad Ishvi wasn't around to slap some sense into me," he added, stepping out from under the terebinth. "I was the one complaining about not having enough time to do what I needed to do. And when

You give it to me, I go storming off because it wasn't what I expected to happen. As I said before, Yah, why do You bother?" He sighed. Now he'd have to find some way to apologize to nearly everyone he knew. Especially Immi.

Streaks of dawn lightened the sky as he wrenched the arrows from the pine and olive trees. Then he stood there, staring at them. Send some meat for the *king's* table! Suddenly he laughed aloud. And he'd bet when his meat reached the king's table, Abner would be there! Trust his Immi! As he headed back to Zelah he thought that he should be able to find a deer, but hopefully one closer to home so he wouldn't have to carry it so far.

¥ ¥ ¥ ¥ ¥ ¥

Sar Ishvi sniffed in the fading light as he entered the fortress. That smelled like venison. If they had some special visitor tonight, he hoped he was dressed properly. Immi hadn't mentioned anything, though. He wondered what she was up to. By noon yesterday, everyone in the town had heard of the way Shaul had dismissed the hassar. It seemed odd under the circumstances that Immi would have a feast, even if only a family one.

Abner's voice caught his ear as he went into the passage to hang his cloak in his old room. It made him frown. He'd gotten the impression that Immi had even less use for Abner now than she ever had. Why would he be invited for dinner? When he emerged, he met Malchi in the passage.

"Do you know what's going on?" his brother asked.

"No," the sar replied.

In the upper room they gathered around the low table, and, taking their cues from Immi, Ishvi and Malchi kept the conversation pleasant and light. Michal was there, a closed look on her face that said something was in the wind, but that she'd never reveal what. Immi seemed her usual self, but Ishvi sensed the hardness of bronze underneath that exterior.

"This is very good venison," Shaul said, cutting another piece. "Who brought it in?"

"Oh, Jonathan sent it especially for the meal tonight," Immi replied. "He killed it just this morning and sent it immediately so it wouldn't spoil. So nice of him to honor us with food, don't you think so, Abner?"

Hastily Ishvi looked down, swallowing his mouthful too quickly and trying not to choke.

The general slowly turned red, staring at the food he'd been eating.

Immi waited for his reply, and the king concentrated on his food, trying to suppress the smile on his face.

"Of course, Hassarah," Abner finally managed to say.

"I'm sure you'll find some way to repay him, General," Immi went on sweetly. Her eyes widened at the way Abner jerked his hands from the food. "Don't hesitate to finish what you have, otherwise I might get the idea you don't like our hospitality."

"I don't see how he could do that, Immi," Malchi said. "This is the best venison I've had in years."

"I thought so, too," Immi said, keeping her eyes on the general until he began eating again.

Suddenly Ishvi had to struggle to keep a straight face. Abner was caught no matter what he did. If he refused to eat, he'd offend both the king and queen. On the other hand, Jonathan had indeed honored the family by sending the food, and because the general had eaten some, he also was honored. That put him under the obligation of returning the honor, and doing that after the way he had disgraced the hassar in court would be nearly impossible. He was, therefore, left with an honor debt to the hassar.

Ishvi made a bet with himself that Jonathan would go hunting as often as he could, sharing his success with his family as a dutiful son should, and Immi would be certain that Abner was at the table, thereby piling the honor debt ever higher in the hassar's favor. He relaxed. The spectacular departure of the hassar had not boded well for Elihu's plans, but it looked as if Jonathan had accepted the situation and would stay at his estate, right where the scribe wanted him.

Later, he and Malchi walked together down the darkened streets, their guards leaving enough space so they could talk in private. "Whatever made Abbi send Jonathan away?" Malchi asked in a worried voice.

His brother shrugged. "Abner would have managed it sooner or later. That accusation of the king's could have exploded anytime. Elihu decided it would be better to control when and where it happened. Now seemed the best time."

"What does your scribe have to do with this?"

"He's been quite busy, Ishvi. There is a lot that Jonathan needs to be doing, but as long as he was distracted by ruling the country, he had no time. Elihu figured Abner would jump at a chance to ban the hassar from court, so he inserted a report of Dahveed's ancestry into a message, and let the general take it from there."

"Did Jonathan know Elihu's plan?"

"No. I agreed with Elihu's assessment that Jonathan's reactions would have to be genuine or Abner would suspect something. After he stormed out like that, though, I was afraid he'd do something to interfere and put himself back into the court."

"And?"

"And our brother is going to find himself extremely busy by tomorrow afternoon."

"I hope he won't be too busy to go hunting."

Ishvi laughed. "I doubt much of anything will keep him from that!"

¥ ¥ ¥ ¥ ¥ ¥

Jonathan woke the next morning with the feeling that he'd forgotten something. Then he remembered everything and relaxed. He wasn't supposed to be at the fortress, but right here, next to Taphath, and he didn't have a particularly busy day planned, so he could lie here and wait until she woke up. Or maybe he'd lie here until he couldn't wait any longer and wake her up. Or maybe she'd wake up and he wouldn't have to wait at all.

Then again, maybe he should get up and go hunting. He looked back at Taphath. She hadn't been upset over the way he'd acted when he arrived. But after she heard what had happened in court, he'd had to calm her down. That had been fun, he thought with a grin. Hunting could wait. Yes, he'd better stay around in case she woke up upset. Staying at his estate had distinct advantages.

When he left the room much later, he was surprised to see two couriers waiting in the courtyard.

Peleth came to him as he descended the outside stairs. "Adoni, these messengers have come from Gibeah for you."

"Gibeah?"

"Yes, adoni. From Sar Ishvi and his scribe Elihu. They said they have a lot of messages."

Jonathan frowned. Normally, he conducted business from his

upper room, but with Taphath here, he couldn't do that anymore. Quickly he looked around at the rest of the complex. "Peleth, is there a room that can be emptied out so I could see them in private?"

Peleth looked surprised. "We already did that, adoni. A message said you'd be staying here for some time and that you'd need a business chamber. We prepared one right away."

"When did that message come?" Jonathan asked curiously.

"About a week ago."

"I see," the hassar said slowly. "Which room did you prepare?"

"The one on the far side of the courtyard to keep things as private as we could."

"Very good, Peleth. Give me a minute there, and then send the courier."

"Yes, adoni."

He crossed the courtyard and entered the room. It had a table with a chair for him. A couple stools stood in the corner, and it had places for two scribes and some smaller tables for food to offer visitors.

Someone had known he'd be sent here. Ishvi? More likely Elihu, he decided. This felt like something Dahveed would be mixed up in, and just as exasperating. But then, since Ishvi had gone south, he'd picked up a few of Dahveed's habits. Still, he'd bet it was Elihu. He grimaced ruefully. Well, he'd told the man that he had a free hand, so he'd better get used to being moved around like a game piece. For certain, Yahweh didn't do things as he'd expected.

As he sat down, he felt the brass earring bump against his chest. Nimshi had returned it to him yesterday when he'd gotten back to the estate. The door opened, and two scribes walked in hurriedly. They stopped short when they saw the hassar.

"Your pardon, adoni," one gasped, bowing.

For a moment Jonathan thought he was seeing double. "You've been assigned to me?" he asked, eyeing the two look-alikes.

"Yes, adoni," the same one said, looking at him in frightened awe.

"Where from?"

"My brother and I worked with Geber Elihu under Sar Ishvi," the man replied. "I am called Bunah, and he is Bunni."

A smile quirked the hassar's mouth. Only Dahveed, or someone in Dahveed's family, would send him two scribes so much alike that it would be impossible to tell them apart. Or two scribes so frightened of him that they couldn't move in their tracks. But then, his arrival wouldn't have exactly been reassuring to newcomers, and if he remembered correctly, these two had found themselves in the midst of it.

"Did Sar Ishvi ever bite you?" he asked abruptly.

They both blinked at the same time. "No, adoni," Bunah said carefully.

"Neither will I. Sit down."

Looking a bit sheepish, they moved to the two tables and sat down, arranging their writing materials. Interesting. The one on the left was left-handed, and the one on the right was right-handed. Before he had time to ask anything more, the door opened, and the guard outside asked if he was ready for the first courier.

"Send him in," Jonathan ordered.

In little under an hour the hassar was deep in reports from his brothers, amazed at the amount of information that had not managed to reach him while he was in the fortress. By the time the afternoon was half over, he gave serious consideration to sending Abner a present for getting him banished. Then he grinned. He'd settle for dispatching some special wine to Immi in the morning. One of the reports had been about the meal the previous night, and he could just imagine Abner choking down that venison!

¥ ¥ ¥ ¥ ¥ ¥

"Sar, there are some visitors in the courtyard."

Malchi eyed his steward. It was long after dark, and he was enjoying a small cup of wine before retiring. "Who?"

"They keep their faces hidden, adoni."

The sar debated. After Jonathan's banishment, he had little trust for Abner. The general might try to remove him next. But using assassins seemed a little much, even for Abner. "Send them up," he decided.

When the steward left, he moved the lamp to the end of the table nearest the door, and seated himself at the far side of the room in the shadows. Then he placed his battle sword beside the stool close to hand.

Three men entered when the steward opened the door and then uneasily looked around the seemingly empty room.

"I prefer to know with whom I'm speaking," Malchi said from the shadows.

The men started a little, and he noticed all three automatically reached for a sword. The first one pushed his cloak hood back, revealing the face of Commander Zorath. The others were Ram and, surprisingly, Pasach.

Malchi rose and stepped up to the table. "This must be serious if you hide your faces from my steward," he commented.

"Yes, adoni," Zorath said. "We have come to ask you to do something."

The sar pushed the plate of bread toward his visitors, then sliced off some of the cheese before sliding that dish toward the others. Picking up the bronze cup, he sipped the wine, and the others took a swallow from it when he passed it along.

"That's good wine, adoni," Ram said wistfully.

"Some that the hassar purchased," Malchi replied. "He's stingy with it."

"I can see why."

"It's about the hassar that we've come," Zorath said after a short silence.

Pasach spoke. "Since Nob, the men are afraid of what might happen next. They think the demon has returned to control the king, and when they come to us with questions, we don't know what to tell them. The men were willing to wait until the hassar returned, for they know that he can restrain the king, even when the demon comes."

Malchi kept his face expressionless. Only Dahveed could restrain the king when the demon attacked. "Go on."

"But now, the hassar has been sent away, and the men are afraid the demon will have a free hand, and they are upset, adoni," Pasach finished.

The sar stroked his beard. His visitors had told him only things that everyone already knew, so what did they really want? "How upset are they?"

"Some of them are thinking of leaving, adoni. The others are hesitant to follow a demon into battle," Zorath explained.

Very adroit, Malchi thought. Don't blame the king, blame it on a demon controlling the king. But sometimes when he looked into his abbi's eyes, he didn't think the men were far from wrong. Shaul had changed since Nob. "Have you gone to General Abner?"

"Yes, adoni," Ram replied. "But his loyalty to the king will not let him consider another attack by the demon. So all the commanders chose us to speak to you."

"You represent the entire professional force?"

"Except Libni," Ram said bluntly.

Malchi wanted to sit down but knew he couldn't. All the units except Libni's? If he handled this correctly, he would have the entire army at his command, which meant at the hassar's command. On the other hand, he must be certain that Abner wasn't somehow behind this.

"This is quite a change for you, Pasach," he said softly. "You normally stick very close to Libni."

"Yes, adoni," the man said, paling a little. "But that was before Nob." His fists clenched. "My sister and her little ones died there. They were not in rebellion against the king, nor would they have been."

"Ram?"

"Will the sar be offended if I speak plainly?"

"No."

"The men might have accepted the slaying of the priests, adoni. But taking the ban to Nob was too much. The demon in the king has brought Yahweh's wrath down on the entire nation. After the miracle at Gibeon, the one hope the men have is Jonathan Hassar. They are certain that if he will stand between them and Yahweh, they will live."

The sar paused in thought, setting the wine cup back in its place. He'd wager that Abner had never imagined that he'd lose control of the professional force when he threw Jonathan out of court. Even so, he carefully phrased his question. "Commanders, will the army give whatever aid requested by the hassar as he works to protect the king from this demon and whatever it might urge him to do?"

"Yes, adoni."

"They are gathered on the training ground, now," Pasach said.

"All but Libni," Ram added. "Will you speak to them?"

In reply, Malchi reached for his cloak.

They walked to the training ground in silence, and again Malchi wondered if this was an elaborate trap set by Abner. He'd have to be very careful what he said.

The training ground appeared empty, but when Zorath led him behind the equipment sheds near the sparring circle, the rest of the commanders were gathered around a single lamp.

"Your messengers told me of your concern," Malchi began.

"Yes, adoni," Natan of the fifth unit answered. "The men are afraid of what the demon might force the king to do next, and thus anger Yahweh even more. They know that the people stand before Yahweh as the king does. When we informed General Abner, he just laughed."

"I am not laughing, for darkness has come to Shaul again. I have already told Jonathan Hassar that I will do all in my power to help as he works to save him."

"We would swear to do the same thing, adoni," Dishon, the eighth unit commander, spoke up quickly.

"Then we are in agreement," Malchi said.

Some of the tension left the air, and Ram stepped forward. One by one the commanders knelt, taking the sar's hand and giving their oaths to help Jonathan protect the king.

When they had finished, Malchi said quietly, "Go back to the units. Reassure the men and remain ready. The hassar will have need of you."

"What of Libni?" Pasach asked. "I'll not let anyone stand in the way of turning aside Yahweh's wrath."

"Libni may be of use just as he is," Malchi said with a slight smile. "Leave him alone. I will take your concerns and your support to Jonathan Hassar. He will be glad to know that you are so concerned for the king's welfare."

"Thank you, adoni," the men said, bowing again.

Ram lingered behind to accompany Malchi back to his house in town, and when the others had gone, someone stepped from the shadows.

"I wondered if you'd come, Libni," Malchi commented.

Ram's hand flashed to his sword, and Malchi clamped down on his wrist.

The tenth unit commander came and knelt also. "I would give you my oath also, if you will take it," he said, uncertain of his reception.

"I will take it. You have served the hassar well and still can."

"Thank you, adoni," Libni said, a catch in his voice.

Malchi held out his hand, and in the last sputtering light of the lamp, Libni joined the others in giving his oath. Ram watched as the officer melted back into the darkness.

"I'd never have thought it of him," he said.

"Neither will Abner."

Ram chuckled drily. "True enough. Can the hassar really do something?" he asked in an undertone.

"Out on the estate, he has no distractions, Ram, and lots of time."

The commander smiled grimly. "Our good general might have miscalculated there."

"In more ways than one, Ram."

CHAPTER 35

Hassar Jonathan had never been busier. While only two couriers came each day (to reduce suspicion), the pouches they carried were packed full.

This morning, Bunni had handed him the sorted messages from the fortress first, the ones the scribe thought most important on the top. Jonathan scanned them quickly. He was learning to trust the scribe's judgment. The first one was from Immi and had bad news. The man on the king's guard who gave the most extensive reports to Commander Sheva had received word that his abbi was very ill and had left. Jonathan frowned. The reports from Sheva about the king's moods and off-hand comments would be much less useful now. Besides that, Abbi had chosen a new personal attendant. Someone from Naphtali who hadn't heard that the call to arms was cancelled until he'd arrived.

He set that message aside to remind him that he had to find a good way to keep a discreet eye on Abbi. Experience with Balak had taught him that just a few private minutes alone with the king at the right time could make an enormous difference.

The next message said that Abner had come to his consultation with the king looking pleased. Jonathan set that one aside also. He would check to see if the messages from Elihu offered any explanation.

The rest were routine, and he handed them off to Bunah to record and store.

"What's next?" he asked Bunni.

The scribe silently handed him two papyri, and Jonathan raised his eyebrows. Normally, he got a whole stack. The top one from Elihu said that he and Ishvi believed they had discovered how the king could collect information on Dahveed without anyone knowing about it. Local people from towns and villages listened for any information in the market place or wine shops, reporting to a few key individuals who discreetly handed out silver. The agents then wrote up the information and sent it to Jaasiel's estates where the scribes winnowed out anything that might pertain to Dahveed. This they passed to Abner. The reports at the estate were then burned. One pile had been rescued before it was destroyed, and Elihu had compiled a list for the hassar's perusal.

Turning to the second papyrus, Jonathan read the various items on it, becoming more and more intent. Grain prices had gone up in Adullam, Keilah, and Nezib, the three towns on the Shephelah east of Gath. The heavy rains last fall had damaged the Way of the Sea, and repairs to it had gone slowly, if at all. Some north-bound caravans were taking a more inland route as a result. A caravan up from the south brought the news that Edom had a new gebirah, and the adons were already jockeying for the chance to be her husband and Edom's next king. Ahlai of Jezreel was down to just the son of his favorite wife, having somehow disposed of an older son and selling off the daughter of the earlier marriage to a rich northern adon. A farmer in Hebron had caused a stir when he appeared in town claiming that the Philistines were raiding and that an entire army had passed his house the night before. Nabal of Carmel had been unusually easy-going this year, having reaped a large profit from the good harvest he'd brought in. Roeh Shamuel's health was worse. His new servant had sent a message to the roeh's sons, Joel and Abiah, both of whom refused to leave Beersheba to attend him.

When Jonathan finished reading, he sat deep in thought for some time. The list was a treasure trove, and he couldn't believe most of it would be thrown away, but Elihu said that only notices of the new gebirah in Edom and the phantom army in Hebron had been passed on.

He leaned back in disgust. If grain prices on the Shephelah had gone up, there was either a shortage or someone was buying. If Carmel had a good harvest, so would the Shephelah, thus someone was purchasing everything available, probably Gath since all three towns were close to it. Was Gath re-supplying or stockpiling?

Caravans willing to take a more inland route north meant an opportunity to lure more into the highlands if there were good roads and places to stay. If the Edomites had a new gebirah, the best warrior would get her, which meant trouble on the southern border and opportunity for Habiru employment, and the army going through Hebron could very well have been Dahveed. And who was Ahlai of Jezreel, and why did the roeh have a new servant?

As he slapped the desk in frustration, the two scribes jumped. Jonathan could see a use for every bit of information on that papyrus, yet Abner had thrown it all away! How could he and Abbi be so focused on Dahveed that they would ignore something as important as the grain prices near Gath? And after Gath had raided Keilah? The situation cried out for investigation!

In addition, this was just the sort of information that Tanhum was asking for to help him with the set-up of the internal trade system. If Ahlai was someone to be gossiped about in Jezreel, he was probably a large landowner and would have commodities to sell. The same applied to Nabal of Carmel, if one could stand to trade with him.

The morning passed, and he was ready for a rest when he climbed the stairs to the upper room for the noon meal.

Taphath looked up from her seat on the stool by the table. "Good, you came right away. I'm hungry." He sat down beside her, and they shared the bread, parched grain, and dried fruit. "Didn't I smell chickpeas?" he asked.

"They're for tonight," his wife replied. "Are you still hungry for something?"

"That's a leading question, Sahrah," he said, smiling.

"Now where could that possibly lead to?"

"If you haven't learned that by now, perhaps I should tell you again." Jonathan kissed her, bringing that little contented smile that he loved to her lips.

Her eyes twinkled. "Do lead on, Hassar!"

He did.

A quiet knock on the door brought Jonathan out of his lazy doze. "What is it?" he asked, stretching.

"The scribes are waiting, adoni," one of the guards said apologetically.

"All right."

The man's footsteps retreated, and Taphath stirred beside him. "Before you go, there's something I need to tell you," she said, turning over to face him. "That overseer at Abner's estate decided that he's only going to hire day laborers from now on. The only servants still there are the ones who've been there for years."

Jonathan sighed. "It's almost as important to keep track of Abner as it is the king. I don't want to coerce anyone on his staff if I can help it. Messing with clan families gets ticklish. But if he's only using day laborers, I guess I'll have to."

"You shouldn't need to," she said. "Ahinoam thinks the same. The day laborers should be enough."

"Taphath, different ones will be hired on any given day."

"That won't make any difference. I doubt there's a laborer in town who won't tell me if they notice anything."

The hassar stared at his wife's closed eyes. Had she somehow enthralled the entire town of Zelah? "Why is that?"

"The people are afraid, Jonathan." She shifted to a more comfortable position. "They know what they will suffer because of the king's sin, and once the word got around that Yahweh had accepted you at Gibeon, there's not a person in the whole of Benjamin who wouldn't do anything you asked. You bring them Yahweh's hesed. It's even been whispered that Roeh Shamuel said that Yahweh had given the kingdom into your hand."

He sat there, wondering if she was really correct. "Anyone?" he asked incredulously.

"Well, any of the farmers and townsmen. Or the servants. Ahinoam says Abner's the only one in Shaul's clan who opposes you, and Ner is upset about that. Rizpah sent word that her clans in Gilead don't like the situation, but would probably support you if you don't humiliate the king."

"I see."

Taphath gave him a sleepy smile and turned over.

That night, after his wife firmly told him she needed to rest, he gave up trying to go to sleep and threw on an old kilt. Taking his cloak and hunting bow and quiver, he went outside, sending one of the guards for Nimshi. The Habiru startled him by coming over the wall instead of through the gate.

The younger man eyed the bow. "It's a little late for deer. Did you want a good tree for target practice?"

"Yes."

"Come this way then." The Habiru took him around the compound and headed north. Not long after, they came to a small clearing with a tree whose lighter bark stood out against the darker background.

Jonathan fitted an arrow, sighting in the dim light of the stars. The arrow thunked into the tree. With a single smooth motion, he pulled another, notched it, drew back, and released.

What should he do? If Taphath was right, he could rouse the entire countryside with just a word. Another arrow sped from his bow. He hadn't really thought about what that meant until this afternoon. But if all the townsmen and servants and farmers supported him, he could carry out any plan he wished in relative safety since anyone who tried to stop him would be reported.

The arrow half-cocked, he paused. The scope of the information in that single stack of reports amazed him. The arrow thudded home. Most of it undoubtedly came from common people talking in the market. If Ethan was tapped into these same sources as well as the caravaneers, it was no wonder he knew most of what happened anywhere he was interested in. And maybe that was how Immi always knew what was going on. She listened to the servants. He knew how important it was that his personal guards not talk, but the full implications hadn't struck him until now.

The next arrow flew from the bow. If he was to build a solid base for Dahveed, such information would be essential. And Abner had been thorough in setting this up. Did he have to destroy it? Could he use it instead? Expand it into the north? He lowered the bow. If the system worked like his brother and Elihu thought, all they needed to do was replace a few key people at the top and redirect the information flow to him.

Finally, he put the bow down. "Bring back the arrows, Nimshi," he said absently.

While the Habiru obeyed, he stared into the darkness. "It could be done, but it needs to be done all at once," he said out loud. "Remove the people who know and have someone else ready to take their place right then. And we'd have to be certain we had the name of everyone who knows the king's objective."

Nimshi appeared beside him.

"Let's go, Nimshi."

The next morning, he was up early, writing up the message to Elihu himself, outlining what he wanted done. Then he sat back to wait.

¥ ¥ ¥ ¥ ¥ ¥

"Adoni, is it possible this was misdirected to us?" Elihu asked, respectfully.

Sar Ishvi took the offered papyrus which had his name on it, reading the seal. Atarah. He frowned in thought. The Jebusite healer had faded from sight since Jonathan's marriage to Taphath. Why would she be sending a message to him?

"Why didn't you open it?" he asked Elihu.

"It's from a woman, adoni."

Ishvi smiled. "You have a nice sense of privacy, Elihu."

The scribe bowed and left the room. The sar opened the message, surprised when a second fell out onto the table. Fingering it, he read Atarah's message with interest.

"Greetings to you, Ishvi ben Shaul, Sar Israel.

"I send the enclosed message hoping you will know how it should be handled. Now that Keturah is no longer here to tend to the needs of her friends, I have taken on the task. They gave this to me, saying it was from a relative of theirs. Please let me know if you are unable to handle the message, and I will try to get it to its destination another way. I would not want Keturah to worry about the friends she left behind.

"In gratitude,

"Atarah bat Tanhum."

Intrigued, Ishvi broke the seal on the second message, reading rapidly. His mouth dropped open, and then he laughed.

"Elihu!"

His door opened and the scribe entered. "Yes, adoni?"

"Find out who this seal belongs to." He showed it to the man.

Elihu darted a quick glance at his face. "Yes, adoni," he said expressionlessly, leaving the room.

Though crudely written, the message was still readable. He'd had no idea that Abner had such trouble keeping servants on his estate, or that he could be so touchy about the way his records were kept, or that he paid his overseer so generously. Of course, if this was what he thought it was, Abner didn't do any of those things. However, he'd bet that Abner did receive visitors late at night, and the names listed should be investigated. Setting the message aside, he waited impatiently for Elihu to find out where it had come from.

Work had been dismissed for the day before Elihu reported back. "What about the seal?" Ishvi asked immediately.

"It comes from a house in Zelah, adoni."

"Which one?"

The scribe kept a straight face. "A house of prostitutes, adoni."

Ishvi stared at the seal in surprise, then laughed again. Abner's overseer seemed to have become quite the man about town lately. "Send a message to my esteemed elder brother. Tell him that we now have a very reliable source for General Abner's household! But before you do that, tell me how this message got here."

"It seems that one of the local prostitutes in Gibeah has a sister in Zelah in the same line of work, adoni. The message was sent to her, and she apparently gave it to Atarah."

"All right. Send a message to Atarah. Tell her that we will have no trouble getting the message she sent where it belongs, and that we can pass along any others that might come. Then read this message and make arrangements to send something appropriate to the person who originated it to express our gratitude for her efforts."

"Yes, adoni."

Ishvi chuckled again as Elihu left the room. Abner seemed surrounded by women interfering with his carefully laid plans at every turn. Then he sighed with anticipation. Jonathan had gone hunting again, and Immi had planned a very nice evening meal around the meat that he had sent. Abner would be there, he knew, forcing himself further into honor-debt to the hassar under his immi's cold stare.

He glanced at the ceiling of the room. "Yahweh, if I ever offend my immi, just kill me, would you?"

¥ ¥ ¥ ¥ ¥ ¥

Sar Malchi wandered among the second and fourth units as they sparred on the training ground, assessing the strengths of the men while Abner watched from the sidelines. They were tired after a full day, and many of them were getting careless, the perfect time for bad fighting habits to come to the fore.

A sharp cry behind him made the sar whip around. Areli dropped his wooden practice sword, holding his arm tightly. He grimaced as Malchi came over. "My apologies, sar. I'm more tired than I thought."

Pallu stepped up, his face worried. "Did I hit too hard, Areli? I thought you'd block that one."

"Wasn't quite quick enough. It should be all right in a couple days."

Since most of the other pairs had stopped to see what had happened, Malchi turned to them all. "Enough for today. Put the practice swords in the shed. You're dismissed."

The men drifted off, Pallu taking both swords as he left.

"If you would check it over, Sar?" Areli asked.

"Hold it out," Malchi said, a bit puzzled.

Areli looked down at the arm, his voice low. "My cousin, Cheran, is the new personal attendant to the king, sar, and the king likes him."

The sar's hands paused a moment, and then kept up their probing.

Wincing a little, the man added, "Dahveed saved the life of his older brother at Birzaith, and he is grateful. What information would be most useful to the hassar?"

Keeping his face calm, Malchi bent Areli's arm a couple times. "Who the king sees and what is on his mind when he is alone." Then he stood back. "It's just bruised, Areli. Everything should be fine, but keep me informed."

"I will, adoni."

¥ ¥ ¥ ¥ ¥ ¥

The list of key people in the king's network grew slowly. Decisions had to be made about each name, how much they actually knew, how much they might guess, and whether they would need to be removed or not. If they were removed, what was Jonathan going to do with them?

"It worries you," Taphath observed.

Her husband paused, adjusting the set of the robe on his shoulders. She always looked inviting in the morning, but lately she seemed to have a special glow. "Yes," he sighed. "The most expedient thing would be to kill them, but most of them are Benjamites, and it would split the tribe if I did."

"Why don't you just enslave them for six years?" Taphath asked. "Sell them to someone you can trust further north or something. By the time six years have passed, whatever they know won't be important anymore. In fact, I suspect anything they know won't matter within just months. They'll be under your control, but still in Israel. That should avoid any tribal repercussions."

"Did you or Immi think up this one?" the hassar demanded, disgusted with himself for not arriving at the obvious himself.

"I thought of that all on my own," she said with a smile.

Jonathan leaned down to kiss her. "I feel very sorry for any sons I might have. You're going to be worse than Immi!"

Taphath laughed.

Bunni had the messages sorted and ready when he walked into his business chamber, but Jonathan shoved them aside. First, he dictated a note to Elihu, explaining what he planned on doing with the people they removed, and specifying that he should find out from Tanhum if Atarah would be willing to have them on her estate near Shechem. He stressed that the men he sent could not be sold, and must be freed at the end of six years if they had not bought themselves free by then, or been redeemed by clan members.

Then he picked up his messages. The top two were from Ishvi and Malchi telling him of the people now reporting on Abner and Shaul. For a moment he just held them. Yahweh used anything, from Balak's arrogance and Dahveed's hesed to Keturah's loyalty and a man's lust. Prostitutes, Habiru, craftsmen, kings, even mulish sars. They were all the same to his God.

"Yahweh, guide us," he whispered.

Another week passed. Reports reaching the hassar said that Abbi had shoved all the court business onto Ishvi and Eshbaal and spent his time seeking Dahveed. It wouldn't be long before he found him. The information crossing Jonathan's table suggested that Dahveed was in Ziph, and Abner would soon pick that up. It was what would happen next that worried the hassar. But everything was in place. Malchi had been informed to keep six units available at all times. Ishvi had increased his staff by the appropriate number of people waiting to be placed. He just needed a chance to strike.

¥ ¥ ¥ ¥ ¥ ¥

Sar Ishvi glanced at King Shaul. Today was a judgment day, and he knew the king had heard nothing of the case just presented to him. He turned back to the petitioners. "The king will now consider your case," he said. "If you will wait below."

The two men left the room, and Ishvi signaled the guards to escort the rest of the people waiting outside also. When the doors closed, Shaul looked up.

"Is court finished?"

"No, adoni, but you must make a decision about the latest case. Everyone is waiting outside for you to do so."

The king waved his hand impatiently. "You heard it. Decide what should be done."

"The decision will need to be sealed with your seal, adoni."

His abbi pulled the seal from his finger and held it out. "Take it," he said annoyed. "Do whatever you want. Just send Abner to me."

The sar took the ring, managing to get it on his trembling finger. "Right away, adoni." He looked at one of the guards. "Send a messenger for General Abner. The king requires him."

"Yes, adoni," the soldier said, ducking his head and hurrying down the stairs.

"Eshbaal, write up a judgment for the merchant. He had every right to expect that the adon would purchase his pottery, and since the set was smashed due to the adon's carelessness, charge the adon with twice the price."

"Yes, adoni." Eshbaal wrote swiftly, putting a blob of clay on the papyrus to seal it, and Ishvi pressed the king's ring into it.

"Adoni?"

"What, Ishvi?"

"When will you require the ring back?"

Shaul turned on the throne, annoyed. "I said keep it. Don't bother me with things you can do yourself!"

"Yes, adoni. Will you hear any more cases today?"

"No."

"Then I will dismiss court."

Intently staring into space, the king waved him away.

Ishvi sent the judgment to the two petitioners and directed that the court had been dismissed for the day. As he and Eshbaal were finishing up, Abner entered the room.

"What have you learned?" Shaul demanded.

"Ziph. But the man was not hopeful. He said it was wild country down there."

"No one is hopeful," Shaul said, annoyed. "One would think that country was covered with darkness all the time, and that the people in it were blind as well. How can 30 people disappear like that? Shall my slave flee, and I not recover him?"

"We are doing the best we can," Abner said.

"No, we are not! I am tired of all the excuses and the reasons and the messages of failure. Get seven units from Malchi, Abner. I shall lead them myself, and we will go to Ziph, and there will be an end of Dahveed. He is a son of death, and I will make him so."

"As you wish, adoni," Abner said, satisfaction in his voice. "When do you want to leave?"

"In the morning."

"The men will be up most of the night, getting ready."

"They can stay up all night if they must," Shaul said, his eyes glittering. "I am their king, and they will do as I command."

"Yes, adoni." With a bow the general departed.

A bit later as Sar Ishvi and his brother left the throne room, he did nothing to hide the seal ring as he passed through the anteroom. He rode his mule to the house by the west gate that he used for estate business. Elihu waited as usual, and he immediately noticed the seal ring.

"Send a message to Jonathan Hassar that the king and Abner will take seven units to Ziph in the morning. The king expects to find Dahveed there."

A faint smile crossed the scribe's face. "He will find that

surprisingly difficult."

"That will be all, Elihu."

"Yes, adoni."

As he expected, Jonathan replied to his message within the hour.

"In one week."

CHAPTER 36

Sar Ishvi sat on the mule, watching the last of the seven units leave the west gate. His abbi and Abner rode at the front of the column, and the king's personal attendant accompanied him. Abner had taken the fourth through the ninth units, adding the eleventh and leaving the commanders known to support Dahveed behind with Libni.

Once the men were well down the road, Ishvi went up to the fortress, planning to send a messenger for Malchi, only to find his brother waiting for him in the anteroom. "Come," he said, leading the way.

"I assume you notified Jonathan," Malchi said when they had closed the door.

"Yesterday. He said things will happen one week from today. You have all you need?"

"Yes. I'll send the units out tomorrow. What excuse are we using?"

"That since the king is going personally after Dahveed, we are guarding the roads and countryside in case Dahveed tries to head north again."

Malchi nodded. His eye caught the seal ring on Ishvi's hand, and he quickly glanced at the other sar's face.

"He shoved it at me yesterday, annoyed with having to seal more documents. Said I should do whatever I wanted to with it."

With still another nod, Malchi started for the door, only to pause, his back toward Ishvi, before opening it. "I didn't think this would hurt so much. But I suppose it's too late to stop now."

Ishvi sighed. "When Abbi handed me this yesterday, I nearly knelt and told him everything, but I couldn't forget holding the Hakkohen Haggadol's body in my arms and seeing his family dead around him."

"Did you go to Nob?" Malchi asked, still staring at the door.

"No."

"I did. That's what keeps me going. We knew those people, Ishvi.

They welcomed us and served us and brought us Yahweh's blessings. And I can't let their deaths go without some recompense."

"Then we go on."

"Yes."

¥ ¥ ¥ ¥ ¥ ¥

Taphath turned over. "You're not sleeping, Jonathan."

"The units left today. We're committed. You're sure you won't go to Jabesh?"

"No."

"You may die."

"So may you."

He stroked her face. "You have made me very happy, Taphath. I don't know how I could have gotten through this without you."

"Then do me a favor, Hassar. Take some ashes, and your bow, and go somewhere alone where you can mourn," she said gently. "I will be visiting Sahrah Ahinoam tomorrow, so don't feel as if you have to be home right away. Stay until your grief is relieved."

Suddenly, Jonathan couldn't wait to be gone. After kissing her gently, he hurriedly dressed, taking his cloak and hunting bow.

Immi's oak tree waited, silent and solid, rooted to the ground that held his ancestors and bound him to his God. He would need all the connections he could find tonight, for the pain of this betrayal was tearing him apart. Dry-eyed, he leaned back against the tree, wondering how he could mourn what was not gone. Abbi hadn't died. Yet he grieved. For what? Yes, he could smear the ashes on his forehead and hands, but to what end?

Jonathan nearly hurled the ash pot from him in frustration. It was all so unnecessary! Yahweh had sent Dahveed to bring light and joy back into their family, and the zammar had done just that. Abbi had loved him for it, and Dahveed had loved the king. The last thing Dahveed would do was to take the throne from the ones he loved. That's why he was down in Ziph right now! But Balak had spoiled everything because of a childhood grudge and a thirst for power.

Remorse and pain welling up inside him, the hassar hunched over. There was so much he could have done, but hadn't. So many things Abbi could have chosen, but didn't. And now Jonathan mourned what could have been, but would never be. In a way, his abbi *had* died. The man he remembered no longer existed, taken over by unnecessary hatred and the stubborn pride that would not let him accept Yahweh's will for Israel, rejecting in the process everything which could have made this time of his life the happiest of all. Instead, his family had split in two, people who should have supported and helped each other seeking to do harm in order to control him. Pulling his knees into his chest, he rocked from pain too deep for tears. "Yahweh, do not leave me! I do not know that I can bear the consequences of what I have done."

He was still there when the dawn's rays found him, and someone walked up the hill.

"You, too?" Michal asked, her eyes red with weeping.

"If it wasn't too late, I'm not sure I could continue, even though I know that not doing this will cost more than doing it."

"Are you sure this will work, and Abbi, well, we won't have to do anything more?"

"I don't know. Does Merab know?"

"Immi sent a message."

She leaned against his chest, and he put his arms around her, tightening his hold. "I needed someone with me," he admitted, "and we've shared this so long, Michal."

"Then why doesn't it hurt less?"

The hassar bent his head, his only reply the tears that finally fell from his eyes.

Three days later, Nimshi pushed open the door to Jonathan's business chamber. "They're coming, geber."

The hassar let out his breath slowly. He'd given a lot of thought to what he should do. But Taphath's comment about the Jabesh clans respecting his coup as long as the king was not humiliated had stayed in his mind. His time here at the estate had taught him that power was not tied to an ebony chair. Nor was a king's honor made up of royal attire. But his abbi needed the trappings of kingship, and Jonathan had decided to leave them with him. It would be a little inconvenient, but it would honor Abbi. Something that he had to do, as much for himself as Shaul.

Taphath looked up from her sewing as he entered the upper room. "They are coming?"

"Nimshi just brought word."

"The robe you picked out is ready," she said, indicating a clothes chest.

Opening it, he pulled out his favorite dark blue, this one with long white fringe that had silver threads in it. There was a worked silver headband, earrings, and arm bands. Taphath set the headband on his hair, then stood back.

"It sets the right tone," she decided. "Kingly, but not blatant."

"Will you come out with me?"

"As long as I can stay on the balcony."

He held the door, and they settled under the awning, Taphath still with her sewing. "Which relative is having a baby?" he asked, noticing the small size of the garment she was working on.

"Oh, there's always someone," she said vaguely. "I believe that's Ishvi on his mule."

Jonathan turned. Yes, his brother was approaching, along with Malchi and two units, the first and second if he saw correctly. Along with them came a line of nearly 20 men, not one of whom looked very worried, he noted with interest. His brothers rode into the courtyard and dismounted, two of the soldiers taking the mules. The others passed through the gate as the hassar descended the stairs.

"Shalom, Ishvi, Malchi. I see you were successful."

"Yes, hassar," Ishvi replied. "We took everyone quietly in one night, and our substitutes are in place. The men from the units will remain for several more days, then return to Gibeah."

"Well done."

"There is one more thing," his brother added. Kneeling, he held something out. "I was instructed by abbi to do whatever I wanted with this."

Jonathan looked at the king's seal. If he took it, he was irrevocably separating himself from his abbi. Could he? Somewhere in the back of his mind, he heard again the ravening darkness howling in triumph over him, and he saw the explosion of fire that had sheltered him from it. He owed highest loyalty to the one with highest honor. Accepting the ring, he slipped it on his own finger again. "This was unexpected," he commented.

"But essential." Ishvi smiled in relief. "I have worn it long enough. You are welcome to it, adoni." Then he touched his forehead to the ground, irrevocably committing himself also.

Jonathan turned to Malchi who, with tears glistening in his eyes, joined Ishvi, bowing to the ground also. The hassar helped them both stand.

"Your men do you credit, Sar Malchi. Tell them I am pleased with them, and with you."

Malchi half smiled. "Thank you, adoni. It is small comfort, but it is comfort."

Jonathan briefly gripped his brother's shoulder, and then turned to the prisoners, now staring at him, wide-eyed.

"You took the king's seal!" one of them gasped, voicing an accusation of treason.

"Yes, and I have also taken the king's authority since it should no longer belong to him," the hassar said quietly. "You have been taken because you betrayed Yahweh by aiding Shaul ben Kish in his rebellion after he killed the priests and destroyed a sacred city. You did this knowingly. You have also conspired against the life of an innocent man, Dahveed ben Jesse. This you also did knowingly."

One or two of the prisoners who had looked ready to protest now shifted uneasily.

"You all know that the penalty for treason is death, and treason against Yahweh means the death of your families also."

"And when the king's general comes and announces that our families will die if we don't do the king's command, what do we do then?" one man demanded angrily.

"According to the information I have in my records, you didn't take much coercing. I would imagine Abner had to give several of you something to tell me just in case you ever fell into my power. Nor has it escaped my attention that not one of you is from the same clan in Benjamin. Abner is not a fool, as I well know."

The men shifted, and one or two looked frightened.

"Abner is right about one thing," Jonathan said, walking down the line. "I have no intention of starting a tribal war. On the other hand, I have no intention of allowing Shaul to trample on Yahweh's covenant either. I am, therefore, going to leave you to the hesed of Yahweh and your clans, neither of whom is very pleased with you. You have been sold to a landowner up near Shechem. This land owner is not an Israelite and has little reason to like Shaul. You will serve there for the required six years, unless your clan decides you deserve to be redeemed sooner, or I grant you permission to buy yourselves free.

"Your families have all been notified to apply to me about your welfare. You will leave immediately."

"Adoni?" one man said, his face glistening with sweat.

"Yes?"

"My clan is poor and my wife is heavy with child. How will she live?"

"If this is true, I will see what can be done. Ram, take them to Shechem."

"Yes, adoni," the commander said.

Once the men were gone, Jonathan took Ishvi and Malchi into his business chamber, receiving their reports on everything that had happened. It was close to the evening meal when they finished.

Taphath had prepared a quiet dinner. She had made things special without the trappings of a feast, and Jonathan was grateful. They all felt the need for some ritual to end the day, and his wife had struck just the right note. Malchi seemed very attentive to her, making Jonathan glance his way a couple of times. But the two of them were chatting, and Jonathan still had some questions for Ishvi, so he was rather glad they entertained each other.

"What about Jaasiel?" he asked. It was the first chance he'd had to find out what had happened to Abner's son.

"Elihu sent him to Dahveed's abbi, Jesse."

"Remind me to stay on that man's good side," Jonathan said half seriously. "Abner won't know what to do if he finds out that his son is in the hands of Jesse! To say nothing of King Yira."

"Hopefully he won't have to know. But Elihu is more concerned with Dahveed's well-being than Jaasiel's."

It was late when the two sars left. Both felt they should be in Gibeah in the morning to handle any reactions that might result from the past days' activities.

Jonathan sighed as he blew out the last lamp and settled down by Taphath on the bedrolls. "Today went quieter than I expected. Now the only thing I have to worry about is Dahveed. I hope he got that last message in time."

"I'm sure he did," his wife said. "You sent it as soon as Ishvi told you the king was going to Ziph. What do you think about Joarib?"

"Who's he?"

"Not a person--the name."

"I don't know," Jonathan said, yawning.

"Or maybe Michal or Merab. Your sisters would like that."

"Like what?"

"The names. I hope you don't want Obed, because I don't," she said positively.

"Do I know anyone called Obed?"

"Not a person--the name. Do you like the name?"

"Why should I?" he asked, a bit exasperated. He wanted to sleep.

"Because we've got to call the baby something."

"People usually do. Whose baby?"

"Yours."

Jonathan's eyes popped open. "*Mine?* You're carrying a child?" he nearly shouted, flipping over to face her.

"Yes."

"But what--I mean how did--I mean, what should I do?"

"You've already done quite enough, Hassar. Malchi had some good ideas for names, but we'll have to review them."

"Malchi! How does he know?" Jonathan sat up on the bedroll.

"He knew as soon as he saw me, Hassar, which means Ishvi knows by now too. We'll have to send a message to my family in the morning."

"Are you sure you're all right? You feel fine? Does Immi know? Did she say you were supposed to do something special, or do you need anything now? What will happen-"

Taphath reached up and put her fingers over his lips with a sigh. "Your Immi warned me you might go flying off like this, so she gave me specific instructions on what to do."

"What? What are they?" he asked anxiously.

"She said I was to very firmly pull you down onto the bedroll, and tell you that the most important thing you can do is hug your wife!" she answered, suiting actions to words.

Jonathan found himself holding Taphath close to him, dizzy with the thought that some day he'd be called Abbi.

CHAPTER 37

Abigail entered her husband's garish business chamber in Carmel. With the addition of the hanging silver lamps, the place looked like a storeroom for unused items belonging to the Pharaoh. She shuddered. It was all that she could have hoped and more.

"You requested I come?" she said, seeing Nabal on the chair on the dais.

"Yes, Gebirah! You will never guess the news!"

His voice was a little thick, and she studied him. Into the wine so soon today? She raised her eyebrows. "It must be good news. You have celebrated already."

Nabal laughed. Picking up the silver goblet beside him, he swallowed more wine. "My source in Jezreel says Ahlai is furious because I saw through his deceit and refused to buy the woman he tempted me with. News came that his son is building up debts again. Tokhath left to see what he can buy up. Oh, this is a wonderful day!

"While I was celebrating, two more adons came. Properly impressed with the wealth I control, they will long remember seeing me in this place."

"What gifts did they bring?"

"Those little trinket boxes over there for you. And this rather dull black pelt of some kind. But not a single piece of gold!"

Abigail went to the large table, seeing the inlaid boxes. Her breath caught. Spice boxes? Two of them would fit comfortably on her palm. She opened one, staring at the contents a moment.

"Did you open these?" she asked, setting them down.

"No. They were too small to bother with," he said sourly.

"What did you give in return?"

"I sent for some silver, and gave them each a suit of clothes. Good-quality wool, but not too fancy. What can I do with skins? They were speechless with my largess. I hinted next time they should bring gold."

Abigail would well believe they were speechless. Even though Tokhath encouraged Nabal's greed, the scribe had enough sense to keep her husband from giving this serious of an offense. But with him absent, as now, one never knew what Nabal would do.

"Who were they?" she asked, her voice a bit unsteady.

"One was called 'Hadar,' I think. They didn't bring much, and they interrupted me."

Hadar! She didn't remember the trader previously dealing in spices, so this must be something new. He'd probably stopped by to give her a sample of the wares, and Nabal had treated him like a subservient adon with inferior gifts! "Well, since you don't like what they brought, I'll have Hezro take it out," she said, gesturing to the guard commander. "I will expect you for the evening meal, Nagid."

As he waved his hand absently, she slipped out. "It was Hadar," she told Hezro as soon as she gained the courtyard. "Find him! I dare not let this insult pass."

As she waited, she slipped the spice boxes into her girdle and inspected the skin. It was more than 40 inches long, and as the sun gleamed on it, she could see what might be spots in a darker black than the background.

"Hadar is leaving the inn, Gebirah. He is furious," her commander said, hurrying back into the courtyard.

"As well he should be," she replied, walking swiftly out the gate. She sped through the streets, getting to the inn yard just as Hadar and his companion were leaving it. After pausing a moment to collect her thoughts, she then approached the angry trader with her chin up and an embarrassed smile on her face. "I'm so glad I found you before you left, Hadar! I'm afraid I must ask you to pardon my forgetfulness."

That stopped him. "Your forgetfulness?"

"Yes, geber. I heard that you went to the nagid today. He is very absent-minded when he is at business, and I meant to tell you that you should always come to me with anything you have. I do hope you have not met with inconvenience because of my faults." Opening her eyes wide, she bowed slightly.

"Uh, well, the nagid was a little, uh, absent-minded as you say," Hadar said, gulping a bit.

"Oh, then you have had some trouble. I do apologize, geber! Please allow me to make things right with you. You have taken so much trouble on my behalf that I hardly know how to express my gratitude as it is." She smiled invitingly. "Would you be willing to accompany me, geber? I see you are ready to leave, and I wouldn't inconvenience you more if I can help it. Please tell me what happened as we go."

The merchant looked down in confusion. "Baalah, you are most gracious."

"Then let us go," she said, walking down the street toward the town gate.

Hadar fell in beside her.

"It is so pleasant to see you again, geber. How is your family? Didn't you mention that you had a wife and some children?"

"Yes, Baalah. They are well, and are waiting for me at my next stop in Beersheba."

"How has trade been? Were the bandits troublesome this year?"

"Not more than usual. Although I have heard that the Amalekites are becoming bolder again. It has been many years since King Shaul defeated them and killed their Agag."

She managed to keep the conversation going until they reached Maon. Once there, she invited Hadar onto the roof of the house and ordered food and wine for his refreshment. She noted with relief that he ate and drank without hesitation.

"Now, Hadar, I'm afraid I must impose on you to help me," she said, taking one of the boxes from her girdle. "Nabal didn't have time to look in these, and when I did, I found your new wares somewhat overwhelming. I believe this is frankincense, correct?"

"Yes, Baalah. That is how it comes from the trees, so it is pure and unmixed with anything else."

"Hezro, have someone bring some coals. Do you mind if I burn a little of it now?"

"Not at all," the trader replied, pleased.

When the coals arrived, Hadar shaved some of the hardened sap off a lump and soon the scent drifted around them.

"You did not carry such things before, did you?"

"No. But El blessed us, and Adon Jether was able to help out a fellow caravaneer who carries goods from Sheba."

Abigail opened another box. "And these are pepper corns?"

"Yes. They become black and wrinkled when they dry. They are best eaten ground up and sprinkled on food."

"I think I remember that. Someone sent some to my abbi many years ago." Taking out the third box, she inhaled the scent. "I'm afraid to say what I think this is, for I might be wrong." She smelled again. "Dare I say it is a clove?"

His smile widened, and he bowed. "It is a clove, Baalah."

"You have done me very great honor, Hadar. I have never received this rarest of spices before. I do not know that I can repay your trouble for bringing these wonderful things to me."

"You do not have to repay. It is our privilege to show you the value we place on your custom."

"You must let me give you something, Hadar. I'm afraid, however, that anything I give will be inferior to your generosity."

"Your kindness and time will make whatever you grant us of great value." Again he bowed.

"And now, Hadar, I must know, what is this pelt?" Carefully she unrolled it. "I've never seen one like it. Where does it come from?"

"The south of Sheba, Baalah. It is from a large predator, the black leopard. They are the fiercest of cats and the strongest. The pelts are rare."

She stroked the skin. "It is beautifully tanned, and so smooth. We are very honored indeed."

The trader and his companion stayed for the noon meal, and

during the noon rest Abigail ransacked the treasure room to find something to send to Hadar's wife, as well as appropriate gifts for the man himself, finally settling on a small dagger of the new hardened iron, an embroidered girdle, and a purse of gold ingots.

¥ ¥ ¥ ¥ ¥ ¥

"He died, Dodi."

"When?" I asked.

"Just a few minutes ago. Keturah said he didn't want to live. Why would anyone feel that way, Dodi?"

"The Gibeonites have had a very different kind of life than you have, Asahel," I replied, knowing that only time would explain this to him. It wasn't something that I really understood either.

I looked around the encampment. It sprawled out carelessly, the men knowing we'd only be here for a day at most. I hadn't said anything, for the heat and the constant watchfulness had made the men's tempers short and unpredictable. Bickering was almost constant, and when it stopped, as now, the tense silence grated on everyone's nerves.

Then one of the Gibeonite bearers had sickened. He had said nothing, and only when he fell carrying the ark did I realize that anything was wrong. Because Gad was consecrated as a prophet, he had taken the man's place, and Keturah had helped the sick Gibeonite the last couple miles to this campsite yesterday.

Shagay's son emerged from the forest. "We can't spend more than a few hours here, adoni. We're cut off from the west now, and the fifth unit will search this area soon."

I looked around again, near despair. Shaul and Abner had driven us for weeks by the simple expedient of having all seven units advancing in different directions at all times. At first, I'd thought the pattern of movement was random, but I quickly realized otherwise. It was the height of summer. Abner had someone with him who knew the country, and he was remorselessly driving us into a track of forest with no permanent springs. The situation would only be worse if I fled south to the Negev at this time of year. I could go east to Moab, but while Yira might protect me, I didn't think his hesed would extend to my men. I had 30 mouths to feed, and the only reason we had anything to eat at all was because of kills made on the march as we twisted and turned through the forest, staying alive only because we were constantly on the move. Alone, I could have found a place to hide and stayed there until the king got tired of hunting for me. But even if I could find somewhere to conceal everyone, we still had to eat and drink.

Not that things had always gone the king's way. Two units had to fight off a pride of lions, one had their supplies ravaged by a passing bear, and the wolves' howling at night made all of Abner's men uneasy. I'd scouted them a few times, myself, and they were as tired as we were, discouraged with uselessly roaming the rough, dark forests after someone they really didn't want to catch, with no idea how close to us they'd come on several occasions.

Hours, Jonathan ben Shammah had said. Where could we go?

"Is there any other water near here?" I asked. The little spring we had used yesterday barely supplied our needs, and would be dry by tonight. I'd been awake half the night, wondering what to do when that happened.

"I'll ask Abbi," Jonathan replied, turning away.

I knew that meant he had no idea either, but didn't want to tell me.

Eliphelet hurried by, casting a quick glance behind him, and disappeared in his tent.

I looked around, wondering where we would find a quick grave for the dead man. It bothered me that we must bury him without the proper rites and mourning, but if the fifth unit found us, there would be more than one grave.

Zelek strode by, his face a thundercloud. He walked into Eliphelet's tent and dragged the man out after him.

"Geber, please," Eliphelet protested. "This is unnecessary!"

"I don't think so," my half-cousin snarled, bringing him to me and practically throwing him at me. "I've had enough."

"No, please," Eliphelet begged. "I didn't mean to-"

"He's stealing, Dahveed," Zelek said angrily. "I'll bet nearly every man in camp has lost items to his sticky fingers, and Yahweh alone knows where he's hidden them, or if he still has them and they're not lost in this cursed forest while we slink away from the king's patrols."

"Is that where my gold ring went?" Shammah said, advancing on Eliphelet. "You took it?"

"Well, I can't say for certain," he hedged, backing away a little.

"Well, maybe it's time you did say," Zalmon added, hearing the commotion. "I didn't want to say anything, but if there's going to be a reckoning, I want my silver earrings and cloak brooch back!"

By now, everyone else had gathered rapidly, and Shagay and Ahiam appeared, standing on either side of me.

"It's time it stopped, Dahveed," Elika shouted. "I've lost most of the spoils that I could bring with me from Keilah."

"He's taken some of my things, too, Dahveed," Elhanan put in, eyeing the thief balefully.

"Cut off his hands," Zelek suggested. "Then we'll have some peace."

"No!" Eliphelet cried, wrapping his hands around himself and curling into a ball on the ground. "Adoni, no!"

Igal turned away, followed by Jaas.

"What's the matter? The sight of blood too much for your delicate northern sensibilities?" Zabad asked sarcastically.

Igal turned back. "I really shouldn't dignify that with an answer," he said coldly. "But I've had enough of your sly remarks about my place of origin. Just because I don't eat my meat in large chunks, or insist on the entire world knowing the misfortunes I've suffered, doesn't mean that I'm incapable of taking offense or doing something about it. Fortunately, I don't have to defend my honor to a slave."

I winced, stepping forward. Blood would flow if this didn't stop. "Any complaints will be directed to me," I said in the ensuing silence.

"Then let's start with this thief!" Zelek said, shoving Eliphelet toward me with his foot.

"Yes, and my spoils!" Zalmon added.

A general babble arose as the men angrily shouted at me all the things that Eliphelet had taken from them during the past few weeks.

"Adoni, protect me," Eliphelet moaned, crouching at my feet. "I didn't mean to! I'll give it all back! Please, adoni, let me keep my hands!"

My head pounded, and Josheb had stepped up beside Zelek. Uzzia watched from the back of the group, towering over the others. Uriah stood off to one side, arms folded, staring at Zabad.

I held up my hands for silence, and the men quieted. Before I could say anything, another voice spoke up.

"I suppose I couldn't have expected any respect for a countryman's death," Naharai said bitterly. "He was, after all, just a Gibeonite, someone bound to serve such as you with no hope of release. Never mind what he might have suffered. And while he waits for burial, you snarl about spoils like dogs over a bone. Or did you intend to just leave him for them?"

Every face went white, and I felt the wave of rage that grew from the men at Naharai's insult. Nothing was lower than a dog.

From the door of the tent where the dead man lay, Keturah stared at her brother with her hand on her mouth. Ahinoam was behind her, and Gad and Abiathar had emerged from their place also.

Zabad's hand slowly pulled his sword, and Naharai watched cynically, his arms folded. As an ark-bearer, he had no weapons.

I had no idea what to do. The men were hungry, beaten down from hard travel and inadequate rest. The Gibeonite's sickness had underlined how vulnerable we were, and my decision to avoid Shaul rather than fight him had galled on the men's pride. Eliphelet's petty stealing had ignited their tempers and Naharai had just provided a target. The wrong one.

I stepped between him and the men, facing them.

"Get out of the way, Dahveed," Zelek said. "No one can speak to us like that."

"Naharai is a Gibeonite, covered by the ancient covenant sealed by Yahweh himself," I replied. "In addition, he spoke the truth. Shall I see a man killed for that? And more, his judgment falls on me, not you, for I have failed and stand shamed before Yahweh. I will die before he does."

No one spoke. Then Gad appeared on one side of me, and Abiathar on the other.

After a few moments, Uzzia left, followed by Gareb and Ira, the three of them going to their tents. Jonathan and Abishai went next, then Ittai, casting an anxious glance at me. One by one, the others turned silently away. When they had all gone, I took out my sword and thrust it into the ground, barring the way to the Gibeonites' tents.

Shagay and Ahiam still stood on either side of Eliphelet, who cowered on the ground.

"You'd better keep him here," I said as I walked by.

"Yes, adoni," Ahiam replied.

I went to my own tent, slung the harp case over my shoulder, and walked into the forest. Climbing the hillside, I found a rock that jutted out toward the east over the ravine below. Sitting down, I laid the harp aside. The morning sun felt warm, and a butterfly or two flitted below me. I said nothing. Yahweh had seen the conflict this morning, and there was nothing I could tell Him about it. My glaring failure to lead the men weighed on me heavily. Roeh Shamuel had said I was to teach them to follow Yahweh's ways, but I couldn't even keep them fed or from each other's throats. We squabbled like children, and the only reason I hadn't joined in was because no one directed any comments to me.

I took the harp from the case, tuning the strings. It had been a long time since I'd played, and my fingers were stiff and a little clumsy. The harp slipped out of tune as I plucked the strings, and I patiently tuned it again, noticing a small crack developing from the heat and dryness close to the inlay on the upright. As soon as I got back to camp I needed to oil the harp. Looking out over the dry land that awaited the early rains, I played randomly. Weary, and thirsty, I yearned for the comfort of somehow knowing what to do. My first time as a melek for Yahweh hadn't turned out well.

A dry and weary land where there is no water. The words fit the tune under my fingers, and I closed my eyes, forgetting all the trouble that pressed on me to pay attention to the music. It had been too long since I'd felt Yahweh's presence.

The three parts of this song formed quickly in my mind as I played quietly, but the words took longer. I rearranged them more than once, humming under my breath, listening to how the harp and the melody and the words all sounded. Then I eased back and sang softly, mindful of how sound could carry sometimes.

"God, my God are You. I will seek for You. My soul is thirsty for You. My flesh yearns for You in a dry, exhausted land, without water.

Thus in the holy place I saw You, seeing Your strength and Your splendor.

Because Your divine loyalty is better than life, my lips will glorify You.

Thus I will bless You with my life. At Your name I will raise my hands.

Just like marrow and fat, You satiate my life, and with lips of joyful shouts my mouth will praise You.

"Whenever I remember You on my bed in the night-watches I ponder on You.

For You have been help to me, and in the shadow of Your wings I shout with joy.

My soul clings behind You. Your right hand has taken firm hold of me.

"But they, for devastation, seek my soul. They will enter in the lowest parts of the earth.

They are hurled down by means of a sword. A portion of foxes they will be.

But the king will rejoice in God. Everyone who swears to him will boast, for the mouth of the ones who speak deception will be stopped."[15]

I liked it. After playing it twice more to remember it, I then set the harp aside. "What do I do now, Yah?" I asked. "We have no water, the men are ready to kill each other, and I don't know how to solve either problem." Somehow I didn't think if the hassar was here, the men would be grumbling like they did with me. Too bad he couldn't have taught me the secret of that.

"Teach. I will teach you the fear of Yahweh. Depart from evil and do good. Seek peace and pursue it."

I grabbed for the harp. The words weren't another verse to the song I'd just finished, but the last verses to the acrostic one.[16]

"Come you children, hearken to me. The fear of Yahweh I will teach you.

Desist from evil and do good. Seek peace and pursue it."

The phrases spun in my mind, but I didn't have time to sort them out. I would have to finish the song later. I looked up at the sun, now past its zenith. "Thank You for leading me here, Yahweh. Show me now what I am to do."

Let Me lead you all the time.

The thought had come clearly to my mind. "What do you mean, Yah? You do lead me."

Silence.

Puzzled, I frowned. Yahweh led. The ark was here with us, and--. The ark. I had not been following, I'd been protecting, placing the ark in the middle of our march as if Yahweh was not capable of taking care of Himself. When Yahweh led, the ark went first. As it had with Moses. I sighed. How many different ways would I have to learn this lesson

---

15 Psalms 63

16 Psalms 34

before it finally stayed with me?

"Forgive Your servant, Yah," I said. "From now on, You will lead."

Sliding the harp into its case, I started back down the hill to the camp. We had a burial to attend to, and then we must move. I didn't want to fight Natan.

The camp was silent when I returned. My sword remained in the earth, and I saw no tracks passing it. Shagay and Ahiam had moved Eliphelet to my tent.

He looked up at me anxiously when I entered. "You will protect me, adoni?" he asked. "I can give everything back! I won't do it again. I just got started this time and couldn't stop, and--"

I halted him with a gesture. "We'll deal with that later. Right now, we must bury our dead."

"Dodi, there is a cave on the hillside that might make a suitable grave," Abishai said.

"All right." I went to the Gibeonites' tents.

Ahinoam came out to meet me.

"Is the body prepared for burial?" I asked.

"Yes, geber."

"Bring it, then. We have found a place."

Gad helped carry the dead man, using his cloak as a stretcher. I could feel Naharai's eyes boring into my back as I followed Abishai down the draw to the cave that he'd found. By the time we got there, every man in camp had followed silently. Abiathar spoke a few words of blessing, commending the name of the dead man to Yahweh's care, and asking for His hesed on us all.

When we returned to camp, the men gathered in front of my tent, looking as if they didn't know what else to do, but really didn't want to do this either.

"Eliphelet," I said.

"Yes, adoni," he replied, dropping down in front of me.

"Bring the things you've stolen to me."

He hurried off, emerging from his tent almost immediately, carrying a carefully wrapped bundle with him. Opening it with shaking fingers, he put it on the ground, backing away to kneel once more.

"Zelek, come take what is yours."

My half-cousin picked through the items, selecting two.

"Zalmon."

The Benjamite took his silver.

"Shammah."

The man from En-Harod got his gold ring and a bracelet.

I called the others, and when I was done, all the items had been claimed.

"Eliphelet, I will have to consider what to do about this," I said. "Your stealing from band members causes trouble, and we don't have time for that. Nor do we have time for much else, either," I added, noting Jonathan's uneasy glances at the sun. "The fifth unit is closing on us, and we must be away from here."

The men remained silent, but I could see the weariness in their eyes. It would mean another all-night march, and they wanted nothing so much as rest.

"However, there will be a difference in the march from now on," I went on. "Starting this afternoon, the ark will go first, and I will follow. If it stops, I stop. If it turns, I turn, and if it continues, so do I.

"Naharai's words this morning brought judgment on me for my failure to allow Yahweh to lead us as He wills, and your lives have been made hard because of this. You were justly angry. I will leave it up to you, then, whether you will depart in peace or remain with me. Shaul's men have blocked us from the water on the uplands. Those of you wishing to depart will find the Arugot gorge about 12 and a half miles east and a little north. It will take you down to the springs of En-gedi. As I said, you may depart in peace, released from your oath, or any enslavement, if you go.

"Those of you choosing to remain must be ready to travel within an hour. I regret that I cannot give you more time to come to a decision. The king's units press on us closely."

Bowing slightly, I went into my tent, collecting my things and beginning to pack them.

"That is my job, adoni," Ahiam said reproachfully.

"My speech applied to you, also. I've made a poor adon to you more than once."

"Yes, but life would have been quite boring, and I'm interested now in your life, so I think I will stay around to see how it ends."

"It might end soon, with a thrust from Shaul's spear."

"He'd try, anyway."

Keeping myself busy helping pack, I deliberately did not watch to see who had decided to leave. I knew Zabad wanted to, for I'd seen him talking to Ahinoam, and his slavery galled on him. Uzzia might, though he'd surprised me once before. Uriah could do very well on his own, and if he left, I hoped some of the others went with him. They'd have a better chance of slipping away from Shaul that way. Yet, while a smaller band would be much easier to lead, I'd been through a lot with these men, and I would be sorry to see any of them go.

When the time came to break camp, they all waited, even Zabad, who looked at Ahinoam in disgust. She kept her face turned away, staring stubbornly straight ahead. Gad again served as an ark bearer with Naharai and his fellow Gibeonites. Abiathar took his place behind the sacred object followed by the two women. I came next, Eliphelet sticking so close that he might have been chained to me.

"Show us the way, Adonai," I whispered.

To everyone's surprise, the ark bearers turned and started back the way we'd already come, headed west, directly into the approaching fifth unit. I followed, determined to go wherever Yahweh might lead me. My first three retainers, my nephews, covenant son, and Jonathan came next, then to my surprise, Igal and Jaas fell in line. Zelek shrugged, loosened his sword, and led his donkey into the column. Zabad threw up his hands, and Elika and Shammah and the rest joined in.

We went silently, ears alert, knowing that somewhere ahead men combed the forest to take our lives. The ark-bearers suddenly turned, following a winding gully with barely room to pass. There was no trail, and we stumbled along in the dry stream bed that dipped deeper into the hillside. The trees closed over us, and the ark bearers halted.

The men bunched together, stirring restlessly.

I held up my hand for silence.

"What do you think?" we heard a voice say.

"What I think doesn't matter. It's what the king thinks!" another replied.

On the hill above us, two scouts tramped through the woods. "It's a waste of time, if you ask me. Look at this place! All Dahveed has to do is scatter his men, and who's to know if they haven't slipped behind us again?"

The men froze, hardly even breathing. Zelek had his hand around his donkey's muzzle.

"Well, that Habiru seems to think he's still in front of us, and cut off from water now. Says the only place left is En-gedi, and three units are waiting there."

"And I don't like that either," the other replied. The two men were directly above us now. "That only left four units back in Gibeah keeping an eye on the Philistines. What if they decide to invade? Think we'll have time to get back?" He stumbled, cursing. "And if we do, we'll be lame from wandering around in this haunt for lions!"

"That's right. You saw one," his companion muttered as they went on past us.

"Saw one! Nearly stepped on it! How was I to know that ledge was a sunning place for them? Didn't smell the beast until too late."

"You yelled loud enough," the other one chuckled.

"It jumped clear over me when I ducked! You'd have yelled, too!"

Their voices faded, and we stayed still until the ark bearers turned around and headed back the way we'd come. The men waited until it passed, then pulled the donkeys around after it. After the gully widened out a little, the ark-bearers again reversed directions, and went back up it. The men looked at me in bewilderment, but I motioned them to follow, and again they urged the donkeys in that direction. This time the ark-bearers walked faster and faster while we struggled to keep up. They swung into a side gully leading toward the north, trees and brush growing so close that they whipped in our faces and nearly snagged the covering from the ark. After we climbed onto the hill the ark turned back east, leading us into a clearing not far away. Once in the open, the men bunched together, facing outward, hands on their swords, ready to fight whoever found us. We heard the voices on our right first.

"Check the gully," Pasach's voice ordered.

Not 500 feet away we heard soldiers clambering down into it. Then came the sounds of another unit on our left, combing the gully that we'd just left.

"Any caves?" Natan asked.

"Not yet," someone answered.

"Keep a close lookout," the commander added. "The king thinks we've got Dahveed pinned in front of us with nowhere to go but the cliffs to the Salt Sea."

"Yes, and when we find him, then what?" the man growled. "You going to be the one to grab the lion's tail, commander?"

"No, I think Abner's planning on doing that," Natan answered grimly.

I caught a glimpse of him as he pushed his way through the trees, staring intently down into the gully, as did everyone else not already down there.

"Something's been by here, commander," a man yelled. "Lots of broken branches on the bushes."

"Be careful, then," Natan warned. "If he tried to get by and found the way blocked, he won't be much further down the ravine. Move on, though. Push him, if we can. Dishon is supposed to be south and east of us."

"As if Commander Dishon is going to lay a hand on him," the man grumbled.

"I didn't ask for your opinion," Natan said coldly.

"Well, my opinion is if Dahveed wants this cursed place, he can have it!" another man just passing said. He stumbled and cursed again.

"Commander! Looks like he's close! Lots of tangled tracks here. He had to turn around and head back east!"

"And may Yahweh save him," Natan said. "Forward, then," he added more loudly.

My men crowded closer, watching in amazement as both units passed us, every man among them staring down into the gullies rather than looking our way. When the ark started up again, the men followed quickly, willing to walk around in circles now if the ark led. We angled toward the west, and soon the road from Carmel to Hebron appeared. The ark bearers nearly ran across it. The men urged the donkeys on, and the animals broke into a trot under their loads, some of them trying to turn down the road when we crossed, and having to be pulled back by brute strength. We'd no more gotten into the shelter of the trees on the other side when the ark stopped, and we froze in place again.

The beat of mule hooves on the road reached my ears.

"Adoni!" a man called from the other side of the road.

The mules stopped.

"What is it?" Abner asked.

"Natan reports he found where Dahveed had to turn back. He was trying to head west again."

"Good," Shaul's voice said with satisfaction. "We have him now, Abner. That Habiru was right. He was just east of us, and we have him boxed in. The only way he can go is east!

"What is the Habiru's name? We must be certain to reward him."

"Hiddai, adoni."

"Some decent clothes and a good sword should satisfy him.

"What do you think, Abner? This close to Carmel, should we pay our respects to Nagid Nabal?"

The hoofbeats of the mules resumed, and we remained still until we could no longer hear them. The ark advanced northwest for nearly two miles, forging straight across the highland to some hills. Tucked into the fold of the hill on the north side was what looked like a small hole.

"Check up there," Gad said, pointing.

Abishai scrambled up, then called down, "It's not small, dodi! It just looks like it from the ground. But there's room for everyone!"

By nightfall we were settled comfortably in the large cave. All the activity to the east had driven game west, and our hunters came back with more than enough. Abiathar offered up a prayer of thanks for our deliverance, and then sacrificed a turtle dove on the rock he set up as an altar, while the men bowed in worship. Once that was done, they grouped around the cloths spread on the floor of the cave, and Ahiam, Keturah, and Ahinoam passed out the food. We all missed having bread, but no one complained, and the men relaxed and enjoyed themselves for the first time in months.

When everyone had finished eating and talk had died down, Abishai brought me the harp. "Play for us, Dodi, the one you just composed."

Startled, I accepted the harp, wondering how he knew what I'd been doing.

Abishai grinned. "You've been humming under your breath and wandering around with your head cocked!" he explained.

I tuned the harp and began the melody, closing my eyes.

"Be gracious to me O God, be gracious to me for in You my soul took refuge. And in the shadow of Your wings I took refuge until destruction passed over.

I will call to God Most High, to God the one who completes things for me.

He will send from heaven and He will save me. He reproaches the ones hounding me. God will send His divine loyalty and His truth.

"My soul is amidst lions. Let me lie down among those who burn. Sons of men whose teeth are a spear and arrows. And their tongue is a sharp sword.

Be high over the heavens, O God, over all the earth is Your glory.

A net they prepare before my footsteps. My soul bows down. They dig before me a pit; they fall into it.

"My heart is steadfast, O God, my heart is steadfast. Let me sing and let me make music.

Awake, my glory! Awake, harp and lyre! I will awake the dawn.

I will praise You among the peoples, my Lord. I will make music among the nations.

For great unto the heavens is Your divine loyalty, and unto clouds is Your truth.

Be high over the heavens, O God, and over all the earth Your glory."[17]

The walls of the cave threw my voice back at me, surrounding us with the sound of praise. As it died away, the men sat, completely silent, for several moments. Then they burst into chaos, shouting and applauding, most of them with tears streaming down their faces.

"It's just as I remembered it," Jonathan said, as he crowded close with the others. "It's still the same!"

I touched as many of the men as I could, knowing that they needed some emotional release. Yahweh's presence permeated the cavern, accepting their cries of rejoicing and wonder.

After the men had bedded down, I went to the alcove where Abiathar had put the ark, kneeling there for some time. For the first time in weeks we slept without fear, with full stomachs, and with hope that we would survive this endless summer.

CHAPTER 38

"Gebirah, Nagid Nabal comes with two strange adons!" Tirzah said excitedly, rushing into the outer room where Abigail was finishing up the accounts with Jotbah and Oholah.

"Quickly, prepare the roof for them," she said, looking around in dismay. She hadn't expected Nabal for another hour. Usually he stayed late the day before Shabbat.

"Jotbah, clear this away. We'll have to finish after Shabbat. Where's Matred?"

"At the loom, Gebirah," the handmaid replied.

"Tell her to start two more cooking fires in case the adons stay for the evening meal."

Namea emerged from the inner room. "Here, put this in your hair," she said, handing Abigail a gold headband before combing back

---

[17] Psalms 57

the Gebirah's dark auburn hair and straightening her robe.

Abigail stepped outside, waiting in the courtyard as Nabal and his guests entered through the gate. She stiffened a moment. Surely that must be King Shaul of Israel dismounting from his mule. What was he doing this far south?

"Shalom, Nagid. Who are our guests?"

"Shaul of Israel and his general, Adon Abner, have come to celebrate Shabbat with us," Nabal said a bit pompously.

"Welcome to you and those with you. May Yahweh bless you."

"Your kind words are most gracious after a tiring day," Shaul replied, a quick smile crossing his face. "I am looking forward to a quiet comfortable rest."

"We will do our best to see that you have it, adoni," she replied, bowing. "Do come up to the roof. The breeze is cooler, and refreshments will be served shortly."

The king turned to the stairs, followed by Abner, who tried not to stare at her. Nabal went up also, his thin voice drifting down as she hurried back into the house.

That night after the guests had bedded down on the rooftop, the nagid came to Abigail.

"They will stay tomorrow and leave the next day. We must have a feast for them tomorrow night. I will show them how I am honored here. We will have it in my business chamber in Carmel. There is room, and the setting is impressive."

"This isn't a state visit, Nagid," Abigail replied slowly. "Shaul specifically said he was looking forward to a quiet rest. Maybe something that formal would not be to his liking."

"He will surely want something more than what we can offer here in Maon! He is nagid, after all, just like me. I must uphold my position and status and serve him appropriately. He will expect to be honored."

"Just the same, Nabal, I do think having something here would be--"

"Gebirah, I would not think of serving Nagid Shaul here! We will go to Carmel for the feast."

Abigail raised her eyebrows at his tone, and he reddened slightly, glancing away. "If that is what you want, Nagid, we shall do so, of course," she said coldly. "I would like to retire now."

As the sun declined the next afternoon, Abigail waited in the courtyard of the compound in Carmel. Having chosen her clothing carefully, she wore a cream-colored robe made from undyed linen with a matching fringed girdle that she had embroidered herself with undyed linen thread. She wore gold earrings, headband, and bracelets. Her dark auburn hair was bound back with a gold brooch in the back. The neutral color of her garments would not clash with anything in the room, and would be a rest from the garishness of the chamber.

Since Shaul and Abner would eat at the large table upstairs with Nabal and herself, she had prepared a table in the courtyard for the four guards accompanying the king. The smells of the roasting meat drifted by, and she kept a small amount of the precious pepper, now finely ground, in the box in her girdle.

She couldn't bring herself to use the clove, sealing the box carefully as Hadar had directed to preserve the flavor until an occasion arose that might be worthy of it.

Shaul rode through the gate, followed by Abner, and then Nabal, looking disgruntled at being last. He hurried into the lower part of the house after dismounting. Abigail wondered what he was doing, but turned to welcome her guests again. She had barely greeted them when Tokhath whispered that the nagid was ready to receive his visitors.

"If you are ready, we can go up," she said with a smile. "The nagid is quite pleased with his chamber here in Carmel, and likes to have visitors see it. It is a rather unusual room."

"I am prepared to admire it, Gebirah," Shaul said, gesturing her to walk by his side up the stairs. "We missed your company today, and I hope to make up for it this evening."

"I will be delighted to entertain you if I can. Do come in," she added at the top of the stairs as a guard there opened the door, bowing politely.

Shaul stepped inside, and as his eyes adjusted to the dimmer light, he paused a moment, looking around. Nabal stood in a king's banqueting robe on the dais, sweat already beginning to cover his face from the hot clothing. Glancing this way and that, taking his time, Shaul crossed the room while Abner followed, struggling to hide his disgust at its ostentatiousness.

Abigail walked beside Shaul, pausing when he did, saying nothing.

"Truly, a most unusual chamber, as you promised, Gebirah," the king said at last. "I can well imagine that it is much talked of."

The Gebirah glanced at the king's face, noticing the wicked gleam dancing in his eyes. She kept her face calm, knowing that her husband would rue the day that he decided to show his chamber to Israel's ruler.

Nabal hadn't moved or spoken from the dais, standing haughtily while Shaul looked everywhere but at him. At last, the king held out his hand to Abigail, and she took it as he handed her to a seat by the low Egyptian-style table. Then he looked around one last time. "Ah, there you are, Nabal! I thought you might have deserted us. Do sit down. This feast smells quite wonderful."

Eyes wide, Abigail struggled to keep from laughing. But as the king seated himself, there was nothing left for Nabal to do but sit down also. He took so long settling himself that Shaul picked up the bread in front of him, tore off a piece, and passed it to Abigail. She accepted it, taking some and passing it to Abner, who cut a large slice with the meat knife at his place and then handed the loaf to Nabal.

Abigail nodded her head at the servers waiting by the door, and food began to arrive from the cooking pit below. The meat had cooled to a comfortable temperature, and the spiced lentils and couscous were warm also. After everyone had their portions, she took the spice box from her girdle and opened it. Taking a pinch of the pepper, she sprinkled it on the food, passing the box to Shaul.

"And what is this specialty?" he asked, following her example.

"It is pepper, adoni. A caravan master was kind enough to send some to us as a sample of his wares. I thought you might enjoy the taste. I've only had it once before in my life, and I've never forgotten it."

Shaul took a bite of the meat, chewing carefully. "I can see why!" he exclaimed. "It has a bite to it, but pleasant, and very flavorful."

Next she passed the box to Abner, who dubiously sprinkled some on his meat only. Nabal took the box, recognizing it as the gift brought to Abigail, and his face reddened. But he tried some. Abigail set it down by the king should he want more, and when he took more lentils, he added a bit of the pepper.

Abner talked very little, his attention on his food. Shaul carried on the conversation with her, turning to Nabal if he said something, but otherwise ignoring her husband. The nagid got angrier and angrier, finding it hard to choke down the food as Shaul focused on Abigail.

The king's conversation was so pleasant that she relaxed and enjoyed herself, refusing to think about the scene she'd have to endure when Nabal vented his spleen. Nevertheless, the Gebirah felt a moment of triumph. The first part of her plan had succeeded. Nabal was so wrapped up in upholding his honor that he failed to realize that he had none in other people's eyes. Obviously Shaul regarded him as a fool and therefore paid no attention to him.

As they left the room in the darkness much later, Abigail sighed with contentment. It had been the most pleasant evening she had had in years. Shaul was an attractive man, and with his charm and wit, she could see why he was honored in the north as king.

In the courtyard her litter waited, and guards brought the mules. During the ride back, she wondered about the rumors that she'd heard about Shaul's erratic behavior. She couldn't reconcile the amusing, considerate guest with the stories of his madness and the execution of the priests of Nob. Having seen no sign of anything like that tonight, she wondered if the rumors hadn't gotten twisted on their way south. As they approached the house in Maon, she pulled the curtains aside, noticing that torches lit the courtyard. Had someone else arrived, she wondered.

Hezro handed her out in time for her to see a man report to General Abner. He looked like a unit commander, and the expression on his face said that his news wasn't good.

She stood quietly as Abner approached Shaul as the king dismounted. "Pasach has reported, adoni," he said in a low voice.

"Good news, I hope," the king said absently.

"No, adoni."

Shaul halted. "No?"

"When the units closed the trap, Dahveed had vanished."

"We had him, Abner!" the king said, his voice deadly. "How could he have slipped away?"

"The men don't know, adoni. Pasach said the units have spent the day combing every inch of the country. The Habiru we hired can trace Dahveed's trail into the trap. He was surrounded by our units; Pasach said he saw that for himself. But when they closed in, he was gone. They are still searching, and Pasach came to report."

Dahveed? The king was here with army units hunting Dahveed Israel? Abigail stood motionless. In all the excitement she had never thought to ask Shaul why he had come south.

"I'll have someone's head for this, Abner," the king said softly, making Abigail shiver. "Bring that lying Habiru to me."

"Yes, adoni."

Abigail saw the hatred and rage on the king's face as he crossed the courtyard and climbed the stairs to the roof. She gripped Hezro's arm tightly. Something about Shaul's look made her believe that he had actually been possessed by a demon and might still be. In fact, she could even believe that this man had indeed ordered the destruction of Yahweh's priests.

¥ ¥ ¥ ¥ ¥ ¥

Sar Ishvi sat on his mule at the west gate, watching the returning units straggle up the road from the highway to Jebus. People welcomed them with cries of greeting, but not much cheering, for even at this distance, he could see the weariness and defeat in the men. His abbi rode as tall as always, but he didn't smile at the people when he nodded at them. Abner looked sour. Ishvi suppressed a smile. Dahveed had escaped again.

Not that he needed this to tell him so. The brass earring had come back to Jonathan over three weeks ago, relieving his older brother's mind so that he could concentrate on the final consolidation of his hold on the kingdom and enjoy his wife's pregnancy.

Another smile played at the sar's lips. He didn't know how Taphath managed Jonathan. He hovered over her like a mother duck with only one duckling. Ishvi was very glad the hassar had been banished to his estate. He'd be no earthly good here in the state he was in. But being within constant call of Taphath allowed him to attend to the administration of the kingdom.

His abbi reached him, and he bowed in greeting, noting how the king checked his hand for the seal ring. What he wore now was a copy of his own personal seal, which looked enough like the king's that no one knew the difference, and his abbi turned the mule to face the road, satisfied. Abner swung his mule around also, and the three of them stayed until the last of the men had passed by.

Ishvi relaxed a trifle. One hurdle down, two more to go.

The next day, Sar Ishvi bowed when his abbi entered the throne room. "Shalom, adoni. You slept well?"

"Yes," Shaul answered. "What is scheduled for today?"

"Mostly court business, adoni. We knew you might want to rest after the trip back, but Eshbaal would like you to approve some of the new procedures that we've tried since you were gone. They have worked well, and we would like to continue them."

"What are they?"

"We have found it easier to listen to cases, petitions, or requisitions in the mornings. They are dealt with in the afternoon and replies given the first thing the next morning. Scribal reports and routine business take place after the noon rest. It is much easier to close court on time that way. Also, more afternoons would be free for you to meet with people as you need to, adoni."

The king's eyes lit up. "That sounds good. Continue to do this. What is next?"

"First is a requisition from Quartermaster Nadab for more carts for the supplies. Since the Philistines didn't raid this year, he's asking that the carts be purchased using treasure that would normally have gone to pay the militia."

As he talked, Ishvi relaxed again. The new procedures allowed all the business of the court to be recorded and sent to Zelah, where Jonathan spent the afternoon attending to it. It was then returned to Gibeah, and Ishvi and Eshbaal reviewed it before retiring for the night. The afternoon reports arrived in Zelah early the next morning, and Jonathan looked them over before noon, sending them back with any questions he might have, which Eshbaal would handle that afternoon. It kept the road between Zelah and Gibeah busy, but Jonathan had been firm about remaining in Zelah until the king, or an emergency, called him back.

They finished in good time, and as the noon rest began, a courier found Ishvi in his house.

"What is it?" he asked, hoping it wouldn't be an emergency and he'd get some rest.

"Cheran says Abner has been summoned this afternoon."

"Very well."

Relieved, he lay down again. He would need to interview the king's personal attendant soon. Cheran couldn't write. It was the only drawback to the situation.

Thus Ishvi wasn't surprised when Abner later came up the stairs to the throne room.

"Shalom, General. Are you here to speak with Abbi?"

"Yes," Abner said, looking around, his eyes sharp.

"The king should be here soon."

"Seems like there's a lot of new faces today," the general said, frowning.

"There are. Hassarah Ahinoam is now maintaining a house outside the fortress, and we had to hire more personal servants. Then some complaints came in from Asher and Zebulun that will take weeks to straighten out, and problems cropped up with trade in Dan that required several more scribes from my group. It's been an annoyance," he added, letting irritation enter his voice. "The new people have to get used to the way things are done here."

A guard opened the door, and King Shaul entered, followed by Cheran, who took his place behind the throne when the king seated himself.

After bowing to him, the two sars moved to Eshbaal's table and began their review of the routine reports. Ishvi listened to the conversation between his abbi and the general with only half an ear, knowing that he'd get a full report later from Cheran.

"I hope you handled that Habiru appropriately," Shaul said in disgust.

"He got away before we could, adoni," Abner confessed uncomfortably.

"He deserved a beating," Shaul snapped. "And why can't anyone tell me how Dahveed escaped?"

The general moved restlessly. "The men weren't very careful with their search," he admitted. "I found one unit literally slashing away at the bushes with their swords, calling Dahveed's name at the top of their lungs! They claimed they thought you wanted him found because he was lost, not because he'd run away and raised a rebellion."

The sars exchanged a quick glance, suppressing their amusement, and bent over the reports again.

Shaul frowned. "I did notice the men seemed to drag their feet. Perhaps we should be more selective whom we take next time."

"I would recommend it, adoni."

"I hadn't realized what the country was like down there," the king added. "It will not be easy to displace Dahveed from it. What people we found were not helpful." He paused. "Some of them were not even respectful," he said, irritated. "I am king after all."

"And they were dealt with, adoni. They will be more respectful the next time," the general said shortly. "Adoni, did you order six units into Benjamin?"

Shaul turned. "Eshbaal, did I order any units anywhere after we left for Ziph?"

"Not that came to my notice," the sar replied. "Sar Malchi would know for certain."

"Send for him."

Ishvi studied the general's face covertly. Abner was noticing a lot, and sooner than Jonathan had expected. He turned back to the reports, calling an under-scribe to remove the stack they had completed.

Before long, Sar Malchi's quick steps rang on the stairs, and he entered the throne room.

"You sent for me, Abbi?" he said, bowing.

"Yes. Did I order any units anywhere after I left for Ziph?"

"Yes. You requested three to be sent to En-gedi. I ordered the twelfth, thirteenth, and fourteenth there as Abner specified."

"What about before that? Any units to Benjamin?" Abner interrupted.

Malchi didn't respond. "Is there anything else, Abbi?"

Abner's face turned a dull red, and the king stroked his chin, his eyes glinting a moment. "Did I order any units into Benjamin?" the king repeated.

"No, Abbi."

"Then why do the quartermaster records show that six units requisitioned equipment and supplies for destinations in Benjamin?" Abner growled.

Sar Malchi kept his eyes on the king, who studied his son, his hand still hiding his mouth.

"Answer him, Malchi."

"The records show that six units went into Benjamin because that's where I ordered them to go."

Abner swallowed and took a deep breath, but Shaul held up his hand. "Why?"

"The last time Dahveed fled, he went north, not south. I thought having some army units barring the way might be helpful in case he decided to try it again."

"A possible happening you didn't think of, Abner," the king commented, stroking his chin once more, that wicked gleam appearing in his eyes. "How long did they remain in place?"

"Until I got your message requesting units in En-gedi, Abbi. I assumed that you had located Dahveed and that he was headed east, not north. I recalled the units, sent the requested ones to you, and put two out on patrol of the Shephelah."

"May I remind you, Sar, that during the war season, the units are mine to command," Abner said.

"They are yours when we are at war, General," Malchi replied, looking at him for the first time. "We are not at war, and I will direct them as I think best."

Sar Eshbaal's hands stilled. That chilling wrath had entered

Malchi's tones, and Ishvi hoped his brother had the self-control to contain his anger at the general.

"Including undermining my authority?" Abner continued, his own voice cold. "I overheard more than one unit commander muttering that he'd never have gone south if you hadn't ordered him to. At what point did my orders not become sufficient?"

Malchi looked shocked. "When a commander comes to me with questions about his orders, did you expect me to tell him to go against them? Of course I said they must be followed! I serve Melek Israel, Abner. And if he wishes the units to go south, they go south!"

"A commendable attitude, Malchi," Shaul observed. "And in light of recent events and your foresight, I believe it would be best for you to have oversight of the army at all times, even during war."

The sar jerked his head up, surprised, as Abner gritted his teeth, standing rigid, his fists clenched. Malchi touched his knee to the floor. "Thank you, Abbi," he replied, his tone a little wooden. "I will do the best I can to serve you. Will there be anything else?"

"No. You may go."

His face an expressionless mask, Malchi left the room.

Later that afternoon as Ishvi accompanied his abbi back from the throne room, he spoke. "Abbi, may I make a suggestion?"

"What is it?"

"It must have been a nuisance to have Eshbaal and me working around while you were trying to confer with Abner today. How about using the upper room of the residence in the afternoons for interviews? It would be more private for you."

The king looked a bit startled. "What about Ahinoam?"

"She has most of her things in the new house just west of the fortress wall. In fact, she suggested the idea to me, and after what happened today, I think she is right. You need someplace private. The residence is still fully staffed, and if you need anything, Cheran is always available."

"I like the idea," Shaul said after a moment's thought. "We will do that."

"I'll tell Eshbaal, then," Ishvi said, leaving his abbi at the passage door. He sighed as he turned away. The last hurdle had just been jumped.

That evening the four sars held their semi-weekly conference. "Everything is in place, Jonathan," Ishvi reported. "The king hasn't questioned the seal ring, the new procedures were approved, and he will use the fortress residence in the afternoons."

"Immi was inspired on that one," Jonathan said in satisfaction. "Now we can work unhindered." He turned to his second brother. "You've been quiet, Malchi."

The sar leaned back against the wall, his face white and eyes closed. "Abbi promoted me today. I'm in charge of the army now all the time because I did such a good job with the units while they were in Ziph. It was all I could do to thank him. Does this ever get any easier, Jonathan?"

"It hasn't yet for me," the hassar said softly. "How did Abner take it?"

"He was furious, and he's already wondering about things, Jonathan. Some of the men were quite open about their feelings about hunting Dahveed, and he overheard certain commanders complaining. He immediately picked up on the six units we sent out, too. If he gets to thinking about their destinations, he'll put some things together."

"He questioned me about all the new faces," Ishvi added. "I didn't think he paid that much attention to the scribes and servants. It caught me by surprise."

"We'll have to let him investigate," Jonathan said. "After all, we knew he'd get suspicious sometime."

"Yes, but not this soon," Malchi commented. "Do we have a firm enough hold to handle him?"

"He's not going to put everything together tomorrow, and we can slow down the flow of information he gets, so we have time yet. So far he's centered mostly on the army, right, Malchi?"

"Yes. Are we willing to forfeit any commanders over this?"

"No. We need all of them. But we can afford to lose men in the units if necessary."

"And he'll probably start with the second unit," Malchi sighed. "That strikes at both Dahveed and me. We've got some good men in that unit in spite of the odd assortment."

"Do the best you can, Malchi," Jonathan replied. "Now, how are Elihu and Tanhum getting along?"

Ishvi chuckled. "They love each other! They've had to work with people who can't keep up with them for so long that now that they've found someone who can, they can't get enough! Elihu passes along all the information coming in and Tanhum runs his organization plans for the trade network past Elihu. There are times when I'd swear we don't rule this kingdom, Jonathan! The scribes do, and those two head the list."

"Good," the hassar smiled. One of his scribes came in with some papyri and left.

"How do you tell them apart?" Malchi asked from curiosity.

"If he never speaks, it's Bunni, unless Bunah doesn't feel the need to talk."

"Which one was that?"

"Probably Bunni. Bunah might have greeted this many of us, but I could be wrong."

"They must be twins."

"Actually they aren't. They're four years apart. But they deliberately do everything alike just to confuse people. It's their one amusement in life." His eyes glinted. "I think I've found a way to tell them apart when they aren't at their scribe's tables, and one day I'll start calling them by name and see how long it takes them to figure out how I do it."

"And how is Taphath," Ishvi asked.

"The short version, please," Malchi hastily added. "I haven't got all night."

"She's fine. The mid-wife came today, and said she's never seen an easier pregnancy."

"Does Abbi know?" Eshbaal inquired.

"Not yet. Taphath plans to visit Immi tomorrow in Gibeah, and she'll break the news then."

No, it wasn't going to take Abner long to discover who now ruled Israel, Jonathan realized as he read the reports from Jaasiel's estate the next day. The king wanted to know more about Dahveed's family, and Abner was asking his people to tap the sources for Dahveed's ancestry for more information. Should he let that request go through? He had long since learned what had happened when he was banished and recognized the wisdom of his brother and Elihu's decision, but feeling used was a new experience for him. That, and Yahweh's giving him a choice, had made him alter his own plans once or twice to avoid using other people against their will.

Well, if his goal was delay, he decided, it would take the longest for Abner to discover that no one in the network had given that information. "Bunah, send a note to Elihu to let Abner ask about Dahveed, but not to insert any of the information he asks for."

"Yes, adoni," the scribe replied, dipping his brush in the ink again.

Jonathan picked up the next message. It was a list of all the scribes that Abner had inquired about in the last two days. He stared at the wall. With the general asking about his communications network already, he'd better be prepared for a visit from the man himself at any time.

For the next two weeks, Jonathan followed Abner's activities through the reports as the general requested information about people and accumulated responses about Dahveed. When the last part of the network reported that none of them had been the source for Dahveed's ancestry, he wasn't surprised when Malchi reported that Abner had taken the tenth unit with him on an "inspection" tour for the king. As expected, the general visited each place where he should have someone collecting information for him.

What was unexpected was that not one of the clans told the general anything about the missing individuals, although they all knew where they were and why. The hassar's hand trembled a little as he set that report down. This alone told eloquently how the people felt about what the king had done, and also the level of support he, himself, had garnered.

Still nothing happened, and when his brothers gathered for the next conference, he questioned them about it.

"He's been quieter than normal," Malchi observed. "But I expected that. He's got a lot on his mind. What was odd was that he apologized just today for what he'd said in the throne room. Even bowed and took my hand. I had to accept it, of course."

Eshbaal had a strange expression on his face.

"What is it?" Jonathan asked.

"Abner apologized to me, too. Yesterday as I was crossing the court, he apologized for not getting out of my way soon enough. Bowed and everything, just like Malchi said."

"That is odd," the hassar mused. He glanced at Ishvi. "Has he said anything to you?"

The sar shook his head. "No, but--well, wait. Not long after he got back from his tour, he stopped me as I was going home to thank me for putting through a requisition he'd sent in. I was in a hurry, and tried to wave it aside, but he insisted on a formal expression. It felt awkward having him bow over my hand."

"What's he doing?" Eshbaal asked. "I've never had Abner bow to me like that in my life."

Jonathan groaned. "He's looking for this," he said, holding up the king's signet. "He knows it's in use, and if Ishvi doesn't have it, who does?"

"That means he's headed your way, brother," Malchi said with a grin.

CHAPTER 39

"Geber! Geber!"

Jonathan jerked his head up from the petition, standing so abruptly that the chair fell over. He stepped out of the door.

"Geber!"

The voice came from the direction of the compound wall.

Nimshi appeared atop it. "He's coming," the youth panted, jumping easily to the ground. "He's got the tenth and eleventh units with him. Sars Malchi and Ishvi are nearly here. Ishvi said to tell you that Abner has not spoken to the king."

"That makes things easier," Jonathan said. "Get my mule ready to go hunting, Nimshi. Bunah, you and your brother will attend Sar Ishvi in the business chamber. Abiezer, get the rest of my guard. Only Abner is to come into the courtyard."

"Yes, adoni," the scribe said.

Jonathan heard the rapid hoof beats of the approaching mules, and walked toward the gate. Ishvi came through first, dismounting immediately.

"Abner's nearly here," he began. "I'd guess he wants to make his accusation publicly."

"He would," Jonathan said sourly. "Malchi, you and I are about to go hunting. Ishvi, you're working in that room with the scribes. You'll need this." He handed the king's seal to his brother.

Sar Ishvi stuffed his own seal into his girdle and slipped on the king's.

"Malchi, my guard will keep the units outside the gate. As soon as you can, get over there and dismiss the units to Gibeah. It might help if you'd be impatiently waiting for me to go."

Nimshi led the readied mule toward the hassar, and Jonathan noted the lad had already fastened on a bow and quiver. "You'd better change, Geber," he said. "Abner won't believe you're hunting in that robe."

Jonathan hurried across the court and up the stairs.

Taphath waited with an old shirt and kilt. "Nimshi told me Abner is coming. What are the two units for?"

"He's hoping to make an arrest," her husband replied, dressing swiftly. "I hope to foil him."

"You will," she said with a smile.

He was heading down the stairs when the units stopped at the compound gate.

"I'm here to see the hassar," Abner announced.

"He's still here," the guard said, opening the gate. As soon as Abner had entered, the guard swung the gate shut again, and the unit commanders, unwilling to be here anyway, shrugged and directed their men back a little.

"What did you wish, Abner?" Jonathan asked, swinging up on his mule. "I'm about to go hunting. Malchi wanted to know where I'm getting the venison you've been enjoying lately."

Abner flushed at the mention of the honor debt he owed, which had grown steadily larger. "I've come for the requisition for the new carts Nadab wanted. I thought I'd save you the trouble of sending it back to Gibeah."

The hassar turned the mule. "Bunah!" he shouted.

The business chamber door opened, and the scribe emerged. "Yes, adoni?"

"Did Ishvi bring a requisition for carts for the army? Abner's here to get it."

Malchi kneed his mule toward the gate. "I've got to get back tonight, Jonathan. Don't take too long."

Jonathan waved his hand at him as the guard opened the gate. Malchi's mule stood half in and half out.

As Bunah paced sedately across the court, Jonathan heard the two units retreating down the road.

"You really didn't need two units just to come for this," he said, taking it from the scribe. "A simple messenger would have been sufficient."

"If that's all I came for, that would be true," Abner said, easing back on his mule. "I happen to know that requisition wasn't sealed when it left Gibeah this morning, and I see it now is. I've also come for the king's seal, Hassar. I do hope the two units won't be necessary."

"I don't see why they would," Jonathan said, puzzled. "Ishvi!" he called.

His brother appeared in the door way. "Yes, Jonathan?"

"Abner says he's come for the king's seal. Did Abbi say anything to you about giving it back to him?"

Ishvi walked forward. "No," he said, keeping his hand in plain sight. "But if he wants it back, I'd better give it personally."

"Let me see that," Abner demanded, pointing at Ishvi's hand.

The sar held up his hand so the general could plainly see the seal.

"You gave it back to him!" the general said, turning on Jonathan. "I know what you're doing, Hassar, and it's treason! Commanders!"

"Those commanders, General?" Malchi drawled from his spot by the gate, indicating the men now quite far down the road.

Abner turned white. "How dare you dismiss them!"

"How dare you question my orders," Malchi said softly, shifting the position of his mule until he faced the general. "This wouldn't be insubordination, would it?" he added, that cold fire in his eyes as he now nudged the animal forward, its head down and legs bunched under him as he came.

"No, Sar," Abner bit out. "My apologies."

"I'll let it pass this time, General, because none of the men witnessed this. Do not count on another chance." The sar's voice was chilly.

"Yes, Sar." Abner backed his mule away.

"Abner?" Jonathan said. "Don't forget the requisition. That is what you came for, isn't it?" He held it out.

Swallowing his rage, the general snatched the papyrus as he went by, the mule racing by the time he left the gate.

"He'll be back," Ishvi said, returning the king's seal, and watching the mule speed down the road toward the general's private estate.

"I know," the hassar said grimly, slipping the signet on his finger again.

It was past dark, and Jonathan had dismissed both scribes, knowing that he would be up a while with the latest pouch from Jaasiel's estate and his thoughts. Abiezer still stood outside, for the hassar reluctantly concluded that he'd better keep a guard with him until the matter with Abner resolved itself. He had the contents of the pouch spread across the table when his body guard opened the door, and Abner stepped in.

Glancing up, Jonathan said, "You've returned, General." He

motioned for Abiezer to remain.

"And this time you haven't been able to get rid of the king's seal," Abner replied. "I had to see if you'd be arrogant enough to let me see it on your hand. Did you really think you could toy with me and make a fool of me? No one takes my honor, Hassar."

The hassar started to say something, but Abner wouldn't let him.

"I found out that you planted the information about Dahveed's ancestry to get yourself dismissed from court so you could come here and plan your coup in peace. No one uses me like that!"

"I didn't, General," Jonathan replied coldly. "I had no idea you'd learned of Dahveed's parentage until you faced me with it before Abbi. It was entirely your choice to do so. And I was thoroughly enraged when I left Gibeah. Only later did the advantages of my banishment come to mind. At that point, I very nearly sent you a gift for what you'd done."

"Don't bother," Abner snarled. "I came back tonight to give you fair warning, since you are a kinsman. If I see that seal ring back on Ishvi's finger by tomorrow morning, I'll say nothing to the king about what you've done. You extended me that courtesy once, as I recall."

"And shall I tell him a half-truth someday to get back into his good graces?" Jonathan retorted. "There's one big difference here, Abner. I have proof for the whole story of my near demise. You have none for your story of treason."

"I mean what I say, Hassar," Abner went on, leaning over the table. "No one takes honor from me and gets away with it."

"Would that be a threat to me, my brothers, or the king?"

"Unlike you, I would never threaten the king, Hassar."

"Since the king has stripped you of honor, and not that long ago, you'd better reconsider that comment."

"Don't condescend to me, Hassar. I take care of myself and my house above all else."

"A most revealing statement, Abner," Jonathan said, wishing that he had worn a sword. He braced himself against the wall, ready to shove the table into the general's mid-section if necessary. All he needed was a moment, for Abiezer was alert, his spear held for a quick strike.

Suddenly still as a stone, Abner didn't answer, his eyes riveted on a papyrus on the table. "This has Jaasiel's seal! What is it doing here?" he demanded, snatching it up.

"All Jaasiel's communications with you come to me first,"

Jonathan replied, his voice neutral.

"Both scribes were gone," Abner muttered, "but everyone said he'd taken them away on business. But if he did that--" His fist crashed on the table. "You dared to touch my son?" he roared, his eyes burning.

"Hassarah Ahinoam did that," the hassar said calmly, getting up. "By the time she was done with him, he came to me quite willingly. He'd learned there were a few things you neglected to tell him, and when he realized where those omissions had led, he offered to do whatever he could to make up for it."

"Jaasiel would never go against my wishes!" Abner thundered.

"That might have been true had you not sided with the king after he turned against Yahweh. If you are trying to preserve your family's honor and status, you should not have backed the king against our God."

"Where is he?" the general growled. "The clan will not condone your taking a clansman's son hostage!"

"They were indeed incensed at hostage taking, especially a young boy like Azmaveth's son. The fact that you forced his abbi to betray me disgusted most of them thoroughly."

Abner's eyes widened, and he pulled back.

Jonathan leaned forward a little. "I can tell you exactly the reception you'll get, Abner. I not only took Jaasiel, I seized every man of Benjamin you hired to feed you information. After I took them, I told the families to come to me about the reasons why I had done so, and they did. But only one clan bothered to redeem their man, the rest deciding instead to let them serve the sentence I passed. The one clan that did, desperately needed his labor, so I allowed him to serve the sentence under the hand of his abbi."

As Jonathan stepped around the table, Abner faced him. "All those clan elders you questioned not long ago were instructed to send you to me if you should ask about the missing men. But I noted with some surprise that *not one* clan gave you any information at all. Neither did the people on your estate, who know full well that I had Jaasiel and the two scribes. Indeed, Abner, your own abbi would have turned you over to me if you had gone to him. Slaughtering Yahweh's priests is not something that is acceptable in this land. You should have remembered that."

Abner's teeth were clenched, and he backed up again. "I suppose Jaasiel will live as long as I say nothing to the king about what you've done."

Jonathan shrugged. "What would you tell him, Abner? That while you took him south on a wild goose chase for Dahveed, his son slipped the kingdom from under his hand? You'd better have proof, General, or he might decide you were trying to destroy his family."

"There is the seal on your finger!" Abner snarled, but he backed up a little more.

"And just this afternoon, before witnesses, you saw it on Sar Ishvi's finger. You'd lose more ground with the king than you already have and look an even bigger fool."

The general's face churned with emotions. For a moment Jonathan feared that the man would sacrifice his son to his pride and love of honor, but at last Abner looked away, forcing himself to touch one knee to the floor. "What am I to do?" he asked, his lips tight.

"Dampen the king's enthusiasm for chasing Dahveed, General."

"And if he commands me to go, then what?"

"If he never gives that command, you do not have a problem."

"You're a hard man, Hassar," Abner said bitterly.

"Only as hard as you have forced me to be. Why do you hate Dahveed so? He's never brought harm to you."

Abner laughed harshly. "Depends on how you look at it, Hassar. I've watched him since he first sang for the king, and I've seen how the people react to him. He would have taken Shaul's place in the people's hearts. And once that happened, he could have seized the kingdom. He's of Judah, Hassar. What place would there be for me and mine under his hand?"

Jonathan stared at him. "Are you so blind, Abner? Dahveed understands your talents and worth! He respects you, and you would have had his gratitude if you served under him! You will bring about the ruin of your house if you go against him or seek to harm him. He is under Yahweh's hand."

"At least until Yahweh tires of him and turns to another," Abner said with a cynical smile. "I can wait." He bowed. "I will do as you say, Hassar, for the love I hold for my son. But do not ever rest easy, for the day will come when I will have my honor back, and everyone will know how you have betrayed your abbi and king."

The hassar stepped back. "You have indeed given me warning, General. I will remember it, and when the time comes, Yahweh will be my advocate."

His face tight, Abner rose and left.

A little later as Jonathan lay beside Taphath, he reached for her hand. "Sahrah?"

"Uhm."

"What do you think of 'Meribbaal?'"[18]

"'My advocate is Adonai?'[19] It's a nice name."

"If we have a son, shall we call him that?"

"Yes, Hassar."

¥ ¥ ¥ ¥ ¥ ¥

Abigail sat in the shade of an awning in Hebron's largest square late in the afternoon of the third day of the New Moon Feast. She'd been unable to convince Nabal to remain in Carmel during the celebration, and now faced the possible ruin of everything that she had worked toward for so long. After the sacrifices and rites at the Hebron high place the first day, Jotbah had stayed in the square through the evening hours keeping track of which adons in the clans gathered the most pledges from the farmers, householders, and townspeople.

With that information in mind, Abigail had sat with Nabal at his place the second day while the adons pledged to nagids. The custom was a farce for her own clans since Nabal had enslaved nearly everyone during the famine, but he insisted that the rite be played out every year. He had received the gifts brought to him, handing out gold jewelry from a small chest on the table in return.

Watching the square now as the nagids gathered, Abigail kept her calm mask in place in spite of the turmoil inside. With the exchange of gifts this evening as the nagids formed alliances, Nabal would realize

---

[18] Meribbaal is the name of Jonathan's son. 'Mephibosheth' came to be associated with Jonathan's son when later scribes altered the name to disparage Shaul's house, incorporating 'bosheth' meaning 'shame' into the name. The exact meaning of Mephibosheth is unclear. Rizpah's son, Mephibosheth, was probably also named Meribbaal, but to avoid confusion, I've kept Mephibosheth for her son since we have no other name given for him.

[19] Please keep in mind that during Jonathan's time, the word "baal" was a generic term for "lord" and could apply to humans or gods. Only later did it come to only mean the god of the Canaanites. However, since our association of the word is so strongly connected to the later meaning, I have substituted "Adonai" to help readers understand the true meaning of the name.

how much honor he'd lost, and if he didn't, Tokhath certainly would. How she would handle her husband then, she didn't know. The fact that he had insisted on coming, and also refused to discuss what gifts he would bring for tonight, meant that he had followed Tokhath's suggestions. Tirzah reported that the scribe was more and more successful in influencing her husband's decisions. It worried her.

Jotbah joined her at the three-legged table to the side of the larger one set up for Nabal's use. "I am ready when you are, Gebirah," the woman said quietly, her keen eyes already taking note of who was present and talking to whom.

"Be sure to record everything," Abigail said unnecessarily. She folded her hands in her lap to keep them still, determined not to let her worry show. Her assessment of the pledging indicated quite a change. Always before, Carmel had held the most powerful alliances, with five or six small groupings clustered around the edges. But Nabal's concentration of personal power and open attacks against Ahlai of Jezreel, among others, had spawned a radical alteration that she expected would create a three-way power struggle between Jezreel, Hebron, and Carmel.

Namea appeared beside her. "Gebirah, Adon Ahlai is now a nagid, already holding pledges from three Jezreelite adons."

"Very good, Namea," Abigail said, smiling to hide the sinking in her heart. Nabal would be furious over this, and unless Ahlai showed great restraint--something never known before--the two would be at each other's throats. And unless Dathan was stronger than she expected, the Hebron clans would be ground to death between Carmel and Jezreel. Nor could she imagine that the Edomites, still jockeying for a decision on a new king, or the Amalekites, would ignore such an obvious opportunity for raiding. She closed her eyes a moment, her head beginning to pound and her stomach knotting.

Dathan appeared at his table across the square, and before he was settled, Nabal arrived with Tokhath, one of the guards setting the same small chest in front of Nabal's chair.

"You are here early, Gebirah," her husband said, wiping the sweat from his brow.

"Yes, the market amused me," she replied, turning her calm face toward him. Nabal wore another of the banqueting robes, this one an odd-looking yellow, more ill-fitting than the green one worn yesterday. The heavy wool material bunched up everywhere as he sat, and the sleeves nearly hid his hands. He wore a gold headband, gold earrings, and several finger rings that caught on the inside of the sleeves every time they slid down over his hands.

Tokhath served a cup of wine, placing another by her own hand. She sipped it briefly. Plain wine. She wondered what Nabal was drinking. Would it be better to have him belligerent or grandiose tonight?

Since Hebron was hosting the celebration, Dathan began the exchange of honor gifts, five or six of his adons carrying them to various nagids and gebirahs. Soon the place was filled with adons coming and going and Abigail caught sight of Ahlai, sitting at a small table with a scribe accepting honor gifts, and one adon carrying reciprocal gifts around the square.

Nabal nearly choked on his third cup of wine when he noticed his rival. "How dare Ahlai be here!" her husband hissed, turning to Tokhath.

The scribe bowed. "Ahlai of Jezreel holds three pledges by clan adons given yesterday, Nagid. His rank has therefore advanced."

"He is nagid now?" Nabal's voice rose.

Abigail turned quickly to silence him, her eye catching an adon beyond him handing a gift to a nagid, not the scribe. An alliance, not an honor gift!

"He should not have such honor--" her husband was sputtering, his face growing red.

Torn, she hesitated an instant.

"--after the way he acts and the debts we hold, I should--"

Biting her lip, she turned swiftly to Jotbah. "Alliances have begun to form."

Several adons were walking toward Nabal's table as Tokhath tried to distract him with more wine, and Abigail kept her eyes on the square, speaking name after name to Jotbah who wrote as swiftly as she could.

"Nagid, please, refresh yourself," Tokhath's voice rose slightly, and Abigail saw the vial disappear in his girdle as he handed her husband another cup. She gave two more names to Jotbah and someone knelt in front of Nabal.

"Nagid Nabal, Dathan of Hebron humbly requests that you accept this small gift from him," the adon said, holding up a silver serving dish.

"Your nagid is indeed generous," Tokhath said while Nabal leaned back in the three-legged chair, sipping the wine.

"Accept these in return," Nabal said shortly as Tokhath took the dish, recording it on the papyrus. Staring icily at the kneeling man and hitching the sleeve of his robe out of his way again, Nabal put two mis-matched gold earrings on the table.

Abigail felt a wave of disbelief wash over her. Nabal was handing out the same gifts to the nagids as he had to his enslaved adons yesterday? Was he *trying* to lose every alliance Carmel had?

But the adon picked up the earrings respectfully, bowing twice, voicing his gratitude while backing away.

Then the adon assisting Ahlai stepped up, also kneeling in front of the table with a small sandalwood box of myrrh.

Silently Nabal threw a small pendant without a chain on the table, ignoring the adon's profuse but humble thanks as Tokhath accepted the box and recorded it.

More adons gathered around, forcing Abigail to lean to the side, trying to see the rest of the square. It was more important now than ever to know how the alliances shifted, for if Carmel lost allies, she must know who collected them, and she feared that it would be Jezreel.

Then an adon from Dathan blocked her view. "Gebirah, please accept this gift from Dathan," the man said, handing a spice box to Jotbah.

Before Abigail could speak, the man moved away, to be replaced by one of the two Maon nagids. "Gebirah, please accept this small gift," he said, handing her a little silver ring.

"You honor me more than I deserve," she managed to say, knowing how much the person had sacrificed to get this gift.

"Gebirah." An adon from Debir approached. "Please accept this token from my nagid," and he handed her a gold bracelet, stepping aside into the crowd before she could reply.

A quick glance at Nabal's table showed her husband's eyes gleaming as man after man knelt, presenting gifts while he parceled out the jewelry from the chest. Tokhath was barely able to accept and record gifts fast enough. Then someone else demanded her attention, an adon from the Carmel clans this time, with a gift of scented anointing oil. The other nagid from Maon came, followed by an adon from the outskirts of Carmel, then someone from near the hill of Hachilah. By the time the crowd thinned, it was too late to learn anything more of the alliances.

The next day, shielded from the mid-morning sun by an awning,

Abigail waited anxiously for Jotbah to bring the records for her to review. "How much of the pledging did we catch?" she asked the scribe when she arrived.

"Less than half, Gebirah. There were simply too many people around us."

Abigail pressed her hands against her temples, rubbing them a little. She was tired from the late feast, and her headache hadn't gone away during the night. "Were you able to see how many allied with Nabal?"

"No. But Namea watched for us. No one did."

"Not one?" Abigail echoed faintly.

"I questioned her closely, Gebirah, and she insists that the nagid was never handed a gift. They all went to Tokhath. And the Carmel and Maon nagids never came at all."

Trying to assimilate the magnitude of the disaster, Abigail could only stare at her handmaid. "They had to have!" she finally said breathlessly. "Nabal owns them! They can't go anywhere else. I remember them there!"

Jotbah checked her records. "It appears they did come to *you*, Gebirah, but not to Nabal."

To her? Why? Think, Abigail, she said to herself. Be calm and consider what this means. "There were so many crowded around," she said slowly. "Did you record who else came to me?"

"I got most of them," Jotbah replied. She read the list aloud.

Abigail inhaled shakily. All but two of the Carmel nagids had sent adons to her. The two who hadn't were not enslaved, and she hoped that they had both allied with Hebron. In addition, many of the nagids who normally allied with Carmel had sent adons also, and the gifts had been given to her. Did she *personally* hold the alliances now, sidestepping the nagid and his vanity?

"Jotbah, I think we need to consult with Dathan," she decided.

They waited only a short time in Nagid Hebron's courtyard.

"Shalom, Gebirah. How may I serve you?" the nagid asked as he emerged from the house.

"Shalom, Dathan. I need to discuss something with you that I'm not certain I understand."

"Then come to the arbor where we can sit out of the sun," the man said, leading the way.

Once settled and supplied with wine and some fruit, Abigail presented her situation. "I have come because this must have been agreed on beforehand," she finished. "I do not want to misinterpret what was done."

"Yes, this was discussed among the clans, and the nagids felt that allying with you personally was an acceptable solution."

"I am undeserving of such honor as you and the others have granted me."

The Hebron nagid smiled. "Last year, many would have agreed. Then we realized you were stripping your own house of honor in order to control the excesses of Nabal. And we have learned from the nagid's behavior that much of the security of the clans rests with you, for Carmel is the central point around which the clans circle. Without that, we will fragment and lose our strength. With the Amalekites growing bold again, we must press together, not pull apart."

"I will do my best to be worthy of the trust you have placed in me."

"I know, Gebirah. Do you have a list of all who came to you? I can supply one if you need it."

"It would be welcome, for I was unprepared for this, and I do not wish to slight someone."

Dathan sent for a papyrus, and Jotbah took it gratefully.

As they hurried back down the street, Abigail knew that she would have to take some of the treasure from the Carmel treasure room in order to reciprocate the gifts and pledges she had received. But she had no idea how she could gain access to the treasury there.

She also didn't know what to expect from Tokhath anymore. Obviously he hadn't told Nabal about Ahlai's change in rank. Did that mean he would say nothing of the lost alliances? Her husband hadn't noticed. If he had, he'd be raging about them right now.

They had almost reached the gate of the house when she stopped short, Jotbah almost bumping into her.

"What--"

Abigail silenced her scribe with a gesture, watching Parai walk swiftly from the house and disappear into a nearby alley. Something about the way he moved told her that he did not intend to return. By the time she got to the gate, she had decided what to do. "Hezro," she called.

"Yes, Gebirah?"

"I am returning to Maon immediately. Leave a couple guards to escort the nagid when he wakens, but I depart within the hour. And Hezro, put that litter on a donkey to take it home. It's too hot to use today--or any day. And if you should find anything belonging to that litter missing, we don't have time to concern ourselves about it now."

The commander of Nabal's guard studied her a moment. "As you wish, Gebirah," he agreed slowly.

As they left the city gates not long after, Abigail glanced back briefly. "May Yahweh go with you, Parai," she whispered.

CHAPTER 40

"Convince her yet?" I asked as Josheb walked by the entrance to my tent from another conversation with Keturah.

He grinned a little. "No, but I'm a lot closer to it."

I chuckled, and he sat down beside me. We were on a hillside in the midst of Horesh, the dark, wild forest covering 25 square miles southwest of the cave where the ark had first led us, and north of the towns of Debir and Eshtemoa. I had no idea how long we'd stay here, or what we would do to make a living, but with the ark truly leading us now, we all felt more confident of survival.

The encampment was neat and orderly, and the men had done much to make it into a stronghold in spite of the early rains that interrupted our work. I'd built an altar on the top of the hill with my own hands. There we met every morning and on the evening of the sixth day. Shabbat we rested.

We trained every day, even Gad and Abiathar, Uriah's teaching of the shalishim growing more advanced as we worked. Only Eliphelet failed to improve, puzzling the Hittite. As fast as the thief's hands were, he should be one of my best warriors instead of my worst. While he worked hard, he didn't seem to respond at the level Uriah knew was there. Naharai fit right in since he'd trained with me in the second unit, and Ishmaiah, one of his fellow ark-bearers, would soon catch up to his skill level. The other Gibeonite would probably never be more than adequate with weapons.

We kept scouts out, for we weren't the only band of Habiru in the area, and several of my men were gone, mostly to Eshtemoa where we were unknown. They had hired out to work in the fields, but our income was still below our needs. I could feel the pouch of ingots that Nahash had given me and that I kept in my girdle always rubbing against my back, but I didn't want to use any of them except for a real emergency.

"How's the cistern coming?" Josheb asked.

"Shagay said it'll be ready in another day or two. It's small, but it should supply us with water for two weeks if we're careful. Gareb and Ira started a garden terrace. I just wish I were sure we would be here to use it. Fresh vegetables would be nice."

All of us had discovered that a constant diet of meat palled quickly. I dearly wished for Immi's lentil stew, and some melons and dried apples. Thinking of her cooking made my mind wander to the recent news from Bethlehem. Eliab was a good steward. The fields were all planted and the vineyards pruned and ready for another year of grapes. Lahab had sold much of his latest pressing to the court in Gibeah again, and sent the rest to Jericho for sale to the caravans. The olive harvest had been indifferent, providing enough oil for Eliab to store, but not much to sell.

Josheb sighed. "Ahinoam looks nice today," he said, watching her leave the tent where she had been helping Keturah sort and dry the herbs they'd gathered.

I nodded absently.

My bodyguard cocked his head at me. "Don't you notice her?"

"She's pretty."

"Are you going to find a husband for her?" he asked right out.

Startled, I glanced at him.

"She's yours, adoni. It's your responsibility to tend to that, you know."

"Does she want one?"

Josheb turned away. "According to Keturah, she does," he said in a strange voice. "You could have her."

I shifted uneasily. Yes, I supposed I could. But somehow the thought of having a woman who *had* to come to me wasn't that inviting. Maybe I'd been spoiled by Michal--I didn't know.

"That look on your face says no," Josheb broke into my thoughts. "Do you mind if I ask why?"

I shrugged. "If I took her, I'd always wonder if she really desired to come to me, and I guess after Abbi and Immi, and then Michal, I don't want to have that on my mind."

He turned to me. "You do see things differently," he said slowly. "I'd never have looked at it that way."

Just then Eliphelet hurried past, followed by Zalmon, and I got up to see what had happened now.

"Eliphelet!"

"Adoni," he said nervously, his hands twitching.

"Give it back."

Reaching into his robe, he pulled out an earring. "I wouldn't have kept it, adoni. I swear."

I handed the earring back to Zalmon, who grunted in disgust as he walked away. Eliphelet gave me a sick smile, wondering if I'd beat him again. I had twice already, and he always promised that he'd stop, but he never did. However, he always readily gave up anything he'd taken.

I frowned at the thought. The man didn't seem to steal to acquire things, he seemed to steal just to be doing it, or because he could, or something like that. Maybe that could be dealt with. Pulling my belt knife, I cut off about eight inches of his girdle. Eyeing the knife, he tried to pull away a little. I handed the cloth to him, and then gripping his free hand by the wrist, held it up in front of me.

He paled.

"I need your blood oath on something," I said, holding the edge of my knife against one of his fingers.

With a scream he jerked his hand and beat at me with the cloth. Josheb instantly leapt up, grabbing Eliphelet's arm, twisting it behind him, and forcing him to his knees. The commotion brought every man in camp charging over, most with weapons in hand.

Too startled to do anything else, I hung on grimly while Eliphelet twisted and yelled, throwing himself around while locked in our grip, words of some foreign language pouring from his mouth. When he finally stopped, exhausted, I said calmly. "Care to tell me what this is all about, Eliphelet?"

"Don't do it, adoni," he pleaded, eyes shut. "Let me live!"

"People do not normally die from giving a blood oath," I said drily.

"Please, adoni, no! I can't stand it!"

"Can't stand what?"

He gulped. "B-blood. Don't make me, adoni, please!"

Nonplussed, I paused. Well, this might explain his deficiencies as a warrior, but it also might provide the way to break his habit of theft.

"Open your eyes, Eliphelet."

"No, I don't want to see," he moaned.

"Does your hand tell you there's anything to see?"

His eyes cracked, then opened.

"It would seem that taking your blood oath will help you remember not to steal from your companions. Press your finger into the blade."

He jerked away, but Josheb tightened his hold. "He'll break my arm," Eliphelet groaned.

"Then press your finger into the blade. You'll have to watch or you might really cut yourself."

The men watched tensely, wondering what I was doing.

Trembling, the thief managed to force his finger tighter. I tipped the knife a fraction, and the point pierced his skin, a drop of blood welling up. His eyes got huge, and sweat stood out on his face.

"Cover it with the cloth," I ordered, taking the knife away.

Josheb let go so that he could obey.

"Squeeze it tight," I added, without letting go of his wrist. "Take it off," I directed after a moment or two.

Eliphelet did. There was a little smear on his finger, but that was all. He stared at the small red patch on the fabric. "It stopped," he said, stunned. "It didn't keep bleeding."

"What made you think it would?"

He shut his eyes again. "I saw someone die once," he whispered. "I was small. There was a sword."

"It must have been a severe wound, then. Now, that's your blood on the cloth, and it's there to remind you of what you are going to swear."

"Yes, adoni," he said, eyes fixed on his finger again.

"This cloth will be outside my tent all the time. Anything you steal, you can keep overnight, but the next morning you will put it on the cloth."

"I swear," he said, hurriedly.

"Good, because if you don't, we will keep adding blood to this cloth."

"You won't need to," he assured me in a shaky voice.

I let go and pointed where I wanted him to spread the cloth, then looked at those gathered silently around. "From now on, anything that Eliphelet steals is lost to you until the next morning, when you can come here and get it." I grinned. "I'm going to be interested to see who has to come the most often."

The men withdrew, looking thoughtful. Eliphelet escaped to his tent, stumbling a couple times because he kept examining his finger.

The crisp, chill air of early morning stung my nose and toes as I emerged from the tent. Winter was here, and it was cold enough that we'd likely have a little snow before long. I expected Shagay and his Jonathan to return today. Shagay's wife, Puah, had decided that she preferred to live in an encampment with her husband and son in Horesh rather than without them in Bethlehem. Unable to blame her, I could hardly refuse to have her come. Besides, she would be company for Keturah and Ahinoam, and could teach them many things about living in the forests, to say nothing of the rest of us, I thought wryly, looking around at the odd ways the men had invented to take care of their things.

My men in Eshtemoa had found a job guarding flocks from predators, whether animal or human, and when Elhanan had come to tell us of this, Asahel and Ittai had gone back with him to work at delivering messages. Those that remained here had continued to train with Uriah, and had started a second cistern and completed more small terraces that Ira and Gareb planned to use for garden crops.

Silently I walked through the trees, making my rounds of the sentries. All four challenged me before I could approach them, and I was pleased. Other Habiru had raided twice in the past month, and while neither attack had been successful, the experience had sharpened the men's awareness of the forest around them and kept the sentries alert while on watch.

When I returned, Ahinoam was lighting the cooking fire in front of the Gibeonites' tents. Since Josheb had spoken to me about finding her a husband, I'd been unable to get her off my mind. She was pretty, and it seemed every time I looked up, she was somewhere about.

Ahiam had our fire started, and as I sat down by it, I glanced at Eliphelet's cloth. There were two more stains on it, along with a pair of earrings and a bracelet. I'd not seen the bracelet before, but the earrings looked like some that Josheb had had. If our personal thief had finally managed to steal something from my third retainer, the whole camp would get a chuckle. So far, Elika and Uzzia had retrieved their belongings the most often.

Late in the afternoon, we welcomed Puah to the camp, and, to my surprise, Zabad returned also. He had been in Eshtemoa. "I would have a word with you after the meal, geber," he requested after we exchanged greetings.

"All right," I said, wondering what he would have to say.

Later, both he and Ahinoam came to the fire, carefully dressed.

"Shalom, Zabad, Ahinoam. Please be seated," I said formally.

They sat down, and Ahiam offered them some bread. After we

had eaten a little, I asked, "What did you wish to speak with me about?"

"As you know, my sister and I are both your slaves," Zabad began. "My abbi gave me to you, and then you purchased Ahinoam in Hebron."

I nodded.

"You spoke once of this, telling me that one gold piece for each of us would buy our freedom."

"I did. And that is still true."

"Then we would like to buy ourselves, geber."

"You have the purchase price?"

"Yes, geber."

"Then a bargain can be completed, and you will both be free."

"Thank you, geber," Zabad replied. Both he and Ahinoam knelt. "You have said that two gold pieces is our price. I give you now this amount," he said, bowing as he placed two gold earrings on the ground in front of me.

I picked them up. "I have received your payment, and you are no longer my slaves. May Yahweh go with you as you go out from here in peace," I responded.

"And may Yahweh bless you for your kindness and generosity to us," Zabad answered. He and his sister stood and bowed again.

As I tucked the jewelry into my girdle, I glanced up at Zabad. "If I may ask, where did you get the gold?"

"From our Immi's dowry."

"But Abbi took that!" Ahinoam exclaimed, turning to her brother.

"No, Lael took it originally," Zabad explained, speaking of their younger half-brother. "He used it as surety for his debts. Abbi couldn't actually bring himself to rob us of it, so he simply continued the practice of using it as surety. When I heard the debts were paid up again, I visited Jezreel. Lael had the marriage contract and list of the dowry, and I made sure every piece was there before I left with it."

"Be sure and tell Gad of this for his chronicle," I reminded them, nodding my dismissal.

"Yes, Dahveed."

Ahiam emerged from our tent as the two left.

"What do you bet Zabad will be gone by morning?" I asked.

"He won't go, adoni. His sister is content right here."

"At least she's one thing off my mind," I said with satisfaction. "Finding a husband for Ahinoam is now Zabad's worry, not mine!"

"Yes, adoni," Ahiam responded with an expressionless face.

¥ ¥ ¥ ¥ ¥ ¥

"You're certain that's all we have left?" Gebirah Abigail asked.

"Yes," Oholah replied. "Everything else we must keep reserved for our needs in the spring."

"Jotbah?"

"We drained the Maon treasury to nothing for reciprocal alliance gifts, and even then we had to send out some of the gifts given to you. We do not have enough to pay for cloth and leather."

With a sigh Abigail closed her eyes and lifted her face toward the weak winter sunlight. What could she do? Since the entire town of Maon belonged to her, she was responsible for clothing the entire town, and the wealth she needed was locked in Nabal's treasury in Carmel.

The clip-clop of a mule on the road made her look down from the balcony of the house in surprise. Her husband rode in, followed by Tokhath, a bound man, and three guards. A couple children peeked in at the gate, all of them ready to run at the slightest hint that the nagid noticed them.

Nabal slid off the mule, waiting while a guard brought the captive. "Did you really think you could run away from me?" he said angrily to the kneeling man.

Run away? "No, Yahweh, not Parai!" Abigail whispered, hurrying to the stairs.

She was too far away to hear what the man replied before he spit.

The nagid erupted in fury. "You dare to show such disrespect to my very face?" he shouted, kicking the man in front of him.

Tokhath said something and even put a restraining hand on the nagid's arm, but Nabal shook him off, turning to the prisoner again.

"You dog! Before I am through with you, you will cower before my face and howl every time I look at you! I am nagid, and no one shall flout my commands or my wishes!" He swung his fist at the man's face, his rings leaving slashes across the skin.

"You are nothing! Do you hear?" he yelled, his voice rising to a near scream. "The spawn of bitches, seed of a wanton woman and conceived during her flow, do you raise your eyes to my honor?"

The names that her husband then used made the blood drain from Abigail's face and even the guards turned white. She gasped for air, telling herself that she dared not leave now no matter what, for the man held there was indeed Parai! She refused to think of how he'd been caught. Somehow she had to get him away before her husband killed him, but she had no idea what to do. Stopping beside the tanner, she stared at her husband, desperately trying to think of something to say.

Tokhath edged away, turning an expression of helplessness toward her, and the guards backed up a little. Nabal glanced at her, his fist raised to slash across Parai's face again, curses still pouring from his mouth at full volume, spittle flying through the air. For an instant he hesitated, and, not knowing what else to do, Abigail raised her chin and deliberately stared straight into the nagid's eyes, the smell of wine on his breath advertising the reason for his explosive belligerence.

His words once again stumbled, losing their shrill quality as they lost volume until they gradually died away into nothingness. Under her unrelenting gaze, he flushed, averted his face, and tried to wipe off his mouth.

"Nagid, will you speak with me in your business chamber?" she asked icily, starting for the room without waiting to see if he followed. Hezro fell in behind her, and she clenched her fists to keep her arms from shaking as she stalked toward the door. Once inside, she faced it, suddenly furious.

Her husband entered the room. "And shall I not demand respect in my own house?" he began defensively.

Once again, the Gebirah stared him into silence. "May I remind you, Nagid, that Parai belongs to me. *I* will take any disciplinary measures necessary to see that he properly respects you. As for you, if you ever come into my presence again in such a passion, shouting such things in my hearing, you will never see my face thereafter!"

Nabal paled. "Gebirah!" he gasped.

"Hezro!" Abigail called sharply. "Send Tokhath here."

"Yes, Gebirah."

In moments the scribe hesitantly joined them.

"Tokhath, the nagid requires refreshment. Mix some wine for him immediately."

Bowing hastily, the man hurriedly obeyed, passing the cup to Nabal with a barely steady hand.

Once she was certain Nabal would stay in the business chamber, emptying another cup of wine, Abigail went outside and found Hezro. "Commander, take Parai out of this compound and lose him someplace where the nagid will *never* find him again!"

"As you wish, Gebirah."

The commander of the guard didn't return for three days, and during that time, Abigail refused to see her husband. On the fourth day, the nagid sent a messenger to her with an expensive ring, asking if he might speak with her.

After dressing carefully, Abigail entered the business chamber. "You wished to see me, Nagid?" she asked coolly.

Nabal bowed. "Yes, Gebirah. You are gracious to come to me. I regret that I have greatly offended your honor, and I wish to know how I may recompense you for this. I will do whatever you require. I would have brought something for you from Carmel today, but I did not know what would please you most. Please tell me."

Thinking quickly, Abigail nodded slightly. "I would have to see what you have to offer," she heard herself say.

"You may have anything you wish," he said eagerly. "The treasure room will be open to you!"

Giving him a slight smile, she nodded once more. "Your sensitivity to my honor does you credit, Nagid. I will come tomorrow morning if that will be convenient."

"I shall welcome you at any time, of course," he replied, offering her his arm.

With another smile, she took it, and they went to the house.

The next day, Jotbah and Namea accompanied her to Carmel. Graciously telling Nabal that he need not stay with her since he had someone waiting to see him, she spent hours in the room, giving Jotbah a chance to take a comprehensive inventory. Finally she chose some things after the noon rest, and when she departed for Maon, Namea carried a duplicate key to the treasury door that Abigail had had made while she was there. She made certain Nabal knew how pleased she was with what she had taken from the room, wearing the gaudy jewelry as often as possible when he was around.

¥ ¥ ¥ ¥ ¥ ¥

It was past midnight when the most blood-curdling yell I'd ever heard filled the air, and I found myself standing outside my tent, sword in hand and heart pounding before the echoes had faded. Complete silence reigned for barely a moment before a battle cry erupted from the same place as the yell, and something hurled itself out of a tent to my left, landing on the ground.

"Torches!" I shouted, running forward, dodging the men boiling from the rest of the tents.

"Stay back, or I'll kill him!" a stranger's voice yelled as the figures on the ground stilled.

"Igal, are you all right?" Jaas shouted.

"I said stay back!" the stranger warned as a torch flared.

The men hesitated in the dim light. I stopped by Jaas. "What happened?" I asked the trembling man.

"A nightmare of that horrible coming--like before, and I couldn't run fast enough, so I woke up, and it was *real*, and I must have yelled, and then Igal--he jumped over me yelling too--and--and they were outside the tent! He didn't even *know*, he just jumped on it, and--"

His teeth were chattering so, I wasn't certain I understood everything he told me. What was clear was that an unwelcome visitor had been in his tent and now held one of my men.

Ahiam arrived with a brighter torch, and I surveyed the scene. A husky stranger sat astride Igal, one knee pinning my man's arm, a hand grasping the other wrist, the other holding a knife against his throat.

"I'm fine, Jaas," Igal said, "but if you would just tell me next time you, Jaas--"

The moment Igal said his name the second time, Jaas suddenly stepped forward, and the stranger's head shot up. In that instant, Igal twisted his arm out of the stranger's hold, grabbing the hand with the knife and squirming, throwing the stranger off balance and precipitating a wrestling match that was all in Igal's favor.

They rolled by Eliphelet, who'd been watching intently, and the next thing I knew, Eliphelet had the knife, and Igal twisted and slipped his way free, rolling away, leaving the stranger lying face up, staring at the point of Shagay's sword just inches from him.

I walked over. "What did you want?"

"Food," he said sullenly.

"Ahinoam, give him some bread."

Shagay backed off, and our unwanted guest climbed to his feet, a bit dazed. Silently, Ahinoam brought a loaf of bread and some raisins, handing them to him.

He seemed to wake up when he saw her. "Ahinoam bat Ahlai," he gasped, jerking his head up. His voice trailed off as he stared around, making me suddenly conscious that we were standing out in the cold in our loincloths, every scar on my own body clearly exposed.

"Dahveed Israel!" he gasped, eyes fastened on me now.

I nearly cursed. I didn't dare send him out of here now unless I wanted to move again. But before I could say anything, he took the decision from me.

"Let me stay with you, adoni!"

I clenched my teeth. I did not want another man! "What is your clan and how are you called?" I finally demanded in disgust.

"My clan is of Hebron, and I'm called Parai."

I pointed to the ground by a fire. "Sleep there. I'll make a final decision in the morning." Then I turned my attention to the sentries who had somehow missed a man entering our camp! It seemed proper to let Jaas and Igal set the punishment for them, and Gareb and Zalmon had their weapons confiscated for three days, and then would have to redeem them.

Since I could do little else, I allowed Parai to remain. But I didn't tell him that he could stay until I finally got the truth from him. I wasn't happy about sheltering a runaway slave of the Gebirah's, but I knew if we returned him, Nabal might very well kill the man.

When the men discovered that Parai knew tanning, they brought him more skins than he could handle. I insisted that they pay for his work and told Parai that I expected him to save enough to buy his freedom from the Gebirah. Also I stipulated that any tools or supplies he used must be instantly portable, since we might have to leave at any time. He had to try several ways of making frames to stretch the larger deer skins, for instance, before he found one that would do the job and still be transportable.

As with everyone else, part of what he earned went to me for the common treasure. I was careful to keep this wealth separate from my personal gains, which were quite small since I now spent most of my time as leader.

The tanner also proved handy with weapons and was remarkably fearless. Uriah welcomed him with open arms, and spent much extra time catching him up to the level the rest of the men had attained.

As winter progressed, I spent some of the band's treasure on warmer clothing for us. We also had to restock our supply of olive oil and salt. Not much remained when I had done that. Puah had quickly made friends with Keturah and Ahinoam, and with three women here now, it began to look more like a Habiru camp than a military one.

Hanan checked in every day or so, informing me that Shaul's agents were still looking for us, but so far had been unable to find a trace. Every day at the morning sacrifice, I silently prayed that Yahweh would somehow send us plenty of warning if we were discovered.

Then one morning, Josheb waited for me when I emerged from my tent. He was kneeling on a blanket and when I appeared, he touched his forehead to the ground.

"What is it, Josheb?"

"I would make a request of you, adoni," he replied, placing two silver earrings on the blanket for me.

I sat down, picking them up. "What is your request?"

"I would like permission to marry," he said with a smile.

"You finally convinced her!" I exclaimed.

His smile grew, and his eyes twinkled. "Yes, adoni."

"And her brother, Naharai?"

"He agreed also."

"Of course you have my permission! And may Yahweh bless you with His richest blessings."

"Thank you, adoni."

"When do you plan on marrying?"

"In two weeks."

"That's not much time for her to get ready."

My retainer smiled again. "I'm not willing to wait any longer, and neither is she!"

I laughed. "In two weeks then."

The camp buzzed with activity while everyone prepared as well as we could for the wedding. Keturah and Puah consulted often, and Ahinoam looked thoughtful, speaking with Zabad about something nearly every day.

I found it harder and harder to keep her out of my thoughts, and the atmosphere before a wedding only intensified it. At last, I decided I needed to get away, and I took Hanan with me on a trip to Eshtemoa to see how things were going with the men there.

Elhanan assured me that things were fine, and handed me the band's portion of the earnings. It was more than I'd spent on the supplies and clothes, so I purchased a little bit of perfume for Keturah for her wedding night. Josheb appreciated things like that, and I suspected Keturah would also.

It was late when I got back, and after checking that everything was right in the camp, I sleepily undressed in my tent and eased into my warm bed. *Warm?* My eyes opened wide, and I tried to sit up, but an arm slipped over my chest.

"It's too late now," Ahinoam said.

"Uh, what are you doing here?" I asked inanely.

"Well, since nothing else seemed to work, I consulted with Ahiam and Shagay, and they all said that in some ways you are just like your great-grandfather, and should therefore be treated like him. It was very nice of you to leave today so I could slip in here while you were gone."

Her fingers were playing on my chest, and I somehow couldn't get angry as I knew I should.

"What does your brother think about this?" I heard myself ask.

"I believe he's waiting outside the tent to see if you come out or not."

"And if I do go out?"

"He'll demand recompense for my honor." She moved closer, and I couldn't help turning my head toward her.

"Well, I guess I'll have to carry on family tradition," I capitulated, reaching toward her in the dark. "Ahinoam, will you be my wife?"

"It took you too long to ask," she said.

We celebrated both weddings on the same day, but Josheb, Keturah, Ahinoam, and I had very little time to enjoy our marriages. Three days after the wedding, Hanan ran into camp bringing the twisted earring and the news that the king's men had arrived in Horesh.

"We must leave, then," I said, turning to Shagay's son. "Jonathan, go to Eshtemoa, tell Elhanan what has happened and that they should remain there working as long as they can. Stay and act as scout for him. You should be able to trail us if you have to bring the others to me. I have no idea where the ark will lead us next."

"Yes, adoni," he said, and hurried away.

"Shagay, bring the men."

When everyone had gathered, I told them of the warning. "We are leaving as soon as we are packed," I added. "Abiathar, we will be following the ark. Uzzia, you and Azmaveth cover the cisterns tightly. That water may come in handy some day. Zalmon, bring the donkeys here."

Everyone scattered, and I had time to get the harp in its case and put on my cuirass before the inevitable questions began. When tents and weapons had been packed, there was little room for much else, but we took as much of the grain and food supplies as we could. Unfortunately, we could do nothing to hide our presence here; the terraces and excavation of the cisterns precluded that. But I did everything possible to disguise which direction we went when we left.

The first arrow hit one of the ark bearers as he stood waiting to pick up his end of the carrying pole, and he fell with a cry. The second whistled passed me, thudding into a tree.

"Raid!" I yelled. "Into the trees!"

The men scattered.

"Check the trees for archers!" I shouted, seeing one aiming an arrow at Abiathar. "Down, Hakkohen!" I added, brushing the sling loops up and reaching for a stone. The archer hesitated when Abiathar dropped to the ground, and I whipped my arm, the sling unwinding in an instant. The stone whumped through the air, smashing into the side of the archer's head. He fell from the tree without a sound.

Cries erupted in the trees down the line from me. "There's another, Gareb!" Ira shouted.

I glanced around behind me. Eliphelet lay on the ground down the trail. "Anyone in the trees?"

He looked at me, but didn't reply. Abiathar had pulled back onto the side of the trail with Gad, and Naharai was chasing someone, so I ran to the thief. He was pale, and trembling.

"Where are you wounded?" I asked.

He couldn't answer, and I checked him over, not finding anything immediately. Among the trees a raider tugged one of our donkeys away with him, and I picked up a stone from the trail, sending it after him. It struck the back of his shoulder, and he dived into the brush, abandoning the animal.

Then I turned back to Eliphelet.

"Forgive me, adoni," he said, closing his eyes. At that instant I realized that he wasn't wounded. He was afraid.

Leaving him there, I started down the trail, but the raid was over. It took more than an hour to reorganize, and I struggled to keep my chagrin to myself. I should have known that the best opportunity to run off with our things was after they were all packed on donkeys, and those two previous raids should have been warning enough. I'd not thought to have anyone on lookout while we packed, and as a result, we had lost two donkeys, one with all our oil, and the other with one pack of weapons, something that we could ill afford to lose. Uzzia, Zabad, and Naharai were wounded, the first two not seriously. But Naharai had a broken rib from a sling stone that hit his chest.

The raiders had lost three men, the one I'd hit in the tree, one which Ira and Gareb found, and Shagay had taken another, rescuing two of our donkeys in the process. In addition, I knew the one in the brush wasn't going to use his arm for some time.

Once everyone had reassembled, I went back up the path to the ark and the wounded bearer. "How is he?" I asked Keturah.

She raised tired eyes to mine. "He's dead, Dahveed."

I bowed my head. "I'm sorry, Keturah."

"The raid wasn't your fault."

"No, but--" I stopped, knowing that I should have been much more prepared for it. But there was no time to do anything now, however, for the king's agents were still coming, and we had to leave. We had a dead man to bury, and a problem even bigger than that. Who was going to help transport the ark? Naharai and Ishmaiah were the only two bearers left, and Naharai now had a broken rib.

That thought was on all the men's minds as the news passed down the line while Gad and I hurriedly unpacked a blanket to wrap the body in and made a quick stretcher to carry it on. Abiathar said he would take the dead bearer's place, but we needed one more man.

"I should--" I started to say.

"No, adoni," Shagay interrupted, his tone forbidding any argument.

"Abiathar, can we consecrate someone?" I asked.

"I have nothing to do the rite with," he replied.

"Let me."

The voice had come from behind me, and I whipped around.

Eliphelet stood there, shaking, the determination in his eyes backed by shame and guilt. "I'm the most disposable," he added.

"Wait over there," I said to him, motioning the others around me to leave.

"Abiathar, I would inquire of Yahweh," I said softly.

"Yes, adoni."

I knelt, and he stilled.

"What is your request, Dahveed ben Jesse?" he asked in that distant voice.

"Adonai, forgive Your servant for my carelessness. There is no one to carry the ark because one bearer is dead and another wounded. Eliphelet ben Ahasbai has offered himself to You for a bearer, but we have no way of performing the rites required for his service to you. Is he acceptable to You even so?"

"Yes. I have drawn him for this purpose."

"Thank you, Adonai. Lead us now, for the king seeks us again."

"Go in peace, Dahveed."

Moments later Abiathar touched my shoulder. "What is Yahweh's answer, Dahveed?"

"Eliphelet can carry the ark," I said, rising. I walked to the waiting men. They shifted, not meeting my eyes, knowing that one of them must take the risk of death to touch the ark.

"Eliphelet ben Ahasbai, Yahweh has called you to serve Him," I announced.

A gasp went through the men, and they stared at the thief.

"Yes, adoni," he replied, coming forward. He touched his forehead to the ground to Abiathar, and then took his place by one of the carrying rods, his legs visibly shaking.

Knowing that it was useless to ask the men to fall in line until they saw if anything would happen to Eliphelet, I said, "Let us go, Abiathar."

The priest gave the order, and the four bearers picked up the ark, raising it to their shoulders awkwardly. Nothing happened, and they started forward, the rest of us following behind, the men very quiet. After about a mile of travel, that ark turned to the south, down a ravine, stopping before the entrance to a small cave. We placed the body in it and blocked up the entrance. Abiathar said some words of consecration, again commending the man's name to Yahweh, and we continued on our way, following the ark into the rain that now began to fall, once again fleeing from the wrath of the king.

For days we marched, Shaul's agents always at our heels, until those days turned into weeks, while we dodged from place to place in Horesh and the wilderness of Ziph, never staying anywhere longer than two nights. The tents were constantly wet, making the loads on the donkeys far beyond what they should have to carry. All of them were footsore and several lame. Most of the time we wandered without seeing anyone, but we had to hide enough times while searchers passed around us that the men were thoroughly convinced to follow the ark without question.

"The donkeys can't go much farther, Dahveed," Shagay said now in the gathering dusk.

Too tired to speak, I nodded, wondering how Shagay found the energy to catch up to me from his place back down the line. The ark still moved, and we plodded after, uncaring if it rained or not, if it was cold or not, or if the king found us or not.

"Look, a road! Such things exist after all!" Igal said in amazement.

Despite my weariness, I smiled. Igal's irrepressible sense of humor had cheered us all. And we were all here. The others from Eshtemoa had joined us almost a month ago after barely escaping town ahead of Shaul's agents. Shagay's Jonathan had brought them through, but nearly at the expense of his life. He and Abishai had shared some harrowing experience that had cemented their friendship and which neither would talk about. The young Abishai who had gone to Eshtemoa to run messages had come back a man with serious eyes and a quiet manner that commanded instant respect.

Jonathan's manner hadn't changed, but there was a reserve about him now that reminded me of Ethan. Not long after he'd returned, I had overheard him ask Abiathar to perform a sin offering for him. Maybe someday I'd learn what happened.

Night came, and still we plodded on. Rain plastered against our backs, whipped by the wind from the sea.

Eliphelet stumbled, and the ark lurched. He recovered his balance, his face white even in the darkness. His left arm hung limply by his side. The constant pressure of the rod on his shoulder had all but paralyzed his arm, and he had to hold the rod of the ark with his right hand. But he'd said nothing about it, and when I ventured to ask him once, he had turned to me, his eyes intent.

"I'm a thief, Dahveed, a thief! And I'm carrying the sacred ark. Do you know how amazing that is? For the first time in my life, I'm doing something that has meaning, even if I don't know what it is. I won't give that up."

"Maybe Yahweh has a special place in His heart for thieves," I had said softly.

Eliphelet had smiled and stood so that Naharai could fit another pad on his shoulder to ease the weight of the ark.

The rain suddenly came down harder, pouring over us in long waves, and I somehow found the energy to step from the line, urging everyone to keep together, helping the stragglers lead the limping donkeys on into the night. We were climbing again, another ridge. I stumbled up the slippery height after making sure the last man and donkey had gone ahead of me. When I reached the top, the line had stopped, and one by one the donkeys folded their legs, falling under the loads. The ark bearers had set the ark down.

"We're here," Abiathar said dully.

"Then we'll stop," I replied. As soon as I'd spoken, the men sat down right where they were. I made one more count to be certain that all were present, and then I lay down on the wet ground in my soaked cloak and fell instantly asleep like everyone else. I do remember thinking, Yah, You set the guard tonight, before sleep closed over me.

CHAPTER 41

"She's doing fine, Jonathan," Michal said absently as she hurried by carrying another water jar.

The hassar stared helplessly after her. If his wife was doing fine, why was everyone running around looking tense? Taphath cried out again, and he started automatically toward the storage chamber that had been cleaned out for a birthing room. Peleth, his overseer, blocked his way.

"You should wait here, adoni," the man said, putting a restraining arm on him.

"But something happened," Jonathan protested.

"Yes, this is a first child, and they are the hardest."

Michal hurried back into the room, and Jonathan shifted impatiently. Immi came out looking at him in exasperation. "Nimshi!" she called.

His young armor-bearer materialized beside him. "Yes, Hassarah?"

"Get the hassar's mule ready. He's leaving."

"I'm staying right here," Jonathan protested.

"No, you're not," Immi replied, her eyes flashing. "Your hovering is interfering with Taphath's concentration. She's more worried about you than giving birth. You are going into the forest to hunt, and *you will not return until sundown.*"

The hassar's mouth dropped open.

The hassarah turned to his guard. "Abiezer, escort him to the house, see that he changes into something suitable for hunting, and then throw him out of the gate!"

"As you command, Hassarah," the guard replied. He took Jonathan's arm and pulled him toward the house.

"How dare you lay a hand on me!" Jonathan said, astonished.

"Begging your indulgence, Hassar, but I'm much more afraid of your Immi right now than I am of you."

"I'm not going anywhere," Jonathan said stubbornly, planting his feet.

"Oh, I think you are," Abiezer replied, glancing at the gate.

Jonathan turned his head. His brothers had just arrived, and Immi was speaking tersely to them, gesturing toward him. Both the sars bowed as Immi turned back into the house, and then walked toward him, trying to hide the smiles on their faces.

"Come on, brother," Ishvi said gently, taking his arm from Abiezer. "It seems you have been acting mulish again."

"You should know better than to do that with Immi," Malchi added, seizing his other arm and propelling him up the stairs to his house.

"But what if something happens?" the hassar protested.

"I'm sure something will happen, and we'll find out soon enough about it. In the meantime, you have been banished from the place of your banishment. Keep acting like this, and you won't have any place left to go. Are you going to take off that robe, or do Ishvi and I cut it off?"

Glaring, the hassar stripped off the robe and put on the shirt and kilt that Sar Ishvi handed him. "Now, if I promise to be quiet, can we stay right here?" he asked.

"No," Ishvi answered. "Immi was quite specific. You are not to be on the estate. The last time she used that tone was after you got sick in the fortress that winter. I'm not about to risk what Abbi got."

"You? What about me?" Jonathan pleaded. "That's my wife in there, and--"

"--and you are making it harder for her," Malchi put in, grabbing his brother's thickest cloak and ushering him firmly out the door. "Sometimes the things you want, brother, are not the best for everyone else." Then he turned to Ishvi, a smile of complete satisfaction on his face. "You don't know how long I've waited to say that!"

Nimshi stood at the bottom of the stairs with the hassar's mule. "Have a good hunt, geber," he said with a grin.

Jonathan groaned. If his armor-bearer was against him, there was no hope at all, at least, not here. But maybe . . . Mounting, he rode out the gate, leading the way down the road toward the path into the forest, ignoring the comments of his brothers. Then he quickly turned off it, winding his way down smaller and smaller paths, twisting and turning, until he was nearly lost himself. But when he tried to take a path that would point him back to Zelah, Malchi barred the way.

"You shouldn't have taken my bet, Ishvi," Malchi said, a half smile on his face as he regarded his oldest brother. "You owe me two gold pieces."

"Only one," Ishvi said. "This was the second path he could have taken, not the first."

"Two," Malchi insisted. "The path back there goes to the top of the next hill, and disappears. Doesn't it, Jonathan?"

"Yes," the hassar conceded with a sigh.

Looking annoyed, Ishvi reached into his girdle and took out two gold pieces, passing them to Malchi.

"Going to make me any richer?" the sar asked. "Ishvi and I have two or three more bets on what you'll do."

The hassar turned the mule around and rode off in dignified silence.

By sundown each of the sars had brought down game, and they headed back. Much as Jonathan hated to admit it, the hunting had made the time pass and allowed him to relax. The forest dripped with moisture, and a late winter fog hovered close to the ground. The latter rains would come soon, and before long the full warmth of spring would return, and he'd have a child to watch grow. He urged the mule forward.

All the bustle and activity in the courtyard had stopped when they rode into the gate. Jonathan dismounted, looking around. The door to the birthing room opened, and Michal stepped out.

"There you are," she said with a smile. "Taphath is waiting to see you."

"I can go in?"

"Certainly."

"She's still doing fine?"

"She couldn't be better."

Taking a deep breath, the hassar walked into the room lit by three lamps. Taphath lay on a pile of bedding on the floor, her hair carefully combed, and holding something close to her chest.

His wife smiled at him. "It must be sundown."

Staring, he nodded. Weren't there supposed to be other people here helping his wife?

"Come here," she said, patting the floor beside her.

He settled down gingerly, bewildered.

She turned toward him. "Meet Meribbaal," she said, uncovering what she held.

The hassar looked down in wonder. That tiny thing was the baby? "Meribbaal?" he asked, jerking his head to see Taphath's face. "I have a son?"

"You do, Abbi."

Tears streamed down his face as Jonathan reached out and touched his son for the first time.

The next morning, the hassar rode out to inspect his flocks and cattle, choosing two ewes and a cow to take to the tabernacle as a thank offering. Immi, who was staying for several days to help Taphath, supervised the preparation of the unleavened breads and oil to go with the sacrifice.

When he arrived at Gibeon the next day, everyone he met congratulated him on the birth of his son. He hardly knew what he replied, but no one seemed to mind anything that he said. The tabernacle was busy, so he didn't linger.

It was on the way home that he remembered General Abner's words, "Do not ever rest easy, Hassar." The memory brought him down to earth instantly. First order of business was to find a personal guard for Meribbaal. Then there was the future to look to. How could he protect his family from those like Abner, as well as his clan and tribe, when Dahveed took the throne? Killing Dahveed was not an option for him. What did that leave?

He dismounted slowly when they returned to the estate. The idea that had formed in his mind might work. But it required a great deal of risk at the moment. Since he'd already decided he would be going to see Dahveed, this was just one more reason to do so. But could he hide his absence now? And he'd have to have Elihu's help. Smiling wryly to himself, he didn't think Dahveed's brother would hesitate for an instant about it.

"I'd like to see your abbi," he said, turning to Nimshi.

"All right, geber," his armor-bearer replied, leading the mules away.

Time flew by, and Hassar Jonathan hurried through the court business each day. Spring had finally arrived, and people were too busy planting gardens and getting ready for grain harvest to bring much work to the court. Most of what he handled was routine, and Eshbaal left little for him to do after his review.

Eagerly he looked forward to meals, when Taphath would hand him Meribbaal, and he could forget about eating and hold his son until time to go back to work, or the baby fell asleep. Members of his family found excuses to visit nearly every day, and Shaul had come twice, staying overnight so that he could have more time with Meribbaal.

More than six weeks had gone by since he gave his thank offering. Ishvi and Elihu had made all the arrangements for his trip south, and he waited impatiently for Ethan to arrive. Then late one afternoon, the man stood in the courtyard.

"Shalom, Ethan," he greeted the Habiru warmly.

"Shalom, adon. I understand there is a new little sar in the family."

Jonathan grinned proudly. "Come up and see him."

Ethan followed up the stairs.

Taphath handed the baby to her husband, looking with surprise at the stranger who entered with him.

"Shalom, Sahrah." He bowed courteously.

"Shalom," she replied, recognition dawning in her eyes. "You are the Habiru who came to my wedding."

"You have a good memory, Sahrah," he chuckled. "The hassar has graced me with his favor as long as I find things for him."

"Something tells me there is much more to it than that," Taphath said, studying him. It was long after dark when she took Meribbaal to bed. After she had gone, Ethan sat back. "You have a fine son, Hassar."

"For which I thank Yahweh every day. I suppose I've done nothing but talk about him since you came."

The older man smiled. "Most new abbis do. What did you want of me, Hassar? Are you looking for something again?"

"Yes, Ethan. Take me to Dahveed."

The Habiru sat motionless for several seconds.

"You know where he is," the hassar went on in a low voice. "And if you don't know exactly, you know how to find him. Having my son won't be complete until Dahveed rejoices with me. Please, take me to him."

After several moments Ethan let out a long breath. "The things you ask me to find get more and more difficult, Hassar."

"In what way?" Jonathan challenged. "It can't be that hard for you to locate him."

"Maybe. The biggest problem comes in dodging the king's men and making certain that we leave no trail to him coming or going. That means walking, Hassar."

Jonathan smiled crookedly. "I'd crawl, Ethan. I've got to see him."

"And you'd go down there on your own, wouldn't you?"

"If I must. But I'd much rather have you guide me. I'm even willing to rack my mind for an acceptable reward for your services."

Ethan chuckled drily. "You are desperate, aren't you? Would you be going alone?"

"I don't think so. I'll need some armor and weapons from Dara, and if I ask for them, he'll know I'm going somewhere and won't remain behind."

The Habiru leader considered. "All right. I'll take you and Dara. Understand, Hassar, I cannot guarantee we will find him. There is that with Dahveed which covers him. He vanished about six weeks ago, as if Yahweh had picked him up and taken him to the realm of the Elohim. We will not find him unless Yahweh wills it."

The next day when he and Taphath sat alone eating the noon meal, a courier brought a small bundle from Elihu. Jonathan set it aside and turned to his wife. "I'm doing more than going hunting tonight," he said. "I cannot say when I'll be back, either."

Her dark eyes widened at him. "Then I'll take Meribbaal to Gibeah a couple times to keep the king from coming here and finding you gone. You haven't been feeling all that well, have you?"

Jonathan's lips quirked. "How did I get so blessed as to have you, Taphath? Truthfully, I have not been feeling as well as I might. I'm sure Immi will want me to stay out of the wet and get lots of rest."

His wife smiled a little. "You be sure to tell Dahveed I wish him Yahweh's blessings." At Jonathan's startled look, Taphath laughed. "Oh, Jonathan, sometimes you're as obvious as a thunderstorm. No one else could make you defy the king!"

"And I thought no one could be worse than Immi about knowing things," the hassar sighed.

On the morning of the fourth day, Jonathan doubted they would ever find anything down in this dark forest with a gully or twist in the hills every place one looked! No wonder his abbi couldn't find Dahveed. About all he knew was that they were somewhere west of Ziph, and maybe a little south. Standing at the seasonal spring he'd just drunk from he looked up at the leafy covering over him. "Grant my request, Yah. Show us the way," he whispered.

Toward mid-morning, Ethan took them to the top of another hill to study the country again. The hassar scanned the terrain, his eyes drawn again and again to a notch in the hills across from him. "There," he said finally, pointing north.

Ethan studied the place. "What is it?"

"It shines, sort of, behind that hill. What's over there?"

They descended the hill, and Ethan led them to a short ridge offering a side view of the place that Jonathan had indicated.

At the base, a youth stepped from the trees, startling them all as he barred the way.

"What did you want, gebers?"

"Shalom, Hanan," Ethan said. "We are looking for the Dahveed."

"He does not wish to be found."

"He will wish to see the hassar, as you well know. We bring no harm to him, Hanan."

"It is still well to be cautious," Hanan replied, bowing gravely. "Do you vouch for those with you?"

"Yes."

"Then come. You might be interested in what is happening today." A mischievous smile crossed his face. He led them along a trail on the northwest side of the ridge, overlooking a rectangular valley below. Near the north end seven groups of three men faced each other down a battle line. "Everyone ready?" Dahveed's voice drifted up to them. "Then begin."

Jonathan watched as the groups advanced toward each other cautiously, and when the mock battle started, he put the bow down and removed his cloak, his gaze more and more intent as the groups engaged.

"Look at them," he said in admiration. "Is that Josheb in there?"

"It has to be, adoni," Dara replied. "I had no idea he could handle a spear that way!"

"He always had talent with it, but he's improved. I never should have let him out of my guard!"

"Who's the demon using a javelin like a spear?" Ethan inquired. "Have you seen what he's done with it?"

Hanan smiled. "That's Igal, the man who brought your wedding gift."

"Look how they work together," Ethan commented, watching closely. "Each unit is almost one man."

"Shalishim!" Jonathan exclaimed. "How can this be? Dara, what else can we be seeing? Come on," he said, loosening his sword. "I can't miss this. Get us down there, Hanan. Where did Dahveed find someone who could teach shalishim?"

"That would be Uriah, the Hittite," Hanan replied. He looked at the hassar. "With Dara on your left, and Ethan on your right, you might be able to challenge them."

The hassar chuckled in delight, his eyes lighting up. "Shall we?" he asked.

Dara already had the shield he'd brought on his arm, and Ethan took off his cloak.

"I just thought of something. If you wait a little, you can join up on the south end," Hanan said to Ethan. The youth disappeared ahead of them.

Down below, the battle was called to a halt, and Jonathan saw a thickset man making some changes to the groupings before they resumed.

Hanan appeared beside them again, carrying a long infantry spear, and handing it to the hassar. "It's Josheb's," he grinned.

Jonathan's eyes glinted, and he hefted the weapon, turning it in his hands. "Ready?" he asked.

They walked out, slipping into the line opposite Josheb. At Jonathan's first thrust, Josheb leaped back, the two men on either side of him following suit automatically.

"Need a little challenge?" the hassar asked.

His former body guard froze, eyes unbelieving, and then they quickly looked to the right, where Dahveed fought, oblivious, on that end of the line. A slow smile spread across his face. "Come on, you two," he said to his companions, "we just ran into something you've never seen before." They stepped forward, and the duel began.

Jonathan had sparred with Josheb often in training, but he'd never seen the elegance of the dance he faced now, and it summoned all his skill. He wished Malchi could be here, he'd have loved this. Thrust, counter-thrust, parry, step aside, and thrust again. Wait for Dara to shield, push back the man threatening Ethan--watch that spear! Thrust again, drive forward, pull back. Then Ethan lunged, and the man on Josheb's right took a hit.

¥ ¥ ¥ ¥ ¥ ¥

Uriah had put Shagay on my right and himself on my left. So far we'd worked smoothly together, and I had the time to look down the line, watching how things were going. At the far end, something was keeping Josheb busy, but with Igal as center against me, I didn't have time to think about it. Jaasiel and Zabad sided Igal, and we went back and forth several times, driving each other's shalish back only to have to retreat again.

During a slight pause, I glanced around and saw Josheb drop out. It looked as though one of his men took a hit from someone with a very fast sword. I ticked in my mind to find out who had faced Josheb today. That shalish continued to spar, and soon a second team withdrew in defeat. The men who were out cheered for the rest of us, and I jerked my attention back to Igal when he nearly knocked me out!

Another shalish fell before the team headed for us, and the gift touched me as I grew more intent, my concentration sharpening until I blocked out everything but the three men in front of me. Shagay saw an opening and thrust forward. I blocked a blow from Igal against him, depending on Uriah to cover me from Zabad's attack. Jaasiel backed away, his sword on the ground, and Igal and Zabad retreated. Uriah, Shagay, and I turned to the next shalish. Uriah had said this would be an exercise to see which group could outlast everyone else, so we had to defeat anyone still on the field.

Shagay gave a little gasp.

"Steady, Shagay," I said encouragingly. "We can take this one."

"Yes, adoni," he said in an odd voice, and we drove forward. A spear point appeared in my face.

I jumped back in surprise. I thought Josheb had dropped out, but I didn't have time to think about it, because that spear just kept coming, thrust after thrust! *I hated spears!*

And then Uriah leaped backward, caught off-guard by the left-hander facing him. Who did we have who was left-handed like that? That spear sprang at me again, but from a different angle, and I slipped to the left, slapping it aside with my sword, my left hand reaching for the handle. A blade appeared before I could retreat and reverse my swing. It touched my left cuirass shoulder, next to my neck. I froze, my eyes traveling up the sword to the person behind it.

"After staring up my own sword into your face, it's so satisfying to stare down it at your face!" Hassar Jonathan's rich voice said.

I couldn't move. This couldn't be! My mind must be playing tricks on me. I looked down. He held the spear in his left hand, fully half the handle behind him, so that I would have to approach close to respond to his thrusts, thus putting me within reach of his sword.

I looked again at the face. The hassar's eyes gleamed with that wicked delight that could only come from him or his abbi, and this certainly wasn't King Shaul! Dara stood on his left, and Ethan waited patiently for me to say something.

It was Jonathan! Hassar Israel stood right here, his eyes dancing at me, pleased as he could be about the way he'd surprised me. "I believe this also repays you for the way I woke up the morning after my wedding," he added.

"Nahsi," I whispered.

Lowering the spear, he thrust it into the ground and sheathed his sword. "Yes, Dahveed. I thought it had been quite long enough since I'd seen you."

I turned to face him, still trying to make myself believe that he was really here. "Nahsi," I said again, but I couldn't think of anything else to say, so I dropped my sword and walked into his embrace.

CHAPTER 42

When Jonathan and I finally let go of each other, I could tell the news of who had come had spread to everyone, and many of the men didn't know what to make of it. If King Shaul was seeking to kill us, what could his oldest son be doing here? I decided to make my position in relationship to Jonathan clear to everyone.

Stepping back, I touched my knee to the ground. "We are honored by your visit, adoni," I said. As soon as I knelt, Ethan, Ahiam, Shagay, and Josheb all did the same, and in moments, the entire band bowed with me.

"Dahveed!" Jonathan growled, his eyes promising all sorts of trouble for what I had just done.

"Yes, Hassar?"

Hands on his hips, he glared at me. "You are still the most exasperating hill man ever to come out of the south! Where is that earring?"

"Right here, adoni," I said, straightening up so that he could see it hanging on my chest.

"I can see it will take a while yet for you to fully appreciate why I gave that to you. That being the case, I will have to instruct my son in the proper behavior he is to show you and pray Yahweh that he will live long enough to see that you learn the lesson!"

"What son?"

"The one which, between Yahweh and Taphath, arrived in my house more than a month ago and has done almost as much as you did to turn everything upside down," he answered. "And so, Dahveed, in payment for what you have just done, you will have to hear all about Meribbaal, the newest disruption to my life." Reaching down, he grasped my shirt, hauling me to my feet, that wicked smile on his face.

"You have a son?" I asked again.

"Yes, I do. Come along now."

The men erupted into cheers and shouts of congratulations as Jonathan and I walked across the clearing to the path that led around the spur of the hill on our left. Once we were in the trees, I turned to him. "Congratulations, Hassar! Yahweh's blessings on you and your house!"

He gripped my forearm hard. "It's like a miracle, Dahveed," he said, his eyes shining. "It's almost more than I can take in."

He talked on as we climbed, and as I listened, a stab of fear went through me that I would lose my place in his affections now that he had a blood son. That familiar feeling of unworthiness flooded into me. Then I was suddenly disgusted with myself. Jonathan Hassar had come all this way, defying his abbi again, just to see me and share his rejoicing, and I couldn't even listen properly to him! Yahweh, forgive my foolishness, I thought. Let me share fully in Jonathan's joy.

I led him up the hill and past the entrance to the same cave the ark had led us to last year when we had escaped Shaul's trap. It now sheltered the ark again, along with those of my band who served it. The rest of us had tents on the crest of the hill in the thick trees that covered it. By the time we got up there, the hassar's gladness had filled me, and there was a melody forming in the back of my mind. But I put it aside. Right now, I needed to listen. A long time passed before he had finished telling me things, and I had run out of questions about them. Tears appeared in his eyes again. "Even Abbi is pleased," he said at last.

The ironic tone of voice wormed its way into my mind, and I replayed the conversation as I watched the way the hassar stared at the king's signet on his clenched fist. "What happened between you and the king?" I asked.

"Nob."

"It doesn't sound as if you've been in Gibeah lately," I commented after a pause.

"I haven't been there at all. Abner made sure Hassar Israel was banished from the king's presence."

"Then how is it that Hassar Israel wears the king's signet?"

"Abbi doesn't know I have it. He thinks Ishvi does."

I settled down on the bedroll. "Sounds as if you have a lot more to tell me."

He eased back also. "I guess I do, since you're in the middle of it," and in a low voice he briefly outlined everything that had taken place since I'd left him at Ezel more than two and a half years before.

"So you met Tiras!" I laughed. "How much trouble did he get into with you?"

Jonathan told me in more detail what had happened. "That reminds me, Dahveed. Tiras asked me to intercede with you for his brother Uzzia. He was worried you would be harsh with him."

"Uzzia is no longer bound to me," I said. "He stays because he decided to. I'll have to see that he contacts Tiras some way."

"I can take a message when I go."

"And you finally found the Steward of the House of Tahat! Did he agree to help you?" I asked next.

An odd smile crossed his face. "Yes, and Tanhum is working closely with the House now to increase trade from the south. How are your parents doing in Moab?"

"Fine, last I heard. But living on Yira's largess is wearing on them, and they all want to come home."

"Maybe they can, soon," the hassar said, looking at the signet again. "Now, tell me about Balak."

When I finished the tale, he shook his head. "I never would have thought he'd get that far with Yira!"

"Yira understands him very well. He knows he's no fool, and a dangerous man."

Ahinoam stuck her head into the tent. "We'll be serving in about half an hour, Dahveed."

"Who is that?" Jonathan asked when she left.

"My wife."

He sat up, looking interested. "Sounds as if you have a lot to tell me, too! How did you meet her?"

"She showed up in Adullam looking for her brother, Zabad, who had been given to me by the Jezreel elders, and then her abbi turned up also, looking for her brother who wasn't Zabad. He ended up giving me his son when I wouldn't let him leave with my nephew who nearly killed him. Then he decided to sell Ahinoam, and Josheb bought her in Hebron with one of the gold pieces you gave me, because we didn't think she'd like Nabal."

"I see talking about women still confuses you," he said, his eyes twinkling. "Now, if Josheb bought her, how did she happen to marry you?"

"Because Josheb married Keturah."

Again he chuckled, a contented smile on his face, and lay back on the bedroll. "Start at the beginning, Dahveed, and tell me in simple words what happened!"

It was time to eat when I finished, and when I sheepishly confessed how Ahinoam had "persuaded" me to marry her, he was holding his sides, gasping. Once he'd laughed himself out, we joined the others where Ahinoam had a blanket spread in the middle of camp, with food for me and our three guests on it.

It surprised me a bit that no provision was made for others to eat with us, but Ahinoam gave me a look that said, "Don't ask," so I said nothing. She had prepared some quail, and there was parched grain and some rather dry raisins. A water skin hung nearby for us to drink from.

When he'd finished, Jonathan said, "Take me around, Dahveed. I'd like to meet your men."

I obeyed, and he spoke to each one, finding something about them to speak of or compliment them on. As usual, before he was half done, he'd charmed the entire camp. Dara and Ethan followed along, and when we got to Eliphelet, Ethan looked at him closely. "Is your family from Ur?" he asked.

"Yes, adon," our thief replied.

"It's quite an experience to meet you, since your name is so well-known on the caravan routes," the Habiru said with a touch of irony in his voice.

Eliphelet flushed. "You make too much of my reputation, adon."

"I don't think that's possible. I wouldn't advise you to stray very far from Dahveed."

"I won't!"

As we walked away I asked curiously, "You know him?"

Ethan sighed. "Every caravaneer from Egypt to Ur knows of him. If you were to put him up for auction in Damascus, you could buy a kingdom or two with what they'd pay to get their hands on him."

"He's just a thief!" I exclaimed.

The old warrior laughed. "Calling him 'just a thief' is like calling the Great Sea a rain puddle. He is "*the thief,*" Dahveed. He's been known to steal entire caravans, sell them hundreds of miles away, and then do it again on the way home. If you ever tell Jether you have him, make sure he's too drunk to understand. How did he end up with you?"

"He stole the purse the hassar gave me, but made the mistake of staying in the market after he'd done it. When I found him again, I greeted him like a long-sought friend and asked what he was trying to buy this time with the rocks in his purse."

"How did you back up that bluff?"

"It wasn't a bluff. I'd taken all the gold from the purse and put in a sling stone with the silver. He was somewhat chagrined when the Geshur merchants saw that rock."

"Somewhat?" Ethan gasped. "Oh, Dahveed, you have no idea what you have done!" He stopped, barely suppressing his laughter. "I assume he got away?"

"From the town, yes. But then he showed up at my camp to get that purse again, along with anything else of value. He insisted on having it, so I dropped it into the sling and returned it that way."

An incredulous mixture of emotions struggled for control of the Habiru's face. "You *slung* that purse back to him?"

"It did have a sling stone in it, Ethan. It hit him in the chest and knocked him down. He woke up after a while."

Slowly Ethan collapsed, sitting on the ground, laughing too hard to stand. "I can't wait to start this story on the caravan routes!" he finally managed to say. "I want every detail, Dahveed. This will be the best news in years!"

"Just be certain you also add he's sworn to me, and I'll take exception to anyone who interferes with him, to say nothing of what Yahweh might do," I said drily.

"What does Yahweh have to do with it?"

"Eliphelet is one of the ark bearers now."

Jonathan's head swung toward me. "The ark? The ark of the covenant?"

I nodded. "Mahesa sent it to me along with Abiathar."

"Then the tabernacle at Gibeon is empty?" he asked in a strange voice.

"I guess so," I said slowly.

In a moment or two we continued on, and Jonathan greeted Puah warmly, making her face light up. Shagay's Jonathan stayed close to camp now, for Puah was ill, and we all knew she would not get better. The trek this winter had brought on a wasting illness that Keturah recognized and could not cure. We did everything possible to make her comfortable, and Puah tried to teach Ahinoam and Keturah as much as she could while she still lived. The three women had become very close.

That night I sat up late, talking with our guests, and Ethan dug all the details about Eliphelet out of me, including how carrying the ark had affected his arm, which was now much improved. "I'll tell Jether first," the Habiru said. "The first caravan that Eliphelet stole was his. It was his first trip as his own caravan master, so you can imagine what he feels about the man. Telling this may satisfy his honor enough that he'll give up the idea of torturing the thief to death."

"Dahveed?" Ahinoam whispered when I finally came to bed.

"Yes?"

"How long is the hassar likely to stay?"

"He'll probably leave day after tomorrow or day after that, why?"

"We don't have any more food."

"What are we out of?" I asked, not surprised by what she said.

"You ate the last of the grain and raisins tonight. We have half a jar of oil, and some salt. That's all, Dahveed. Anything we eat from now on comes from the hunters."

"All right."

She dropped off to sleep again, but I couldn't, wondering what I was going to do now.

In the morning Jonathan agreed to a hunting trip, and he and I set out together. I headed east, crossing the Hebron road and gradually descending toward the Arabah.

"Was the Gad I met last night the roeh's servant?" he asked after we'd walked for some time.

"Yes."

"And Ahinoam's abbi is Ahlai of Jezreel?"

"Yes. Why?"

"Just putting together some bits of information," he said absently.

We kept going, crossing a seasonal brook. The sun came from the clouds after a while, and Jonathan stopped in a little clearing.

"How much food do you have left, Dahveed?"

"We hunt a lot," I hedged.

"We ate all you had last night, didn't we? That's why no one else ate with us, why there was no evidence that anyone else had eaten when I toured the camp. There's nothing left, is there, Dahveed?"

Knowing it was useless to deny anything when he used that relentless tone, I sat down on one of the large stones nearby, realizing that I was shaking. "From now on, we eat what we hunt," I said.

"You're still afraid, aren't you?" he asked quietly. "He said you were."

"Who?"

"Mahesa. He threw you at me at Nob to keep me from killing myself."

"Jonathan!" I gasped.

His hand resting on his belt knife, he looked grim. "After seeing what happened there, it was the only thing I could think of that might shield the people from Yahweh's wrath. Mahesa, and then Yahweh, showed me otherwise." Then he told me the full story of how he came to carry the king's signet.

"You took the kingdom?" I asked in disbelief.

"As king in place of my abbi, I can stand between the people and Shaul's sin." He sat down on another stone with a sigh. "Yahweh has taken us up for his use, Dahveed," Jonathan continued. "I never dreamed that I'd fulfill the roeh's prophecy and seize the kingship from my abbi. I've had my heart torn out, and I've lain shaking in the mud beside it, but instead of death, my God spoke to me personally. I rule Israel. The son of my choosing will take the throne after me. And now, I have a second son, of my body this time. Nothing happened like I expected, but there's not much more I could ask for."

He rested his chin on his hands. "And think of your life, Dahveed. A shepherd saving the kingdom in war? A southern hill man married to a sahrah? The king bowing at your feet?" His eyes laughed at me, and I flushed.

"And now the king's favored zammar is running for his life, but what fugitive ever had Yahweh lead him personally? Or had a brother working in the king's court to protect him? Or had his own roeh and a personal priest to inquire of at an instant's notice? Yahweh has told you how enemies will strike and planned your battles for you. He has protected you and hid you and sent you men who can do things long thought lost."

Eyes gleaming, he shook his head. "Shalishim! I still can't believe it! Any one of them could defeat an army unit now, and Yahweh will send you more. With fighting men like that, you're not going to rule just Israel, Dahveed. You will have an empire!"

"Not if I can't keep them alive now," I said, shifting restlessly. "I don't know what to do, Jonathan! Ahinoam went right to sleep last night after she'd told me the food was gone. She's sure I'll find some way to feed everyone, but I can't magically conjure up supplies. I can't even figure out a way to buy some without exposing our encampment to the king!"

The hassar half smiled. "But Yahweh is leading you, remember, in the same manner He led our people from Egypt. He fed them then; He will feed you. It sounds as if you're kicking yourself for some mistakes."

"Two men have died," I confessed. "One because I didn't notice he was ill until too late, and the other because I forgot to do something as basic as set a guard. I don't know why the men still trust me."

"Somehow, Yahweh uses everything," Jonathan said, staring into the surrounding forest. "Even hardships and mistakes and mulish attitudes. We need to stay close to Him, Dahveed. I've felt His hand protecting me and teaching me, and He's doing the same for you. That's why I don't think you should worry overmuch about Abbi. He knows you'll be king someday and that I'll serve under you. And as hard as he's trying to kill you, I think Yahweh is more than a match for him, even with Abner urging him on. They'll never win."

I put my head in my hands. "That's hard to believe right now while we hide from the king's men, with the camp empty of food."

"I know. I get up some days wondering why I'm the one who has to do everything. And then I remember that I understand so much now that I didn't years ago, and that gives me hope that someday I'll understand why this is happening."

"And maybe we'll never know."

"Maybe," he said, facing me again. "But maybe leaving some things in Yahweh's hands is the most important thing of all."

"What do you leave there?"

"It's the only place I can leave my abbi, and the choice of who rules Israel," he said, looking down at his hands.

"That's why you called your son Meribbaal," I added with sudden understanding.

Wiping his eyes, he nodded. "All I can do now is trust that Yah is leading me as He did our ancestors in the wilderness."

After he picked up his bow again, we went on in silence. But learning that Jonathan struggled with questions and troubles just as I did, and hearing the ways that Yahweh had answered him, gave me hope that our God would also lead me through the wilderness and that someday I would understand.

I was glad for something to encourage me, because hunting was poor, and we started back empty-handed. I hoped someone else had more luck, or it would be a hungry night. But as we approached the hill, I sniffed the air. "That smells like bread," I said, picking up the pace. More aromas reached us as we got closer, and I wondered if I'd wandered into someone else's encampment by mistake.

Ahinoam beamed at me when we walked to the fire. I stared at the pot of lentils cooking with garlic and onion. "Elika and Shammah found an abandoned farmstead about a mile west of here," she explained. "The granaries and storerooms were full and now we can have a proper feast to celebrate the hassar's son! I hope you don't mind that we don't have meat," she added, turning to Jonathan. "But we've had so much of that lately!"

He laughed. "This will be the first feast I've celebrated that way, but I think it's appropriate."

While we washed up for the feast, Jonathan commented, "It's odd that Yahweh's presence filled the tabernacle in Gibeon when the ark wasn't there."

I thought for a minute. "I don't know. The Hassarah always said Yahweh can be anywhere. I don't think Yah needs an ark. But I doubt my men would have been able to trust His leading without it, even though Yahweh could have led us just the same. Maybe that's why it came."

"I hadn't thought of it that way," the hassar mused.

When we sat down, everyone huddled together, and stories flew back and forth while we ate the most tasty feast that we'd had in months, singing and talking and enjoying the single jar of wine until long into the night.

In the morning Jonathan, Dara, and Ethan joined us on the training ground, and the men had a taste of the teamwork between the hassar and his shield-bearer and the speed of Ethan's sword. Then I suggested archery practice, knowing a demonstration of the hassar's skill would prove invaluable to the men. Ittai watched intently, and the hassar spent considerable time teaching my covenant son.

After the noon rest, Jonathan came to my cooking fire, watched as the sars always were, by anyone in the vicinity.

"Adoni Dahveed."

I straightened from my work on my cuirass at the formality of his address, standing up. "Yes, Hassar Jonathan?"

He touched his knee to the ground. "I would speak with you, adoni."

Everything around faded to total silence, and I looked down at his bent head. "You just had to do this, didn't you?" I said in a low voice, seething. "By all means, come into the tent where I can strangle you in peace!"

His grin was totally unrepentant, and he followed as I stalked into the tent. As soon as the tent flap fell, Josheb took up his station outside the door, spear in hand.

The sight of the hassar's personal bodyguard on duty stilled my sense of irritation. "What did you wish, Hassar?"

"Let us cut a covenant, Mashiah."

After two previous experiences, I knew better than to argue with that request. Then I cocked my head. This wasn't a request.

"Your invitation will require some thought," I said slowly, watching the approval in his eyes as I picked up the nuances of his statement. "Josheb?"

He opened the flap. "Yes, adoni?"

"We will require some food and drink, and a suitable place for a discussion."

"Yes, adoni."

Within moments, Ahinoam came in, looking curious as she spread a blanket for us to sit on and went to get some food.

"Sit down," I said, my mind trying to fathom what the hassar was up to now.

After we'd had the obligatory food and drink, I looked at him. "You have proposed a covenant between us. What sort of covenant?"

"Two covenants of Yahweh stand between us, adoni, one of hesed between you and me, and one of hesed between our houses. Let us cut a covenant now between Yahweh's melek and my kingdom, so that when our God fulfills His promise to you, each will know his place."

Startled, I sat up. How could the hassar call me a king when I had no kingdom? The only territory I controlled was very small and portable. So far it hadn't covered the same two acres twice. I ran his comment through my mind again. Jonathan hadn't asked for a covenant between kingdoms, but between me, as Yahweh's king, and *his own kingdom*. His proposal was between equal kings, but he granted me the place of higher honor before Yahweh when he suggested the covenant.

I eased back in thought, praying that Yah would show me what was acceptable in this and what wasn't.

"Any kingdom that I have is in Yahweh's hands, Hassar."

"You hold more than you know, Mashiah. I would ally myself with Yahweh and with you. You will be melek to Him one day. If I live, grant me the second place after you when Yahweh calls you to the throne."

He must be very certain that I'd survive and come to rule. More certain than I was myself. I glanced down, catching sight of the earring on my chest. He'd always been more certain of some things about me than I had. And he'd been right, too.

What he proposed had wisdom in it. Such a covenant could make an easier transfer of the kingship and might well avoid a war. It would also protect his position and authority now, I realized. If I agreed to this covenant as Mashiah, and thus his superior, I was confirming his displacement of his abbi as king because I was superior to Shaul as well.

As far as I could tell, it was Yahweh's will that Jonathan's hand guide Israel. I trusted the hassar's honor enough to accept his recounting of Yahweh's words at Gibeon.

"I believe such a covenant would be beneficial for everyone involved," I said at last, silently asking Yah to let me know if I'd missed something.

"Josheb?" Jonathan called.

"Yes, Hassar?"

"Tell Dara I need the pouch he brought."

The shield bearer entered, handing the hassar a bundle carefully wrapped in hide. Jonathan unwrapped it and placed two small parchments on the blanket in front of me. I recognized Elihu's swift, sure writing. Scanning them, I saw they were a formal covenant outlining the terms the hassar had just proposed to me. As I read, I realized that my brother had carefully safe-guarded my position as superior in this covenant, while still assuring the hassar of his place and authority under me as long as I wished him to hold it.

My hand shaking as the ramifications struck home, I set it down. This covenant was an abdication of the throne by Jonathan on behalf of his house, even if it was to take place in the future.

"Have you read these?" I asked.

"Yes, adoni. They were written according to my specifications."

Once again, he forced me to step up to the honor that Yahweh had said was mine. And once again, I asked the same question. "Why are you doing this?"

He smiled. "Because there are still some things you will only learn from me, Dahveed. Yahweh will give you control of people's lives, and you must begin to know what that means. If you start with my life, I know you will think about what you are doing now and what it might mean for the future, something that you must do when you are king."

With a sigh I picked up the parchment and read it again. Second place in the kingdom. There was a great deal of power there, as he well knew. Slowly a still larger picture formed in my mind of what this covenant was. "This would also assure the protection and status of yourself and your house, even your tribe." I said slowly.

"It does. I would not lose more honor than I can help," he added wryly.

Again I fell silent, wondering what it would be like to rule with Jonathan standing in second place. Would I always be wondering whether he approved, or whether he could do a better job? Would there be conflict between us sometimes? I went back to the terms again. Elihu had evidently thought of that, for the authority granted the second place was subject to whatever changes I might decide. I remembered when I had assumed the place of superiority to Ethan. That had gone smoothly because my old mentor had yielded gracefully.

I sighed in exasperation. Jonathan was way ahead of me again, for he was doing that very thing right now! Leaning back, I gestured to the blanket. "Tell me, Hassar, just what do I get out of this?" I asked in mock irritation. "So far, you've insisted that I take the place of Mashiah before my men, you've pushed me to face up to more aspects of the kingship, insured my confirmation of your coup, abdicated the throne even though your abbi still sits on it, and you're stepping into second place right now, thereby guaranteeing that place for your family and honor when I rule. Have I missed anything?"

That wicked grin flashed across his face. "You've summed up my position quite well!" he drawled, looking just like King Shaul had when he first lounged back on the throne and demanded whether I was objecting to his rewards. Then he sobered. "But what do you see that you are getting?"

"I see a chance to receive the kingdom from Yahweh's hand with no blood being shed. And it is worth the price you have set down. Let us cut this covenant, Jonathan, Melek Israel."

"Then let us go out and swear," the hassar said. "I would have witnesses to a covenant, even if not the exact terms."

I ducked out of the tent first. "Bring the blanket to the fire, Josheb," I directed.

He obeyed, then stood several feet in front of us as we knelt opposite each other. The men grouped together, keeping their distance, watching. I took out my belt knife and laid it down, the point toward me and stilled myself, waiting. Yah remained silent.

"I, the Dahveed ben Jesse, Yahweh's Mashiah, swear before Yahweh that I will keep this covenant between me and Jonathan ben Shaul, Melek Israel, to set him as second after me when Yahweh shall call me to Israel's throne. May Yahweh require this from my hand, and may I be cut as an animal if ever I do not do as I have sworn."

Jonathan had waited with his head bowed while I swore. He took the knife next, pointing it toward himself, and said, "I, Jonathan ben Shaul, Melek Israel, swear before Yahweh that I shall keep this covenant between me and Dahveed ben Jesse, Yahweh's Mashiah, to take second place after him when Yahweh shall call him to Israel's throne. May Yahweh require this from my hand, and may I be cut as an animal if ever I do not do as I have sworn." Then he bowed to me, and I picked up the knife, sheathing it.

Early the next morning, Ahinoam urged some parched grain and a few dates on our guests as they prepared to go, and the hassar and Dara took another tour of the camp, speaking to everyone. He spent some extra minutes with Puah, and she was beaming when he left.

We accompanied them for a little way into the forest, until Ethan planned on turning east to lose his trail in the rough country so as to protect the location of our camp. I waited until the last minute, then took the earring off.

"You forgot something, Hassar," I said, holding it out to him.

"What's that for?" he asked suspiciously.

"Shall we say it's for coercing me into cutting a covenant? Take it, Hassar!"

For a moment he glared, then suddenly grinned. Coming forward, he knelt in front of me taking the earring. "As you command, adoni!"

¥ ¥ ¥ ¥ ¥ ¥

Abigail closed the gate to the garden. The pool had water in it now, and would until summer's heat dried it up again. She set the basket down and took out the meil. Not much had been done since she'd started it. Rarely did she have time to embroider anymore, but she was truly Gebirah now. The harvest this year had been exceptionally good, the fields the nagid could see from the road producing enough to satisfy him that all had been done as he directed. The farmers said nothing about the fields planted out of the nagid's sight, which had also yielded well, and the store rooms and granaries were full for the first time in years.

Abigail suspected that Nagids Ahlai and Dathan were working in concert to keep Nabal distracted, and she was grateful for whatever help she got. Many times in the past two years she had nearly given up, overwhelmed with the enormity of her task and the amount that she had to learn in order to preserve the people of her land.

As she created the twining vine down the meil with her green thread, she thanked Yahweh that whatever Hezro had done with Parai had been effective. He had never told her where he had taken the man, and she never asked. Nabal no longer tried to cross her, but he drank more, and Tokhath encouraged him to do so, while he advised the nagid in his business deals, thus increasing his own influence.

However, now that she had the routine of administration worked out, she could turn her attention to what she must do about the nagid's oppression of the people in Maon and Carmel. The other adons were dealing well with his interference in other places, keeping her informed of what he did and their responses to it.

But here, with nearly all the land and people belonging to the nagid, the problem was much harder to resolve, and she was unwilling to have her people suffer from the nagid's increasing viciousness. It was time to work on the second part of her plan. She could see only one road open to her, and it would leave her a pauper, but it would break the nagid's power completely. And not just Nabal, but any nagid who followed.

Taking a deep breath, she steadied her hands on the needle. It must be done, and that was the end of the argument. What she'd do after that she didn't know. But she would think of that later.

Tirzah's voice rose in the compound, distracting her. She was the one who brought the unusual news lately. While she didn't put much credence in some of the stories the handmaid told, it was still amusing sometimes to hear the gossip of the market. There were always stories of Dahveed Israel, some of them so fantastic they couldn't possibly be true, others just enough odd to make you wonder if they might have happened. What was certain was that Dahveed had vanished again, like the mist in the morning.

Shaul had chased him most of the winter. Rumors of the numbers of men that the Israelite king had brought spread across the countryside, and Abigail wondered how Dahveed managed to remain free. But while the patrols would locate where Dahveed had stayed, they never found the man himself. Then in the unusually constant heavy rains between winter and spring, he had vanished, and no amount of searching could pick up a trace of him.

Smiling a little, she remembered the expression on his face when he'd first seen her. People said that when he liked something, his eyes glowed. Or was that when he was angry? She could never remember. But Tirzah had come home with one piece of information that might explain Dahveed's skill in avoiding Shaul. He had both a prophet and a priest with him. And not just any prophet, but Gad, the right-hand of Roeh Shamuel himself, as well as the last surviving priest of Eli's line. Abiathar supposedly brought more than just himself to Dahveed after the slaughter at Nob. Some of the tabernacle treasure came also, enough to make Dahveed the richest man in the kingdom.

Knowing the nature of rumors, she doubted that. But it did seem fairly certain that Dahveed had both Gad and Abiathar with him. Her needle slowed. What might that mean? By sending Gad, the Roeh Shamuel had given Dahveed his blessing. And with Shaul rejecting Yahweh as his God, it appeared that Yahweh had sent His priest to Dahveed also, showing His blessing, too. But for what?

She sat a long time, until the fading light made her put up her needle and fold the meil. It might behoove her to learn more about Dahveed. Not only was his clan distantly related to her, but chances were that he'd run across her path sooner or later. If he had the blessing of both the roeh and Yahweh, she should treat him with care. Picking up the basket, she left the garden.

CHAPTER 43

Cheran stood behind the throne while the torchlight in the room flickered and King Shaul studied the three rough-looking men bowing in front of the dais. As personal attendant, he remained quietly in the background, having already filled the silver cup next to the king's left hand with wine.

General Abner spoke. "Your pardon, adoni, for the lateness of the hour, but I thought you'd want to hear what these men have to say about Dahveed as soon as possible."

"Do you know where he is?" the king demanded, leaning forward.

"He is at the hill of Hachilah in the south," the center man replied, glancing up briefly.

"Why tell this to me?"

"Everyone knows the thing you crave most is to find Dahveed, O king."

"And as a result, everyone comes to me with lies about where he is, hoping for a reward," Shaul snorted in disgust. "How am I to know you are any different from the two I heard from just yesterday?"

"We are from Ziph, adoni. Why should we want Dahveed among us?"

Cheran pricked up his ears. Was that bitterness he heard in the man's tone? Since he'd become the king's personal attendant, he'd learned that Hassar Jonathan valued such indications highly. Under pretense of checking that the bowl by the king's hand had fruit, the servant shifted his position so he could watch the king's face as well as the messengers.

Shaul raised his eyebrows. "So you would use me to remove an annoyance from your land? Someone who is too strong for you to challenge?" he asked sardonically.

The Ziphite's face hardened. "No, adoni. But if you come down, we will see it as our duty to surrender him to you."

Abruptly Shaul laughed. "Surrender him? Do you expect to have him bound and in your power when I get there?"

The man shrugged. "Why not, adoni? He has retreated far from any aid, and we know the country better than he does."

The king leaned back on the ivory inlaid chair, resting his hands on its arms. "Do you, now?" he said softly. "What else do you know?"

"We know that he hunts food with only one or two companions, and that he will often go out at night completely alone."

Cheran saw the glance that passed between Shaul and his cousin. "It appears as though your encouragement of the south to aid us is producing results, Abner," the king smiled. "Stand up," he said to the Ziphites.

They obeyed, their spokesman the only one brave enough to look the king in the face.

"How are you called?" Shaul asked.

"Rinnah, adoni."

"May Yahweh bless you for this news, Rinnah. It seems you have more compassion for me than my own court did when the priests betrayed me."

Cheran clenched his hands behind his back. The king dared to use Yahweh's name after Nob? When there had been no compassion in his heart for the priests? Was Shaul's compassion reserved only for such as these men and the Amalekite Agag who flattered him and encouraged him to go against Israel's God? The attendant's eyes narrowed a little. Roeh Shamuel had made short work of the Amalekite king. Would the same happen to Israel's ruler?

"Go back to Ziph and investigate thoroughly," Shaul said, bringing Cheran's attention back to the three men. "Dahveed has proven impossible to catch so far. I want to know every place he hides, or might hide, and who has seen him. Once you're certain you know everywhere he might go and how he might get there, let me know. I'll go down after him, and I'll find him, if I have to search every clan in Judah!"

The three men bowed again. "As you wish, adoni," Rinnah spoke for them.

¥ ¥ ¥ ¥ ¥ ¥

Shagay appeared beside me. "Those Ziphites are back, watching us again."

I sighed, looking over the encampment. Less than a week after Jonathan's departure, I'd grown more and more uncomfortable that close to the town of Ziph, and we moved the camp south and east of Maon near the hill of Hachilah. But barely three weeks later, Yahweh spoke to Gad, telling him the Ziphites had informed Shaul of our presence. We had left the day after, again following the ark down into the wilderness east of Maon and to our present camp.

"It's rather hard not to notice us, Shagay."

"I know," the Habiru said. "But it's not just the encampment. They are watching everything we do, where the hunting parties go, the approaches we use--everything. And they have followed you every time you leave."

"It's me they want. How is Puah?"

"My wife won't live much longer," he said, looking away.

When we reached the camp, Ahinoam greeted me with a smile, but I saw the frown marks between her eyes. The supplies from the abandoned farmstead we'd found were nearly gone, and hunting enough to feed everyone took most of every day. We needed a place where we could stay long enough to plant crops and gardens for food, and I had until fall to find one.

"Did you see Hanan?" I asked just before we parted.

My retainer shook his head.

Ducking into my tent, I hung up my bow and quiver. Where could the Habiru youth be? It wasn't unusual for me not to see him for days, but it was not normal for me to feel a total lack of his presence.

¥ ¥ ¥ ¥ ¥ ¥

Jonathan stretched, arching his shoulders backward to ease the tension between them. "Is that it for the day, Bunah?" he asked.

"Yes, adoni," the scribe replied, packing the message pouch with the decisions the hassar had made on the judgment cases brought before the court that morning. Jonathan smiled to himself at the startled look the scribe gave when he called him by his correct name. He knew how to tell them apart now even when they weren't sitting at their tables.

He sat back a moment, glad to be done early. Rarely did he have special messages to attend to any more. The last one had been Cheran's report more than a week ago informing him when the king and Abner would leave for Hachilah and Dahveed's camp. Jonathan had sent a messenger south with the twisted brass earring within the hour, giving Dahveed plenty of time to get away.

Walking out the door, he saw the courier leave for Gibeah. It might be more convenient if he could rule the kingdom from the fortress, but then he wouldn't get to spend nearly as much time with Taphath and Meribbaal. He sniffed. It smelled as if there would be beans for supper, and he was hungry.

Later that night, Jonathan stirred on the bedroll, turning on his side. Meribbaal whimpered next to him. It must be nearly time for Taphath to feed the baby. The sound of a sword coming free from a bronze sheath jarred though him, fully wakening him instantly. His eyes swept the room even as he realized the sound came from the balcony outside the door. His hand slipped under the bedroll, gripping the battle dagger he had kept there since the night General Abner had threatened him.

Faint footsteps outside slowly circled the balcony, and then stopped by the door. The hassar rolled to his feet, edging silently forward, ears straining to hear.

Someone scratched on the wood. "Hassar? Hassar, it's Abiezer."

Jonathan went to the door. "What is it?"

"I'm not sure," his bodyguard whispered. "I thought I saw someone."

"Wait." Quickly pulling his under-garment on over the loincloth, he slung a kilt around his waist, and substituted his sword for the dagger. Opening the door as quietly as he could, he stepped over the threshold, pulling the door shut behind him. Abiezer stood near the middle of the balcony, facing the stairs and the courtyard.

"Anything further?" Jonathan whispered.

The man shook his head. "It was a shadow, near the stairs. And then I realized no shadow should be there, but when I looked again, it was gone."

Shifting uneasily, the hassar surveyed the empty courtyard. Then he checked the balcony. As he did so he felt the unmistakable shape of the twisted brass earring pressed against his left hand.

"I'll stay here," he said softly. "Go get the guards at the gate and search the courtyard."

Abiezer warily descended the stairs.

"Who are you?" Jonathan asked.

"Hanan, adon," a voice replied from the shadow directly beside him, but low enough that the hassar realized the youth must be kneeling. "What message did you send? I found a courier's mule in the hills about three miles south of here. It had taken a misstep on the trail and thrown the rider onto the rocks. The messenger was killed. When I found the earring on him, I came directly here."

Jonathan's heart nearly stopped beating. "Hanan, the king and Abner left for Ziph four days ago! The Ziphites knew exactly where Dahveed was. Shaul will be on top of him by now!"

"I will warn him," the youth said, rising swiftly.

"You'd never get through in time. It's 30 miles, and the king took five units." Jonathan started pacing, thinking frantically. Suddenly he swung around. "Don't go to Dahveed, Hanan. Go to the king."

"The king?"

"Yes. Insist on seeing Shaul himself. Tell him-tell him that the Philistines have invaded with 10 full units, and it looks like another thrust directly toward Gibeah. Tell him Malchi and I are on our way to meet them with what we have of the professional force. We'll try to trap them in the hills somewhere and hold them off until he can get here with the rest of the army.

"Do you understand, Hanan?"

"Yes, Hassar." The youth jumped toward the low wall surrounding the balcony.

"Wait, you'll need this," Jonathan said, slipping the king's signet from his finger and handing it to the young man. "Just be sure you tell the king you come from Sar Ishvi, *not me*. And Hanan, don't lose that!"

The young Habiru's teeth flashed in a quick grin. "I won't, Hassar."

He disappeared over the outside wall of the house, and in moments the hassar saw him jogging into the forest. "Yahweh go with you," he muttered. Then he started to pace. He knew his message would bring his abbi back as fast as he could. What he didn't know was how to explain the absence of Philistines once the king got here!

¥ ¥ ¥ ¥ ¥ ¥

I looked around in the early light of dawn. The camp was nearly packed, and Zalmon was bringing the last of the donkeys. Uriah had all the weapons that we weren't wearing already loaded, and Ahiam and Igal were balancing the loads on the donkeys carrying our food supplies. Gad had come to me late yesterday with word from Yahweh that we must leave immediately. Knowing that we were watched, we'd packed everything we could without being obvious about it, intending to slip away in the night. But I'd delayed our departure in deference to Puah, Shagay's dying wife.

Rubbing the back of my neck, I checked the trail to the west. With Hanan still missing, Shagay and Jonathan were the best scouts I had, and they were both in the one tent still standing. Josheb, my third retainer, walked over. "Who's out on sentry duty?" I asked.

"Uzzia and Zelek."

Moving restlessly, I flexed my fingers. Although I knew that I'd let our best chance of leaving unnoticed slip away, I couldn't bring myself to disturb Puah. I wished I knew what was out there in the forest. Uzzia would be alert for anything unusual since he'd lived as a Habiru all his life. But Zelek, as a grandson of King Nahash, had been raised near Rabbah, Ammon's capital. He had been a city dweller and was not as familiar with wild places.

Just then Uzzia burst through the trees. "Dahveed, Shaul comes!" he shouted, breaking the morning's silence.

"Get whatever is left loaded and moving," I snapped at Josheb, who hurried off. "Where is the king?" I asked as Uzzia came panting up.

"Heading down the north ravine leading from Hachilah, Dahveed. He's got at least three units and several guides. They'll be here within the hour!"

Stunned, I glanced at the sun, barely above the hills descending into the Arabah behind me. That meant Shaul had been waiting on the uplands just west of us all night! I never should have delayed our leaving, but I'd thought the king was on his way, not already here! "Yahweh, save us," I groaned. "Uzzia, tell the others that whatever isn't on the donkeys gets left behind." The huge man rushed off and I turned to my nephew. "Abishai, tell Abiathar to be ready with the ark. We leave as soon as possible."

While my nephew dashed away, I reluctantly turned to Shagay's tent. I had no choice now. I only prayed that I had not delayed too long.

"Dahveed! Dahveed, it's Abner!" Zelek charged into what was left of camp. "Two units at least. He's coming down from the headlands in the big ravine just over a mile south," he finished, panting hard.

"Elhanan, you and Jaasiel carry Puah," I directed. "Zelek, tell Abiathar to lift the ark."

The men obeyed instantly, and Ahiam and my wife already had Shagay's tent half down. Gad, Naharai, Eliphelet, and Ishmaiah, the last Gibeonite bearer, walked swiftly past and headed directly down the ridge east into the Arabah.

I counted the men as they urged the donkeys along, making sure that all 30 of them were accounted for. With Shaul coming down north of us, and Abner to the south, it would be a race to see who got to the Arabah first. I wondered which way the ark would turn at the end of the ridge. The long hill down there barring our way wasn't that high, but it was covered with so much underbrush, most of which had thorns of one sort or another, that it was impossible to cross unless there was a path. And there wasn't.

No one looked at me as they hurried by. Only Ahiam seemed relaxed as he went by at the end of the line, his Habiru-trained donkey following along four feet behind him. I sighed. That was something else I should do. If all our donkeys were trained to follow that way, we wouldn't have half the trouble we did keeping them moving. I swung the harp case across my back, checking around the area one more time as I trotted toward the trees, bringing up the rear.

The blow on my mid-back sent me flat on my face. Automatically I pushed myself up, scrambling forward the last few feet into the shelter of the trees. I'd nearly caught up to Ahiam before the pain registered in my thoughts. Gasping, I reached around with my hand. It came away bloody, and every move made me clench my teeth. "Faster, Ahiam!

Their scouts have seen us!"

The Habiru broke into a run, and the donkey put his head down, cantering after. By the time we came in sight of the others, moving nearly as fast as we were, I'd felt enough to realize that I'd been hit with an arrow that had driven clear through the harp case! Someone back there had a compound bow. They weren't as powerful as composite bows, or I'd be dead, but they were much more powerful than the usual wooden ones. The blood had already flowed all the way down my right leg, increasing in volume with every move I made.

Gritting my teeth, I managed to keep up with Ahiam. We practically slid down the last of the ridge to the Arabah, turning left to the north. I sighed in relief. If we were caught, I had a slim chance of begging hesed from Shaul, at least for my men. There was no possibility at all from Abner. Not after the scene in King Nahash's throne room.

The pain making me dizzy, I stumbled. Come to think of it, there might not be any hesed from Shaul this time either. That arrow in my back might be evidence that the king had ordered me killed, not captured. He must truly be after my blood this time. And he was getting it, too, I thought grimly, stumbling again and blinking to clear my vision.

Ahead I could see Shagay and Jonathan on either side of the litter carrying Puah, doing their best to steady Elhanan and Jaasiel on the rough ground. The ark was out of sight in the thick trees and forest, but I could hear the sounds of those up front, and we were leaving a trail a babe could follow.

When we reached the end of the hill, the ark had turned east again. Faint shouts reached my ears, and I glanced behind me, up on the ridges. We'd been seen! And not just by the scouts. The soldiers were hurrying upon us, some of them sliding down the slopes into the water courses now that we'd been spotted.

"We've got to close up the line," I shouted to Ahiam. I suspected that the watercourse we followed would continue to curve until it pointed us south again, which was probably why the Ziphites brought Abner down on that side of us. We didn't dare run into him spread out along half a mile of trail. He'd cut us to pieces.

Then a shout, followed by a scream of pain up ahead, reached my ears. Fear thrilled through me. Had Abner come on us this quickly? Gasping, I lurched ahead. Zabad, Ahinoam's brother, appeared in front of Ahiam and me.

"Zalmon broke his leg. What do we do?"

Ahiam yanked his healer's bag from the donkey and charged ahead.

"Is the ark still moving?" I asked.

"Abiathar says we are not to stop."

"Then we don't. Get two men on either side of him and support him."

"He's unconscious, adoni."

"Good. Load him across Uzzia's shoulders, and follow the ark," I said shortly.

Giving me a strange look, Zabad ran back.

I shook my head. Another gush of blood flowed down my leg, and, groaning, I grabbed onto the donkey beside me to stay upright. The creature started forward, taking me with it.

"This way! Adoni Shaul, this way!"

The shout behind me spurred me on, clearing my head a little. I glanced at the sun, on my left now. We were headed directly south. The men had bunched ahead of me on the trail, getting Zalmon settled.

"Move on!" I shouted.

"Adoni! We must turn back," Zelek yelled, crashing through the trees into view from the south. "We're headed into Abner's units! They've rounded the ridge and are coming right for us."

Breathing hard, all the men turned to me. I swayed a little, still clinging to the donkey's pack. "Where's the ark? Follow it! I don't care if it takes us into a pride of lions. We go where Yahweh leads!" I said savagely. "Move! Now!"

Abiathar and those carrying the ark nearly ran down the trail south, and the men turned and followed. It was still in my sight when it swung to the right, dropping down off the trail, the bearers clinging to the rods. The donkeys didn't hesitate, plunging down after it, one after the other, the men following single file through the narrow path created as they forced their way through the undergrowth. The ground gradually rose, and the underbrush cleared a little on the up-slope until I saw that we were in a natural amphitheater, surrounded by the arms of the hills. The steep rise of cliffs across from me would protect our backs, and any attackers would have to come uphill to meet us. The ark led straight toward the far side, and I let go of the donkey, swaying until I could steady myself against a tree.

The pain nearly drove me to my knees, and I could hardly hold the water cruse to my mouth as I tried to slake my burning thirst. The men were safe now.

"Thank You, Yah," I muttered, nearly falling. I turned and went back the way I'd come, barely managing to get back on the trail outside our haven. I knew if I wasn't around, Shaul wouldn't be either, and my men would soon be left in peace. They had the ark, and Ahiam and Shagay would know what to do.

I staggered north until I couldn't see the place behind me where the ark had turned. Then I leaned against a large tree near the trail, waiting for Shaul to arrive.

"Adoni Shaul, adoni Shaul," the shout reached my ears, and I raised my head. "Messenger for the king! Make way!"

I shook my head. I must be weaker than I thought. That sounded like Hanan's voice.

"Here! The king is here," Natan cried from just out of sight around a bend in the trail ahead of me.

I froze.

"Adoni Shaul, turn back!"

Struggling to stay upright, I waited.

"Bring him here," the king commanded.

"Adoni, I come from Gibeah," the courier panted, hardly able to get his words out. "Sar Ishvi sends to you in haste. The Philistines have invaded!"

"When? How many?" the king demanded.

"They are in the land now. Ten full units," the messenger replied, still gasping for breath.

I clung to the tree. That had to be Hanan's voice. What was happening? How could he be bringing a message from Sar Ishvi?

"Adoni, this message may be false," someone interrupted. "This lad is a Habiru, and you know how they favor Dahveed. Remember, he is cunning, and will mislead you any way that he can."

I closed my eyes, biting my lips, gathering strength to start down the trail. They would kill Hanan for this!

"My message is true," the youth retorted. "I am to give you this, adoni."

"What does Ishvi say," the king asked after a moment of silence, his voice urgent now.

"He says you must come immediately. Sar Malchi has taken the units to meet the Philsitines. They seem to be headed right for Gibeah again."

"What of the hassar?"

"Adoni, he has risked your displeasure and gone with Sar Malchi."

"He would, and the men will fight all the better for it," the king said grimly. "Since he will be fighting against full units, I hope that he can confront them in the hills. Has a call to arms gone out?"

"I do not know, adoni," Hanan replied. "I stopped for nothing on the way."

"Natan, send a message immediately to Abner with this news. We will not wait for him in the uplands, but go straight to Gibeah. He is to follow as fast as he can."

"Adoni, you are doing exactly as the Dahveed wishes," that other voice said. "We have him. You saw him for yourself. We cannot leave the chase now!"

"When Sar Ishvi entrusts the royal signet to a Habiru, and Hassar Jonathan goes against my orders, the situation demands my attention. Or do you wish me to risk my entire kingdom to clean up your back courtyard?"

The ice in the king's tones sent shivers down my spine. Moments later a man dashed by me on the trail.

I labored to think. I didn't have to save Hanan. He'd brought proof from Ishvi. The king's signet. But Ishvi didn't have the king's signet. Jonathan did. Hanan must have come from Jonathan, not Ishvi. Now, what did that mean? My knees hit the ground. Was Jonathan *lying to his abbi* in order to protect me? "Yahweh, grant him hesed," I muttered before the blackness gathering at the edge of my vision closed in around me.

CHAPTER 44

"Forgive me, Ishvi, but it was the only thing I could think of that would bring Abbi back," Jonathan finished, while his next younger brother stared at him, shocked.

"He *will* kill you this time. Or if you do manage to keep your head, he'll never trust you again. Not after a lie like this, especially if it kept him from capturing Dahveed."

"I know. And that means when the king gets back, you'll be hassar. We've got a day or so for me to tell you what I've been planning," Jonathan replied, trying to pace in the cramped space of his business chamber at the Zelah estate.

"That'll never work, either," the sar said. "The only thing we can do that might save you is to bluff this out all the way. If we did that, we might be able to convince Abbi we got incorrect information, but didn't dare ignore it."

The hassar regarded Ishvi in surprise. "What do you mean?"

"I mean, we bluff. When did Hanan leave?"

"Just before midnight, I think."

"It's well past dawn now. I'll send out a call to arms to every town within 10 miles of here. Malchi can tell the units here to be ready to leave within an hour, and then you and Malchi march them west as fast as you can go. Once you get to Kiriath-jearim, spread the units out northward as if you're looking for raiding parties in the ravines of Gaash. Leave me with at least one unit. I'll need some professionals to be officers for the militia as they assemble."

"Ishvi, if Abbi finds out you've helped me in this, he'll turn against you, too."

"Then we can keep each other company. If we move fast, you and Malchi can be out there by late afternoon."

"Are we going to tell our younger brother that we're both lying to Abbi?" the hassar asked.

"Too late for that," Sar Malchi replied, opening the door. "I heard the whole plan. What unit do you want left here, Ishvi?"

"The third if possible. Zorath favors Dahveed more than all the other commanders, so he may be willing to save my neck if it needs it."

Malchi snorted. "You haven't seen Commander Ram when he gets worked up about Libni. But if you want Zorath, you can have him. Come on, Jonathan. You have to say good-by to Taphath and that son of yours, and Ishvi and I need to get back to Gibeah. I'll be here with the army before noon, and I don't want to wait for you to dress!"

With that the younger sar stalked out the door, and they heard the hoof-beats of his mule moments later.

"If he's galloping, he's really in a hurry," Ishvi grinned, following him out the door.

"Ishvi, there's no need for all of us to go against Abbi this time."

"Only if we sacrifice you, older brother, and we don't seem willing to do that. Although Yahweh alone knows why. You've got the most mulish attitude sometimes," the sar finished, closing the door behind him.

Jonathan pulled up the mule just off the road near the first land stair to the Shephelah, and squinted in the late afternoon sun. "Is that smoke?" he asked, pointing to a spot against a far hillside.

"Looks like it," Malchi agreed, raising a hand to halt the column of units moving rapidly behind them.

"Someone is approaching, adoni," Commander Ram added from his position behind the two sars.

A young boy raced from the trees. "Please, commander," he cried when he got close enough. "Philistines! They raided our farmstead. We were able to get away since Abbi had seen smoke further north, and he was worried and took us from the house. He sent me to find help."

"How much farther north?" Jonathan asked.

"The next farmstead is just over half a mile, adon," the lad replied.

"When did he see smoke?" Sar Malchi put in.

"The sun was mid-afternoon, the ninth hour."

"We'd be too late to track them down now," Jonathan sighed.

"Ram, send a man with this lad to see his abbi. Bring back what information you can," Sar Malchi directed. "It looks as if you'll have some ground to stand on when Abbi gets back," he commented in a low voice as the lad led a soldier back the way he'd come.

"A farmstead or two won't help much," Jonathan replied absently, staring at the land falling away before him. "Malchi, does anything look odd to you down there?"

"Odd how?"

"Well, dark sort of, in the ravines."

"No," the sar replied, glancing at Jonathan.

Another figure stepped from the trees. Pasach of the eleventh unit drew his sword, but Jonathan held up his hand, watching the Habiru approach.

"You are the hassar?" the man asked, studying him.

"Yes, geber."

"You'll need all the units you've got here. I'm Dahveed Heber, allied to Jeshua of Gibeon. My men report a good many Philistines are filtering up the ravines of Gaash for the next four miles north."

"Can you supply guides for us?" the hassar inquired.

"If you've got men who will listen to them, adon."

"When did the raiding begin?" Malchi asked again.

The Habiru dahveed eyed the sar a moment. "Late in the day, mid-afternoon or so."

Jonathan and Malchi glanced at each other.

"Isn't that unusual for them?" the hassar continued.

"They've never done it before that I know of," the Habiru replied.

"I think we'll be able to use all the guides you can provide us, Heber," Sar Malchi said thoughtfully. "When can you be back with them?"

"My own band within the hour, and I can have Jeshua's band here by dusk."

"Very good, Heber. I'll expect you both."

"I don't recall the Philistines ever starting the war season this early," Jonathan mused, watching the Habiru dahveed trot away. "Threshing isn't half over yet. How many do you think are out there?"

The sar gave his brother a disgusted look. "I'd guess about 10 full units. Let's go find a good place to set up headquarters. I'm anxious for more information."

Jonathan started his mule silently. Ten units? This early in the year? Then he caught sight of another column of smoke, and his hands tightened on the reins. Was it possible that by Yahweh's hesed, his "lie" hadn't been one at all?

Before the sun had set, messengers began arriving, each one bringing news that the Philistines had sent multiple raiding parties into the highlands, and that scores of farmsteads and some towns had been robbed and/or destroyed, the grain either carried off or burned, water sources fouled, and in some cases fields sown with salt.

"Someone is either very angry, or desperate," Jonathan commented grimly to his brother as they waited in a tent for the next messenger to arrive.

"I noticed," Malchi replied. "Ruining fields seems counterproductive. There will just be less grain to steal next year. Will we try to track down the raiding parties as we learn of them, or did you have something else in mind?"

"Abbi left you in charge of the army, Malchi. The decisions are yours."

The sar was silent a moment. "Does that mean you consider yourself under my command?"

Jonathan bowed his head slightly. "It does, brother."

A small smile quirked the sar's lips. "In that case, here's what I'd like to do. I think the Philistines plan on spending the night here in the highlands. All the raids are limited to places near the ravines, leaving the impression they have gone back to the Shephelah. But if they actually stay up here, they would have most of tomorrow to lay waste the countryside before we could respond *if we had only learned of the raiding tonight.*"

The hassar thought a moment. "You may be right, Malchi."

"They also know that Abner has no use for Habiru, so the last thing they will expect is cooperation between our units and Habiru guides."

Jonathan's eyes glinted. "And?"

"Tonight, I want to break up our force into as many small groups as we have guides for and quietly drop in on those Philistine camps."

The hassar smiled. "And waking up with several of their companions dead will certainly dampen their spirits about raiding tomorrow! Especially if we target the professionals."

"Buying us some badly needed time," Malchi added. "I want you to take three units at least four miles north, then work your way back south. I'll advance north from here. And if we leave a few men with a guide every half mile, it'll be that much easier to respond quickly to any raiding that does begin in the morning."

"As you wish, Sar," Jonathan said.

It had been one of the strangest nights of his life, Jonathan reflected as he watched the sky brighten in the east. Probably the only one odder had been the night he first betrayed his abbi, went to Ramah, and met Ethan.

This night, too, had been filled with silent twists and turns in the dark forest, punctuated by pauses and whispered instructions about where the Philistine camp lay, whether there were tents or not, where the men lay around the fires, and if any guards were still alive.

Sometimes they could creep up and simply stab a man sleeping too close to the trees. Other times a quick slash opened up a tent, and moments later a soft cry might signal the death of another invader in the land. More than once, Heber held them back while his men stole weapons or supplies they needed, leaving the dead behind as a warning to their fellows.

During the noon rest of the day after, Dara woke him. "Adoni, Sar Malchi sends for you at once."

"Malchi, or Sar Malchi?" Jonathan asked, unwilling to pull his mind away from his sleep.

"The messenger said Sar Malchi, adoni."

"It's an official summons then," the hassar sighed, rolling to his feet.

"Nimshi has your mule ready."

Getting into the clean kilt Dara had, Jonathan managed to wake up while his shield-bearer quickly combed and re-bound his hair. Once his cuirass was on, he kept the mule at a trot to Malchi's tent.

He slid off, giving the reins to a guard. Pulling the flap back, he entered. "You sent for me, Sar?"

"Yes. Someone wanted to see you."

Jonathan followed his brother's glance to see his abbi standing to the side, watching him. Instantly, he knelt, touching his forehead to the ground briefly. "What is your wish for me, adoni?"

"How it is that your younger brother summons you and you come?" Shaul asked curiously.

"He is your representative, adoni. Why would I not come?"

The king stroked his beard. "As I recall, I confined you to your estate in Zelah until such time as I sent for you. When did I bid you come from Zelah?"

Jonathan tensed a moment. He had no idea how much Malchi had told the king. "Sar Malchi told me that he would be coming to Zelah with the army, and he didn't want to wait for me to dress, adoni. I took that as a summons. If I was mistaken, I beg for pardon."

"He wasn't mistaken, Abbi," Malchi interjected.

"He usually isn't," Shaul replied, amusement in his voice.

Jonathan glanced up, catching the twinkle in his abbi's eyes. Seeing it there brought years of memories flooding into his mind, and he trembled with the overwhelming yearning to be loved and honored by him again. He wanted to see that half smile the king could give when something amused him. To hear his abbi's laughter when he played with Merab's sons, and share the events of the day in court, and know the fierce bond between them as they fought side by side to drive the enemies of Yahweh from their land.

Strangely, it was Mahesa's eyes that kept him from crawling forward and begging for acceptance and approval. Those dark blue eyes that had pierced his soul, telling him as he knelt there by the smoldering ruins of Nob, that his abbi had brought Yahweh's anger and curse on the entire land. Sorrow such as he had never known welled up in him, a deep, aching longing for what could never return.

A shudder went through him, and he swallowed at the lump in his throat, his very soul torn at what was ending in this tent. His act of obeisance had drawn forgiveness from his abbi, he could feel it in the air between them, and at the same time, he knew that he could never again give Shaul this gift of high respect, for his abbi no longer ruled

Israel. Jonathan could bow from his knees only to Yahweh and the Mashiah. Suddenly he understood why it had been so hard for Dahveed to accept his rank as second only to Yahweh. He himself knelt here, yearning with all his being to remain Hassar Israel, rather than become fully Melek Israel as Yahweh had named him at Gibeon.

The tent flap behind him opened, and Abner stepped in, his voice breaking the silence. "Where are all the supposed Philistines?"

"A good many are running for the barred gates of the five cities, General," Malchi replied. "They discovered that staying the night in the highlands can be fatal, and trying to raid in the land the day after wasn't any healthier."

The king's cousin snorted. "What happened here, an early raid by three or four over-eager mercenaries?"

"If so, pray you do not meet them, General," Malchi drawled. "If only three or four of them left two dozen farmsteads in ruins along four miles of our borders, to say nothing of the occasional town, they are much better fighters than you and I will ever be."

"And how much of this destruction have you actually seen, adoni?" Abner said irritably. "The message bidding us here came at a very opportune time for the Dahveed!"

"Would you be accusing my sons of deceiving me?" Shaul asked, his voice chill.

"Dahveed was surrounded, adoni, and his entire band with him, trapped between us with nowhere to go!" the general retorted. "And right at that moment, a message arrives? Brought by a *Habiru*? That strains my belief, adoni."

"Since I've seen more than five ruined farmsteads and one town so far, and heard the commanders tell of many more, my belief is not so strained. I hope you are not implying that the units destroyed the farms themselves just to give me something to see. Or would you have me believe that every commander in the army would lie to me?"

Jonathan thought he would die from the irony pulsing through him. He dared not look at Malchi, for the commanders would indeed lie to the king if Malchi ordered it, something that Abner might very well be suspecting by now.

"It's too early in the season for raids like this," Abner protested.

"And the Philistines must do only what we expect of them? You yourself told me that their tactics have shifted lately and were wondering why! Abner, you seem very willing to accuse my sons of disloyalty."

"Maybe I know them better than you do," the general snapped back, his face hard with rage.

"And maybe I know you," Shaul replied, his voice very quiet.

Jonathan glanced around in time to see Abner stiffen. The color drained from the general's face, and he bowed stiffly. "You do, Nahsi. With your permission, I will assess the damage done in the raids, while you deal with that disobedient cur on his knees." Abruptly, Abner stalked from the tent.

"Let him go, Malchi," Shaul commanded, his voice amused. "We shouldn't begin a clan war while the Philistines are within our borders."

Struggling to control the rage coursing through him at the general's insult, Jonathan waited for Shaul to decide what happened next.

"Stand up, Jonathan," his abbi finally said.

The hassar obeyed.

"Do not take insult over what your cousin said. I've found Dodi Ner quite effective when his son gets the bit between his teeth and lets his tongue run wild. I'll be interested to see just what Dodi will come up with this time to remind the general to keep to his place."

Jonathan had to chuckle. "Come to think of it, I've used Dodi Ner that way myself. I wouldn't imagine Abner is looking forward to his visit!"

"He's not. You will take no insult?"

"I will not, Abbi. Ner will deal with it far better than I could. What is your wish regarding me, adoni?"

"You will remain here under Sar Malchi's command for the war season. It encourages the men to know that you are here, and I believe they will need all the encouragement we can give them. I'm afraid this kind of beginning bodes no good for us."

Jonathan bowed. "As you wish, adoni. Sar," he added, nodding to Malchi before leaving.

¥ ¥ ¥ ¥ ¥ ¥

"Where are we?" I croaked.

"En-gedi."

"Then there must be some water around."

"There is," Ahiam replied, holding a cruse to my lips. "How do you feel?"

"Like I've been dragged up a tree and chewed by a leopard. When did we get here?"

"Two weeks ago."

I thought for a moment. "I don't remember coming. Should I?"

"No, adoni. You were more dead than alive."

"What happened after Hanan arrived?"

"Shaul headed back for Gibeah faster than he came after you, and Abner followed, although I'm told he cursed your name every step of the way."

"Puah?"

"She died the night we stayed in the circular valley. She roused just before the end, and Jonathan and Shagay said farewell. We didn't find you until nearly nightfall. How long was that arrow in you?" my retainer asked tightly.

"I got hit as I was leaving our old camp."

Ahiam went rigid. "Adoni, if you ever fail to tell me when you are wounded again, I won't answer for my actions."

"There was nothing you could have done. There wasn't time."

"There would have been time to get the arrow out and bind the wound. As it was, that wound was four times as bad as it should have been, and you nearly bled to death. If you'd fallen backward under that tree instead of on your face, Hassar Jonathan would be king now."

"King?" I asked puzzled.

"Do you think Shagay would have let Shaul live if you had died? As it was, he and his son disappeared once we found you. I doubt there's a Ziphite guide left living from the Arabah to Hebron."

I tried to sit up but couldn't. "What about Hanan?"

"He haunted this camp day and night. When he left yesterday afternoon, I knew you were going to recover. He gave me this," Ahiam added, handing me the twisted brass earring.

It was more than three weeks before I could do anything beyond sitting in the sun for a while before going back to my bed. Ahiam sent the harp case across the Salt Sea to Abinadab in Moab for repairs, and I did what I could to smooth the gouge across the bottom of the instrument where the arrow had scarred it.

By then Hanan had returned with the news that fighting was constant along the western border, with Hassar Jonathan commanding the units south of Kiriath-jearim, Shaul and Abner holding the center, and Sar Malchi at Aijalon. He also added that Dahveed Heber's band was getting rich running messages among the sars at camp and those in Gibeah.

While I worried about the situation out there, I was also thankful for the peace it afforded me and my men. Fortunately, the hunting here was good, due to the abundant water, and we smoked and dried as much of the meat as we could. Ahiam and Shagay had come half a mile north of the town to a triangular depression in the land more than half a mile across at its widest point. The entrance at the point faced slightly south of east toward En-gedi, and it was quite a scramble up the nearly 900 feet from the water below. I had the men start terraces and walls for fields, and we kept a constant watch on top of the cliffs that rose an additional 700 feet at our backs.

Within the confines of our haven, I had found a private retreat, a grotto in the rocks with water spraying down on one side, the profusion of ferns and mosses growing from the rock walls making a cool, green oasis for my soul. I came here often while I recovered my strength, for I had much to think about.

I went there today, taking the harp with me. The ache of my wound reminded me of Maon, and I'd had verses to another song intruding on my thoughts since the day I'd wakened here. I wanted to finish it now if I could. Sitting on the rocks in the cool, green nook made it easy to remember how Yah had saved me again. I'd given a sacrifice yesterday and the welcome feeling of Yah's presence with me humbled me. In the quietness as I played, the melody finally arranged itself properly and I sang the short song[20].

"O God, by Your name save me and by Your strength bring justice to me.

O God, hear my prayer! Listen to the sayings of my mouth!

For strangers have risen against me and violent ones seek my soul. They do not put God before them.

Behold, God is the one who helps me. My Lord is among the ones who support my soul.

He will turn back the evil to my enemy. In Your faithfulness destroy them.

With willingness let me sacrifice to You. I will praise Your name, Yahweh, for it is good.

For from all distress He rescued me, and on my enemies my eyes looked."

---

[20] Psalms 54

As the soft sound of the music drifted upward in the confined space, I closed my eyes. "Show me the way, Yah," I whispered, fingering the deep scratch on the harp that the arrow had gouged. I'd been running from Shaul for three years, driven from one end of the land to the other, rarely getting more than a few weeks of rest, barely managing to keep myself and those bound to me alive. I simply could not continue. Never knowing if Shaul's men would descend on us made it hard to contract for work, and there was much we could not supply ourselves with by hunting. In another year we would be little more than beggars.

Praying again for Yah's wisdom, I returned to my tent. I was already tired and beginning to wonder if I'd ever recover my strength. Settling myself outside the door, I waited for Ahiam to bring me camp business that I needed to attend to.

The Habiru pulled back the tent flap. "Adoni, I know you are tired, but there is someone to whom you must talk. He is waiting outside."

With a sigh, I held up my arm, and Ahiam helped me to my feet. Outside, a strange man knelt.

"This man is called Ithmah of Heshbon, adoni," Ahiam said. "He joined us on our trip here from En-gedi, and wishes to become part of your band. He was beaten and banished from his town and has no one to help him."

"Let me see your face," I said softly.

Raising his head, he hesitantly met my eyes. His were haunted, and I somehow got the impression that there was something he greatly feared.

"Has he worked with Uriah yet?" I asked, noting the nearly healed bruises on his face, which looked more compatible with a scribe's room than a warrior.

"Yes, adoni. Uriah said he was more trainable than some of the others you've picked up."

Ithmah flushed.

"Coming from Uriah, that's a compliment," I explained. "You said you were from Heshbon. There was an Ithmah of Heshbon who was married to Shimrith, the temple singer long ago. Is that your clan?"

Surprise crossed his face. "Yes, adon. I am descended from their daughter Orpah and Sakar, son of King Hissil."

"Then you are welcome indeed," I said warmly. "My blood owes yours, for I am descended from Ithmah's other daughter, Ruth."

His smile lit up his whole face. "Adon, you tell me good news indeed. My abbi lost contact with Ruth's descendants, and often prayed for Kemosh's protection on them in the land of Yahweh!"

"Yahweh has been good to us here. We have our lives, even though Shaul has turned against us. My clan is now in Moab, under Yira's protection until I know what Yahweh has in store for me. Our lives are hard sometimes, and there is always danger, but you are welcome to stay as long as you wish."

"Thank you, adoni," the man said, lowering his gaze and hesitating. "Adoni, there is one more thing."

"Yes?"

"I left family across the Jordan, and I must go to them periodically. I am all the support they have."

"Do not let that concern you, Ithmah. Just let me know when you need to leave."

He bowed again. "Thank you, adoni," he whispered.

¥ ¥ ¥ ¥ ¥ ¥

"There's Immi," Hassar Jonathan said in surprise as he and Sar Malchi rode their mules up to the gate of Jonathan's estate in Zelah at the end of the war season. He slid off his mule to greet her, wrapping his arms around her. "Spoiling Meribbaal again?"

Hassarah Ahinoam laughed. "Not as much as I should, but I try. When you and Malchi didn't return with the king two days ago, I decided to wait for you here. What kept you?"

"Since I'm now in charge of the army, Abner dumped all the administrative details on me," Malchi said in disgust.

"I see," his immi replied, her eyes twinkling.

One of the guards brought the mule that Ahinoam had ridden and helped her mount. "Catch up to me on the road, Malchi," she said, waving good-by to Taphath, who watched from the balcony of the big house.

"Did Abbi say anything more to you now that the war season is over?" Malchi asked as they watched her ride down the road.

"No."

"I hope he brings you back to Gibeah soon. Ishvi has more than he can handle."

"I'm not certain I want to go," the hassar said, looking up at his wife. Staying in war camp had been hard, even though Malchi had used him as a courier more than once so he could stop by here on his way to Gibeah and back.

"There's still a kingdom to rule," the sar reminded him.

"Only through Yahweh's hesed. This had to be the most determined push into the highlands the Philistines have ever tried. There's got to be something behind it, Malchi."

"That's *your* puzzle, brother. *I'm* afraid our esteemed cousin is up to something again."

"Abner's been courtesy itself since Ner sent him back to Abbi."

"And he's also been reminding Shaul of Dahveed whenever we're not around. Cheran says that abbi is set on going after the zammar just as soon as he can get the units out."

Jonathan slumped down on the mule. "That's why he hasn't invited me back," he sighed.

"I think I'm going to speak to Abner when I get home," his brother said. "Well, Taphath's been waiting long enough, Jonathan, so you are dismissed."

"I thought you'd never say it!" the hassar grinned, kneeing the mule through the gate.

¥ ¥ ¥ ¥ ¥ ¥

Sar Malchi eased back in the chair in Sheva's chamber on the east wall of the fortress in Gibeah. He'd just sent a messenger to Jonathan's estate for the earring, which had arrived back north in mid-summer, returned to the hassar in a military dispatch pouch. Malchi had been greeted upon his return by Cheran with the news that the king would leave in the morning for the south.

"It was the same man," the king's attendant had said. "That Ziphite, Rinnah, who came before, and who guided the king last spring. He brought word that Dahveed is at the springs of En-gedi. And he spoke with Abner, Sar. Rinnah was extremely bitter about Shaul abandoning the pursuit before the war season. He said had they gone even 100 feet farther down the trail, they would have captured Dahveed, who was badly wounded from an arrow Rinnah had shot."

"Has Dahveed recovered?" Malchi asked grimly.

"According to Rinnah, he still isn't completely well."

"Has Abner done anything to discourage the king's plans?"

Cheran had looked at him in amazement. "Discourage them? He has done all he can to encourage them!"

Just thinking about that answer made that icy wrath well up in Malchi. Once again, Abner wasn't listening. It didn't seem possible that he would risk his son, Jaasiel, like this, and as soon as the general got here, Malchi intended to find out just what Abner had in mind.

The footsteps stomping up the stairs told Malchi that the general was not any too pleased to be summoned from his bed so close to midnight. The sar smiled grimly. He wasn't any too happy either.

The door opened, and Abner burst in. "You dared to send for me at this hour?" he nearly snarled.

Malchi raised his eyebrows, regarding the angry man calmly. "As your sar, let alone your commanding officer, I will send for you whenever I please. Some news has reached my ears which I find very puzzling, and I needed an explanation before you left in the morning with the king. I was forced, therefore, to summon you now."

"Which of the commanders came running to you with word of our leaving?" Abner growled.

"The commanders have said nothing, which is quite in line with your commands to them, I would guess. But hand-picking men to make up three units, without giving them a rest from the war season, was not a popular decision, General. They were quite vocal about their disgust. All I had to do was walk through the barracks once to hear about the entire expedition."

Abner looked sour.

"I wasn't surprised to hear that the king wanted to chase after Dahveed again. What did surprise me is that you would risk the life of your son to encourage him. Did you think Jonathan was bluffing?"

Abner stood stiffly. "Jaasiel is safe enough. There's not a man of Benjamin who would kill my son, and Jonathan dares not risk a clan war to protect that southern shepherd."

"That might have been true before Shaul attacked Yahweh, Abner. Or didn't you understand how deeply that affected everyone? Your son is not the only hostage. Jonathan took hostages from nearly every clan in the tribe, remember? And not one voice was raised in protest."

The general snorted. "Did they need to? Every man of them is on an estate north of Shechem, alive and well. I admit, it surprised me that Jonathan would send them that far, and for a full six years, but I've already made arrangements to redeem Jaasiel, and by now, he's on his way home."

Malchi leaned back against the wall, staring at his abbi's cousin. "I take it that courier hasn't returned yet," he said in an odd voice.

His tone made Abner pause. "No."

"I can't imagine he's in much of a hurry to report. Did you really think Jonathan would be so naive as to send your son with the rest of them to Shechem?"

"He wouldn't dare risk anything really happening to him!"

"Abner, when the king murdered the priests, he brought Yahweh's curse down on the entire kingdom!" Malchi shouted, smashing his fist into the table in front of him. "And when Jonathan himself went to Ner about the man he took from your clan, your abbi personally guaranteed that there would be no ransom. Ner was so incensed he wanted to execute the man himself! The hassar can demand any life he wishes from Benjamin, or any of the tribes of Israel, and it would be given him! So don't delude yourself about Jaasiel being protected by your clan! Your son isn't even in Israel any longer."

"He wouldn't dare send him that far!"

"He did dare, ben Ner. Think about it. Who would be the most perfect person to watch over your son in order to ensure your cooperation?"

The general stared at Malchi for several moments, then his face gradually paled. "He wouldn't," he choked out. "He couldn't! He doesn't know where Dahveed is!"

Malchi raised his eyebrows. "Oh? The Ziphites seem to have found him for you easily enough."

"Dahveed wouldn't dare touch him!" Abner snarled, his eyes wild.

"Probably not," the sar conceded. "But are you so willing to trust Jaasiel's life in the hands of Dahveed's Habiru?"

Abner staggered a little, looking sick.

"Allow me to suggest, General, that while you're marching those picked units of yours down south to En-gedi that you figure out some way of discouraging the king's search when you get there."

"Yes, Sar," Abner croaked.

"You are dismissed."

As the officer left the room, Malchi leaned back again, watching him go. He hadn't meant for the king's cousin to jump to the conclusion that Dahveed had Jaasiel, who was actually over in Moab under the hand of Jesse, Dahveed's abbi. But the general had had enough shocks for one night, and it would be unkind of him to supply another one. Maybe he would correct the man's misapprehension later. The sar smiled. Much later.

CHAPTER 45

Emerging from my tent, I paused to scan the sky. Clear and blue, it arched overhead, and far above an eagle rode the wind, circling lazily. Just to the east, I caught sight of hundreds of dark specks in the sky. The fall migrations of birds up from Egypt had begun. Good. It would give us some variety in our meals.

"Shalom, adoni."

"Shalom, Igal," I replied. "I didn't expect you until tomorrow."

"Shagay was anxious to let you know that we've finished terracing the hillside and have three large fields in the valley all ready to plant. He sent me to ask about seed."

"This is good news, Igal," I said, pleased. Several weeks ago, remembering that Ethan's band maintained at least three strongholds scattered around the land, I had sent Shagay and seven men back to the hill in the Forest of Horesh to continue the work we had started there.

Then I sent Ira and Gareb back to the abandoned farmstead near the camp where the hassar had visited. They came from a very small clan, and when Gareb had brought his abbi to me a month ago with the news that they had been driven from their land by debt, I sent them all to the farmstead with instructions to make it as productive as possible, and I gave them the last of Hassar Jonathan's gold pieces for expenses. Ira had reported yesterday that the two granaries I wanted constructed were done, and that his abbi said the fields should be productive enough to fill them. With the news which Igal just brought, I began to feel as though our lives might not be so precarious anymore.

When I looked up again, Ethan walked toward me.

"Shalom, Ethan! What brings you here?" I asked, rising to welcome him.

"En-gedi is one of my usual stops," the Habiru said, smiling. "And I have something for you to keep track of." He tossed me the twisted brass earring.

I looked up in surprise. "When did you see the hassar?"

"I happened to be at his estate when the message came from Sar Malchi that Shaul was on his way south again. The king left Gibeah this morning."

"You made a quick run!" I exclaimed. "Shaul won't be here until tomorrow afternoon at the earliest."

"I had a mule for most of the way," Ethan admitted, easing down on the cushion Ahinoam set out for him. She brought some bread and raisins for him also, and I handed him a cruse of water.

"Does the king know exactly where we are again?"

"No. Just that you are somewhere near En-gedi."

"Well, that's some comfort," I sighed. "The Ziphites must not be helping him this time."

Ethan's smile was cold. "The forest is no longer a safe place for Ziphites. Rinnah hasn't been home for a while, and he'll be surprised at the changes that he finds. He's joined Shaul's service for all practical purposes."

"So I don't have to worry about them any longer?"

Ethan considered. "I wouldn't say that. Rinnah seems to be related to nearly any Ziphite alive, and they are a very close clan. If you are in their territory, news of it will reach him sooner or later."

Leaning back against a cushion, I stared at the tent ceiling. "So Shaul will be hunting me on his own?"

"For the most part."

"That presents some possibilities."

"You don't plan on running."

"Not unless Yahweh tells me to. We've been busy this summer. Found a couple places for hidden cisterns so we can get water without actually having to come to the springs, and some caves where we can cache supplies. There are two valleys where we plan to put in some garden crops, and Zalmon wants to plant a couple grape vines."

"You're also learning to look ahead," the Habiru leader commented.

"And I'm tired of running," I added. "If Shaul doesn't have guides, I'm going to go up on the plateau and lay a trail into the Arugot gorge. That should keep him chasing his own tail until he gets tired and goes home."

"The Arugot! There are more goats and caves in that gorge than any place I've ever seen! I'd take my oath those cliffs are more hollow than rock!"

I smiled. "Yes, and I'm going to make Shaul think he's got to search every one of them!"

Well, King Shaul was certainly persistent, I thought, watching the unit under Libni's command wait impatiently while Rinnah worked out the trail that Ahiam and three of my men had laid for him early this morning.

"It comes from the gorge, and goes back into the gorge," he said for the third time.

"But we've just been down there, and there's no one there!"

The Ziphite shrugged. "Every trail I've followed so far goes into the gorge at some point. They have to be down there."

"Yes, but where?"

Rinnah shrugged again.

Behind me, Abishai laughed silently. The Arugot was more than a mile south of our true camp, and the bottom of it was mostly rock, leaving no trail once my men got down there. With a little care, it was possible to escape the canyon in several places with no sign of our passing. Shaul, Abner, and the three units with them had spent the past three weeks combing the entire two miles of that gorge, only to go down there and do it again, and now once more!

Ahiam, Shagay's Jonathan, and Abishai usually guided the small groups of men who trooped around the forest and down into the Arugot every third day or so to keep the king's interest keen. Shaul got occasional glimpses of men, once or twice a donkey, and they left a few old fires outside of caves where they had eaten a meal. Four of his sentinels had reported seeing fires burning down in the gorge from the rim, but by the time the army reached them, no one was there.

King Shaul was so frustrated that Rinnah dared not show his face to him, and the men were nearly in open rebellion against the fruitless searching of empty caves day after day. Rinnah was angry, and Hanan reported that the man had cast about for signs of us on the uplands as far as a mile on either side of Shaul. But I only allowed the most skilled men on the uplands, having the others leave the gorge by its mouth and return on the well-traveled road that came up the Arabah to En-gedi. We had to be careful the last half mile north, since the road turned west into the uplands just outside of town.

In spite of our success thwarting Shaul, I still felt a sense of irritation. Planting season was here, for the first rains had softened the ground. I wanted my men to be working the fields we'd made, not playing "chase me" with the king. But it looked as if Shaul was willing to stay around all winter, and I couldn't afford the time or the men to keep him distracted.

All 12 of the warriors here at En-gedi waited with me in the trees, leaving only Keturah, Ahinoam, Gad, and Abiathar back at our camp. We'd planned on splitting into four groups and leaving trails all over the plateau south of the canyon, then heading off into the hills to the west. I hoped Shaul would get the idea that we'd left the area that way.

Just then a messenger appeared. "Commander Libni, Shaul comes," I heard him announce.

Shaul himself strode from the trees shortly, followed by Abner, who looked exhausted. I frowned. If I didn't know better, I'd say the king's cousin was very worried about something. But I'd never seen that expression on the general's face, so I couldn't tell for certain. The wind blew past, and I turned my face to it, drawing in a deep breath. Rain.

Hanan appeared beside me. "Adoni, if you mean to cross the gorge, you should start now. Rain is on the way."

"I smelled it."

"You know, adoni, we are on the north side of the gorge, and the only way out of the gorge at the mouth is on the south side of the watercourse."

Jonathan chuckled beside me. "So if we take Shaul's men down there and time it right. The water from the rains could trap them for a day or two!"

I considered. With rain approaching, leaving a trail on the plateau would be useless. "Maybe it's time to use that double-cave you found down there by those old sheepfolds, Jonathan," I said. "We could lead them down and hide in the back part of that cave until they've searched past us. Then we'll cross the watercourse and head out of the gorge. What do you think, Ahiam?"

"It could work, and it might disgust Shaul's men enough that they will force him to leave. Abner looks ready to abandon the chase as it is."

"All right, let's do it. Jonathan, give us an hour to get down the gorge. I don't want to hurry on that path down the cliff face. Then lure Rinnah to our trail. He'll do the rest. Just be sure you give yourself time to get to the bottom without getting hurt. And remember, Rinnah has a compound bow. Stay out of range!"

Both Jonathan and Hanan disappeared, and I briefly outlined the plan before leading the men to the cliff face. The path was little more than a ledge that clung to the vertical face of the cliff, descending nearly 200 of the 1,000 feet to the bottom before it widened out to cross and re-cross a watercourse that had cut itself into the cliff as it twisted down the rest of the way.

We descended carefully, most of us keeping one hand on the rock beside us for whatever support it could provide. Zabad came right after me, and I listened carefully to his breathing. When it got too rapid, I'd pause a little, giving him time to lean against the cliff and relax. My brother-in-law feared heights nearly as much as Jaasiel, Igal's friend, feared the dark. He'd never said anything to me, and he never hesitated at times like this when he was required to climb around high spots, but I knew he'd be the most thankful man in the land if he could leave En-gedi and never see another cliff again.

Once that first descent was over, his breathing evened out, and I went faster, making it to the bottom in good time. We drank at a small spring, and I kept my eye on the top of the cliff. Soon, Jonathan started down the first part of the trail, going faster than I liked, but he made it to the wider part of the watercourse before anyone else appeared at the top.

"Let's show ourselves," I said, walking away from the canyon wall. Once we were well out, the men gathered around as though they were listening to something I was saying. A couple walked closer to me as if giving a report. Jonathan was nearly at the bottom by the time we broke up the group and started west up the canyon, disappearing around a bend.

Once out of sight, we waited. Soon Jonathan trotted up, a huge smile on his face. "They're coming, adoni. All of them. Even the king!"

"Abner won't be happy about Shaul taking that trail," I commented.

"From what I could see, Shaul didn't care what Abner thought. He's very determined, adoni."

I nodded. "Where's that cave you found?"

"Keep going up the canyon past the next two bends. There's a jumble of huge boulders behind the old sheepfolds. The entrance is on this side of the boulders. Some ferns have grown over it."

The breeze again brought the scent of rain as we hurried forward, leaving only one or two indications of our passing. The sky above me was still cloudless and blue, but I knew how fast that could change.

We found the cave without delay, and Jonathan and Abishai made certain that we left no indication we had turned off the trail at this point. Even inside the cave, I made the men stay only on rocks around the edge of the room beyond the entrance. The area was dimly lit, the ceiling only 11 feet over our heads, with a tumble of rocks and debris on the right side. One of the boulders jutted out from the back wall, concealing a passage that led back into a second room. Likely the two rooms had formerly been one, until an earthquake had shaken down part of the ceiling. Very little light filtered into the side-room from the passage, but there was a hole or two near the ceiling that illuminated the place a little.

Jonathan checked the first room carefully to be certain that nothing indicated our presence, and then we settled down to wait until the units went by.

"They're just coming into sight, adoni," Jonathan whispered, carefully stepping from rock to rock along the side of the cave to where I waited by the boulder.

"Are they searching the caves again?"

"Yes."

I went back to the men, quieting them while we waited. Silence rose around us, seeming to press into our ears as if we could actually hear it. In a couple moments we heard sounds from the other room.

"We will be outside, adoni," Commander Libni said.

I rose, silently stepping to the boulder, listening as someone moved around in the other room. The noises grew closer, and I shrank back against the rock, waiting until they stopped. When I heard nothing more for several moments, I cautiously peered around.

King Shaul was not 10 feet from me, his girdle, meil, and loincloth lying closer to me, his robe and undergarment hiked up as he squatted by the rocks to relieve himself!

A bit dazed, I pulled back quickly.

"What is it?" Jonathan breathed, puzzled. Before I could say anything, he looked around the boulder. Jerking back nearly as quickly as I had, he stepped away, fighting to contain his laughter.

I tried to stop Zabad from looking, but couldn't move quickly enough, and I dared not make a sound. His reaction was just as marked as Jonathan's, but in an entirely different way. He drew his dagger and edged forward.

My hand clamped down on his arm, and I risked the noise of forcing him back. By now, everyone wanted to see, and I had to pull my belt knife before I could herd the men to the far side of the room.

"What is it?" Josheb breathed.

"Shaul, alone," Zabad barely whispered. "This is your chance to end this chase, Dahveed! Otherwise, he'll just keep after you."

"Roeh Shamuel did say this day would come, adoni," Zalmon added.

"I heard that, too," Azmaveth, another former bodyguard to Jonathan, whispered as the rest strained to hear. "Shamuel prophesied that Yahweh would deliver your enemy to you, and that you could do whatever you wanted with him."

I remained silent.

"Yahweh has given him to you," Zabad put in again. "He's trying to kill you, and us as well. And there's only one way we'll really be safe again. Don't scorn what comes from Yahweh's hands!"

Something drew me back to the boulder, and I looked around it again. Shaul was still there, obviously not paying attention to anything around him. What should I do? I well remembered Shamuel's prophecy, uttered the day the king had stripped himself at Navyoth when he arrived to kill me there. He had come seeking my life now, and stripped himself again, fulfilling even the circumstances under which the prophecy had been given. But what should I do with the man that Yahweh had placed in my power?

Drawing my belt knife, I edged out from the boulder. I did have the safety of my men to consider. For years he'd chased us, and even now was making it impossible for us to do what was necessary for us to live. Shaul had indeed become my enemy. I paused. But was I his? I looked down at the belt knife, the blade forged generations ago to protect Boaz's bloodline. It didn't feel right in my hand. Glancing at the man uncovered before me again, I knew that in spite of everything he had done, I still loved him. He had needed me as no one else had. His gratitude and acceptance had filled my thirsty soul more than once, enabling me to lift my head with honor for the first time in my life, his need holding me close until Hassar Jonathan could take me under his wing.

The day might come when I would have to kill him in battle, but I could not do it here, like this. I might be able to teach him a lesson, however. Silently, I stepped forward, kneeling by the king's meil. Keeping one eye on Shaul's back, I bunched the edge in my hand, pressing my belt knife against the damp earth on the cave floor to slice off a portion. Then I faded back to the boulder, the fringe I held falling over my hand.

Shaking a bit in reaction, I eased back into the side room and turned to my men, who had gathered around the entrance once more. I glanced down at the cloth in my hand. Suddenly, I caught my breath, dizzy. My heart had quit beating! Then it gave a great leap in my chest as it had when I was struck by Yahweh's fire while fleeing from Gath. I had to bend over to ease the painful pounding, gritting my teeth against the flash of pain from the burn scar on my arm.

"What is it, adoni?" Josheb whispered anxiously, steadying me as I staggered to the far side of the room again.

"I never should have touched it," I whispered in reply. "Yahweh forbid that I do such a thing again!"

"Do what?" Zalmon breathed.

I held out the cloth I'd cut from the meil. "He is my master, and it is not for me to touch anything of his!"

My heart had eased, and I straightened up, breathing easier.

"You killed him?" Zabad pressed.

"I cut off part of his meil. It was on the rocks close to me."

"Is that all?"

"It was enough," I whispered, my voice shaking. "It was his *meil*! The symbol of his authority and throne! When this becomes known, it will weaken the king's position, and that will make it harder for him to protect Israel. I had no right to touch him!"

"Then let me kill him," Zabad urged. "He's still out there."

"No. He is Mashiah, belonging to Yahweh. Yah's power has flowed through him. He is not to be harmed!"

"And what about us? Are we here to be harmed? Dahveed, that man out there would slaughter us all! Can't we protect ourselves?" Jaasiel hissed.

I motioned for silence again. "If he attacks, we defend ourselves. But he's not attacking now. He doesn't even know we are here. All we had to do was sit still, and he would have left, none the wiser. I have sinned in what I have done!"

"We are to let our enemy go free?" Zabad demanded bitterly.

"When Shaul comes against us in battle, you may kill him if you can, Zabad. But we will not murder Yahweh's anointed nagid for any other reason! I have already done enough by taking this," I held up the cloth. "I might as well have laid claim to his throne. I've no doubt that more than one person will see it that way!"

Zabad wasn't the only one angry. Jaasiel had his fists clenched, and Naharai and Ishmaiah gripped their swords. Josheb shifted closer to me, subtly reinforcing my authority with his acceptance of my command. When the others looked around, Uriah had his arms folded, leaning against the cave wall, watching them steadily.

Silence descended on us again, and we became aware of the sounds from the outer room as Shaul dressed himself. Zabad could hardly keep himself still as we listened to the king leave.

Suddenly I realized that I was thirsty, and that the gift must have taken me some time during our nearly silent discussion. Shaking my head, I stepped back a bit. Ahiam handed me his cruse, and I drank gratefully.

"This is a hard thing to accept, Dodi," Abishai spoke softly. "He has chased us all over this land. Must we continue to endure it?"

I looked at the piece of the king's meil. "No," I said slowly. "You should not have to. Shaul's displeasure is for me to endure. Stay here a moment."

Without saying anything else, I left the side room, moving swiftly since I wanted to be outside before the men realized where I was going. Yahweh had been very clear with me. Previous to this, I had never done anything against Israel's king. But I had now. I'd been in court long enough to understand the seriousness of my actions. Hassar Jonathan protected the king's honor so fiercely for a very good reason.

The king held the tribes together. And only together could they hope to keep the kingdoms surrounding us from plundering the land. Therefore, *anything* that weakened the king's authority and power endangered all of Israel. A good portion of the army came from the tribes north of the Jezreel valley, and the sole hold that Shaul had over them was the power of his reputation. Something like this would make him look like a fool, and if that happened, the kingdom might literally fall apart.

I paused at the entrance to the cave, making sure that I could step out without being seen. While I had only wanted to demonstrate to the king that I was not a threat to him, by overstepping the bounds, I had created a situation that could destroy the very thing I was anointed to protect. It was a wonder Yahweh hadn't struck me dead!

I could think of just one thing to do that might repair the damage and show Shaul that I meant him no harm. It might cost me my life, but Yahweh had demonstrated that in touching Shaul, I had already endangered my own life.

Stuffing the cloth of the meil into my girdle, I walked out to the path that followed the water course in the bottom of the canyon. The units had already rounded the next bend and were out of sight. Picking up my pace, I caught up to them.

Not far around the bend, Shaul watched with Abner while Libni directed soldiers as they searched another cave. Taking a deep breath, I went forward, still unseen, for everyone's attention was on the cave entrance. When I was close enough, I stopped. "Adoni melek," I called out.

Shaul whipped around.

I dropped to my knees and bowed to the ground, then flattened myself all the way down. Total silence greeted me. After several moments, I rose to my knees, then got up and walked closer. No one moved or spoke as I knelt again. "Adoni, why did you listen when someone told you that I was trying to kill you?" I asked. "Surely you can see now that it isn't true, for Yahweh gave you into my hand in that cave. My men urged me to take your life, but I refused, for you are not only my abbi, but Yahweh's mashiah."

I pulled the meil cloth out of my girdle. "Look at it, abbi. Check the edge of your meil."

Automatically, Shaul glanced down, pulling the garment around until he found the place on the hem where it had been cut. He jerked his head up to stare at me again.

"See this? I cut off this piece of cloth in that cave instead of your life. I haven't rebelled against you, or wished you any harm, or done any sin against you. Why did you come here to ambush me?"

It was almost as if no one was capable of speech. Or maybe the shock of my appearance after so many days of fruitless searching still held them, for no one answered me.

"Yahweh judge between you and me, adoni," I continued. "Let it be His job to avenge me for what you've done, for I will never avenge myself. Like the ancients have said, 'Wickedness only comes from the wicked,' and my hands will not bring you harm."

A couple soldiers to one side appeared about to draw their swords, and strangely, it was Abner who stopped them with a quick gesture. He seemed ill-at-ease, glancing around constantly, his face nearly gray. Getting to my feet, I approached a little closer and knelt again.

"Adoni, you are king of Israel! Why did you bother to bring the army down here to make war on me?" I begged softly. "You're chasing nothing more than a dead dog, or even a flea on that dog!"

Abner's eyes searched the rocks, following the watercourse, but he kept his hand up to restrain the men, who waited in silence. The king moved for the first time, advancing closer, still staring at me.

"If you wish, adoni, let Yahweh judge between us," I repeated. "He can see my heart, and plead my cause, and vindicate me now in your hand." I bowed again to the ground and remained there.

"Is that really your voice, Dahveed, my son?" the king finally said, his own breaking. Suddenly he wept openly, holding out his arms to me, and I went to him, kneeling again and giving him my hands.

"You're in the right, Dahveed," he said at last, "for in spite of all the wicked things I have done to you, you've done only good things to me. You always bring the light."

His grip on my hands tightened. "As you have done now. Yahweh must indeed have put me in your power and yet you still didn't kill me." He looked down at the cloth in our clasped hands. "You cannot be my enemy, for no one is so foolish as to find his enemy at his mercy and then let him go. I should not have come against you, Dahveed, and may Yahweh reward you with prosperity for what you have done for me today."

Tears fell from my eyes also, and I returned the tight grip he kept on my hands. I didn't trust myself to speak. It had been so long since I had felt the king's approval and good-will!

Shaul quieted himself, staring at the piece of his meil. "You will indeed be king, Dahveed, and the kingdom of Israel will be established under your hand." Then he looked into my eyes, and his hands trembled. "Swear to me, Dahveed! Swear to me now, by Yahweh, that you will not kill my family when I am dead, that you won't destroy my name from my abbi's house."

I looked up in surprise.

"Give me that comfort, Dahveed," he added softly, his eyes pleading with me.

"Adoni, you know what the hassar means to me! I could never harm him, or anything of his!"

"Swear this to me, Dahveed," he pressed, trembling more. "Swear that they shall live."

"Adoni, by Yahweh's name I swear that I will not raise my hand against your descendants, or destroy your name when I am king over Israel."

"You cannot break that oath, my son," Shaul said.

"I would never want to, abbi. I owe you too much."

The wind swept down the canyon, sending a chill through me, and I glanced up. Black clouds covered the sky, racing toward the east.

"Adoni, you must cross the watercourse immediately," I said, rising, "or the rains will soon block your passage."

"My son, do you come with me?"

"I do not know what Yahweh has planned for me, adoni. He will send me to you if He wills." I glanced again at the sky, the roar of the wind swelling in the canyon. "Do not delay any longer," I urged. "If rain has already fallen in the uplands, the watercourse can fill without warning."

Thunder crashed overhead, and the wind whined through the rocks. I pulled the king to Abner. "General, get the king and your men to the other side immediately. Once over there, you should have a clear way to the mouth."

Abner nodded, glancing apprehensively at the sky. I turned to go, but his hand stopped me. "Dahveed, is Jaasiel all right?" he asked in a low voice.

I looked at him, startled. Why would he be concerned about Igal's friend Jaas? But he looked as if he wasn't going to budge until I answered his question, so I did.

"He's fine, although when I left him last, he was probably still angry with me. But you must go quickly, Abner," I added. And in the rush to get the units to the other side of the canyon, I slipped away.

¥ ¥ ¥ ¥ ¥ ¥

"Geber, Shaul is coming," Nimshi called, scrambling up the courtyard wall to the roof of Jonathan's business chamber, then swinging down from the beams protruding outside. "They left the units at Gibeah, but Shaul didn't stop there, and Abner's with him!"

Why would the king be coming here, the hassar wondered, hastily stripping the king's signet from his hand and tucking it into his girdle. "Nimshi! Do they have Dahveed?" he gasped.

"No, geber."

"Did they kill him?"

"Couldn't have, geber. If Dahveed was dead, Shaul would be, too."

At Jonathan's startled glance, Nimshi gave him an unsettling smile. "We are not called Yahweh's Arrows for nothing, geber."

The guard at the gate opened it for the king as Jonathan stepped outside. "It's good to see you, Abbi," he greeted, striding over to take the bridle of the king's mule.

"Jonathan, I must speak with you."

"Then come to the upper room, Abbi. Taphath is visiting in Gibeah, and my business chamber is quite small."

The hassar expected that Abner would accompany them also, but the general remained by his mule, looking pale and drawn. Maybe Malchi knew why, he thought. As he followed the king up the stairs, he saw the gap in the meil, cut off, not torn. What could have happened?

"Sit down, Abbi," he said when they entered the room. He pulled a stool back from the table and pushed the stone bowl of fruit closer to the king. Abiezer came in with a cruse of wine and two goblets.

"You are well?" Jonathan asked as his abbi sipped some of the wine.

"At present. How is Meribbaal?"

"Getting into everything now that he's discovered he can get places on his own!"

A brief smile crossed the king's face. "You were that way. Ahinoam never knew where she'd find you next." Shaul paused. "Jonathan, how long have you had my signet?"

Jonathan froze in his chair and glanced quickly at the man across the table. His abbi studied the brass goblet, turning it around and around in his hands, his shoulders stiff. How much dared he tell? Did he have the right to endanger his brothers by saying anything at all? But saying nothing would be just as bad. However, the king only seemed subdued, not angry or suspicious. Jonathan clenched his hands together. He would answer questions, but nothing more. "Nearly a year and half."

The king's tension lessened, and he let out his breath. "Why did you take Jaasiel?"

"Immi did that," his son replied softly.

Jonathan's lips quirked as Shaul's head jerked up in amazement. "Ahinoam? Why?"

"Abner took the young son of one of my personal guards to force the man to report everything I did."

"He compromised your personal guard?"

"Yes."

Shaul's face darkened. "Abner's been busier than I thought. He's getting bold now that Ner is aging."

When the king said no more, Jonathan spoke. "Do you require the signet back, adoni?"

"No, Hassar. I came here to be sure you had it, one way or the other. You are to keep it. If you have it, perhaps he will go gently and leave me in peace."

Jonathan eyed his abbi, wondering if he was prophesying again, but Shaul seemed calm enough.

"Whom are you speaking of?" he finally asked.

"Dahveed. He said Yahweh would send him, and it will probably be soon." The king looked down at the goblet again, his dark hair liberally laced with gray, his eyes tired. "I have failed, Jonathan. You should be king after me, but it will never happen now. But at least you can rule until Dahveed comes to take the kingdom."

"Abbi, Dahveed will never *take* the kingdom."

"It is his, Jonathan. Roeh Shamuel was right. Yahweh has rejected me, and my house, from holding the throne."

"I know, Abbi, but Dahveed will never take the throne so long as you live."

"I made him swear to keep you alive, Jonathan. I did that much for you all."

"Abbi, you don't understand," the hassar said, taking Shaul's hand, worried at the despondent tones in the king's voice. "Dahveed will never *take* the throne."

"No, Jonathan, you don't understand. I cannot keep the throne for you. You will never rule after me. Shamuel said it would not be so, and it won't!"

"Abbi, please look at me," Jonathan pleaded, gripping his abbi's hands.

The king looked up, and his son held his gaze. "Abbi, I know I will not reign after you. I know Israel's throne is not mine to keep. Just as Dahveed knows that *it is not his to take*. It belongs to Yahweh, who will give it to His king when He wills. Believe me, Abbi, Dahveed will never go against Yahweh by coming up here and demanding what is not yet his."

"Then there is time yet?" Shaul asked softly. "There is time yet for you to rule?"

"Yes, Abbi, Yahweh has still left the kingdom with our house."

The king frowned. "And Abner is restless." He looked at Jonathan again. "Remember this, Jonathan Hassar. When Ner is dead, do not trust his son."

"I do not trust him now, adoni."

"You are wise," his abbi replied, easing back in the chair.

"Now, Abbi, tell me what happened at En-gedi. You must have spoken to Dahveed. Is he well?"

"He looked well," Shaul said, his voice trembling. "He called me 'abbi,' Jonathan. After all I have done to him, he called me that."

"He loves you," the hassar said. "He always has."

A sad smile crossed the king's face. "He must. You have always spoken truth, Jonathan. He held my life in his hands, and I still live because of his hesed."

The next day, Jonathan returned to Gibeah with Shaul, resuming his place as Hassar and the duties that Sar Ishvi gladly relinquished to him.

Tamar bat Dahveed

Shaul has again parted from Dahveed in peace. But even so, Dahveed did not trust himself to him, but to Yah. He has learned caution in his relationship with Shaul and not to place his own wisdom above Yahweh's. The near tragedy at Maon taught him that! His humility before the king in response to Yah's pointing out his sin brought about the necessary reconciliation between them, for it is time for Dahveed's focus to change. He has looked to the north, to Israel, for the years of his exile, but the culmination of Yah's work in Carmel is at hand, and it is time for Dahveed to pay attention to his homeland, Judah, and the people in it. There must be security here first, for the tribes further south in the Negev and beyond are growing stronger and more restless. The time of their judgment is nearly at hand, and Yah knows that wars are best fought one at a time.

Abigail and Carmel

CHAPTER 46

I wiped the sweat from my forehead and looked across the field and down the valley. Shammah and Elika were already out of sight. After the king left us at En-gedi--and I had endured Ahiam's opinion of my decision to show myself to the king--Yahweh had sent word through Gad that we were to leave the springs. When I had asked where I should go, Yahweh had said Horesh, so we had joined Shagay at the stronghold.

Shammah and Elika, however, remained at En-gedi. They were used to farming in areas with a constant water supply, and I was unwilling to lose all the effort that we had put into the place. They also needed to tell Ithmah of Moab where we'd gone. He had crossed the Jordan the day after I reconciled with Shaul.

The two men from En-harod had established themselves quickly, and I'd given permission for them to send for their families. The report they had just brought surprised me. Their families had come already, bringing enough people to work the farmstead. I told them to be careful, for we'd found at least one traveler dead on the west Hebron-Beersheba highway, and stories circulated about robberies and theft.

Probably a small band of robbers now roved in our area, and I had debated whether or not to do anything about it. But it seemed more important to get the crops in the ground. I worried about the approaching winter. Until we harvested our first crop, we had to live by hunting, and even though I sent the men miles into the forest so as to keep game available close to us, I knew that by the time winter ended, food would be scarce in the stronghold. Zalmon's wife and four children had joined us, increasing the pressure on our food supply.

I had to spend another gold ingot for oil, salt, seeds, and leather, and we'd already lost to wolves one of the sheep that Zalmon's wife brought. I turned back to my work. This was the last field to be planted, and it needed to get done before Shagay's Jonathan arrived with the grape shoots that we'd purchased.

"Dodi, there's someone hurt down there," Asahel called, trotting up.

"Where?" I asked, straightening.

"Over the hill in the big valley east of here. There are four of them, and I think they are shepherds. I overheard them saying that someone else should be here soon with a flock of some sort."

"Go get your healer's bag," I directed.

Once on the other side of the hill, Asahel and I stayed in the trees, looking the situation over. The men had made a fire and were tending their companion. Finally I walked out into the open and toward them.

"It looks bad to me," one was saying, "but I don't know enough to be sure."

"Perhaps we can help," I said.

The men whirled around, their faces blanching when they saw me. "Habiru!" one exclaimed. They bunched closer together, facing me.

"Habiru, yes," I said drily, "but I'm feeling lazy today and don't want to exert myself fighting anyone."

"We don't have anything you'd want," one of them protested.

"True," I replied, looking them over thoroughly. "But I might have something you want."

They stared in surprise.

"Asahel?"

My nephew trotted out, making the shepherds jump back again. "He knows something of wounds, if you're willing."

"We have to do something," one of them hissed to the spokesman. "We can't let her die."

Her? I pricked up my ears. Given the presence of robbers, what was a woman doing out here without guards?

The man finally stepped back and Asahel hurried over. I retreated a little way. The shepherds warmed up to him quickly, my nephew's easy way with people putting them at ease.

In a short while, Asahel hurried over to me. "It's a stab wound, Dodi. They say she's a scribe coming to meet with them, and a Habiru attacked her."

We walked over to the shepherds. "Where is your master's house?"

"Carmel."

I raised my eyebrows. "You belong to Nabal, then."

Bitterness crossed the man's face. "Yes. But she belongs to the Gebirah," he indicated the scribe.

"Can she be moved, Asahel?"

The young man shrugged. "I don't see why not. Whoever stabbed her was either the worst hand with a knife in the land, or in a hurry."

"All right. I'll send Elhanan and Zalmon with a donkey."

"You've shown us much kindness, geber," the spokesman said. "What name shall we give our Gebirah, for she will want to know."

I bowed slightly. "Give her the compliments of the Dahveed."

"Dahveed Israel!" one of the shepherds gasped. "Forgive me, adon, I did not recognize you. I am called Mibhar ben Hagri. I served in your unit the season you earned Sahrah Michal."

"Then you can reassure your companions that my band will not harm them," I said, smiling.

They looked at each other.

"Adon, please, cover us with more of your kindness," Mibhar said, dropping to his knees. "Oholah is not the first of us to be hurt, and we have little way of protecting ourselves. The attacks are sudden and always from ambush. Adon, let us remain here by you with our flocks. The nagid does not care enough to send guards for us, but the Gebirah will be grateful."

Indeed, she might, I thought, considering the idea. It might also create some good-will for my band. I was beginning to understand why the dahveeds allied to Ethan coveted the title of Yahweh's Arrows so much. Survival was much easier with a reputation of trustworthiness. Besides, now that I was reconciled to Shaul, I wanted to establish myself and my men within honorable society. Here might be a very good place to begin.

"Remain here, and I will cover you," I agreed.

"Thank you, adoni," the men said gratefully.

It turned out that Elhanan had gone hunting, so I decided to accompany Zalmon myself. Mibhar offered to guide us to Maon where the Gebirah was. As we threaded our way through the forest paths the shepherd steadied Oholah on the donkey and told me much of the news in the area. I gleaned a great deal from his passing comments about the Gebirah and the nagid. He certainly didn't seem to have much respect for his adon, and I wondered what the situation might be around here.

The atmosphere near Maon was worse than I remembered from my previous visit. I kept fighting the urge to glance behind myself. The way everyone nearly cringed reminded me of the Gibeonites, and I had to restrain my growing sense of anger.

Mibhar had fallen silent as we went through the town, finally turning into a gate at a large compound. Two guards straightened as we entered, the one on the balcony of the house notching an arrow as he hurried down the stairs.

"Thank Yahweh you are here, Gebirah," Mibhar exclaimed, seeing her emerge from the house and move gracefully toward us. Her face was just as stunning as I remembered it, and Zalmon stared so hard that he couldn't get his mouth closed.

"Oholah was hurt on her way to us, and these men helped us tend her and bring her back," Mibhar explained as he eased the fainting woman from the donkey. She had stood the trip well, but now that she was here, she collapsed.

"Quickly, get her inside!" the Gebirah commanded. "Please wait," she threw over her shoulder as she followed the shepherd into the house.

"A young man tended her and said the wound wasn't too bad . . ." Mibhar's voice faded as they entered the house. Moments later, a rather plump woman hurried from the house to a storeroom.

Zalmon and I retreated to the wall by the gate, and I took the time to study the compound thoroughly. It had several storerooms on the left and a large two-story house on the right shaded by an oak in the private courtyard around it. Between it and the storerooms there was a grape arbor with a bench and what was probably the original house with something walled off on the right and a squat room made of stone on the left. My eyes sharpened. The walls looked especially thick and the roof was of heavy timber. A treasury?

Shouts from the road made Zalmon and me turn to see what was happening.

"Way! Make way for the nagid," a man cried, trotting into view, throwing his admonition to both sides of the road for the benefit of two caged ducks, a dove on the compound wall, and a goat that glanced over its shoulder, several blades of grass disappearing gradually into its chewing jaws.

"Way! Make way for the nagid!"

Switching its tail, the goat grabbed another mouthful while the nagid, surrounded by four guards, rode into view on a mule, sitting stiffly, staring straight ahead. His chin was pointed with a beard at the end, and his hair receded from his forehead, circled with a gold headband. There wasn't a human being in sight, and I glanced around curiously.

"Weren't there people in this town, Zalmon?" I asked.

"I remember some, although they were quite shy."

"They seem non-existent now," I said, lounging against the wall, watching the nagid progress past.

"Way! Make way for the nagid," the man cried again, turning into the compound. When he saw us, he stopped. Nabal continued forward and halted his mule several feet away. He was draped about with several clashing colors, and I finally realized that he had on a robe made of long vertical panels of cloth. Rings glittered on every finger, and a gold clasp caught back his hair in addition to the headband.

"I am Nagid Carmel. What are you doing in my compound?" he demanded.

I straightened up from the wall. "Shalom, Nagid."

"Account for yourself, Habiru."

I bowed slightly. "I am returning the Gebirah's possession, and she bade me wait on her out here. I obeyed, of course."

"There is nothing of hers that you could possibly have found! Guards, beat these two dogs and drive them from the town." The foremost two guards started toward us.

Zalmon and I both straightened, moving apart. It was the fact that we separated instead of crowding together that made the guards hesitate. Neither of us had drawn a weapon yet, and we both watched the approaching men steadily. I'm not certain what would have happened next if the Gebirah hadn't appeared at that moment.

"Nagid, why have you troubled yourself about these two?" she asked, emerging from the doorway of the house.

Nabal's head swivelled to stare at her. "Gebirah!" he gasped. "You should not be giving your attention to these riffraff!"

"And even less should you be giving yours, Nagid. These men returned one of my people who was attacked out near the sheep pastures. But that is far beneath your notice. Others can reward them, although they have been honored already by the sight of your magnificence. It would not be meet for you to stay overlong since it will take your time from much more important things."

I managed to make myself bow, as did Zalmon.

"There is much in what you say," Nabal agreed. "They have indeed been rewarded by the privilege of seeing me. That should be reward enough for their service."

"Indeed, it will," I said, my voice hard.

Nabal jerked the mule's head around, and the guard followed him to the room against the far wall.

Gebirah Abigail turned her attention to us. She met my gaze, and froze an instant, her eyes suddenly wide and dark. Then calmness settled across her face, and she nodded graciously. "You have our gratitude for your consideration," she said in a steady tone that tugged at my memory some way, but I couldn't quite bring anything to mind. "I hope you will accept some reward for your service. What may I offer you?"

Standing there, so calm and collected after the way her husband had exhibited himself, she earned my admiration. I bowed. "When I think of something, I will let you know, Gebirah." Before she could respond, I left, forcibly removing Zalmon as I did. I wanted out of this town. Even the gebirah here wore a mask. But I couldn't help wondering what might be behind it.

The weeks passed, and the wheat and barley sprouted and grew, giving promise of an abundant harvest in the spring. We had three large flocks of sheep and one of goats to guard out in the big valley, and in spite of the rain and occasional snow, the men had finished a wine press, and dug out an even bigger cistern than the two small ones we'd made the first time we had been here.

Ira and Gareb, as well as Elika and Shammah, reported in regularly on progress at the farmstead and the springs. Uriah kept up a strict training schedule for the men here with me. I'd been restless, wandering the camp at night, checking that the guards on duty stayed alert.

More stories of robberies circulated along the roads, and no one traveled alone south of Hebron. Once again, I considered the possibility of hunting down the men responsible. The last time Elhanan had gone to a town to purchase some badly needed cloth, the shopkeeper had practically accused him of stealing the silver he had with him.

At last, I could stand the restlessness no longer. "I'll go out hunting with you tomorrow," I told Shagay.

"As you wish, adoni."

Just at first light, I strapped on my sword and cuirass, took my bow and quiver, and Jonathan, Shagay, and I left the camp, running along the spine of the ridge, which pointed northeast toward Ziph. We shortly turned down a watercourse into the deep intersecting valley on the north side, following it west to the Hebron/Beersheba highway. Once on the west side of the road, we jogged about a mile farther, and then spread out to hunt. Hanan had joined us by now, and in the early morning light we drifted northwest in a long, loose line, intent on finding deer.

The others were out of my sight in the forest when I paused, an unexpected odor briefly tickling my nose. I slowed, moving silently forward, eyes alert. The sun's rays shone brighter in the foliage ahead of me, indicating a small clearing. The back of my neck prickled, and I stopped between a sycamore and an oak, studying the space ahead that had nothing but a tall post in it. I had circled around to my left before I realized there was a man tied to that post. He was on his knees, half leaning on the post, half hanging from his hands which were bound over his head. I studied him a while longer. Either he was asleep or faint from the wounds on his naked upper body.

Through the trees farther around to my left I glimpsed two ragged tents. Most likely I'd just stumbled on the men responsible for the robberies in the area. I guessed it was time to clean up the forest. But first I needed to get that captive safely away.

Pulling my belt knife, I silently crossed to the post and sliced through the rawhide binding his hands. His arms dropped, and I reached out to steady him.

With incredible speed, his arm flashed forward, pulling my sword from its sheath, swinging it around to slice into my leg. I leaped away, ducking around the post, and he lunged after me, my sword biting into the wood at neck level.

Instantly, I was plunged deep in the gift, the air rushing around me as I faced him, stopping his downward stroke with the blade of my belt knife, shedding it to the side. A battle cry burst from my mouth, and I jumped at him, making him retreat, his eyes wide with astonishment. My knife flashed in the light, leaving a score of red across his chest as he desperately tried to give himself enough room to use the sword effectively.

Pressing close, my right hand brushed off the pan of the sling, then dipped into the shepherd's bag and grabbed the sling stone there.

My opponent hit my chest with his fist, trying to shove me away and swing the sword up, but I brushed it aside with the knife, leaving another score of red down his arm. Then I whipped my right arm around, and the sling unwound, smashing the stone into the back of his head. He reeled back against the post, and I drove my belt knife into it, that hand flashing down to tear my blade from him as I leaped back.

The man froze, watching over my shoulder, a bitter smile on his dark face. Some of the foulest curses I'd ever heard spilled from his mouth, making me ache to continue the battle.

Then a sword point pricked the back of my neck. "You defeated him, you get to kill him," a voice said behind me. "Do so, now."

He had barely finished speaking when I drove my left foot backward into the speaker's legs, whirling left so quickly that my sword swept his to the side long before he even knew what I'd done. The speed of my turn brought my right fist smashing into his face. I'd driven that same fist into his mid-section before he hit the ground.

A second man ran toward me, and I hurled the stone still in the sling at him, hitting him in mid-chest, sending him tumbling. A third man jerked to a halt by the second, pulling back his bow to shoot. He died where he stood, pierced by three arrows from three different directions.

The captive hadn't moved. I turned my blazing eyes on him, and he stared back, body braced against the post.

"Adoni, take a drink," Shagay said off to one side.

I turned my head, backing up a bit, reaching for what Shagay held out to me.

"Adoni, does he live or die?" Shagay asked, indicating the man at the post.

I fought to find my voice. "He lives," I said, and drove my sword into the ground, gasping for air.

"What about the others," Jonathan asked me a bit later after I'd drained the cruse.

I looked over the two men still alive who had attacked me. The one who had held a sword at my neck was Hiddai, the man who had tried to abduct Sar Ishvi's foster son. The one I'd stoned looked like a fit companion for him. "Strip them to their loincloths, take everything they have, and burn it with their camp," I directed.

Ahinoam had a meal prepared by the time we got back to the stronghold. She saw my surprise and laughed. "Hanan," she explained.

After eating gratefully, I went out to deal with Hiddai's captive. Shagay hadn't trusted the man an inch, binding him securely before bringing him in. I wasn't certain that I trusted him either, and thus couldn't decide what to do about him.

Shagay had taken him to a lean-to we had by our fields in the valley. He lay on the ground, his hands bound over his head to a young tree used to make the shelter. When I stepped in, Asahel was just finishing tending the man's wounds.

The fighter's eyes blazed when he saw me. "Was his care supposed to make me grateful?" he snarled.

"I don't much care if you're grateful or not since I haven't decided whether I'm going to keep you or sell you," I said coldly. "How are you called?"

"I am not called anything for you!" he replied. "Hiddai took great delight in telling me what I could expect when you came, Qausa! So don't think you can fool me with talk of keeping me alive!"

"He called me Qausa, did he? It's been a while since I've heard that name," I said, curious.

"Stopped using it?" the man sneered. "If half of what Hiddai said is true, your name isn't fit to come from a demon's mouth! He just didn't tell me that you could fight," he added grudgingly.

While he'd been talking, I'd remembered the way that he had braced himself against that post, and I looked him over carefully. Just the way he breathed and kept his hands clenched made me wonder if he wasn't worse off than he seemed.

"Since Hiddai didn't know I could fight, you can hardly blame him for the oversight," I said. "Also, Qausa the Habiru has been dead for years. He took silver for King Shaul's life, and Shaul left his body to rot in the forest."

Bitterness flashed again across the man's face. "Trying to win me over with lies, now?" he taunted.

Without a word, I whipped his belt knife from the sheath lying inside the shelter, and slashed the tether tying him to the tree. Using his bound hands, I yanked him to his feet and sent him stumbling into the open. He tried to whirl to face me, but fell halfway around. I threw the knife into the ground beside him. "That way is north," I said, pointing. "It's the one direction I won't be going for a while. Pick up your knife, go that way, and pray Yahweh I never see you again!"

Somehow he managed to twist around and retrieve his knife. One arm gripped his mid-section, and sweat dripped down his face. I watched him struggle, barely able to keep from grabbing his bound hands and dragging him north myself.

Unable to move more, he stared at the ground, his back rising with every hard-drawn breath. "I am called Sibbecai, and my clan was from Hushah above Hebron."

I clenched my teeth. After insulting me this much, he now expected me to take him in? Only the memory of Roeh Shamuel's admonition not to despise the men that Yahweh sent to me, enabled me to speak to him again.

"There is a Hushah west of Bethlehem."

"I was born there."

"Your clan?"

"Dead, or sold by Nagid Nabal for debts to him that we could not pay."

"You're still here."

That bitter smile crossed his face. "I was up north, fighting with Shaul's army when the nagid sent his men for my clan. He would not have dared otherwise."

"How did Hiddai capture you?"

"I slipped on a trail after a rain and woke up tied to that post."

"You're a long way from the land that holds your dead."

"I was going to kill Nabal, or join the Dahveed. I didn't much care which." He squeezed his eyes shut, gasping a little.

"You found me," I said sourly, walking away.

That evening Sibbecai swore to me, and once I held his oath, I assigned him a tent and told him he was confined in it until he could breathe without wincing. Although he didn't look exactly grateful, at least he didn't snarl at me.

¥ ¥ ¥ ¥ ¥ ¥

"Gebirah, would you mind if I went with Mibhar to the sheep pastures today?" Hezro asked. "He says there is something there I should see."

Abigail considered a moment. "I don't see why not. Oholah and I have much to do here in the compound, and the nagid will remain in Carmel until this evening as usual."

The commander of the house guard still hesitated.

Abigail smiled. "I'll be fine, Hezro. There are plenty of guards here, and the attacks were all closer to Hebron. Besides, there have been no reports of any more for some time now. I'll look forward to your report this afternoon."

Once Hezro had gone, she turned back to her second scribe. Oholah had nearly recovered from her wound, which had not been as serious as it looked, but she still tired easily, and when noon came, Abigail insisted that the woman rest for the remainder of the afternoon.

After eating the noon meal, she went to her garden. The meil she was embroidering was nearly done, and she wanted to finish it. She was still there when Hezro knocked at the gate.

"Gebirah?"

"Just a moment," she replied, laying the cloth in the basket of embroidery thread. "What did Mibhar want you to see?" she asked as they walked to the private courtyard of the big house.

"I'm not certain of what he showed me, but if it's what I think it is, the balance of power in the Cabelite clans may not matter any more."

"How so?" the Gebirah asked calmly, setting the basket on a bench under the grape arbor and sitting down beside it.

"You know Mibhar asked the nagid for guards for the flocks, and he refused?"

Abigail nodded. "I haven't found a way to hire more guards since Oholah was attacked. Has Mibhar said anything more?"

"No, because he asked to shelter under the wings of the Habiru band west of the pastures."

She raised her eyebrows.

"The band is led by Dahveed Israel, Gebirah. Mibhar served in his unit under Shaul one war season, and recognized him."

"Then it was the Dahveed himself who brought Oholah," she said softly. "He looked familiar." She should have remembered sooner, she thought to herself. But she'd been too far away the first time to see his eyes, though his glance had affected her the same way both times, producing a disturbing response in her that she'd never felt before. "If Dahveed has settled that close to us, we need to take that into account," she murmured.

"There is more to it, Gebirah. He doesn't just have Habiru. Mibhar wanted me to see how they fought. He discovered where the men with Dahveed train, and he's watched more than once. Gebirah, he's training shalishim! In a year or two, Dahveed Israel will be able to outfight anything brought against him!"

"It is good to know this," Abigail said slowly, once Hezro had explained further. "I must consider it."

The commander bowed and left. Leaning back against the courtyard wall, she reviewed everything the man had said. If Dahveed was sheltering the nagid's shepherds, what might that imply? Was Dahveed trying to ingratiate himself with Nabal? Trying to make a place for himself here? While her husband might be despised by most people now, he was still the most powerful ruler in the south.

The thought of what her husband would do if he realized the military potential that had made contact with him frightened her. There wouldn't be a clan in the south left free of her husband's control. She must prevent any sort of alliance between the two at all costs! At the same time, she should not offend the Dahveed. Not only was he distantly related, but he might become the only factor that would make it possible for the other clans to resist Nabal's control. Dathan in Hebron was hard put now to keep his clans fed this year, and Ahlai of Jezreel would probably have to sell the surplus from his harvest to pay once again the debts of his son, Lael.

As hard as it had been the past two years manipulating Nabal into keeping the people of Carmel and Maon fed, she had to give thanks for his parsimony now, which had left a good surplus in the storehouses. She just had to keep the nagid under control until the New Year this fall. Furthermore, she must have the additional wealth that the sale of the surplus crops would bring before she could carry out her plans. She only needed a few more months' time.

"Yah, grant me wisdom," she whispered, realizing that she wouldn't be able to eat tonight.

CHAPTER 47

Full winter brought one man after another to my tent door, every one of them begging for shelter for themselves, and a couple wishing to bring their families. I had no idea how the news spread, or how these people found me, but all of them seemed to believe that once they had, I wouldn't turn them away. They were right, although with every addition to my band, it became harder for us to survive.

The hunters were already hard pressed to bring in enough for us to eat, and any supplies the newcomers brought were soon exhausted. I'd had no idea there were so many people who were indebted, driven from their land, without food, or just discontented. Uriah had enough men now that he could divide out the ones best suited to work in shalishim from those who could not. The latter group got standard military training, while the former worked doubly hard coming up to Uriah's exacting standards.

The hours not spent in training I filled with various work projects. I had several men who came to me expecting a lazy life, and they soon learned better, or left, looking for an easier adon.

Taking another idea from Ethan, I had, using the lay of the land, the natural growth of thorn bushes, and deliberately made "deadfalls," created defenses around us. Shagay and Ahiam planned most of this, and by the time they were done, I doubt anything less than a dozen army units could have overwhelmed the place.

In addition, I ordered the construction of granaries and had another cistern dug. The men lived in tents for the most part, although we had put up three houses in the valley among our fields for those with families. I offered to have a house built for Zalmon, but he and his wife decided to stay on the hill with me.

I was completely unsuspecting, then, when Igal came to me from his place on watch and said someone had approached camp and apparently wanted to see me. As I descended the hill on the north side I hoped it was just a single man and not someone with another family.

I stopped short when I saw Hiddai waiting for me. Why would he be coming to me? Then I realized that he hadn't really seen my face either time we'd met in the past. "What do you want?" I asked brusquely, staring at him.

He bowed quite deeply. "I have not come empty-handed begging for something, adon. I would offer something of value to you."

I studied him. His clothes were better looking this time, and he had a battle dagger and sword. Something about his appearance made me suspect that he'd come up from the south.

At first I was about to refuse him, then curiosity took over. "What do you have?"

"I noticed that you have many working for you now," he said. "I bring the opportunity to add another strong back to your slaves."

I stiffened from distaste. I preferred retainers to slaves. "Let me see him."

Bowing again, the robber went into the trees and returned, half dragging an unwilling victim with him. Hiddai was right about one thing, I thought, watching. This one would have a strong back. He was shorter than I, but had large bones, like Eliab and Abinadab did. Wearing only a ragged loincloth, he had an Egyptian slave collar with a chain running down his chest to two manacles holding his wrists at waist level. Furthermore, he was also hobbled. Hiddai was so rough with him that the man nearly landed on his face instead of his knees.

Grabbing his chin, I pulled his face up so that I could see him. Both of us froze, and then he opened his mouth. Instantly, I squeezed, digging my fingers into his jaw, and what came out was only an agonized groan.

"What makes you think I'd accept him," I said to Hiddai, while staring directly into my nephew Joab's wide eyes. When he again started to say something, I squeezed once more. "I'm not pleased to see you," I went on, more to Joab than Hiddai. "I've half a mind to drive you all the way to Beersheba. I'll bet the Egyptians down that way could use him better than I could."

Abishai's brother stared at me, his expression anguished, and tears streamed from his eyes before I let go.

"Adon, please don't be hasty," Hiddai said, hurriedly, while Joab bent toward me, trembling. "He is very strong, as you can see from the way I've had to bind him. He will do much work for you."

"He would be nothing but trouble to me," I said, "just as he's undoubtedly been trouble to his family." Just thinking of the disgrace he'd brought on our house, and how his wild ways had driven my half-sister Zeruiah to an early grave, filled me with anger.

"But adon, he is young and will serve you for years. This is a bargain not to be passed up. Only a few silver pieces will purchase you his labor for the rest of his life. You can see from his features that he's Ammonite."

"You will accept skins for him, not silver," I said, knowing that no matter how angry I was, I couldn't leave my blood in Hiddai's hands. "Igal?"

Hiddai looked up in surprise as his former companion emerged from the trees. "Yes, adoni?"

"Tell Sibbecai to bring two of the large buck skins, and five--no, four--of the hyrax skins, the full winter ones."

"As you wish, adoni," Igal said, retracing his steps back up the hill.

"Where did you find him?" I asked, nudging Joab with my toe.

"Just chance, adon, or the blessing of the gods."

Joab's neck turned red, but he didn't move. The filthy state of the loincloth was rather in contrast to the rest of my nephew, who looked reasonably clean and relatively unscathed. He hadn't been in Hiddai's hands for long, and he'd been dressed much better not long ago. I glanced again at the clothes Hiddai wore. They looked a little big. Chances were, he was wearing Joab's clothes. Somehow I couldn't find much sympathy for my nephew.

Sibbecai appeared, carrying the skins. He dumped them on the ground by Hiddai. The bandit shifted nervously under the man's bitter gaze.

"Take your payment and go," I said.

Hiddai hesitated. "I want my collar back."

"I'm sure you do."

Although he waited, I said nothing more. Finally, looking very uncomfortable, he bent down and collected the skins. Sibbecai's foot twitched.

"Don't," I said softly.

The back of Hiddai's neck was as red as his face when he straightened up. Igal stepped into view and slowly advanced. Looking from one man to the other, Hiddai backed into the safety of the trees and ran.

"Igal, have Zabad bring a file to get this collar off this man. He is to be given a belt knife, a shirt and kilt, and then be sent from this camp!" Turning on my heel, I started to leave.

"Dahveed! You can't!" Joab cried, trying to follow me.

I whirled around, grabbing his chin again and bending over him. "An Ammonite face, with an arrow-shaped scar on the cheek," I said, digging my thumb into the scar. "Not only did you drive your immi to an early grave, and bring more disgrace on Boaz's bloodline than it ever bore before, but you thought to steal from Malchi-shua, Sar Israel, son of the man who showed our house royal honor. Do you expect me to ignore that affront? To say nothing of the fact that the sar nearly died an hour later following the directions you gave him to my supposed camp! Get out of my sight, Joab!"

I strode away.

¥ ¥ ¥ ¥ ¥ ¥

Nabal watched her admiringly across the low Egyptian-style four-legged table in the upper room of the house. Abigail turned her face to him. Around her neck she wore a gold chain with a single small pearl hanging from it. "The necklace is lovely, Nagid, and it is nice to sit and enjoy a meal with just the two of us."

Her husband leaned back a little on the cushion. "Yes. It is a rest from the inferior company I have to put up with during the day."

"Did someone in particular annoy you?"

"Some man from Ziph," Nabal snorted. "He was hardly dressed fit to come before me, and he took his time about answering me when I gave him leave to speak. He was called Rinnah. I'll speak to Hezro about him tomorrow. He can take five guards and teach Ziph a lesson. I deserve more respect!" he ended belligerently.

Abigail clenched her hands. Nabal must have been drinking before the meal for him to react this badly after only one cup of wine. "What recompense do you feel they owe?" she asked.

"I do not know that I shall ask for recompense," he replied angrily. "I should simply send Hezro there to burn a farmstead or two!"

Abigail felt her head begin to pound. With Ziph allied with Hebron, such an act by Nabal would force both clans to respond. "The Ziphites would certainly remember a visit such as that, and cause trouble in our northern territory. Remember, Abbi warned that they were difficult to deal with."

Nabal snorted again. "Your abbi didn't gain as much honor as I have," he said, draining the wine cup. "As Nagid Carmel, I must be respected!"

The Gebirah stilled. This was the first time Nabal had failed to comply with a directive her abbi had given. What could she do? She had to stop him from attacking Ziph somehow!

"Here, let me have Tokhath bring the spices for the wine you like so well," she said, beginning to rise. It might be easier to deal with Nabal's grandiose mood.

"You do not need to serve me," Nabal said, looking gratified just the same. "Call one of the servants."

Abigail nodded at Tirzah, and the handmaid left the room, returning shortly with the scribe, who prepared the wine. She noticed that he put more of the spices in the cup than he usually did.

Her husband drank several swallows, and Abigail frowned thoughtfully, waiting for the additive to take effect. "What did the man say once he talked?"

"He wanted me to deal with that runaway slave Shaul has been so eager to find. Something about a clan relationship and the two of us being a match for Israel."

His wife caught her breath. Waiting a moment to still her heart, she looked at Nabal.

"And what did you say?"

"I told him no, of course. Does he think I am a fool? I'm not yet strong enough to face Shaul. I'll need control of the entire south first."

Abigail let out her breath. Apparently, it hadn't occurred to Nabal that Dahveed might be helpful in uniting the south. But from the flash of contempt that crossed Tokhath's face, she realized that the scribe had. Why hadn't he mentioned it to Nabal? "Very true, Nagid," she said, thankful that, for whatever reason, Tokhath had held his tongue. "You answered him properly, and you saw through his trap as well. You are indeed no fool."

A satisfied smile crossed her husband's face, and he lifted the cup of wine to his lips again. "You think Rinnah tried to trap me?" Nabal asked after a bit.

"I don't see how you can come to any other conclusion," she replied carefully. "Such a venture would be dangerous for you, for if you threatened Shaul too soon, he would come here and destroy the country, leaving it all for the Ziphites to take over."

A worried frown appeared on his face. "Do you think Shaul would be that angry?"

"Wouldn't you be?"

Nabal paled a little, and his hands began to shake. "He would be very angry. He might have come down here and killed me! No, it is not yet time to deal with Shaul."

"Indeed not," Abigail said, startled. She hadn't expected Nabal to be afraid after drinking the hard wine. Well, fear was better than anger right now. "There was more to it than that, as you must have seen," she went on. "After all, who is this man Shaul is chasing? Didn't I hear he has some men with him?"

Nabal laughed, the tension in his shoulders relaxing. "Rinnah tried to tell me that runaway had a whole band of trained fighters following him!"

"Perhaps he does. Some men will follow anyone, you know. But even if he did have men, they would only be Habiru, and you know how treacherous they are. If you allied with them, they would turn on you and kill you as soon as it was convenient. This was a narrow escape, Nagid."

"Yes, well, I saw through it," he said shortly, drinking more. "He dared to try to entrap me! I will have to do something about the Ziphites."

Abigail leaned back in relief. The wine had just taken longer to be effective tonight. "The Ziphites can be dealt with anytime. But this Habiru runaway may be the real danger. After all, Rinnah did try to connect you to him, and what good would that do Rinnah? He would only profit if you were dead."

Nabal considered, and Abigail tried to unclench her hands under the low table. She must wait for the right moment.

"Yes, Rinnah must be plotting against my life! It is the only thing one can think. I will not listen to him again!"

"It might be best to bar him from your presence, Nagid. Besides, what good would Shaul's runaway slave be to you? Even though he is related, he is disgraced and a Habiru. It would not be appropriate for you to have mere Habiru fighting for you. They should not presume to even be noticed! When you go against Shaul, you must have a properly trained army, something worthy of Nagid Carmel. There must be some Egyptian troops also. The best to be had. Perhaps a unit or two of archers."

"Yes, yes," Nabal said, spreading his arms wide. "A fine army to do my will."

"And the archers would be sworn to you, Nagid, for once they see the glories of your rule, they will want to come to you at once! Being connected to a mere runaway might hamper your plans, and keep you from ruling as you wish." Abigail glanced to the side to see Tokhath watching the nagid cynically. When he noticed her, she couldn't suppress the shiver at the look in his eyes.

"I can see that now," Nabal said, drinking more. "When he bows to me and cringes in my presence as the Agag did before Shaul, I will deal with this runaway! I will be merciful to him, since he is kin, but they all shall bow at my feet, and will bring the best of everything to me. And I shall give it to you! For you are Gebirah!" he finished, turning to admire her again.

"You do me too much honor, husband," Abigail replied absently, watching Tokhath leave the room without being dismissed.

¥ ¥ ¥ ¥ ¥ ¥

"Jonathan, you should go back to Zelah tonight," Michal said quietly as her brother returned to the throne room after the noon rest.

"Is Taphath worse again?" he asked quickly.

"Immi says so. The pain in her lower right abdomen is so bad she could hardly get up. Immi sent for Judith to help care for Meribbaal while she tends to Taphath."

"I'll go as soon as court is dismissed," he promised.

Michal nodded.

Jonathan worried all afternoon, barely able to keep track of the reports given by the scribes. When he left, he kept his light gray mule at a gallop all the way to his estate. He spent the night at Taphath's side, stroking her head while she lay curled in pain on the bedroll in spite of the willow bark tea Ahinoam gave her.

¥ ¥ ¥ ¥ ¥ ¥

I was watching Uriah and Elhanan working with the regular warriors when Gad found me.

"Adoni, I must speak with you," he said urgently.

"What is it?" I asked, swinging around to face him.

His lips trembled. "Adoni, I have just received word that Roeh Shamuel is dying." He paused a moment to regain control of his voice. "Please, adoni, let me go to Ramah! I cannot bear the thought of not seeing him again!"

I started up the hill to the stronghold. "We should take Azmaveth," I said as I walked. "This will give him a chance to see his wife and sons. We'll leave as soon as we can pack."

"We can go, adoni?"

"Unless Yahweh says no."

After telling Ahinoam what had happened, I went to the part of camp that we had marked off as sacred to the ark. Abiathar, assisted by Naharai, was just finishing up a sacrifice for Eliphelet. Out of the corner of my eye, I noticed movement back in the trees, and Asahel hurried away in the other direction. I frowned. Although I had made it plain that Joab was not welcome to stay, I suspected Zeruiah's second son had remained close by.

Abiathar gave my personal thief a blessing, then turned to me. "What is it, Dahveed?" he asked, a slight smile on his face as he watched the northerner leave.

"I would inquire of Yahweh, Abiathar."

"Come then," he said, taking me to the shelter that we had made for the ark.

I knelt, and in a couple moments Abiathar's voice became distant. "Why have you come, Dahveed ben Jesse?"

"Adonai, we have received word that Your seer, Roeh Shamuel, is dying. Gad's heart yearns to go to his former master. I would accompany him. Is this good for us to do?"

"Go, for I have sent Gad to comfort my servant Shamuel, and you to comfort Melek Israel."

"We will go, Adonai."

It was past noon of the next day before we entered Ramah after a hard trip of more than 30 miles with only a few hours of rest during the night. I had to smile as we made our way down the narrow streets to the roeh's house. This would be the first time in all my visits that I wouldn't enter his courtyard over the wall.

Since Azmaveth had already left us for his home, only Ittai remained with Gad and me. Ahinoam had suggested that I take my covenant son, and I was glad that I could leave the donkey in his care while I followed Gad into the roeh's house.

The roeh's current personal attendant recognized Gad and welcomed him gratefully. The man was less sure of my welcome, but when I remained in the outer room, he assumed that I was Gad's attendant. He was a bit surprised, therefore, when Shamuel sent for me.

When I entered the familiar room I found the old prophet seated on his cushions, incense lingering in the air. He wore the meil as always, and his long silver hair coiled on the floor beside him. I knelt to him, then touched my forehead to the ground.

"It is not for you to bow to me, Dahveed," he said in his deep voice.

"Perhaps not," I replied. "But it is well for me to show proper respect toward Yahweh's voice."

A smile touched his lips. "Well, we will let this pass, then, since I see from your eyes that you have begun to accept the honor which is yours."

As I reddened a little, Shamuel's smile grew. "What has brought about the change?"

"Yahweh's hand," I answered ruefully. "He insists on sending me men, and I've become sar to them. I have nearly a full band now."

"Ah, what they call a 'six hundred?'"

"Yes, Roeh."

"There will be more who come, Dahveed. Rule them well."

"I am trying, Roeh. But sometimes it is difficult to know what is best."

"Is not Abiathar there for you?" Shamuel questioned, his eyebrows raised. "You inquired of Yahweh regularly when Hassar Jonathan sent you on his errands. Did you think Yahweh would be any less inclined to help you with your own concerns?"

"Sometimes in the press of responsibilities, I forget to ask Him, Roeh," I confessed.

"And yet, Dahveed, that is your main task now. Yahweh has given you all you need to become Melek for Him. But you must remember to use what He has provided. Learn to follow Him closely in every responsibility that is yours. Take time every now and then to think about how Yah leads you, just as you used to discuss your actions as Jonathan's representative with the hassar after you returned. As the hassar did, Yahweh will help you know how best to carry out His wishes."

With a polite cough, the prophet's personal attendant reappeared. "Roeh, the elders have arrived."

"Then we must go out to them. Dahveed, as soon as I am finished speaking, you must leave."

"Adoni, I would not part from you," Gad protested.

"You no longer serve me, but Yahweh's Mashiah," Shamuel reminded him sternly.

"Then may I not bid him remain here as he wishes?" I asked.

"You are indeed learning, ben Jesse," the roeh said with another smile. "He would be a comfort to me should he remain."

"Then he will remain until you no longer have need of him."

"You are kind to an old man, Dahveed," Shamuel said, his hands gripping Gad's.

"Given all that you have done for me, how can I do any less? Where am I to go, Roeh?"

"Take the road west to Kiriath-Jearim. Yahweh's Arrow will meet you on it. He knows where to take you."

"I will obey, Roeh," I said, bowing to the floor again.

When I stood, the roeh's attendant stared at me with wide eyes before hurrying to the prophet's side, helping him to his feet. Aided also by Gad, Roeh Shamuel shuffled out the door and through the outer room. I held the door there, and Shamuel stepped out into the late afternoon sunshine.

The sight in the courtyard startled me. I'd expected just the elders of Ramah, but the place was packed with representatives from apparently every tribe. I'd never be able to obey the roeh if I left by the front of the house, so I went back through the storeroom and out the stable, climbing the wall to the back alley. Not far from the roeh's gate, I found Ittai waiting with the donkey.

Since the road in front of the courtyard gate was full also, I remained where I was. The roeh's voice was still deep and penetrating, though his body was weak, and Ittai and I heard every word.

Beginning with Hakkohen Haggadol Eli's death, Shamuel recited the events of Israel's history, reminding them how Yahweh had led them and given them His hesed even when they had gone against Yahweh's wishes and plans for them. The courtyard was completely silent when he ended with the destruction of Nob and Eli's blood line. I suspected some of the oldest men there had been elders when the tribes had demanded a king of Shamuel, and they couldn't be feeling very comfortable now, given the act of treason that the king had committed.

"I am about to go to my fathers," Shamuel said, "and there is but one more thing for me to do to fulfill Yahweh's commands, now that the nagid has brought Yahweh's curse down on Israel by his slaughter of the consecrated priests."

Their faces pale, several of the elders sank to their knees, and in moments the entire crowd had done the same. "Intercede for us, Roeh, that Yahweh will grant us His hesed, and we do not die," they begged.

"Yahweh has heard your plea," Shamuel replied. "He has found for Himself a melek who will be faithful to Him, and who will rule over you."

As soon as the words were out of his mouth, I grabbed the donkey, and started down the street for the alley that led to the Habiru's back way into Ramah, the roeh's ringing voice following us.

"Yahweh has anointed the Dahveed ben Jesse from Bethlehem in Judah to be melek for Him. By Dahveed's hand, He will deliver His people in Israel and Judah from the hands of the Philistines and from the hands of all your enemies. But He will give you into Dahveed's hands, and you and your sons will serve and obey him and his sons for as long as Yahweh shall ordain. Thus says Yahweh!"

An excited babble of voices rose, but Ittai and I were already in the alley, and I nearly ran down it, realizing that to be found now might lead the elders to try to instate me as king immediately, and I knew that so long as Shaul lived, the throne was not mine.

In the gathering dusk we headed north toward the close shelter of the forest, finding the familiar Habiru trails with the shortest route across the forested plateau to Gibeon. We reached Gibeon in less than an hour, and picked up the road west to Kiriath-Jearim as Shamuel had commanded.

I hadn't gone much more than half a mile when Nimshi appeared out of the forest. "Dod, you are here!" he exclaimed. "I didn't know whether to believe the message or not! Did the roeh send you?"

"Yes, Nimshi. He told me you would know where I am to go. What has happened?"

"It's Taphath, dod," Ethan's son said, leading us off the road to a trail south. "She has been in pain for some time. Hassarah Ahinoam came, and then Atarah came."

"What did she say?" I asked, keeping the pace to a jog.

"After she examined Taphath, she talked with Ahinoam alone.

She told her that if the pain got worse, fever would come, and once that happened, Taphath would probably die. Atarah said her immi had only known of one person who had survived the fever from this illness." His voice shook.

I stopped. "Nimshi?"

He halted also and turned to me, and I saw him wipe his face with his arm in the dim light.

"She died late this afternoon, Dod."

"Jonathan?"

"He wouldn't leave her. He was holding her when she died, then he just sat there, not doing anything. He looked so empty."

"He would be empty," I said, my own voice trembling a little.

Jonathan had waited so long for a wife and family, and he had come to love the woman from Jabesh that Shaul had picked for him. She had responded with the same kind of loyalty and love, and when the hassar had visited me in Horesh, he had spent nearly as much time talking about Taphath as he had about his baby son, Meribbaal. To lose her so soon would tear the heart out of him.

Yet I dared not go to him publicly, for the announcement of my anointing that Shamuel had given the elders would now make the political situation unstable, and I had no idea how Shaul would react. Even though he had privately acknowledged me as the next king, he might feel that a public acknowledgment threatened Jonathan, and would respond accordingly. The hassar didn't need any more upheavals around him at the moment.

"I have to see him, Nimshi. Where can I meet privately with him?"

The Habiru youth wiped his face again. "There's an oak on the hill north of Zelah where he goes sometimes. I'll take you there and then I'll try to bring him. But no one can get him to move, Dod."

"Let's go. I've got an idea that may help."

The three of us covered the trail to the hill above Zelah as swiftly as we could. Leaving Ittai to find a suitable place to camp, I took the harp from the donkey's pack and Nimshi led me the rest of the way to the oak.

¥ ¥ ¥ ¥ ¥ ¥

Jonathan stared down at his empty arms. Taphath was dead. This morning she had been alive and had smiled at him and said that she felt a little bit better. She'd played with Meribbaal and then gone to sleep. And then--and then--

He shuddered. She had screamed out in pain, and his immi had come running, and he had held Taphath while her body got hotter and hotter in his arms. Immi had given her more and more of the medicine until the pain eased, and then she had become so still and so cold. First Immi and then Michal had tried to get him to leave. But he couldn't leave, not with Taphath so cold. He had to keep her warm. Finally Ishvi and Malchi arrived, and they made him let go because Taphath was dead.

The hassar shook his head. She couldn't be. Meribbaal needed her, and they were going to have three more children at least. If there was another boy, they were thinking of naming him after the zammar.

"Geber? You must come," Nimshi said.

No, he must stay here. Taphath was here, and he couldn't leave her.

"Just for a little while, geber. Get up and come."

He didn't move.

"Geber! Please, just come with me a little way," his youngest armor bearer persisted, tugging at his arm. "It's important, and-and the Mashiah said you shouldn't be mulish!"

Jonathan glanced at Nimshi. The Mashiah? Something pressed into his hand, and he closed his fingers over it. It was the twisted brass earring. Dahveed needed something. He had to find out what. And help Dahveed.

Pushing himself up, he blindly followed Nimshi into the darkness outside. People were moving around in the middle of the courtyard, and Ishvi stood by Abner, who was talking about something that the roeh had said. He hoped he wouldn't have to talk to the general, not with his head aching like it did. Thankfully, Nimshi led him around the edge of the courtyard, staying in the shadows, and they went out the gate unnoticed because another courier had arrived, announcing that he had news of the roeh from Ramah.

The quiet of the fields and the darkness relieved him. Jonathan gripped Nimshi's shoulder tighter. Maybe it was a good thing he had left. He didn't want people. What he needed was the silence, and the night, and the stars, and a place to rest.

"Take me to the oak tree," he said hoarsely.

"I am, geber. We're going as fast as we can."

His body numb, he stumbled up the path.

"We're almost there, geber."

The hassar stopped. "Did you hear something?"

"Yes, geber. Come on."

Jonathan followed, more quickly now. He hadn't been mistaken. But he must be dreaming. Only one harp in all the land sounded like that one did. Yet he didn't know how it was possible. Dahveed could not have known, could not be here. But the music didn't go away.

"Dodi," Nimshi called softly as they stepped under the spreading branches of Ahinoam's oak tree.

Someone rose from the old stump, and Jonathan felt the familiar grip on his shoulders.

"Nahsi," Dahveed's voice said.

The hassar swayed, his hands finding Dahveed's arms as the bottom dropped out of his life, and he knelt there in the dead leaves and Dahveed held his wrists again while he emptied himself of tears.

"How did you know to come?" Jonathan asked as the first red streaks of dawn touched the sky.

"Yahweh sent me to you and Gad to Shamuel."

"What's wrong with the roeh?"

"He is dying."

"Were there a lot of elders there?" the hassar asked. "Seems as if I remember hearing about a summons to Ramah a few days ago."

"Are you sure you want to talk about this now?"

He nodded. "Yes. I need something to occupy my mind before I go back and--" he stopped, rigidly controlling his thoughts.

"Yes. There were elders there from most of the tribes, I think. The roeh spoke to them yesterday afternoon. He recited Yahweh's dealings with Israel. The elders were frightened when he stopped with Nob."

"Rightly so," Jonathan said grimly, easing himself into a more comfortable position by the fire in Dahveed's hidden camp.

"They all begged Yahweh's hesed, and Shamuel told them that Yahweh had heard their repentance. Then he announced who had been anointed king."

"Did he name you publicly?" he gasped.

"Yes. That's why I didn't dare come to the compound. If the elders knew I was in the area, they might try to make me king now."

"Maybe it is time that you were," Jonathan said soberly, watching the man across the fire.

"No. The roeh told me one time that when Yahweh expected me

to take up a task for Him nothing would stand in my way. I would only have to accept what was coming from Yah's hand."

The hassar thought a moment. "And Shaul still lives."

"Yes."

"Your hesed piles around us again, Dahveed."

"You are Melek Israel, and it is not for me to say when you will be otherwise."

"You still don't want the throne, do you?"

The younger man shook his head. "No, Jonathan. It is more than I can handle being dahveed to the men I have."

The light had strengthened, and Jonathan reluctantly stood. "I must get back, Dahveed," he said heavily. "Taphath must be buried. But you have done my heart good. I will be able to face the others and care for Meribbaal now."

"May Yahweh comfort you, Jonathan. I will have to leave this afternoon."

"Yahweh guard you."

Nimshi appeared from nowhere to escort him back to the compound. Immi embraced him in relief when he walked in. "When we found you gone, we didn't know what to think," she said, hugging him again.

"Yahweh knew what I needed. Is she--I mean, is everything ready?" he asked, swallowing the lump in his throat.

"Yes, son. Do you wish to sit with her a while?"

He nodded.

At mid-morning they carried Taphath from the house to the cave in the hillside containing the bones of Kish, his wife, and two brothers of Shaul who had not survived childhood. Judith carried Meribbaal so that Jonathan could help ease the body of his wife onto the hard stone floor of the cave. Once back outside, Ishvi and Malchi closed up the cave.

It looked as if the entire town had come, Jonathan thought, seeing the crowd gathered outside. He took Meribbaal from Judith, hugging his son close as his grief brought tears to his eyes again.

"We will all miss her, Jonathan," Shaul said, embracing both of them. "But at least there is Meribbaal to comfort us."

"I know, Abbi."

The elders of Zelah came to express their condolences, followed by others from the town. It seemed people would never stop arriving, for gentle Taphath had touched everyone she met. When only the immediate family members were left, he looked around again for his abbi. He might want to hold Meribbaal. But Shaul was gone also.

"Abner," Malchi said grimly in response to his unspoken question. "He took Abbi away as soon as he could."

Jonathan looked down, angry that the general would intrude on their grief at such a time, yet knowing he could expect nothing else from his cousin given the situation between them.

Then, carried on the light breeze, the sound of a harp reached their ears. The family stilled. With a sob, Michal ran to Jonathan, and he held her while they listened as, hidden from sight, Dahveed sang.

"Yahweh is the one who tends me. I shall not want.

He makes me lie down in pastures of new fresh grass, and leads me beside the waters of rest.

He restores my soul; He guides me in the ruts of righteousness for His name's sake.

Even though I walk through a valley of dangerous darkness, I will not fear evil, for You are with me. Your rod and staff comfort me.

You prepare before me a table fit for a king in the presence of my harassers; You have anointed my head with oil and my cup overflows.

Surely prosperity and hesed will chase after me all the days of my life, and I will dwell in Yahweh's house forever."[21]

When the last notes died away, Ahinoam turned to Jonathan. "Yahweh did indeed know what we needed," she said.

CHAPTER 48

"Did you find out what the summons was about?" Gebirah Abigail asked anxiously.

"Yes," Tirzah said. "All the elders in Israel were called to Ramah."

"Ramah? Not Gibeah?"

"Ramah, Gebirah, for they were summoned by Roeh Shamuel, not King Shaul."

"What can the Roeh of Yahweh want with them?" her mistress

---

21 Psalms 23

asked softly.

"Gebirah! Gebirah!" The faint call came from outside the courtyard.

"That sounds like Mibhar," the handmaid said, rising. "I'll go see what he wants."

Abigail went to the door after her, and in moments, Hezro accompanied the excited man to her. He dropped on his knees. "Gebirah, the news just came to Carmel," he panted. "Roeh Shamuel is dead. He died day before yesterday, and they buried him in his house in Ramah. The entire land is in mourning."

"Perhaps that is why he summoned the elders. If he knew he was going to die " She hesitated.

"No, Gebirah!" Mibhar said, still breathing hard. "He gathered the elders to hear his final prophecy. Yahweh has anointed a new king for Israel!"

"Who? Did he say who?" Hezro demanded instantly.

"Yes, Commander, and the whole land is buzzing about it! He didn't choose anyone from the tribes of Israel. It's someone from the south! From Judah! He chose my commander--Dahveed Israel! The Dahveed is to be the next king!"

While Mibhar was clearly delighted with the news, it took Abigail's breath away. Yahweh had chosen a *southerner* to be king of *Israel*?! The elders must be in a complete quandary.

"Was Dahveed there to be anointed?" Abigail questioned.

"No, Gebirah. The word is that Shamuel anointed Dahveed years ago when he was still a youth. No one knows what to do. They say Abner is beside himself with rage, but Shaul refuses to do anything without the hassar, who is in mourning for his wife. No one has told Hassar Jonathan anything about this yet."

Her thoughts raced. The key, of course, was what the hassar would do. Many of the elders would consider Dahveed a foreigner and thus unworthy to rule Israel. But if Yahweh had anointed him, how could they refuse the man? Yahweh must be very angered at Shaul's treachery at Nob, she decided, to reject anyone from the Israel tribes as the next king. On the other hand, Dahveed had served Shaul for years, and the people up there knew him well. Shaul had even married him to his daughter, although with the king angry at Dahveed, that might have to be discounted. It was possible, however, that many elders would favor him and be glad of Yahweh's choice. Chances were, the balance between the two sides was equal, and that meant whatever side the hassar supported would prevail.

She wondered what Jonathan would think when he heard the news. And how would this affect his patronage of Dahveed? If Dahveed was now his rival for the throne, what would he do? Abigail bit her lip. The situation was ripe for war. And Dahveed was sitting right next door to Carmel. It looked as if he would need those shalish things that Hezro had told her about. And if Shaul came down against Dahveed, how would Nabal react? Two years ago, he would have fawned all over Shaul's feet, supporting him. But now? He could just as easily endorse Dahveed as Yahweh's Mashiah, and she didn't know enough about the man to count on his restraining her husband's excesses.

"Tirzah! Tirzah!" the nagid's nasal tones drifted down from the upper room. He'd gotten very drunk last night, only just now wakening. He'd want her next, for after his drinking bouts, he needed her to soothe his head.

Abigail closed her eyes, her own head aching. She had to think, but there wasn't time. Her husband would notice the excitement in the compound, and once he heard the news, he might decide to ally with Dahveed, especially with Tokhath, who fully appreciated the services Dahveed could provide, advising him to do so. She no longer knew how much the scribe influenced him.

"Mibhar," she said suddenly, interrupting the man's excited discussion with Hezro.

The shepherd turned to her. He was still kneeling, too caught up in the news to get to his feet.

"Mibhar, you are to run back to Carmel as quickly as you can. Tell everyone there that the Nagid is *not* to know of Shamuel's prophecy! No one is to tell him. Do you understand?"

The man stared at her. "Yes, Gebirah," he finally stammered.

"Make sure every man, woman, and child in the town understands as well. Hezro, you will see that no one here, or in Maon, mentions this either. If the Nagid asks, tell him that Roeh Shamuel has died. Nothing more!" she commanded.

Hezro bowed. "Yes, Gebirah."

The men left, and Abigail sat down again, her thoughts whirling. Then she steadied herself. So long as Nabal remained ignorant of Dahveed's future, she could control her husband. And she must maintain control until the New Year. But what could she do about Tokhath? A shudder ran through her. She hated the way that man watched her.

¥ ¥ ¥ ¥ ¥ ¥

I was tired when Ittai and I sighted the stronghold on the hill. Once we had come to Hebron, I went south by way of the big valley in order to check on the guards covering the Nagid's flocks.

"Shalom, adoni," Elika and Shammah greeted me when I found them.

"Shalom. Has all been well here?"

"Yes," Elika replied. "Since you drove Hiddai away, the roads are much safer, and only animal predators have threatened the flocks. We killed a wolf the day you left, and Uzzia swears there is a bear eyeing the goats."

While Ittai took the donkey back to the stronghold, I looked for Uzzia. Mibhar saw me talking with the giant man, and he hurried over to greet me and express again the gratitude of the shepherds for our protection.

On the way to the stronghold, I stopped at our fields in the small valley. The grain was thick, green, and abundant. We'd have a good harvest if nothing intervened. Looking at the children running around the three houses down here, I knew we needed that crop.

Just outside my tent, Asahel laughed, talking with someone by my fire. All I had to see was his back to rouse my anger. Silently, I strode forward, grabbing Joab by his shirt and hauling him to his feet. He turned like a snake, belt knife slashing. I managed to avoid the worst of it, but the blade bit into my thigh.

Wrath flooded me. I could hear Asahel breathing, and the smell of my own blood made me tremble, the light intensifying around me. Seizing my nephew's girdle with my other hand, I lifted him off the ground and threw him away from the fire. He landed several feet away, rolling twice. I walked toward him, and when he saw my face, he scrambled back, yelling, "Dodi! Dodi! I didn't know it was you!"

"What does that matter?" I roared at him. "Every man in this camp is sworn to me, and you would try to kill them?"

"Dodi, please! I thought--"

Reaching down, I grabbed him again. "I sent you from this camp because you showed yourself unwilling to live honorably within Yahweh's commands! You are a murderer, polluting this camp with the innocent blood dripping from your hands. Am I to let you remain, and bring Yahweh's curse down on us all? Shall we die because of you?" I shook him, then heaved him away from me again.

He cried out when he landed, rolling over. "Dodi, no!" When he scrambled back again, I stalked toward him. Sobbing with fear and pain, he retreated, the men scattering before us as I drove him before me, heedless of his pleas for hesed.

And then I ran into a wall. I started forward again and could not go. Trembling still, I backed up, shaking my head a little. I had my belt knife in my hand, and Joab lay half inside a shelter not far away, clinging to the ground. Abiathar stood in front of me, his hands outthrust in front of him.

"Come no farther, Dahveed," the hakkohen commanded. "Joab has sought refuge in Yahweh, and you will not harm him."

Realizing I was at the boundary of the area for the ark, I pulled back a little more, then again unsuccessfully tried to reach toward him.

"He will bring Yahweh's curse on us all," I said hoarsely, shifting restlessly.

"You have fulfilled your duty to El Shaddai's demand for justice, Dahveed. But if Yahweh wishes to grant hesed, that is His right."

Breathing hard, I backed up once more. "How am I to know if Yahweh's hesed is given to him?"

"Return in the morning, and see if Yahweh has spared his life."

Pain returned to my leg, the blood flowing down from the stab wound, and I was awkward when I knelt. "It shall be as Yahweh ordains," I said, sheathing my belt knife and bowing to Abiathar. Eliphelet stepped up to help me to my feet, and as I left, Naharai covered my nephew with a cloak.

The next morning Ahinoam had to waken me, and I groaned when I sat up. My leg throbbed. I limped to the fire, being careful not to break open the wound. Joab's belt knife lay not far away, and neither Abishai nor Asahel was in evidence. I glanced at the sun. It was late, not early.

"Where is everyone?" I asked.

"It's Shabbat," Ahinoam reminded me. "They are at the altar for the morning sacrifice, although the entire camp may still be clinging to Abiathar for safety."

"I'm not angry with them, just Joab," I said sourly, taking a drink from the cruse and dipping my hand into the bowl of figs that we'd dried from a tree growing wild.

"You may have a hard time convincing anyone of that. You didn't see yourself raging through this place like a lion with your eyes practically glowing. You roared like one, too. I've never seen Shagay shaking from fear before."

"You don't seem to be shaking," I said, catching her arm and pulling her down to steal a kiss.

"I've noticed Yahweh only uses your gift against enemies, or to get someone's attention. As far as I know, I don't fit into either category," she said, supplying me with a wine skin.

I washed and dressed in clean clothes before I presented myself before Abiathar later that morning. The camp was unusually quiet today, and the men who saw me quickly bowed as I went by.

Pausing at the boundary line to the sanctuary area, I waited until the hakkohen emerged from his tent, which was pitched to one side of the shelter for the ark. I touched one knee to the ground briefly. "I have come to learn Yahweh's will for Joab ben Zeruiah."

"Come," Abiathar said, and I followed him to a stool placed by the shelter.

I eased down on it, glad to take the weight off my leg. The rest of the men gathered around silently, staying away from the boundary around the ark. Josheb came out of his tent, pitched by the hakkohen's, and Keturah followed. Then Naharai led Joab, who clung to him, toward me. My nephew had been washed up, but the only thing he wore was a loincloth.

Face averted, Joab followed Naharai to me, then flattened himself on the ground and waited. I regarded him in silence for a while. "Ahinoam mentioned that Yahweh uses me on occasion to get someone's attention. Was His voice sufficiently loud for you to listen this time?"

"Yes, Nahsi," he whispered.

"You know the risk we will be taking by accepting you into our band? You are outlawed by the Pharaoh, Joab."

"Yes, Nahsi, but killing the Egyptian courier was an accident, and I wasn't anywhere around when the second one died," he said, his voice trembling.

"You not only bow before me but Yahweh, Joab, for we are in the presence of the ark."

My nephew flinched a little. "I know, Nahsi."

"You still say to me that you were outlawed for an accident, and for a killing not your own?"

"Yes."

"Get on your knees, Joab. Eliab said you had killed before."

The young man obeyed. "The first time I was out in the forest, and a man attacked me. That's how I got the scar," he said, touching his face. "Had I not killed him, he would have killed me. I tried to tell Geber Jesse this, but he wouldn't listen. Dodi Eliab had already stated his opinion," he ended, his voice bitter.

"Is that all?" I asked, studying him.

He hung his head. "No, Nahsi. There was one other time. After Jesse banished me."

My lips tight, I reminded myself to hear him out before making any decisions.

"What happened then?"

"I had gone to Jericho, and a man there mocked me at the inn. He was from Beersheba." He flushed a little. "I followed him the next morning and confronted him on the road up to Jebus. I-I killed him there," he admitted, trembling. "I-I hid the body, and then I came back south."

"How did you meet up with Hiddai?"

"He was servant in a caravan to Egypt, and I was a guard. When it returned to Beersheba, we left together. Once we were in the uplands, he gave me a drink of wine. I woke up in that slave collar."

It apparently wasn't safe to be within miles of Hiddai, I thought to myself, glancing at Sibbecai.

Joab bowed. "What is to become of me, Nahsi?"

"You will keep your life, since Yahweh Himself has granted it to you. As for the rest--" I hesitated.

"Please, dodi, don't send me away," he whispered.

Yah, what is best? I wondered. Keeping him here might cause any amount of trouble. On the other hand, driving him away now could force him to become a hardened murderer in order to survive.

If there is one thing I've learned from the hassar, Abishai, it is that if hesed can be granted, it should be.

My own words ran though my mind. I stood. "You may stay, Joab, but--" I said as he wilted in relief.

"--but you stay here without honor from clan or family. And because of your shameless action in attacking someone you knew to be either kin, or belonging to kin, you will be servant to anyone who speaks to you, from the youngest child to myself. This is my will for you."

"Yes, Nahsi," Joab said, his face white as he bowed again.

I limped away.

"It's not ready," Zalmon insisted.

I looked at Ahiam.

"I told you it wasn't, adoni," he said patiently.

I stared at the fire in front of my tent. I knew the barley wasn't ready for harvest, too. But we had nothing left to eat. "How long?" I asked, hoping they would tell me something other than what I had already estimated.

"At the least, three weeks," the Benjamite answered. "And that's only if the sun is out all day every day."

"Ahiam?"

"I would say a month, possibly more. Again, it depends on the weather."

"And the gardens are at least that long from producing their earliest crops," I sighed. "Did Shagay say anything to you about hunting, Ahiam?"

From the expression on the Habiru's face, Shagay had probably said quite a lot about my inquiry, the third in as many days, but my retainer shook his head. "There is no change, adoni. We have hunted this area out."

I turned to my old friend from Bethlehem. "Elhanan, is there anything available to purchase?"

"Nearly every town is down to their last supplies as well, Dahveed. Last year's harvest wasn't the best, if you recall."

"What do you mean, 'nearly,'" I asked. "Have you heard of some place that has something we can buy?"

"I've heard of one place with some extra this year," he admitted. "But the price is exorbitant." He named it, and I winced. Even the last of the gold ingots I still hoarded wouldn't buy enough to feed the band for the required time. "Who's got it?" I asked.

"Nagid Ahlai of Jezreel."

"Pekah, go get Zabad," I called to Zalmon's oldest child, who was usually close at hand. He raced off and soon my brother-in-law arrived.

"You sent for me, adoni?"

"Yes. Elhanan says your abbi has some extra food that we might purchase. He's asking a tremendous price, however. What are the chances he would be willing to lower it a little?"

"He's sold it already, adoni. Lael had run up debts again," he explained, speaking of his half-brother.

I sighed. "You can go, Zabad. I'll have to consider this," I said to the others.

A little later I went down to the fields. "All we need is food for four to six weeks, Yah," I said. "Then we'll have plenty. But what can we do until then?" Continuing on east, I climbed the long hill separating us from the huge valley beyond. It was empty now, for the flocks had returned to Carmel and Maon. The ewes were heavy with lambs, and it was time to shear them. It was easier for the lambs to find their mother's teats without hunting through all the wool, and paradoxically, the ewes were only able to keep their lambs warm after they had been sheared. Their wool was too thick otherwise.

Leaning against a pine, I rubbed the scar on my leg from Joab's knife. What could I do to feed the people with me? More had arrived during the final weeks of winter, fortunately mostly single men, but one other family had come, and the men had just finished a fourth small house for them. They were busy putting in a late garden with the last of our seeds.

I was going to have to ask someone for help. And there was only one source available. Nabal of Carmel.

"Yah, how am I to approach him?" I asked, remembering the sort of man he was.

You are kin to him, and he is shearing his sheep.

The thought was distinct in my mind. Sheep shearing was always a time of rejoicing in a household, just as harvest was, and therefore, it was also an occasion for distributing to the needy, something that Abbi had done faithfully every season of feasting that we had. I sighed. Never had I thought that I would be the one begging for food during a feast.

I stayed there on the hill while I decided just what I should say. Abbi had said there in Moab that the nagid would keep them as long as it was worth his while to do so. But the only thing of value I had to offer was myself and our fighting skills. Could I stand to place myself under that man's hand? Did I have a choice? We must eat. I couldn't swear loyalty to him, but I could serve him as I had Shaul. I would have to at least hint at that.

And I must be prepared to follow through on my offer. The fact that I would almost rather starve than deal with that fool made me clench my fists. But I had other lives to consider than my own, and they must come first. Just as the sheep must come first for the shepherd.

Being covered by Nabal would mean that we were no longer Habiru, but retainers under an established ruler. That would bring the chance for many of the men to obtain land and live a respectable life under Yahweh's covenant with Israel. So I would kneel to him if I must, and be his servant if it was required of me.

Back at the camp, I had Abishai begin preparations and called Asahel to give him my instructions.

CHAPTER 49

Abigail watched as Nabal, accompanied by four guards, left the compound for Carmel, and the second day of sheep shearing. Hezro said a canopy had been erected over the dais that her husband had requested. The nagid had not been pleased yesterday because he had to sit in the sun. She sighed. If he would wear a linen robe instead of those heavy wool ones made for tall kings ruling from the tops of mountains, he would be much more comfortable. Then she shivered. The wind was very chill today, so maybe the thing would keep him warm. At least she hoped that he wouldn't trip over the dragging hem on his way to the dais.

"Are you ready, Gebirah?" Jotbah asked.

"Yes. What were we going over today?"

"Oholah has the list from Maon. She recorded each household, what lands they held before selling themselves to the nagid, and how long they have been slaves."

"Did she find out how many injuries or deaths have occurred?"

"Yes. That is a separate list. And she appended the usual recompense owed for such injuries."

"Good. Then we can figure up how much recompense my house owes to them. Does Oholah also have a current total for what's in the treasury for Maon?"

"Yes, Gebirah, although remember, we may have to buy seed in the fall."

"'Then set that aside." Turning from the door, Abigail settled down to the work of the day.

¥ ¥ ¥ ¥ ¥ ¥

Dragging his gaze from the strangers approaching, Mibhar picked up the new tally for Tokhath. The nagid sat on the black leopard skin draped over a three-legged chair resting on the raised dais that had guards standing at each corner. The shepherd shivered a little. Even though the colors on Nabal's robe were highly out-of-place, it was probably very warm. As he approached, he saw Tokhath pouring the spices into a wine cup. Was the nagid drinking already? Wondering how much he'd had, the shepherd bowed to the man on the dais and then went to the scribe.

"The flock at the far enclosure has 10 more sheared ewes, and a yearling ram, Tokhath."

"Very good, Mibhar," the scribe said, jotting the numbers down.

The shepherd turned to Nabal. "Nagid, there are strangers approaching, and I believe they will seek for you."

"You dare to speak to me?" the man snapped, staring at him.

"Your pardon," the shepherd replied immediately, bowing low. "I will tell the scribe."

As Nabal regally ignored him, Mibhar backed away. Obviously the nagid had had more than enough to drink already.

"Where are they?" Tokhath asked softly.

"They are beyond the sheep folds yet. About 10 of them with donkeys."

Tokhath left his table and knelt before the dais. "Nagid, some strangers have come in search of you. I know you are extremely busy. Is it your will that they be sent away?"

Nabal inclined his head. "I will receive them. Bring them here," he commanded.

"Yes, Nagid."

Mibhar bowed again before going to the visitors. He recognized a couple of them. "Shalom. Are you from the Dahveed?" he asked in surprise.

"Yes," the foremost one replied, a slender, likeable young man with a quick smile. "We have a message for Nagid Nabal. Where can we find him?"

"I'll take you to him. He's by the sheepfolds. Is your adon well?"

"Yes. And is the Gebirah well?"

"She is, although she's in Maon today."

The crestfallen look that quickly crossed the young man's face made Mibhar smile. He had probably hoped to see her.

"How are you called?"

"I'm called Asahel."

Mibhar looked the men over. "Asahel, may I make a suggestion?"

"Of course."

"Whoever talks to the nagid probably shouldn't be wearing weapons.

"Oh, I hadn't thought of that!" With a smile, he removed his sword and gave it and his bow to another man. Two others followed suit.

The shepherd led them to the dais, and they approached close enough that Nabal frowned with irritation.

"Just three of you better go forward from here," Mibhar warned quietly, halting the others.

Nodding, Asahel left the donkeys, and two other men followed him to the dais. All three bowed before Asahel spoke. "Nagid, in the name of Dahveed ben Jesse of Judah: Life to you." He bowed again. "To you and to your house and all that you have, shalom," he said formally.

Nabal nodded silently in reply, and the young man continued. "When my adon heard that you were shearing your sheep, he sent us to you. Your shepherds in Carmel stayed with us under our protection all season, and we kept anything from being stolen from the flocks."

The expression on Nabal's face turned to a frown, and he stared at Asahel.

"Ask your shepherds, and they will tell you what we have done for them," he added quickly, bowing again. "My adon says, 'Let us find favor in your eyes, Nagid. According to custom on a festive day, please give whatever food you have close to hand to your servants, and to your son, Dahveed."

All three of the men bowed again and waited.

Mibhar stared. Had he heard correctly? He glanced at Tokhath. The scribe looked just as startled. But Nabal's face was turning red. Tokhath started up from his seat, giving a quick glance at the seven men waiting with the donkeys. Then a calculating look crossed his face, and he settled down again.

The nagid pushed himself off the chair. "Just who is this Dahveed? Does this son of Jesse dare to think he has honor enough to come begging to me?" he said, his voice rising. "He's just another Habiru, a runaway slave like all the others fleeing from their rightful masters! And he expects me to feed him?" Shouting now, he stepped forward. "Am I supposed to take *my* bread, and *my* water, and *my* meat slaughtered for *my* shearers, and waste it on someone whose family hasn't enough honor for me to know them?

"How dare any of you appear before me! Get out! Go, before I set my sheep dogs on you all!"

With horror Mibhar watched the amazement on the men's faces turn to rage. One man toward the back of the group started forward, and one of the others pulled him back.

Asahel inclined his head slightly. "I will inform my adon of your reply." Turning on his heel, he walked stiffly to the donkeys. The group departed in complete silence. In a daze, Mibhar looked at Tokhath. The scribe's face was a mask as he walked forward to help Nabal back to his chair. But it was the sight of the frightened glances that passed between the guards that set his heart to racing. He returned to the sheepfolds, where the shouts and calls of the men had prevented them from hearing what had happened. The shepherd glanced back to see Dahveed's men again. They weren't walking now, they were jogging, covering ground rapidly. Mibhar turned and fled as fast as he could toward Maon.

¥ ¥ ¥ ¥ ¥ ¥

I paced outside my tent, waiting for Asahel and those with him to return. Maybe I shouldn't have sent Elhanan. Had Zalmon prepared the others sufficiently if they saw the Gebirah? Had my message been understandable to the nagid? Was I going to have to bind myself and my band to Nabal?

"Adoni, adoni, they're coming," Pekah called, running toward me.

Puzzled, I looked at the sun. It was only five hours high, too early for them to be already back.

"Are you certain?"

Zalmon's son nodded. "All of them. Very fast."

I hurried down the ridge to see for myself. As soon as I saw them, I knew something had gone very wrong. The donkeys had no loads.

"What happened?" I asked Asahel.

"We arrived in good time, adoni. He's shearing at Carmel. Mibhar took us to him. And we gave him your message." He paused, his hands clenching.

"And?"

"Did you want his reply word for word?" my nephew asked tightly.

"I think so."

He gave it to me.

I stood there, stunned. I don't know what came welling up inside, but I could hardly speak.

"Go get your swords!" I commanded, turning to my tent to retrieve my own.

¥ ¥ ¥ ¥ ¥ ¥

"Gebirah! Gebirah!"

Hearing the faint call, Abigail looked up, seeing out the chamber door that the sun was about five hours high. "Jotbah, go see what they want," she said, turning back to the list. If she read it correctly, the Maon treasury had nearly enough to cover all her recompense to the town. And with the income from harvest, there should be sufficient. Now she needed some way to safeguard what she had set aside until she found the opportunity to complete her plans. She looked outside again thoughtfully.

"Gebirah!" The voice was closer now.

To begin with, she had thought she could quietly make things right, but Tokhath would undoubtedly notice what she was doing. He might tell the nagid, and with wine of any sort making him unpredictable, she dared not risk that. All she needed was a few days, four at most. What if she got him drunk and kept him that way for the time required? Maybe suggest a feast? During the harvest celebration Feast of Weeks perhaps? Certainly a celebration of some kind would be necessary, and . . .

"Gebirah!" Mibhar burst through the door, throwing himself down in front of her. "You must do something!" he gasped. "He sent men--and the nagid refused. They will kill us all, Gebirah!"

"Calm down, Mibhar," Abigail said quickly. "Catch your breath, and then tell me from the beginning. Who sent men?"

"Dahveed Israel, 10 of them, with donkeys. They came all the way from their stronghold, I'm sure, and brought greetings to the nagid." He paused gasping in more air. "The nagid was drinking already, and he scorned them, Gebirah! You can't believe what he said! And that was after they told him that we had asked for their protection out there, and they gave it without requiring anything in return. They were like a wall for us the entire time we were at the pastures!"

Mibhar grabbed her robe. "I saw their faces when they left, Gebirah. Please, you must do something! Disaster is coming down on the nagid, and all of us with him. And he is such an idiot that no one can get through to him!"

"I'll do something, Mibhar, but I must know precisely what happened. As nearly as you can, tell me exactly what the Dahveed's men said, and what Nabal replied."

The shepherd stumbled a bit at first, but soon had told her the entire message from Dahveed. When he started to go on, she stopped him, still untangling everything in that message. It had appealed to Nabal's conceits, the only possible way to elicit from him the help requested, to which Dahveed had a claim on two accounts, she realized. He had performed a service at the request of the shepherds, and through them at Nabal's request, and he was from Judah, therefore related to the Calebite clans. But it was the last part of the message that frightened her.

"He said, 'your servants,' and 'your son'?"

"Yes, Gebirah. And it was his nephew who gave the message."

The closest blood kin that Dahveed had with him! Abigail stiffened. Her worst nightmare had just happened. Dahveed had offered to place himself under Nabal's control, and with Tokhath right there to advise him of what Dahveed could do for him, she couldn't imagine her husband ignoring that kind of power!

"How much did he send?" she asked hopelessly.

"He didn't send anything, Gebirah! That's why you have to do something! He refused!"

"He refused?" Hope lit up in Abigail's heart. "Didn't Tokhath advise him?"

"No, Gebirah, why would he?" Mibhar replied, confused. "He didn't say anything. It was the nagid who spoke, and it would have been better if he hadn't!"

"What did he say?"

"He jumped out of his chair and yelled at them, asking who Dahveed was and how the son of Jesse dared to think he had honor enough to come begging to him!"

Abigail stared at the kneeling man in dismay.

"Then he called him a runaway slave like all the others fleeing from their rightful masters!"

She closed her eyes a moment. The next king of Israel had just begged her husband for food and had been slapped aside! How could Nabal have refused to honor the clan relationship?

"And then he threatened to set the sheep dogs on them!" Mibhar continued.

Abigail froze in disbelief. Nabal had dared to treat Dahveed's men like the predators they had protected his sheep from? Her stomach squeezed into a hard knot, and she swayed backward. "Go get Hezro," she said faintly.

"Yes, Gebirah," the shepherd said, leaving the room at a run. As soon as he was gone, Abigail groped for the chair and sat down. Disaster didn't begin to describe what had just happened! She'd never dreamed that Nabal could be so--idiotic was the only word--as to insult anyone like this! In addition, she had expected that if Dahveed wanted anything, he would send to her, not Nabal. That day he had returned Oholah, he'd said that was what he'd do!

An ironic smile crossed her face. Well, the Dahveed would never ally with Nabal now. For a moment, she was tempted to do nothing and let Dahveed kill her husband and get him out of the way. But she rejected the thought. Too many other people would die, and Nabal had dragged her family's honor in the dust enough already.

But what was she to do? She could only imagine what it had cost Dahveed to offer himself to Nabal after seeing personally the kind of man he was. They must be in desperate need. He'd sent 10 donkeys to transport the food he had requested, after all.

Food. Abigail straightened a little. Think, she said to herself. What would Hassarah Ruth have done? She would have sent food immediately. And she would have taken it herself. When Hezro and Mibhar dashed into the room, she was ready. "Mibhar, how many men does Dahveed have?"

"A full band, Gebirah. And there are some women and children with him, and at least three families that live under his protection."

"All right. Mibhar, get donkeys. Hezro, gather some servants. We need to load a lot of food in a short time. All the bread we made for the feast tonight needs to be packed up. While we're gone, the women can make more. Open the storerooms," she said to Jotbah who had appeared in the doorway. "I want two large pithoi of wine, the dried raisin clusters, and dried figs. Load all of the sweet ones from Tekoa."

"But the nagid likes those," Jotbah protested.

"If we don't send them, the nagid may not be alive to eat anything," Abigail said sternly. "Take all the dressed sheep ready for roasting. There must be at least five. Load up all the roasted grain we have on hand. Hezro, I'll need you and an escort to lead the donkeys."

"Gebirah, you don't mean to go to him!" the commander of the house guard gasped. "He must be furious by now!"

"I can't imagine that he would be any other way. But I'm hoping the sight of all that food will get his attention. It worked for Jacob with Esau. Let's hope it works for us."

"Gebirah," Jotbah protested, "You've ordered that all the food for the feast be sent to Dahveed. What will we do about tonight?"

Abigail paused. "The only people invited were the elders from Carmel and Maon, correct?"

"Yes."

"Tell them I request them not to come. Hezro, send a messenger to Tokhath. He's to ply the nagid with wine. I want him to return here so drunk that he can't see straight. Then have the servants load his table down with every possible dish that can be prepared before then. Have the entertainers start playing as soon as he sits down. If all goes well, he won't remember in the morning that he was the only one there."

"If he starts to ask questions, I'll have some of the servants pretend to be elders," Jotbah said quickly.

"All right. Now go. I have to get ready."

Everyone scattered, and Abigail went to her room. Tirzah had heard the news, and had one of her best robes laid out, along with a selection of jewelry. Once she was dressed, Abigail let her maid brush a little bit of red on her cheeks and apply a hint of it to her lips. She carefully darkened a line under her eyes, and decided that was enough after checking in her silver mirror.

Then she went out to mount the waiting donkey.

"You've told your men where we are going and why?" she asked Hezro.

"Yes, Gebirah. They know that if we meet Dahveed, they are to surrender instantly."

"Very good. Send the food out first. I'll come after."

"They have already left, Gebirah. I will escort you. We can easily catch up."

"Then let us go," she said, glancing at the sun. Could only two hours have passed?

"Where do you think he'll be?" she asked as they hurried up the road toward Carmel.

Her commander glanced back grimly. "If it was me coming against the nagid, I'd find a hill where I could see both Maon and Carmel since Nabal lives in one but keeps his business in the other, and I'd be ready to destroy both towns."

"Is there such a place?"

"Three-quarters of a mile away, with hidden approaches toward either town. I sent the food that way, and told the men to be as obvious as possible about their passing."

"So close?" she gasped.

"Gebirah, Dahveed's stronghold is less than three miles west, and most of that is easy traveling across the sheep pastures. If he's even half as angry as I think he is, he's already staring down his sword at Nabal's heart, debating which body part he's going to cut off first."

"Oh. That's why you sent the married guards home," she added.

Hezro nodded. "We probably won't survive this. But you might. As Parai said, you can make any man living do whatever you want."

Remembering the few times she had seen Dahveed's eyes on her, Abigail wondered about that. Dahveed might not be so besotted with her looks. She needed more than that; she needed an argument that would persuade him to spare her people. What was she going to say to the man?

Hezro turned off the road onto a path, and Abigail clung to the donkey automatically, her mind racing over any possible way she could appease Dahveed's anger. As she struggled to think of anything to say, she suddenly realized that Hezro had stopped. They were atop a hill, and her commander studied the country intently.

"You don't think he's at Carmel yet?" she asked.

"It's not burning," he said shortly. "There's the food," he pointed to the valley below them. "I told them to head north from here and try to get between Dahveed and Carmel. And there's Dahveed," he added softly, pointing into the valley to where a group of men were approaching from the west. "They're less than a quarter of a mile away. Are you sure you want to go down there? He may be angry enough to do anything at all, and I'll only be able to protect you for a short time."

He didn't expect to live. The thought drove into Abigail, making her tremble a little. "Let me go down alone," she said impulsively.

Amazement flashed in his eyes, and then he smiled and bowed his head. "That offer means more to me than you know," he said quietly. "And you also know that I will not accept it."

The Gebirah raised her chin. "Then let us go down."

"We'll end up right in the middle of them," Hezro warned. "His scouts have already found the trail of the food donkeys."

Abigail's mouth suddenly went dry. All the things she might say to save her people whirled chaotically in her head. "Yah, grant us hesed!" she breathed as the donkey took her down into the valley after her guard commander.

As the watercourse they followed approached the western valley, Abigail tried to calm her pounding heart. Not far from them in the little dell where the watercourse met the valley, she saw Dahveed listening to one of his men.

¥ ¥ ¥ ¥ ¥ ¥

"First you tell me that I'm supposed to accept honor, and then you tell me I shouldn't defend what I have? What do you expect of me, Ahiam?" I exploded when my retainer finished urging me to leave Carmel in peace. "Did I guard that man's livelihood all winter for nothing? I've been such a wall to him that he hasn't lost a single sheep! And he thinks he can treat me this badly? May Yahweh do the same to me, and more also, if I leave anything alive of his that pisses on a wall, *especially this wall*, by morning!"

As I stalked away, a donkey suddenly appeared by me, led by an armed man. Instantly, I pulled my sword, the blade flashing toward the man.

"Please, adoni, on me," a cry stopped me as someone slid off the animal and fell on her knees. "Let the blame be on me," the woman added, bowing to the ground.

In the sudden silence the guard stood absolutely still, his head slightly bent, but his eyes never left me, and one hand remained on his sword hilt. I shifted my sword point a little, but did nothing more. I had the feeling that I should recognize the man.

Hastily, the woman got up and knelt practically under my sword. "Let me speak to you," she begged.

Motionless, I kept watch on the soldier, my hand ready to pull my belt knife if this was a trick of some kind.

"Please, listen to your slave."

I took a quick glance down and eased back a little. The soldier slowly removed his hand from the sword hilt.

"Please, adoni, don't pay attention to anything that Nabal has said! He's worthless and wicked," her voice, calm now, went on. "He is his name, a fool, and folly is with him."

And nobody listens to a fool, my mind added in Grandmother Ruth's tones. This woman's voice curiously echoed my grandmother's. Startled, I really looked at who knelt in front of me. Gebirah Abigail! I backed up a step, and the soldier--Hezro, I remembered now--knelt. But he didn't take his eyes off me.

"When your messengers came to Carmel, geber, I didn't see them," Abigail continued, "so the fault is mine, geber. Do not let your anger fall on the innocent. By Yahweh's life and your own life, geber, can't you see that He has intervened to stop you from avenging yourself like this? Would Yahweh that every enemy who sought your life was as foolish and insignificant as Nabal!"

She certainly had my attention now, as well as that of all my men.

Then Hanan trotted from the trees. "Adoni, we found the donkeys. They are for us, and they are loaded with food! Here they come now."

I looked up as Shagay appeared, leading a whole caravan of animals. "They say they are from the Gebirah, adoni," he said, then caught sight of her kneeling in front of me. The look he gave me said plenty, and I flushed, sheathing my sword and offering her my hand to help her up. Hezro nearly collapsed with relief, bringing a slight smile to my face.

"Please, geber, take this gift for your men, and forgive my offense toward you," Abigail repeated, gesturing toward the food. The pulse pounded in her neck despite the calm expression on her face. Feeling my gaze, she raised her chin slightly and met my eyes.

Just as I had seen Grandmother Ruth do time and time again. The memory made me melt inside. "Go see what's on them," I said, nodding toward the animals.

Smiles broke out on everyone's faces, and they crowded forward to investigate what was in the packs, although their comments remained quiet and subdued.

As I turned back to Abigail I caught the relief on her face. "Yahweh will surely give you an enduring dynasty, adoni," she said gratefully. "We hear how you are fighting His battles, and that you have never done evil."

She paused a moment, looking down at my right hand which, strangely, still held hers. "Not that you need to worry about enemies seeking your life. Yahweh must keep it safe in His shepherd's pouch. But He'll sling the lives of your enemies away!" she added, a giddy smile flashing across her face.

Hezro stared at his gebirah in amazement, and Ahiam started coughing.

I dragged my eyes from her face. Speaking of giddy, I should probably let go of her hand. I did that somehow, making Ahiam cough again. "Yahweh has already shown me much hesed," I managed to say.

"And thank you for yours today, adoni," she said, composed again. "It will be good that what happened today will not cause you grief when Yahweh fulfills His promises to you and you become Israel's nagid. You have not shed blood without cause, and we are grateful!" She bowed again. "And, when Yah deals well with you, please remember your maidservant," she added softly.

As I looked at her bowed head, I finally woke to what I had almost done, the deed I had been leading my men into. I could have killed this woman! And scores of innocent people with her!

"Thank Yahweh He sent you to meet me!" I said, rubbing a hand across my face and backing up a little. "And bless you and your good judgment for keeping me from bloodguilt!" Taking a deep breath, I managed to pull myself away from the unclean anger that still clung to me. "Yahweh indeed kept me from bringing harm to you, Gebirah, for by His life, if you had not come this quickly, I would have slaughtered every male in Nabal's house!" I shuddered again, shaking the last of the unreasoning fury from my mind. "You have my gratitude, and your gift is most welcome. I'm sure my men will enjoy it."

"Mibhar will bring the rest of it tomorrow," she said as Hezro helped her back on the donkey. "We didn't take time to get the grain from the granaries."

I stopped, meeting her eyes again. What else could I do now but accept this, too? Her chin came up again, and I smiled. It was just the way I could imagine the Hassarah handling a similar situation! This time I bowed my head. "That part of your gift will be most welcome, also. Go back to your house in peace. I have heard and accepted you and your request," I said formally.

"You are very gracious to me, adoni," she replied, and Hezro led the donkey back up the watercourse.

CHAPTER 50

When Abigail arrived back at Maon, Nabal was in his business chamber as she'd hoped he would be. She immediately dismissed the guards for the day, and they gratefully trooped away to rest. Abigail felt so exhausted that she was unsteady on her feet, and she accepted Namea's arm when her maid came running to her.

"Did you find him?"

"Yes, and all has been put right," the Gebirah answered. "Tell the others that. I have to rest now. Hezro, you go rest also."

"Are you going to tell the nagid about this?" he asked before he left.

She glanced at the business chamber. The entertainers were in the middle of a wild, rousing song, with Nabal shouting and clapping in time, already too drunk to speak with.

"No," she said tightly, sudden anger sweeping over her. At least Dahveed had acknowledged his wrong when it was pointed out to him. She doubted that Nabal would ever recognize the irony of his feasting like this after refusing to feed those with no food at all.

¥ ¥ ¥ ¥ ¥ ¥

Our return to camp was heralded at first with some trepidation. But when the loaded donkeys came into view with enough food packed on them for a feast, the apprehension melted away, replaced by cries of excitement, and everyone rushed to get the meal ready as quickly as possible.

Ahinoam stood beside me as I watched the men unload the food. "How many died?" she asked.

"None. Yahweh sent Gebirah Abigail to meet me and to talk some sense into my head." I put my arm around her. "You didn't want me to go, did you?"

"It didn't seem right, somehow, for you to be set on such vengeance."

"It wasn't right. I'll have to take a sin offering to Abiathar tomorrow. What do we have?"

With a wry smile, she gestured to the food being unloaded. "Whatever is there."

"I'll catch a turtledove then."

"How much are you going to let them eat?"

I pulled her to me. "As much as they want. This is only part of what is coming. More will be here tomorrow."

"The Gebirah always did know what people needed."

"As does Yahweh," I said. "I knew Nabal was a fool to start with. I never should have paid any heed to him. Ahiam tried to tell me that, but I wouldn't listen either."

Ahinoam went to help with the food preparations, and I climbed to the top of the hill, leaning against the oak at the top. I stayed up there until dark, thinking about the sin that I had nearly committed. Then I went back to camp, and Ahinoam's welcoming arms.

¥ ¥ ¥ ¥ ¥ ¥

Abigail woke up late the next morning. When she finally emerged from the house, she was gratified to see that Mibhar had the grain loaded and ready, waiting only for her approval and dismissal. After sending them on their way, she turned her thoughts to what she should do about Nabal.

"When did he finish his feast last night?" she asked Namea.

"It was after midnight, Gebirah. He left only when the entertainers were too exhausted to play anymore, and by then, he was so drunk, two of the guards had to carry him to his bedroll."

Staring out across the courtyard, Abigail realized she was sick to death of dealing with Nabal. Yesterday had been just one more in a chain of events stretching across her entire married life. And it wouldn't stop. She couldn't muzzle her husband every minute of every day. For a while she had tried guile. Maybe it was time for something else.

"Let me know when he wakes up," she said, heading to her own business chamber.

It was nearly noon when Tirzah appeared at her door. "Gebirah, he is rousing."

"All right. I'll be there." She put aside the report she was working through. Maybe a little shock would help the nagid limit his drinking of strong wine. She left the room and walked to the spot by the courtyard wall where she knew the nagid would come.

Helped by Tirzah, her husband stumbled from the house, squinting in the sun even though it was partially covered by clouds today. He managed to adjust his loincloth himself, and as the wine left him, Abigail spoke.

"Do you know what the Dahveed did yesterday when his men reported how you replied to his request?" she asked him.

Nabal turned his head in surprise. "Gebirah?"

"When he heard how you insulted him, he gathered his entire band, armed them for war, and came to Carmel, vowing to slaughter every living thing in our household that pissed against a wall!" she said, glaring at him.

Nabal's mouth dropped open, and he looked down at what he was doing, then back at Abigail.

"Starting with you!" she finished, walking away.

"Gebirah! Gebirah, please," he said, trying to follow her. "Why would you need to be concerned with him?"

She stopped, and then swung around to face him again. "Were you so drunk even at that hour that you don't remember how you scorned him?"

"But Gebirah, he is beneath me!"

"He did not come to you as an equal, but as a suppliant asking bread for those under his care. Are you so blind to duty that you would despise Yahweh's command to feed even the beggars at your gates, let alone those from a kindred clan? You could have at least ordered your lowest servants to do that!"

"He did not deserve even that!" Nabal said passionately, his face red. "He did not come to me himself, but sent servants, and they did not show proper respect when they appeared before me, standing and bowing as if I was some ordinary adon, and not Nagid Carmel, ruler of the richest Calebite clan!"

Her husband would never understand, Abigail realized. His greed for honor had made him as blind, deaf, and hard as a stone. She approached him. "Standing and bowing?" she repeated. "Do you know what I had to do yesterday? I had to scrape the ground before him to plead for your life!"

"You went to him?" Nabal shouted.

"I didn't have to go very far. He was less than a mile from your gates when I found him, and managed to turn him back from his vow." She looked at him with loathing. "You are not to come into my sight again, Nabal. I will have nothing more to do with you!" Without another word she walked away.

"How dare you speak to me this way?" he shouted after her. "I am Nagid Carmel! You will see my greatness. Everyone will see!"

She had never felt such anger as now raged inside her, and Abigail went directly to her bedchamber. She was still there when Tirzah timidly requested entrance.

"What is it?" Abigail snapped.

"Gebirah, the nagid has gone to his business chamber and locked himself in. He has called for food and wine, saying he will give such a feast as has never been seen before that all may come and look on his greatness. What should we do?"

"Give it to him," Abigail answered softly. "Give him whatever he asks for, so long as he doesn't come out of that room!"

"Yes, Gebirah," Tirzah whispered, disappearing.

Her thoughts whirling, Abigail stared after her. Then she hurried to the nagid's bedchamber, hastily searching through the careless toss of bedroll, robes, and sashes.

"It's in the pouch under the stool in the corner," someone said. "That's where he always keeps it, no matter how drunk he gets."

Abigail froze a moment, her heart suddenly pounding. First things first, she thought, getting the pouch and finding Nabal's signet ring. Only then did she turn and face Tokhath. "You have saved me considerable time. I will remember," she said.

He stood in the doorway, his gaze running over her. "I hope so. Do you remember also the other favors I have done you?"

She did not look away. "Of course. That's why I haven't called for the guards."

The scribe stepped forward. "I've wanted you for years," he said, his voice thick, "and now that you have banished that fool of a husband, you'll be happy with me!"

"Tokhath, I haven't called the guards because if I did, you'd die. I owe you that much for holding your tongue when Dahveed's men came with his offer of servitude."

The man smiled. "Nabal was so caught up in his offended honor that he never even realized what Dahveed had done. But I knew, and so did you. I've been planning this for years, letting you destroy him. We will rule together, Gebirah. With the Dahveed under our hand, we will rule all of Israel!"

"I do not intend to rule all of Israel. I intend to save my family's honor, and return to the people what is rightfully theirs."

"An honorable, but useless sentiment," Tokhath smirked. "What would the people do with recompense? To live, they need land, and they would have to use your recompense to buy that land, leaving them with nothing to live on again. No, it's better that the land and people are kept as they are.

"I know you, Abigail, and I am aware how you manipulated Nabal, twisting him around your fingers until he didn't know he even had a mind. But let us get something settled right now. You cannot do that to me."

She straightened up to her full height, staring at Tokhath. "What makes you think I intend to do anything at all with you?"

"Who else is there? You must have a husband; the clans will demand it."

"And you think I will accept you?"

"No, Gebirah. I think I will take you." The scribe moved more quickly than she had expected, and she had to jump back to stay out of his reach.

He stopped, a small unsettling smile on his face. "Don't worry, Abigail, I have no intention of marring your perfect beauty. I need it too much. But I will take the lands of the richest Calebite clan in the south."

The picture of Dahveed's face when she had mentioned the extra grain came to her mind, and an answering smile crossed her own face. "I would rather they went to a despised Habiru, than you," she said softly.

"You cannot mean that," he laughed.

"Oh, I think she does, and I agree with her," Hezro said as the expression on Tokhath's face swiftly shifted to one of fear.

"I rather thought you might," Abigail said, keeping herself from showing her relief. Having never faced such a situation before, she hadn't known how to make her escape.

Tokhath edged toward one side of the room, shuffling his legs awkwardly, letting Abigail know where the point of Hezro's sword was at the moment.

She went to the door, then paused. "Hezro?"

"Yes, Gebirah?"

"If you, or any of your men, ever see Tokhath again, make him a eunuch."

"I may not wait until I see him again," her commander of the guard said, twisting his sword a little as she left.

Sometime later, Hezro found her in her business chamber. "He is gone, Gebirah."

"Very good, commander," she said, her voice shaking. "I have one other thing that must be attended to," she added. "Post a guard at the door of the nagid's business chamber. Whoever wishes to may go in, but the nagid may not come out."

For a moment, Hezro simply stared. Then he bowed his head. "As you wish, Gebirah."

Day after day, isolated in his business chamber, Nabal shouted and sang of his greatness, drinking jar after jar of wine, adding the spices himself now. Tirzah had found three juglets of the additive in Tokhath's room, and the nagid promised to make her the second baalah of the land when she gave them to him.

While Jotbah helped her review Nabal's records to acquaint herself with all that her husband had been doing, Abigail kept in the back of her mind the conundrum that Tokhath had thrown at her. She had thought only of recompense for the people's slavery and injuries, but now the problem of the land itself reared its head. She couldn't simply give the land back, for each household had voluntarily sold it, even if under famine conditions. It must, therefore, be purchased back somehow.

After she had reviewed every record of Nabal's that they could find, she still didn't have a solution to the problem, and finally turned to the one thing she knew she had to do no matter what, determining the recompense that she owed the people themselves.

Everything in the treasury had to be valued, then sorted according to how much recompense she owed to which families and pouches made up ready to distribute. A week had passed when the second consequence of her rejection of the nagid forced itself into her mind. She had yet to produce a girl child to be gebirah after her, and as Carmel was the largest clan, no one could afford to have ownership of her land in question. Not with the attacks from Amalekites still increasing along the southwestern border. That meant she must marry, and Tokhath's comment reminded her that any future husband might not agree with her decision to deplete her riches. Therefore, everything must be done very quietly. For the first time, Nabal was useful for something! So long as he lived, she could work toward her goal in peace.

Three days later, Namea came to her at the end of the noon rest.

"Gebirah, the nagid is dead."

She raised her head. A strange silence emanated from the business chamber. Abigail closed her eyes again, tears of frustration running down her cheeks. The only thing she had needed from Nabal now was that he live. And he couldn't even do that.

They buried him within the hour, the household following silently to a cave in a nearby hillside, and just as silently returned to the compound.

"It's strange," Tirzah said. "I suppose we should be sad, but I feel more like celebrating Jubilee!"

The Gebirah stared at her handmaid. Jubilee? Jubilee came every fiftieth year and Yahweh had commanded that all land be returned to the original owners to restore the covenant . . .

"Your pardon, Gebirah," Tirzah gasped at the look on her face.

"But Tirzah, that's the answer! I will declare a Jubilee!" Abigail said, smiling for the first time in days.

¥ ¥ ¥ ¥ ¥ ¥

"Dahveed?"

I looked around from my discussion with Ahinoam over how much longer the supplies from the Gebirah would last.

Hanan bowed. "Nagid Carmel is dead."

"Was he buried at Carmel or Maon?"

"Maon, adoni. Why?"

"I should send something to the Gebirah while she is in mourning."

The Habiru youth shook his head. "She is not in mourning, Dahveed. I have watched for more than a week. Messages and business documents still enter and leave the estate with the nagid's seal."

"All right, Hanan," I said thoughtfully. "We will respect the Gebirah's wishes as we understand them. Tell the men to say nothing of the death until she does."

"Yes, Dahveed."

That evening I took the harp to the top of the hill. Finding a place to sit, I flexed my hand around the sling, remembering the flash of humor in Abigail's eye there in the valley. Yahweh had indeed slung away the life of my enemy. I should have trusted him. I was, after all, first and always a slave to Yah, and it was His responsibility, not mine, to guard my honor.

Setting the harp to my chest, I plucked a tune that was half dirge, half rejoicing. Then I leaned back and sang.

"Blessed be Yahweh
who pleaded the case of my abuse from the hand of Nabal.
And who withheld his slave from evil.
But the wickedness of Nabal Yahweh returned on his own head."

I looked to the heavens. "May you never have to return any evildoing on my head," I prayed, my grip tightening on the harp. As I stood to leave, I felt the brass earring pull away from my chest, then fall back. I had squeezed the harp so tightly that the earing had left a small indentation in the chest piece.

Harvest came a little later than we had hoped, but the grain from Maon lasted longer than we expected, too. All of us worked from dawn till dark getting the barley cut, threshed, and stored. Then we did the same for the wheat. The gardens produced in plenty, and we held a one-day celebration of Feast of Weeks.

The day after that, I ordered the camp to prepare to leave. We had over-hunted the land, and it needed time to recover. I planned on returning to the wilderness east of Maon, near the hill of Hachilah, six miles away. There was a good place near there that had caught my eye, and I wanted to set up another stronghold.

The day that we moved I lingered behind as I liked to, just checking that we had left nothing important. It wasn't really necessary, for all four of the families with houses in the small valley were staying here to look after things, tend the gardens, and continue with improvements.

Standing atop the hill, I gazed out across the larger valley before going down to it. The Gebirah's flocks were back in the pastures, provided with guards this time, so we would not be missed. Some birds flew up north of me, and I waited to see what had disturbed them. A figure on a mule rode slowly along, wandering a little from the path among the sheep, not really lingering anywhere, but I got the impression that whoever was on that mule was paying close attention to what he looked at.

When he glanced toward the ridge his eyes paused a moment. Likely he'd seen the smoke from the fires at the houses behind me. The mule kept coming, and in spite of the slow pace, its ears were twisted back to its rider. As the animal passed below me, a slight breeze whispered through the trees, and one ear on the mule twisted toward me. The rider halted, apparently searching around. He wore good-quality clothes, nothing showy, but he'd be wealthier than most, I decided. Although he didn't look like a northern adon, I couldn't think of anyone around here with enough wealth to be on that good of a mule in those clothes.

The stranger urged his mount forward a little, then halted again, studying the trees. I waited. Something about his carriage reminded me of Josheb, but the cut of his clothes wasn't usual. From Jebus maybe?

"My mule says you're still there," he said in a pleasant voice.

"You've got a good mule," I replied. "Were you looking for something in particular?"

"I'd heard there was a large band of Habiru in this area."

"Geber, why would anyone riding that much of a mule be looking for Habiru? Isn't that rather like a goat walking into a lion's den?"

The man smiled. "Depends on whether or not the lion's hungry, doesn't it?"

I laughed. "Have you ever known Habiru not to be hungry?"

"Well, I once saw a Habiru dahveed refuse to kill someone, and then pass up the opportunity to rob and hold for ransom two wealthy men, all for the courtesy of a woman."

"The dahveed must have been moon-struck!"

"No, he just wasn't hungry, and that has never left my mind."

"And how is your son Eliam?" I asked, smiling to myself, my memory producing the picture of this man and his son frozen on that mule the day that Ahlai gave Zabad to me four years ago. Eliam had asked a lot of questions as I escorted them back to Giloh.

"What do you know of him?" he asked warily.

I stepped into view. "I know he likes to ask questions."

"I've never forgotten some of your replies, either, or of your courtesy in escorting Eliam and me home," Ahibaal[22] said, nodding a greeting to me.

I shrugged. "It was my pleasure. What may I do for you today?"

He eased his seat on the mule, and the animal shifted in response. "You mentioned that day that you knew Dahveed Israel."

"I do."

"He's said to be in the south somewhere."

"I'd heard that."

"If possible, I'd like to talk to him."

"Why?" I asked, startled.

"Because the Amalekites are restless, and so is the south. And I have heard nothing of Nagid Carmel in too long." The man looked around him intently. "But everything seems fine."

I studied him. His words elicited a vague uneasiness from me.

"Do you know anything of him?" he continued.

I shrugged. "I've only seen him once, and didn't like what I saw."

"You've heard nothing of him then?"

"Geber, I keep myself and my band out of trouble as much as I can, and Nabal seemed like nothing but trouble!"

Ahibaal smiled. "You judged his character very well." As he

---

22 Likely Ahithophel's real name. See A Word About . . .

shifted his weight the mule shook its head, stepping restlessly. "If you would pass on my message about Dahveed Israel, I would be pleased."

"I will." As I stepped aside, the mule started down the trail. I let him go a ways, then called, "Geber?"

A tinge of annoyance on his face, he swung his mount around.

"The Dahveed has many eyes in the forest. If you ever want to get another message to him, just wander down this way on that same mule." I hesitated a moment. "If it's urgent, notch the right fore hoof."

Ahibaal nodded, then continued on his way. When he was out of sight, Hanan appeared beside me.

"That man sees a long way, Hanan," I said. "I want to know everything there is to know about him before I let him get anywhere near me."

The Habiru youth disappeared again.

¥ ¥ ¥ ¥ ¥ ¥

Gebirah Abigail leaned back from the table. Harvest had kept her too busy to tend to recompense, and since she had decided to declare a Jubilee, every payment must be re-figured to include the production value of every field, garden, and grove that Nabal had taken from the people. That had to be multiplied by how many years he had held them to determine the payment owed. In addition, personal injury and/or death recompense had to be added in.

The only thing she had done already was to free those slaves her husband had taken by fiat. She was just now finding the time to turn her attention to recompense again before the grapes ripened.

Namea entered. "Nagid Ahlai from Jezreel is approaching on the road."

Abigail rose. "Coming here?"

"It seems so."

She bit her lip. Given Ahlai's grasping nature, he of all people, must never suspect that Nabal was dead, or what she was doing. But if he insisted on seeing her husband, what could she do?

"I want to see Nabal," Ahlai immediately announced after she had greeted him in the courtyard.

"My husband is not here," she said calmly. "Is there some way I may serve you?"

"This is a matter which I must take up with him," Ahlai said brusquely, looking everywhere but at her.

On impulse, Abigail put her hand on the bridle of the man's mule to get his attention, then opened her eyes wide as she looked up at him. "Would you be pleased to come into the business chamber? It is a poor enough place for someone of your status, but since the proper chamber is in Carmel, I hope you will forgive the discomfort."

Ahlai couldn't take his eyes from her face, and sweat began to bead on his. "Well, I suppose I could, if that's what you want." He flushed a little as he slid off the mule. Abigail stayed close to him, and by the time they had entered the business chamber, Ahlai had the dazed, admiring look in his eyes that she had hoped for, and he stumbled over himself sitting down.

Namea brought fruit and wine, and Abigail served Ahlai herself, talking with him while he refreshed himself. He didn't eat much; he kept forgetting to chew.

At last, she leaned toward him. "I really must apologize, Nagid, but Nabal is on an extended absence until the new year. Was your business with him very important?"

"Uh, uh, no, not much. Just a trifle, really. There was this debt he claimed, but I can work that out with him any time."

"Just a small debt then?" she prodded, widening her eyes at him again.

He swallowed. "Well, not that small. Actually, I don't remember it at all, but this can't concern you," he ended.

"But I am concerned," she assured him. "This was obviously important enough for you to come all the way from Jezreel. That's quite a journey."

"It was nothing, Gebirah. Really, no trouble at all."

"Well, we can't have you going all the way back without an answer. After all, what would you think of us? Do you have a record of the debt?"

"Well, no, actually. That's why I had come. Tokhath delivered the request for payment, and he wanted to take the silver right away. Lael nearly gave it to him, but I got there in time." As he spoke he pulled a papyrus from his girdle.

"Isn't Lael your son? That nice young man who spoke to me one day?" She smiled again, reaching out and taking the document from his hand, brushing his fingers while she did.

Ahlai gulped. "Y-yes, Gebirah, that's the one. He has told me often of his admiration for you. I-I share it, Gebirah."

She looked down modestly. "You are too kind. I don't think you need to worry about the debt. Tokhath no longer works for Nabal."

"Oh? He-he's not here anymore?"

"No. He was--untrustworthy--and forced to leave. It was quite distressing," she said, unable to suppress a shudder.

"You should not think of it," Ahlai said quickly, nearly touching her hand in reassurance before snatching it back. "Don't let it trouble you at all. I'm sure Nagid Carmel would never let anything happen."

"You are so kind," she repeated. "I guess that concludes our business then. There is no debt for you to pay. See, this isn't even sealed by the nagid's signet."

"No, I can see it isn't," Ahlai said, looking around vaguely.

"Then let me help you to your mule again. You must be getting back to Jezreel. Who knows what Lael will have gotten into now?"

"Jezreel? Oh, yes, Jezreel. Or course." Awkwardly he rose to his feet. "I should check up on my son."

Hezro appeared and helped Ahlai mount the mule, leading the animal out of the gate, and giving it a slap to start it down the road. Ahlai still hadn't taken his eyes off her, and she watched until he was out of sight.

"Hezro, is there anyone we know who can find out what Tokhath was doing in Jezreel?" she asked.

"I can try to find someone," he said doubtfully. "But Jezreel is far outside your clan."

Abigail returned to her business chamber. At least Ahlai hadn't suspected anything! Now she should have until the new year's New Moon to complete her plans.

CHAPTER 51

The rest of the summer passed quickly. Uriah looked more and more pleased with the fighting quality of my men, Gad and Ittai had time to fill in the chronicle, Ithmah came and went from Moab so regularly that I used him as a courier to my family and Ahiam's wife, Jemima, who was now Immi's maid. Rinnah didn't seem to care what I did anymore so long as I stayed away from Ziph, although Shagay said Ziphite scouts had checked on us once or twice. I forbore from asking him what had happened to those scouts once he had noticed them.

I had made one or two trips around our strongholds, going up the Arabah to En-gedi, then visiting the farmstead west of Ziph before heading down the ridge to Horesh and back to Hachilah in Maon. Summer was nearly over now, and I was making one last trip, trying to decide if we should stay in Hachilah for the winter or return to Horesh.

Just as I left the farmstead, Hanan joined us. "Adoni, the mule with a notched hoof is in Hebron."

"Did Ahibaal ride it?" I asked.

"Yes."

I stared into the trees, thinking quickly. During the past two months Hanan had brought me a great deal of information about Ahibaal. His estate in Giloh came from his wife, who was now deceased. Himself a Jebusite, he was apparently very well connected there. Hanan said the family fortunes had taken a turn for the worse with Debir's coup, but they had managed to stay alive and were slowly making their position secure again.

He was well-respected in both places for his sensible viewpoint and even-handed treatment of people. Even Habiru, I smiled to myself. The one odd thing Hanan had learned was that his clan elders treated him as their equal, if not superior. I wondered why.

His son Eliam had recently married a well-connected young woman from Jebus. Everything I had learned pointed to a respectable, well-off man, with very good prospects for the future. What I couldn't figure out was why such a man would be bothering with Habiru in the south, unless he wasn't as much interested in Habiru as he was in the announced heir to Israel's throne. And I had learned enough from the hassar to be very wary of that possibility.

But--I was curious. Sending Uzzia and Jaas, who had accompanied me on this trip, back to Hachilah, I set off at a run for Hebron seven miles away. I wanted time to linger around the town before I met with Ahibaal.

After entering the north gate, I loitered at the community well in the market long enough to hear that all the Calebite nagids were meeting at Nagid Hebron's compound tonight. And I'd bet my sling that meeting had something to do with why Ahibaal wanted to talk to me, although I couldn't begin to figure out why.

Since the town was a crossroads for the trade routes up from Beersheba and across to the coast of the Great Sea, it had three inns. I found the mule in the stables of the second one I checked. As soon as I spoke to the animal, its ears swivelled around to keep track of me, and I found my brother Shammah's brand the first thing. Running my hand down the back and foreleg I clucked my tongue, and the mule shifted its weight and picked up the leg to check the hoof. The notch wasn't large, and done so that it looked as if the mule had broken the hoof on a rock.

The stable man stood in the doorway when I straightened up. He didn't look too welcoming, and I knew I didn't look very respectable after my run. "I noticed the track outside of town," I said to him. "Tell the owner he's got a crack on the right fore hoof. That's too good a mule to let go lame for something like that." Then I walked straight toward him, and he moved out of my way by the time I reached the door.

At dusk that evening, I leaned against a wall in the shadows and watched the nagids gather at Dathan's compound. Ahibaal arrived, riding his mule, and the way he glanced around let me know the stable man had told him about the Habiru who had inspected his animal.

Dathan gave him a special welcome, so the nagid was probably Ahibaal's connection here, and from the place given at the tables, he was much honored. I waited longer, wondering when the Gebirah would arrive, and when it became clear that she wouldn't, I got even more curious. I hadn't seen anyone who could be a representative for her either. Then I noticed the middle-aged woman lingering around the gate.

Hanan appeared beside me. "If you want to get in, adoni, there are always lots of strange servants at such feasts. They come with one guest or another."

"I'm armed, Hanan," I said.

He shrugged. "You're just another of the guards who hold the heavy dishes they serve food from."

"The server being you, I suppose?"

Another shrug.

I pushed myself off the wall. "Lead on, Hanan."

Adjusting his clothes, he transformed himself into a rather poor, but respectable, youth. I put a patient, bored expression on my face and followed him to the gate. The woman that I'd noticed drew closer to us when we stopped.

"I was sent to serve here, geber," Hanan said, looking his most harmless.

"Come in, then," the guard said. I stepped back a bit to allow the woman to approach.

"You are here to help also?" I asked.

She nodded and entered the gate ahead of me. Once inside, no one questioned our presence, and as Hanan said, we easily blended in. I lugged around a huge wooden platter that had a variety of fruit, dried and otherwise, on it. Hanan had obviously done this before, moving quickly from table to table, his quiet voice asking the occupants what fruit they would like, signaling me to bring the platter within reach if a guest wanted to choose their own. We were quite busy at first, but after the guests had eaten their first fill, we dallied at the edges of the tables and listened to the conversations.

The reason for the Gebirah's absence soon became clear. The nagids had gathered to discuss her. The news had circulated that Nagid Carmel was apparently too ill to leave his house, and as the illness continued, everyone assumed he would not recover. The topic on everyone's mind was who would marry the Gebirah when Nabal died. Every nagid here either wanted to, or to have someone in their clan do it. Aside from her personal beauty, the connection to the richest of the Calebite clans was invaluable.

While we listened, Hanan and I hurriedly ate something, and the other servers cleared away the brass meat platters and polished stone dishes from the tables. I switched from the wooden platter to a large wooden bowl, and Hanan carried parched grain.

At Dathan's table I offered the bowl of fruit to the nagid first. "Another piece, adon?"

"Are there any of the figs left?" he asked. I tilted the bowl so that he could look. "There should be one or two," I told him. Hearing my voice, Ahibaal froze, then relaxed before I moved to him.

"May I serve you, adon?" I inquired, giving him a polite smile.

He nodded slightly. "I believe you may," he replied, selecting an apricot.

Bowing again, I moved on, Hanan following me. Once we'd been to all the tables a second time, Hanan led me to a corner and pulled out a jar of wine. We waited with it at the edge of the tables, where we could listen again.

"No one has a chance except Dathan and Ahlai," a man said to his companion near me. "The rest of them may dream of it, but will never get it. The Gebirah will have to pick one or the other."

"I don't know," the other man replied. "Clan alliances were about equal between Hebron and Jezreel last year. Seems to me that if she picked one of them, the one left out would make trouble, and either of them have enough resources to make a lot of trouble. If she picks someone from a lesser clan of her own alliances she could maintain a three-way balance of power."

The first man frowned. "Maybe, but I don't think Ahlai will be content with that, not with that much power up for someone to take."

Just then, Hanan saw a signal for wine, and I followed him, and we were busy thereafter. But by the time the feast ended, it was clear that Nabal's imminent death would have a disrupting effect on the relationships between the clans, and the nagids were worried.

The guests were taking their leave when Hanan and I slipped out of the gate, the woman who had come in with us going out with us. She looked tired and worried, and she hurried away as soon as we were at the next corner.

At the inn where Ahibaal stayed, I sat in the courtyard to wait for the adon to arrive. It didn't take him long, and as I rose from the shadows, the inn guard came forward also.

"Is everything all right?" he asked, stationing himself by the adon.

"Yes, guard, although you are correct to inquire," Ahibaal replied. "I asked this man to meet with me."

The guard bowed and went back to his post.

"You have many talents," Ahibaal said drily.

"I have to live as best I can, adon," I replied similarly. "May I assume this meeting of the nagids was the reason for the notched hoof?"

"You may. The situation could explode at any time, and I would like to discuss it with Dahveed Israel. Can you arrange a meeting?"

"I'm afraid I'm as much of a meeting as you get," I said apologetically.

"I really would prefer to speak to him directly," the man pressed.

"You've made that plain, adon. But I am here, and he does not appear to be," I said with a shrug.

"And if I speak with you, how can I know the report will get to him as it should?" he demanded, irritation in his voice.

I backed up a step and bowed a little. "Shalom to you, adon," I said, turning away.

"Wait," he commanded.

I paused.

"You misunderstood me; I meant that it is very important this news reach him as soon as possible."

"Then you only need to say the message is urgent, adon," I said stiffly.

His faced tightened a bit, and then he made himself bow slightly.

"If that is all that is needed, then my comment must have seemed rude."

I didn't move.

"Please disregard it."

"As you wish, adon. What am I to tell Dahveed Israel?"

"That unless the right person marries Gebirah Carmel, the clans will go to war, inviting the Amalekites and Edomites into the south. And that could destroy them all."

He could be right, I thought to myself. "But won't the same thing happen no matter which nagid she chooses?" I questioned. "If I understand the alliances correctly, Hebron and Jezreel are about equal this year."

"Of course it will be the same," Ahibaal said impatiently. "That's why Dahveed Israel has to marry her!"

I blinked.

"He's the only one who can take her without risking a war. As an outsider, he's not involved in this internal struggle, but at the same time because he's of Judah, he's related, and can be accepted as such. He has proved his military ability beyond question, and also his goodwill toward the clans in the south when he protected them from Philistine raiding. The only nagid who might be unwilling to accept that solution would be Ahlai, and he would challenge whomever she married. But given Dahveed Israel's prowess, he would be virtually alone, or at most draw two or three small clans after him. The nagids can easily deal with that.

"Besides, the Dahveed will need a strong, united south behind him when he turns to Israel, or he will never get further north than Bethlehem, and if the clans fragment, Dahveed will never sit on Israel's throne."

I tried to get my mind to think. Marry Abigail myself? The thought had never entered my mind! Well, not seriously anyway. I'd dreamed of having her as a wife as much as the next man, but become nagid? Unite the south?

"You will tell him?" Ahibaal asked somewhat impatiently.

"Yes, adon," I said automatically, bowing.

I left him, disappearing into the forest, my mind whirling with too many thoughts to rest. Turning southeast, I simply ran, covering mile after mile until the feeling of the wind across my face and the flashes of moonlight between the trees had soothed me. The rhythm of my running brought a melody to mind, one that I realized would accommodate the acrostic verses I'd composed during the past three years. While I jogged along, the song came together in my mind.[23]

"Let me bless Yahweh at all times. Continually His praise is in my mouth.

In Yahweh my soul will boast. The afflicted will hear, and they will rejoice.

Extol Yahweh with me, and let us exalt His name together.

I sought Yahweh, and He answered me, and from all of my horrors He delivered me.

They looked to Him and were radiant, so let not their faces be ashamed.

This afflicted one called, and Yahweh heard. And from all his distress He saved him.

The messenger of Yahweh encamps around about the ones who fear Him, and He will deliver them.

Taste and see how good is Yahweh. Blessed is the man who will take refuge in Him.

Fear Yahweh, O His holy ones, for there is no lack for the ones who fear Him.

Young lions suffer want and they hunger, but the seekers of Yahweh will not lack any good thing.

Come you children, hearken to me. The fear of Yahweh I will teach you.

Who is the man who takes pleasure in life? Who loves days to see good things?

Guard your tongue from evil and your lips from speaking deceit.

Desist from evil and do good. Seek peace and pursue it.

The eyes of Yahweh are toward the righteous and His ears are open to their cry for help.

The face of Yahweh is against doers of evil to eliminate from the earth mention of them.

They cried and Yahweh heard, and from all their distresses He rescued them.

Yahweh is near to the broken of heart and the crushed of spirit He will save.

Many troubles have the righteous, but from all of them Yahweh will deliver him.

He keeps all his bones. From them not one was broken.

---

[23] Psalms 34

Evil shall slay the wicked, and the ones who hate the righteous will incur guilt.

Yahweh ransoms the life of His servants, and they will not incur guilt, all the ones who seek refuge in Him."

Finally, my mind settled on the conversation that I'd just had with Ahibaal. And as it did, I realized there was a third side to the situation that Ahibaal hadn't mentioned. The Habiru. And I must give as much consideration to them as the Calebite clans and the struggling few of Judah and Simeon who eked out a living in this dark forest. And how, as king of Israel, I was going to fit both north and south together into a union under Yahweh, I hadn't any idea.

"Yah, You will have to show me the way," I whispered, standing on the bald rock of a hilltop looking down over the land spread out below.

CHAPTER 52

"What did you learn, Jotbah?" Abigail asked late that night when Hezro helped the scribe off the mule that she had ridden back from Hebron.

"It is as you thought, Gebirah. The main topic of discussion was the nagid. But it wasn't about his absence, but about what would happen when he died."

"They think he's sick, not still away on business?"

"Yes, Gebirah. I got in with some late servers. I spent my time around the cooking fires. Everyone believes the nagid came back from his trip with a serious illness, and the women there were all saying that you must marry either Nagid Hebron or Nagid Ahlai when Nabal dies. But they were afraid that no matter which one you pick, there would be a split among the clans, if not a war. They are frightened, Gebirah."

So am I, Abigail thought. If people assumed that her husband was ill, not absent, and with the clan nagids worried about a war, she could have messengers arriving at any time to find out just what the situation was, with Ahlai likely coming first of all! And the Jezreelite would start a war with her rather than let her empty the treasury. Not for the first time, she silently cursed Nabal for his greed. He had married the richest Calebite clan, and then turned it into a concentration of power just waiting for someone to pick up and use. Well, if she was poor, her political usefulness would be much less, and she might find some peace.

Still, she had made some progress. She had repaid Maon--every clan, every family, every man--but she was not done with Carmel. For that, she needed more time and more silver, for the treasury in Carmel had not contained enough to pay for the use of the land given back in Jubilee.

While Jotbah had gone to Hebron, she had worked with Oholah to value all the land she had personally inherited from her abbi. When that wasn't enough, she hadn't known what to do next. And now she had run out of time!

¥ ¥ ¥ ¥ ¥ ¥

My run from Hebron had taken me nearly to Hachilah, so I continued the rest of the way, arriving in camp after midnight. I summoned Ahiam, Josheb, and Zabad the first thing after I broke my fast in the morning. Bringing them into my tent, I told them most of what had happened over the past couple days. The threat of clan wars in the south was very material to our survival, and I gave as many details as I could, but kept Ahibaal's suggestion to myself.

When I had finished, Zabad spoke first. "Pray Yahweh Ahlai doesn't marry the Gebirah! Abbi will be worse than Nabal, for he is no fool."

"Dathan would be the best candidate," Ahiam agreed. "Something I imagine the Gebirah will know as well. But he is not a warrior and would be lost in the middle of clan wars." We discussed the situation for some time before I turned to Josheb.

"You haven't said anything," I prodded.

His handsome face thoughtful, he studied me. "What is the Gebirah doing?" he finally asked.

"What do you mean?"

"We know more than the nagids do. We *know* that Nabal is already dead and how long ago he died. So what is the Gebirah doing? She has been working at a nearly frantic pace all summer. Just the volume of correspondence going in and out testifies to that. And yet, there hasn't been a whisper from anyone in Maon or Carmel about anything unusual, which is itself unusual!"

I remembered Ahibaal's comment about not hearing from the nagid at the beginning of summer. He had seen the importance of that, way back then. It was almost frightening, and I still wasn't certain that I wanted him near me.

Josheb looked at me. "I think everyone is missing the key piece to this situation, because Gebirah Abigail holds it, and she isn't letting it go."

"Which means we have to learn what she is doing," I concluded.

"I think so," Josheb agreed.

"Any ideas?" I asked.

"Send someone to her household," Ahiam suggested. "Ethan's band has been getting information that way since Meshullam's time, and it has paid off."

"Who?"

"It would be best if they could at least read," Ahiam said thoughtfully.

"That narrows the field considerably," I observed. "Zabad, go ask any man who can read to wait outside the tent."

"And they must also seem uninterested in what we want to know," Josheb added. "It would help if they didn't look as if they could read."

When I went outside to see who answered my summons, Elhanan, Uriah, Abishai, Asahel, Zelek, and Eliphelet waited for me. Sibbecai stood a little to one side, arms folded, watching with a hard face, as did some of the others.

I couldn't afford to send Uriah, for I didn't know how long this was going to take, and the military training of the men couldn't be neglected, particularly if clan wars loomed on the horizon. Abishai had become nearly indispensable to me, and I dared not send Asahel, for the youth was too likeable where women were concerned. He'd already given me more problems than I cared to handle in that line. I'd seen him eyeing Keturah once or twice, and I deliberately left that up to Josheb, who proved more than equal to the task of educating my nephew.

Eliphelet would steal the Gebirah blind in three days, so he had to stay here. That left Elhanan and Zelek. Elhanan looked too intelligent for our purposes, and Zelek was obviously an Ammonite, thus unlikely to be welcomed into a Judahite household.

Reluctantly, I dismissed them all. As the others left, Sibbecai slouched closer. "You still need someone who can read?"

"Yes."

"I can," he admitted roughly, his chin thrust out in challenge.

For a moment I didn't know what to say. The thought of the profane, bitter man being able to read had never entered my head. Then

I grinned. "Come into the tent, Sibbecai. I think you're just the man I need!"

Once he understood what I wanted and why, he stood up. "I'll go," he announced and started out of the tent.

"Sibbecai, we need to decide how you should enter her household," I said, stopping him.

He glared at me. "I already know how to do that! Now may I go, or do you want to waste any more of my time?"

I sat back, looking him straight in the eye.

His glance never wavered.

"Come back when you know what we want," I said finally.

His face turned just a bit red, and he hinted at a bow before he left. He departed the camp in less than half an hour, only delaying to consult with Keturah about something.

¥ ¥ ¥ ¥ ¥ ¥

"You're sure there isn't anything else?" Abigail asked Oholah hopelessly.

"I'm sorry, Gebirah, but this is absolutely everything you own," her scribe replied in a tired voice.

"How much more do we need?"

"Payment for lands to two families, and recompense for personal injury for five family members. There is also one death, but the family has not listed it."

"We will pay it anyway, somehow."

"Gebirah! Come quickly," Mibhar shouted from the front courtyard.

Abigail jumped up and rushed out the door, seeing the shepherd running to the gate where a man clung to the wall, obviously ready to fall.

He landed on the ground before anyone reached him, Hezro making it before anyone else. The first thing the commander did was to strip the weapons off him. The stranger's face was pale as death, and he wore rough clothing that had seen heavy usage. As they carried him into the shade of the house, Abigail decided that he was the hardest looking man that she'd ever seen.

There he started coughing, then twisted on the ground, retching painfully. When he eased back, Tirzah felt his forehead. "He's burning with fever," she said, and went to get her herbs. Abigail drew back with

Hezro. "Have you ever seen him before?" she asked.

The commander shook his head. "But he's fought, probably a lot. I'd not like to meet him in a back alley at any time."

"Send Mibhar out to scout around before he returns to the pastures today. Maybe he can see if any travelers have come through."

By noon Mibhar had reported no one on the roads, so she sent him back to the flocks. The man seemed near delirium all that afternoon, and only toward nightfall did his condition ease. Hezro locked him in a storeroom for the night, making sure that two guards accompanied Tirzah when she checked him.

Abigail inquired after his condition the next morning.

"He's better, Gebirah," her maid reported. "The worst seems to be over, but he's very weak still."

"What do you think it was?"

"If I had to guess, I'd say he got some bad meat or something. Once he had emptied out, we got him to drink, and he emptied that out also. But it seemed to ease him."

"I'll talk to him now. Maybe we can find out what clan he belongs to and how he's called."

Tirzah had washed him up a little, and he lay in the shade of the house again. Abigail knelt by the blankets.

"Geber?" she said.

Opening his eyes, he shifted his head toward her. For a moment he stared blankly, and then an expression of complete awe filled his eyes. His gaze traveled to her clothes, and one hand stretched out to touch the bracelet she wore as if he couldn't believe what he saw. Then his hand dropped, and he averted his face. "Yes, baalah?"

"How do you feel?"

A grim smile crossed his lips. "Like I will live this time."

"What's your clan?"

"I have none."

"How are you called?"

"Sibbecai, Baalah." He looked at her again. "Where am I?"

"At my house in Maon. I am called Gebirah Abigail."

"Thank you for your kindness."

"It was the least we could do for one so ill. Do you travel alone?"

"Who would want the likes of me?" he asked bitterly, turning away again, and Abigail left him alone.

It was during the noon rest, thinking of how the stranger had touched her bracelet, that the answer to her need for more silver came to mind. As soon as the rest was over, she summoned Oholah to her bedchamber.

All her jewelry was spread out on the blankets. "How much is all this worth?" she asked. "Would it be enough to cover what I owe?"

Her maid and scribe fingered the items. "I don't know for certain. We would need to get it to a jewel merchant for valuation. And we'd probably have to go to Jebus for that."

Abigail pressed her lips together. It seemed as soon as she solved one problem, another arose. One thing at a time, she told herself. It took three more days to get the name of a jewelry merchant in Jebus. In the meantime, Sibbecai rested, doing what he could to help around with things before he had to return to the blankets spread for him by the house.

The afternoon of the third day he found her in her business chamber.

"Baalah?"

"Yes?" She looked up.

"You have done much for me. What may I do in return?"

"You do not need to repay me for tending someone who was ill, Sibbecai."

"You have done more than just tend me. I want to repay what I can." His chin jutted out.

Abigail looked him over. "Your strength has returned?"

"Mostly," he shrugged.

"All right. I am waiting for a messenger to carry a package for me. Will you accompany him as guard?"

"If you wish."

"He will be bringing something back as well. Could you come back here also?"

"If you wish."

"Then we will consider your debt paid."

"You will not regret it, Baalah."

¥ ¥ ¥ ¥ ¥ ¥

"Dodi, Sibbecai is back," Abishai said nearly a week after I'd sent the man to Abigail's house.

"Bring him to my tent," I replied. "Run to Geber Ahiam, and ask him to come to me," I told one of Zalmon's children.

Ahiam arrived first and looked questioningly. "Sibbecai is

returning," I explained.

The man entered the tent and handed me a bundle that I had to reach for with both hands. He gave me a terse report of the past few days.

"What made you so ill?" I asked, alarmed.

"Keturah. It's this that is important," and he gestured to the bundle. "She sent it by messenger to be valued in Jebus. I was the guard."

"Why is it here?"

"The courier guessed what it was and decided to keep it for himself. I disagreed."

I rather suspected what I'd find, but I opened the bundle anyway, exposing the glittering contents.

"It's everything she has," Sibbecai stated. "I thought you would know the best place in Jebus to take it."

"Surely the messenger knew where to go?"

"The messenger thought to steal from her, adoni. Shall I trust him?"

"Besides, he's dead, isn't he?"

My retainer shrugged again.

I looked at Ahiam. "Do you know of anyone?"

"Well, Ethan dealt with one or two merchants there, but the one he used the most was a man named Gabri. Take them to him and mention Ethan's name. He should give you an honest valuation."

Without a word, Sibbecai bundled up the jewelry again and left.

¥ ¥ ¥ ¥ ¥ ¥

"It's been a full week, Gebirah. I don't think he's coming back," Hezro said quietly. "He killed the messenger, you know."

"We don't know that," Abigail said. "You only found the man's body. And it was south of here. I didn't tell Sibbecai where the messenger was going, so if his body was south, the man was already heading the wrong way."

"And likely Sibbecai took what he carried and kept right on going," the guard commander muttered, leaving the room.

Abigail remained silent. She had more to think about than her lost jewelry. The message in front of her was from Nagid Hebron and was a direct request about the health of Nabal. As a result she would be unable to delay any longer. And once she admitted that Nabal was dead, she had an idea that it wouldn't be long before the clans demanded that she marry again. Probably no later than after the traditional week of mourning.

A sigh welled up from deep inside her. The women in Hebron were right. No matter whom she picked, clan wars would inevitably develop. "Yahweh, send someone!" she pleaded. Ahlai was the best fighter, but there had already been trouble between him and three other clans. Although she wished that Nagid Jezreel could keep him under control, she well knew that would never happen. The nagid was old, feeble, and about to die, and the only male able to replace him was Ahlai himself.

Finally she summoned Jotbah to write the message to Dathan. She might be able to stall a day or two longer, hinting that they were standing Nabal's death watch.

Two days later, Sibbecai waited for her in her business chamber in Maon after the noon rest. He bowed when she entered, and she sat down, pushing aside all the papyri pertaining to the last recompenses she had to pay, wondering how to ask this man what had happened. Her bundle sat on the desk, with a papyus folded on top.

"Shalom, Sibbecai. We expected you sooner," she said calmly.

"The merchant in Jebus was gone, Baalah. I had to wait for his return."

"So the messenger was able to tell you where to go before he died?"

The man's face hardened. "I didn't wait for him to finish. He wanted to rob you."

"I see," she said, stilling her trembling hands. "What did you do?"

"I knew the name of an honest merchant in Jebus, and he valued all the items," he explained, gesturing to the papyrus.

"You have served me well, Sibbecai," she said, a bit stunned.

"You were kind to me, Baalah."

Without another word, he disappeared out the door.

Abigail opened the papyrus with trembling hands. She looked at the total at the bottom, and nearly cried. "It is enough! Yahweh, it is enough!" she whispered.

¥ ¥ ¥ ¥ ¥ ¥

Sibbecai came directly to my tent when he returned the second time to camp. I gestured for him to sit with me by the fire, and

Ahinoam brought some parched grain and water.

"She has nothing left," he said.

By now, I was getting used to the terse way Sibbecai reported things. "What did the Gebirah do with it all?"

"She declared a Jubilee."

I sat up abruptly, turning to him.

"She returned every piece of land that Nabal had taken, paid rent for the usage of it, and added in recompense for injuries and death. Nabal's treasuries did not have enough to cover the costs, so she used her personal land and then her jewelry. Even her compound in Maon is no longer hers."

"Yahweh above!" I said, stunned. "There is nothing left to her?"

He shrugged. "She may have some clothes."

My wife gave up all pretense of not listening and sat down beside me. "What will she do?" she asked, her face worried.

"She will marry. The nagids are sure now that Nabal is dead or nearly so, and they will press their suits."

"Only until they find out that she has nothing!" I said. "And Yahweh only knows what will happen then!"

Ahinoam turned to me. "Nothing?" she said in amazement. "She is richer now than she has ever been! And if my abbi gets his hands on her--"

"What do you mean?" I asked in bewilderment.

"Dahveed, she just gave *everything she had* to honor her people. If you want to know how rich that makes her, you just ask the men who were with you in Nahash's throne room when you gave yourself to Abner in exchange for them! Every man in this band knows what you did, and they will follow you to Sheol and back because of it!

"The nagids may only be thinking of her land and the power that brings, but the farmers and the vine dressers and the women and householders of every clan in the south will be longing to belong to a Gebirah who cares that much for them! They will do absolutely anything she wishes now. Don't let my abbi get his hands on that much power, Dahveed," she said fiercely. "Do whatever it takes--marry her yourself if you can--but don't put her into Abbi's power!"

Not knowing what to say, I just stared at her.

"She's right, adoni," Josheb said from where he stood a little way away. "Whoever marries the Gebirah now will rule all the south. I think it should be you."

"But I--"

"It won't look like it at first," Ahiam added, stepping up beside Josheb. "It will take a couple years for clan alliances to re-arrange, but in the end, the Gebirah will hold them all either directly or indirectly. Ethan has told me more than once that you will need a united south in order to take Israel's throne. It's here now. And I think, if you offered for her, she would accept."

"I'm Habiru!"

"You are Dahveed Israel and Yahweh's Mashiah."

"I must think about this," I said, dazed. I took the harp and wandered out of camp, finding a comfortable seat under an elm. Tuning the instrument, I plucked the strings idly. "Yah, what should I do? I have a wife."

The Gebirah needs the shelter of your wings.

Later that night, I lay down beside Ahinoam.

"What did you decide?" she asked.

I took her into my arms. "I haven't decided. What about you, Ahinoam?" I could feel her start to tremble.

"You will be king of Israel, and more besides, Dahveed. That means alliances, and alliances mean wives. I have my place with you already, even though I tricked you into making it for me!"

I squeezed her closer.

"I've always admired and liked the Gebirah, even if she does make me look like a carp from the river! If she can give up everything for those in her care, I won't begrudge her the peace she deserves, and if she marries anyone else, the clans will wage war."

I loved Ahinoam very tenderly that night.

CHAPTER 53

"The situation is worse than we thought, Gebirah," Hezro announced as he entered Abigail's chamber in Maon. "According to Hanan, the young man I told you of, the nagids are on their way, with Ahlai nearly here. He said Tokhath told Ahlai that you planned on repaying Maon and Carmel for Nabal's injustices now that Nabal is dead. Ahlai has 10 soldiers with him to keep you from 'wasting all that Nabal has done.'"

"They didn't even wait out the week of mourning, did they?" she asked, her stomach tightening.

"No, Hanan said Ahlai is about an hour away, so you have time to leave."

She smiled faintly. "What good would that do, Hezro? Should I let him chase me all over the south?"

Her commander grimaced. "No, but it might give Nagid Hebron time to get his representatives here."

"And that would start the war immediately. No, Ahlai is the best one to settle a war among the clans quickly. Besides, many nagids will hesitate to attack him, and that might buy enough time for things to settle and maybe prevent a war after all."

"But he'll be worse than Nabal! And you can't control Ahlai as you did Nabal."

"I wouldn't try, and I may not have to. His own self-interest will keep him from doing much that Nabal did. Besides, what would he do it with? The treasuries are empty. Who is left in the compound?"

"Myself, Mibhar, and your maids."

"I told them to go this morning!"

"They don't appear to have listened," Hezro said, smiling.

"You don't have to stay," she said, looking down.

"I'll be with you until Ahlai manages to kill me," he said simply.

Namea entered, looking frightened. "Gebirah, there are armed men outside. They-they want to talk to you."

"Very good, Namea. I'll be right out."

"I guess my source underestimated how long it would take Ahlai to get here," Hezro commented. He offered his arm to Abigail. "Shall we go, Gebirah?"

"Certainly, commander," she replied, raising her chin and taking his arm.

Outside, she faced the 10 men, who all bowed when she appeared. A tall, elegant-looking man stepped forward and bowed again. "Shalom, Gebirah. I am Josheb ben Zabdiel. We have come from Dahveed Israel. Having heard of your misfortune in the loss of Nabal, he wishes to know if you would consider him as your husband."

Had she heard correctly? "You are from Dahveed Israel?"

"Yes, Gebirah."

"And *he* is offering me marriage?"

"Yes, Gebirah. He was much impressed with your concern for your people and for his reputation the day you met him in the valley."

Suddenly dizzy with relief, she swayed a little, clinging tightly to Hezro's arm. He quickly steadied her. "You're not from Ahlai, then?" she said.

"No, Gebirah," the man said, watching her closely. "Were you expecting him?"

"He is supposed to be on his way."

A faint murmur ran through the men, and they glanced at each other.

"Then it seems you have a choice, Gebirah," Josheb commented. His tone told her that he perfectly understood the position she was in, which meant that Dahveed Israel did, too. "Are you willing to come with us?" he asked softly.

"Am I willing?" she repeated a bit unsteadily. Then she bowed deeply. "Josheb ben Zabdiel, I would be willing to go with you if all I could hope for was to be a slave to Dahveed's servants!"

Amazement crossed the man's face, and then he smiled in delight. "Gebirah, you are most welcome to our band, and I don't think you will have to be a slave!"

Abigail smiled in return. "You bring good news to me. Namea, we must leave at once!"

"Yes, Gebirah," the handmaid replied, staring at the men. "Are we all to go with them?"

"If you would," Josheb answered with a courtly bow. "Unless you would rather wait here for Nagid Ahlai?"

"No!" Namea said, whirling around.

"Get them up on the donkeys," the man ordered, and Abigail saw that the delegation had brought six donkeys with them.

In only seconds it seemed, Hezro helped her mount, taking her donkey's bridle a little defiantly. Josheb courteously gestured him to lead the animal away. Once they were out on the road, a young man appeared. "They're coming into town," he told Josheb.

"Keep an eye on them, Hanan."

"Yes, adon." The youth vanished.

"Your pardon, Gebirah, but we must hurry," Josheb said, turning to her.

"By all means, go as fast as we must, adon."

She was barely out of sight of the compound when she heard the clatter of mule's hooves and then Ahlai's voice raised in anger.

Josheb studied the street briefly, then hurried the donkeys down an alley, across the next street, and down still another alley. They stopped briefly. "Sibbecai, you and Zalmon get the Gebirah and her maids to the stronghold," he ordered quietly. "I think the rest of us will remain here to make sure Ahlai stays busy for a while."

Sibbecai reluctantly nodded, looking rebellious.

"Let Hezro, Mibhar, and Zalmon lead the donkeys," Josheb added. "I want you in the rear. I saw at least one Ziphite with Ahlai, and you know what they're like. Don't let anyone get past you to the Gebirah."

Sibbecai straightened. "As you command, adon," he said, his voice flinty.

Just then more shouts rang down the streets. Abigail glanced behind her.

"Looks as if Nagid Dathan's men just arrived," Josheb said, grinning. "Maybe we won't have to do anything but watch. Get her safely to Dahveed, Sibbecai."

The man who had rescued her jewelry turned away without a word, and the donkeys soon trotted as fast as they could between the walled vineyards, headed toward the watercourse that began just southeast of town. Once the trees closed over them, Sibbecai paused, watching the way they had come.

Then he turned abruptly to Hezro. "Follow Zalmon. One of the Ziphites picked up our trail."

Abigail jerked her head up to stare back at the town, seeing a flash of movement between two vineyard walls. Hezro started out after Zalmon, the donkeys trotting rapidly along the watercourse. It joined a larger watercourse, one coming in from the right, then turned back southeast, climbing up onto what Abigail realized must be the high hill that her guard commander had said was two miles from the town.

"Hezro, can we rest a moment?" she asked quietly, indicating Tirzah's flushed face and plump form.

"Zalmon," he called quietly. "A rest, perhaps?"

The Habiru looked around. "You're tired already?" he asked in surprise.

"The Gebirah is."

Zalmon looked abashed. "Your pardon, Gebirah. I didn't think. Certainly, we can rest for a little."

"I would appreciate it," Abigail said, contriving to look tired. "And I'm sure my maids would also,"

"I, for one, would," Namea agreed.

Mibhar helped her down, then Tirzah, who nearly collapsed on the ground the moment she stood on it. They had only been there a short time when Sibbecai emerged from the trees.

"We've thrown them off the track for now, but Josheb said to get to the stronghold as soon as we can. Those Ziphites have no love for Dahveed," Abigail heard him tell Hezro.

"Tirzah, would you prefer to ride or walk?" Abigail asked. "These men say we must go quickly."

"I'll walk if I can," her handmaid said, eyeing the donkey with disfavor.

"I will, also," Namea added. "Come on, Tirzah, I'm tired of my donkey, too."

Hezro seated Abigail again, and they continued southeast across the ridge top, still descending until the ridge split into two fingers, and the trail turned sharply down into a hollow backed by a steep hillside. When she saw someone running ahead of them, she knew that she must be close to the end of her journey. She looked around at the trees closing around them, dimming the light from the bright blue sky above. What sort of a place was a stronghold, she wondered. How did one live in one? Where did one get water? Would she have to sleep on the ground? Suddenly she realized that she had left so quickly that the only robe she had to wear was on her back. Everything else had been left at the house unless Namea or Tirzah had remembered to pick up the bundle.

As the donkey descended farther into the ravine, its walls shutting out more of the sky, she shivered a little. Just how much of her situation did Dahveed know? What would he do when he realized she brought no lands, no silver, no riches of any kind? How many men would there be, and what were they like? From what she had seen of Josheb, he deserved the title of adon. His graceful elegance shouted of a high status family. Zalmon seemed a cheerful, reliable man, the kind she would have hired to work for her without a second thought. But Sibbecai was an entirely different matter. Never would she have dreamed that he could be trusted with all of her jewelry. She stared hard at Hezro's back in front of her. Would Dahveed let him stay with her? The thought of facing so much unknown made her stomach tremble.

Suddenly, she wanted more than anything else to whip the donkey around and run it back up the hills into the sun again and the familiar walls of Carmel and Maon. What had she done when she accepted Dahveed's proposal? She hadn't really thought about any of this. She'd only seen him three times, spoken with him twice, and now she had agreed to be his wife out of complete desperation, because there was nowhere else to go that might avoid disaster for her people. But how could she protect them out here in the wilderness? What was happening to them back in Carmel? Would they think that she had deserted them? What on earth had possessed her? Panic swept over her, and she clenched her hands to stop them from shaking. As always, she turned to her memory. What would Hassarah Ruth have done? Had she ever felt this way?

But she must have, Abigail suddenly realized in wonder. Ruth hadn't just left a house three miles away on the plateau. She had abandoned her home, family, and her dead to throw herself on the hesed of a strange God in an unknown land where everyone would regard her with suspicion and distrust.

As she straightened on the donkey she knew that she didn't have to face half of what Ruth had endured. Everything would work out. Ruth had become the most honored person in Bethlehem, and-and she was going to be too scared to see straight by the time she got to wherever they were going.

¥ ¥ ¥ ¥ ¥ ¥

"They are coming, adoni," Asahel said. "But only Sibbecai and Zalmon are with them."

"She agreed?" I gasped, staring at my nephew. When I'd sent Josheb with my offer of marriage, I hadn't really believed it might be accepted! I had thought that she would just use it as a bargaining chip against the other nagids.

"And what do you mean only Sibbecai and Zalmon are there?" I asked, waking up to what Asahel had said.

"They are the only ones escorting the Gebirah, five handmaids, and two retainers."

"Who are the retainers?" I asked instantly. I hadn't expected that even if she accepted the proposal she would come with servants. That might be a problem, for I couldn't afford to have anyone here who wasn't trustworthy. The political situation in Israel was still explosive, and I didn't want people to know where I was.

"One is Mibhar, the shepherd, and the other is her commander of the guard, I think."

Hezro. I sighed in relief. Mibhar had proven to be a good man, and I personally knew that Hezro would give his life for his baalah. I glanced at the tent that Ahinoam had insisted on getting ready. It was a little way away from the rest, and large enough for her handmaids to stay with her if she wished. There wasn't much in it, we didn't have much, and I wondered what she would think of the sparseness of our lives after the comfortable life she had known since birth.

Well, she had faced me down in that valley by Carmel, so she couldn't be the whining, useless type that made more of a burden than anything else. And she would have to be a strong woman to have survived Nabal. But how could she possibly accept me when all I had to offer was a promise made by Yahweh? I couldn't keep her comfortable, might not be able to feed her, would certainly tear her away from everything she knew, and just might get her killed. How did I get myself into these messes?

¥ ¥ ¥ ¥ ¥ ¥

Abigail tried to keep from gasping for every breath as the donkey slowed, climbing a little toward a stand of pine trees. She looked around, wondering where the stronghold was, and caught sight of two women. When Hezro stopped the donkey, they came forward.

"Shalom, Gebirah," one said, her accent different from any Abigail had ever heard. "I am called Keturah, and this is Ahinoam of Jezreel, Dahveed's wife."

Somehow Abigail managed to control her expression as her handmaids clustered around her. Dahveed was already married? Was he only taking her as a concubine? Having never considered being a second wife, she didn't know what to say. Should she bow? She guessed that she had better. Somewhere she'd heard that northerners from the Jezreel valley were very formal. As she started to bow, Ahinoam put out her hand.

"No, Gebirah, there is no need for that," she said kindly, her accent soft and familiar.

"Oh, you're from Jezreel in the south!" Abigail exclaimed in relief.

"I am, Gebirah, and I've always admired you, now more than ever before."

Tears pricked Abigail's eyes, and she couldn't stop them from streaming down her cheeks.

Ahinoam turned to Keturah. "I knew she'd be exhausted. Keturah, take the maids to their place, and I'll get Gebirah Abigail settled in hers. Zalmon, bring the Gebirah's things," she said crisply.

A blank look crossed his face. "Her things?" he said, looking around, puzzled.

"Don't tell me you threw her on that donkey and dragged her down here without her possessions, did you?"

"Well, Geberet, it was sort of--I mean--we had to come right away and--"

"Zalmon ben Ahoh, how could you do such a thing?" Ahinoam exclaimed in horror.

"Well, Josheb said we had to go and--"

"Josheb did this? He should know better! Where is he? He can just go right back and--"

Abigail had to smile through her tears at the look of helpless chagrin on Zalmon's face as he meekly listened to Ahinoam's scolding.

"Please, Geberet, don't blame him or Josheb," she said, interrupting. "We had to leave in rather a hurry and there wasn't time or opportunity to take our things. Surely they can be sent for later, can't they?"

"They most assuredly will be." Ahinoam glared at Zalmon. "Now, come with me. You must be dropping with fatigue and everything must be so strange after getting dragged out of town without the chance to even--"

"It was more like pushed," Abigail said thoughtfully, following Ahinoam up among the trees that shielded a little clearing.

"What was that you said?" her guide asked.

"Pushed, not dragged. They stayed behind us to make sure we got away safely."

"From whom?" Ahinoam asked, turning to her.

"Nagid Ahlai. He arrived at my gate just moments after we went out of it. So there really wasn't time to get anything to take with us."

"So Abbi got there first," Ahinoam said grimly. "He would."

"You're Ahinoam bat Ahlai?" Abigail exclaimed, startled. "But I heard you were sold-um, taken north by a northern adon!"

"That was Josheb. He purchased me to help Zabad and Dahveed get me away from Abbi, who was trying to sell me to Nabal. Once Zabad and I got Immi's dowry back, we bought ourselves from Dahveed, and have stayed with him since." The woman turned to her. "I know exactly what Ahlai is like, and there was no way at all that I was willing for you to end up married to him, especially after what you've just done!"

Abigail looked into her fierce gaze and read there a great deal which the woman would never say to her. "Thank you, Ahinoam," she said gravely, bowing slightly. "Thank you for your kindness toward me. I'm not certain I deserve it."

Ahinoam straightened. "It is the least I could do, Gebirah, after you left yourself with nothing to repay those whom the nagid had wronged."

"How did you know I did that?" Abigail gasped. "No one in Carmel or Maon said a word, and the other nagids only know that I was considering something like that."

Dahveed's wife started for the tent again. "We knew a little more than the nagids," she smiled. "We knew when Nabal really died, you see. Josheb suspected that whatever you were doing was important, but it wasn't until Sibbecai went to you that we discovered the extent of what you'd done." She pulled back the tent flap. "It isn't much, but we did what we could," she said, gesturing her inside.

As Abigail looked around, she realized that Ahinoam was correct. It wasn't much. Still, it had a couple cushions to sit on, some reed mats on the floor, a short, round three-legged table, a bedroll, and a battered chest to store things in.

"I know it's not what you're used to," Ahinoam said, looking away.

"No. But it's a great deal more than I have now!"

Ahinoam looked at her in surprise, and then the tight embarrassed expression on her face faded into laughter. "Shall I leave you alone for a bit? I know you must be tired."

"I'd prefer if you stayed for a while if you can. This is the first time I've stepped inside a tent in my life, and I have a great deal to learn. Do you mind if I ask you some questions?"

"I know the feeling," Ahinoam said, sitting down while Abigail settled herself on the other cushion. "I felt so lost about what to do about so many things until Puah came. I think I drove her to distraction with all the questions I asked."

"Who is Puah?"

"Shagay's wife. Shagay is Dahveed's first retainer. Puah died about a year ago, but she taught Keturah and me a great deal. Keturah is a Gibeonite," Ahinoam went on. "She's married to Josheb, who is Dahveed's third retainer. He used to be part of Hassar Jonathan's body guard."

Relaxing for the first time in hours, Abigail listened while Ahinoam told about the people who made up the band of which she had now become a part. She would never forget the welcome this woman had given her, and she knew that because of it, she would find a place for herself here.

¥ ¥ ¥ ¥ ¥ ¥

I had watched from the doorway of my tent while Ahinoam led the Gebirah to the tent prepared for her. She did look tired, and if she was half as frightened as her maids were, she probably wouldn't emerge from it until next week.

Keturah had such a hard time soothing the women in her charge that I had sent Asahel over to help. He was willing enough, and it wasn't long until his way with the female half of the population had exerted itself, and the handmaids no longer looked as if they expected to be eaten for the next meal. What puzzled me, however, was why I hadn't seen any bundles or baggage arriving with them.

The evening meal was nearly ready when Hanan trotted out of the trees, a fresh bruise on one side of his face and a cut bound up on his arm.

"What happened?" I asked.

He touched the bruise. "Ahlai. Josheb needs to talk to you."

"Go have Keturah and Asahel look after that cut."

Before long Josheb and the rest of the men arrived. "Did the Gebirah get here all right?" were the first words out of his mouth.

"Yes. Ahinoam is still talking to her. What happened?"

"We barely got out of her gate before Ahlai arrived. He'd heard rumors the Gebirah was thinking of freeing Nabal's slaves and paying out recompense, so he hurried over from Jezreel to stop her. Dathan must also have heard the same thing, but I don't think his representatives were thinking of stopping her, just asking her to give her hand to him in marriage.

"Things got a little tense in town. Dathan hadn't sent soldiers as Ahlai had with him, but after Hanan implied that Ahlai had abducted the Gebirah, Dathan's men were ready to fight."

"I suppose Ahlai won?" I asked sourly.

"Honor was pretty even all around," Josheb said seriously. "Dathan's men didn't have the same skill that Ahlai's had, but then they didn't have to worry about what might be happening behind them. I'm afraid Ahlai's soldiers got a few nasty surprises."

"Supplied by you?"

"Not necessarily. Those townspeople love their Gebirah, and they didn't appreciate the way Ahlai stormed around in the Gebirah's house, throwing things. So we let the townspeople handle most of that. It was the Ziphites we worried about."

I jerked my head up. "What were they doing there?"

"Siding with Ahlai. He had three guides. One of them found our trail, but he ran into Sibbecai."

"And the other two?"

"Hanan found one and knocked him out, and the other disappeared. It was Rinnah, I believe."

I frowned. That man had a nose for my whereabouts that I couldn't afford to ignore. "How long do you think we have?"

Josheb thought for a moment. "It might take Rinnah a while. Between Sibbecai and Hanan, the impression is that we are south and maybe a bit west of Maon. But I think that's the least of your problems, Dahveed."

Most everyone had gathered around now, and Ahinoam and Abigail had also emerged from the tent.

"You need to be worrying about the nagids," he said. "By the time we left town two more had arrived, and we avoided another as we left. The only thing keeping them from killing each other is that none of them knows where the Gebirah is and each of them suspects that one of the others does."

"Do they know yet what the Gebirah did with Nabal's wealth?"

"No. And the people in Carmel and Maon will never tell them."

I saw Ahinoam and Abigail glance at each other. "Can you keep my whereabouts a secret until the New Year's new moon?" Abigail asked quickly.

I looked at Hanan and Shagay.

They nodded.

"Yes," I replied.

"Then we can plan on attending the usual gathering at Hebron. I had intended to announce whom I would marry at that time, and I know the nagids expected that. But it seems the situation has changed."

"It has," Josheb agreed. "Nagid Ahlai wouldn't wait, and now none of the others can."

"Then there is only one thing to be done," Abigail said, looking at Ahinoam again.

"And it must be done tonight," my wife added.

Seeing the two of them standing there side by side, I wondered just what I'd let myself in for. The expression on Josheb and Shagay's faces said they had a glimmering of it and were vastly amused.

"What would that be?" I asked cautiously.

"I must be married tonight," Abigail said. "We dare not wait even a day longer."

"Tonight?"

Ahinoam nodded. "You know Rinnah, Dahveed. All he would have to do is hint to Ahlai about where you were, and he'll come charging down here with all the nagids right behind. We'd have war on our hands with all the clans."

"How could he possibly suspect that the Gebirah is with me?" I asked, bewildered.

"Because of something she said to Tokhath," Hezro interjected. "He, well, he got a little eager after the Gebirah before Nabal died, and she told him she would rather her lands went to a Habiru than to him."

"You did?" I said, turning to her.

A faint blush crossed her cheeks. "And I meant it," she said. "It's the only way, adoni. If I am actually married, the other nagids will no longer contend for me. And you should be able to handle Ahlai and however few he might get to follow him. But you must become my husband tonight, just in case the Ziphites know more than we think they do."

"But there won't be a wedding feast, or any preparations, or--"

"Dahveed, we can feast anytime," Ahinoam interrupted. "What we can't do is take the chance of the Ziphites learning where Abigail is."

Bewildered, I looked around. This was so sudden.

"Are you, by chance, objecting to the proceedings?" Ahiam asked with a straight face.

I felt myself flush and Abigail's eyes flashed with amusement as she looked at me. "May we at least have something to eat first?" I asked plaintively.

CHAPTER 54

My men roared with laughter, but I noticed Hezro and Mibhar glancing anxiously at their mistress. Abigail had a little smile on her face, however, which seemed to reassure them.

Turning to her, I bowed formally. "Abigail, Gebirah Carmel, would you do me the honor of becoming my wife?"

She bowed back. "It would be my honor to become the wife of the

Dahveed Israel," she replied just as formally.

"Then, as circumstances seem to have restricted our choice of wedding times, perhaps we should pledge our houses immediately."

"I am willing."

Abiathar came forward with a cup of wine and some bread and stood beside us.

"I, the Dahveed ben Jesse, do swear before Yahweh to support and honor you as my wife in all things," I said.

"I, Abigail Gebirah Carmel, do swear before Yahweh to honor you as my husband in all things."

Abiathar handed me the cup, and we both drank from it. Then I broke off a piece of bread, and we both ate.

The men cheered, and I offered my arm to her, leading her toward the tent we'd put up for her. Keturah slipped out of it as we arrived, and when we went in, there was food for a meal spread out on a reed mat.

I helped her sit on a cushion, sat down on the other, and we began to eat.

"I know this is very sudden, Abigail. I wish there was more time for us to get acquainted," I said before the silence became strained.

"We don't have time, adoni. Not yet. And if marrying now will avoid war in the Calebite clans, it is worth the price."

A little shaft of disappointment went through me. Somehow being accepted as husband as a duty didn't appeal to me.

"Is that what you were thinking of when you spoke to Tokhath?" I asked, looking at her.

She blushed a little in the light of the two oil lamps burning near us. "No."

"What were you thinking of?"

"The way your face looked when I said there was more grain coming from Maon there in the valley."

"How did it look?" I asked, startled.

"A little surprised, a lot relieved, and very much trapped into something," she said. "About how you looked out there a bit ago."

"Is that a good thing, or a bad thing?"

Her smile grew. "It's a good thing. It makes you look very appealing."

I reached across and touched her face. "And when you drop that calm mask you wear, and let your eyes twinkle, you look very appealing, too. You won't need that mask here, you know."

Her eyes grew dark, wide, and startled, and I ran my hand down her hair, gently pulling my fingers from the tangles. "I'd like to see more of that twinkle. I wanted to there in the valley when you talked about my sling."

"I'll try to put it there, adoni."

"No, I'll try to make it safe for you to have it there," I corrected, kissing her palm.

She shivered.

"Are you cold?" I asked.

"No, adoni. I don't think so."

Helping her lie down, I pulled a blanket over us anyway, but she still shivered.

"I don't want you to be frightened, Abigail," I said quietly, stroking her face again.

"I'm not. I-I've never felt this way before."

"Is that a good thing, or a bad thing?"

She looked at me, her eyes wide and dark as I kissed her palm again. "I think it's a good thing, Dahveed. A very good thing," she added as I covered her mouth with my kiss.

It seemed best to wait for our wedding feast until after the New Moon festival in Hebron, which would begin the day after tomorrow. Abigail wanted to arrive the second day of the festival, planning on announcing our marriage at the feast after the pledging by adons to nagids had concluded. This would allow her to answer any questions that nagids might have regarding her lack of land and pledges, all of which would impact the various clan alliances.

The entire band gathered in the Maon stronghold the first day of the New Moon, and we had a simple rite there for everyone to swear to me for the next year. After the men already sworn to me renewed their vows, Parai stepped up. Once he'd taken his oath, he stopped in front of Abigail. I noticed Hezro tense behind her and put his hand on his sword.

Parai pulled a pouch from his girdle, then knelt, holding out the pouch. Before my wife could reach for it, Hezro took it, feeling it quickly before he handed it to her. Although Parai flushed slightly, he remained motionless.

She opened it, spilling the silver into her palm. "What is this for, Parai?"

"I would buy myself back from you."

Abigail glanced at the silver again. "There is much more here than is necessary."

He looked up. "If you remember, I promised you recompense for what you had done."

That calm mask settled on Abigail's face. "I remember."

The tanner looked down again. "I find that I cannot give the recompense I promised you, so I hope you will be gracious, and accept what is there instead." Bowing, he then prostrated himself on the ground.

Abigail didn't say anything for a moment or two. "What you have given here is more than adequate, Parai," she said quietly. "The purchase price is accepted. Go out from here in peace."

The tanner rose from the ground and walked away and the rite continued, but I got the distinct feeling that more had been said between Parai and Abigail than I knew. I'd have to ask what had really happened sometime. The next interruption to the ceremony was extremely unwelcome.

Hiddai showed up, all but crawling to me, begging to swear also.

"He'll betray you for the first man with better food!" Sibbecai said caustically, fingering his sword.

Igal just looked at him with contempt.

But the roeh's words rang in my mind. "It is not even necessary that you like them, Dahveed. Just respect them as Yahweh's tools to be used by Him as you are."

I hadn't any idea what Yahweh could possibly want this man for, but I let him swear. He was gone the next morning to no one's sorrow, but I wondered if I'd let an enemy into the camp.

Those of us going to the festival left immediately after the noon rest for the seven-mile trip to the stronghold in Horesh. I wanted to check on the place, and it broke the trip to Hebron up into something that the Gebirah's maids could tolerate.

We avoided all roads both to Horesh, and then to Hebron the next morning. Abigail told Josheb that Dathan had a small house close to his compound that he normally reserved for her use every year, and when my third retainer returned from the town to say the house was not occupied, she was pleased.

"Ahinoam, the maids, and I can stay there," she said. "It's too small for everyone."

"I should probably be there, also," I said. "What do you suggest, Ahiam?"

"Hezro, Zabad, Josheb, and Sibbecai should accompany you as

guards. Pekah can serve as a courier. As for the rest of us, we will be around."

We entered town during the noon rest, Hezro leading the way, and Abigail sent Pekah to Nagid Dathan to let him know that she had arrived and would be attending the feast tonight.

It didn't take long for Dathan to appear at our gate, and Abigail went to greet him.

"Gebirah! It is so good to see you well! No one knew what had happened in Maon, and we feared some harm had come to you!"

"As you can see, I am perfectly fine, Nagid," she said, smiling.

"But Gebirah, where have you been?" he asked, noticing Sibbecai and Zabad obviously standing guard. "These men have not hurt you?"

"Quite the contrary. They have been very kind. I have a favor to ask, if you would be inclined to grant it."

"Anything, Gebirah," Dathan said, bowing.

"Please don't mention that I am here to the other nagids. I would prefer that they not know until the feast. And if you could be certain that there are two places beside me at the table?"

"It shall be as you wish." Then he hesitated a little. "Gebirah, if I may be so bold, one of those places wouldn't be for Nagid Ahlai, would it?"

"No," Abigail said firmly.

"Then my mind will be at ease. I am so thankful that you are with us again, Gebirah. There will be much praise tonight for your safe return. I would stay to see that you are comfortable, but I have business that cannot be put off. Please pardon my rushing away like this."

"I will be resting now anyway. Shalom, nagid."

"Shalom, Gebirah." Dathan hurried out the gate.

I hadn't decided yet whether I should escort Abigail into the feast, or stay in the background a while to see what developed after her arrival. It was nearly time to get ready when Ittai came through the gate.

"Adoni, may I speak with you?"

"What is it, Ittai?"

"Adoni, there is much unrest in the town. Rumors are everywhere about the nagids and the Gebirah. The people are . . ." he hesitated. "They are not worried exactly, but could easily be roused to violence."

"Over what?"

"What happens to the Gebirah. It's not the nagids who are this way, but it seems nearly everyone else is. If I may say so, adoni, there will be trouble unless the people like the Gebirah's new husband."

I studied the still face of my covenant son. "Did you have any ideas?"

"Yes, adoni. Only the nagids will be at Dathan's compound. The householders, adons, retainers, and servants will be feasting in the market place again tonight. I think you should go there first. Play for them. Then go to Dathan's."

I smiled. "In other words, I should win over the common people."

"There are enough to bring pressure on the nagids if necessary."

"All right, Ittai. I'll tell Ahinoam and Abigail what to expect."

At dusk, Abigail left our house, dressed in clothing that she and Ahinoam had conjured up from somewhere. I wore the robes Nahash of Ammon had given me. For my foray into the town market, however, I had mine covered by a light cloak, although I wore all the gold jewelry.

Once the food was brought out in the market square, I emerged from an alley, and wandered around a little, following Ittai while he identified for me the principal adons here.

"Geber, can you play that?" Someone pointed to my harp strapped to my side as I walked past a table.

"I've been told so," I said, smiling. "Are you willing to give me your opinion?"

He laughed. "I don't see why not, and I might add some coppers into the bargain."

"Ah, a generous patron!" I laughed. "I'll have to do my best." By now, the tables nearby were listening in as I tuned the harp. "Was there any song in particular you wanted to hear?"

"Do you know the Traveler's Song? My son here loves to guess what the traveler saw on his journey, but he can never make up his mind about some things!"

I winked at the half-grown boy sitting solemnly beside his abbi. "I'll have to make it very plain then," I said, and started the song. It didn't take long before both tables on either side competed with each other in the guesses. They identified the donkey going by, the hoof beats of a courier's mule, the tramp of an army unit, and then the pounding of pestles as the local women made flour. But the little ticks I played next puzzled everyone until a young woman clapped her hands. "It's loom weights!" she exclaimed. "He's passing a loom, and the woman is weaving!"

The young boy's face lit up. "That's the one I never knew. But that's just what it sounds like!" I finished the song, and the man gave three coppers to his son. His face beaming, the lad held them out to me.

"I predict you will grow up to be as generous as your abbi," I said, accepting the coppers.

His delighted grin, and the way he leaned against the man next to him, amply repaid me. The next tables I visited had a request already in mind, and I played the Answering Song there, leaving everyone chuckling behind me as I moved on. There were children again at the next tables, and I played the Goat's Song, describing the trouble a goat kid got into when it wandered away from the flock, and how the shepherd found and saved it. The children demanded coppers from their parents, insisting that they each get to give some to me. When I had collected them all, I stood back. "Now, what am I going to do with such riches?" I asked while they giggled at me.

"Put it in your girdle, zammar, before a Habiru takes it!" someone suggested.

I turned to him solemnly. "An excellent idea, geber. But I've met one Habiru who is quite capable of extracting coppers from a purse, and then returning the empty purse without anyone knowing!"

Sympathetic chuckles followed me as I left. I stayed longer than I'd expected, but when it seemed that I would leave, the entire crowd demanded that I remain. I held up my hand. "One song for you all," I called out. Then I played "The Dahveed," the song Grandmother Ruth had written for me about a shepherd boy who saved his flock from wolves.

After the shouting and clapping died down, I made my way through the square, headed for Dathan's compound.

¥ ¥ ¥ ¥ ¥ ¥

Abigail's presence as the guests arrived had caused a great deal of commotion as the nagids, gebirahs, wives, and attendants all welcomed her. Most of them were genuinely relieved to find her well, she decided in surprise, and their good wishes and concern warmed her heart. She hoped the sentiment would last once all her actions became known.

After most of the guests seated themselves, Namea slipped up to her.

"Gebirah, there is talk around the cooking fires of nothing but Nagid Ahlai," she said quickly. "During the pledging yesterday he made accusations against most of the nagids regarding you. It's whispered that the nagids decided to do something, but I've not been able to discover what or when."

"Very good, Namea. Keep your ears open."

Jotbah sat down in her place, and Ahiam arrived at the same time, escorting Ahinoam whom he seated on the other side of Dathan's place before taking the cushion behind the spot that Dahveed would occupy.

Dathan sat down and glanced at the woman on his left. "Ahinoam bat Ahlai?" he asked in amazement.

She nodded. "Yes, nagid. I am here with Gebirah Abigail. I understand my abbi was quite troublesome to you yesterday. I hope you were able to restrain him."

The man looked a little dazed. "Yes, I--we did," he said, then hurriedly turned to Abigail, looking at the empty spot between them inquiringly.

"Do not wait to serve,"Abigail said in a soft voice.

After bowing slightly, he surveyed the guests to be certain that everyone had arrived. Some people hurried in, exclaiming about the zammar out in the market place whom they had stopped to hear. Once they were seated, Dathan clapped his hands and the servers spread out, taking the food to everyone.

As she ate, Abigail wondered what the nagids had done to restrain Ahlai. After nearly an hour passed, she also had begun to wonder where her husband had gone before she saw him come through the gate. A nagid spoke to him, and he readied his harp and began to sing. At the applause when he finished, Dathan looked up, a puzzled expression crossing his face as the zammar responded to another request, and nearly all of the guests quieted to listen.

Abigail turned to him. "Your guests are enjoying the singing, don't you think?"

His face relaxed a little. "Yes, they are. He has a captivating voice."

"I think so," Abigail said, smiling to herself. Several people offered him silver when he was done, and he tactfully refused, saying that he had already been paid for coming. Then he performed the Answering Song, and his mimicry of the haughty baalah's silly excuses for refusing to meet her suitor made everyone forget to eat while they laughed.

Dathan enjoyed the song with the rest, but he looked a little uncertain when the zammar walked toward the head table, then swung around behind it. Abigail watched him, a welcoming smile on her face.

Her husband handed Ahiam the harp and removed his cloak. At the sight of his rich clothing, the courtyard stilled. As they had planned, he turned to Ahinoam first, kissing the hand she gave him, then he sat down between Abigail and Nagid Dathan.

In the stillness her voice was audible to everyone. "Sar, may I present Nagid Dathan of the Hebron Calebite clan. Dathan, this is my husband, Sar Dahveed Israel."

CHAPTER 55

"Your husband!" Dathan gasped. "You married?"

"I believe that's what the nagids wished of me, wasn't it?" Abigail asked, her eyebrows arched.

Dathan hastily averted his stare, gulping a little. "May I offer my congratulations, Nagid?" he said a bit unsteadily, turning to me.

I smiled. "I am called Sar, Dathan. And your congratulations are most welcome."

To give the nagid time to pull himself together, Abigail spoke. "There is bread here, and some couscous, Dahveed. I'm sure you haven't had a chance to eat yet."

"I haven't," I replied, then turned to Dathan. "I must ask for your pardon for my lateness. I was delayed longer in the market than I expected."

"Think nothing of it," he said, still a bit dazed.

I'd eaten my fill, under the covert stares of the entire assembly, before Dathan found the courage to speak to me again.

"Sar, please forgive my forwardness, but I understood you to be leading a band of Habiru."

I smiled at him. "Yes, I am dahveed to a band. Four of them are in your courtyard now, and there are others around."

Faintly alarmed, he glanced around.

"Don't worry. They are here as a precaution only. They like the Gebirah a great deal, and would take serious exception to anything happening to her. Nagid Ahlai made a nuisance of himself once already, and they didn't want anything similar to occur again."

Dathan snorted. "Nagid Ahlai made a nuisance of himself once too often. Your men do not need to worry about him any more."

"That's good to know," I said.

"Since you married the Gebirah, you must be settling down."

I glanced at Abigail, and she nodded fractionally. "I'm afraid it takes land to do that, adon," I said. "That is something that has not yet come our way."

"But the Gebirah's lands will surely provide for you."

"The Gebirah has no land," I said nonchalantly. "It has all been let go."

The nagid turned to me. "But surely you can talk her out of that. We'd heard that she had planned on trying to recompense--"

"You misunderstood me, Nagid," I interrupted him gently. "It is already done. It was accomplished before I married her."

"All her land?"

"Her house and possessions also. Everything is gone. Therefore, calling me nagid is rather an empty title."

Dathan sat back in silence.

Not long after, Abigail turned to him. "I would guess some of the nagids wish to speak with me again. I would like to circulate a little."

The nagid seemed to wake up. "Of course, Gebirah." He helped her stand and escorted her around the table. While she greeted friends and replied to questions, I watched Dathan go from table to table, speaking to every nagid here.

Eventually he escorted Abigail back to her seat. Then he turned to the courtyard and clapped his hands for attention. "There is one more piece of business to attend to tonight," he announced. He nodded to a very elderly man, who had to be helped to his feet, and who shuffled forward to the head table.

"The Nagid Jezreel," Abigail said softly when I raised my eyebrows questioningly at her.

The man bowed as best he could to Abigail. "Gebirah, the elders of Jezreel feel that we owe recompense for the way one of our nagids troubled not just you, but nearly every other nagid in this courtyard. We have agreed, however, that since the offense toward you was the greatest, recompense will be paid to you."

The nagid's aged voice quavered a little. "Nagid Ahlai has troubled Jezreel for some time by his neglect to properly restrain his son Lael, whose loose tongue and continual debts have disgraced us all for years. Finding that Lael had again incurred debts that could not be paid, the elders declared Ahlai's estate forfeit and sold it. The day of the sale, Ahlai absented himself in pursuit of Gebirah Abigail, nearly causing war among the clans. His false accusations just yesterday against nearly every Calebite nagid have brought such dishonor to

Jezreel that the elders decided the only appropriate punishment is enslavement for him and his house. He and his son were sold this morning to a caravan headed for Damascus."

The elderly nagid turned to Abigail, bowed shakily, and handed a purse to the younger man attending him. "Here is the purchase price for the estates and persons belonging to Ahlai of Jezreel as well as for the man himself and his son. May it be enough to restore your honor."

After a final bow he was helped back to his seat.

Abigail accepted the purse. "Let me express my gratitude to the nagids and elders of Jezreel. Your goodwill in regard to my honor would have been recompense enough, therefore I am more than amply repaid."

She sat down and turned to Dathan. "Is there any other business, nagid? If not, I would like to retire."

"We have finished for the evening," he assured her. "You have graced us with your presence, Gebirah."

Abigail led the way through the courtyard, and I followed, escorting Ahinoam, who was trembling from what she had just learned. Once we were back at the house in town, she ran into Zabad's waiting arms.

We had barely finished breaking our fast the next morning when a visitor appeared at the gate.

"Gebirah, it's someone to see you," Hezro announced.

Abigail went out to see who it was, and the commander of the guard looked over at Jotbah, a smile on his face. "I think you will be needed out there," he said.

"I wondered," she replied, getting her scribal materials. "I heard enough at the feast last night to suspect that all didn't go as the Gebirah expected."

"It didn't," the commander replied.

I looked at Ittai who had stayed in the square last night. "What's happening?"

"None of her adons pledged to other nagids," he explained. "The householders only gave conditional pledges to the adons, which would not be approved unless the adons and nagids pledged to the Gebirah again."

Namea nodded. "I heard the same thing. And some of the other women were saying that several adons farther out from Carmel learned what was happening, and they did the same with their nagids."

"How much territory does Carmel cover?" I asked.

"Traditionally, all the area around Carmel and Maon and spreading northwest from there. But I heard of adons nearly to Ziph waiting for her. Even Dathan lost a few, and every Calebite clan to the southwest of Maon waited also," the handmaid reported.

"And with the adons going to her, the nagids will have to follow! She covers more territory now than Nabal!" Ahinoam said in delight. "Next year, it will probably be the clans around the south and west borders, because Dathan is well liked. And now that it's known she married Dahveed Israel, the people of Judah and Simeon will be considering giving support also!"

By that evening Gebirah Abigail was the most powerful figure in the Calebite clans.

¥ ¥ ¥ ¥ ¥ ¥

"Hassar!"

Jonathan looked around, puzzled that anyone this far north would be calling him. He was nearly to Shechem, on his way to check on the hostages he'd sent there. With the new moon feast over, he'd decided to get out of Gibeah for a while, and checking on the hostages was as good an excuse as any.

"Hassar!"

He reined his mule to a halt. A rider galloped toward him up the road leading down to the Arabah.

To his amazement, Ethan pulled up. "You're a hard man to find. What are you doing this far north?"

"Traveling to Shechem."

"Is it urgent?"

"No."

"Good. Let's go. Dahveed is celebrating his marriage, and I don't want to miss the feast."

Jonathan stared. "He's getting married again?"

"He sort of had to, otherwise the south would have erupted in war. Are you coming?"

Jonathan looked to see if the Habiru was joking. "War? What did Dahveed do to precipitate war?"

"There would only have been war if he *didn't* do something. Hassar, we've got to leave now, and your escort will never be able to keep up."

Suddenly Jonathan couldn't wait to hear whatever tangled story Dahveed would have for him this time, the details of which he'd have to drag from that exasperating zammar one at a time in order to understand. Besides, he had to go down there and be sure Dahveed was wearing that brass earring.

"Wait for me at Gibeah," he told his escort recklessly, turning his mule. Without a word, Ethan led the way, rapidly picking up speed until their mounts raced down the road, their riders' cloaks flying in the wind.

In just more than an hour the mules covered the 15 miles from the highlands down to the Arabah, and Jonathan was having second thoughts about this mad rush. When Ethan swung off the road toward a small farmstead, he was relieved that he'd have time to send a message or two. But the Habiru passed the house and went into the trees ahead. Out of sight of the road, he slid off his mule.

"We need to change mounts, Hassar." As he spoke, a man led two long-legged mules from the trees, already harnessed with riding cloths strapped tight to their withers. Ethan jumped on one and held out the reins of the other to Jonathan.

"Ethan, it's nearly dark."

"Yes, and we've got a long way to go. Get on."

"But-"

"Your mule will be back at Gibeah by the time you get there, Hassar. We're wasting time we haven't got."

"Ethan, I only have the travel clothes I'm wearing, I haven't told anyone where I'm going, and I don't have a wedding gift!"

The Habiru smiled. "Hassar," he said softly, "you *are* the wedding gift. Now, are you coming peaceably?"

Something about the very madness of this whole thing reminded him irresistibly of Dahveed. And the look in Ethan's eye said the man just might take him bound and gagged and dump him outside Dahveed's tent if he didn't get on that mule.

He mounted, and as soon as he did, he looked at the Habiru in amazement. "What kind of a mule is this?" he asked as the animal shifted around impatiently.

Ethan laughed. "All you have to do is hang on, Hassar. Zelek had some ideas about breeding mules that appealed to me, and you're riding one of the results."

"It's warm enough that you won't need your cloak," the Habiru leader said, removing his cloak and fastening it behind him. Jonathan followed suit.

The mules started for the road. As soon as it flattened out on the floor of the Arabah, Ethan called to him. "Grab a handful of mane," doing the same himself. Then he bent low over the neck of his animal and loosened the reins.

Jonathan barely had time to comply before the animal under him put its head down and took off, his grip on the mane the only thing keeping him astride it at the sudden explosion of speed. The hassar gasped, the wind bringing tears to his eyes. He'd never known anything could run so fast, and it wasn't long before he realized that the mule wasn't going nearly as fast as it could.

"What did Zelek do, harness a storm wind?" he yelled to Ethan.

"Just about," the Habiru yelled back. "They'll slow after a while, but if we don't let them get it out of their system now, they'll be too hard to handle the rest of the way. That's why we use them at night. Can't let them go like this with caravans and travelers on the roads."

The stars emerged in the blackness above them, and he never even knew when they passed Jericho, the hoof beats of the mules pounding in his mind as he followed Ethan through the night, speeding south. Hours later, the Habiru chieftain pulled his mule to a relaxed trot, and Jonathan's mount followed suit.

"How far have we come?" Jonathan asked.

"We're right at the beginning of the Salt Sea. We've got another 10 miles yet. There's a farmstead where we'll sleep for a while and change mules."

Jonathan shook his head in amazement. They would have traveled 50 miles by the time they reached the farmstead, and more than half of that would have been on this incredible animal he rode now.

"What about tomorrow?"

"We've got a 25-mile run, most of that across the hills in the wilderness of Maon. There should be some bundles for us there, too. Jether said that he'd see they arrived in good time. You've always said that Sahrah Michal had good taste, so whatever she sent for your wedding gift should be something Dahveed will like."

"You haven't even told me who Dahveed is marrying."

"I'll let you find out when we get there," Ethan chuckled. "Shall we go?"

"Do I have a choice?" Jonathan asked as his mount tugged at the bit.

"No, Hassar, you do not!" And the mules took off again.

For the rest of his life Jonathan remembered that wild night ride down the Arabah. They only slept about four hours before Ethan put him on another mule, with shorter legs, but the most powerful stride the hassar had ever ridden. Up to the first hills above the Arabah, they climbed, the mules fighting the bits the entire way up the Hever gorge until they reached the first plateau. When the Habiru loosened his reins, the mules snorted and leaned into a run, the men clinging low over their necks as the trails passed into trees. Once in the dense, dark forests that crowded down from the higher hills, they slowed to take the climb at a saner pace. At last they reached the top of a ridge, and Ethan dismounted.

To Jonathan's surprise, Hanan appeared. "You made it in good time, adon," he told the old warrior.

"Zelek's bred some good mules," Ethan replied, slapping the one he'd ridden affectionately. "Take care of them. We'll need the bundles tied on the back before evening."

As Hanan led the mules off, Ethan indicated a spot under a pine, thick with dead needles. "Your bed awaits, Hassar. We can sleep a few hours before the feast tonight!"

It was just before dusk when Ethan wakened him. "Time to get dressed, Hassar." Jonathan stretched and rolled over, expecting to be stiff from sleeping on the ground, but the thick pine needles had made a bed nearly as comfortable as the one he normally slept on. He washed in a small pool from a spring and found clean undergarments waiting along with his best robe.

Ethan grinned, tying the girdle he wore. "Hassarah Ahinoam sent whatever she thought you'd need."

"Seems as if everyone knew Dahveed was celebrating a wedding except me," he said testily.

The Habiru chuckled. "I said you were a hard man to find. Took me a day and a half to track you down, and Jether barely got the word to me in time to do that. It wouldn't have been such a race except that local politics took a hand, and Dahveed had to rush the actual marriage. That happened before the New Moon, I believe."

"Just what are these serious local politics?" Jonathan asked, trying to work the comb Immi had sent through his long tangled black hair. He winced as he accidentally pulled some hair from his scalp.

"Once word got out that Nagid Nabal had died, everyone stampeded for his Gebirah."

The hassar paused. "Are you telling me Dahveed married Gebirah

Carmel?"

"The day he took her out from under the noses of every nagid in the Calebite clans!"

Jonathan managed to get his hair into a presentable state while Ethan explained the political situation in the south, including the use that Abigail had made of Nabal's riches. He considered what he'd learned while he fastened the gold arm bands and put on the gold earrings and headband. What the Gebirah had done would probably result in a united south.

He stared into the deepening dusk. "Yahweh plans very far ahead, Ethan. I think you and I are part of something that He's been building for generations."

"May we be worthy of His notice," the Habiru said quietly.

"May we, indeed. I think I'm ready. Didn't you say there would be a gift around here for me to give?"

"It's already been delivered," Ethan chuckled. "Sahrah Michal sent jewelry for both Dahveed and Abigail, and Jether and his wife supplied robes. That's what the wedding couple are wearing now. So I guess you'll just have to settle for being a gift yourself."

"Did anyone ever tell you that your son comes by his impertinence naturally?" Jonathan asked, irritated.

"What else did you expect from us southern hill men, Hassar?" Chuckling at the expression on Jonathan's face, Ethan started across the ridge, and before long, the hassar heard the sounds of laughter and singing.

"We're late, Habiru."

"And if I showed up with you earlier, do you think the feast would have ever begun?" Ethan retorted.

Despite the fact that it was a time of rejoicing, they were still challenged by sentries. Down in the camp torches and a large fire provided light for everyone grouped around in a small glade. Dahveed stood to one side of the fire in a red robe with yellow fringe as long as the fringe on the robe that Jonathan himself wore. A panel of embroidery covered the chest, the gold threads flashing in the firelight every time he moved. He had narrow gold arm bands, gold earrings and headband, and his mantle was a rich chestnut brown that matched his hair, fastened at both shoulders with gold brooches. And something about his carriage and the way he held his head made him seem too good for the clothes.

Instead of going forward, Jonathan remained in the shadows of the trees, drinking in the sight of the zammar he had come to love more than his own life. Then, for a short time, the darkness vanished, and sunlight streamed through windows and Dahveed appeared just as he was now, in the same color robe, only a crown circled his head, and he stood in front of a throne holding a scepter, backed by magnificent hangings instead of the night's darkness. The vision took the hassar's breath away, and he stared as hard as he could. Dahveed's face was older, and he had met some great sorrow, for his eyes held a shadow that only seemed to heighten the rejoicing in them, and the shouts of some great triumph echoed in his ears.

The sunlight faded, night coming again, and Jonathan realized Dahveed was singing and playing his harp, accompanied by a drum, tambourine, and a single wind instrument. There were many more people than when he'd visited last. The hassar saw several women and children. Wiping the tears from his eyes, he listened to the familiar song "Rejoice in Happiness," a short song describing how the bride and groom delighted in each other. Only there was a twist to it he'd never heard before.

With every repetition, the tempo increased, the crowd clapping in time, all of them laughing while they sang, only to listen breathlessly while Dahveed drew out the last syllable of the word "happiness" longer and longer every time they came to it.

At last, they were singing so fast they could hardly get the words out, and Dahveed took a huge breath, throwing his head back, his eyes closed, his glorious voice taking that long note up a third, and letting it spill out clear and true, until it seemed that he would never stop.

Beside him, Ethan suddenly chuckled and nudged Jonathan forward. Eyes glinting, the hassar walked into sight, standing where Dahveed would see him the moment he opened his eyes.

¥ ¥ ¥ ¥ ¥ ¥

I held the note longer than I ever had before, counting my heartbeats to keep track of time. Something about the atmosphere around me changed, a ripple of amusement running through the rest of the people singing with me, and I opened my eyes.

The first thing I noticed was a rich blue robe with a meil over it, and the torchlight glinting on wide gold armbands and a worked headband. The second thing I saw was Jonathan's fascinated gaze, his eyes laughing as he waited for my note to end. The shock of seeing him here, now, took over my mind, and left me drawing out that note until the edges of my vision began to go dark. Somehow I managed to bring the note down, and with shouts of laughter, the crowd rushed the song to its end. I just stood there as everyone cheered. Jonathan walked toward me, stopped and touched one knee to the ground, then bowed all the way down before getting up again. The harp dropped from my grasp.

"And what was that for?" I asked softly when he stopped in front of me.

"That was for what I have seen tonight of what will be," he replied, and for a moment his black eyes carried the same look Mahesa's blue ones did.

"Then this is for what still is," I said, touching my own knee to the ground and bowing my head.

His hands reached for mine. "Get up, Dahveed, and let me see you. Yahweh has done much since we talked last."

I stood. "He has," I agreed, as we embraced, then gripped forearms tightly. "And you're late!"

"Ethan wouldn't let me come into camp earlier," the hassar shrugged. "Something about the feast never getting started if I did."

I had to laugh and looked around for my oldest friend. He emerged from the shadows, wearing clothes nearly as rich as the hassar's, decked out in dark green and silver, and we embraced also.

"Come and sit down," I said. "You need to meet my wife."

"I've had the pleasure once, and it is well worth repeating," Jonathan said, taking Abigail's hand and bowing to her also.

"Your house honored mine greatly that night, Hassar," Abigail said. "I have never forgotten it."

Once everyone was seated, Keturah directed that the food be served. I looked around at the happy faces reflected in the torchlight, listening to the laughter around me, and gratitude flowed from my heart. The king I loved no longer sought my life, we had abundant food, were blessed with the presence of our God in our midst, and Jonathan Hassar sat beside me celebrating with me the marriage that brought security to the south and our lives.

I glanced up at the stars. I had been a fugitive for so long that it was hard to believe the position I had now. But then, I'd been Yahweh's fugitive, and His hand had guided. "Thank You, Yah." I whispered.

Tamar bat Dahveed

There. Our story is done for now. All has been accomplished. Dahveed has gained the core of his future army and has learned the essentials of trusting Yah in everything and of governing men. Jonathan rules in Israel, and the two of them have set in place the things necessary for the peaceful transfer of the kingdom. Gebirah Abigail has saved her family honor, and the people of the south have found a way to unite, bringing together Judah, Simeon, Caleb, and the Habiru in the union between Gebirah Carmel and Dahveed Israel. It is truly a time for rejoicing!

Pass the harp back here to me now. Did everyone get to feel the indentation in the chest piece from the brass earring? You can tell the wine stain on the bottom if you look closely. It stops about half way across and the wood is just a little darker. Yes, my abbi had an instrument maker put that inlay in the spear gouge several years ago. The one from the arrow at Maon was filled with pitch. See the dark line?

What was that you asked, young geberet? Is there more? Oh yes, there is much more to the story, although the next part of it is hard for me to tell. It is the story of Baalah Hazzel defending Gath against Dahveed, of the hassar's new zammar, of the saddest triumph in Israel's history, and the breaking of my abbi's heart.

Now then, you've got me crying already. Abbi never could tell it without tears either. Put the signet of Moab back in the case also. I know-- if Dahveed gave it to Yira, why is it here now? You asked that last time, I believe. That's even further along in our story, and yes, Balak is a part of it. Well, go on now, and may Yahweh hold you close to His heart.

Tamar bat Dahveed
Second year of Solomon
(968 B.C.)

Maps

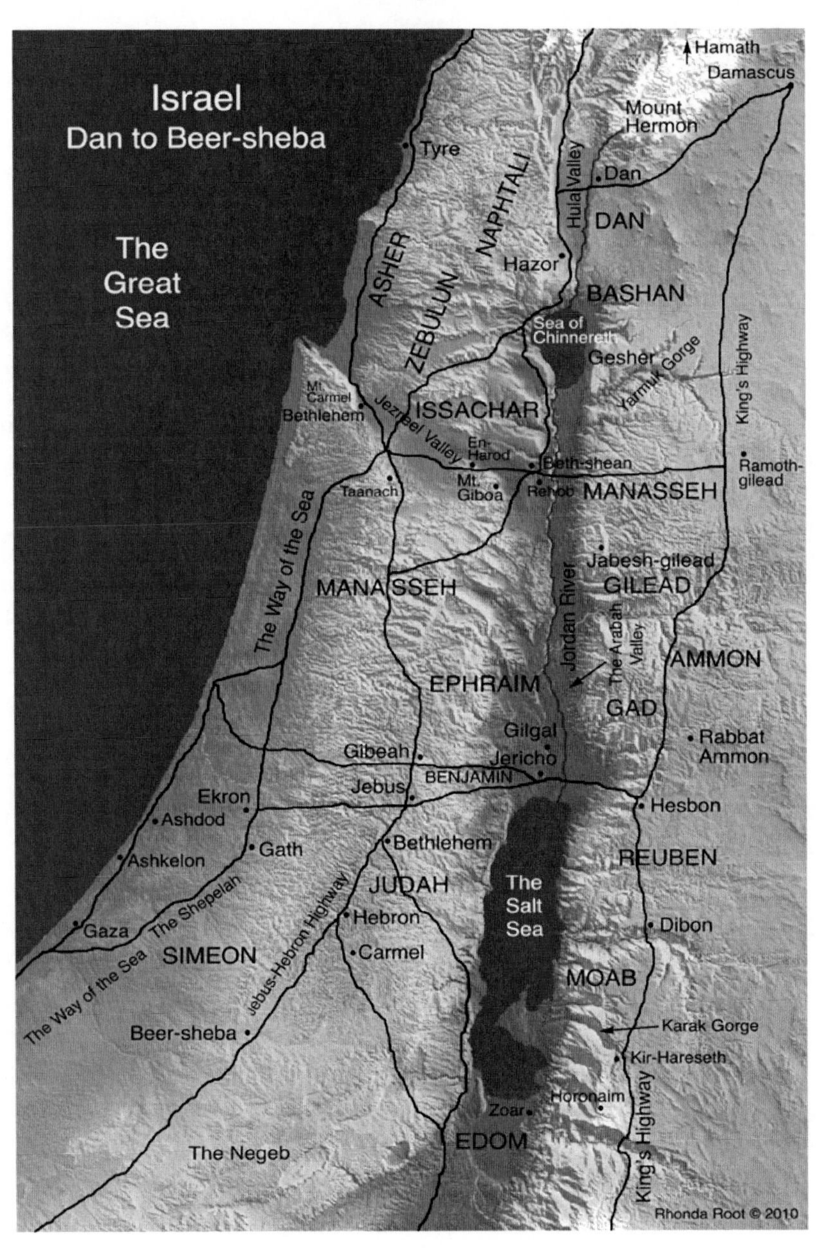

Israel
Dan to Beer-sheba
The Great Sea
Hamath
Damascus
Mount Hermon
Tyre
Dan
Hula Valley
DAN
NAPHTALI
ASHER
ZEBULUN
Hazor
BASHAN
Sea of Chinnereth
Gesher
Yarmuk Gorge
King's Highway
Mt. Carmel
Bethlehem
ISSACHAR
Jezreel Valley
En-Harod
Beth-shean
Ramoth-gilead
Taanach
Mt. Giboa
Rehob
MANASSEH
The Way of the Sea
Jabesh-gilead
GILEAD
MANASSEH
Jordan River
The Arabah Valley
AMMON
EPHRAIM
GAD
Gilgal
Rabbat Ammon
Gibeah
Jericho
BENJAMIN
Jebus
Ekron
Ashdod
Hesbon
Bethlehem
Gath
Ashkelon
REUBEN
The Shepelah
JUDAH
The Salt Sea
Jebus-Hebron Highway
Hebron
Gaza
Dibon
Carmel
SIMEON
The Way of the Sea
MOAB
Beer-sheba
Karak Gorge
Kir-Hareseth
Horonaim
Zoar
EDOM
The Negeb
King's Highway
Rhonda Root © 2010

Israel

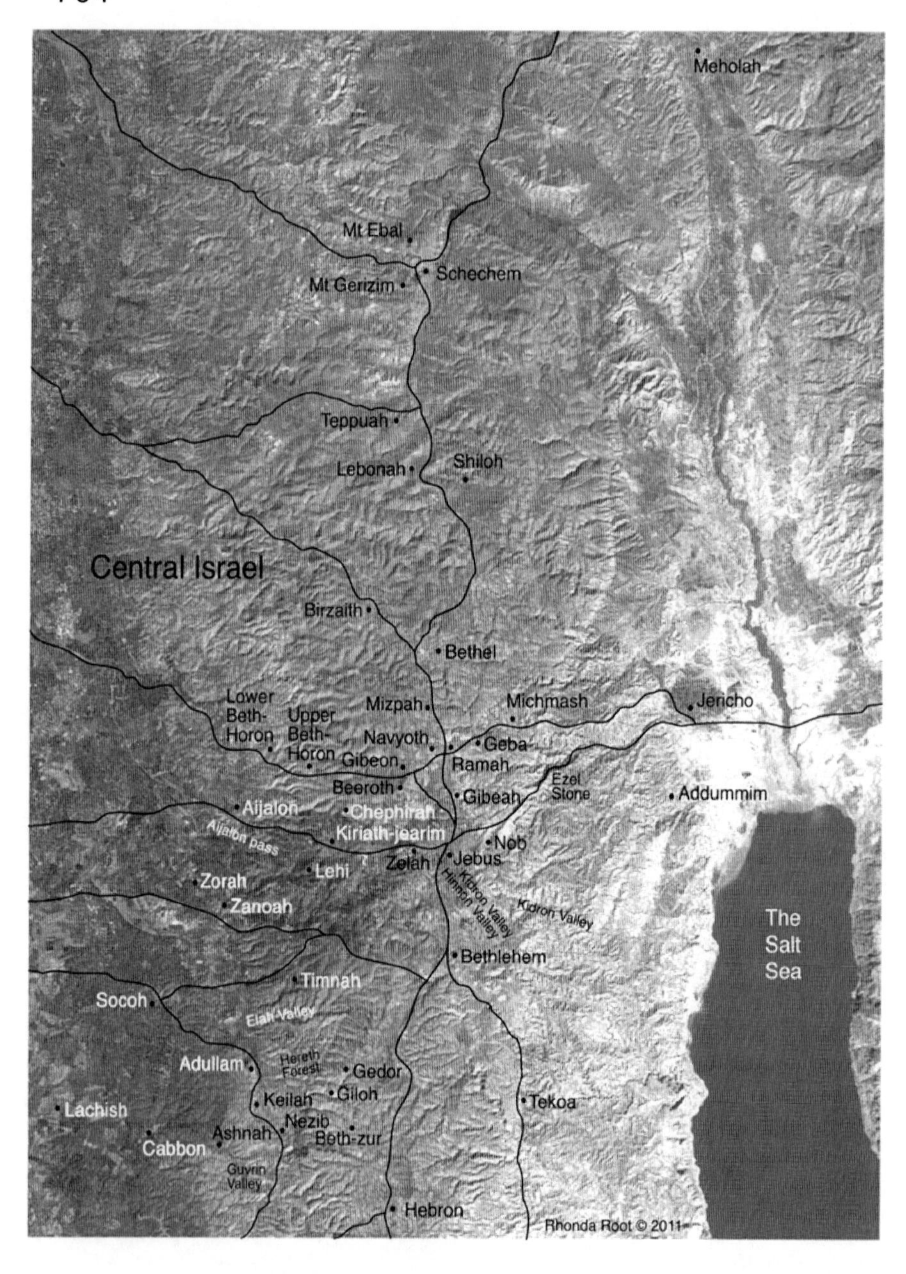

Central Israel

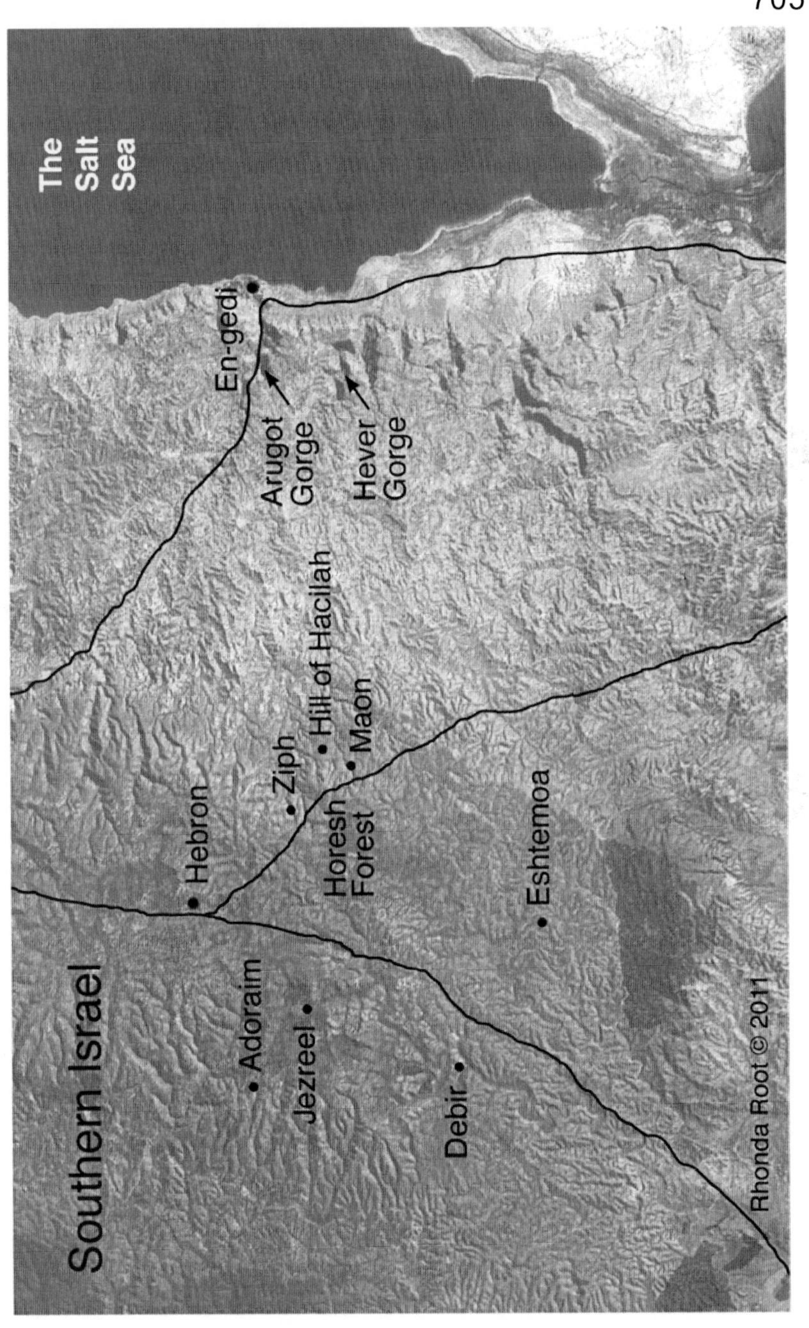

Southern Israel